L. E. Modesitt, Jr.

MAGE-GUARD OF HAMOR

TOR®
fantasy

A TOM DOHERTY ASSOCIATES BOOK
NEW YORK

This is a work of fiction. All the characters, organizations, and events portrayed in this novel are products of the author's imagination or are used fictitiously.

MAGE-GUARD OF HAMOR

Copyright © 2008 by L. E. Modesitt, Jr.

All rights reserved.

Maps by Ellisa Mitchell

A Tor Book
Published by Tom Doherty Associates, LLC
175 Fifth Avenue
New York, NY 10010

www.tor-forge.com

Tor® is a registered trademark of Tom Doherty Associates, LLC.

ISBN-13: 978-0-7653-5882-0
ISBN-10: 0-7653-5882-4

First Edition: July 2008
First Mass Market Edition: March 2009

Printed in the United States of America

0 9 8 7 6 5 4 3 2 1

For Tom,
who understands those who cross oceans for love

CHARACTERS

Emperor of Hamor	Mythalt
Empress of Hamor	Emerya
Administer of Merowey	Golyat
Triads	Fieryn—Mage-Guards
	Jubyl—Emperor
	Dhoryk—High Command

High Command

Overmarshal	Berndyt
Sea Marshal	Chastyr
Land Marshal	Valatyr
Marshal (Merowey Command)	Charynat
Marshal (Merowey Command)	Byrna

Mage-Guards

Overcommander	Kurtweyl
Administrative Director of the Triad	Cyphryt
Overcommander, Cigoerne Region	Welleyn
Triad (former)	Taryl
Assistants to Triad Jubyl	Klassyn
	Serita
Assistant to Triad Dhoryk	Medora
Assistant to Triad Fieryn	Kielora
Assistants to Director Cyphryt	Vladyrt
	Saulya

HAMOR

Dolari

Northpoin

Swartheld

Luba

Guasyra
Cigoerne

Heldya

Highpo

Quarries

SWARTH RIVER

Westyr

CLYAN RIVER

Jabuti

Kysha

Clyanaka

Alsenyi

MEROWEY

Dawhut

Elmari

Sastak

Nubyat

SOUTHERN
OCEAN

NORTHERN

CANDAR

Gulf of Murr

Gulf of Candar

RECLUCE

EASTERN OCEAN

The WORLD

Nylan

I

Rahl stood on the port wing of the fast frigate's bridge, looking out at the seemingly endless gray-blue waters of the Eastern Ocean. Even in midocean, the early-fall air seemed hazy and cool, and the cloudless green-blue sky held a hint of silver. Below the iron decks, he could sense the controlled chaos of the boilers and engines of the E.S. *Ascadya* as she steamed northeast—toward Recluce. He could also feel the latent chaos of the powder in the locked iron magazines below the forward gun turret with its twin guns.

He glanced toward the covered center of the bridge where Captain Jaracyn stood beside the officer of the day, both slightly back of the helmsman. Although the captain had been polite and courteous to both Rahl and Taryl—particularly toward the older mage-guard—Rahl could sense Jaracyn's distaste for his mission. As a fighting commander of the Hamorian Navy, the captain would have preferred a more active role in dealing with the rebellion in Merowey than to transport two mage-guard envoys to Nylan, even though the mission was designed to keep the black ships of Nylan from becoming involved in hostilities against the Emperor.

Rahl glanced back as the frigate pitched forward, slicing through a heavy swell that sent spray flying back from the bow. Two ratings in khaki trousers and collarless khaki shirts didn't even duck as the cool spray showered them.

Rahl couldn't help but shake his head at how his life had twisted since he'd left Land's End more than a year before. He'd been exiled from the north of Recluce to the Black City of Nylan, and from there to Hamor because he could not control his abilities with order. He'd been drugged with nemysa to destroy his memory after he'd discovered the thefts by the director of the Nylan Merchant Association, and ended up as laborer in the ironworks of Luba, where he'd been rescued and trained by a self-exiled mage-guard—Taryl—who had once been the Emperor's Mage-Guard Triad. Then Rahl had been posted to Swartheld as a junior mage-guard, where he'd uncovered the Jeranyi pirate plot to destroy the merchant sector of the harbor—and killed his superior and destroyed the entire Nylan Merchant Association in the process of saving the rest of the merchant houses. As a result, he and Taryl were now being dispatched to Nylan to explain all that had happened.

Yet, because Rahl had not learned enough about handling order, he knew he could not return permanently to Nylan. After his exile from Nylan and the conditions set forth for his return, if it were not for Deybri, the healer whose image and warmth he could not forget, he would not have been looking forward to returning at all—because he had little more control over his abilities to handle order than when he had been dispatched and because every time he thought about the events leading to his exile, he had to fight the anger and rage those memories sparked.

"You're looking somber," observed Taryl. The thin-faced and angular mage-guard stepped to the bridge railing inboard of where Rahl stood. "You're concerned about the reception you might get?"

Rahl nodded. He was concerned about two reactions—that of the board of magisters in Nylan and that of Deybri.

"You're an official envoy of the Emperor," Taryl said. "The most they can do is tell you to depart once we've delivered our messages."

"You're really the envoy, ser. You're a former Triad, and I still don't see why anyone really needed me."

"I suppose Jyrolt told you about the Triad?"

"Yes, ser. He didn't tell me much, except that all the rumors were wrong, and that I was to tell anyone who suggested such that they were."

Taryl shook his head. "They won't believe you. Rumors are far more attractive, as you will discover."

"Ah . . . ser . . . you didn't say why anyone needs me."

"Because, as I've told you several times," Taryl replied patiently, "they know who you are, and what you are, and they'll be able to tell that you're telling them the truth. Also, you're the only one alive who has firsthand knowledge about the way the managing director of the Nylan Merchant Association in Swartheld was linked to the Jeranyi."

Rahl supposed that was true, but what difference would it make? The magisters hadn't ever really listened to him before. Why would they now, especially since he was a mage-guard of Hamor?

"The engineers aren't the Council of Recluce," Rahl pointed out.

"Exactly." Taryl smiled. "But they are the real power on the isle. Most of the trade comes through Nylan. They have the only warships that can challenge Hamor. By dealing with the magisters of Nylan, we will foment a certain amount of internal unrest in Recluce. That may focus their interest internally, rather than on Hamor, because the Emperor is suggesting that the true power lies in Nylan and not at Land's End."

"You said that Fairhaven might be aiding the rebels in Merowey. If that is so, why would Recluce want to get involved? They wouldn't want to do anything to help Fairhaven."

"No, they wouldn't. You're right about that. But . . ." Taryl paused. "If they thought that they could weaken us by restricting trade or some other means, they might. That's why we need to point out that the Jeranyi were behind the attack on Swartheld and that the Jeranyi were willing to sacrifice the Nylan Merchant Association and all its goods and revenues in order to strike at Hamor. That confirms the Jeranyi as an enemy of both Recluce and Hamor. That's also why the captain is making speed. We need to be the ones to explain what happened first, to show good faith and concern."

"The Council in Land's End has already declared the Jeranyi as an enemy and restricted trade," Rahl said. "They did that more than a year ago."

"But Nylan still trades with them, according to our people there. That embargo only applies north of the black wall."

Rahl hadn't known that.

"Most trade comes through Nylan now, remember," added Taryl. "You'll need to make the Jeranyi role clear. I will tell them the truth. They will be skeptical, and they will ask you. You are to convey what you know completely truthfully. You will tell them exactly what happened, and you will also tell them that the Emperor will announce that the Jeranyi were acting to cripple trade in Swartheld, but that they were stopped before they could complete their efforts."

"What if they ask about what I did?"

"You tell them. If you'd done nothing, the merchant association still would have lost everything."

Rahl nodded. That was certainly true enough, but he wondered if the magisters would see it that way, and, even if they did, whether the traders would.

He put his hand on the bridge railing to steady himself as the frigate pitched forward slightly, then rolled a bit to starboard on the recovery before righting herself. His eyes took in the port lookout, standing at the outboard end of the bridge, five cubits beyond the two mages. The rating had not even budged while Rahl was grasping to keep his balance.

"You had said that Swartheld would not be suitable for

my further training, but you did not say what that training would be," Rahl finally ventured.

"I did not," replied Taryl.

Rahl waited.

"Most of the mage-guards one sees are white and handle chaos. I assume you have noticed this."

"Yes, ser."

"The reason for that is obvious. They can deal with malefactors quickly, and the way in which they do also inspires fear and respect. One does not build a land on fear alone. Order is also required, but mastering order and understanding its uses takes far longer and much more work. In your case, because you are a natural ordermage, it will take even longer.

"On our return, you and I, as well as a number of other ordermages, will be sent to Merowey and placed at the disposal of Marshal Charynat to assist him in dealing with the rebellion there." Taryl's lips curled into a wry smile. "I am certain we will both learn a great deal."

"The rebellion is still continuing? Against the Emperor?"

"It is likely to continue for a considerable time," Taryl replied. "It appears that the Emperor's elder brother is behind it."

"*Elder* brother?"

"All the Emperor's offspring are trained as leaders and administrators. Those who are unqualified are exiled. The one who succeeds is not necessarily the oldest, but the one in the bloodline who the Triad and the High Command feel is best qualified." The older mage laughed. "There have been mistakes, but not so many as when the Emperor's successor was always the eldest son."

"The older son was the administrator in Merowey?" asked Rahl.

"He still is, and he has trained and raised his own army."

The more Rahl learned about Hamor, the less he knew . . . or so it seemed.

He glanced out to the horizon. Even though there were no clouds in sight, he had the feeling that there would be storms ahead.

II

The voyage back to Nylan aboard the *Ascadya* was far swifter than had been Rahl's trip to Swartheld aboard the *Diev* more than a year earlier. Upon occasion the glasses passed more quickly, particularly when Taryl was working with Rahl on sharpening his order-senses and abilities. Rahl also wrote a letter to his parents, explaining what had happened in general terms, and that while he would be in Nylan, it would only be for a few days before he had to return to Hamor, since he had certainly not gained the control of his order-abilities required by the magisters. He thought he had enough coins to have the letter sent from Nylan.

Writing the letter, careful as he was, did not take all that much time, and all too often, Rahl found himself somewhere at the railing, staring out at the seemingly endless Eastern Ocean and wondering if he would ever gain full mastery of order-abilities. Or would he always be limited to little more than what he could now accomplish?

Then there was Deybri. What could he really do except talk to her? He had no future in Recluce, at least not anytime soon, and she was years older. Yet . . . he shook his head. He could only see her . . . if she'd even agree to that.

Early on fiveday morning, a long, dark shape appeared on the horizon, and shortly thereafter Captain Jaracyn ordered the envoy ensign to the top of the mast—an oblong white flag bordered in green.

By midday, the southern end of Recluce was clearly visible dead ahead, but Rahl was more concerned about what he sensed approaching. Aft on the starboard side of the *Ascadya* and a good kay to the east, Rahl could sense a concentration of order, a blackness that he could not see with his eyes.

At that moment, Taryl climbed the ladder to the starboard wing of the bridge, joining Rahl and nodding to the junior mage-guard. "You can sense we have company?"

"Yes, ser. It must be one of the black ships."

Taryl nodded. "I'd judge so."

For a time, they both were silent, but Rahl could not help but keep trying to see the Recluce vessel, even as it quickly drew nearer, despite the speed of the Hamorian frigate.

"It's faster than I'd realized," admitted Taryl. "It's a good thing we're here, although they wouldn't have as much of an advantage as they'd think."

"Ser?"

The older mage gestured in the direction of the unseen vessel. "The closer they get, the easier it is to calculate where they are. Look aft. You can see the wake. They've probably got their screws set deeply to minimize it, but if they get close enough, a good gunner could calculate where they are. They're most dangerous at dusk and at night, when you can't see the wake clearly."

That might be, reflected Rahl, but as he watched the wake of the unseen vessel, roughly abeam the *Ascadya,* he could sense it abruptly increasing its speed and pulling away from the Hamorian frigate. Before its wake vanished, Rahl could see that it was headed toward the southernmost tip of Recluce and the black city and port of Nylan.

"It's fast, though, much faster than anything we have," Taryl added.

"Are we running at top speed?" Rahl refrained from mentioning Khalyt, the young engineer he had met briefly in Nylan, and his ideas for developing an even faster warship.

"No. That wastes too much coal, but even at flank speed, we couldn't match them. Still, they don't have anywhere near the numbers of vessels we do, I don't believe." With a laugh, Taryl added, "They don't need as many, either."

By the time the *Ascadya* neared the entrance to Nylan, a pilot boat was waiting, accompanied by one of the black ships—without a sight shield. It might have been the same one that had earlier scouted the Hamorian frigate, but Rahl had no way of telling. It also had turrets fore and aft, but they were lower, and the twin guns shorter, with an iron tube mounted in the center of the turret above the guns.

Captain Jaracyn slowed the frigate to mere headway as the pilot boat came alongside.

With Taryl beside him, Rahl listened as the pilot used a conical tube to amplify his voice. For a moment, Rahl didn't understand a word, before he realized that the pilot and the captain were speaking Low Temple and not Hamorian.

". . . diplomatic mission to the magisters and engineers of Nylan . . ." replied the captain.

". . . welcome . . . you'll be berthed at the first set of piers on the north side of the harbor . . . the pier will have a berthing flag on the end—green square on white . . . deeper water there . . . would you like a pilot?"

"No . . . that's a negative."

"We'll lead you in . . ."

"Thank you . . . we'll need as much headway as we're now making."

"You'll have it, Captain."

Within moments, the pilot boat pulled away, and the frigate followed, picking up slightly more speed as they followed the boat toward the main channel into the harbor.

"The piers where they're berthing us are the ones where the black ships are docked." Rahl pointed to the northwest end of the harbor.

"That makes sense. They want to keep an eye on us, and have the ability to make sure we behave ourselves." Taryl offered a half smile. "They shouldn't know what happened in Swartheld yet, anyway. That was one reason why the captain pushed it. The Emperor wanted us to deliver the news before anyone else, but that also means that the magisters will be skeptical of our appearance under a parley banner."

Rahl glanced northward, at the black-stone buildings and dwellings rising from the harbor onto the long, sloping hill. He thought he could see the training center and the small park below it. In the distance, he could make out a faint dark line. "You can see the black wall. It runs across the entire isle."

"Is it as great as they claim?" asked Taryl.

"All the stones are the same size, at least in the parts of the wall I've seen, and it's order-protected for its entire length." Rahl did not wish to mention his own difficulties with the wall, those that had been the final element in assuring his exile. "It is impressive."

As the *Ascadya* neared the piers, Rahl noted that there was no sight shield in place and that the four long piers were totally empty. "They've moved out all the black ships."

"Or the one that scouted us was the only one here," replied Taryl. "That's more likely. They don't have that many of them."

Rahl had to wonder how Taryl knew that when he didn't, and when he hadn't even been able to see how many of the black ships had been berthed in Nylan in the whole time he'd been in the city.

"There are ways," Taryl answered the unspoken question. "The sea marshals analyze all reports of the sightings of the black ships. Even if they can't identify them, or know for certain, it's a pretty fair wager that a wake from an unseen high-speed vessel is from a Recluce black ship, and most of the time when they're at sea, they don't hold the sight shields except when they're close to

Hamorian warships or pirate vessels. It's too hard on the mages, and they can't have that many."

"Doesn't Recluce have more black mages than many lands?"

"That's true. There were far more mages among those who founded the isle, but even so, Hamor is hundreds of times the size of Recluce and doubtless has hundreds of times the number of people, even with the great eastern desert and the high grasslands." Taryl smiled faintly. "And Hamor does not exile any of its mages. We find uses for almost all of them, including those from Recluce and elsewhere, as you know."

Rahl had to admire the way in which Captain Jaracyn eased the frigate into the pier—a black-stone structure far narrower than those in Swartheld—perhaps a mere fifty cubits in width.

"Lines out!"

The line handlers on the pier wore dark gray uniforms, Rahl noted, and all were dressed the same. Unlike the Hamorian crews and dockworkers, though, several were women.

"Double up!"

Only after the frigate was secured to the heavy bollards, and the fenders were all in place, did the captain order the gangway lowered. By then, it was late afternoon, and the sun was not that high over the Gulf of Candar to the west of Nylan.

Almost immediately, a thin man in the same dark gray as the line handlers appeared on the pier, walking down it toward the *Ascadya*.

Rahl followed the captain and Taryl down from the bridge to the quarterdeck, standing behind them as they waited.

The lanky figure who walked up the gangway also wore silver insignia on his collars and a visored cap with a silver emblem of a trident crossed with a cannon—clearly an officer. "Permission to come aboard?"

"Granted," replied Jaracyn in accented but correct Low Temple. "You're more than welcome. Jaracyn, captain and commanding."

"Senior Captain Haerylt."

"Senior Captain," Taryl said politely in precise Low Temple. "I am Senior Mage-Guard Taryl, assigned as envoy to the magisters of Nylan, and this is Mage-Guard Rahl, assigned as assistant envoy."

"It has been some time since a Hamorian warship has sought port here on a peaceful mission," observed Haerylt. "I assume that with the parley ensign your mission is peaceful."

"We are here to convey information to the magisters that we sincerely hope will assure continued peace between Recluce and Hamor," replied Taryl. "Past hostilities have proved costly to both lands, but there have been some recent events in Swartheld that suggest others would pit us against each other, and the Emperor would like to make certain that the magisters of Nylan understand the background of such events."

Haerylt frowned.

"As far as we are concerned, Senior Captain," Taryl went on, "you are more than welcome to be present when we meet with the magisters. We have no secrets, but, obviously, we would prefer to inform all those concerned at one time."

The senior captain's frown became a scowl. "You are suggesting . . . less than welcome news."

"I can assure you that no vessels of Recluce have been involved, nor are there any hostilities that have taken place, but we wish to inform the magisters of certain events involving Jeranyi pirates and their attempts to attack the merchanting sector of Swartheld."

Haerylt's scowl was replaced with an expression half frown and half puzzlement.

"I trust that you can convey our request," Taryl said politely. "We would not have traveled the breadth of the

Eastern Ocean if the Emperor did not believe that the magisters of Nylan should be informed of these events as soon as possible."

"I can convey your request, Envoy, but I cannot make any commitments for the magisters. In the meantime, we welcome you here, and we will be more than happy to provide water and arrange for any coal or provisions you may require—at the same rates as those for our vessels."

"Thank you."

"If there's anything else you need, you can check with the piermaster. He's in the study in the building at the end of the pier." Haerylt frowned again. "You and your men have the freedom of our base here, but I'd like to request that they remain within the gates until we've conveyed your request to the magisters and received their instructions."

"We understand," Taryl said politely. "I trust that will not be long."

"I imagine they already know you have ported here," Haerylt said dryly, "and I will be conveying your request as soon as I leave."

"We appreciate your courtesy," replied Taryl, "and we look forward to their response. Thank you." He inclined his head slightly.

Haerylt did as well, then turned and walked down the gangway.

Jaracyn glanced to Taryl. So did Rahl.

"We have them concerned," observed Taryl, using Hamorian once more. "That's always useful. Let's hope that will be enough to get them to grant us an immediate audience or hearing."

"The senior captain would just as soon have us gone," added the captain. "He might press for an early meeting."

"It's more likely to be a hearing or a meeting with the magisters, I'd guess," said Rahl, "but I don't know. I only met with the magisters for the training center, and I don't know if those are the same magisters, or if others are in charge of the city."

"How soon will the magisters in Land's End find out about our arrival?" asked Taryl.

"I don't see how they could find out before next three-day at the earliest, and I doubt that the magisters here will press a messenger that hard."

"That soon?" asked Jaracyn.

"The high road from Nylan to Land's End is said to be one of the best in the world," Taryl said. "The Great Highway being built from Cigoerne to Atla is based on its design."

Jaracyn nodded, but Rahl could tell that the captain was skeptical.

Rahl just wondered what the magisters would do.

III

After an early breakfast in the mess on the *Ascadya*, Taryl and Rahl stood on the pier side of the bridge. Taryl handed Rahl a small square of iron. "Study it as you can with your order-senses."

Rahl did so, but so far as he could tell, there was nothing unusual about the iron.

Then the older mage handed him a second piece. "This one. What is the difference?"

With one in each hand, Rahl could immediately sense a difference, if not exactly what it might be. The second one was the slightest bit heavier, but that wasn't all. He tried to probe it. "It's a bit heavier and more resistant to probing."

Taryl offered a third and far more irregular square, one clearly blacker than the other two.

"This has to be black iron," Rahl replied. "It's resistant to order-sensing, and it's much harder."

"It's also more resilient to force and impact." Taryl paused, then asked, "What about the first two?"

"They're iron of some sort, but I'm not a smith or engineer."

"The first is a good steel; the second is iron ordered by pattern welding or forging."

"The second is stronger," observed Rahl.

"It is. It came from a broken blade. The last square came from Candar, although it was created in Recluce generations ago."

"Is Recluce the only place that forges black iron?"

"It is, but not because it could not be done elsewhere." Taryl smiled faintly, as if offering an unspoken question.

Rahl pondered for several moments. "Is that because Hamor needs too much iron and has too few mages to devote to it?"

"Partly. It's also because most uses of iron don't require the strength of black iron, and you can't cut or rework black iron without a mage. Hamor has engineers also, and they've been able to create an iron alloy that's stronger than most, without requiring magery."

"What about Fairhaven? Do they avoid black iron?"

"In Fairhaven, but their warships are iron-hulled as well." Taryl looked up and then out at the pier. "I believe someone is coming in response to our request."

Rahl turned. A silver-haired magister was striding toward the gangway. Rahl recognized him. "It's Tamryn. He was one of the magisters at the training center, and one of those who sentenced me to exile."

"Good."

Rahl wasn't so sure about that.

Taryl headed down the ladder to the quarterdeck, and Rahl followed.

Tamryn came to a halt short of the quarterdeck. "Permission to come aboard?"

"You're most welcome, Magister Tamryn," replied Taryl.

Rahl could sense Tamryn's surprise, but the silver-haired mage merely said, "Thank you."

Taryl gestured, and the three moved onto the main deck forward of the quarterdeck and outboard of the turret.

As Rahl studied both Tamryn and Taryl, he could see that within Taryl was far more power than within Tamryn, of a *depth* that Rahl could not have described exactly.

"I presume that you are here in response to our request to address the magisters of Nylan," Taryl prompted.

"That I am." Tamryn's eyes drifted to Rahl momentarily before he continued. "The magisters will receive you at the training center at the second glass past noon." Tamryn's eyes strayed to Rahl once more. "They will hear whatever you wish to convey from the Emperor. They asked me to inform you, however, that they can only represent the black city, and that anything involving more than that upon Recluce must be brought before the magisters in Land's End."

"That is understood," replied Taryl. "What information we bring is concerned with Nylan." The ordermage emphasized the word *we* ever so slightly.

The silver-haired Tamryn inclined his head to Taryl. "As an envoy of the Emperor and as an ordermage, you are welcome in Nylan for the duration of your visit, and the city is open to you." His eyes traveled to Rahl. "Rahl, however . . ."

Rahl could feel himself stiffening, and he tried to relax. Even before Taryl or he could explain, Tamryn was jumping to conclusions, just like the magisters always had. No wonder he'd gotten so angry at them so often.

Taryl cleared his throat gently. "Rahl is not here for pleasure. Nor is he seeking a revocation of his exile at this time. He would not be here were his presence not absolutely necessary, as affirmed by the Emperor. You can see that he harbors no chaos, and he is my aide. It would be to your benefit, and admittedly to Rahl's, that he be allowed the same access as you have granted me. As a mage-guard, he will remain in uniform, and thus there should be no misapprehensions that the intent of the orders of the magisters is being disregarded." The older ordermage smiled politely.

"I suppose, under those conditions . . . but we would ask that Rahl refrain from any active order-magery."

Rahl inclined his head. "Except in self-defense or as requested by Taryl or the magisters."

The hint of a sour expression crossed Tamryn's face. "That would be acceptable."

"What about the crew?" asked Taryl.

"With the exception of any chaos-mages—"

"There are none aboard," replied Taryl. "We understand those limitations."

". . . we would suggest that they remain close to the harbor area, but they can travel where they will within the black wall."

Taryl nodded.

Tamryn did not quite look at Rahl before he continued. "Either I or another black mage will be here for you both with a wagon at one glass past midday." He inclined his head to Taryl. "Good day, Senior Mage-Guard, and welcome to Nylan." He did not ever look directly at Rahl.

"Thank you."

Rahl merely nodded. Tamryn's presence had rekindled his anger at the close-mindedness and arrogance of the magisters, particularly the rage against Puvort, whose deception and smugness had triggered all the events that had led to Rahl's exile.

Once Tamryn was on the pier and headed toward the trap he had driven down, Taryl looked to Rahl with an amused smile. "He wasn't exactly pleased with you."

"No. I was a problem for them, especially after I exploded a section of the black wall by accident." He paused. "I'm not exactly pleased with them, either."

"That was obvious." The older mage looked hard at Rahl. "How did you do that to the wall?"

"I was just poking around, trying to see how they'd

used order to link all the stones together. They kept telling me to investigate things."

Taryl shook his head. "Telling that to a beginning natural ordermage is about as smart as having a beginning gunner play with cammabark or powder. Do you know why?"

"I felt that, but I couldn't explain why."

"When a true ordermage creates black iron or something like the black wall, what he's doing is essentially confining chaos within order. The more order and chaos involved, the stronger the structure or material, but . . ." Taryl looked to Rahl.

"The more it can explode if the order's unlinked?"

"Exactly." Taryl shook his head again. "Idiots . . ."

"You don't have much respect for them, do you, ser?"

"As individuals, yes, but not as a land. They work as much against each other as against other lands, although they would claim otherwise."

Rahl wasn't so certain about that. He thought it might be true of the magisters he'd known, but some of the engineers and even Anitra the machinist had seemed to work together, but then, he hadn't actually worked with the engineers.

"I need to go over what I will say about matters, Rahl, and how best to address the magisters," Taryl said. "I'll meet you in the mess later."

"Yes, ser."

While Rahl had thought about leaving the frigate, he decided against it, at least until after their mission was completed. Instead, he spent the time reviewing in his mind exactly what had occurred in Swartheld with Shyret and Daelyt.

Then, after a quick meal, he donned the dress mage-guard uniform he had never worn. The trousers were still khaki, but of a far finer grade of wool, rather than cotton, and the shirt was crimson, rather than khaki, with khaki shoulder straps holding embroidered mage-guard insignia.

The visor cap was the same as his working cap, except that the bill was high-gloss polished black leather, and all the insignia were gold-plated, rather than bronze.

He met Taryl on the quarterdeck, and they walked down the gangway to meet Tamryn.

The silver-haired magister's eyes again slid away from Rahl, and he said little to either mage-guard on the drive up to the training center. When he brought the wagon to a halt, Rahl studied the long, black-stone building, with the black-slate roof tiles. It was much as he remembered it, save that it looked smaller than he recalled.

"This way, envoys, if you please."

As Tamryn stepped into the building, Taryl murmured, "Remember, don't use any shields when you speak. They have to feel as well as hear the truth of your words."

"Yes, ser."

The chamber to which Tamryn escorted them was the same hearing chamber in which Rahl had been exiled. The same long, black-lorken table stood at one end, with the four chairs behind it. This time all were occupied.

Tamryn stepped to one side and bowed before speaking. "Magisters Lecoyat, Severyna, and Myanelyt, and Magistra Leyla, might I present Envoy and Senior Mage-Guard Taryl and his assistant Mage-Guard Rahl."

Even before Tamryn had made his introductions, Rahl recognized one of the magisters and the magistra—the gray-haired Myanelyt and Leyla, although neither looked directly at him.

Taryl stepped forward, bowing slightly, if gracefully. "Greetings. We are here on behalf of the Emperor and in the shared interests of assuring that our lands remain on amicable terms, and on behalf of His Majesty, we offer his felicitations and best wishes." Taryl smiled, and paused before continuing. "If you have not already received word from your own traders, you will shortly, I am most certain. The Nylan Merchant Association compound in Swartheld was totally destroyed by an explosion and fire as a result of actions by the Association director there and Jeranyi merchant vessel crews smuggled into the compound. Many of the Jeranyi died in the explosion, and the subsequent explosion of one of their vessels, but before they did, these same Jeranyi had earlier killed all those in the Nylan Merchant Association to cover their trail. When I am done, Rahl here, with whom some of you are familiar, will explain how this happened in detail, since he is the only one left alive who was a witness." Taryl paused just long enough to clear his throat. "That destruction was only the first part of a Jeranyi plan to burn the entire merchanting district of Swartheld and possibly even to set Hamor and Recluce against each other."

"But . . . what would they gain?" murmured Lecoyat.

"What you may not know is that the Emperor is dealing with an insurrection in the province of Merowey, and that insurrection is tacitly being supported by the white mages of Fairhaven, we believe, as well as the Jeranyi. Had the destruction of Swartheld's harbor structures and warehouses been accomplished, the prices of Jeranyi goods would have increased markedly in value. More important, had you sent the black ships to Hamor, there would have been far fewer patrols to deal with Jeranyi pirates. As it is, the Emperor has been forced to cut back many of our patrols in order to shut down efforts to supply the rebels in Merowey."

"So you want us to take up the entire burden of dealing with the Jeranyi cutthroats?" asked Severyna.

"The Emperor would not wish to imply or impose any duty on Recluce. All we can say is that at present Hamor cannot deal as aggressively with such pirates as we have done in the past." Before any of the others could speak, Taryl stepped toward the long table and extended an envelope to Myanelyt. "This contains a more elaborate written version of what we have conveyed to you. It is a copy of the official and complete report on what occurred.

The Emperor felt that you should have a copy as well."
He turned toward Rahl. "Now, Mage-Guard Rahl will
provide some of the details. These should be of particular interest to you." Taryl inclined his head to Rahl.

Rahl gave a polite half bow before speaking. "Magisters and magistra, as some of you know, I am an exile
from Nylan, and I was sent as a clerk to the Nylan Merchant Association in Swartheld. At that time, Director
Shyret was in charge there. I had not been there more than
two eightdays when I became aware that the director was
declaring excessive spoilage, then selling these 'spoiled'
goods in local markets and pocketing the golds. The
amounts were not small. At least, they did not seem so to
me. On a single cargo, the director might declare two
kegs of madder or indigo as spoiled, along with a bale or
two of prime black wool. This was never less than thirty
golds a cargo, and could be in excess of a hundred."

"Between thirty and a hundred golds a cargo?" asked
Leyla.

"Yes, magistra." Rahl paused. "In addition, I discovered something else rather unusual. Director Shyret was
receiving barrels labeled as Feyn River pickles and storing them at the warehouses, but these barrels were never
shipped on Recluce vessels, but always on Jeranyi vessels . . ." Rahl went on to explain how he had been attacked one night, then drugged with nemysa only days
later and lost all his memories and ended up in the ironworks, before Taryl had helped him recover his memories, then trained him and sent him back to Swartheld.
He also told how he had realized that the barrels of
"pickles" had actually contained cammabark packed in
vinegar to keep it from exploding . . . and finally what
had occurred after he had discovered the Jeranyi raiders
and set off the cammabark in the Merchant Association
courtyard. ". . . I managed to set off the powder in that
one ship, but I had to jump into the harbor, and it took a
while for me to recover."

The four exchanged glances. Finally, Leyla spoke.

"You're admitting that you killed a superior officer and effectively destroyed our merchant compound?"

"Yes, magistra. Undercaptain Craelyt had already killed the captain, and he was working with the Jeranyi. If I hadn't set off the cammabark in the Merchant Association compound, we might have lost much of the harbor area."

After that, there were more questions.

"Can you be absolutely certain that Director Shyret was involved?"

"How did you know the Jeranyi were using these . . . pickle barrels?"

"Wasn't there any other way to stop them?"

"Why didn't you bring this to the attention of your superiors earlier?"

"Were there other indications that might have allowed earlier actions?"

Rahl answered each question as thoroughly and honestly as he could, trying not to become even more irritated by their skepticism and arrogance.

And finally, "Do you honestly expect us to believe this?"

At that point, Taryl cleared his throat. "You are all black mages. You all *know* that Rahl and I are telling the truth. You also should know that the Emperor would not send us across an entire ocean if he did not respect you and believe you should know the facts. We could easily have claimed that the fire and explosion were accidental and sent no one. Such fires do occur."

"Why *are* you here, then?" asked Myanelyt.

"To confirm for you that the Jeranyi were working through your own director, and, as Rahl tells me the magisters in Land's End have already acknowledged and acted upon, that the Jeranyi do not have the best interests of Recluce in mind. We also wished to confirm by our presence, and by our allowing you to question us as necessary, that they were using your facilities to strike against Hamor. We thought you should know this and that you should learn of it in a manner in which you could verify the truth for yourselves. It is well-known that no one can lie to the magisters of Nylan without it being more than obvious to them."

Finally, Myanelyt rose and bowed. "Envoy Taryl, you have been more than patient, and we appreciate your forbearance. We will convey these findings to the Merchant Association as well. While it is premature for us to make any decisions, not until we have evaluated what you have presented, if matters are as you have indicated, it would seem unlikely that we would wish to engage in any actions that would be interpreted as hostile. We wish you a speedy and safe return to Hamor."

"Thank you," replied Taryl. "It is likely that we will depart tomorrow, but that will depend upon the weather and whether Captain Jaracyn has been able to fill all the bunkers."

All the Nylan mages rose, concluding the meeting. Rahl followed Taryl from the chamber.

Tamryn was waiting in the corridor outside. "I would be happy to drive you back to your ship."

"I will avail myself of that offer," Taryl said.

As they walked out of the building, Rahl looked to Taryl, and said in a low voice, "Would you mind if . . . ?"

Taryl laughed softly. "I thought you might. Just remember that Captain Jaracyn will wish to leave close to dawn tomorrow."

"Because the *Ascadya* is needed in Hamor? To deal with the rebellion?"

"And more, I fear." Taryl smiled. "There's a lady, isn't there?"

"She's a healer."

The older mage reached into his belt wallet, then extended a coin. "Take her to dinner, and be back on board before midnight."

Rahl almost swallowed as he realized Taryl had given him a gold. "You . . ."

"No, I don't, but you conducted yourself well, and we

were provided coins in case of need. This is a need." Taryl nodded. "Nothing in life is certain, and you may never see her again. So give her something she can remember."

Rahl could sense Tamryn's amazement and concern, but he just smiled, then watched as the magister drove Taryl back toward the black ship piers. After a moment, he turned and began to walk toward the infirmary.

He could sense the puzzled gazes as he passed the mess and turned westward on the stone walk. When he entered the foyer, he recognized the younger healer. "Kelyssa?"

She looked at him, staring at the unfamiliar dress uniform, as if she could not remember but should. She started to frown, as if to suggest that he was not welcome.

"I'm Rahl. Is Deybri here?"

"Rahl?" Kelyssa's mouth opened, but she said nothing for several long moments. "Rahl?"

"The same one you had to pick up off the weapons training floor," he added. "Is Deybri around?"

"Is someone asking for me?"

Rahl turned at the sound of her voice.

As Deybri walked toward him, Rahl just watched, taking in the brown hair, the gold-flecked brown eyes, and the warmth within.

She stopped two cubits from him, then laughed, abruptly, but warmly.

Rahl could sense that she was pleased, but not exactly why, and he found himself smiling, if quizzically.

"Oh, Rahl . . . that look was the greatest compliment I've ever had."

He found himself flushing. "You deserve it."

"That's a Hamorian mage-guard uniform, isn't it? You didn't mention that in your letter." Her eyes did not quite meet his.

"I wasn't a mage-guard then. I was working to be one, but I didn't know if I'd make it, and I wrote as soon as I could . . . after . . . everything happened."

"Everything?"

"Is it possible that I could take you to dinner some-where? I only have tonight. Then I could tell you . . ."

"I . . ." Deybri turned and looked at Kelyssa. "Would you?"

"How could I not?" The younger healer grinned. "It'll make a great story."

"Kelyssa . . ."

"Someday, anyway," added Kelyssa.

Deybri looked hard at the other healer.

"In a few years?"

Deybri nodded.

Rahl managed not to grin as he turned and accompa-nied Deybri. Outside the infirmary, he glanced sideways at her once more. If anything, she was more beautiful than he recalled.

"Before I forget," Deybri said, "I did send a letter to your parents—"

"Oh . . . can I post one from here, if I pay for it? I wrote one to them on the ship."

"We could stop by the bursar's study," Deybri said. "It might cost a copper or two more, but it would be easier than going down to the Merchant Association."

"That might be best, for several reasons."

"Oh?"

"That's part of the everything I'm going to tell you."

Deybri led the way back to the main building and down a side corridor off the main corridor and on the east side—well away from where Rahl and Taryl had met with the magisters.

The bursar, an older woman in dark gray, looked up with a clearly startled expression on her face as Rahl and Deybri appeared in the door to her study.

"Elyssa?" Deybri said with a smile. "This is Rahl. He was trained here, and he's now a mage-guard in Hamor, but his ship is in port here. He wanted to send a letter to his parents in Land's End. He can just pay you, can't he?"

"Oh . . . that won't be a problem." The graying bursar tilted her head. "From what I heard, he's not just an ordinary mage-guard."

Rahl found himself flushing as he extended the envelope. "How much will it be?"

"Oh . . . not that much. Four coppers. We'll just put it in with everything to the portmaster at Land's End." Elyssa took the envelope and the coppers from Rahl. "Good hand, best I've seen in years."

"I was once a scrivener," Rahl admitted.

"It shows."

"Thank you." Rahl inclined his head.

"That's what we're here for . . . among other things."

Deybri was smiling and shaking her head as they walked back outside into the late-midafternoon sunlight filtering intermittently through scattered clouds to the west.

Rather than ask what Deybri was thinking, Rahl took a half silver from his wallet. "Thank you for letting my parents know. I said I'd repay you when I could. Will this do?"

"It's more than enough. It's—"

"It's not," Rahl said. "I can't thank you enough." He pressed the small coin on her.

Deybri finally took it. They walked on the west sidewalk of the stone-paved road that led down to the harbor, leaving the training center behind.

"You don't mind walking, do you?" Rahl asked, after they passed an older large stone dwelling he did not remember. "I'd thought we could get an early meal at the place where your uncle took us . . ."

"If you let me pay for myself."

Rahl shook his head. "I was given coins for a meal here. There's enough for both of us."

"So long as you're not paying. Mage-guards aren't wealthy. I do know that."

"The pay's not bad, better than what I would have

gotten as a journeyman scrivener in Land's End." And far better than he'd gotten as a clerk at the Merchant Association or as checker at the ironworks. "How have you been?" He really wanted to tell her that the past did have a hold on him, but something told him not to rush that, and not to blurt it out—much as he wanted to do just that.

"I'm fine. Nothing much has changed here. Thankfully, we haven't had anything like that boiler explosion since you left. I understand that the harbormaster has refused landing to several older ships. They've had to moor offshore."

"Did they ever fix the black wall?"

Deybri laughed. "About a season after you left. Tamryn and Kadara were muttering about it for weeks after that."

Across the road from them, a patroller stopped and stared, clearly startled by a couple where the woman was in the green of a healer and the man in a Hamorian dress uniform.

"You still do manage to startle people, I see," Deybri said.

"They're just not used to seeing Hamorian mageguards. We might be the first ever actually to walk through Nylan."

"That's possible. Where is your ship?"

"At the naval piers. The engineers moved out all the black ships. We came on a frigate—the *Ascadya.* I think the idea was to get us here quickly on a warship to convey the presence and concerns of the Emperor, but on one that wouldn't be seen as a threat."

Rahl glanced to his right, toward the small park he had often passed on his way to the harbor. He had thought he might see children playing hoop tag, but the only person in the park was an elderly man feeding bread crumbs to the traitor birds.

"You've been through a lot, haven't you?" she asked softly.

"It has been a long year," he admitted. "The hardest part was finding out that Shyret was betraying Recluce and not being able to do anything about it."

"Oh?"

"The Hamorian Codex doesn't look at things in the same way. There are great penalties for selling shoddy goods or spoiled ones, or for misrepresenting them. But there are no penalties for things like what Shyret was doing. He was telling the Association here that a portion of the goods had spoiled, and then selling them on the side. So the Association had to take the losses . . ." Rahl tried to explain what had happened and why it wasn't against Hamorian law, and how he had had no real proof of what Shyret was doing. ". . . and it would only have been my word against his. That was why I'd decided to see the mage-guards on oneday." He shook his head wryly. "You'd think I'd have learned not to wait on something like that. That was how I ended up in Nylan, you know. I waited till oneday to see Magister Puvort in Land's End."

"There's a fine line between when to wait and when not to," Deybri said quietly.

That, Rahl had learned, but he wasn't sure he could always discern when to wait and when not to. He gestured toward the lane on the east side of the road. "Your house is down there, isn't it?"

"It is. Well . . . it's not really mine. It's Uncle Thorl's, and I pay him rent. Healers at the training center don't make that many coins, either."

"Oh . . . I didn't know."

"You wouldn't have, Rahl. I never told you."

There was so much about her that he really didn't know, Rahl reflected, and yet . . . beyond all that, there was something beyond her warmth and beauty that drew him to her. But, to say that would be so presumptuous . . . but would he ever have another chance to utter such words in person?

As they entered the restaurant, Rahl saw a slender

graying man with his back to the entrance talking to a server. Even so, Rahl recognized him. As before, the proprietor was dressed in spotless khaki trousers and shirt, but this time his vest was chartreuse edged in silver thread.

"Kysant, I know you may not have a table," began Rahl in Hamorian, with an apologetic smile, "but I would be most grateful . . ."

The proprietor turned . . . and froze, looking at the mage-guard uniform. After a long moment, Kysant looked from Deybri to Rahl and back to Deybri.

"He's from Recluce, Kysant," Deybri said softly. "He's eaten here with Thorl, and he was exiled for a time. So they sent him back as an envoy to the magisters."

"Would it help if I spoke Temple?" Rahl asked in that language, accompanied by a sheepish grin.

"You . . . startled me, ser. You . . ."

"Could we just have a table?" Rahl asked. "The last meal I had here was so good . . ."

"Oh . . . of course . . ." Kysant escorted them to a corner table, one with no one seated nearby, not that there were many in the place, not when it was still late afternoon and not an end-day. He seated Deybri.

Rahl sat across from her.

"Can I get you something to drink?" asked Kysant.

Rahl looked to Deybri. "Leshak?"

She nodded.

"Two, please."

After the proprietor hurried away, Deybri looked to Rahl. "You scared Kysant. He saw you in that uniform, and it terrified him."

"I think his parents must have told terrible stories about the mage-guards," reflected Rahl. "He didn't grow up in Hamor, from what your uncle said."

"That's true." She paused, as if uncertain what to say next.

Rahl could see Kysant preparing a pitcher and two tall

goblets. "Kysant will be back with our drinks before long. Why don't you order for us both?"

"You trust me with that?" The words were accompanied with a smile.

"I'd trust you with far more than that, and you know it."

"You do make things difficult, you know?"

Rahl wasn't quite sure how to respond to that. So he just shrugged . . . helplessly.

Kysant returned with a tray that held the glass pitcher of leshak and two crystal goblets, then set a goblet before each and half-filled both goblets.

"Kysant," said Rahl with a smile, "you can tell people that your place is so good that a Hamorian mage-guard traveled all the way here to eat."

"Ah . . . yes, ser. Have you decided . . . a light lunch . . . or more?"

Rahl nodded to Deybri.

"The pashtaki and kasnya for appetizers, and the cumin fowl with sweet rice, with a side of biastras . . ."

Rahl watched and listened. Once Kysant had left, he lifted his goblet. "To the loveliest healer in Recluce."

Deybri actually blushed. Then she shook her head. "You're impossible."

"You already knew that."

She sipped the leshak, and so did Rahl. It was better than he recalled, smooth and cool, bearing hints of pear-apple, greenberries, honey, and an even tinier trace of pine.

"How did you know that I was an envoy?" he asked after several moments. "I hadn't gotten around to telling you."

She smiled. "You've changed. Once that would have been one of the first things you said."

"It didn't seem so important. Not now." Rahl waited for her to go on.

"Tamryn told everyone that the Emperor had sent two

envoys to Nylan, and that they were both black mage-
guards. Everyone was cautioned to be most courteous."
Deybri laughed. "I had no idea you were one of them."

"They sent me because I'm the only one who knew
about the smuggling and the theft in the Nylan Merchant
Association in Swartheld. That was how I ended up in the
ironworks at Luba. Director Shyret dosed me with nemysa because he didn't know I was a sort of mage . . ."
Rahl went on to outline quickly his progression from
loader to clerk to mage-clerk and finally to mage-guard.
". . . couldn't have done it if Taryl had not found ways to
help me regain some of my abilities, and to train some of
the others."

At that point, he stopped because Kysant arrived with
a large circular platter bearing the deep-fried pashtakis
and what looked to be small pastry crescents.

"Uncle Thorl doesn't like kasnya." Deybri picked up
one of the crescents. "He thinks they're bland, but their
taste is just more subtle."

Rahl took one and nibbled it. After a moment, he nodded. The taste was a combination of almond and other
spices that he could not identify, but he enjoyed the flavor. "It's good. I like it."

"You're not just saying that?"

"No. Especially with you, I wouldn't do that."

Rahl enjoyed the appetizers, but not so much as just
looking at Deybri.

At that moment, Kysant escorted three men into the
room, seating them at a round table in the corner farthest
from Rahl and Deybri. One was clearly a trader, and he
kept looking at Rahl, finally murmuring something to the
others.

"You'll have everyone in Nylan talking for eightdays
after you've left," said Deybri in a low voice.

"It might help Kysant." Rahl didn't really want to think
about leaving.

Before he could say more, Kysant arrived with the main
course—the cumin fowl and the biastras.

The fowl breasts had been cut into thin strips, then braised and laid on a bed of sticky rice. Deybri served them each several strips and rice.

Rahl found the meat tender, moist, and piquant—as well as slightly smoky and pearapple sweet. The rice carried the same flavors, with a hint of crunchiness. "I like this."

"I'm glad."

While Rahl was careful to wrap the spicy biastra in the thin flat bread, after a mouthful he realized that it was nowhere near as hot and spicy as he had recalled. Then he glanced across at Deybri, who had taken a cloth and was blotting her forehead.

"These are spicier," she said, "and you're not even noticing." She laughed softly. "That's another way you've changed. I still remember the expression on your face when you took the first bite of a biastra."

"I've had to eat hot food for more than a year. Some of it wouldn't have been edible if I'd been able to taste it."

"Luba? That must have been awful."

"I wouldn't recommend it to anyone," Rahl said slowly, "but it wasn't as bad as people say. The guards and over-seers were more patient than you'd think. I once watched a mage-guard tell an overseer that if he didn't take better care of his men, he'd be one of them."

"I wouldn't be surprised if it was every bit as bad as they say," Deybri replied. "You just learned how to handle it."

"I suppose I did, but I only saw one or two cases where the overseers were cruel, and I wasn't the only loader who got promoted to checker."

"Checker?"

"A low-level clerk who keeps track of the iron shipments. That was how Taryl found me." Rahl went on to explain, concluding, ". . . and I was reading about Recluce and the magisters when the rest of my memories came back, and I sent word to Taryl, and I became a clerk at the mage-guard station. As soon as I had enough coins, I wrote you."

Deybri just nodded.

After several long moments of silence, Rahl said, "Thank you again for letting my parents know." He managed a smile.

"You could have sent a letter to them . . . rather than me."

"I could have, but I could only afford one letter," Rahl said slowly, looking across the table into her gold-flecked brown eyes. "You told me that the past had no hold on me. That might have been true once. It's not any longer. It hasn't been for a long time, now."

Deybri met his eyes without looking away. "I know."

"And?"

"Rahl . . . you have come back to Nylan, and you may again . . . but already, you are not truly of Recluce . . . or even of Nylan."

"You might be right, but why do you say that?"

"You're different. Stronger within. I don't mean in order, although that is also true, and it may come that you will become even more powerful in time." She paused as Kysant arrived to take the empty plates and platters.

Rahl realized that the light had dimmed in the room because it was twilight outside. He hadn't really paid any attention.

"Any sweets?" asked the proprietor.

"The orange cake, if you have it. Two slices," replied Deybri.

"An excellent choice, lady." Kysant bowed, but his eyes avoided Rahl.

Once Kysant had left, Deybri added, "I like it because it's sweet, but not cloying."

"And there's no aftertaste of the rest of the meal?"

She nodded.

"I'm different now," Rahl prompted her. "That's what you were saying."

"You think you love me. That's obvious, and I can't tell you how flattering it is to have someone as talented and handsome as you are in love with me. But . . . it won't work out."

Rahl could sense the turmoil within her. What could he say? "I'm not asking that. I'm only telling you what I feel."

"Rahl . . . I told you I had to spend time as a healer in Hamor. I was in Atla. I can't tell you how unhappy I was. I kept counting the eightdays, and I almost ran to the ship that took me back to Nylan. You . . . you're strong. I'm not. I know I'm not. I'm not worthy of you." Her eyes were bright in the dimming light of the dining chamber.

"You're more than worthy of anyone. Not feeling comfortable in a strange land when you're young isn't exactly weakness. I didn't feel at all comfortable in Swartheld for the whole time I was first there." He offered a smile. "Besides, you feel something for me."

"I always have." She looked down for a moment. "That doesn't change anything. You won't come back to Nylan, and I can't live in Hamor."

"Healers are always welcome there," he said mildly.

"I don't feel welcome there." Her smile was strained. "Can we leave it at that?"

"Until after the orange cake." Rahl forced a smile.

"You don't deceive any better than I do." An unsteady laugh followed her words.

"I'm not trying to deceive anyone. I couldn't come here and not tell you how I feel. The letter . . . I didn't want to say too much, or not enough . . ." He shook his head.

"You said enough."

"Too much?"

Deybri was the one to shake her head. "If you were an engineer here, even a stevedore on the docks, I wouldn't hesitate a moment to consort you."

Rahl could sense the cost of the admission. "But I'm not, and you're not someone who can do things halfway or partway or with an ocean between us."

"No. I can't. I just can't . . . and I hate myself for that weakness . . . but I can't."

Rahl considered her words. Her ability to recognize where she was weak was another strength, and held an honesty he had not considered.

Kysant reappeared with two small plates. "Would you like a brandy or something hot, as well?"

Rahl looked to Deybri, catching the slightest shake of her head before replying. "No, thank you."

Neither Rahl nor Deybri said anything as they slowly ate.

"The cake is better than the khouros, I think," Rahl said after finishing the last moist crumbs on his plate.

Deybri smiled. "I think so, too, but Uncle Thorl doesn't. But he's never liked oranges. That might be because his father had an orchard, and Thorl's job was to take care of the spoiled and rotten ones."

"I can see that might give him less liking for oranges," replied Rahl with a laugh.

"That's just the excuse he gives." She paused just slightly. "He does ask if I hear from you. He said you were one of his best students, that you had the gift for languages."

"He has the gift of teaching them."

"He's never asked about anyone else."

"That's because he's never had another student in love with his niece," Rahl answered lightly.

"Please . . . Rahl. No more. Not now."

"For now. How is Aleasya?"

"She's close to becoming an arms magistra, I think. Before she does, though, she'll have to learn more about order and how it affects weapons."

"Has she started building that house yet?"

"Not so far . . ."

In the end, the dinner cost three silvers, with a tip, and Rahl felt strange keeping the seven, but he'd return them to Taryl the next day.

He did offer Deybri his arm once they left the restaurant, and she took it, gently. They walked through the early evening, uphill toward her small dwelling. Rahl tried to keep his words away from what he really felt.

". . . never realized how small Recluce is . . . almost as far from just Swartheld to Cigoerne as it is from Land's End to Feyn . . ."

Deybri fell silent, and Rahl quickly went on. "I saw my first Kaordist Temple in Swartheld . . . all the words about twinners suddenly made sense. You know that they have twin spires, one that's twisted and strange . . . and that's the female one . . ."

"Why doesn't that surprise me?" She shook her head.

"Men think of women as chaotic everywhere, you think?"

"In most places, from what I've heard and seen."

"I don't."

"You're one of the few," she said dryly.

All too soon, they reached the low stoop before her front door.

Deybri let go of Rahl's arm and stepped back. "I know I must be a disappointment to you. You've crossed an ocean and laid your heart at my feet. But . . ."

Rahl could sense the unshed tears as he looked at her standing before the doorway . . . so strong, and yet, in ways, so fragile. "Thank you for this afternoon and to-night." What else could he say? That there would be no one else? That sounded stupid. That without her, life seemed empty. True as it felt, that was almost as bad. He swallowed, then took her hands in his hoping, that she would not mind. "You know how I feel . . ."

"Rahl . . . I can't . . . I can't do this." Tears streamed down her face. "When will I see you again? A year from now? Five? Ten?"

He had no answer to that. Mage-guards, even senior ones, had neither the time nor the coins to make personal voyages across the Eastern Ocean. And—after having seen Tamryn's reaction to his presence—he doubted that he would ever meet the magisters' criteria for returning permanently to Recluce. Yet . . . how could he leave Deybri?

He wanted to shake his head. He knew she had some feeling for him, more than just some feeling, or she would not be crying, but . . .

She raised her hand, and her fingers touched the side of his face and then his cheek. "I told you before . . ."

"You did." His voice was ragged. "But . . . it didn't help much. Not to forget you. When I was in Luba, even before I remembered who I was, I had dreams of you." He forced a laugh, but the sound was shaky. "I kept hearing and seeing you say that the past had no hold on me, and it was so strange because you were all I could remember of the past."

Abruptly, her arms were around him. "Hold me. Just hold me."

He did.

In the end, that night, it was all he did, except mingle tears with her, before he finally left and walked the long and lonely way back to the *Ascadya*.

IV

Although Rahl took a long time to fall asleep in the small ship's cabin he had to himself, he did not sleep well and was up close to dawn. He washed up, dressed in his everyday uniform, and made his way to the bridge, to watch as Captain Jaracyn readied the frigate for departure from Nylan. A faint mist lay on the harbor's surface, but it ended only a cubit or so above the water, and there was no sign of fog or mist out in the Gulf of Candar west of the harbor.

As the gangway was hoisted aboard and smoke began to issue from the funnels, Rahl lifted his eyes from the ship and the piers to the black city, lit by the orangish first rays of the sun. The expanses of green between the black-stone roads and buildings seemed more vivid in the early light, and the shadows somehow both darker and more indistinct. From where he stood, he could not see Deybri's small cottage, a dwelling he had never even entered.

He could understand how she felt. His first eightdays in Swartheld had been difficult, and they hadn't gotten any easier for almost a year, no thanks to the magisters in both Land's End and Nylan. In one respect, both sets of Recluce magisters were alike—they didn't want anyone different around, and they didn't want to change their ways.

He pursed his lips, thinking. He hadn't seen that people were that much different in Hamor. So why were the mage-guards more tolerant? Was it because Hamor was so much larger that there were places for different people? Or was it because all mages were closely supervised? Or because there were fewer mages for the number of people, and they were seen as more necessary? Or were they really more tolerant? Was he just seeing what he wanted to see?

"You're deep in thought," observed Taryl, joining him on the open wing of the bridge. "Did you have a good dinner?"

"Dinner was good. So was the company." Rahl fumbled with his wallet. "I owe you some silvers. It didn't take nearly so much as you gave me."

Taryl held up his hand. "Keep it. We were each given a gold for incidentals. Usually, what we get for these sorts of expenses is never enough. Just be thankful that it was."

Rahl sensed the truth of the angular mage's words, but keeping the silvers bothered him.

"Believe me, Rahl, you'll spend more out of your own wallet for the mage-guards than you'll ever get back." Taryl smiled. "You weren't out that late."

"No. There wasn't much point in it. She wasn't terribly

impressed with Hamor when she was there, and Recluce isn't exactly impressed with me."

"If you keep working on your order-skills, you'll gain enough control to meet even their standards. You can already meet many of them, in areas such as shielding yourself from sight and making your way in total darkness."

What Taryl wasn't saying, but what Rahl understood, was that the magisters would probably find another reason to keep him from returning to Nylan.

"Do you think you'd be happy and useful in Nylan," asked Taryl, "especially when the magisters in the north might not allow you to return there?"

"I thought so."

"And now?"

"Probably not. If it weren't for Deybri, I wouldn't be considering it."

"Do you know how she feels?"

"She's torn between me and not wanting to leave Recluce."

Taryl nodded. "That could be a hard decision, especially for a healer."

Rahl almost said that she shouldn't have had to make such a decision, and wouldn't have if the magisters had been fair, but he curbed the words, only saying, "I don't think she'll leave Nylan."

"If you love her, don't give up on her," Taryl said.

Rahl had the feeling that far more emotion lay behind the older mage's words, but he wasn't about to ask.

"Lines in!" came the order from the ship's duty officer.

Slowly, the *Ascadya* eased away from the pier, stern first, until she was out into the main channel.

"Forward a quarter . . ."

For several moments, the ship seemed not to move. Then she gained headway, straightening on a westward course that took her out the center of the channel, past the black-stone pillars that marked the ends of both the north and the south breakwaters. Rahl wanted to look back, but did not.

Standing well to the west of the harbor was one of the black ships, its lines low and menacing. From what Rahl judged, it was slightly longer than the *Ascadya,* but nowhere as large as the Hamorian cruiser he had seen at the naval piers in Swartheld.

"Do they have larger black ships?" he asked Taryl.

"Not that we know of. Some of the newer ones are slightly larger in length and beam than that one, but they're all effectively about the same size. That makes it easier to maintain and supply them. The shells and rockets are the same for all vessels."

"Rockets?"

"They use incendiary rockets when necessary. That's probably one reason why the Jeranyi pirates have gone to iron-hulled vessels." Taryl smiled wryly. "There's word now that the black ships are using black-iron-penetrating tips on some rockets."

"They're working on a new kind of engine, too," Rahl said. "I don't understand it, but one of the engineers said it would be lighter and stronger and allow a ship to move faster."

Taryl frowned. "Are they actually building it?"

"No, ser. They weren't when I left. It was something one of the junior engineers had thought up."

Taryl laughed, ironically. "It will be years before we see it, if then."

"Why?"

"Even if it's a good idea, turning it into hard metal takes years, and that's if there aren't any problems with it . . . and if the junior engineer doesn't have to argue with those who know better."

"Like the senior engineers?"

Taryl shook his head. "Most of the time, those who get to be senior engineers are willing to look at a new idea. They'll be skeptical, but they'll look. It's the ones in the middle. They'll either try to stop it or steal it. The same

thing is often true with armsmen and other military officers." He paused. "Not exactly. Very junior undercaptains
usually don't know what they're doing, not unless they're
former rankers, but older and senior majers from distinguished families with Imperial connections are to be
avoided as much as possible. So are older senior mage-
guards. They have a great similarity to the magisters of
Land's End."

Even in Hamor?

"Now . . . I have another exercise for you." Taryl
smiled. "We're headed aft to the fantail, and you're going
to attempt to 'tag' some pieces of wood and follow them
with your order-senses when I drop them off the stern."
At that, the senior mage-guard turned and headed for the
ladder down to the main deck.

Rahl saw that Taryl was carrying the satchel that usually meant some other exercise. After a moment, the
younger mage followed. Why did Taryl keep pushing
him?

Cigoerne

V

If anything, Captain Jaracyn pushed the *Ascadya* even more on the return voyage to Swartheld. The seas were rougher, and Rahl was a touch queasy, for the first time.

Late on threeday, the northwestern cliffs of Hamor came into view, and before long Rahl could see the late-afternoon sun reflecting off the great northwest lighthouse, a spire above the white cliffs. The swells were high enough that a wide line of white foam marked Heartbreak Reef.

"I'm glad we're almost back," Taryl said from where he stood on the wing of the bridge beside Rahl.

As he took in the lighthouse, Rahl recalled what Captain Liedra had told him on his first trip to Hamor. "The merchant captains think that Hamor's never recovered from what Creslin did after he founded Recluce. Is that true?"

Taryl laughed. "It is, but not in the way they would think. Hamor's never forgotten the lesson he taught us."

Lesson?

"Good tactics, magery, and new ways of doing things will usually defeat someone who merely relies on what has worked in the past. Why do you think we keep improving our ships? Or trying to use every mage we have, rather than just exiling or executing the ones who are difficult to train or don't fit into predetermined roles and patterns?"

"I don't think they see it that way."

"All the better for us. They think we avoid conflict with them because we fear their black ships, but that's not the real reason. Oh, the black ships could cause considerable damage, but we could build a score of these frigates in the time it would take them to build one black ship, and a half score of our new fast frigates could probably take out two of their ships."

"Then . . ." Rahl wasn't sure he wanted to ask the question.

"Why don't we attack Recluce and remove a problem? Because we'd gain nothing and lose a great deal. They provide goods we want. They send us black and white mages, and while they complain a lot, they don't attack our shipping, and they buy our goods. A war would cost us golds, ships, and trained men, and in the end, we'd either have to rebuild Recluce the way it was or lose more coins." Taryl shook his head. "Our navy's best use is to keep trade free and open, and to track down pirates and raiders. Or to keep people from attacking us or meddling."

"Like in the rebellion?"

Taryl snorted. "It's not true all the time, but most of the time, lands have far more problems within their borders than without. Often, even when they are attacked, such attacks come because of the problems they have within and have failed to address."

"Might I ask what problem caused the rebellion?"

"The failure of the previous emperor and of the present emperor to recognize that Golyat was not qualified to be emperor and too self-centered and ambitious to serve his brother for longer than it would take him to raise an army and golds enough for him to attempt to seize the throne."

"What would you have done?" asked Rahl.

"Had him perish as a young man while hunting some dangerous beast, then inform the Emperor of the unfortunate accident. Golyat is the kind who would only chafe in exile until he could find someone to back an invasion."

Rahl swallowed at the matter-of-fact tone—and the conviction within the older mage.

"You think I am cruel? That I have deceived you about who and what I am?" Taryl shook his head. "Hundreds have already died, and thousands will yet die. Crops and grasslands will be devastated. Hundreds, if not thousands, of women will become widows, and children will become orphans. Golds that could be spent on roads and reservoirs and other good works will be spent on weapons and supplies that would not be needed otherwise. The prices of food will rise, and the poor will become poorer. All this because a father and a son would not face the fact that a son and a brother cared for nothing but his own power and pleasure."

"But . . . to order the death of his own son?" Rahl protested.

"A ruler has a responsibility to those he rules, and one of those responsibilities is to assure that those who follow him provide good and just governance. Rebellions and civil wars do not do so, particularly when they are caused by an emperor's offspring."

Rahl just looked at Taryl.

The older mage sighed, then took a deep breath. "You killed Undercaptain Craelyt and at least a score of Jeranyi. Why?"

"Because the Jeranyi would have killed hundreds more."

"And the undercaptain?"

"Because he had killed the captain and . . . it wasn't right. You know that, ser."

"I do, indeed," replied Taryl, "and so does the Triad. Your actions prevented far greater harm. Now . . . is the Emperor more or less responsible for Hamor than are you?"

"More . . ." Rahl grudged.

"Then he has an even greater responsibility than you

do. If he is unwilling to do, or have done, what is best as a ruler, what right does he have to request that others behave honorably?"

"But . . . murder . . . fratricide? How is that just?"

"It is not just. That, I admit, and that is why the Emperor could not and should not do such," Taryl said. "If emperors are allowed such latitude, all too soon they will see anyone who opposes them in anything as a threat to be removed, and they will become corrupt."

Rahl realized, then, exactly what Taryl had said and meant. "The Triad and the High Command? They should have acted? Was that why . . . ?"

"The Triad and the High Command are supposed to act as a check upon the Emperor."

"You were involved, weren't you?"

"Let us just say that is why one member of the Triad died and one stepped down after recovering from his injuries. All Hamor will now suffer from that lack of resolution." Taryl looked directly at Rahl. "A good mage-guard always does his best. Sometimes, it is not enough. That does not mean the effort was wasted, for it must always be made. Bitter as it can be, those who risk all and fail, or only partly succeed, have held true to themselves. Those who weigh the odds and never try unless they have absolute certainty . . . they never know their true worth." The older mage-guard offered an ironic smile. "That's enough philosophy for now. Just remember that all loyalties have their prices, and make sure you understand what those prices are before you act."

Taryl gestured toward the southeast. "We'll be porting shortly, and I need to finish writing my report to the Emperor." He turned and headed down the ladder.

After Taryl had left, Rahl looked toward the stone lighthouse and the white cliffs beneath it.

VI

Fourday morning found Rahl following Taryl onto the
Khamyl—a river steamship headed for Cigoerne. The
two had spent the night before at the naval mage-guard
quarters in Swartheld, a space largely deserted, since
there was only one other warship ported at the naval
piers—an older coastal patroller—and two broad-beamed
iron-hulled cargo transports.

"The transports will be dispatched once we have word
that we have control of a deep-water port in Merowey,"
Taryl had said. "Golyat's forces control Sastak and
Nubyat."

Rahl had merely nodded, knowing only that the two
cities were ports in the southwestern part of the continent
that was Hamor. Still, the fact that the rebel chief held two
major ports suggested that the Emperor faced something
more like a civil war than a mere rebellion.

The *Khamyl* was smaller than the *Ascadya,* and Rahl
and Taryl shared a small room with two bunks. Taryl suggested that the upper was more appropriate for Rahl, and
the younger mage-guard had to agree. Small as their room
was, it was on the upper deck, the one reserved for those
passengers who were either wealthy or on official business of some sort.

Rahl and Taryl had taken a position on the starboard
railing of the upper deck, from where Rahl was observing the various commercial buildings on the south side
of Swartheld and trying to see if he could pick out where
the Nylan Merchant Association had stood.

"Rahl," Taryl said quietly, "in a moment, I'll be intro-
ducing you to someone."

As the older mage-guard spoke, Taryl tightened his
order shields to the point that Rahl could not determine
in the slightest what Taryl was feeling. Even before Rahl

turned, he followed Taryl's example, although he doubted
his shields were as effective.

A slender but muscular mage-guard walked along the
deck toward them. Those near him, the men in their ornately embroidered fharongs and the women in silks and
with head scarves of even more sheer shimmersilk, eased
away with a swiftness that they had not evidenced when
Rahl and Taryl had taken their place at the railing. From
more than twenty cubits away Rahl could sense the tight-
ness of the newcomer's shields, as well as note the quality of the cloth of his uniform. He did not seem to notice
Taryl or Rahl until Taryl cleared his throat.

"Cyphryt," said Taryl pleasantly, "what a pleasant surprise. It's rather distant from Cigoerne, and I would not
have expected to see you here."

"Nor I you," replied the round-faced and cheery-
looking mage-guard, who carried a strong aura of white
chaos. "But one must occasionally review rather unpleasant situations. As I am sure you know."

Taryl smiled and gestured. "Oh . . . this is Rahl. He's
been transferred from Swartheld to be my assistant."

Cyphryt gave a nod slightly more than perfunctory.
"You will learn much from Taryl, in more ways than most
would believe."

"And in more ways than I would have as well, ser,"
replied Rahl.

Cyphryt tilted his head slightly. "For an Atlan, you're
remarkably well spoken."

"As you suggested, ser, I've already learned a great deal
from Senior Mage-Guard Taryl." Rahl sensed that Cyphryt
harbored the same kind of arrogance as Puvort did . . .
and roused the same kind of anger within Rahl. Rahl nodded politely.

"That's always for the best." Cyphryt continued to
smile cheerfully. "I wish you both well. I understand
that, after the untimely and unfortunate death of Marshal
Charynat, the Emperor and the High Command have settled on Marshal Byrna to command the campaign. I would

have expected you to continue doing penance in Luba, Taryl, but the vast expanses of Merowey will do as well, I assume, after you do what you must in Cigoerne."

"We've been requested to report on our last commission."

"Ah, yes. Placating the black barbarians. So troublesome, but necessary. You do deal with unpleasantness so well and so patiently."

"As do you," replied Taryl.

"I can see that your . . . sabbatical . . . has done you well, Taryl, and that is for the best." Cyphryt nodded pleasantly. "I am certain I will see you in Cigoerne." With a continuing smile, he walked toward the rear of the upper deck, where he joined two younger mage-guards—both chaos-mages—at a table under the awning overlooking the lower rear deck. One was a striking red-haired woman.

Even Cyphryt's bearing and walk reminded Rahl of Puvort, although the two looked not in the slightest alike.

"I take it that Cyphryt is to be treated with the same care as . . . I did with Undercaptain Craelyt?"

"I would suggest even greater care. For all his outward cheerfulness, Cyphryt can muster more chaos with one finger in an instant than the late undercaptain could have with his entire being in an eightday."

"He is highly placed, also?"

"He is the administrative director of the Triad. Officially, he's not in the chain of command. That suits him and his approach, but in practice he has close to the same authority as the Mage-Guard Overcommander—without the accountability."

Rahl didn't know quite what else to say. It was clear that Taryl and Cyphryt disliked each other intensely.

"You will have to watch for him, now," Taryl went on. "He takes any remark that offers the slightest disagreement with him as a personal affront. He won't deign to deal with you personally, but it's more than likely that one of those who wishes to please him will attempt to make your life less pleasant. It will most probably be a woman, one such as Saulya—she's the redhead there."

Rahl kept his head lowered, as if he continued to study the shore, behind the *Khamyl,* but let his eyes and order-senses focus on Saulya. Like all the others at the table, she held firm shields, and there was a sense of coolness behind those shields. "She's cold."

"Others have not found her so," Taryl said dryly, "not until they tried to do her a favor of some sort, generally against the rules, and ended up in places where they did not wish to be."

"But . . . that sort of enticement . . . ?"

"As a mage-guard, Rahl, there is only one reason to break the rules or the Codex, and that is to prevent a greater harm. Anything else is just an excuse, and excuses are not acceptable." Taryl's voice softened as he went on. "You've already broken more than a few provisions of the Codex, if with reason and provocation, but it would be best if you avoided any minor infractions for some time to come." He laughed gently, but ironically. "Often the minor infractions cost more than the great ones."

Rahl had already come to understand that. He looked at Taryl. "Was Cyphryt correct about where you'll be assigned?"

"I'm certain he is. He prides himself on that." Taryl grinned, almost mischievously, and yet sadly. "That was one reason why I spoke to him. I'd only been told that we would be assigned to the land campaign under Marshal Charynat, and that the details would be forthcoming when we reached Cigoerne."

"You don't think Charynat's death was coincidental or accidental, do you?"

"I'd be very surprised if it happened to be," Taryl admitted. "He was an honest and capable commander. Such are always regarded with suspicion by rulers and would-be rulers, and by those who would manipulate both."

Such as Cyphryt, surmised Rahl.

"We will do what we can, as we can."

Rahl nodded slowly. Taryl had told him that he would not have learned more in remaining at Swartheld, but the older mage-guard had not pointed out that gaining greater knowledge and experience was going to be far more dangerous. But then, Rahl realized, he should have known that.

VII

Late on eightday afternoon, the *Khamyl* ported at the river docks in Cigoerne. As Rahl studied the gleaming white-limestone piers and the colonnaded walkways roofed in red tile that led to the transportation rotundas west of the piers, he wondered if there happened to be a word more appropriate than *dock* for such magnificent facilities. The structures he could see beyond the riverside area were also all of white stone, and many were three or four stories in height, all roofed with the same brilliant red tile.

"We'll watch from here while everyone leaves the ship," Taryl declared from beside him on the upper deck. "It's always useful to see who's coming to Cigoerne. Just watch and try to pick out anything that feels noteworthy. Write it down, if you must, but don't say a word to me until I speak to you again."

"Yes, ser."

Rahl turned his attention to the gangways as they were run out to the piers. Cyphryt and his entourage were among the first taking the gangway from the upper deck. The red-haired mage-guard was the closest to Cyphryt, and while they did not hold hands, they might as well have, Rahl thought. As always, even those in shimmer-silk and gold-embroidered fharongs deferred to the mage-guards. At the same time, Rahl noted that several of the gray-haired men stiffened as they watched Cyphryt. Two shapely women beside them looked away. Had Cyphryt taken liberties with them, or merely encouraged them? Or had he taken some action against their consorts?

The gray-haired men, attired as wealthy merchants, let a good score of well-dressed younger men depart before nodding to three husky young attendants. The servants, dressed in pale blue trousers and shirts, immediately picked up the heavy trunks and followed the two men and their consorts. After the merchants came several Imperial tariff enumerators, but their attire was of finer quality than that of those Rahl had seen in Swartheld. Each also wore a bronze collar insignia that Rahl could not make out clearly, although it looked to be something like a sheaf of wheat crossed with a staff.

Last to leave the upper deck were functionaries of various sorts. At least, Rahl presumed that they were because they wore khaki trousers and shirts, black belts and boots, and blue visor caps without the crimson of the mage-guards or the tariff enumerators. They also carried their own gear, all in black satchel-like bags. Two of them looked sideways at Taryl, and one woman murmured something to another. The second woman shook her head and moved down the gangway even more quickly.

Taryl nodded and straightened, then looked at Rahl. "We'll have to take a carriage-for-hire to the Mage-Guard Headquarters. If there happened to be a mage-guard duty carriage, I'm most certain that Cyphryt commandeered it. You can tell me what you saw later. Remember that in Cigoerne, even the walls have both ears and eyes."

"Yes, ser."

Carrying his tan canvas kit bag, Rahl walked down the gangway beside Taryl. The senior mage-guard set a brisk pace along the colonnaded walkway to the southernmost rotunda. There were no peddlers and no vendors anywhere—unlike the piers in Swartheld, but there was an older mage-guard patrolling the rotunda. When he caught sight of Taryl, he froze for an instant before bowing respectfully.

"Good afternoon, Salastyr," Taryl said cheerfully.

"Yes, ser. Ah . . . there's no headquarters carriage here. Senior Mage-Guard Cyphryt . . ."

"I thought he might. We'll find a good hack." Taryl inclined his head toward Rahl. "This is Rahl. He was the assistant envoy on our mission to Recluce."

"Ser." Salastyr inclined his head to Rahl.

Rahl was about to protest that he shouldn't be addressed so formally, except that the cool feeling and quick glance from Taryl stilled his protest. All Rahl said, stifling his irritation, after a silence that seemed too long, was, "I did what I could to assist."

"Yes, ser. We all do. Have a good day, sers." Salastyr bowed again.

Taryl continued across the polished white-stone floor of the rotunda to the right, where several hackers waited. As the two mage-guards stepped out onto the concourse, Taryl said in a low voice, "Nicely done. I'll explain later, if you need it."

Why had Taryl warned him against explaining his relatively junior position? Because perception was important, and perception of position strengthened one's actual position? Or was it something else?

Rahl could sense something about the first hacker, but before he could say anything, Taryl bypassed him and gestured to the second, an older woman, whose rig and horse were immaculate, if older, Rahl felt.

"Where to, sers?"

"Mage-Guard Headquarters. East entrance."

"Yes, ser. We'll be on the way once you're settled."

Taryl gestured for Rahl to enter the coach first, then followed. No sooner had the older mage-guard closed the door than the driver flicked the leads, and the coach began to move.

"This is the Northern Boulevard," Taryl said, once the

hired carriage headed away from the mounting blocks in the rotunda concourse and across another avenue that ran north and south. "The avenue we just crossed was the River Road. The Northern Boulevard runs due west from the river piers and eventually becomes the west highway. Some twenty kays beyond the city, it becomes a minor road, paved but narrow. Oh, roads and avenues run north and south, and boulevards and streets go east and west. Lanes and ways go where they will."

Rahl tried to take everything in, but not to gawk as he did. If Nylan were the black city, then Cigoerne was a city of white stone, but not of stark white, as some said Fairhaven was, but a warmer white, perhaps because of the reddish light reflected from all the bright tile roofs and the brightly colored awnings. The other thing that he noticed was that while he could smell various odors and scents, none of them were unpleasant, and in that respect, the city was much like Nylan.

At one intersection of an avenue and a boulevard, Rahl made out five different eateries, all with awnings or overhanging roofs, but otherwise open to the light breezes that swirled around the city—and all were nearly deserted. In Land's End or Nylan, so late in the afternoon, there would have been some patrons. Clearly, people in Cigoerne ate far later.

Warm as it was, Rahl was more than glad that the side curtains of the coach windows and door were tied back.

"What did you notice?" Taryl asked.

"The red-haired mage-guard with Cyphryt is very close to him, perhaps a lover, or one who would be. Two of the wealthier men—they looked to be merchants—do not like him at all, and their consorts share that dislike. Two women who were some sort of Imperial functionaries that I did not recognize noted you and made some comments. Oh . . . and everyone is wary and respectful of mage-guards."

"That is acceptable. The two you noted are actually landowners as well as holding the controlling interests in several factorages with facilities in most of the major cities in Hamor. They are reputed to owe some of their success to Cyphryt's indirect influence. Undercaptain Craelyt was a distant cousin of Cyphryt, by the way."

"Is it possible—"

"It's more than probable that Craelyt's involvement in the events in Swartheld and his relationship to Cyphryt are less than coincidental," Taryl said dryly. "It would have been interesting to see which trading houses in Swartheld might have been spared from the Jeranyi attempts to burn them, but the cost of discovering that would have been far too high."

"You know this? Don't others?" asked Rahl.

"I suspect it, but there is no proof, and one cannot act on suspicion alone." Taryl laughed ironically. "If the Emperor and the Triad did, a score of senior mage-guards would be dead, you and I among them, as well as most of the wealthy landowners and factors in Cigoerne. That is how those such as Cyphryt survive and prosper. There is never any proof, and the advantages accrue to those who have no interest in pursuing matters to develop such proof."

"But . . ." Rahl wasn't quite sure what to say. "Cannot the mage-guards find such proof?"

"Only if it exists. Often it does not, not by the time it comes to anyone's attention."

"You make it sound . . ."

"Hopeless?" Taryl shook his head. "The mage-guards, particularly those of the order persuasion, have one advantage, and that is that all schemes are chaotic at heart, and thereby hold weakness. Consider this. If a plan, whether in administering or in commerce, benefits all, and creates profit, there is little need to scheme. Whoever begins may need secrecy before he or she implements such a plan, but once implemented, such a plan does not have to be kept secret. Since something that must be kept secret has weaknesses, and since effort must be spent to keep it secret, sooner or later, the weaknesses will do in such plotting. The one problem is that, often, such weaknesses appear so late that great damage is done."

"Like this rebellion?"

Taryl nodded.

"You're not saying that the rebellion would fail even if the Emperor did nothing, are you?"

"No. I'm saying that in the end, little would change for most people—those who survived. Even if the revolt succeeded, there would be an emperor, and sooner or later, he would be succeeded by another. If the new emperor did not retain the systems now in place, or devise others that accomplished the same ends, he would fail and be overthrown. The reason the revolt needs to be put down quickly is that both a revolt and a bad emperor create more chaos and more suffering, and Golyat will be a bad emperor."

While what Taryl said made sense on the surface, Rahl needed to think about that. The same argument could be made about Recluce, and that suggested that his own personal revolt against bad magisters like Puvort was useless and meaningless, because he could do nothing to change the system.

"We've been traveling some time," Rahl ventured after another period of silence.

"The Mage-Guard Headquarters is on a low hill on the western side of the city. The Imperial Palace is in the center of Cigoerne. Both the early emperors and the early Triads felt that some separation was desirable."

"I suppose the High Command is well to the north?"

"A good five kays to the south, along the river. They have their docks, their own steam transports, and their garrisons there." After a moment, Taryl added, "Our engineers design their equipment and train their mechanics."

Rahl considered Taryl's last comment. While delivered offhandedly, the older mage-guard never spoke or acted without consideration. Finally, Rahl replied, "That's your way of assuring some control over the . . . military?"

"Call it our form of balance. The people need a single

figure to respect and to hold accountable—that is the emperor. Hamor needs a single decision-maker as well. His power is balanced partly because the mage-guards screen out the most unsuitable heirs. The High Command is balanced because the number of troops in arms in Hamor is limited. Ships and crews are not, but the draft of most vessels is too deep to reach Cigoerne. The mage-guards are limited by their traditions and by the fact that there are never that many mages—and that people never truly trust mages." Taryl took a deep breath. "The limited number of troops has now become a liability in dealing with Prince Golyat's rebellion. The Triad has acceded to expanding the army, temporarily, but it will take seasons before some of the new recruits are truly ready for battle, and we do not have seasons if we are to prevent total disruption."

As the carriage drew up to a halt, Rahl peered outside. The building was of the same white limestone as most structures in Cigoerne, but was only two stories tall.

Taryl stepped out of the carriage, kit bag in hand, and tendered four coppers to the driver.

"Thank you, ser."

As the hack departed, the older mage-guard looked at Rahl. "What do you think?"

"It's . . . rather modest."

"What would you expect? It's very simple in layout," Taryl said. "The building is a rectangle of four wings around a central garden courtyard. The front wing is for the Mage-Guard Triad and his staff and clerks. The west wing is for the Mage-Guard Overcommander and his staff and support. The east wing is the quarters wing, and the rear wing holds the kitchens, and the dining and banquet areas. Each wing has an outside entry, and there is no internal entry from the other wings to either the Triad's wing or that of the Mage-Guard Overcommander." He motioned toward the square archway up three low stone steps from the mounting blocks.

Rahl followed.

Getting settled in Mage-Guard Headquarters on eight-day evening went smoothly enough. Taryl had produced dispatch orders. The quartering clerk had assigned rooms, giving Rahl one on the far south end of the second level. Rahl had made his way there, where he hung out his gear, and then gone down to the mess.

Taryl was nowhere to be seen, and from the entry, Rahl glanced across the long tables. The two in the center bore white linens trimmed in crimson, while the two adjacent and outside of those had linens of a pale tan—or faded khaki—but also trimmed in crimson, if with a thinner banding. Two other long tables set perpendicular to the other four bore plain khaki linen.

"The center two are for the seniors, and the two at the base are for the clerks and juniors," said the mage-guard who had appeared to Rahl's left. "I don't think we've met. I'm Laryn, or as all the seniors say, Laryn the younger. You new here or transient?"

"I'm new and probably transient. I've been assigned as Senior Mage-Guard Taryl's assistant." Rahl could sense that the other was an order-type mage-guard, but one without particularly strong order-skills.

"Triad Taryl's back?"

"Not as a Triad, I don't think," Rahl replied. "He says he's a senior mage-guard."

"That's . . . interesting." Laryn gestured. "We're a bit early, but we might as well sit down." He walked toward the far table. "This is the men's table, for all those not seniors or juniors. You're not a senior, are you?"

Rahl just shrugged. "No. I did a tour in Swartheld, and I've just been assigned to Taryl."

Laryn laughed. "If that's the case, sooner or later, you will be."

After they seated themselves near the middle of the long table, Rahl asked, "What do you do here?"

"You can probably tell. I'm not that good a mage, but I've a talent for numbers and things like that. So they put me in charge of supplies here at headquarters, and sometimes, they send me to stations that have messed up their accounts to straighten them out, but that doesn't happen often. Usually doesn't take long to fix them either. Oh, I'm also part of the bookkeeping auditing team that reviews the Emperor's accounts."

That was another surprise. "How often do you do that?"

"Twice a year, at the turn of summer and at the turn of winter. Usually we don't find much." Laryn turned to the server. "Ale."

"Do you have a light beer?" asked Rahl.

"Golden lager, ser," replied the server.

"I'll have that."

"What will you and Triad Taryl be doing? Do you know?"

"It has something to do with the rebellion, but that's all I know. You probably know more about it than I do."

"Prince Golyat has stationed patrols and armsmen at all the major entry points to Merowey—in the port towns, anyway." Laryn stopped and nodded to another mage-guard who was seating himself. "Devalyn, this is Rahl."

"Good to see you."

"And you, too," replied Rahl.

In the entry to the mess, Rahl could see Taryl, talking to an older mage-guard. Both walked to the senior's table for men. Taryl glanced at Rahl and nodded, then continued on.

After that, more mage-guards appeared, and Rahl spent the rest of the meal being introduced. He only talked about Swartheld, and no one else asked about Taryl—or about Recluce or the attempted Jeranyi attack in Swartheld.

VIII

Breakfast on oneday was little different from the evening meal on eightday, save that Rahl was introduced to even more mage-guards. Unlike the mess in Swartheld, Rahl found that there were fully as many mage-guards who had order-skills as chaos-skills, although he did not sense any who approached Taryl in strength . . . unless some of the older mage-guards had such subtle shields that he could not ascertain their true strength, and that was certainly possible. Once more, he only mentioned his vague assignment to Taryl and did his best to talk about Swartheld. After he had eaten, and Taryl had done so with the seniors, Taryl joined Rahl in the foyer outside the mess.

"I'm meeting with Triad Fieryn shortly," announced the thin-faced and angular mage-guard. "When I know more, I'll get back to you. I've already arranged for you to spar with Khedren this morning. He's the headquarters armsmaster, and he should be able to teach you something about how to handle a falchiona with less strain."

Rahl wondered if that could be possible.

"There are techniques. Physical techniques, not order techniques," Taryl added.

"Besides," Rahl replied with a grin, "I'll get into less trouble if I'm working hard and no one can ask questions."

"There is that." Taryl's face was expressionless.

Even so, Rahl caught the sense of amusement.

"You'll need all the practice you can get," Taryl added. "After you finish, wait for me in the library. I trust you can find some suitable reading material to pass the time."

"What would you consider most suitable, ser."

"I'd suggest one of the histories of the mage-guards. It

might give you a better feel for the traditions, but try to read between the lines and the words. What is not written is often as important as what is. Try the most slender volume first."

"Yes, ser." Rahl had to wonder how he was supposed to determine what had not been written. Taryl was sounding like Kadara, and that bothered him.

"Off with you. The armory and exercise chambers are in the smaller separate building to the south, across the paved rear area and next to the stables."

Rahl nodded and headed for the main entry foyer, passing several other mage-guards and nodding politely as he did. Outside, even as early as it was, the air was warm and nearly as damp as it had been in late summer in Swartheld. The green-blue sky was faintly silvered with a thin haze that did nothing to reduce the heat and glare of the sun.

Unlike the main headquarters, the armory was a low one-story building with two entrances. Rahl took the eastern one and found himself in a foyer with three corridors branching from it. In the middle of the foyer was a table with a fresh-faced mage-clerk seated behind it.

"Might I help you, ser?"

"I'm supposed to meet with armsmaster Khedren."

"Yes, ser. He said he had a sparring session."

"That's what I'm supposed to be doing," Rahl admitted.

"He's in the main sparring chamber. If you'd take the right corridor to the second set of double doors halfway down."

"Thank you." Rahl smiled and followed the mage-clerk's directions down the empty corridor. He passed one door, and he could sense a number of people beyond it. He also heard a strident voice.

". . . juniors! All of you . . . the next one who makes that mistake gets to spar with a senior . . ."

A faint smile crossed Rahl's lips.

When he reached the second set of doors, Rahl paused,

taking a long, slow breath and wondering exactly what to
expect. Then he opened the right-hand door and stepped
inside. The stone-walled chamber was well lit by four
large skylights, but each had what looked to be a black
shade to one side and a rope dangling from one end.

Rahl nodded. The arrangement was similar to what
Taryl had used in Luba to train Rahl.

"Taryl said you'd be here." The man who stepped forward wore a worn khaki uniform of a mage-guard, but
without insignia. He was the only one in the chamber besides Rahl.

"Yes, ser. You're armsmaster Khedren, ser?"

Nodding, Khedren picked up two staffs, extending one
to Rahl. The armsmaster was one of the few men in
Hamor taller than Rahl, yet even in the few moments Rahl
had observed him, Rahl saw a spare grace in his movements and gestures. He bore only the slightest traces of
white, but Rahl suspected that was because of the effectiveness of his shields.

Rahl set aside his visor cap, hanging it on one of the
polished wooden pegs on the rack beside the door, then
took the proffered staff.

"You might as well strip down to your undertunic,"
suggested Khedren. "Taryl said to give you a workout."

"Yes, ser." After leaning the staff against the stone
wall, Rahl took off his shirt and hung it on another peg,
then took out his truncheon and laid it across the space
between two of the pegs. He reclaimed the exercise staff
and turned.

"Taryl said you were tolerably good with a staff and
truncheon. I'd like to see how tolerably good that might
be. Let's see your defenses, first. No attacks." The armsmaster took his staff and walked to the center of the exercise chamber without waiting for a response.

Rahl followed and then squared off, waiting for whatever attack Khedren might offer.

For several long moments, Khedren did nothing, and

Rahl waited, shifting his weight from foot to foot, trying to keep loose, yet alert. More time passed, but Rahl waited, knowing that Khedren was simply trying to unnerve him . . . or get him to attack and thus fail to follow instructions.

The armsmaster finally moved, with a graceful jab that was half feint, followed by an undercut that Rahl slid. Khedren then thrust directly at Rahl from below, and Rahl slipped sideways, keeping his attention on the armsmaster's body rather than his eyes. Eyes could deceive, but body weight was harder to use as a feint or deception.

Once Khedren seemed to realize that Rahl was not open to the normal openings and feints, the armsmaster's next efforts were based on his greater height and physical strength. Rahl countered by moving and slipping the blows, always sideways, rather than retreating.

Then came the more complex movements, some that Rahl had never seen, but he managed to avoid being struck, although, at times, Khedren nearly managed it . . . but not quite.

Rahl was sweating profusely when Khedren finally stepped back and lowered his staff. He laughed, softly. "Taryl always did prefer understatement. If you're tolerably good with a staff, how are you with a truncheon?"

"Actually, ser, I'm just a trace better with the truncheon."

"I'll take your word for that." Khedren paused. "You must have had training before you came to Luba, even before you went to Nylan."

"My father put a truncheon in my hands almost as soon as I could hold it, ser. He had no order-skills, but he wanted me to be able to defend myself in a way that would not encourage me to be a bravo." That was partly a surmise on Rahl's part, because Kian had never quite said that, but Rahl felt it to be so.

"Wise man. We'll work on the blades, now, since Taryl asked me to give you instruction in falchiona techniques that are most useful for an ordermage. If you'd put the staffs in the rack over there, I'll get the weighted wooden blanks."

Khedren walked to a chest set against the far wall, which he opened, and from which he extracted two blades. He walked back to Rahl, displaying both blunted practice weapons. They looked almost identical, but one felt far less threatening to Rahl.

"You can tell the difference, can't you?"

"Yes, ser."

A faint smile appeared on Khedren's lips. "The one you'll use is of heavy oak with small lead weights set in the wood to approximate the weight and heft of a fal-chiona as closely as possible. Even a blunted blade strains a good ordermage, and the better the ordermage, the more the strain. There's no reason to create unnecessary strain." Khedren paused. "What we'll work on with you is a series of moves designed more to keep an opponent from even crossing blades with you. From that basic set of moves, you'll learn three or four single strikes. Obviously, you only want to use them when you're facing a single opponent, or when others aren't too close, be-cause if you're successful, you'll be frozen for a moment after a blade kill, and a good blade can strike in that in-stant."

Rahl took the weighted wooden blank. As Khedren had said, it had the weight and heft of a falchiona, but it was easier to hold and didn't contain the ugly reddish white of a true falchiona.

"Now . . . watch this." Khedren stepped to one side and began to demonstrate.

Rahl concentrated, knowing that he well might need to know everything that the armsmaster could teach him.

Once more Rahl found himself sweating heavily by the time Khedren called a halt.

"That's enough for today. You'll need more practice before they become natural."

Rahl could tell already that the techniques would be

helpful, although he hoped never to have to discover exactly how useful. "Thank you."

"My pleasure." Khedren smiled. "In return, I have a favor to ask of you. After you have some bread and cheese, and some rest." He gestured.

Rahl followed him to a small adjoining chamber, which held a small table and several straight-backed chairs. He was glad to sit down, but surprised when Khedren sliced several small wedges of cheese off a wheel and set a loaf of bread on the table, along with two mugs of ale.

"Thank you."

"I enjoyed it. Unless Taryl or Jyrolt or a handful of others come through, I don't really get a chance to work out with someone of skill. You could be among the best in years—with the staff and truncheon."

Rahl wondered about the favor. "Ah . . ."

"Oh, the favor. It's very simple. I'd like you to spar with some of the older mage-clerks, and I'd like you to disarm them as quickly, but painlessly, as possible. As you may know, the mage-clerks have this tendency to think that they are better than they are, and they dismiss my efforts because they feel that I'm an armsmaster and that they'll seldom come up against anyone that good."

Rahl couldn't help grinning.

"Finish up eating while I have Fientard bring them over here."

Rahl tried not to hurry, but he still felt nervous, and was waiting at the end of the chamber when Khedren returned with another arms-mage and five mage-clerks. As he walked toward the group, Rahl couldn't help but be aware of his disheveled appearance and the aura of near contempt from the dark-haired youth who was taller than the others and even slightly taller than Rahl himself.

Rahl stopped and listened as Khedren addressed the five.

"Some of you seem to have the mistaken impression that you are of equivalent ability to the everyday

mage-guard. I have told you that is not so, but you seem
not to have understood my words." Khedren inclined his
head to Rahl. "Rahl here became a full mage-guard less
than a year ago, and he has been stationed in Swartheld.
He is an ordermage, as some of you should be able to
tell, so that he will not be able to use chaos against you.
Each of you will have an opportunity to attack him with
your own weapon of choice. He will use a truncheon."

Rahl decided to use his own weapon, rather than a
practice truncheon, and reclaimed it from where he had
placed it on the pegs.

Khedren turned to the mage-clerk who still radiated a
slightly veiled contempt. "Viencyr, you seem eager to
prove your worth. You can go first."

The would-be mage-guard lifted a blunt-edged falchiona.

Rahl emulated Khedren's earlier example and walked
to the center of the chamber, where he waited for Viencyr.

The youth followed, then took a stance, with his feet
slightly too far apart, raising his falchiona to a guard position.

"You may begin," Rahl said quietly.

Viencyr began to circle, and Rahl angled into the
youth's trailing side. When Viencyr turned and flicked
out the blade, almost as if as a warning, Rahl leaned and
darted in behind the blade, bringing his truncheon sharply
across Viencyr's elbow. The falchiona clattered to the
stone.

Rahl could sense that he'd been too quick for what he
had done to make an impression. He stepped back. "Pick
it up."

Viencyr scooped up the blade and attempted to attack
as he came up.

Rahl was waiting, and beat down the blade, stepped
on it, and jammed his truncheon into Viencyr's gut. The
youth doubled over, letting go of the blade. Rahl stepped
back.

"You're next, Xeryt."

Xeryt was more cautious, but the results were the same, if with different moves by Rahl.

Rahl didn't raise a sweat in disarming all five.

After the last, Khedren turned. "Thank you very much, Mage-Guard Rahl."

"My pleasure, ser."

Rahl began to collect his gear, deciding, although it might not be approved, merely to carry his shirt back to the quarters and not to wear it until he washed up. He also managed not to smile as Khedren spoke to the mage-clerks.

". . . hope this little demonstration has given you all an idea of how much you still have to learn about arms. I would also point out that Mage-Guard Rahl could easily have killed each and every one of you with no more effort than he used in disarming you. There are a number of Codex breakers in Swartheld who are no longer with the living as a result of his truncheon . . ."

How much had Taryl told Khedren? Rahl slipped out of the arms exercise chamber and made his way back to his quarters. By the time he had cleaned up and was back in full uniform, it was early afternoon.

As he walked along the main-floor corridor toward the library, he noted large pale green glass hexagons set at regular intervals between the stone floor tiles, something he had not seen before. The hexagons ended at the door to the library, located in the corner spaces between the quarters wing and the mess wing.

Only a few older mages were in the chamber, but one glared at Rahl as he entered. Rahl merely smiled politely in return and made his way to the floor-to-ceiling shelves. In time, he located the shelf that held the histories, and he found four different ones. Following Taryl's advice, he picked the thinnest volume—*Historie of the Mage-Guards of Hamor*. From the binding and the letter styles, he suspected it was also the oldest.

Then he settled into one of the comfortable armchairs best placed to catch the light from the long and narrow windows and began to read.

The historie of the Mage-Guards of Hamor is old and illustrious, for the Mage-Guards form one pillar of the three that support the Empire, and the most vital pillar of those three . . .

He read almost thirty pages, learning little more than what Taryl and Jyrolt had already told him, except for names and accomplishments that meant little to him and the fact that the Triad was actually composed of a senior mage picked by the senior mages of the mage-guards, one chosen by the High Command, and one picked by the Emperor.

His stomach was beginning to growl, when the faintest sound of steps . . . and the aura of another mage-guard, definitely female, neared. She carried a larger volume than Rahl's and eased into the chair beside him. Although she did not look at Rahl at all, he could sense that she had order-skills and was employing them. He left his order shields as they had been, low enough to protect him from casual probing and intrusion, and continued with the book. He turned the pages, slowly, not so much reading as looking for facts that would help him better understand the mage-guards.

She finally coughed, and Rahl looked up.

The blond mage-guard pointed to his volume and shook her head.

He raised his eyebrows.

She stood, still carrying the large tome, then motioned for Rahl to follow her.

Rahl rose and walked after her, out into the foyer of the library. The history was not that intriguing, and he wanted to know why she was spying on him. He couldn't believe it was just casual interest.

"I'm Edelya," she said. "I noticed that you were reading a mage-guard history. Everyone picks that one up because it looks short, but it's not very good, and it's harder to read than almost any of the others."

"Rahl," he replied. "The language is . . . stiff, I guess I'd call it. How did you know that?" He looked at her closely. While she was small and wiry, petite, her face was smooth, almost chiseled, and her eyes were like gray granite, and looked about as hard. Behind the pleasant smile, she felt cool, almost shallow, compared to Deybri, or even Kadara or Leyla. With a shock, he realized that her bearing and attitude were more like Fahla, the factor's daughter that Puvort had sentenced to indentured slavery because she had refused to betray her father.

For a moment, Rahl's anger flared, but he caught himself. The faintest hint of puzzlement escaped Edelya's shields. Rahl decided it was better to explain than let her think the anger was directed at her.

"I'm sorry," Rahl said. "You reminded me of someone to whom a great wrong was done, and it kindled anger at those who did it."

"Someone you cared for?" Her eyebrows lifted.

He laughed softly. "She was never more than a friend, but it was still a wrong." After a moment, he added, "Which history would you suggest?"

"Aliazyr's—it's the one in the brown-and-black binding."

"How do you know so much about the histories?"

"We all have to read them sooner or later. The training mages force them upon mage-clerks here, and those of you who are trained elsewhere . . . usually someone 'suggests' you read them when you come here."

Rahl nodded. "Where are you from?"

"Cigoerne." Edelya paused. "Chalamer, actually. It's about ten kays from here, but I always have to explain."

"What are your duties here?"

"My . . . you are formal, Rahl."

"More like curious." Rahl offered a grin. "I haven't

really figured out why the Emperor and the mage-guards need so many mages here."

"There really aren't that many." She frowned. "There might be twoscore, not counting the trainee mage-clerks. There are about twoscore and a half of those right now, but you won't see most of them. Only the senior mage-clerks get to eat in the mess with the mage-guards. The senior clerks are the ones within a year of their evaluation."

"And you? Are you one of those who helps train them?"

"Sometimes I help with the exercises for those who are ordermages, but I'm actually an assistant to the weather mage. Before long, I'll probably be sent south." She shook her head. "Knowing what the weather might be is something people overlook, but it can determine when to fight and when not to."

Rahl hadn't thought about that. "Can you affect the weather?"

"I'm not that good, not yet, anyway. If the air's really damp, sometimes I can make it rain, and at times in the mountains, I can make fog. What about you?"

Rahl shook his head. "I'm just a patrol mage."

"You wouldn't be here if you were just a patrol mage."

"I'm just following orders." Rahl smiled, politely. "I'll take your advice about the histories . . . but I do need to get back to reading one of them, or I'll be in trouble."

"I hope I'll see you around." Edelya smiled warmly, although the feelings beneath the expression were cooler and more calculating. "Some nights, some of the regular mage-guards go over to the Staff and Blade. It's just half a kay west."

"Thank you. Some of that depends on my duties and when I'm ordered off somewhere else."

"It always does. Do you know where?"

"No, I don't, and I've learned there's not much point in asking until someone's ready to tell me."

She laughed. "There is that. Good day, Rahl."

"Good day, Edelya."

Rahl nodded and stepped back, moving back into the

library, where he followed her suggestion and exchanged the history he'd been reading for the one bound in brown and black. After reading twenty pages in a fraction of the time it had taken him to read the same amount in the first book, Rahl had to admit that Edelya had been right. Aliazyr's history was far better—not to mention more readable—than the one he'd been reading before.

He had read through another forty pages by the time Taryl arrived and motioned for him to leave the library. He also noted the veiled surprise from the two older mage-guards—both ordermages—who were reading.

Taryl did not speak until they were out in the corridor beyond the library foyer. "We'll be here for several more days, if not longer, while Marshal Byrna gathers his forces. We will be going to the High Command for a briefing tomorrow afternoon. I was invited, but you're coming as well."

"Yes, ser."

"How was your day?"

"I sparred with Khedren and learned some of the techniques. He said I was better than tolerable with the staff and truncheon, and he had some of the older mage-clerks go against me. He said I'd be doing him a favor if I disarmed them quickly without damaging them permanently."

"I assume you did."

"Yes, ser."

"Good. Did anything else of interest happen?" Taryl raised his eyebrows.

"Just what you warned me about. A pretty mage-guard named Edelya approached me. We talked for a while, but I did my best to play dumb and dutiful."

"You probably did well with dutiful, but I doubt you deceived her about your intelligence. You can't play dumb well, Rahl." Taryl turned. "We have some time. I'm going to try another set of exercises on you, and then we'll visit the stables. This way." He walked from the foyer back along the corridor to a narrow door.

When Taryl opened the door, Rahl saw an equally narrow staircase leading downward to a landing, then doubling back.

"Close the door behind you."

"Yes, ser."

There were no lamps in the corridor below—roughly half the width of the main-floor hallway—but it was still dimly lit with faint greenish lights set in the ceiling at regular intervals. Rahl glanced up at the nearest, slowing and trying to make out where the light came from that emerged from the hexagonal glass faces. He'd seen them before . . .

Taryl stopped and looked over his shoulder. "It's an elongated prism set in the corridor floor above. It catches the light and diffuses it down here. That's enough for most mages, and that means we don't have to worry about lamps and lamp oil. They use them on ships, too. Come on."

The concept was simple enough, Rahl realized, and he should have realized that the green hexagons in the floor above were for more than decoration. Still, he didn't recall seeing anything like them being used anywhere else.

Taryl stopped before a closed door and turned to Rahl. "I want you to wait outside in the corridor until I call you. Then I want you to close your eyes, and use your order-senses to enter. You won't be attacked. This is something else." The senior mage-guard's voice was dry.

Rahl waited, then closed his eyes and pressed the door lever after he heard his name.

"Close the door firmly. Then you can open your eyes."

When Rahl opened his eyes, he could see nothing. The room was pitch-black. Not more of Taryl's exercises in the dark!

"There's a table in front of you," Taryl said. "Pick up the block on it that feels most orderly. Don't feel around for it. Pick it up on a single attempt."

Rahl could sense Taryl standing behind the table.

"Go ahead. Don't waste time."

Rahl concentrated, but each of the three blocks felt so small that he had a hard time determining which had the most order. Finally, he picked the one farthest from him. It was iron, but tiny enough that two of them could have rested on his thumbnail.

"Now, without letting any of the blocks touch, take the one you have and set it as close as you can to the one with the least order."

Rahl managed that, although he actually set it slightly farther away, then nudged it nearer to the least orderly block.

"Line them up as close as possible, with the least orderly to your right and the most orderly to your left . . ."

The exercises went on for a time before Taryl said, "Now, use your order-senses to make a triangle of the blocks with the most orderly at the point facing me. Don't move them with your hands, and don't let them touch."

Rahl was sweating by the time he moved the tiny blocks without using his hands, but he did manage the task.

Taryl set another block on the table. "Make a square with all four."

That seemed easier.

Two more tiny blocks went onto the table.

"A hexagon, now."

Even with six blocks, Rahl arranged them more easily than he had at first with only three.

"Just stand there and relax for a moment while I set up the next exercise. Don't ask any questions."

Rahl took a slow deep breath in the darkness and blotted his forehead with the back of his hand. He couldn't help wondering what was in the bucket Taryl lifted and tilted. Something poured out with a rustling sound. Sand?

Taryl lifted another bucket, but this time Rahl could sense that it held water. The second bucket was only partly full, and Taryl set it on the table.

"Use just enough water to moisten the sand. I want

you to make a small square wall with the wet sand. Use your hands and fingers for the first side."

Rahl had an idea what was coming, but he separated the sand into two piles, moistening one, and saving the other in case he used too much water inadvertently. When it felt damp enough to hold together, he formed a crude wall the length of his hand.

"Support the inside of the next wall with order, but use your fingers on the outside . . ."

When Rahl finished following Taryl's instructions—completing the last wall strictly with order—he was not only sweating again, but his shoulders ached.

"Now . . ." continued Taryl. "I assume you've seen what happens when sand castles dry in the sun."

"Yes, ser. They hold their shape in a way, but if there's any wind . . ."

"Good. I want you to use order to move the water, just the water, out of the sand in the walls you built on the table. Don't ask why or how. You can do it. Just do it."

Rahl didn't even know where to start, but he thought of the water as if it were made of little tiny boxes, and he concentrated on moving it a "box" at a time. Surprisingly, to him, it seemed to work, but it was a tedious process. Finally, he straightened. "I think . . . I think I did it."

"Good." Taryl sounded pleased, for the first time. "That's all you should do here today."

Rahl had to agree. He felt as though he'd walked kays and kays carrying half a score of his father's heaviest tomes.

Taryl walked around the table past Rahl and opened the door. "We're not done."

Rahl didn't ask who would clean up the mess, but turned to follow Taryl.

At the door, Taryl extended his hand. "Here are the blocks. You'll need to practice every night for a while."

"Yes, ser."

"Do you understand what you've done?" Taryl asked as he walked toward the narrow staircase.

"I've used order to move things around."

"Exactly. You know how, now, but you'll have to practice to gain strength. Not many mage-guards can do what you just did. Do you know what was important about the water and the sand?"

"Besides moving it? No, ser."

"You proved you can sense and handle water. That means you have some ability with the weather."

Rahl frowned. What did water have to do with weather?

Taryl stopped. "I can see that we'll have to work on certain parts of your education. For the moment, I'll just say that all weather is created by just two things—the heat and light of the sun and the water in the oceans and the air. You've seen a kettle boil, haven't you?"

"Yes, ser."

"Well, that's what the sun does to the ocean except it's slower, and we can't see it. If you put a piece of cold, cold iron over a kettle spout, do you know what happens?"

"Water appears."

"That's what happens when warm air from the oceans meets the high mountain peaks or cold air coming from somewhere else. That's the basis of weather."

"I could be a weather mage?" Like Creslin?

"I don't know, but you certainly should be able to learn to read the weather."

Taryl hurried up the steps, and Rahl had to scramble to follow him, but Taryl said nothing more until they were outside the building and headed toward the stables. Then he glanced toward Rahl. "What about the healer in Nylan? Are you still interested in her?"

"I was thinking about writing a letter, but I didn't think posting it here . . ."

Taryl nodded. "You're already understanding. Don't post it here, not if you don't want everyone to know what's in it. Oh, no one will open it, but some of the chaos types have skills that can reproduce the writing without breaking the seal, and as my assistant, those beholden to

Cyphryt, or some others, will certainly wish to know your thoughts. You can post it somewhere on the way when we leave here. That would be best."

"I'd wondered."

"You won't return to Recluce, you know?"

Rahl looked hard at Taryl.

"I didn't say you wouldn't be able to," replied the older mage. "I said you wouldn't, and you know that as well as I do. It's too small for you already."

"She said that, too."

"Your healer?"

"She's not mine."

"But you wish she were."

Rahl thought for a moment. "Not in that way. I can't ask her to join me here." He laughed, ironically. "I don't even know that she could."

"Like mages, healers are always welcome, and while the mage-guards sponsor them, they don't have to become mage-guards."

"If I wrote her that . . . that would be a request."

Taryl nodded. "It would be. Especially now, but don't hesitate to let her know how you feel."

Rahl caught a sense of what almost felt like regret from Taryl, but he didn't wish to pry. "I'll have a letter ready for when we leave and can post it."

"That would be best."

Neither spoke as they neared the stables. Then, as they passed through the open doors, the older mage-guard nodded to the ostler who stepped forward. "We aren't riding. Rahl just needs to get more familiar with the horses."

The woman nodded and stepped back. "You might try the big chestnut gelding in the corner. That stall makes it easy to get to the manger. He likes almost everyone."

"Thank you." Taryl smiled, turning toward the southeast corner of the stables.

Even before they reached the farthest stall, the chestnut was turning his head, trying to greet them. Taryl moved along the wooden side of the stall. "You like company,

don't you? In a moment, you'll get a treat. Yes, you will."
He looked to Rahl. "I want you to try to sense what the
horses feel. It will help you with riding, and I have the
feeling that we'll be riding more than a little in the seasons ahead." Taryl produced a pearapple and a small
knife. He cut a slice off the pearapple, most carefully,
then handed it to Rahl.

"Offer it to him on the flat of your palm. You're less
likely to get nipped that way. Don't force any feelings.
Just leave your order-senses open."

Rahl stepped forward, pearapple ready.

The chestnut's muzzle was soft, and he lifted the slice
of pearapple almost delicately.

Rahl thought he could sense . . . something.

"Wait a moment before you give him another." Taryl
handed another slice to Rahl. Rahl held it in the hand
away from the chestnut.

The gelding tossed his head, then nuzzled Rahl's empty
hand.

Rahl smiled. He could definitely sense something akin
to impatience.

IX

Even before breakfast on twoday, Rahl practiced with
the small iron blocks. He also put small droplets of water
on top of the blocks and tried to move the droplets. That
was harder, but he managed. Was it because water embodied more order than moving water that was dispersed,
as in the sand, was easier? He didn't know and wished
that he now had a copy of *The Basis of Order*. At that
thought, he laughed.

When Rahl walked into the mess for breakfast, he saw
Edelya sitting at the women's table next to Saulya and
another older mage-guard. He nodded politely to all

three and took a seat beside Laryn and across from another mage-guard he hadn't met.

"Rahl, this is Rhyett. He's the assistant to Triad Fieryn."

Rhyett grimaced. "I'm really the assistant to Kielora, and she's the principal assistant to the Triad."

Rahl sensed the whitish aura of chaos around Rhyett. "That means you do everything that no one else wants to do?"

"That's absolutely right."

"What sorts of things?"

"I get to read all the routine dispatches and reports and sort them. I work with Laryn here to prepare the draft reports on past and projected expenditures—we have to track what the stations and regions are spending, and compare them. That way, we can see if anything's out of line . . ."

Rahl half listened to Rhyett, but he was also aware of a conversation at the juniors' table that had begun after two of the juniors had glanced at Rahl, then looked away. Rahl extended his order-senses.

". . . he's the one. Not a senior . . ."

". . . claims he is . . . or might as well be one . . ."

". . . too young . . ."

Rahl just smiled. Let them wonder.

". . . and on top of all that," Rhyett went on, "as if it weren't enough, I'm supposed to keep in touch with Director Cyphryt's assistants . . ." His words died away as his eyes flicked toward the women's side of the mess.

"Saulya?" asked Rahl quietly.

"She's one of them. At least, she smiles when she wants something, and she's good to look at. Vladyrt . . ." Rhyett just shook his head.

Much as he almost instinctively liked Rhyett, Rahl understood exactly why he was an assistant to an assistant. There was such a thing as being too open, especially in a place like Cigoerne. He wanted to snort. Much as Recluce supposedly valued honesty, even in Nylan few of the magisters wanted to hear the truth if it conflicted with what they wanted to believe.

"He thinks he's as important as Cyphryt?" Rahl asked with a smile.

"He's not quite that deluded, but he thinks that the director couldn't do anything without his help," Rhyett replied.

"We'd all like to believe that," said Laryn. "Why, I could claim that nothing would happen here because no one would get fed."

"I can't even claim that," Rahl said, taking a helping of sausage and egg toast.

"Someone said you were an assistant envoy to Recluce," Laryn said. "That's not exactly nothing."

Rahl shrugged helplessly. "I'm just a mage-guard who does what he's told and goes where he's ordered." *And happy to be that, considering what could have happened.* He took a swallow of the pale lager that was becoming a morning staple for him.

Laryn and Rhyett exchanged glances.

Then Laryn laughed and said,

> *"A man who claims nothing of naught*
> *has never for blind honor fought."*

The words were clearly a quote from someone, but Rahl didn't recognize them. He *thought* he agreed with the sentiment if he had heard it correctly. More important, he decided Taryl should know about the rumors, since Rahl himself had told no one. In the meantime, he tried the egg toast and berry syrup.

After breakfast, Rahl and Taryl walked toward the coach waiting for them outside the entrance to the quarters' wing.

"I'm sorry if I haven't kept you more informed," Taryl said, "but we'll have time to talk on the drive to High

Command. It's a good six kays from here, even by the ring road." He gestured for Rahl to enter the coach. "I like sitting on this side."

Rahl settled himself and waited until they were moving before speaking again. "Someone has been spreading the word that I was an assistant envoy to Recluce."

"You were," Taryl replied amiably.

"But I've never told anyone. You told the mage-guard at the river docks, but I don't think he'd be telling people here."

Taryl laughed. "As soon as Cyphryt saw you with me, I'm certain he checked on your assignment—if he didn't already know, which was more likely. He doubtless told his assistants, and they told others . . ."

"But . . . I wouldn't ever have been made that, except—"

"Rahl," replied Taryl firmly, "that's life. None of us would be anything except for something. It doesn't always happen, but sometimes good things do come from trials. You wouldn't be here if Shyret hadn't drugged you and tried to destroy your memories. You wouldn't have met the healer in Nylan if you hadn't upset the magisters in Land's End."

After a moment, Rahl nodded.

"Now . . . let me give you some background. The High Command is the direct authority over both the army and the navy—as well as over the naval marines and the mage-guards assigned to the army. Certain types of mage-guards are always assigned to the High Command. They're the chaos-mages who see things as either black or white. Who they are is better suited to military discipline and operations, but they never serve on vessels as crew, and the navy dislikes transporting them except when absolutely necessary. Chaos has no place in the normal working of a vessel. On the other hand, as the white wizards of Fairhaven have shown, it can be most useful in land battles. That is why you and I and other ordermages have been detailed to the High Command for the duration of the campaign against Prince Golyat and the rebels. The prince has almost no ordermages among his forces. Most ordermages would not be disposed to support a rebellion because it is, at least in most cases, a form of chaos. There are exceptions, of course, but this is not one of them."

"Exceptions?"

"Were Emperor Mythalt a tyrant who acted arbitrarily and murdered and killed and created chaos, then the most ordered course of action might be a rebellion. He is not. Now . . . back to the High Command. The head of the High Command is the Overmarshal. That is Berndyt. Under him are the Land Marshal and the Sea Marshal, and under each of them are marshals with specific military or geographical commands . . ."

Rahl forced himself to listen as Taryl outlined the military chain of command and subsidiary organizations in exceedingly fine detail. At times, he glanced out the window, taking in the paved road and the small steads to the southwest. On the northeast side of the road, the dwellings were far closer together, as though the ring road were a sort of boundary.

After quite a time, Taryl paused. "We'll be there shortly. I doubt you'll remember everything I've told you, but this way, you won't look like a steer blinded by a chaos-bolt when someone mentions something you should know."

"In other words," replied Rahl, "I'm not supposed to look surprised or stunned no matter what."

"Exactly."

The building housing the High Command was markedly smaller than that holding the Mage-Guard Headquarters, just a single-story stone structure, with two wings in a chevron shape coming off a central rotunda.

"It's smaller . . ." ventured Rahl.

"Not really," replied Taryl. "All the dwellings and buildings behind the hill to the west are part of the post. The marshals have large dwellings, and even those of the commanders are not small. The armory is half the size of the Mage-Guard Headquarters, but it's not obvious because much of it's underground."

Rahl didn't see any of those buildings, just the command building on the grassy slope that ran down to the river.

"See that berm to the south?" Taryl pointed. "All the river docks and warehouses are behind that. All the other buildings are to the west and south of the hill that holds the command headquarters. It's a matter of impressions."

Impressions. So the mage-guards wanted an impression of greater presence, while the High Command wanted to create the opposite impression?

"The thing about impressions, Rahl, is that, while we can tell ourselves that they are merely impressions, we still tend to believe what we see and experience. There's a reason why they're called impressions. They do impress themselves upon our mind and feelings. That's why those in power who are wise take care in the impressions they create. It's always harder to deal with opponents when you must not only overcome their physical power, but also the power they create within people and even within you."

Rahl was still considering Taryl's words when the coach came to a halt.

Taryl stepped out, and Rahl followed. The receiving concourse was at the foot of a long set of wide stone steps that rose to the entrance—little more than a square arch supported by plain circular stone pillars. Taryl and Rahl started up the steps.

"This part of the hill isn't natural, is it?" asked Rahl.

"No. They built the hill around the hidden lower levels. I suggest you merely observe unless addressed directly."

"Yes, ser."

Once through the archway, they found themselves in an oblong foyer. A single long desk dominated the space, with two uniformed figures seated behind it.

An undercaptain who looked to be even younger than

Rahl stepped forward from one side of the desk as he caught sight of the two mage-guards. "Senior Mage-Guard Taryl, ser?"

Taryl nodded. "This is my assistant, Rahl."

"Ah . . . yes, ser. Marshal Byrna is expecting you. I'll escort you to the briefing room and tell him that you are here."

As they followed the young officer down the corridor that led from the right-hand side of the entry hall, Rahl had the definite impression neither the officer nor the marshal happened to be expecting Rahl.

After walking briskly for over a hundred cubits—roughly a third of the way down the corridor—the under-captain opened an unmarked door on the right-hand side of the corridor and stood back for the mage-guards to enter, then followed them inside. The walls of the briefing room were paneled in a golden wood, as were the casements of the three tall, narrow windows. There were no window hangings, and the only furnishings were an oblong table close to ten cubits in length, flanked by straight-backed chairs of the same golden wood as the paneling, and a set of cabinets against the wall at the foot of the table. The table was set parallel to the outer wall.

"The marshal and his senior staff will be here shortly, ser." The undercaptain bowed slightly, turned, and departed.

Mindful of Taryl's earlier observations, Rahl said nothing but walked to the middle window and gazed out. The parklike grounds sloped down to the Swarth River, creating a sweeping view that seemed more suited to a grand estate than to a military headquarters. To the south, he could see a haze that suggested the river docks and far more practical and working facilities.

As Taryl cleared his throat, Rahl immediately turned.

A number of officers began to enter the briefing room, followed by a short and squarish man in an immaculate khaki uniform with the gold insignia of a marshal on his collars—a starburst above three crossed blades.

"Marshal Byrna." Taryl's voice was polite, but he did not incline his head to the marshal.

"I believe that only your presence was requested, Mage-Guard." Byrna's voice was a flat high baritone that fitted his triangular face and sparse goatee. His eyes were close-set and brilliant blue, and he stood half a head shorter than Rahl.

Taryl's eyes slowly traveled across the two commanders, the overcaptain, and the two captains who had stationed themselves around the conference table. "You have quite a staff here, Marshal."

"I don't believe the size of my staff is exactly your purview."

"Nor, I might reply," said Taryl mildly, "is the size of mine yours."

"What you do with your . . . staff elsewhere is your business, Mage-Guard. You, and you alone, will be briefed."

"I think you might consider the matter in greater detail, Marshal," Taryl replied, his voice still calm. "If Rahl is excluded, then I will have to spend extra time briefing him. That means I will have less time and energy to devote to assisting you, Marshal, and that would not be good for anyone, but particularly for you . . ."

"Aren't you putting your time above mine, Mage-Guard?"

"No, Marshal, I'm not. It takes nothing from you to include Rahl. It takes time from me if you do not."

"I trust you, Mage-Guard Taryl. I do not even know this Rahl."

"If you trust me, Marshal, then you must trust my judgment. If you question my judgment in this, how can I be certain you will trust my judgment in other matters? Such lack of trust benefits neither of us."

The marshal frowned, then shook his head. "Words . . ."

"Do you wish the assistance of the mage-guards?" Taryl's voice remained calm, but each word was like iron.

"You are not a Triad anymore."

Taryl smiled. "No, but do you think I relinquished the abilities with the title?"

The oldest commander tried to conceal a wince.

"Do what you will." Byrna snorted and gestured toward the table, taking a seat at one end.

Taryl took his seat at the other end. After noting that the senior commander sat to the marshal's right, Rahl took the chair to Taryl's right.

"Before we begin the briefing proper," Byrna said, irritation still in his voice, "I'd like a clarification of what services the mage-guards will provide."

"We're detailed to provide a certain level of protection for you and your staff against rebel mages."

"Except to protect me and my staff, what other services do you provide?"

"An earlier knowledge of where the rebels are placing their chaos-mages, where they have explosives, and, in the case of storms, how long they are likely to last and where they are most likely to have the greatest effect. Also, where their largest concentrations of forces may be." Taryl inclined his head just slightly.

"Helpful, but hardly decisive," snorted Byrna.

"We do not claim to be decisive. We claim to be helpful and useful. Past marshals and emperors have found us so."

"We'll see." Byrna turned. "Commander Eswyt, if you would begin . . ."

"Yes, ser. At the moment, it appears that the rebels hold all the possible deep-water ports from just west of the south Heldyn Cliffs to a point close to due west of Jabuti and Alsenyi. They have fortified and reinforced the ports. A direct coastal assault would be close to suicidal for those involved. Prince Golyat's chaos-mages would be able to concentrate on individual vessels and boats . . . Most important are the facilities at Nubyat and Sastak. The Jeranyi are supplying the rebels, as well as raiding commerce in the area, and there have been sightings of ships reported as bearing Sligan and Spidarlian ensigns, and those are usually vessels under the control of Fairhaven, but the white wizards have been careful to date to keep their warships away from our coasts . . ."

The commander went on to detail the positions of the Hamorian fleets before concluding, ". . . our principal advantage is the loyalty of the navy. To our knowledge, not a single naval vessel supports the rebels."

"Commander Surrylt?"

"Unfortunately, we are not faring nearly so well in terms of troops. Prince Golyat has a minimum of fifteen thousand men under arms, and this does not include irregulars or those locals who may be conscripted and armed. Within a season, we may be facing more than thirty thousand armed men. Currently, our entire army is only thirty-odd thousand, and there are only another three thousand naval marines. . . ."

When Surrylt concluded, the marshal glanced toward the older overcaptain. "Beltryx."

"We have five river steamers that we can use to transport our forces to Kysha. Farther south than that the Swarth River is not navigable. Even so, there will be considerable delays in using the locks around the second and third cataracts. Three of the steamers were requisitioned and refitted quickly, but the *Fyrador* and the *Syadtar* had always been used for supply and company transport. They can each carry four hundred men and their field equipment. The other three are limited to somewhat fewer, around three hundred men each. The trip upriver will take a minimum of five days and the return slightly less than four days. Consider the need for a day at each end . . ."

Rahl tried to calculate the time and requirements. As he figured the numbers, it would take most of a season to move even ten thousand men.

". . . mitigated by the fact that we already had five thousand men in Kysha, and the steamers are now returning from transporting yet another two thousand men, but it must be noted that even by the main roads, which are paved, it is almost seven hundred kays from Kysha either to Nubyat or Sastak, and yet they are each two hundred and fifty kays apart. That means that either we must have two large forces or we must proceed first to one port, then the other . . ."

Not for the first time, it came to Rahl just how big Hamor was. The senior officers were talking about a rebel administrative region that might amount to a tenth of Hamor, and yet probably comprised an area five times that of all Recluce.

When the overcaptain finished, Taryl asked, "How much control do the rebels actually have outside of the ports and the larger towns?"

"Very little, we think," replied Commander Eswyt. "Most of the local Imperial administrators are still reporting and sending their tariffs to Cigoerne. At this point, the regional garrison at Dawhut is still in our hands, and that's halfway to the coast. We've already sent transport wagons and horses to Kysha, enough to transport half the force."

"Is there any way you could use the navy to land forces on the coast?"

Marshal Byrna shook his head. "No way at all. Ships aren't designed except to port, and we don't have enough boats to row or sail troops into land. They could pick off our men easily with their chaos-mages. Now . . . once we take Nubyat, we can pour men and supplies in." He looked hard at Taryl. "What about your mages? How many are there in Merowey? How many are loyal?"

"There were somewhere over a hundred mage-guards in the area claimed by the rebels," Taryl replied. "Of that number, close to thirty are ordermages in smaller towns. We have no way of determining what, if anything, has happened to them, but only a few would have skills of use to the rebels even if they were so inclined, and such inclinations would be extremely rare among ordermages . . ."

At that moment, Rahl realized that his friend Talanyr was one of those thirty, but he could not imagine that Talanyr would throw in with the rebels.

". . . most of the remainder are patrol mages in the larger towns, and half of those are split between Sastak and Nubyat. There are perhaps twenty who have sufficient talents and capability to inflict more than minor harm to our forces. Of that number, seven have already escaped the area and reported their safety outside the rebel area. Reports indicate that about ten are supporting the rebels."

"Half of them! That's insufferable," declared Byrna.

"That's one in ten, Marshal, and not to be unexpected among chaos-mages, who have an exceedingly high opinion of themselves. Nine out of ten of all the mage-guards appear to be loyal to the Emperor, and that is a far higher proportion than among the army troops in the port cities, it appears."

"I would certainly hope so."

For some time, questions and replies continued.

"What is the largest chaos-bolt you would expect, and how many men would it harm . . . ?"

"It is unlikely that any of the mages in Merowey could affect more than a squad at a time, a foot company, perhaps, if they were in a tight formation, fewer from a cavalry or mounted heavy infantry company . . ."

"How many such bolts could they throw . . . ?"

"How long will it take for a sizable force to reach Dawhut . . . ?"

It was well past midafternoon when Rahl followed Taryl back to the waiting carriage.

Taryl did not speak until the coach was well away from the grounds of the High Command and headed northwest on the ring road back toward the Mage-Guard Headquarters. "What do you think of the marshal?"

"I've never met one before," Rahl temporized.

"Don't sound like the functionaries around the Emperor, Rahl."

"I don't think he ever likes to change his mind once he's made it up," Rahl said quietly, "and I feel he's the type to decide before he knows everything that he should. That's just what I feel."

"His history would suggest you are not far wrong. One of the problems the Emperor faces is that the most able officers are in the navy. Our navy has always been Hamor's bulwark. That's because Hamor was unified early by the Cyadoran refugees. That makes it unlike Candar, where most of the fighting is hand-to-hand, rather than vessel-to-vessel. Marshal Charnyat was most capable, and relatively young. After his untimely, and most expected death, Cyphryt and Triad Fieryn both pushed for Byrna to succeed Charnyat as the one in charge of the campaign. So did Triad Dhoryk—he's the senior mage-guard in the High Command."

Rahl nodded. Once more he was having to decipher what was not said. On top of that, he had more than a few impressions to sort through and try to place in a more correct perspective.

"Why would they do that?"

"Why indeed?" Taryl laughed, ironically. "There are so many possibilities that it's difficult to say. The most likely is that they fear the Emperor's plans to consolidate and centralize control of Hamor's administrative regions within the palace." He shrugged. "It could be as simple as fear of the Emperor's Triad. That's Jubyl."

"Why would they fear him?"

"He and Charnyat were most close, and shared many views, particularly in opposing changes in the way in which the army is organized and supplied. There have been many complaints that the goods inspectors and enumerators were being unreasonable in the standards they applied to the large factoring houses."

"Is that why you asked for me as an assistant?"

"No . . . but your knowledge might be useful later. Tomorrow or the next day we'll be going to the Palace. There are some things you should know. In particular, let me fill in a few gaps in what the most respected officers of the High Command said . . . and what they did not. We might even have enough time for me to finish before we reach headquarters."

Rahl had the feeling he wasn't going to like what he was about to learn, but he merely nodded.

X

After a quiet evening meal, Rahl retired to his chamber, reflecting upon the day, and what had happened. Although Edelya had mentioned the Staff and Blade, as had Laryn, Rahl didn't feel like pretending to enjoy socializing while being on guard all the time. During the briefing at the High Command, Taryl had behaved almost as if he were the marshal's superior, and he had gone to great lengths to force the military officers to accept Rahl himself as their equal. Then, Taryl had made the statement about their going to the Palace on the next day, as if it were more like a stroll across the rear courtyard to the stables.

Rahl also realized that there was much more he did not understand. How could an entire administrative district larger than Recluce—or many countries in Candar—stage a revolt without anyone knowing it was about to happen? He shook his head. Obviously, people had known, but whoever had known had kept the news from reaching Mage-Guard Headquarters, the High Command, or the Emperor—or delayed it until the rebellion was in progress. That suggested to Rahl that at least some very talented mage-guards had to have been involved, perhaps even some in Mage-Guard Headquarters, and that Taryl thought so as well, although the angular former Triad had said nothing about that. Still, that was only a guess on Rahl's part. He certainly had no knowledge or even any hints of such.

There was little enough he could do about any of that at the moment, only watch and learn, and try not to reveal anything.

Slowly, he sat down at the small writing desk and took out several sheets of paper and the small portable inkwell and a copper-tipped iron pen. What could he say? How much should he put to paper?

He used several sheets of paper—and burned the discarded sheets in the small brazier that he suspected had been placed in the chamber for the use of chaos-type mage-guards—before he finally had a letter that satisfied him. He'd also had to light the lamp over the desk because composing it had taken so long. While he could certainly detect objects in the dark, so far his skills did not let him read in darkness.

Finally, he read it silently, and carefully.

My dear healer,
I am now in Cigoerne. It might well be called another white city, with its white-stone walls and red-tile roofs. Even the streets are paved in a light-colored stone like a white granite. Many of the buildings are of two and three stories, and all that I have seen are well kept. When the sun reflects off the stone and roofs, there is a warmth to the light. There is also a warmth to the days and nights because Hamor is considerably hotter than Recluce.

At the moment, I am staying in a comfortable room in the Mage-Guard Headquarters on the west side of the city. I was most surprised to discover that there are many ordermages here, and many of them would fit in Nylan—if the magisters did not know from where they hailed. I've also been reading a history of the mage-guards. They date back to the first emperors. I am continuing to learn, thanks in great measure to the teaching techniques of Senior Mage-Guard Taryl. While you did not meet him, he was the envoy I accompanied to Recluce, and he is the one who reclaimed me from the ironworks at Luba and enabled me to become a mage-guard.

From what I have seen so far, Cigoerne is almost as neat and clean as Nylan, if far larger, and everyone appears well behaved and orderly. There are also similarities in the way in which senior mage-guards relate to each other and the way in which magisters relate to each other, although the mage-guards place a great emphasis on the development and application of practical skills by all mage-guards and not just upon those who fit a given mold.

In the days to come, I will be leaving Cigoerne on my next duty, and I will write as I can. I cannot help but think of you, and dream of you, no matter how far apart we are. I know it may be some time before I will have any opportunity or time to return to Nylan, and I know how and what you feel about Hamor. For all that, the past that I found in Nylan does have a hold on me, and it always will. You are usually better at seeing such than I, but in that one particular, you were mistaken. That past—and you—hold me fast.

This time, he did close the letter more affectionately, with the words, "All my love," above his signature.

Now that he had written the letter, he would have to keep it with him at all times until he found a safe place from which to post it. He couldn't help but think about the ironies of life. When it had been perfectly safe to write Deybri, he hadn't often had the coins. Now that he had the coins, he had to worry about where and when he posted the letter.

He folded the letter and slipped it into the envelope, which he addressed to her in Nylan, then sealed.

After that, he disrobed and climbed into his bed. As he lay there, his eyes not looking anywhere, he kept thinking about Deybri and her gold-flecked brown eyes, the soft waves of her brown hair, and the warmth that radiated from her.

Finally, he got up and extracted the tiny iron cubes from his belt wallet. Then he sat down in the darkness before the writing table and set the cubes on the polished ancient golden oak. He closed his eyes and reached for the cubes with his order-senses.

If nothing else, he could practice improving his order-skills until he was exhausted enough to sleep.

XI

Threeday afternoon found Rahl once more in a coach—this time headed to the Imperial Palace with Taryl. He was still warm. Cigoerne in the late fall was often warmer than Recluce in spring or early summer. He'd had to practice falchiona exercises with Khedren much of the morning, and he was happy to sit back and relax—until he realized that Taryl carried his satchel. Rahl looked at the black leather once, then again.

"We do have some time. Sit on the other side as far from me as you can."

As Rahl reluctantly shifted his position to comply, Taryl opened the satchel.

"This is a different kind of training," offered the older mage-guard. "I have some darts in here. They look alike, but some are tipped with quill points, some with needles, and some with needles charged with chaos. In a moment, I will start throwing them at you. Your shields are certainly strong enough to stop all of them, but I want you to try to use only enough order to stop those with the needles and the chaos."

For a moment, Rahl wanted to protest. What difference did it make whether he stopped all the darts instead of just some of them?

"In battle, you won't have enough strength left to last a day if you can't pace your use of order," Taryl added.

Rahl nodded. He supposed that was true.

Taryl flipped a feathered dart, and Rahl blocked it with his shields, before discovering that it was just one of those with a quill tip.

"You have to be faster." Taryl raised his eyebrows. "Much faster."

By the time the coach pulled up in the functionaries' rotunda of the Imperial Palace, Rahl was both tired and frustrated. He hadn't done well at all with Taryl's exercise, either blocking darts that he shouldn't have blocked or not blocking those he should have and getting mild chaos-jolts. Near the end, he had improved, but not nearly to Taryl's satisfaction. Not only that, but Taryl had been so insistent on the exercise that Rahl hadn't had a chance to ask about finding a place to post his letter to Deybri.

Taryl left the satchel in the coach and stepped out onto the wide white-stone mounting block, then moved aside and waited for Rahl.

The younger mage-guard stepped down, trying to mask his frustration and irritation behind personal shields.

Taryl gestured around the exterior courtyard. "What do you think?"

The white-stone walls surrounding the Palace grounds and gardens extended a full kay on each side, and rose fifteen cubits from the ground to the base of the crenelated parapets. While Rahl did not see any guards, he could sense their presence. The exterior of the Palace itself was also of glistening white stone, three levels above its foun-

dations, with three arched domes rising above the highest level of the triangular building, a dome in the center
of the front section of each of the wings that surrounded
a central courtyard garden. The tall-but-narrow exterior
windows were set in clusters of three, and the glass bore
a greenish tint. The roofs were of red tile and gently
sloped.

"Beautiful and impressive, ser."

"It's meant to be." Taryl started up the low steps to the
columns that flanked an entry rotunda. "While I meet
with Triad Jubyl, you'll be entertained and educated in
some fashion or another by his principal assistants. Just
be pleasant and friendly, but listen and watch carefully.
Assume that all you do not know, and perhaps some you
do, are as trustworthy as your former undercaptain."

Rahl had already come to that conclusion. Was it that
way among all who held power?

When the two mage-guards stepped through the arch
into the entry hall, two young women, scarcely more than
girls, stepped forward. They wore identical garments,
flowing trousers of pale green, long-sleeved blouses of the
same shade, and vests of a deep maroon. They also wore
shimmersilk scarves of pale green, clearly able to be used
as head coverings. Their garments suggested that they
were not indentured slaves.

"Honored Mage-Guard Taryl," offered the brunette, "I
am to escort you to Triad Jubyl."

"Honored Mage-Guard Rahl," added the redhead, "I
am to escort you to Mage-Guards Serita and Klassyn."

Taryl inclined his head to Rahl. "I'll send someone to
get you when we're done."

"Yes, ser."

Rahl's guide did not say more, but turned and led the
way toward a vaulted arch that opened onto another corridor. The columns that supported the arch were of a rose
marble, as were the polished floor tiles. She walked less
than fifty cubits down the corridor before turning right
and starting up an open staircase, whose steps and

balustrade were also of the rose marble. At the top of the steps was another foyer.

From down the corridor came the sound of music, not just a single harp or a guitar, or even a lute or a few violins, but a sweeping melody carried by many instruments. Rahl paused to listen, then looked to his guide. "The music?"

"Those are the Emperor's players, his personal orchestra."

Rahl had never heard of such, but he just nodded.

The guide turned and escorted Rahl to the third door on the left, which was open, where she announced, "Mage-Guard Rahl." Then she gestured for Rahl to enter.

He did.

A short hallway of three cubits opened into a larger square chamber with three sets of three floor-to-ceiling windows that overlooked a garden courtyard. The room was furnished as if a parlor in a great house, with settees and armchairs, but with two desks set against the opposing inside walls. Standing in the middle of the thick-piled square mauve carpet that was bordered in gold were two mage-guards.

Serita was small and wiry, and her black hair shimmered in the light from the windows. Klassyn was taller, but shorter than Rahl, and slightly stockier. He offered a broad and practiced smile.

"Welcome," said Serita, with a trace of shyness in her voice that Rahl found more appealing than Klassyn's big smile.

"Thank you." Rahl inclined his head to them. "I appreciate your hospitality."

Klassyn returned the gesture with the slightest head bow and a phrase.

> *"When words spoken come from the soul,*
> *all praise to the man who is whole."*

Rahl wasn't quite certain how to respond, but finally replied, "The most honest ones do."

"Please . . ." Serita gestured in the direction of one of the settees. "We don't see too many other mage-guards often."

Rahl took the wooden armchair closest to the settee, because there was a small side table between the settee and his chair. Serita took the place on the settee closest to Rahl.

Klassyn remained standing. "We'd like to offer you something to drink. A coach ride even from headquarters can be thirsty. What would you like? We have almost anything. That's one of the perquisites of being an assistant to the Emperor's Triad."

"That sounds wonderful," Rahl replied with a smile. "Just a pale lager, if you would."

Klassyn inclined his head to Serita.

"That actually sounds good. I think I'll have one, too. Have Vernya make sure it's the light amber, though. That's the better lager."

"I can manage that." Klassyn's smile was slightly strained. "I might even have one, too. It will make things easier."

"You . . . actually stooping to lager instead of chewy ales?"

"Sometimes, something lighter is good for a change, as you should know." Klassyn turned and walked toward the center corridor.

"You're an ordermage," Rahl said politely to Serita.

Her thin lips formed a crooked smile. "Of sorts. I have some healing talents, and I've had some ability in discovering which plants are useful in speeding healing, especially of injuries and wounds."

"What about Klassyn?"

"Klassyn is a chaos air mage," Serita added.

"Chaos air mage?" Rahl had never heard of such.

"He can use chaos and order to create storms—small

ones anyway." She glanced up as the other mage-guard returned.

"It won't be long," said Klassyn, seating himself in a chair at the other end of the settee and moving it forward and sideways so that he could look more directly at both Rahl and Serita.

"Is it true that you came from Recluce?" asked Serita.

"I don't think that's any secret," replied Rahl as genially as possible. "Recluce exiles a number of good people. The question isn't whether they're good but whether they fit."

Klassyn nodded, tilting his head slightly before quoting:

> *"What holds the storm, suits well the sun,*
> *or even night, when day is run."*

"Please, Klassyn," said Serita. "We know you studied the classic poets."

"So few do." Klassyn smiled politely.

"So few need to," she countered.

"And you were a harbor mage-guard in Swartheld— as an ordermage?" asked Klassyn. "You must be good with weapons."

"I do all right with a truncheon."

"Why did they post you there?" asked Serita. "Do you know?"

"I was a clerk for a factorage house when I was younger. I think someone liked the idea that I understood trade."

"Did you ever kill a Codex breaker?" asked Klassyn.

"Mostly, I disabled them. The captain wasn't displeased, I don't think, because that meant we had offenders we could send to Luba or the quarries."

"Oh . . . I hadn't thought of that, but then, I suppose, with your background," replied Klassyn, "you would have."

"It's more a practical thing," Rahl said, ignoring the dig at his time as a loader in the ironworks. "Killing people shows power, but dead people aren't much use. There are some people who aren't of much use alive, of course, but I've found those everywhere, and not just on the docks. Usually, they think they're far better and more important than they are." He smiled. "What do you two do as assistants to the Imperial Triad?"

"Emperor's Triad," corrected Klassyn.

"Whatever Triad Jubyl wants," replied Serita.

A bell tinkled, and Klassyn rose. "That must be Vernya. I'd better check."

Within moments, he had returned, with a serving girl following him. The girl had a tray on which were three crystal beakers. She served Rahl first, placing the beaker on the low table between him and Serita, then Serita, and finally Klassyn.

"That will be all, Vernya," said Serita.

Rahl lifted the crystal beaker, admiring the graceful lines of the Emperor's initials cut into the glass. There was something about the lager. He could almost sense—he could sense—the unnatural sweetness. Where had he . . . ? He tried not to freeze but smile pleasantly, as he realized that the lager held nemysa. "Beautiful engraving," he said blandly, setting the beaker down on the side table. "Excuse me." He wrinkled his nose, as if it itched. Could he exchange beakers? No . . . he could sense the same sweetness in the beaker that had been presented to Serita. Could it just be the type of lager? He had to trust his feelings that it was not, but what could he do? He'd asked for the drink, and not drinking it would certainly be unfriendly.

Abruptly, he sneezed, violently, and his arm swept out, knocking his beaker into Serita's, and both tumbled onto the stone tiles, shattering and spilling lager everywhere.

"Oh . . . I'm so sorry." Rahl managed another sneeze

as he stood. "I'm so sorry. I don't know what happened." He rubbed his nose, then blinked. "I do apologize. I don't know what set that off."

"Oh . . . these things happen," Serita said, not quite dismissively, as she rose.

"Upon rare occasion," added Klassyn.

"What rarer is to see than what can never be—"

"My dear Klassyn," interrupted Serita, "we all have found ourselves in similar situations. Please don't suggest that we have not. I do believe Rahl has handled himself as well as possible. Let us just resume our conversation on the other side of the chamber. Vernya can clean it up later."

Rahl followed Serita, but found he had to sit on the other settee beside her.

"Would you mind telling us about Recluce?" she asked.

"What would you like to know?"

"Why do they insist on exiling chaos-mages? Is it just because some ancient ruler didn't like Fairhaven?" asked Serita. "That really isn't a very good reason, is it?"

"Creslin supposedly was stripped of his memories and put on a road crew by the white wizards, and they kept trying to kill him and Megaera. For him, I imagine those were very good reasons." Rahl smiled politely. "Then that became a tradition, and it's hard to change tradition. The black engineers in Nylan don't care for chaos because they work with black iron, and they believe that chaos anywhere near would create a great danger." He shrugged. "You don't argue with them."

"Do they really have ships of black iron?"

"Oh, yes. They also have an engineering works of some size."

"You're not a chaos-mage. Why did you get exiled?"

"That's a long story," Rahl temporized, wondering just how much he should say. "There's no point in giving all the details. What happened was that I don't have the kind of order-skills that the magisters in Recluce know what to do with. So they spent some time teaching me Hamorian and a few other things and sent me off."

"No one would ever think you were from Recluce the way you speak," Serita said.

"From Atla or parts of Merowey, but not Recluce," Klassyn added.

"Where are you two from?" asked Rahl.

The rest of the conversation proceeded along relatively innocuous lines until the girl who had guided Rahl to Serita and Klassyn reappeared.

Rahl stood and smiled. "It appears as though I've been summoned. I thank you both very much for your patience, courtesy, and hospitality."

"Your presence and your knowledge have been most instructive," replied Serita.

Klassyn merely nodded as Rahl took his leave.

Taryl was waiting by himself in the functionary's foyer.

"Thank you," Rahl told the guide, before turning to Taryl. "I came as soon as you sent word."

"I've only been here a few moments. Shall we go?" Taryl raised his eyebrows.

They walked out through the archway and down to the duty coach, which had been driven to the forward mounting blocks.

Once they had settled themselves, and the coach was on its way through the outer gardens toward the gates in the white-stone wall, Taryl turned to Rahl.

"What happened? I can sense you're concerned."

"I hope Klassyn and Serita couldn't . . . or not why. They offered me a drink, and both my lager and Serita's were dosed with nemysa. At least, it felt that way."

"You didn't tell them that, I presume?" Taryl's voice was mild, but Rahl could sense his worry.

"No. I had a terrible attack of sneezing and inadvertently knocked over both beakers. After that and many

apologies, I decided that perhaps I'd better not tax their
hospitality further and drink anything at all. We talked
about personal history and Creslin."

"Excellent, but I will warn Jubyl about Klassyn."

"What about Serita?"

"Oh, she won't be in danger immediately. Klassyn
would have claimed that you'd attempted to dose all three
drinks and failed. They were all identical, were they not?"

"They were all pale lager."

"He needed someone else to blame. Or it could be that
you were intended to discover that the drinks were dosed,
and that they were tainted, but not with nemysa, or without enough to have an effect, and they hoped you would
make a scene or act inappropriately."

Was anything simple? "You don't seem that worried
about Serita."

"I'm not. She's loyal to Dhoryk, not to Jubyl or the
Emperor."

"And Triad Jubyl hasn't replaced her?"

"He's aware of her loyalties, or lack thereof, but at the
moment, he needs to play a deeper game. I'd rather not
say more right now, except that I must admit I didn't expect such an obvious move against you and me quite so
quickly. That suggests that Cyphryt is most worried, and
that means we need to move on to the High Command
post. If Jubyl and the Emperor act as they have indicated, we may be able to leave tomorrow, but hopefully
no later than fourday. The quarters won't be as comfortable, but that will reduce the frequency of such attempts
on us. Dhoryk would not wish anything to occur under
his hospitality."

Taryl had used the word *us,* as if the attempted poison-
ing had been against Taryl as well. As he thought about
it, Rahl wanted to shake his head. Of course, Rahl would
have been accused of acting under Taryl's orders . . .
or . . . He frowned.

"Yes?" asked Taryl. "You have a question?"

"Was it just to try to discredit you, or was it also to create problems with Recluce?"

"Both, I'd suspect."

"But why? Does Cyphryt want the rebellion to succeed?"

"Of course not. He just wants to show that Triad Fieryn's judgment, as indicated by his trust in me, as well as in other matters, such as the explosion of the Nylan Merchant Association buildings, proves he is not a worthy Triad."

"But . . . we stopped total destruction of the entire trade quarter in Swartheld," Rahl protested.

"*You* did, but that won't stop Cyphryt from intimating that what did happen was a result of Fieryn's decision to make Gheryk the mage-captain in Swartheld."

"But. . . . Craelyt did it all, and he killed Gheryk."

"Who can prove that?" asked Taryl. "When you're in command, no one cares when something bad happens even if you managed to keep far worse from occurring. In everyone's mind, it's still your fault that anything at all happened."

Rahl fell silent.

"It is most unlikely that Golyat will succeed in making Merowey independent of Hamor, but almost everyone in high circles of power—except Jubyl, the Emperor, and possibly Sea Marshal Chastyr—has an interest in fanning or prolonging the conflict." Taryl lifted and opened the satchel. "The darts that held chaos charges are exhausted, and I don't have the requisite abilities to recharge them. So you'll only have to decide which ones have quills and which needles. Block the needles."

"Ser . . ."

"You need practice, Rahl. Much more practice."

"Yes, ser." Rahl took a deep breath.

XII

Fourday morning found Rahl once more walking into the arms practice area, as ordered by Taryl—after Taryl had upbraided him for not attempting to work on learning to read the weather, even though he had practiced with the iron blocks. Rahl was beginning to feel as though he couldn't do everything that Taryl required . . . and that he never would be able to meet those standards. He had remembered to wear an exercise jersey, though.

With Khedren was another mage-guard, one that Rahl had not met or seen before.

"Rahl, this is Elatyr. I've asked him to put you through a full workout. You'll begin with truncheon and staff, and then you'll don the plated jersey and do your best with a real, if blunted, falchiona."

Rahl inclined his head to Elatyr. "Ser."

"Let's see what you can do." Elatyr extended a practice truncheon to Rahl, then turned and walked toward the center of the chamber.

Rahl followed.

As soon as he took his position, the older mage-guard attacked, with moves nearly as fast as those employed by Khedren. Rahl was slower than he would have liked with the first parry-slide, but he immediately recovered.

After a time, Elatyr seemed to slip and falter, but Rahl sensed the ploy and feinted, as if to take the bait, then used an uppercutting back slash to disarm the other. He stepped back.

Elatyr nodded, but Rahl could sense a certain annoyance. "Let's try again."

The older mage was more cautious on the second round, but Rahl exploited an opening when Elatyr extended himself just a touch too much and managed to beat down the other's truncheon and pin it with his boot.

"Why don't you try the staff?" suggested Khedren from the side.

"We might as well," said Elatyr dryly.

Rahl stepped back and blotted his forehead. He'd had to work hard. Elatyr was almost as good as Khedren and somewhat sneakier.

Khedren appeared with a set of practice staffs and took the two truncheons.

Effectively, Rahl and Elatyr were evenly matched with the staffs, and neither managed a touch on the other. Both were sweating heavily when Khedren called a halt. Again, Rahl could sense a certain irritation behind the politeness of the older mage.

"Sit down and cool off while I get the plated jerseys," Khedren said.

Rahl walked back to the nearest bench and blotted his forehead, then leaned back and let the back of his head rest against the cooler stone of the wall.

Elatyr took the other bench but did not look in Rahl's direction.

Shortly, Khedren returned with two of the plated practice jerseys over one arm and two practice falchionas held together by a leather strap in the other hand. "Here you go." He laid one blade and one jersey on the bench beside Rahl, then carried the other to Elatyr.

Rahl straightened, then eased himself into the heavy plated practice jersey. He wasn't looking forward to what came next, not at all. Still, it would be interesting to see how effective the techniques Khedren had shown him might be. He just hoped that finding out wouldn't be too painful.

Slowly, he picked up the practice falchiona. Unlike the weighted blank with which he had practiced, the weapon felt ugly and reddish white to his order-senses. He glanced toward Elatyr, who stood waiting in the middle of the chamber. From just the way in which Elatyr handled the practice falchiona, Rahl could sense that he was very much at ease with the blade. Rahl just hoped that the plates in the jersey would prove adequate to keep him from getting too badly bruised.

He walked out to meet the other mage-guard.

"No leg cuts, now," Khedren reminded the two. "Just upper body."

Rahl nodded, then lifted the blade into guard position. Even before Elatyr moved his blade, Rahl began one of the patterns Khedren had shown him. For a moment, he sensed momentary surprise in Elatyr, but that didn't stop the other mage-guard from a feint that led to a sliding tip backcut.

Rahl's footwork kept him from having even to cross blades with Elatyr for several moments more, but before long he was having to slide and parry, in addition to circling to the side.

After that, each time their blades crossed, white lances of pain shot up his arm. He managed to avoid any direct hits, but one of Elatyr's cutting slashes angled off one of the jersey's hip plates, and Rahl staggered, then scrambled aside. He barely managed to block the next cut and beat aside the thrust that followed.

From that point on, through a haze of chaos-pain, and physical strain, Rahl had to rely on instinct and training.

"That's enough," Khedren called out loudly.

Rahl stepped back and lowered the falchiona, which he could barely even hold. He was just glad he'd survived without taking a major blow. At least, he didn't think he had.

He walked slowly toward the bench, where he set down the practice blade, glad to have it out of his hand, and slowly struggled out of the practice jersey, soaked with sweat, as was his own jersey under it. Rahl just sat on the bench. Bright flashes of light, like pointed darts, flared before his eyes, and his entire body ached.

Off to one side, a good twenty cubits away, he could see Elatyr gesturing. Despite the pain and effort it required, Rahl forced himself to extend his order-senses.

". . . know he's an ordermage . . . can feel it . . . but no ordermage . . . do that . . ."

". . . not gray . . . not a hint of white there . . ."

". . . how could he . . ."

". . . remember . . . loader in Luba . . . suspect he can handle more pain . . . look over there. He's not feeling all that good."

". . . ought to be stretched out on the stone . . ."

". . . could be, but that isn't what we were asked . . ."

". . . approve his skills . . . no question there . . . awfully young, though . . ."

". . . headed to Merowey . . ."

"That makes more sense . . ."

Whatever it was didn't make any more sense to Rahl, except that someone wanted someone else besides Khedren to assess his arms abilities. He just sat on the bench, trying to recover some strength. He wasn't certain how long he sat there, but he was aware that Elatyr had left and that Khedren was carrying a mug of something toward him.

"You look like you could use this." Khedren extended the mug.

Rahl sipped the heavy ale.

The armsmaster sat on the bench beside him. "You did well. Elatyr is the southeast regional armsmaster—that's in Sylpa."

"Even with everything you taught me," Rahl said slowly, "I couldn't keep him from getting through." Even after a few sips, he could tell that the ale helped, because the worst of the light flashes subsided.

"Only a few times," Khedren pointed out. "Most chaos types wouldn't have done that much better."

"They would have lasted longer," Rahl pointed out.

"Not much," replied Khedren. "You can't last longer if you've been knocked cold or you've been disarmed. Anyway, you've learned enough to stay alive for a while against a good blade. You could kill an average armsman with a falchiona if you had to."

Somehow, that assessment didn't cheer Rahl much. It suggested that a good armsman could kill him, and that angered him, because he knew he could have done much better if he could just have held on to the blade without feeling chaos-pain all the time. He took a larger swallow of the ale. "I think I'd better stick to the truncheon."

"That you should, when you can. But even being able to hold a falchiona can hold some folks at bay."

Rahl knew that was doubtless true, but he didn't have to like it.

"If you're around in the morning, I could use some help with the staff and the mage-clerks."

"If Taryl doesn't have something else planned, I'll be here."

"Good. I need to see to some papers with Elatyr. Leave the mug here when you go."

"Yes, ser."

Rahl watched the armsmaster hurry off, then slowly finished the ale. He could almost see normally by the time he stood and started back toward the main building.

Rahl didn't see Taryl as he walked through the quarters entry and headed to clean up, but he did see Edelya, and there was no polite way to avoid her as she smiled and walked toward him.

"You look like you've had a workout, Rahl."

Rahl managed a laugh. "I did."

"Helping Khedren with the mage-clerks again?"

"No. He had me sparring with another armsmaster. Elatyr. The truncheon and the staff weren't bad."

"He didn't bang you up too badly, then?"

Rahl couldn't help but be irritated by the condescension behind the inquiry. "Not with those. I disarmed him twice with the truncheon. The staff was a draw. No hits by either of us."

Rahl ignored the order-sensing. He was telling the truth.

"Not with those, you said," prompted Edelya.

"I had to use a falchiona after that. I've been working

on techniques for defense in case I didn't have anything else with me. He did hit me a few times, but only glancing blows. Well, except once."

Edelya looked hard at him. "You're an ordermage. You went a full sparring round with a falchiona against Elatyr?"

"Yes. Why wouldn't I?"

Abruptly, she smiled, as if she had discovered something. "Oh, nothing. Most mage-guards don't. Even chaos types."

"If you'll excuse me . . . I really do need a shower."

The calculating smile changed to one that was more like a grin. "Yes, you do. I'll see you later."

As he walked back toward the washrooms, Rahl couldn't help but wonder what she had learned, or what he had revealed. Khedren hadn't hidden the fact that Elatyr was an armsmaster, and it was clear he wanted Rahl to spar against someone else of ability besides himself. That certainly made sense.

XIII

After showering and donning a clean uniform, Rahl returned to the lower level, then to the library. He walked some of the other corridors, and checked Taryl's quarters, but he did not see Taryl anywhere. So he returned to the library and settled into reading more of the mage-guard history. What was more intriguing were the observations on why things had happened. One short section, in particular, caught his attention:

As a result of the loss of the expeditionary fleet to Recluce and the previously unobserved powers of its weather mages, Emperor Cyth'alt resolved to change the very structure of Hamor. So many of what historians

view as changes in lands or societies are nothing of the
sort, but merely the replacement of one set of rulers for
another with exactly the same beliefs and systems of
ruling. Cyth'alt was wise enough to understand this. He
was wiser than that, in that the reforms he put in place
were designed not to change the appearance of existing
institutions but to change their very functions without
changing their outward appearance. By geographically
separating two-thirds of the Triad from the Imperial
Palace, and by creating an independent High Command,
he not only limited the very powers of the emperor, but
strengthened Hamor by attempting to assure that all
decisions would require action by three separate power
centers . . . Yet by reifying these essentially new sources
of power in existing institutions, he also created the
illusion that nothing had changed . . .

Some skeptics suggest that his decisions were based
on the fact that, since he had no sons, he wished to
place checks on his brother's offspring . . . Whatever
the reason, the very structure of today's Hamor dates
from those decisions . . .

Despite such occasionally and too infrequently interesting passages, Rahl found himself nodding off, doubtless because of his efforts against Elatyr, and he finally
left the book open on his lap and let himself doze. When
he woke, he shelved the volume and decided to make his
way to the mess, although he knew he would be early for
dinner.

In the foyer outside the mess, he saw Taryl in the middle
of a group of mage-guards, mostly older men, although
there were several women mage-guards as well. Rahl did
not recognize any of them by name, although he had seen
several at the seniors' table at previous meals.

Rahl started to ease away when Taryl caught his eye.

"If you would excuse me for a moment," Taryl said,
stepping away from the group and toward Rahl.

Rahl realized that Taryl was not wearing the standard

mage-guard starburst, but another insignia—one in which the starburst was set above a crossed staff and lightning bolt.

"New insignia, ser," Rahl offered.

"I've been appointed Mage-Guard Overcommander of Merowey. We'll need to meet after dinner. I don't know how long things will take. If I'm not here when you finish, do some reading, and I'll get you from the library."

"Yes, ser."

With a pleasant smile, Taryl nodded and returned to the others. "You'll pardon me, but this was such an unexpected promotion that neither I nor my assistant had any knowledge of the Emperor's and the Triad's decision, and this is the first time I have seen Rahl."

As Rahl turned away, he maintained a pleasant smile. While Taryl might not have *known*, it was clear to Rahl that Taryl's new position had resulted from the meetings of the previous days.

Once the mess doors opened, Rahl seated himself with the three mage-guards he knew more than just by name—Laryn, Devalyn, and Rhyett. The main course at dinner was burhka, with side platters of goat biastras. As he wrapped the flat bread around the thin tube of goat, Rahl couldn't help but think of Deybri . . . and the letter he still carried with him.

"Taryl's wearing an overcommander's insignia," observed Devalyn, looking to Rahl. "All the seniors are courting him . . . again." After a pause, he offered in a more formal tone,

> *"For those in power all will court,*
> *in seeking softer words of praise,*
> *and bringing harder truths up short,*
> *exalting self and sunlit days."*

Rahl glanced at Devalyn.

"That's Elhazuryn, one of the old Afritan poets."

"Does everyone quote old poets?" asked Rahl curiously.

"Only in Cigoerne," injected Rhyett. "You're considered . . . uncultured . . . if you don't."

Rahl had a suspicion that Rhyett had almost said "Atlan," but he just smiled. "I'd better read a few of them, then. Are there any in the library here?"

"Ah . . . I don't know. I've never looked," replied Rhyett.

Rahl turned his eyes on Devalyn.

Devalyn shrugged. "Me, neither. I just memorized a bunch because my father said they'd be useful. It helps if you deal with Vladyrt. Saulya just laughs, but that helps, too."

"Do you know where Taryl's going?" asked Rhyett.

"He's been appointed Mage-Guard Overcommander in Merowey," Rahl replied, "but I don't know more than that."

"That won't go down well with Cyphryt or Welleyn," murmured Rhyett.

"You think not? I can't imagine why." Laryn's voice was pleasantly ironic.

"Are you going with him?" asked Rhyett.

"Yes. I don't know when we'll leave, though, except it's likely to be before too long."

"Word is that you should have been an arms-mage," ventured Laryn. "One of the mage-clerks said you disarmed every one of them, just using a truncheon."

"There are advantages to having been a patrol mage in Swartheld," Rahl replied. "I can't use chaos, and that meant I had to be good with the truncheon."

"That's why the best mage-guards with the army are those who can handle a blade," Devalyn pointed out. "You get exhausted if all you can do is throw chaos. You'll run out of chaos before the enemy runs out of armsmen."

Rhyett gave Devalyn a hard look.

"That's what Khedren says," added Devalyn.

No one pressed Rahl on what Taryl had in mind for the rest of the meal, and when he had finished, he made his way to the library.

Rahl had read enough of the two mage-guard histories, more than enough, he thought, and he began to peruse the shelves to see if he could find any volumes of the old poets. Most of the verse, he discovered, was rather more florid than what he'd heard, as he read the opening of something called "Remembrances Past."

> *Evening's soft hues seep o'er the hamlet's green,*
> *with magely tints to harmonize the scene,*
> *stilled is the crack that through the village broke*
> *when to the ground crashed down their ancient oak . . .*

Surely, there had to be something that he could memorize and use, as necessary, if sparingly, to suggest he'd read *something*.

One set of lines suggested Saulya to him.

> *You spoke and smiled, and I believed*
> *By every sound and word deceived . . .*

Another set of lines bewildered him more than anything else at first, and he read them several times.

> *As if your deepest thoughts had been screed clear*
> *and in the glass set forth with every fear,*
> *while we stand a hundred kays apart*
> *order links us life to life, heart to heart.*

Could an ordermage actually use a glass to see something hundreds of kays away—or sense what someone was feeling? Certainly, Rahl could sense what someone else felt, but only when they were near. How would such a glass work? Or was it something special that had only existed in ancient Cyad?

He finally left those lines of verse and leafed on through the book.

Rahl had only found two or three sets of lines that he had committed—he hoped—to memory when Taryl appeared. Rahl quickly reshelved the books and hurried out after Taryl, who, in turn, led him back down to the underground chamber.

The older mage-guard did not speak until he had closed the door to the small windowless chamber, lit only by a single bronze wall lamp, and stood behind the small table where Rahl had manipulated sand and water. The table was now clean, without a trace of either sand or water. "Rahl . . . there is a great deal at stake here, and I'll be more than happy to explain matters once we leave headquarters, but not until then."

"What about your becoming an overcommander? Can you explain that?"

"Everyone will know that in a few days. The Emperor made the appointment, but he told Dhoryk beforehand that he would. Dhoryk agreed, because he's been trying his best to discredit Fieryn's leadership and choice of seniors. Dhoryk also didn't want to cross Jubyl, not when Fieryn's already his enemy. While Fieryn didn't like it, with the Emperor and two out of the Triad supporting the choice, Fieryn really had no choice but to accede."

"So Jubyl and the Emperor were the ones who really sent you to Recluce, then?"

"I can't admit that, but I won't contradict it, either. For the moment, those matters are all you need to know."

"I can't reveal matters inadvertently if I know nothing?" Rahl tried to keep the tinge of bitterness out of his voice.

"Your shields are strong enough to hide anything, but you're not yet skilled enough to hide the fact that you're hiding something. That alone, given the right questions, would reveal more than necessary, and there is the difficulty that there are those who would use any tactic to discover certain things."

"Like Saulya or Edelya?"

Taryl laughed softly. "They're gentle by comparison to Cyphryt and Welleyn and some of their enthusiastic subordinates."

"Who is Welleyn? Rhyett mentioned him at dinner."

"Welleyn is the overcommander of the Cigoerne region, and that effectively makes him the third-most-powerful mage-guard and the equal of Cyphryt. They're both vying to succeed Fieryn."

"But don't the senior mage-guards select a successor?"

"They do, and it's usually who's the most powerful, for obvious reasons. Very few of the Triads have been chaos-mages. Fieryn and Dhoryk among the few. Now . . . enough of that. We can talk about such on the way to the High Command."

"Yes, ser."

"I want you to raise full personal shields. You'll need them."

Rahl did so.

"I'm going to ask you questions, and I want you to try to avoid revealing anything . . . or any emotion involved with the answers." Taryl extended a tendril of order and snuffed out the wall lamp.

"Yes, ser." Rahl waited in the darkness.

"Were you really so stupid as to think you could seduce that girl in Land's End with order and not get her with child?"

Rahl tried not to think about Jienela, but why had Taryl used that question?

"Did you honestly think that even a second-rate order-master like Puvort wouldn't have known what you'd done? Or do you just think he's second-rate because he discovered you were breaking the laws?"

Rahl tried just to think of Deybri, anything calming, behind his shields.

"Rahl! You're not paying attention. You never do, not for long enough, anyway." Taryl's voice dripped sarcasm and venom. "Why do you always think you know better? Was that why you killed the undercaptain? Because he really did know better than you, and you couldn't face it?"

Rahl could sense the disapproval, the condescension behind Taryl's words. What had he done so wrong?

"Feeling sorry for yourself now? Is that it?" Waves of scorn washed toward Rahl. "You think you're the only one in the world who's had troubles?"

Rahl knew he wasn't, but certainly more than a few of the mage-guards had led far easier and more sheltered lives than Rahl.

"Do you really think that it was just Shyret's fault that you ended up in Luba?"

The questions seemed to go on and on, as did waves of the condescension, scorn, and disappointment. What had he done to upset Taryl so much? Had he misread the older mage? And Hamor and the mage-guards?

Then, almost abruptly, Taryl stopped badgering Rahl. The older mage-guard walked past Rahl and relit the lamp before turning to face Rahl. Taryl's face was dripping sweat, and Rahl could sense the strain that the "exercise" had taken on him.

"I asked you questions designed to upset you and put you on edge, but that was merely a small sampling of what a truly cruel and disciplined mage-guard interrogator can do." Even Taryl's voice sounded tired. "You didn't do too badly, except you still feel far too guilty, and I could guess your answers to a number of the questions by the fluctuations in your shields and the level of your anger. Several times, whatever you were thinking of, you were totally effective. I think you know when that happened. You need to work on that. I suggest that you practice being very polite at the mess and projecting only friendliness. Keep everything else behind shields. Keep at it until it's a firm habit. I can't do much more with you on this, because now you'll be expecting it, and it won't have that kind of impact anymore."

Rahl could see that.

"Remember this. I like you far too much truly to batter at you, or to deceive or ensnare you. I hope you understand that." Taryl took a deep breath. "I need to wait a bit before heading upstairs. Do you have any questions?"

"I came across something in the library," Rahl offered, wanting to shift the conversation away from the failings that Taryl had exposed. "The writer mentioned screeing, and seeing someone in a glass, and also sensing what they felt through it."

Taryl frowned. "They have it mixed up. It's a rare ability, but some mages can use a glass to see events at a distance. Once it was said only chaos-mages had the talent, but a few ordermages have shown that ability, but it's said they do it differently. I wouldn't know." He smiled. "Like all ambitious young mages, I tried it, but never had any success. As for sensing what others feel, some mages who are consorted develop that closeness. There supposedly is a way to force such a link, and the legends say that it was done to Creslin and Megaera—you should know about that."

"It's not mentioned in any of the readings or the legends, and none of the magisters said anything about it," Rahl replied carefully.

"The more I hear about what they don't teach, the more I have to wonder how long the isle will remain strong." Taryl snorted.

"The engineers teach more, but they're not . . ." Rahl didn't really want to finish that sentence.

"Yes? What?"

"They only see things their way, and if you ask questions that don't fit, they get unhappy."

Taryl laughed. "That describes most people in most lands. We all want things our way."

"You were talking about that link . . ."

"I don't know how it could be accomplished, nor do I wish to know that, nor would any honest mage ever want to wreak such violence on another. It could kill both parties."

"Was that why they died young?"

"It could be. It also could be that they were so linked that one could not survive the other's death." Taryl used a cloth to blot his face.

"What plans do you have for me for tomorrow?"

"Not that many." Taryl smiled. "But you'll need to pack all your gear tonight. We'll be leaving headquarters right after breakfast and traveling to quarters at the High Command. But don't forget to practice with trying to see the weather. I'll expect a report while we're traveling tomorrow."

"Yes, ser." Rahl had forgotten about the weather exercises, although he had actually managed to order-lift one of the tiny iron cubes rather than just to push it across a smooth surface.

XIV

After leaving Taryl, Rahl walked up the narrow steps that led to the small stone-walled platform above the quarters wing. It was late enough that he doubted anyone would be on the platform, and it was easier for him to sense what little he could about the weather when he was outside. He thought it might be easier yet if he were higher. Taryl had only mentioned the platform, but it was no secret, and he'd seen others using the steps.

The door that opened onto the platform was secured only by a latch. Rahl paused, letting his order-senses extend out beyond the closed door, but there was no one on the platform. He opened the door and stepped into the night.

The evening air was still—cool and heavy. The slightest hint of a breeze wafted across his face, coming from the east-northeast. Rahl walked to the stone balustrade on the north side of the platform—a space no more than six cubits on a side—and faced into the light breath of air. He stood there, not so much concentrating as letting his order-senses be one with the air, trying to feel the dispersed water in it, and the various patterns that it created.

More to the east, over the Swarth River, there was a greater feel of water in the air, and beyond that, much higher in the sky, there was even more. He almost laughed. There were clouds there that he could make out because they blocked the stars, and he certainly didn't need order-sensing to determine where there were clouds he could see.

Were there clouds beyond the ones he could see?

He tried to let his order-senses feel what lay beyond the nearer clouds, and while he had a feeling of more water in the air, he could not be certain. Slowly, he let his senses range across the skies, moving slowly around the platform as he did. In the end the only dampness in the air near Cigoerne seemed to be that to the northeast, but he had no idea whether that meant rain, although he thought he had felt some motion toward the city.

When he felt he could do no more, he left the platform, but he was careful to latch the upper door behind him. As he walked down the stone steps toward his single room, he thought about the weather. Taryl had said that weather was nothing more than heat and water. People and animals and everything that lived held some water. Rahl didn't know how much, but there had to be some. And most land, except the deserts, held water. So did most air. So . . . if he could sense weather, at a distance, why couldn't he sense other things? Even sense them with a glass the way Taryl said some mages could?

The second-level corridor to his room was empty, although it didn't seem all that late to him, but it could be that many of the mage-guards were at the Staff and Blade. Abruptly, Rahl had to wonder what had changed. When he'd been an apprentice scrivener, he couldn't wait to go out, either to play plaques with Sevien or just to share talk and redberry or ale. Now, it didn't seem that important.

Once he was back in his room, he slid the door bolt into place, then took the mirror off the wall and laid it flat on the small writing table. He sat down at the table and looked down at the mirror. His own face looked back at him.

What should he do? How did one look for someone or something? Whom could he seek out? It should be someone he knew, but not a greater mage-guard. That might be embarrassing, or even dangerous. He also did not think it wise to seek anyone who might encounter him casually.

Idly, he wondered what Edelya was doing. Then he let his order-senses reach for an image of what he recalled of the blond mage-guard.

The glass silvered, and fog seemed to swirl somewhere beneath the shimmering surface. Slowly, a face appeared in the center of the glass, wreathed in fog, a sleeping face. Abruptly, Edelya's eyes flew open, and a look of fear appeared, and her mouth opened as if she would scream.

Rahl was so startled by her reaction that he released all his order-hold on the glass. It was just a mirror once more. He found he was breathing faster, and he was slightly light-headed. He didn't want to lose the feeling of what he had done, but he certainly didn't want to try to look at anyone—or not another mage. It was clear that Edelya had felt something. Could all mages sense being seen through screeing?

After resting for several moments, Rahl decided just to see if he could view the platform from where he'd sought out the weather. This time, he tried to visualize looking eastward toward the scattered lights of Cigoerne. Once more, the glass silvered over, then showed swirling mists, and slowly, indistinctly, an image emerged, foglike, but clear, showing a section of the ring road and the Northern Boulevard, stretching eastward.

Rahl could feel himself getting light-headed, and he tried to relax, not to use so much effort. That seemed to help, but he could still feel the strain, as well as the sweat beginning to roll down the sides of his face. He stopped, and found he needed to take several deep breaths.

Had he succeeded? Or had he imagined it? He looked down more closely at the mirror. A thin line of frost ran around the outside edge of the glass. He touched the glass there. It was so cold that for a moment, it felt like he'd burned his fingertip. He'd definitely done something.

Rahl smiled. Perhaps . . . just perhaps . . . if he practiced . . . if he worked at it . . . he might be able to obtain a glimpse of Deybri.

He wiped his forehead and blinked. A white oblong caught his eye—the still-unsent letter to Deybri. He smiled, if but for a moment.

Taryl—and the ancient poet—had both mentioned, if in different ways, that consorted mages could develop a link. Was that what he felt with Deybri?

He shook his head. That sort of thing only happened in legends and ancient poems. Anyway, it was just wistful thinking. Or dangerous thinking. Or both. Would he want someone, even someone as warm as Deybri, knowing his every feeling? Yet why did he feel so much for her? It hadn't been like that with any other girl—or woman. But . . . what use was there in pursuing such thoughts? No matter how accomplished he became with order-skills, none of the magisters would let him return to Recluce. In fact, he suspected that the more accomplished he became, the less likely they would be to allow him to return.

If it weren't for Deybri . . . would he even care?

Yet . . . Hamor was far more dangerous than he had realized, even with Taryl's efforts to help him and guide him.

He almost laughed as he recalled that, in its own way, Recluce had also been dangerous.

With a last glance at the letter, he rose from the writing table. Slowly he opened the narrow wardrobe. He bent down and pulled out the canvas gear bag and set it on the foot of the bed.

He took a deep breath. He still had to pack.

XV

On fiveday at breakfast, Rahl sat between Devalyn and Fientard, and, mindful of Taryl's suggestion, even before joining them, had strengthened his personal shields and tried to overlay them with a "wash" of friendliness.

"I have to ask," Fientard said, after eating several mouthfuls, "where you got your arms training. Khedren was impressed, and so was Elatyr, and they aren't often pleased."

Rahl could sense Devalyn's increased attention, as well as that of others, but he just smiled, holding friendliness in front of his shields. "I'd have to say that I owe much to my father. He put a truncheon in my hand almost as soon as I could hold it."

"He was a patroller or mage-guard?"

"No. He was a scrivener, but he was very good with the truncheon and not bad with the staff." Rahl waited a moment before continuing. "I also worked with some armsmasters in Nylan, and then with Khaill in Luba, and then with the armsmaster in Swartheld."

"Nylan?" Fientard frowned. "I thought you were from Atla or Merowey."

Rahl shrugged. "That's just how I learned to speak."

Devalyn frowned. "You didn't mention you were trained as an order armsmaster."

"I wasn't. They tried to teach me about both order and arms. I didn't learn much about order, but I did learn something about arms before I got sent to Swartheld."

Fientard was the one to frown. "And the mage-guards made you a clerk there?"

Rahl laughed, a slight struggle while maintaining tight personal shields. "Oh, no. I was a clerk. I didn't have that many order-skills, but I was working for an outland trading outfit, and I was registered . . ." He explained quickly how he'd ended up in Luba as a loader without any memory and his progress from there.

The armsmaster's assistant nodded slowly. "Makes sense. Also explains a lot."

"What do you mean?" asked Devalyn.

An embarrassed smile crossed Fientard's face before he responded. "More than a few mage-guards only learn weapons because they have to. They think that chaos will always save them. Doesn't always happen that way."

"I don't know about that," Devalyn replied. "Why are there so many chaos types compared to order types?"

"That's only here in Hamor," Rahl replied. "The Balance applies to the entire world. The ordermages in Recluce could ask why there are so many order types as compared to chaos types."

"There's something else to think about," interjected Rhyett from down the table. "Chaos is more suited to attacking, and order more suited to defending. On land, anyway."

"You won't solve that question by discussion," said a mage-guard Rahl didn't recognize. "It's how each is handled. . . ."

Rahl was more than happy to let others debate. He had the feeling that the less others knew about his ability, the better.

Once he finished breakfast, Rahl started out from the mess when Taryl appeared and gestured to him. "I'll be a while. It might be midmorning."

"Khedren asked if I could help him. Would that be all right for a time?"

"Until midmorning. If I'm through before that, I'll get you."

"Yes, ser."

Before going to help Khedren, Rahl went back to his quarters room and made sure that his gear was ready to go. Then he walked back to the arms exercise building in back.

Most of what Rahl did for Khedren was to illustrate specific moves with the staff, then make an attack on each of the mage-clerks of the sort that could be blocked, parried, or countered with the move they had just been shown.

Rahl found it more tiring than he'd thought it would be because there was no telling what some of them would do.

After the group had left, Rahl looked at the armsmaster. "That's hard work."

"But necessary." Khedren grinned. "You've got the makings of an armsmaster, leastwise with staff and truncheon."

"I thought you had to be a chaos type for that."

"Most are, but . . . if you're good enough to beat a master blade with a staff or truncheon . . . there have been a few." Khedren shook his head. "You'll do better than that. That's if you listen close to Taryl." He paused. "You'd better go. Wouldn't want to keep him waiting."

Rahl did have a chance to wash up a bit before he carried his gear down to the waiting coach. He had no sooner eased his gear into the small luggage compartment at the back of the coach, beside Taryl's two larger canvas gear bags, and closed it than the driver appeared to slip a latch clip in place.

"Wouldn't want anything falling out, ser."

"That we wouldn't." Rahl offered a smile, then scrambled into the coach and eased past Taryl to the side away from the door.

Because he sensed Taryl was preoccupied, he said nothing, just watched through the open window, glad of the slight breeze generated by the motion of the coach as it headed eastward on the Northern Boulevard. The area around Mage-Guard Headquarters was meadow, or grass-lands, for almost half a kay in all directions. Then there were dwellings and small shops. Rahl caught sight of the Staff and Blade—the tavern he'd never visited in the short time he'd been at headquarters. Rahl wondered why they were headed back into Cigoerne, rather than taking the ring road as they had before. Doubtless, Taryl had some reason, but Rahl wasn't about to ask at the moment.

They'd traveled slightly more than a kay when Taryl looked up, and asked genially, "What can you tell me about the weather?"

"Ah . . . there aren't any clouds close, except to the northeast, and there are more farther to the northeast. There's some water in them, and the wind is still blowing out of the northeast." Rahl shrugged. "I can only guess that there might be some light rain here by tonight. That's just a guess."

"Keep practicing. You'll get better at it." Taryl nod-ded. "You were carrying stronger personal shields when you got in the coach. That's good."

"It's work," Rahl admitted.

"Did you help Khedren this morning?"

"With staff demonstrations and practice," Rahl ad-mitted.

"He thinks you could be an armsmaster. If you could be more patient."

Rahl thought he'd been very patient with the uppity mage-clerks. "He told me that, ser."

"But what?"

"Ah . . ." Rahl wasn't quite sure what to say.

"Yes?"

"Was I that bad when you and Khaill started working with me?"

Taryl laughed. "No. But you'd already had consider-able training. You were doubtless that bad when you started."

As the coach neared the intersection with another wide

avenue, the driver slowed, then turned southward. Like some of the avenues and boulevards in Swartheld, the one they now traveled held a wide center area landscaped in trees, bushes, and gardens, with a center paved walkway. Larger homes, not quite estates, flanked the avenue, with low walls around them. Most of the small mansions were square or oblong and appeared to have central garden courtyards. From what Rahl could see, there were more impressive dwellings along the Western Avenue than in all of the parts of Swartheld that he'd seen.

After a moment, he spoke. "Ser . . . I do have a favor to ask."

"Yes?" Taryl raised his thin eyebrows.

"I still have this letter I'd like to post."

The overcommander nodded. "I thought you might. I asked the driver to go by way of the Great West Avenue, then the Southern Boulevard to the River Road. We'll pass the south city mage-guard station, and we'll stop there." Taryl lifted his satchel. "In the meantime, I have another exercise for you."

Taryl took out a thin sheet of iron and laid it on his lap. Then came three small iron boxes without tops, and finally came a small square of iron. "While you're not looking, or using your order-senses, I'll put the small cube under one of the boxes, and we'll shuffle them around, and you use your order-senses to tell me which box it's under."

Rahl nodded warily. That didn't seem all that hard, but usually with Taryl what seemed not all that hard was anything but easy. He looked away until Taryl cleared his throat.

"You can try now."

Rahl extended his order-senses—and realized that each of the upside-down boxes had been imbued with enough free order to mask what was—or was not—inside it.

"Well?"

Rahl concentrated, trying to sense any minute variation in the amount of order or . . . something. Finally, he said, "The one closest the window."

Taryl lifted the box. There was nothing under it. "Look away. You can try again."

It took Rahl five attempts before he realized that Taryl had changed the amount of order in the covering boxes themselves to conceal the small metal cube. Then he got the placement right the next three times.

"Good. Now . . . we'll try a different variation."

Rahl had been struggling so hard with Taryl's exercise that he really hadn't paid too much attention to their surroundings, but he could feel the coach slow again as the driver turned back eastward.

"This time should be a little more difficult," Taryl said.

Once more, Rahl was stymied and couldn't discover where the target metal cube was hidden—until he realized that Taryl had placed a miniature order shield around the cube. By probing for such a shield, Rahl could find the cube on the first attempt.

By now, his forehead was damp from the effort.

Abruptly, Taryl looked up, then leaned out the window and called to the driver, "Don't forget to stop at the south mage-guard station."

"Yes, ser. It's about a half kay ahead."

Taryl set aside the metal board and boxes, placing them on the seat across from him, rather than back in the satchel.

As the coach eased to a halt outside a two-story stone building that could have been a duplicate of the Swartheld station, Rahl eased the letter out from inside his uniform shirt and extended it to Taryl. "Here's the letter, ser."

Taryl took the envelope, studied it for a moment. "Everything's on it, and you've got a clear hand. Good."

"Oh, ser." Rahl extended four silvers. "I think this should be enough."

Taryl took the coins. "That looks about right. I'll let you know if it's more or give you the change." He opened the coach door and stepped out. "I'll be back in a bit. I hope it won't take too long."

Why would it take too long? Rahl frowned.

Without even the slight breeze caused by the coach's movement, and even with both windows open, the passenger compartment felt warm and close. Rahl glanced at the metal board and the boxes and the metal cube, then probed them with his order-senses. They were just what Taryl had said they were—worked iron, not black iron, or anything else.

He still had to wonder what the purpose of the exercise might be, although he knew that Taryl did nothing without a reason.

Rahl settled back in the seat and waited . . . and waited . . . and waited.

Finally, Taryl reappeared, followed by a squat mage-captain who stood outside the station as the overcommander reentered the coach.

"I'm sorry, but I had to spend a little time with Captain Myelr. He'll make sure that it won't get intercepted." Taryl settled himself in the seat, and the coach pulled away and back out onto the Southern Boulevard.

"You must know most of the captains."

"Not most, but many." Taryl extended his hand. "Here's your change."

"Thank you." Rahl took the three coppers.

"Now . . . back to the exercise. You've mastered the simple parts. We'll see about the more complex ones, now."

More exercise practice? More complex?

Why was Taryl pushing him so hard? From what little Rahl had seen at headquarters and from his time at Swartheld harbor station, he knew most other mage-guards weren't pressed to improve skills the way Taryl was pressing him, and he also knew his skills were better than those of most mage-guards, especially of those close to his own age.

Taryl grinned. "You could practice keeping your feelings of irritation and resignation behind shields, too."

Rahl did sigh.

XVI

Rahl was almost exhausted by the time the coach reached the High Command. This time, the driver did not stop at the headquarters building but drove on southward and followed the stone-paved road through a gap in the berm into what, at first glance, appeared to be a large town, or small city with rectangular blocks and stone-paved streets. While the buildings were of a gray stone, rather than the white of Cigoerne, the roofs were still of red tile.

"The quarters for the senior officers are those closest to the headquarters, on the higher part of the slope," Taryl said, gesturing to the west. "The piers and loading docks are along the river, and behind them are the storehouses. Then come the barracks for the troops, and farther west, the quarters for the senior squad leaders, and then the junior officers' quarters, and behind them the visiting and senior officers' quarters. That's where we're headed. The armories and ammunition bunkers are farther south, behind another berm."

Ammunition? "The army uses cannon?"

"When prudent. We won't be traveling with any, though. Given the number of chaos mage-guards that support Golyat, attempting to use cannon does not appear practical at this time." Taryl's voice was dry.

"How long will we be here?"

"Much of that is up to the marshal, but not entirely. The Emperor wishes matters resolved so that Marshal Byrna cannot delay excessively."

"Why would he want to delay?"

"To amass as many troops and as much cavalry and mounted heavy infantry as he can. He is one of those who believes that battles are only won by superiority in matériel and numbers of troops. Now . . . there are several matters I haven't mentioned. First, you are a captain. Mage-guards assigned to the High Command have an assumed rank of captain, unless they have an actual rank."

"So you rank as a senior officer?"

"As a mage-guard overcommander, I'm the same as a junior marshal."

"Marshal Byrna doesn't outrank you, then."

"No, but I don't outrank him, and that means we have to work together." Taryl smiled. "There's also one other military custom that's very different. You won't have a problem with it, but, by the same token, remember that it is unusual for Hamor. All officers eat at the same tables in the mess, regardless of whether they are men or women. Now, there aren't as many women officers as there are women mage-guards, and most are captains or majers, but at the mess all seating is by general rank."

"That means I sit among the captains? Do they go by date of rank?"

"No. For seating at the mess, all of the same rank are considered of equal precedence. The second matter is that you are never to discuss anything involved with magery or with whatever tasks you are assigned, except in very general terms. Third, no matter what is said about me, about you, and about mage-guards or mages, or anything else, you are not to take offense. If one of the officers insists on calling you a coward, ignore it. If, however, he demands satisfaction for your cowardice, accept it, demand the right to name weapons, and use a staff or truncheon, and allow him a blade—and then kill him as swiftly as possible."

"Ser?"

"Any officer who is stupid enough to be that insulting to a mage-guard is only a liability to Hamor. At the same time, you must be seen as patient and above it all, until you deal with him as if he were vermin."

"But will any officer . . . ?"

"There are always a few, and what you will do at first will not be obvious nor seem that dangerous."

"Ser . . . I know you have much on your mind," Rahl said quietly, "but I am concerned about my duties."

"Oh?" Taryl did not smile.

"I have no idea what I am supposed to be doing for you. When I was a patrol mage, it was clear enough. Even when I was a clerk and a scrivener, it was clear. But now . . ." Rahl shrugged helplessly.

"You are to do what I tell you. Once we are in the field, you will be doing what I would be thought to be doing while I will be keeping the marshal from doing excessive damage to our efforts. Why do you think I've been pushing all these exercises? They have all been designed to improve your order-senses and perceptions and shields. You will accompany one of the armed mounted heavy infantry companies that will be doing advance reconnaissance, and your duties are to help them gather as much information as possible about opposing forces while also keeping their casualties as low as practicable. You will also send messages directly to me with any strategic or tactical recommendations. You may make tactical recommendations to the company captain about his options. If anyone asks you, just say that you're currently staff but will likely be reassigned."

"Ser . . . I don't know anything about military operations."

Taryl laughed. "Neither does anyone else—not about land fighting. We haven't fought any major battles on land in more than a century, and I have my doubts that all the manuals are that good. Just keep your eyes and senses open and use common sense. And try not to get killed. Troopers can be replaced more easily than mages."

As if to punctuate Taryl's words, the coach came to a stop outside a modest two-story stone structure with the usual red-tile roof.

"One last thing," Taryl said. "Keep working on using those personal shields, especially in the mess."

"Yes, ser."

From that point on, Rahl just followed Taryl.

They were given quarters. Rahl was given a key and directed to a chamber on the main level, about as far as possible from the mess chamber, while Taryl was escorted up the stairs to true quarters—since the quartering clerk was apologizing that the senior officers' quarters only had a sitting room and a bedchamber, along with attached bathing and necessary chambers.

At least, reflected Rahl as he unpacked his gear, he wasn't far from the showers and jakes.

After that, he stretched out on the bed and ended up taking a nap and then having to hurry to get to the mess. He hadn't realized he'd been so tired.

He reached the foyer outside the mess just as a single bell rang once, and the senior officer—who looked to be an overcommander, inclined his head to Taryl. "If you would, Marshal?"

Was the title a reflection of Taryl's effective rank? Rahl wondered. It had to be.

Taryl inclined his head in return. "If you would join me, Overcommander."

Rahl followed the other officers into a chamber set up with a short table set cross-wise to two others, with a fourth table set below the two parallel tables. Just from looking at the officers, he could tell that the short table was for the senior officers, and the left-hand one was for majers—the half closest to the senior table—while the lower half of that table and the adjoining one was for captains, and the fourth table for undercaptains.

From what Rahl could see of the score and a half of officers in the mess, there were perhaps five or six mage-guards, and all were chaos-mages. There were also three healers, two men and a woman, distinguished by the inverted green chevron across the shoulders of their khaki shirts. All but one were seated in the section of the tables with the captains—and Rahl.

The captains around Rahl offered names quickly.

"Sernyt . . ."

"Bleun . . ."

"Sevela . . ."

Seated across the table to Rahl's left was one of the mage-guards, an older man with streaks of gray in his hair. "Tilsytt, assigned to Second Cavalry."

"Rahl, assigned to Overcommander Taryl."

Tilsytt frowned. "The former Triad?"

"The same one."

"You're staff, then?"

Rahl shrugged. "I think that's temporary. He's said I'll be reassigned shortly."

"This isn't your first assignment?"

Rahl shook his head. "My third." That was true enough, even if his previous assignments had been short.

"You wear years well," Tilsytt said with a trace of irony.

"The second assignment was only about a season. The first was in Swartheld, in the harbor station."

"You involved with that mess caused by the Jeranyi?"

"Most of us were, one way or another."

"I mean . . . *really* involved."

"Yes."

"You're an order type. Ever kill anyone?"

Rahl smiled politely, trying to keep his irritation behind his shields. "I couldn't count the number." He let the honesty of that response seep out from behind his shields, especially since it was true. He'd set the explosion that had destroyed the Jeranyi pirate vessel, and he couldn't count how many had died, except he knew it had been more than a score, and that didn't count the others.

Tilsytt frowned. "Where'd you train, if I might ask?"

"Luba. I spent time there as a loader, and then a clerk before the mage-guards found I had order-abilities."

Tilsytt paled, ever so slightly. "I see."

So the reference to Luba bothered Tilsytt. Rahl would have to ask Taryl about that.

"Were the Jeranyi really going to blow up most of the merchant district in Swartheld?" asked Captain Sernyt.

"Did you know that they were backing the rebels then?" followed Bleun, before Rahl could reply.

Rahl took a sip of the lager, then nodded politely. "The Jeranyi raiders had stockpiled barrels and barrels of cammabark that they'd smuggled in. They did so under false pretenses, and then killed the trader whose warehouse they'd used . . ." Rahl gave a short explanation of what had happened, omitting the specifics of his action or the fact that it was the Nylan Merchant Association.

During the meal he tried to find out more about the others, but the captains around him were far more interested in knowing about what had happened in Swartheld and what role the Jeranyi had played.

Between being polite, holding his personal shields, and trying to keep track of who was who and attached to what, Rahl found dinner tiring, and he was more than glad when he could rise with the others and leave.

In the foyer outside the mess chamber, several groups of officers remained, talking more informally and across ranks. Rahl spied Tilsytt speaking to a majer and began to drift in that direction without actually looking at the two. As he neared them, he stopped, turning to look at the portrait of an overcommander in a dress uniform hanging on the wall. Then he extended his order-senses, curious as to what the two were discussing.

". . . asked him, like you said . . . wagering he's the closest thing to an order-type bravo you'll see. Overcommander must have picked him out and trained him . . ."

". . . tell you how good he was?"

". . . avoided it, mostly . . . like the good ones . . . don't have to brag . . ."

". . . confirms . . . sources say he's armsmaster class with order weapons . . . any idea why he's here . . . what he's doing?"

". . . said he's likely to be reassigned, doesn't know where . . . that reads true . . ."

"Could he be deceiving you?"

". . . been reading mage-guards a long time, majer. If he's that good, then he's more like a senior mage-guard, maybe even an overcaptain, but he's too young for that . . . looking this way . . ."

Rahl turned and slowly moved away. Why did the majer want to know about Rahl? More likely the question was to whom the majer reported who wanted to know.

"Captain?"

Rahl turned to find himself face-to-face with one of the healer mage-guards, a square-faced older woman closer to his mother's age than his, he suspected. "I'm still not used to being called 'captain.'"

"You don't look like it will take long. I'm Xerya."

"Rahl. Is there anything . . ." He smiled politely.

"Not really. I heard that Taryl had brought one assistant, and I wanted to meet you."

"I hope you're not disappointed. I'm just a former patrol mage from Swartheld."

Her smile was broader and more open, and Rahl could sense the same type of warmth that Deybri and the healers in Nylan had shown. "I doubt anyone who accompanies a former Triad who is now a marshal is just a former patrol mage."

Rahl shrugged helplessly. "I'm fortunate, then."

The smile faded. "I wouldn't say that. Being around Taryl offers great opportunities and great dangers."

Rahl had already gotten that impression, but he just nodded.

"The other reason I wanted to talk to you was that I'd like you to come to the infirmary when you can. You're an order type, and while you'll never be a true healer, there are some techniques that any ordermage can use, and they can be helpful in battle or in case of injuries. We can show you some of those."

"I'd be happy to learn what I can." Rahl paused. "Where is the infirmary?"

"One block south of here and two blocks toward the

river. It's the only building with green doors and shutters."

Rahl nodded politely. "I'll be there when I can."

"We'll look forward to it . . . Captain."

Rahl realized that she had been the one at the majers' table. "Yes, Majer."

"Save the rank for public use, Rahl." The words were warm, if brief, and Xerya nodded and turned.

Rahl kept a faint smile on his face as he moved across the foyer and toward the doors to the outside. He needed some fresh air, and some time to think.

XVII

On sixday morning, even before Rahl could cross the foyer and step into the mess for breakfast, Taryl appeared and drew him aside.

"What do you have to report?"

"Last night, one of the mage-guards—that was Tilsytt—met with a majer I don't know and reported on what I said. They were concerned that I might be some sort of bravo."

"That won't hurt, so long as it's limited to that. What else?"

"A healer majer named Xerya asked me to visit her at the infirmary so that she could give me some instruction on field healing." Rahl smiled wryly. "The sort that any ordermage could do. I didn't tell her that in some areas I was less capable than any ordermage."

"Not anymore," Taryl said. "What do you think all the exercises were for? Go meet with her after breakfast and spend as much time with her as she'll give you. Learn and listen. After that, I want you to walk as much of the post as you can—slowly. Take in everything. Be friendly and talk to any officer who shows an interest. We'll meet on the weather platform after dinner. If I'm not there immediately, you can work on studying the weather."

"Yes, ser."

With that, Taryl was gone, and Rahl had the feeling that the overcommander had eaten very early and had just been waiting for Rahl. Just what had Taryl been doing? Rahl wished he knew.

Breakfast was far less formal, with officers coming and going, and all eating rather quickly. Rahl sat with some captains he had not met before and asked general questions, just trying to get a feel of what they and their units did, but not probing too intently, except with his order-senses.

After he ate, he left the mess and stepped outside, into a breeze, almost chill, and certainly the coolest he'd experienced in Hamor. He walked briskly southward, and then east. As the majer had said, with its bright green shutters and doors, the infirmary was hard to miss. He made his way through the main doors.

A woman younger than Rahl and wearing a plain trooper's uniform, except with the green healing corps chevron, looked up from the table in the infirmary's entry foyer. "Yes, ser. Might I help you?"

"Captain Rahl here to see Majer Xerya, at her request."

"Yes, ser. This way. She said you might be by. She's on rounds at the moment, but you're to accompany her."

Rounds? Of injured troopers? Rahl didn't ask, but followed the trooper along a narrow corridor, then around yet another corridor. The walls were smooth white plaster, and the stone floors shimmered.

Ahead of them was the healer majer. She smiled as she caught sight of Rahl, but addressed the trooper. "Thank you, Seshya."

Rahl's escort slipped away.

"You're prompt," noted Xerya. "I thought you might be.

The overcommander isn't known to favor laggards. This way, if you would. We're fortunate that we don't have many injuries here at the moment, but I would have liked to show you a wider range." She turned into a larger room with three beds on each side. Four were occupied, with the middle one on each side empty.

A young trooper lay on the end bed, his back propped up with leather pillows and a bulky leather-and-iron splint around one leg.

"Can you sense what happened here?" asked Xerya.

"I don't know," Rahl admitted. "Let me try."

The trooper glanced from the healer to Rahl and back to the healer, puzzlement warring with pain on his face.

Rahl extended his order-senses, finding wound chaos, of a sort, in the splinted leg. He turned to the healer. "There's a spot where things don't quite meet, a broken bone, and there's still wound chaos there."

"Where?"

Rahl pointed to a spot two spans below the knee.

"That's where the bone broke. It just happened last night. There will be wound chaos for several days after a fracture, even if the wound is clean and the skin's not broken, but it should decrease some each day. The dangerous breaks are where the skin is broken, and the bone protrudes."

Rahl managed not to wince at that thought.

"Thank you." The healer nodded to the trooper, who still looked puzzled. She moved to the next occupied bed. The man lying there was barely breathing.

"Brain fever. All we can do is feed him ale and lager and keep him cool. About half recover." She crossed the ward to the next trooper. The man was missing his foot and his leg from just above the ankle. He was moaning, but not really awake.

Rahl could sense a certain amount of wound chaos, but it was spread throughout the man's body. He looked to the healer.

"He stepped on a spike or something and didn't tell anyone. The wound festered so badly we had to amputate his foot and lower leg. Almost any order-type mage-guard could have stopped or slowed the initial wound chaos. That's something you can look out for in the field. The same thing is true of minor blade slashes, thorns, that sort of thing." Xerya studied Rahl. "Can you concentrate order in a small space?"

"For a time," Rahl said.

"That's all it takes for some of the little wounds. Clean them out with something that won't make the festering worse—like lager or strong brandy, but clear strong spirits are the best, then concentrate a small bit of order around the wound and dress it with something clean."

Rahl nodded and followed her to the next trooper.

All in all, he spent the entire morning with the healer—and just hoped he could remember most of what she told him. Her warmth, although not directed at him especially, reminded him of Deybri, and he had to tell himself that it would be eightdays before she received his letter.

After that, he embarked upon Taryl's task, touring the post area, block by block, and taking in what he observed.

He saw more than a few companies of fresh-faced recruits, most seemingly much younger than he had been when he'd been sent to Nylan, being taught to march, and to handle sabres, rather than falchionas.

When he caught sight of two companies of archers launching arrows into skyward arcs toward distant straw targets, he moved closer, with an idea in mind. Could he create a small order shield, one strong enough to stop one of those long arrows? He moved closer, but stopped behind a stone pillar and began to try out his idea.

He discovered that he could halt an arrow in midflight—but that continuing the effort for long left him light-headed. It also puzzled one of the instructors, a grizzled captain who began to look around.

Rahl had discovered what he needed to know and slipped away under cover of a sight shield and headed toward the river docks.

Rahl's feet were sore and his boots dusty by the time he returned to the visiting officers' quarters and washed up for dinner. He tried to say as little as possible in the mess, just smiling, and holding his shields, and asking a question now and again.

Taryl wasn't at the seniors' table, and after Rahl left the mess, he made his way up to the weather platform. Surprisingly, someone else was there—a woman undercaptain. She turned, and Rahl realized that she was as tall as he was, and almost as broad across the shoulders. He'd never run across a woman that large.

"Oh, ser," she said. "I was just taking the evening observations."

"What observations, Undercaptain?" Rahl had to wonder because she was a troop officer, not a mage-guard.

"Wind direction, clouds, mostly, but also if the air feels damp or dry." She paused. "Begging your pardon, ser, but are you a weather mage?"

"No. I have a few small skills."

"Is rain likely? Can you tell me that, ser?"

"I can try. Is it important?"

"If there's a lot of rain south of here, it changes the river currents, and that will slow the freighters. It also means the cargo loaders will have to rig tarps over the hold hatches or some of the provisions will spoil—more, really—on the trip upriver."

"They were loading today."

"Yes, ser, but it will take at least two more days, and a day for troops and mounts. That's without rain."

Rahl smiled politely. "I'm Rahl. You are?"

"Oh, Undercaptain Demya, ser."

"I'm not a weather mage, but let me see if I can tell you anything." Rahl concentrated on letting his senses range southward, toward what might be clouds just barely visible above the horizon in the last fading glow of twilight. There was definitely a touch more water in the air, but not much, and it was concentrated in two or three places, rather than in a broad sweep. He kept studying. Finally, he stopped. He wasn't even light-headed. Was that because he'd just eaten? That made sense.

"Ser?"

"There are some clouds south of here, mainly on the east side of the river. I can't say for certain, but it feels like there might be a few showers coming this way, but I don't think there will be any continuing rain."

Her eyes widened. "You can tell that? Just from looking."

"I was doing more than just looking, Demya. It's work. A true weather mage could tell you when any rain would arrive and how much. An air mage might even be able to move storms or clouds away from the river."

"You're a different kind of mage, then."

"I'm a mage-guard."

"Begging your pardon, again, ser, but all mage-guards are mages of some sort."

"I was a patrol mage in Swartheld. I'm good with staff and truncheon, and I understand something about trade and commerce." He smiled. "I was sent here, and I have no idea where I'll be assigned." Then he shrugged.

"I'm sorry, ser. I didn't mean . . ."

"That's all right."

She backed down the steps, then hurried away without speaking.

Rahl could sense Taryl approaching, but he had to wonder at her implied question. Just what sort of mage was he? The magisters in Nylan had called him a natural ordermage, but that had been as much epithet as description.

"What did you do to that poor undercaptain?" asked Taryl as he stepped onto the platform. "She acted like she'd been dressed down and ripped apart."

"I didn't raise my voice, ser, and I didn't say one harsh word. She kept pressing me about what kind of mage I was, and I finally said that I was a patrol mage who was good with a staff and truncheon who'd been sent here for reassignment."

"That was enough." Taryl laughed sourly. "Word is going around that one of the mage-guards sent here recently is a trained bravo who has killed scores, and that he's here to make sure that the junior officers stay in line."

"I never said anything like that. That idiot Tilsytt kept asking me how many people I'd killed, and I only said something like I couldn't have counted them in the mess at Swartheld." That wasn't exactly what he'd said, but he didn't want to admit his precise words.

"It doesn't matter. You were convincing enough that you've created a reputation that may be hard to live up to."

"Oh . . . frig," Rahl muttered.

"You can't do much about it now. How was the rest of your day?" asked Taryl.

"I spent the morning with the healer majer. She told me a great deal, and had me practice a few simple healing skills, and said that I wasn't that bad, not for an ordermage with no instruction in healing."

"Were those her exact words?"

"Close to it, ser," replied Rahl, smiling crookedly. "She did say that I paid more attention than most mage-guards."

Taryl just waited.

"Then I walked all around. I think I traveled every street and lane. There are heavy wagons coming in, and they're loading supplies on the steamers at the docks, and they're working from first light to darkness."

"They'd better."

"Oh . . . the undercaptain told me that they have two more days of loading supplies, and one to get mounts and troops aboard. That's if it doesn't rain."

"Will it?"

"I don't think so. We might get a shower or two. Maybe. If I'm reading things right."

"What else?"

"I've seen green troopers everywhere, greener than I was when I went to Nylan. Almost all of them look too young."

"You'll find that with each year they look younger." Taryl sighed. "But you're right. We don't have enough seasoned troops, and the only way to get seasoned troops quickly is to train them hard and send them into battle. Those who survive become seasoned."

Rahl didn't have that much more to say. "Is there anything else I should know, or that you'd like me to do?"

"Go back to the healer tomorrow and follow her around, or one of the others, if they'll let you. Do that in the morning. Then practice all of your order-skills in the early afternoon, and check out the docks after that. Tomorrow evening, we're going to a reception at the Palace—wear your dress uniform and best boots. We'll leave before the mess opens for dinner."

"Yes, ser." Rahl had no idea how a reception fit into Taryl's plans or why attending a reception was necessary, but he had no doubt that it was.

"And get some sleep tonight. I plan to." Taryl turned and walked away, down the steps toward his quarters.

Rahl had the feeling that somehow he'd disappointed the overcommander. He shouldn't have been so determined to put Tilsytt in his place . . . but the older mage-guard had been so condescending, just like Puvort and all the magisters in Nylan, as if Rahl were nothing. And he hated that.

Rahl took a deep breath, then headed down the stone steps, his boots echoing dully in the enclosed stairwell.

XVIII

On sevenday morning, Rahl was in the mess earlier and sat across from two captains he had not met before.

"I'm Bertayk," offered the younger one.

"Alfhyr." The older captain nodded brusquely.

"Rahl."

"You're new here. Some of the other mage-guards were talking about a patrol mage-guard who was a bravo . . ." Bertayk looked speculatively at Rahl.

Alfhyr concealed a wince.

"I'm the guilty party, but I never was a bravo. Something I said was taken in a way I didn't mean . . ." Rahl went on to explain briefly what had happened at Swartheld. ". . . and all I meant was that, with Jeranyi everywhere, and explosions, I don't think anyone kept tallies on who they fought and what happened."

Alfhyr nodded slowly and said in a low voice, "You've already found out that the . . . mage-guard . . . you spoke to doesn't always convey matters in the way you meant."

"I have." Rahl smiled ruefully. "But I do appreciate the words of caution."

"Are you from Merowey or Atla?" asked Bertayk.

Alfhyr winced inside once again, and Rahl managed to keep from laughing or smiling.

"I'm not from either, but I learned to speak where that was the way people did." He paused. "Actually, I'm an exile from Recluce."

Bertayk nodded enthusiastically. "They say that many of the mage-guards come from Recluce or Recluce stock. My great-uncle came from Alaren, and the engineers in Nylan sent him on his way. He hoped I'd be a mage-guard." The young captain shrugged. "I don't have any talent."

"I'm sure you have other talents," Rahl said.

"He's good with a blade and getting troopers to follow him," interjected the older captain. "They appreciate his enthusiasm."

Rahl actually enjoyed the rest of his breakfast, passing pleasantries with the two, although he still had to concentrate on maintaining tighter personal shields.

The rest of sevenday morning and afternoon was much like sixday, except that Xerya pressed Rahl into trying to negate some of the chaos in the trooper with brain fever. Rahl thought he might have helped, but he didn't notice much improvement when he left the man.

He did allow himself plenty of time after his casual inspection of the river docks to return to his quarters to polish his boots and wash up and don the crimson dress uniform. In fact, he was the one waiting for Taryl.

When Taryl arrived, the overcommander looked over Rahl, then nodded. "You'll pass." He turned and walked toward the waiting coach—one decorated in tan and crimson.

Taryl said little until the coach pulled away from the quarters. "Tell me about your day."

"I spent most of it with Majer Xerya. She's as demanding as you are, ser."

"She should be. I asked her to be. The more you learn before you're reassigned, the better your chances to survive and succeed. I stopped by later. She said you already know what's required of a senior mage-guard. That's not enough, but it's a start."

Rahl managed to keep a smile on his face and his irritation behind his personal shields. Why was nothing he did enough for Taryl anymore? Had he displeased the older mage-guard that much? "After that, I checked the loading docks. I think they're running behind. They're supposed to finish loading tomorrow, but . . . I got the impression . . . it won't happen."

"You're right about that. We'll be fortunate to leave by threeday." Taryl leaned back and closed his eyes for several moments.

Rahl waited.

After a while, Taryl straightened. "Tonight is a social occasion, as much as any reception hosted by the Emperor is. You are not to approach him. When it's appropriate, I'll present you, or Jubyl will, and the Emperor will make some pleasant comment. You are to give him a bow and thank him, nothing more. If he says more, you reply, but always briefly and courteously. You do not ask him any questions. Is that clear?"

"Yes, ser." Rahl paused. "Might I ask if there is any special reason for the reception?"

"He generally has a reception for senior officials once or twice a season, sometimes more often. There is no special reason for the reception. There is a reason why we were invited. Can you tell me why?"

"To show his support for your appointment as overcommander in Merowey."

"Exactly. Now . . . why were you invited? You were invited by name and will be announced by name."

"Ah . . . I don't know, ser. I have no idea."

Taryl smiled. "By inviting you, as my assistant envoy in Recluce and as my current assistant, the Emperor is making the point that he will brook no disparagement of my decisions and choices."

"Especially since it must be known that I am from Recluce?"

Taryl nodded.

Rahl had to ask himself if he would ever understand or master the intricacies of personal plotting and positioning seemingly required in Hamor. Then he almost laughed. Much as he might dream, he'd never have to worry about the sorts of matters that faced Taryl.

"And Rahl . . ."

"Yes, ser?"

"I know you've memorized some verse. Don't quote more than one or two back at Klassyn. That's appropriate. More isn't."

How had Taryl known that?

"You're letting your personal shields slip. I saw the book you had in hand when you were supposed to be reading the history of the mage-guards."

"I read parts of two of the histories, ser."

"Good. Oh . . . one other thing. You'll probably run across Triad Juby!. He will be there."

"What about the others?"

"Except when the Triad meets officially in council to advise the Emperor, and all are present, there is never more than one in attendance upon the Emperor at one time. Now . . . if you'll excuse me, I'm going to try to get a nap."

Rahl looked out the window. He was feeling almost as frustrated as he had in Nylan. He was supposed to keep his emotions hidden behind personal shields, learn all sorts of new applications of his order-skills, and not let any vital information slip. On top of that, he was just supposed to let insults and slights slide off him and do nothing.

"Rahl," Taryl said in a gentle—and tired—tone, his eyes still closed. "Please stop feeling sorry for yourself and angry. I suspect that combination of feelings has led to many of your problems. Because of your abilities, I tend to forget how young you are. Let me explain. First, if you do not learn to shield your feelings, seniors who are less scrupulous will use those feelings to manipulate you, and that will never be to your advantage. Second, if you do not learn everything possible about your skills, you will be at a disadvantage in dealing with others who have not neglected to develop their skills fully. Third, if you reveal information that you do not wish to reveal, it can and will be used against you. Finally, insults and pettiness are just that. They're usually a reflection of the uneasiness of others and their fear that you might be superior or a threat. While they should never be ignored, responding directly to them weakens you. It's always better to deal with such individuals when it suits you—after reflection—not immediately, and never when it suits them." Taryl sighed. "Please think about what I have said, and if you wish to be angry, please cloak the anger behind your shields. That way, at least you'll get more practice, and I might be able to nap."

Most of Rahl's anger faded as he heard the patient tiredness in the older mage-guard's voice. Not all of the anger, but what remained was not directed at Taryl so much as at Rahl's own situation. Even so, he strengthened his shields.

"Thank you," said Taryl.

Why did people have to be so difficult? From everything Rahl had learned, Prince Golyat was in charge of an area ten times the size of Recluce, and he wasn't satisfied and had to plot a rebellion. Cyphryt was one of the highest-ranking mage-guards, and he was still scheming. Puvort was one of the top magisters in Recluce, and he'd used order dishonestly and unfairly—and Rahl had injured Jienela's brothers—not that they hadn't deserved it—in defending himself, and they'd been hurt, and Rahl had been exiled to Nylan. Everywhere he looked, people were trying to drag others down, often people who were their betters.

He frowned. He had to be honest with himself. That wasn't always true. He hadn't liked her decision, but Magistra Leyla had tried to be fair, as she saw it. Taryl was fair, and Deybri was one of the fairest and most honest people he'd met. Poor Captain Gheryk had been fair, too. But it was hard to deal with so much unfairness and pettiness, especially when he felt it was directed at him.

Then he nodded. He was likely to face some sort of slight or comment from Klassyn and perhaps even from Serita or others. What could he say that would be polite and friendly, without accepting such a slight? For a long time, he considered possible phrases.

Finally, he looked out the coach window, taking in the neatly fenced and bordered fields to the west, and the orchards to the east, stretching down toward the river, almost a kay away from the road. Before all that long, as the twilight began to darken into evening, the fields and olive and fruit trees gave way to small dwellings with garden plots around them. Unlike the buildings in the center of Cigoerne, the houses and cots were of brick, but the roofs were of red tile, if more faded than that Rahl had seen in other places. He didn't think that was because of the dimming light, either.

Despite the growing darkness, Rahl could see the Imperial Palace ahead, dominating the city from its position on the low hill in the center of Cigoerne. The gentle slopes—holding gardens and lawn—that rose from the white walls encircling the grounds were too regular on all sides for it to have been anything other than created for just that effect.

The gateway on the east side of the Imperial Palace, as well as the Palace itself, was lit with lamps seemingly hung everywhere, and behind each was a polished reflector. Several coaches—one of them a gleaming silver— preceded the one holding Taryl and Rahl through the outer gate and up the slight incline of the drive paved in white stone toward the Palace proper. The white stone of the Emperor's gate—and the receiving rotunda—shimmered in the light.

In time, their coach came to a halt, and a crimson-clad footman opened the coach door. "Welcome to the Palace."

"Thank you." Taryl nodded, and so did Rahl.

They walked along a pillared and covered walkway to a wide archway whose gilded double doors were drawn open. Inside was a vaulted entry hall that soared upward into one of the three domes of the Palace. The polished-marble floor was of pale rose, as were the fluted columns. The entire inside of the dome was comprised of pale rose triangles, the vertices alternating up and down, against a white background. Rahl looked again. Some of the triangles were windows of milky rose glass.

The sound of Rahl's boots was lost in the vastness of the circular entry hall—a good fifty cubits across, and more than that to the top of the dome.

Taryl turned to the left in the middle of the hall toward a series of columns framing a hallway with a wide crimson carpet runner. Stationed at intervals along the hallway were guards in crimson-and-gold uniforms. Ahead was another circular hall foyer, but one less than twenty cubits across, where several couples waited to enter through a set of doors to the right.

Taryl and Rahl stopped at the end of the short line.

"This is the Grand Parlor," Taryl murmured.

Ahead were a woman and man wearing a dress uniform of black and khaki, with a crimson stripe down the outside of each trouser leg. The woman wore a black-and-silver gown, with the sheerest black-shimersilk sleeves and a silver scarf. As the couple stepped through the archway into the chamber beyond, a sonorous voice announced, "Land Marshal Valatyr and his consort Chelyna."

Taryl stepped forward, and so did Rahl. After a moment, Taryl nodded to Rahl.

"Mage-Guard Overcommander of Merowey Taryl. Mage-Guard and attaché to the Overcommander Rahl," announced the crimson-clad functionary.

Inside the Grand Parlor, Rahl could see close to twoscore individuals, and it felt as though about half had turned to look at him. He kept smiling, and managed to keep his personal shields strong, as he accompanied Taryl.

Music filled the room, a lush melody of mixed instruments, without a sense of discord. Rahl's eyes traveled to the far end of the Grand Parlor, where he could see a half score of players, including violins, a large floor viol, and two sets of hammered harps, as well as several horns and a flute. The melody was soft, and not intrusive, yet held a harmony.

"The Emperor doesn't like receiving lines," said Taryl quietly. "He tends to wait until everyone is here before he appears. I see Klassyn and Serita over to the right. Since they're the only ones you officially know, except for Marshal Byrna, you should begin by paying your respects. Then, in time, someone will offer you something to drink. Try not to have to sneeze."

Rahl couldn't help smiling. "I'll just set it down somewhere and forget it, if it comes to that."

"Servers will appear with various dainties. Eat what appeals to you because that will be dinner, but eat judiciously."

Rahl nodded. Although Taryl had said all that earlier, Rahl didn't mind the reminder.

Taryl moved toward Marshal Byrna, while Rahl made his way toward Serita and Klassyn, both of whom wore mage-guard dress uniforms—with one addition. They wore gold-braided epaulet cords on their left shoulders. Each held a crystal goblet.

"Good evening," offered Rahl, inclining his head to Serita, then to Klassyn.

"Good evening to you, Rahl," she replied.

"It is a very good evening," added Klassyn, "and good to see you here. You actually look as though you belong."

"One can look as though he belongs when he's properly invited," replied Rahl. "I've found that it's usually discomfort that makes one look out of place." He smiled politely, glad that he'd thought ahead somewhat. He continued to project friendliness. "Still, I imagine it took some time for you to get used to working and living in the Palace. It's quite a change from even the largest of mage-guard stations."

"Oh, not so much a change for Klassyn," said Serita. "His family owns rather a great deal of land in the northwest. Somewhat isolated, I understand, but quite grand."

"And for you?" inquired Rahl. "You seem equally at home."

"We were comfortable."

"More than that," added Klassyn cheerfully.

Rahl could sense a certain coolness beneath the facade.

"Compared to your family, Klassyn, comfortable is appropriate."

"I won't dispute you, not tonight. What about you, Rahl?"

"All Recluce is modest, compared to Hamor, and my background more so than most."

"One would never guess it. You speak and comport yourself like a well-educated Atlan or Nubyatan."

"I suspect that's in my favor," Rahl replied.

Serita laughed softly. "You must have something to drink." She raised a hand, and a server seemed to appear from nowhere.

"Ser, might I get you some refreshment?"

"A pale lager, please."

The server slipped away.

"No leshak or brandy?" asked Klassyn. "The Emperor's leshak is not to be believed."

"And probably what it does to those who are unprepared to drink it is also not to be believed," Rahl said genially.

The server turned and offered Rahl a crystal beaker from a small tray.

Rahl let his order-senses check the lager, but it felt untainted, and he took the smallest sip. "The Emperor's lager is also quite good."

"As it should be," said Klassyn.

Another crimson-clad server slipped up next to the three, proffering a tray on which rested small pastry octagons. Rahl waited for Serita to take one before helping himself.

Klassyn ignored the server, instead continuing, "I understand you're going off to be a hero. As one of the old poets—Remyl, it was, said,

> How brave are they who sleep in earth
> who blessed in death their land of birth.

"Although," he added, "Hamor is not actually your land of birth."

Rahl smiled politely. "I'm afraid I'm not that kind of hero. I think such words reflect another time. Today,

> *The song is strained, the notes are cold,*
> *the strings will break with words so old. . . ."*

Serita laughed.

"Some think times change, but they don't," Klassyn replied. "As the ancient Cyadoran wrote,

> *and the new becomes the old,*
> *with the way the story's told."*

"That's a good point," Rahl conceded.

"Precisely. We all think that we and our times are different, but all situations result from people, and people don't change from generation to generation." Klassyn offered a superior smile.

"Ah . . . but that same poet would not necessarily agree," interjected another voice.

Rahl turned to see a slender man dressed in gold and crimson. It had to be the Triad Jubyl.

"He also wrote some other lines, such as

> *take your desert dunes and sunswept sands,*
> *and pour them through your empty hands.*

"Or," continued the Triad,

> *"I hear the altage souls lifting lances*
> *against what the future past advances . . .*
> *until those towers crumble into sand*
> *and Cyad can no longer stand.*

"And since Cyad no longer stands, and has not for many, many centuries, it is fair to conclude that while human nature may not change, the circumstances do, and at times, the new is indeed new, and not merely a retelling of the past. But the trick is to learn when new is new, and when it is not." The Triad turned to Rahl. "You must be Taryl's assistant."

Rahl bowed. "Yes, Triad."

"Save your bows for the Emperor. A simple 'ser' will do. As you have doubtless surmised, I am Jubyl."

"Yes, ser."

"You are said to have considerable skill with truncheon and staff, enough to be considered as equal to an arms-master with those weapons. Have you thought of seeking such a position?"

"No, ser."

"Why not? It is a most honorable position, and those armsmasters with whom you have worked feel you have the ability to impart skills to others." Jubyl smiled, not coolly, but as if with interest, although his personal shields hid all feelings except a general friendliness, most possibly projected in the way that Taryl had suggested Rahl attempt to cultivate.

"I had not thought of it. It might be because I feel that I still have much to learn, and that handling a blade is painful and difficult."

The Triad nodded. "It is unwise to dream of what cannot be, but it is even more foolish to have no dreams beyond the present."

How could he reply to that? After a hesitation, Rahl offered a smile. "I'm still trying to learn about what is possible and what is not."

"If you can determine that, Rahl, you will have attempted what most never try, and fewer yet can do."

Rahl could sense that both Klassyn and Serita were watching intently. Although they were out of comfortable earshot, both were capable of using their skills to catch every word. "I will keep your observation in mind, ser."

"Oh . . . now you sound like the courtiers who used to flatter Hamylt."

"Ser . . . if I say that I will determine what is possible,

then I sound arrogant. If I say that I will act as I can, I will sound willful and stupid, and if I agree, then I sound weak and seeking merely to agree."

Jubyl shook his head, still smiling. "That is the answer you should have given first."

"I might have, ser, but I couldn't think of it that quickly."

At that, Jubyl laughed. "A most honest answer."

Before Rahl could say more, the Triad turned toward his assistants. "A word with you, Klassyn, if you would."

Rahl watched for a moment as Jubyl steered Klassyn in the direction of the main doors to the Grand Parlor.

"Honeyed biastras, ser?" A server appeared with a tray, offering delicate pastry tubes.

Rahl took one, carefully, and ate it, finding it too sweet for his taste. At that thought, he smiled, knowing that his mother would never believe that he would find anything too sweet. He took a longer swallow of lager from the beaker he still held.

"Mage-Guard Rahl?"

The voice was Taryl's, but the formality of the address alerted Rahl, and he turned immediately.

With Taryl was a personage that could only be the Emperor. Surprisingly, at least to Rahl, the Emperor Mythalt did not wear crimson or gold, but a black-silk shirt with a white vest trimmed in crimson and white trousers with a single black stripe down the outside of each leg. He was not especially tall, a span less than Rahl, but his black eyes were alert, and his smile was warm. So were the feelings behind the smile.

"Highest," said Taryl, "this is Mage-Guard Rahl. He was the assistant envoy on the mission to Recluce, and he acquitted himself well."

Rahl immediately offered a bow. "Highest."

"You are an exile from Recluce who registered as a mage and labored in Luba. Is that not so?"

"Yes, Highest."

"How have you found Hamor?" A faint smile hovered on the Emperor's lips.

"Hamor has been far more welcoming to me than Recluce, Highest, and Overcommander Taryl has taught me much."

"Did he tell you to say that?"

"No, Highest. He told me to keep my replies to you direct and short."

Mythalt laughed. "Would that all those who serve Hamor followed that advice." After the slightest pause, he added, "We wish you well and thank you for all that you have already done for us."

"Thank you, Highest."

With another smile, the Emperor nodded to Taryl and moved toward Jubyl.

Taryl did not follow the Emperor but remained beside Rahl. "A good touch. Short, polite, but not obsequious, and truthful. Now that the Emperor has recognized you, we need to mingle. Just accompany me." Taryl eased toward a man in black and tan who was talking to another senior officer in a similar but not identical uniform.

Rahl realized that the first man was the Land Marshal who had preceded them into the Grand Parlor.

"Ah . . . Overcommander Taryl," offered Valatyr. "Surely, you recall Sea Marshal Chastyr."

"I do indeed." Taryl inclined his head slightly.

"A pleasure to see you back in a more commanding role, Taryl," replied Chastyr. "I understand your mage-guards in Swartheld got rid of more than a few of those Jeranyi vermin. It's too bad that you had to travel the whole Eastern Ocean to smooth the feathers of those self-important engineers in Nylan. Worth the effort to us, though."

"It was worth the effort." Taryl inclined his head to Rahl. "Rahl here was the one who uncovered the Jeranyi plot and managed to destroy the one pirate vessel himself."

Valatyr nodded to Rahl. "A pleasure to meet you, Rahl. I told the Sea Marshal here that there was a reason the Emperor recognized you."

Rahl inclined his head politely. "I've attempted to follow the example of the overcommander."

"A good example, indeed," said Valatyr heartily.

"Likewise, I congratulate you," added Chastyr. "A pity you couldn't have gotten all those Jeranyi in Swartheld. The world wouldn't miss them. We certainly wouldn't."

In turn, Rahl inclined his head to the Sea Marshal.

"Rahl was my assistant in Recluce and will be a part of the land campaign," Taryl added. "We'll not keep you, but it was a pleasure to see you both again."

Rahl followed Taryl away from the two marshals, and toward a woman standing beside two younger women, yet looking somehow alone. The taller and black-haired woman was attired in a deep green that matched her eyes. Her shimmersilk sleeves and scarf were of the same shade, but so sheer that they were nearly transparent.

"My Lady Highest," offered Taryl, bowing deeply.

Rahl followed Taryl's example but did not speak.

"Triad Taryl, I had hoped you would notice me."

"One can never not notice you. That has always been true, and always will be so." Taryl inclined his head. "Might I take the liberty of presenting my assistant, Rahl?"

"Indeed you might." She turned the deep green eyes on Rahl.

Abruptly, Rahl realized two things he should have caught the moment he had first seen her. She was the Empress, and she was a healer.

"Yes," she replied ambiguously, "and it is always a pleasure to meet a mage-guard who holds order."

"Thank you, Lady Highest."

"Emerya. Lady Emerya is required and more than enough." Her eyes and being were lit with a warmth that Rahl associated with the best healers. Without ignoring Rahl, she addressed Taryl. "I wish you well, and thank you for returning." Her eyes returned to Rahl. "I also wish you well, Rahl."

"You are kind, lady," replied Taryl.

"How could I not repay such as you have done?" Her eyes flicked to her left, to the Emperor. "If you will excuse me."

Both Rahl and Taryl bowed.

After that, Rahl lost count of the names and introductions.

When the time came for their departure, he was more than glad to accompany Taryl out through the marble halls and columns and back to their coach—waiting several hundred cubits away from the rotunda concourse, unlike a number of others lined up at the entrance. Most of those were far more ornately decorated than the one that had brought the two mage-guards.

"We don't need to make a departure," Taryl murmured, but he said nothing more to Rahl until they were in the coach and had left the outer gate of the Palace well behind.

Then he turned to Rahl. "What did you think of the Emperor?"

Rahl wondered how he could respond to such a question. "An honest and direct answer, ser?"

"So long as we're in private, Rahl."

"He's intelligent, good-hearted, and he chose his consort well."

"That he did. Better than even he deserved but what Hamor needs."

Rahl could sense something behind Taryl's words, but wasn't sure he should ask or even hint.

"What else? Was that all you noticed?"

"The Emperor is possibly too kind to be as effective as he needs to be. He seems like the kind of man who might give too many second chances."

"He already has, especially to his brother, but he has begun to learn the costs of ill-advised kindness." Taryl leaned back in the coach seat. "One of the hardest things to learn is when to offer kindness and when not to."

"Is there any rule to that?"

Taryl laughed softly in the darkness. "Only that you will always make mistakes."

XIX

Because it was end-day, far fewer mage-guards had been at breakfast, and Rahl had eaten alone. As Taryl had requested, after breakfast, Rahl waited outside the quarters entrance. Before long, a duty coach, one of plain and drab tan, halted. From inside the coach Taryl opened the door and gestured for Rahl to join him. Once Rahl was seated, the driver flicked the leads, and the coach eased away from the quarters.

"We have a short ride," said Taryl.

Rahl managed to conceal his puzzlement behind his shields. "Yes, ser. Might I ask where?"

"We're going to visit an empty powder bunker." Taryl's smile was polite and brisk.

Rahl sensed he would not get any more information, not at that moment, and forced himself to sit back, although he doubted he would find relaxing possible.

The coach turned east and, after a quarter kay, southward, proceeding past the troop barracks and along an older paved road that had been cut through another berm running east and west from the river. Beyond the berm were only grass-covered bunkers, and the coach pulled up at the third one.

Taryl got out and waited for Rahl.

Rahl descended from the coach and looked westward along the short stone ramp that led to the bunker's entrance—an open doorway below ground level.

"This will be another type of examination," Taryl said. "It is obviously to your advantage to do as well as you can. Absolute failure could be quite painful, possibly deadly."

Rahl managed to keep his irritation behind his shields. "Might I ask if this has anything to do with what my future assignment in the mage-guards will be?"

"Anything that you do, or fail to do, will affect your

future," Taryl said dryly. "Generally, total failure in any field of endeavor is painful and often deadly. I can only say that you will be examined through confrontation of all sorts, from verbal through order and chaos. You are to walk into the bunker and close the door behind you. Beyond that, I cannot say."

Rahl thought he might have detected some concern behind Taryl's personal shields, but that could have just been wistful thinking. "Yes, ser."

"When you are finished, I'll be here."

Rahl wasn't exactly cheered by the older mage-guard's choice of words, but he nodded, then walked down the stone ramp to the door, heavy double-planked and iron-bound oak. He stepped through the door and closed it, then turned in the total darkness. The floor underfoot was packed clay, not stone, and he could sense two figures inside standing ten cubits or so from him. Both were shielded, but one's shields were order-based, and the other's bore chaos.

"Step forward."

Rahl couldn't tell which figure spoke, but he stepped forward until he was roughly three cubits away.

"Were you told to stop?"

"No, ser."

"Why did you?" The questions came from the figure who radiated order, rather than the one who held chaos.

"Stepping forward usually means to meet someone, not to walk into or past them, ser."

"You were born in Recluce, were you not?"

"Yes, ser."

"You were exiled, were you not?"

"Yes, ser."

"Explain why. Briefly, and without excuses."

"I was and am what the magisters called a natural or-dermage. I was unable to improve my skills under their teaching, and whenever I attempted to teach myself, I made severe mistakes. They decided that I was too much of a danger to Nylan and prepared me for exile—with the exception that I was not to attempt any active use of order until I departed."

"Did you?"

"Not that I was aware of or that they told me, ser."

"Did not this inability to learn suggest a grave deficiency in you?"

Even though Rahl knew that his interrogator was working to make him angry, he still felt irritation, although he thought he was keeping it behind his shields. "I may have a deficiency in being unable to learn certain aspects of handling order from merely reading—"

"*Merely* reading?" The words were mocking. "Merely reading?"

"From reading by itself without an effort to work out in practice what the words mean," Rahl said evenly.

"Then that is what you should have said. Do you always use words that incite and irritate others, Mage-Guard?"

"I attempt not to, ser."

"Attempting is not succeeding. As a mage-guard, what you attempt matters little if you fail. Effort is honorable, but meaningless unless it leads either to present or future success. Life does not reward pointless and unsuccessful effort. Why should the mage-guards?"

Rahl nodded, but did not speak.

"Answer the question, Mage-Guard. Why should the mage-guards reward pointless and useless effort?"

"They should not, ser, not unless it is useful in teaching a mage-guard or unless it leads to success either by that mage-guard or another."

"You killed a superior officer in your last posting. While you may have felt it was justified, there is a real question as to whether it indeed was. Was it not just because you had failed to follow your captain's orders? Or because you actively flaunted those orders?"

Rahl had thought about that question more than a few

times in the eightdays since he had left Swartheld. "No, ser."

"That is a simple and convenient reply, but one with little meaning—except your conviction. Why did you not follow your captain's orders?"

"Begging your pardon, ser, but I did follow those orders. I did not understand at first the meaning of all that I had seen, and when I did tell the captain, he felt that I was exaggerating the seriousness of the situation. When I observed what was happening in the course of my assigned pier watch, I tried again to tell him, but he had already vanished. I believe, as does Overcommander Taryl, that he had already been killed by the undercaptain. Even so, I told the undercaptain, and he called me aside. There he insisted that I had disobeyed orders. Keeping one's eyes open while on duty and then reporting what one has seen to one's superiors is not disobeying orders. He attempted to kill me. Obviously, to me, and as events later proved, he was attempting to cover up what was happening. I was not skilled enough to disable or to immobilize him, and in trying to remain alive to report what was happening, I did kill him."

"There was no way to stop him? I find that hard to believe."

"There may have been, but I saw no other way at the time."

"No other way? Are you so blind as to think that each situation has but a single possible resolution . . ."

The questions and insinuations seemed to go on forever.

Then, abruptly, they stopped.

"Raise any shields you require to defend yourself against a chaos-attack."

Rahl did so.

A moderately strong bolt of chaos flared against Rahl's shields, then a stronger one. At the same time order hammered at them so hard that he was almost knocked off his feet. Abruptly, the packed clay under his left foot began to disintegrate.

Rahl forced himself to check the ground on both sides, then jumped farther to left and squared his footing.

A chaos-bolt that was more light than flame seared his eyes, leaving them watering, but he sensed that something else was coming.

A dart of iron, propelled by chaos-force, slammed into his shields, and then a small ball of chaos seemed to come from it and began to unlink his shields. Rahl erected a second set of shields behind the first, then collapsed the first around the chaos-worm or -serpent.

The serpent exploded, lifting Rahl and throwing him backward. While he held his shields, he had to scramble back to his feet.

A soundless scream shivered his ears, so loudly that they rang.

He could sense fog growing between him and the two figures, almost a miniature storm of some sort, and a small jagged bolt of lightning flashed toward him. He managed to turn it away from him, although it passed through his shields.

He could sense another forming. Immediately, he used order to gather the heat from the chaos-forces used and create a hot breeze directed at the miniature storm. The storm dissolved into fog—although it was fog he could only feel and not see. Then the fog vanished under the force of his hot wind.

Then . . . there was silence.

Rahl tried to sense what might be coming next, but he could only feel a growing chill, an arc growing larger, an arc that was likely to surround him before long.

How was he supposed to stop chill? He couldn't generate heat from chaos the way a chaos-mage could.

How were they creating the chill?

Order. It had to be order, so structured that it was lifeless.

He could feel the heat being sucked away from him.
What could he do?

Movement!

He recalled Taryl's exercises and concentrated on a
patch of clay on the ground just at the inside edge of the
arc, beginning to move bits of order around, tugging at
the ground under the arc, then linking order. Abruptly, he
realized that the arc was linked together in the same way
as the black wall of Nylan, but not nearly so intricately.
With a smile he began to investigate the linkages, probing their "hooks."

Light flared everywhere, and Rahl was flung backward. His shields cushioned him somewhat as he was
shoved into the stone wall beside the door, but he had to
take several gasping breaths.

He thought the explosion had knocked down both
other figures, but by the time he could gather himself together, they were apparently standing where they had
been.

"You may go, Mage-Guard." The words were cool but
not cold, impersonal but not mocking or indifferent.

As he stepped out into the midday sun, Rahl understood that he had been tested on the limits of his abilities
and personal control. That had been obvious. Why was
another question.

Taryl was waiting, standing beside the coach.

Did he look relieved or worried? Or merely disinter-
ested? Rahl wasn't certain.

All emotion was concealed behind impenetrable
shields, as Taryl said calmly, "The driver will take you
back to the quarters, then return for me and the others.
We will meet in the library after the evening meal. It is
much smaller than the one at headquarters, but it will
suffice. It appears likely that we will embark on the lead
river steamer before long, but I should know more by tonight. In the meantime, I would suggest that you read the
manual on tactics for cavalry and other mounted units.
I took the liberty of leaving a copy on the desk in your

quarters. It is yours to use and keep for as long as necessary." Taryl nodded.

Rahl returned the nod, climbed into the coach, and closed the door.

As the coach pulled away from the bunker, he tried to think about everything that had occurred. First, Taryl had pushed and pressed him to develop every possible order-ability he might possess. Second, Rahl had been introduced to some of the highest officials in Hamor and been recognized by them. Third, he had been effectively examined twice, once in arms and once in order and chaos. Fourth, Taryl had pressed him to learn what he could about healing.

All of that suggested that Taryl was preparing him for something. Was it that the overcommander had deep concerns about what awaited the forces being assembled to deal with the rebellion? Rahl didn't know, but what he did know was that Taryl was being mysterious, and the longer they had been in Cigoerne, the more mysterious he had become.

Taryl clearly didn't trust either Triad Fieryn or Triad Dhoryk, but if he didn't, why had he been recalled from Luba? Or had he asked Jubyl to be recalled? Or was something else happening?

Rahl shifted his weight on the coach seat, realizing something else. He was going to be sore and stiff.

Following Taryl's advice, Rahl returned to his quarters and began to study *Mounted Tactics*. Because he had ridden little and had no military experience, he read slowly, and had only gone through two long basic chapters by dinnertime. He consoled himself that the reading had taken so long because he had actually drawn out some of the simple maneuvers to be able to understand them. He did wish the manual had more diagrams.

He brought the manual down to the mess but kept it tucked inside his uniform.

At the evening meal, Rahl looked to see Taryl, but the overcommander was not seated at the seniors' table, which held but a few officers, who appeared to say little to each other. Rahl sat across from the garrulous Bertayk and another younger captain named Uhlyr. To Rahl's left was Sevala. The place to his right was empty.

"Word is that you went off in a formal coach last night with the overcommander," Bertayk said cheerfully, spearing two slices of mutton marinated in firemint. "Word also is that you went to the Imperial Palace. What's it like?"

Rahl laughed gently. "Big. The halls are wider than the mess. The columns are tall and white, and there are guards in crimson everywhere."

"How did you get that lucky?" persisted Bertayk.

"When you're the assistant to an overcommander, you go where you're told and try not to be obvious."

"Did you see the Emperor?" asked Sevala. "What does he look like?" Her interest was genuine, Rahl felt, and she was less pushy than Bertayk.

"I only saw him in passing," Rahl replied. "I'm just a mage-guard. He wore black and white and a vest of some sort. He seemed to spend a little time with each of the senior officers. Both the Land Marshal and the Sea Marshal were there."

"You were with some powerful officers," observed Uhlyr.

"I was with one powerful mage-guard overcommander," Rahl said with a smile. "I wouldn't have been there if I weren't his assistant. I'm sure all of those officers knew that." Rahl helped himself to the mutton and to the laced potatoes, breaking off a section of the thin fried bread.

"This is your first tour in Cigoerne, you said the other night," offered Sevala, after a sip of what looked to be dark ale. "How does it compare to Nylan?"

Rahl grinned, thankful for the question. "There's almost no comparison. Cigoerne is far larger, and the buildings are far taller . . ." He went on to describe Nylan at great length and in extreme detail. By the time he finished, so was dinner.

Rahl had also drunk a second lager, more than he usually did.

As he rose to leave the mess, he turned to Sevala. "Thank you."

The lanky captain flushed slightly. "Thank you. Bertayk is always pushing to find out anything he can about seniors." Her voice was pleasant, but slightly husky.

"You work with him?"

"I've had to." She smiled. "I did enjoy the description. I don't think anything I've read conveys the sense of the black city the way you did, but . . . I do have some reports to write."

"My condolences."

"It's part of the duty. Good evening, Rahl."

"Good evening."

Rahl made his way to the library, but only read three pages of the tactics manual before Taryl appeared. He closed the book and carried it with him to follow the overcommander down to a musty chamber on the lower level. Unlike the one where Taryl had offered instruction, this chamber was dank with a clay floor.

Taryl lit the lamp, and Rahl closed the door.

"There are few places with privacy in Cigoerne, especially in Mage-Guard Headquarters," Taryl began. "The Triad Fieryn has indicated that he would like to meet with you tomorrow. We'll go from breakfast to his study. When we return, you will spend the remainder of the day with Majer Xerya. When she dismisses you, you are to continue reading the tactics manual. I'd also like you to continue your efforts to sense and forecast the weather. It is possible that we may embark and depart on twoday. I still have much to do, and you will see little of me until we are on board the river steamer. It appears likely that you will be assigned as the mage-captain of a mounted heavy infantry company used for in-force reconnaissance.

That is not certain yet, and I would caution you not to mention it until I can confirm it."

The tactics manual made more sense, not that Rahl doubted Taryl did anything without a solid reason—even if Rahl had no idea what that reason might be.

"Can you tell me more about this morning's . . . examination?" Rahl finally asked.

"Your performance was satisfactory. There was some discussion about whether your last effort was defensive, but since it was addressed at the means of attack and not the attackers, it was considered defensive, if somewhat unique. It was also suggested that I instruct you on a less explosive means of dealing with order strangulation."

"Order strangulation—is that what it's called when they use order to pull all the heat away from everything?"

"It's more complex than that, but that is often the effect." Taryl turned back toward the door. "If you'd put out the lamp."

"Is that all?" asked Rahl.

"For now. You look like you could use a good night's sleep, after you read a bit more, and I have another large stack of reports to read. Among other things."

Rahl didn't quite know what to say. Taryl hadn't really answered his question about the meaning of the examination in the bunker and clearly wasn't going to say more. All manner of intrigue was taking place, from what Rahl could surmise, and yet he couldn't figure out who wanted what from whom or why, and Taryl wasn't saying, and Rahl didn't know enough to figure it out, especially since those involved kept tight personal shields.

So Rahl used a touch of order to put out the lamp and followed Taryl back up the narrow stone stairway to the main level, where each went his own way.

XX

Rahl's back and shoulders were stiff and more than a little sore when he woke on oneday. He hadn't slept all that well, either, because his thoughts had kept circling around the questions of what actually was happening that was so preoccupying Taryl.

The Emperor supported Taryl, and so did Jubyl. Because the Emperor did, so did Fieryn, but Rahl had the feeling that neither Dhoryk nor Fieryn was all that supportive of Taryl, particularly with the selection of Byrna to succeed Charynat. But why would Dhoryk and the Overmarshal want a less effective commander? Or was it that they feared an effective commander's future ambitions? In his brief meeting with Land Marshal Valatyr, Rahl had been less than impressed, although Valatyr had certainly been pleasant. While Rahl could not support his feelings with any real proof, he had the definite feeling that much of the Emperor's decisiveness rested with Jubyl and the Empress and that their influence was no secret. That would also explain why Serita was a tool of Dhoryk and Klassyn of Fieryn and why the allegiances of the assistants were no secret. That way, Jubyl and the Emperor could claim that they were keeping no secrets from the other Triads.

Against that background, Taryl's appointment as Mage-Guard Overcommander of Merowey was a necessity for the Triad, if a grudging one. Taryl's preoccupation and general attitude since they had arrived in Cigoerne suggested that not everyone in positions of power beneath and beyond the Triad accepted that necessity.

Rahl finished dressing and took a deep breath. Just thinking about the intrigue tired him. He could only hope that matters would be less involuted once they reached

Merowey and embarked on the campaign against the rebels.

At breakfast, he sat with Alfhyr, Sernyt, and Bleun, all of whom were speculating on which of their companies would be picked for what specific duties once they reached Kysha. Rahl could offer little information on such and mainly listened and ate.

After breakfast, he had to wait some time outside, standing in a brisk breeze under high, scudding clouds, before Taryl appeared in another timeworn tan duty coach. Taryl did not leave the coach but just motioned for Rahl to climb in.

The overcommander had a large stack of papers in his lap, and Rahl had to ease past him carefully in getting into the coach and the seat on the far side from the door.

"You see that smaller stack of dispatches there?" asked Taryl.

"Yes, ser."

"Start reading them. You don't have to do anything with them. Just read them. Notice how they're written. It's possible you may have to write some."

Rahl began to read. Even though the road was paved, he found concentrating on the dispatches difficult, both because of the style of writing and the swaying of the coach. Although the windows were only cracked, he also had to make sure that nothing blew away.

Reading the dispatches raised more questions than answers, although some of those questions were more irritating than substantial. Why had a Majer Dheryan asked for "additional equine replenishment prior to riverine transport and deployment" when it would have been so much simpler to just say that he needed more mounts before his companies were shipped to Kysha and the campaign got under way?

Rahl only managed about a third of the dispatches before the coach pulled up before the Triad's wing of Mage-Guard Headquarters, and his head was aching.

"How many have you read, ser?"

"That stack I handed you amounts to two days' worth. I've had to catch up on almost a year's worth. You have to read what's not written as well as what is." Taryl climbed out of the coach, leaving the dispatches on the coach seat.

Rahl followed him, but he did not see a single mage-guard or clerk in the corridors through which Taryl led him, not until they reached a foyer off the main corridor, where an older mage-guard sat behind a table desk.

The mage-guard stood upon catching sight of Taryl. "Overcommander, I'll tell the Triad you're here." Even before he could move, the door behind him opened.

"Mage-Guards . . . come in." Fieryn was a slender and wiry man, almost a head shorter than Rahl, with blond hair that clung to his scalp in tight ringlets. His eyes were a watery pale blue that seemed more intense, perhaps because his pale eyebrows were almost invisible. He had an easy smile as he stepped forward. "Taryl, I've been most interested in meeting your assistant. It's good of you to bring him here." His eyes lighted on Rahl.

In reply, Rahl inclined his head. "Triad."

"Do come in," repeated Fieryn, stepping back and gesturing for them to follow him into the study beyond.

Rahl walked behind the two senior mage-guards and was about to shut the door behind him when Fieryn's assistant did just that.

The study was scarcely overlarge, an oblong chamber fifteen cubits by ten, with a single bookcase of golden wood set against the west wall and filled with leather-bound volumes with spines chased in gilt and arranged in order. Rahl suspected none had been read recently. In front of the east wall was a table desk with several documents laid carelessly across it and a wooden armchair behind it. Set before the window in the south wall that overlooked the interior courtyard garden was a circular table with four chairs around it.

Fieryn took the chair on the west side of the table. "We might as well sit down. Everyone will have a long day."

Taryl settled into the chair on the east. Rahl took the

chair that faced the window. As he seated himself, he could sense the faint but thorough probes at his personal shields.

"Good shields, but I wouldn't have expected less . . . if you're working for Taryl."

Rahl wondered at the slight hesitation, but he replied, "I've tried to follow his example."

Fieryn laughed. "I'm glad you used the word *tried*. Few have been able to actually follow that example." His eyes focused directly on Rahl. "So you're the mage-guard who managed to disrupt the Jeranyi scheme in Swartheld?"

"I did what I could, ser," replied Rahl deferentially.

"You're an ordermage, and stronger than the average for a mage-guard, but there's no hint of chaos about you. How did you manage to get the ship to explode?"

"I managed to use a sight shield to get to the ammunition magazines, and I set fuses to the powder, sir. I did fashion a little order around the fuses so that they'd burn steady. Then I hurried as fast as I could to get away. I almost didn't make it, and I had to jump into the harbor and stay underwater."

Fieryn laughed once more. "It's good to hear when a mage-guard has to use something besides his order- or chaos-abilities." The laugh and smile vanished. "I'm curious. How did Recluce let an ordermage as accomplished as you are depart?"

Rahl offered a rueful smile. "It's a long story, ser, but the short version is that they declared that I was a natural ordermage, and could not learn anything, and that I was a danger to Recluce and Nylan. The magisters were relieved to see me depart."

"Yet you worked as a clerk for a time?"

"They did not think I was teachable or knew that much. I didn't know better. I didn't even think I knew enough to be considered any sort of mage until one of the harbor mage-guards stopped me while I was delivering papers and suggested that I register as an outland mage."

"Did you?"

"Yes, ser. Almost immediately."

"Almost?" Fieryn raised his near-transparent eyebrows.

"I finished delivering the papers to the tariff enumerators and went straight to the mage-guard station."

Fieryn looked to Taryl.

"He did, and there's a record of his registry."

Fieryn shook his head. "Sometimes, I have to wonder how Recluce survives. They throw out mages like you, and they threw out the greatest engineer in recent history, and he had to defeat an entire fleet with one ship for them to allow him back—and only if he built a separate city." His eyes flicked back to Rahl. "Are you loyal to the mage-guards or to Taryl?"

"From what I know and have seen, ser, there is no difference." As soon as he spoke, Rahl wished he'd phrased his reply differently.

Fieryn paused, just fractionally, before asking, "Did anyone tell you to say that?"

"No, ser. It's just that everything I've seen tells me that. I doubt the overcommander would have wanted me to say that. It's probably not a good answer for someone who is ambitious or knows Cigoerne well." That was an even worse answer. Why couldn't he just murmur something polite?

"Why do you say that?"

That he could answer honestly without getting in trouble. "Because I don't know Cigoerne, ser, and because I'm most grateful to be a mage-guard after all I've seen."

Fieryn nodded slowly. "I can sense you mean that deeply, and few do, or not for long. I would caution you that innocence will not protect you from evil or corruption. Nor will good will and faith. The only true protection is an understanding that there is no such thing as a little corruption and that all power and fame are fleeting. I doubt that there is a mage-guard anywhere under thirty years who can name the Triad before my predecessor, and less than a handful of Hamorians recall the name of the Emperor before Hamylt. Cyad once ruled the world, and no one is certain where most of her great cities even were."

Rahl sensed that the Triad meant every word, and yet . . . He just nodded. "Yes, ser."

Fieryn stood abruptly. "It has been good to see you again, Taryl, and to meet you, Rahl. I look forward to hearing good things from both of you."

Rahl rose from the conference table with Taryl. He realized that he had not sensed the Triad's intention until Fieryn had stood. That alone told him he still had much to learn.

He also had to wonder why Fieryn had requested such a long coach ride for both Taryl and Rahl for such a short meeting that seemed almost perfunctory, yet he had the strong feeling that asking about it would be most unwise.

Taryl did not speak until they had left the Triad's wing and were back in the coach.

"When we get back to the High Command post, I'd like you to impose on Majer Xerya to show you anything she thinks might someday be within your capability, even if you cannot do it now or in the near future."

"Ser?"

"Rahl . . . think.".

Rahl almost stopped dead in his boots. Why was . . . He shook his head. "Is that because I have to know it can be done by having seen it?"

"After the past year, you have to ask?" Taryl's tone was between exasperated and chiding.

What could Rahl say to that? Although Taryl's words had irritated him, the overcommander was right. It was just that he was trying to learn so much.

"Rahl . . . you have this tendency to feel sorry for yourself when you are overwhelmed with what you need to do and learn. I'm going to say something that I will not say again, but I expect you to remember it."

"Yes, ser."

"First, anyone who has ever done anything of true worth has been overwhelmed. Only the lazy, the incompetent, and the ignorant have not experienced that feeling when working hard at something. Second, no one cares if you feel overwhelmed. They only want the task at hand accomplished. Feeling sorry for yourself just distracts you and wastes time and effort." Taryl pointed to the smaller stack of dispatches. "You have more than a little reading to do."

"Yes, ser."

There were definitely aspects to being a mage-guard that Rahl had never considered. He picked up the dispatches and began to read once more.

XXI

The remainder of oneday and most of twoday blurred together for Rahl, perhaps because his head was splitting by the time he got out of the coach back at the High Command. Trying to read through the dispatches was almost as bad as copying *Natural Philosophies* had been when he'd been an apprentice scrivener. Half the officers wrote too little, and the other half wrote too much in phrases that sounded as though they were trying to please an ancient master of rhetoric, perhaps even an ancient Cyadoran master of rhetoric.

After Taryl left him, Rahl had gone to the infirmary and conveyed Taryl's wishes to Majer Xerya. She had promptly made him accompany her for the entire remainder of the day, which had included using order and a sharp surgical saw to amputate a leg, assisting as he could in setting and splinting a broken lower arm, and lancing and cleaning a number of boils. Rahl managed to get adequately proficient with boils and small eruptions that Xerya had him handle several on his own, if under her watchful eye. He had to admit that he had a far greater respect for the majer—and for Deybri—when he walked slowly back to his quarters to wash up for the evening meal in the mess.

By the time oneday was over, his back, shoulders, head, eyes, and fingers all ached. Still, he did scan the skies and try to determine the weather ahead. He even managed some more exercises with the iron blocks and water.

Twoday wasn't much better. After breakfast, Taryl quizzed him briefly on the tactics manual, then handed him a list of questions on tactics and told him to come up with written answers before the evening meal. The over-commander also handed him more dispatches, asking Rahl to sort out those he thought important and to be prepared to tell Taryl why. He was also asked to write out a report on what he thought the weather would be for the next three days heading upriver.

Rahl finished the weather report just before the evening meal and handed it to Taryl in the library that was little more than a quarters chamber stuffed with shelves, books, a few ancient wooden armchairs, and two battered table desks.

Taryl looked at it and nodded. Then he skimmed over Rahl's responses to the tactics questions and nodded at those. But . . . on every dispatch Rahl pulled out, he asked variations on the same question: "What isn't in this dispatch, and what does that mean?"

By threeday, Rahl was more than ready to carry his gear onto the *Fyrador*. Following Taryl's orders, he boarded slightly after midday and found himself assigned to a cabin that held two bunks and little more. He put his gear in the net above the upper bunk and went out to the upper deck to wait for Taryl. *Upper deck* was a misnomer, because it was actually the third deck, above both the main deck and the middeck. There was a half deck above the upper deck, but that was reserved for the crew.

Rahl stood at the railing under the hazy winter sun that created a warmth more like the spring in Land's End, but the air held the acrid odor of burning coal. He eased his visored cap back slightly, his eyes drifting from the stone piers back aft to the massive paddle wheel. As he had noted earlier when he'd inspected the docks, the river steamers were most unlike the seagoing trading vessels or warships like the *Ascadya*. They were far broader in the beam, and except for the bow, almost oblong in shape. The *Fyrador* and the *Syadtar* were more than a hundred and fifty cubits in length, while the other three were a good thirty cubits shorter. They all had neither the screws of the iron-hulled military vessels nor the side-wheel paddles of the trading ships, but a single rear paddle wheel more than fifteen cubits in diameter. Rahl didn't know exactly how much water they drew, but their draft was far shallower than the sea-going vessels, certainly less than ten cubits.

So far as Rahl could tell, he was the only mage-guard on the *Fyrador*. The upper deck was limited to squad leaders and officers, but Rahl only saw a handful of either.

The overcommander arrived just before the *Fyrador* blew its departure whistle. Rahl watched as Taryl hurried up the gangway carrying two gear bags that bulged in all directions. Behind him came a trooper carrying two more bags. Before long, Taryl appeared on the upper deck and walked to join Rahl. The older mage-guard had deep circles under his red-rimmed eyes, and while his steps were firm, Rahl could sense his exhaustion.

For a time, Taryl just leaned on the railing and watched as the gangway was swung aboard and the lines singled up, then untied and reeled in. Another series of long blasts issued from whistle, and the paddle wheel began to turn, slowly thumping as it churned the water aft of the *Fyrador*. Slowly, the river steamer pulled away from the pier and out into the channel, heading upstream.

The departure whistles of the second river steamer, the *Syadtar,* echoed through the afternoon.

Slowly, Taryl straightened. "I'm going to take a nap. Keep an eye on things, and wake me if you sense anything strange. Otherwise, I'll see you later."

"Should I be looking for anything in particular?"

"If I knew that—" Taryl broke off his words. "I'm sorry. No, I can't tell you what to look for, just anything that feels chaotic or disordered . . . or makes you uneasy, particularly any boxes or bundles that no one is around."

"Yes, ser."

After Taryl left for his cabin, Rahl checked the truncheon at his belt, then walked slowly along the upper deck, pausing every few cubits to let his order-senses range over the troopers on the middeck and main deck. For the first twenty cubits or so, he sensed nothing unusual. Then he could feel a touch of chaos, but he had trouble locating it. Finally, he realized that it was not chaos properly at all, but some sort of vent that carried hot air—probably from the engine or boiler room.

He passed several officers, generally captains, and nodded politely to each. The only one he knew by sight and name was Bleun, but Bleun just nodded and stepped back as Rahl neared him.

Rahl paid special attention to boxes set on the narrow, uncovered, outboard section of the main deck, but troopers were still carrying a number of them toward the forward hold. With the steamer's shallow draft, Rahl could imagine that not all that much cargo could be stored belowdecks, not with the need for the boilers and engines—and the coal that powered them.

With Taryl's concerns and cautions in mind, Rahl took his time in making a complete circuit of the upper deck and probing below with his order-senses. He had found a number of "chaotic" points, but so far as he could tell, all had to do with the actual operation of the *Fyrador* in some fashion or another.

Before making another circuit, he stopped and took a long and deep breath.

He glanced aft. The massive rear paddle wheel left a white froth behind·on the dark water, yet that foam vanished by the time the *Fyrador* had traveled twice its own length, and certainly long before the *Syadtar* reached where the foam had been.

Even hundreds of kays upstream from Swartheld, the Swarth River was far wider than the Feyn—the only river worthy of the name in Recluce—still close to half a kay in width although not so deep as it was near Swartheld. Orchards still lined both sides of the river, planted in neat rows on the slopes above the marshy area at the river's edge.

Rahl spied several wild gray geese in calmer water near a stubby pier on the west side of the river. He thought they might take flight as the ripples from the steamer reached them, but they only bobbed slightly in the water. For some reason, their apparent grace and calm reminded him of Deybri, and the thought that he was traveling toward a rebellion seemed almost impossible.

One of the geese tipped sideways, and Rahl realized that it was only a decoy. He smiled wryly and began another circuit of the upper deck.

Merowey

XXII

Taryl slept most of threeday afternoon, and Rahl saw him only briefly at the evening meal, if overspiced burhka and soggy noodles qualified as a meal. Taryl said little beyond pleasantries, and his thoughts were clearly somewhere else. Because Rahl had learned that trying to get Taryl to say something he did not want to discuss was clearly unproductive, he did not press. Irritated as he was, he kept that irritation behind his personal shields. At least, that was a form of practice at strengthening those shields.

Breakfast was overdone egg toast and dry mutton slapped on a platter with warm ale. Rahl sat at a corner table in the small mess that served both squad leaders and officers. No one asked to sit with him.

Finally, well past midmorning on fourday, Taryl joined Rahl under the awning at the rear of the upper deck. Given the cloudy nature of the day, the awning was unnecessary either as respite from the sun or from rain, because the clouds were high enough—and contained little enough moisture, Rahl had ascertained—that rain was most unlikely. The river had narrowed somewhat, and the current seemed stronger. Rahl could sense that the engines were working harder, and their upstream progress seemed slower.

He'd had time to think more about the revolt, and there were certain aspects of it that made little sense.

"You have that quizzical look, Rahl. Creating effective shields isn't much use if your face reveals what your shields conceal."

"I know I don't understand all the machinations, or the reasons behind them, ser, but I'm having trouble figuring out why there's so much maneuvering and scheming. The Triads are all powerful mages, and the Emperor . . . well, he's the Emperor. Who could stand up to them directly?"

Taryl laughed. "That's exactly why there's scheming. Think about it this way. No one rules except through others who carry out their will. In every land, some group has the power to support or topple a ruler. If the white wizards of Fairhaven do not support the High Wizard, there is another High Wizard. If the magisters just below the council in Nylan do not support the council, the council changes. In Hamor, matters are more . . . mixed."

"That's what I don't understand. The officers in charge of the battalions and regiments seem to support the Emperor. Most of the more successful traders and factors do. The mage-guards were established and govern to support the Emperor."

"That's not quite true, Rahl. Why do you think that there are three Triads, one for the Emperor, one for the High Command, and one for the mage-guards?"

Rahl frowned. "You're suggesting that the Triads were formed to weaken the power of the mages?"

"To channel and restrain that power, yes. A structure that provides equal power to advise the Emperor and to carry out his policies and the law of the land to three powerful mages goes far to assure that no one group or person has too much power. It also assures the people, the troopers and sailors of the High Command, and the mage-guards that they have an equal voice in how Hamor is governed. Equally important, it restricts what the order-mages and chaos-mages of Hamor can and cannot do. In return for certain powers and privileges, they are forced to forgo others. In a way, it's a continuation of the Cyadoran division of elthage, altage, and merage."

Rahl hadn't the faintest idea what Taryl meant.

"Cyador divided its society into mages, military, and merchanters. Hamor's structure is somewhat different, but the Cyadoran system endured thousands of years before the great collapse." Taryl paused. "The problem facing the Emperor is simple. He believes that the mage-guards have enough power and privilege, and that trade and prosperous growers are the keys to Hamor's future. He's right, because neither the High Command nor the mage-guards produce anything. We only protect. The High Command protects against other lands and their fleets. The mage-guards protect the people against themselves. Both protections are needed, but they should serve all people, not just those with coins or power. The problem of ruling in Hamor is that the Emperor needs the support of two of the three Triads. To remain as Mage-Guard Triad, Fieryn needs the support of most of the more powerful senior mage-guards. Dhoryk needs the support of his marshals. The Emperor needs the support of the people. No ruler has ever survived against the opposition of his people. Those who scheme attempt to undermine such support to their own ends, which are their own accession to power." Taryl offered a wry smile. "All lands have schemers, and in all lands, those who wish a fair and honest ruler need to oppose such schemers. That does not guarantee a good ruler, but the success of scheming almost always guarantees poor governing for most of the populace." He cleared his throat. "Enough of that for now. Have you discerned anything out of the ordinary here on board?"

"No, ser. I've been making regular checks. There's chaos heat in places vented from the boilers and the engines, and some of the troops are a little ill—that shows up as diffuse chaos."

"You can sense that?" Taryl seemed surprised, and that didn't happen often.

"Yes, ser." Rahl paused. "I guess I always could, but until I worked with Majer Xerya, I really didn't know what it was."

"She didn't mention that to me." Taryl sounded some-where between amused and slightly miffed.

"I didn't tell her, ser. It was when I saw the patient with brain fever, and there was chaos all through his body, but not all that much in one place, not like the troops with wounds or broken bones. I got to thinking and watching. The majer seemed to know that, and there didn't seem to be much point in telling her what she knew and expected me to know."

Taryl laughed, ruefully. "Just because people expect you to know something doesn't mean that they know you know it. You need to find a way to let them know without being obnoxious or obsequious. But then, that's true of most times when you have to tell superiors something."

True as Taryl's words probably were, they irritated Rahl. Why couldn't he just say something without hav-ing to worry about how people reacted? Most of them didn't seem to care about how he felt.

"You've been assigned to the Third Mounted Heavy In-fantry under Captain Drakeyt. That's normally a position for a longtime mage-guard or one with less time in the mage-guards who's just been made a senior mage-guard. Cyphryt wanted someone else for the position—"

"Vladyrt?"

Taryl shook his head. "Vladyrt isn't suited to that. He'd end up with half the company dead and his throat cut in weeks. I could have just assigned you. That's within my purview, but I wanted Fieryn and Jubyl to un-derstand my reasons. That's why you had to meet so many people and undergo the arms evaluation and the order/chaos-skills evaluation. They had to know that you had the basic skills for the position."

Rahl considered Taryl's words, then looked at the overcommander. Taryl was waiting. "I'm new to all the plotting and scheming, and I don't think I'll ever be that good at it. You're saying that I had to get the position on my ability rather than because you wanted me in that po-

sition. I don't have a problem with that, ser, but . . ." Rahl
paused. "That suggests that there are only so many things
you can order just on your say-so . . . or . . . that everything you do needs to be supported." Rahl could sense
that he didn't have it quite right. "Is all this because there
are mage-guards and officers who are secretly supporting Golyat and who would use any favoritism against the
Emperor?"

"Close enough," replied Taryl. "In something like this,
the more all the officers feel that everything is being
done as well as possible, the more likely that the troops
will feel the same way. That makes them more effective
troops. Making them feel that way consists of two parts.
First, the officers have to do it the best way possible.
Second, they have to make those they command feel that
they've done it that way."

"How many other mage-guards are assigned to other
companies?"

"There are supposed to be two mage-guards for every
battalion. We'll be fortunate if we have one for every
other battalion."

"What exactly are my duties?"

"The Third Mounted Heavy Infantry will conduct
scouting expeditions ahead of the main body. Your task
is to locate enemy forces as you can, find and check water supplies, provide an idea of the weather conditions,
act as a field healer as much as practicable, and advise
the captain who commands the company. You are also
his back-up in case of injury, but not his subordinate, and
you need to keep that distinction in mind."

"Ser . . . what is the difference between mounted
heavy infantry and cavalry?"

"It's minimal these days, but the basic distinction is
that in heavy infantry, the officers and men are trained to
fight as individuals and units both on foot and from the
saddle. We don't use footmen that much for attacks, in
any event, because they're sitting swans for a chaos-mage.

They're better suited to defense behind walls, and we're usually not the defenders."

"Why do they use sabres, instead of falchionas?"

"In combat, except in the hands of a master blade or someone trained as a mage-guard, falchionas can be as much a danger to the wielder as the opponent. They're also much heavier. That means most lose their effectiveness sooner in a pitched battle."

"Is the Third Mounted Heavy Infantry onboard the *Fyrador*?" If Captain Drakeyt were on the steamer, Rahl might as well meet him before they reached Kysha.

"No. They're already in Kysha, and they'll be setting out almost as soon as we disembark. They've been part of the force protecting the city. They're ready to go. The heavy mounted companies on the steamers will need several days before their mounts are ready."

"Then I'll be setting out fairly soon."

"Yes." Taryl smiled. "And if you want to post a letter to your healer, you ought to write it and have it ready to go before we reach Kysha. The *Fyrador* can carry it back. After that, it could take eightdays for anything you write to get back as far as Kysha."

"Is there someone on the ship . . . ?"

"All river vessels have dispatch clerks. Just ask."

"Thank you."

"You're welcome." Taryl paused, then added, "Oh . . . I also have something for you. It's with my gear. I meant to give it to you earlier. It's a black-oak truncheon that's about the length of a cavalry sabre. It might take a little getting used to, but that shouldn't be hard for you."

Rahl suspected that learning to ride well would be far harder than adjusting to a longer truncheon.

XXIII

By midmorning on sevenday, Rahl was more than ready to get off the *Fyrador.* There was little enough to do on the river steamer, besides read the dispatches and keep checking the vessel for any chaos that showed up out of place—which was almost none. He had written several pages of a letter to Deybri, mostly telling her about what he had seen along the river, but he had decided not to finish it or seal it until they had almost arrived in Kysha.

The river had narrowed considerably, so that it was only about two hundred cubits wide, and the river steamer had to follow a narrower channel, marked with yellow-and-maroon buoys. The lands beyond the banks—when he could see over the low hills that bordered the river—were also hilly and mostly covered in browning grasses. On the hillside to the west, half a kay or so ahead was a stand of trees, certainly no more than a half kay in length on the side that fronted the river, and not much more than that in depth.

Rahl didn't recognize the trees, but there was something about them that bothered him. He turned and started forward to find Taryl.

At that moment, a column of water exploded skyward from the water less than fifty cubits from the midships area of the port side of the ship. Three short blasts of the whistle followed, and the ship swung starboard, as if the captain were going to run her aground.

"Cannon!"

Taryl scrambled out of the midships hatch and glanced around.

"It's coming from the trees, I think!" Rahl pointed toward the grove.

Taryl turned. "Can you tell how many men are there?"

Rahl tried to extend his order-senses, but he had trouble reaching that far. Still . . .

"How many?"

"I can't tell exact numbers, but probably not more than thirty, maybe only a score."

"Good!" Taryl turned and hurried forward.

Another column of water spouted, this time within a handful of cubits of the steamer, but still on the port side.

Three more whistle blasts followed. Rahl could tell that the steamer was heading for the shore. What he couldn't understand was why.

"Shore force! Ready on the bow! Shore force!"

Belatedly, Rahl moved forward. Troopers were forming up on the lower forward deck. He could see two distinct groups—archers and footmen. Taryl had just finished talking to a grizzled captain.

Already the *Fyrador* was nearing the shore, and from what Rahl could tell, the steamer would ground almost below the trees.

Suddenly, he sensed . . . something . . . and threw up full shields.

CRUMMPTT!

Rahl found himself being flung backwards and sliding along the railing, then bouncing against a bulkhead. Stars flashed in front of his eyes as he staggered to his feet.

The pilothouse and the front part of the crew deck was a shattered mass of wood, but the steamer stayed on course toward the shore, except he didn't hear the thumping of the paddle wheel. He glanced aft. It was almost still. Then, within less than a hundred cubits of where Rahl thought they would ground, it began to turn—in reverse, slowly at first, and then building speed.

Rahl grabbed the railing.

There was a lurching grinding and a long shudder as the steamer grounded.

After hurrying farther forward, Rahl was able to see that a bow ramp had been lowered and almost a company of infantry was charging uphill. The archers loosed wave after wave of arrows.

Another spout of water erupted, but it was a good fifty cubits out into the river.

Rahl tried to concentrate on finding where the rebels were, now that he was closer.

"Rahl!" yelled Taryl.

"Most of them are in a small clearing at the south end . . . a hundred cubits back on a rise!" Rahl bellowed back.

Taryl turned and relayed the directions to the archer captain, then to a messenger who sprinted down the ramp and through the knee-deep muddy water.

Another cannonball slammed into the water just off the bow of the *Fyrador,* close enough that spray rained down on the port side of the bow.

The shore force had vanished into the trees, and Rahl keep trying to sense what he could not see, occasionally glancing down at the forward main deck where Taryl stood, with two messengers. Beside him, another company was forming up.

Then an explosion and a font of flame rose from where the attackers had been, followed by the reddish white chaos and emptiness of death. Rahl guessed that the attackers had set off the remaining powder when the shore force had neared.

There were no more cannon splashes in the water, or impacts elsewhere, and another company of troopers followed the shore force into the trees. Rahl could sense the continuing chaos emanating from the trees as the number of dead and wounded mounted.

Then, as midday approached, that diminished, and the troopers from the second force returned to the *Fyrador.* Most looked unwounded.

Rahl could sense no more deaths, and he walked aft until he could see the channel downstream. The other four steamers had clearly backed down, awaiting the outcome of the skirmish on the shore.

Once the wounded started returning, Rahl made his way down to the main deck, where they were being treated by the healers—not order-healers, but those trained in dealing with wounds without using order or chaos. Remembering what he had learned from both Deybri and Majer Xerya, Rahl used his limited healing skills only where necessary, and applied as little order as was required. Even so, he had to retire from the area of the bow used as an infirmary after doing what he could for only about a score of troopers.

He managed to get some bread and cold mutton from the mess. Eating that eliminated the light-headedness, but he could still feel that he couldn't do much more order-work until he had rested more.

In midafternoon, Taryl found him sitting on a bench on the upper deck. "Majer Chevaryn said that you helped the healers for a while."

"I tried to be careful, but . . ." Rahl shrugged. "After about a score of them, I couldn't do any more."

"That score are fortunate, and I told the majer that. Most mage-guards don't have your abilities there, and true healers are in short supply. Majer Xerya and two of her assistant healers will be taking the next convoy to Kysha, but three healers for a force of more than ten thousand . . ." Taryl shook his head.

"Why are there so few healers compared to order-mages?"

"There always have been. I can only guess that it's because dealing with living bodies takes a different talent that's rarer. Also, it often comes with other abilities, and some of those are even more scarce."

Rahl nodded.

"You know something about that?"

"I was thinking of Dorrin. He was the smith who built the first black ships and founded Nylan. He was a healer, according to what I read while I was in Nylan." Rahl frowned. "And Creslin had some healing abilities, supposedly."

"Those are anecdotal examples, but they support the point." Taryl smiled wryly. "Before I forget, Majer Chevaryn asked me to convey his thanks for your information. He said it reduced their casualties."

Rahl shook his head. "I sensed something just before they fired, and I was on my way to tell you. I just didn't think about a cannon attack from the shore."

"How would you have known?" asked Taryl. "You've never experienced one." He laughed ruefully. "Neither have I. I've been under attack at sea, but never on a river in Hamor itself. The majer didn't think about cannon, but he did want to be able to make a shore attack if he spotted rebels. It's a good thing he did."

"Why didn't he think about cannon?"

"There weren't any High Command cannon anywhere along the river, and that meant they were either smuggled here by Golyat or carried by wagon from the coast. They must have just gotten them in place because they didn't fire at the earlier convoys."

"That's over seven hundred kays."

"That's why no one was thinking about cannon."

Rahl paused. "I heard Marshal Byrna say that Imperial forces controlled Dawhut. How did they get the cannon past them?"

"That's a good question, but I would be cautious at accepting at full value anything that the good marshal asserts. In any case, the shore force did manage to catch a number of the rebels, and I'll be interrogating them shortly, and you'll be observing. Then, we'll have a better idea."

"Do you think there will be other attacks on the way to Kysha?"

"There could be, but I have my doubts. Before long, we'll be in the area of the river where the High Command forces are patrolling regularly. I'd guess this group set up in one of the few places where they had trees for cover outside the patrolled area. But we'll see what the prisoners have to say before we proceed upstream." Taryl turned and began to walk toward the ladder down to the lower decks.

Rahl followed him down until they met Captain Erehtel, who led them forward along the fore and aft passageway on the main deck until he was roughly amidships.

"The prisoners are confined in a single space here. We've moved one into the adjoining space, as you requested, Overcommander." The captain nodded to the hatch to his right.

"How many prisoners are there?" Taryl asked the captain.

"Five. There were six, but one died of his wounds before they could get him back. We found fourteen bodies, and several of the shore force saw two or three men running through the fields on the far side. They were probably spotters higher on the hill who made off when they saw how many men we landed."

"Because we'll need to question each one separately, this will take a little time, but it's actually faster."

And both safer and easier, thought Rahl.

"Yes, ser," replied the captain.

Rahl followed Taryl into the small windowless room. The first prisoner sat on a stool, his hands bound behind his back. He wore a khaki shirt and trousers, with a four-pointed gray star on each shoulder of his shirt. His face was smudged with dirt, and there were bruises on one cheek. His eyes widened as he saw the two mage-guards, but he said nothing.

"Is that the uniform you all wear?" asked Taryl casually, remaining standing.

There was no response, but Rahl could sense a vague sense of a smothered affirmative answer.

"Or is that just for now, until Prince Golyat can issue gray uniforms?"

There was still no response, but Rahl sensed nothing behind the silence.

"You don't know," Taryl said. "That's often the case, especially when your superiors don't want you to know."

He paused. "So far, we've found fifteen bodies, and there are five of you who are prisoners."

Rahl could sense something . . . perhaps satisfaction that some had escaped.

"The handful who ran off won't be much use. We did capture the teams that hauled that cannon here. How long did it take you, a season?"

Rahl got a definite feeling that it was half that.

"And you had help in getting around Dawhut, isn't that so?" Taryl's voice was calm but forceful.

Rahl could also sense that the overcommander was pressing the prisoner with a mild compulsion to tell the truth, enough that the man's feelings and unspoken words were revealing what he was not saying.

"Was it one of the local garrison officers? Or a mage-guard officer?"

The questioning went on . . . and on.

Abruptly, Taryl stopped. "He's told us what he can."

Rahl watched as Taryl went through the same procedure with the second prisoner, but that took less time. Then the overcommander turned to Rahl. "You do the next one. I'll add any questions if you miss something."

"Yes, ser."

Rahl emulated Taryl's technique on the next two prisoners, adequately enough that Taryl only asked two or three questions. The overcommander did interrogate the last, an older and more hard-faced rebel.

In the end, from what Rahl determined himself, there had only been one group and one cannon that the prisoners knew about. The cannon had actually been an older practice weapon in Dawhut and moved to a stead outside of the city, probably before the revolt. None of the prisoners knew who had done it. They'd just ridden back roads and taken two wagons holding a small disassembled cannon and powder and cannonballs from Dawhut to the attack point. They'd had a map and instructions to return when they used up their ammunition, leaving the cannon behind.

Taryl went to fill in Majer Chevaryn, and Rahl climbed back to the upper deck, where he sat on a short wooden bench set against the superstructure.

Before long, Taryl rejoined him.

"What do you think?" The overcommander sat down heavily beside Rahl.

"They were sent out to disrupt things. No one really cared if they returned. There probably won't be many others, but how would we know?"

Taryl nodded. "They send out a little more than a score with an ancient cannon. It will cost us a full day, and fifteen dead, counting everyone in the pilothouse, twenty wounded, half of it from that powder explosion. Most likely, those they sent are the kind who wouldn't do well in ranks, anyway."

"You think there will be more things like this?"

"I'm certain of it. Pits in the roads, ambushes, poisoned food."

Rahl grimaced.

"Golyat's already shown his colors. He promised loyalty to Hamor and his brother, and he was loyal exactly as long as it took him to build his own treasury and army. He'll do whatever it will take to make this a long and unpleasant war, and if he can't win, he'll try to destroy Hamorian unity. That's what we have to stop, and that means winning as effectively and quickly as possible and with as few casualties among the people as possible— even among those quietly supporting Golyat." Taryl offered a wintry smile. "There is one exception to that. The life of any mage-guard who rebelled is forfeit."

"Ah . . . I think I understand."

"It's very simple, Rahl. There are few mage-guards around who could not escape once he or she knew what was happening. Even if they chose to remain and keep the peace, they don't have to support Golyat. There's also another reason—if the mage-guards aren't held to a higher standard of loyalty, then how can we claim the right to enforce order in Hamor?"

Rahl understood that. He also understood why the Emperor had insisted on Taryl as overcommander, and he wouldn't have wished to be a disloyal mage-guard who fell into Taryl's hands.

XXIV

After the cannon ambush on sevenday, and the delays caused by the counterattack and the interrogation of the prisoners, as well as the makeshift repairs to the *Fyrador,* it was late evening before the convoy resumed its progress upriver. The acting captain of the *Fyrador* had surrendered the lead to the *Syadtar,* given the awkwardness of piloting with makeshift arrangements, and Taryl had fretted the rest of the way, despite his earlier words to Rahl about the likelihood that no attacks would occur much closer to Kysha.

Rahl debated writing about the ambush in his letter to Deybri before signing and sealing it, but, in the end, only added a few words of affection—as well as the observation that the hold of the past was stronger than ever. He really didn't want to use the trite phrase that he missed her, much as he did. Then he gave it to the dispatch clerk, whose eyebrows lifted at the address—and the cost— four silvers.

The *Fyrador* finally steamed into the timeworn and battered timber piers at Kysha slightly before noon on oneday. The sky was gray, and the day was chill enough that Rahl wore his mage-guard cold-weather jacket, the first time that he'd needed to do so. From the upper deck, as the crew doubled up the lines, Rahl and Taryl surveyed the town, perhaps half the size of Land's End, if that.

From what Rahl could see, almost all the dwellings and buildings were of a yellowish brown brick, with gray-tile roofs, and none was of more than two stories. To the southwest, beyond Kysha, he thought he could make out areas of forest.

"How far does the forest go?" he asked Taryl.

"About halfway to Dawhut. From there on it's a mix of trees and grasslands that becomes more grass as you head southwest. It's mostly grasslands beyond Dawhut until you get near the coastal hills, and then you get trees again in most places."

Rahl surveyed the river piers, realizing as he did that they held only the stevedores and dockworkers—and several score armed guards stationed along a recently constructed timber fence separating the piers from the rest of the town. "They've blocked off the piers."

"That's because the local cutpurses were robbing the troopers, and the vendors on the piers were shortchanging them."

"There aren't enough mage-guards, then?"

"There never are," Taryl replied. "But with the troopers here, Kysha has more than twice as many people as it did a season ago. Fieryn doesn't want to move more mage-guards from other cities, because that will leave them shorthanded."

"And, besides," Rahl added, "you're now the Mage-Guard Overcommander of Merowey, and it's your problem."

"There might be a certain truth in that, but time will tell. We need to get to what passes for the campaign headquarters as soon as we can. Marshal Byrna's headquarters is located on the south side of Kysha, in what was the district army center. He's not here yet, and Submarshal Dettyr's in command for now."

Rahl could sense Taryl's disgust, even through the older mage-guard's personal shield, but that might have been because Taryl wasn't that worried about Rahl, rather than because of any increased ability on Rahl's part.

"Most of the troops are to the west, in field bivouac." Taryl shook his head as he turned. "If the submarshal or the marshal doesn't get them moving, before long, we'll have sickness, then more sickness. It would already be a problem if it were still summer or early fall." He strode toward the ladder and the trooper who stood by all his gear.

Rahl had to scramble to pick up his kit. He didn't catch up with Taryl until they were both on the main deck. At least one company of troopers was formed up on the small forward section of the main deck, crowded together, each trooper with full gear.

Just before he stepped onto the gangway, Taryl said quietly to Rahl, "We may have to walk, and I'd suggest that you have your patrol truncheon in hand once we leave the piers."

"How far?"

"Close to a kay."

Rahl wasn't looking forward to that, but surprisingly, at least to Rahl, there was a tan wagon with a squad leader waiting at the end of the pier. "Overcommander! Here, ser!"

The trooper with Taryl's gear eased it into the back of the wagon, then climbed in with the equipment, taking Rahl's single bag and setting it alongside Taryl's. Rahl sat in the second wagon seat next to Taryl.

At the direction of a single mage-guard, two pier-guard troopers opened a turnpost gate that was little more than a long plank attached to a wheel on a vertical axle, and the squad leader guided the two drays and the wagon through the gate and into a crowd of vendors, who eased away from the horses and the wagon slowly and reluctantly.

"Make way or get run over!" called the driver.

Rahl didn't see that his words made much difference.

The first building Rahl saw on the far side of the pier road was a chandlery. The shutters and door were painted blue, but time had faded the color almost to a gray. Next to the chandlery was a tinsmith, and a thin line of gray smoke rose from the soot-covered bricks of the chimney.

At the second street into the town from the pier road, the driver turned the wagon south, and in less than four blocks, they had left the shops and trades places behind and were driving past small brick dwellings, with their gray-tile roofs. Unlike the dwellings in Swartheld or Cigoerne—or even Guasyra, the little town south of the ironworks of Luba—the dwellings were not constructed around a central courtyard but tended to have walled gardens in the rear.

Ahead, Rahl could see a compound of several brick buildings, surrounded by a brick wall little more than head high. There was no gate, just an opening in the wall to accommodate the paved lane leading into the compound.

"Headquarters just ahead, ser." The driver halted the wagon in front of a brick walkway, flanked by a scruffy knee-high hedge, that led to a two-story building, one only about forty cubits across the front and half that in depth. A narrow porch extended the entire width of the structure, its roof supported by six brick pillars. On the south side of the dying hedge was a paved area, where a group of troopers stood in loose formation, as if waiting to be mustered.

"I shouldn't be long," Taryl said as he climbed down from the wagon.

"Yes, ser."

Rahl swung down to the pavement after the overcommander, but only moved a few steps from the wagon before his attention focused on the troopers, sensing both chaos and danger from one man near the back of the score or so.

The single trooper was looking toward Taryl as the overcommander stepped onto the covered porch of the building. Then the man lifted a small crossbow.

Rahl boosted his own shields and stepped sideways to use them to block the shot, reaching for his truncheon as he moved.

Thunk!

Rahl staggered back from the impact against his shields, then straightened, and dashed toward the man who looked blankly at Rahl for several moments. Then the trooper reached for the short-sword at his belt.

Rahl's truncheon was faster, far faster, and the *crunch* of the ironbound black oak told Rahl that the man wouldn't be using that arm anytime soon—even before he felt the chaos-pain from the trooper. Rahl yanked the trooper upright with his free hand. "Why did you fire that crossbow at the overcommander?"

"Don't know, ser." The words were mechanical.

"Did someone order you to shoot?"

"Don't know, ser."

Rahl could sense that the trooper truly didn't know. Then, suddenly, the man collapsed, his weight yanking the part of his uniform that Rahl had held right out of the mage-guard's hand. Rahl could sense that he wasn't dead, but why had he collapsed?

The other troopers edged away.

"Just who are you? What are you doing here? These are my men."

Rahl glanced sideways at the stocky captain who had appeared from around the corner of the headquarters building. "Mage-Guard and Captain Rahl. And you?"

"Captain Helyrt to you. What business did you have attacking my trooper?"

Rahl could feel white-hot anger seething through him, but he managed to reply. "Captain, if you had watched what happened, your trooper fired a crossbow at the over-commander." He gestured at the weapon on the packed clay. "That crossbow. I was trying to restrain him when he pulled his blade. He attacked two officers. I merely broke his arm to keep him from injuring me."

"A likely story."

Rahl offered a cold smile. "Mage-guards don't lie, and they don't ignore evidence in front of their eyes, and they don't immediately offer disrespect to other officers, apparently unlike army officers, who apparently do all three, and who don't seem able to control or restrain their men."

Helyrt's face began to turn red.

At that point, an overcaptain made his way through the squad of troopers and walked up to Rahl. "Enough of this disrespect. You may be a high-and-mighty mage-guard to the civilians, but here you're just a captain like scores of other officers. You're even less than them because you're just an ordermage, and ordermages aren't all that useful in killing rebels. And . . . you're subordinate to overcaptains, and I expect an apology for the way you addressed Captain Helyrt. I expect it now."

Rahl had sensed the presence of chaos even before another mage-guard stepped forward, beside the overcaptain, and he had strengthened his own shields. "One of Captain Helyrt's men used a crossbow against a superior officer—"

"Mage-guards aren't superior officers. They're not in the chain of command," snapped the overcaptain.

Rahl was both angry and amazed. "It's attempted assault in any case, and mage-guards are in the line of command if the officers with whom they work are disabled." He probed with his order-senses, only to discover that the other mage-guard was shielding the overcaptain. As he probed, the other troopers slipped away, leaving Rahl facing a captain, an overcaptain, and an unfamiliar and clearly unfriendly mage-guard. Exactly what was he supposed to do?

"An apology now, mage-guard, or a court-martial tomorrow."

Rahl knew something was wrong. Why did he always end up in such situations? Anything he did would be wrong, if for differing reasons. He channeled as much order as he could into the truncheon and moved—not toward either army officer, but toward the mage-guard.

Chaos flared around his shields, harmlessly, and Rahl could sense the concern and fear in the other mage-guard, even as he jab-feinted toward the other's gut, then slammed upward into his throat and chin, before coming back across his temple. The mage-guard pitched to one side, dead.

The captain looked stunned, but the overcaptain had his sabre half-out when Rahl's truncheon slammed into his skull. Although Rahl's blow should only have stunned him, Rahl could sense his death instantly.

The captain started to run, then froze in place.

Rahl could sense the shields holding the captain and turned.

Taryl appeared, seemingly from nowhere, and Rahl realized that the overcommander had used a sight shield to see at least some of what had happened.

The color drained from the immobilized Helyrt's face as he looked from Rahl to Taryl.

"I'd be within my purview as head of all mage-guards in Merowey to execute you on the spot, Captain." Taryl smiled. "Or . . . I could have Mage-Guard Rahl take you apart with his truncheon. I won't. I'll be merciful."

Before Rahl could say a word, something like a bolt of concentrated order flashed from Taryl to the captain. Helyrt started to open his mouth, then pitched forward onto the ground, dead.

Rahl swallowed. Finally, he spoke. "You were watching the whole time, weren't you?"

Taryl nodded.

"You wanted me to handle it."

"Yes. Everyone has to know that you can handle difficult situations without my being around. They also have to know that you have my backing to act independently without asking my permission. That will be very important."

"There's more," Rahl suggested.

"There is, indeed. What would be the reaction if the overcommander of mage-guards killed three troopers as soon as he arrived?"

"Not very good."

"And if his assistant killed three who had actually fired on him?"

"People still won't be happy, but they'll be asking questions about the officers as well." Rahl paused. "*I* killed all three?"

"It's better that way." Taryl's smile was grim. Then he laughed. "Besides, it doesn't matter. If I dropped dead right now, there wouldn't be any difference. You can only be executed once." After the slightest pause, he added, "Now . . . we'll have to explain to Submarshal Dettyr that his command is riddled with traitors, and he will claim that it's not possible, that we're mistaken, and that if we're not, it's all our fault, or the fault of that traitorous mage-guard who influenced the poor overcaptain and captain."

Rahl bent and picked up the crossbow. "What do we do with him?" He pointed to the unconscious trooper still lying on the stone.

"I'll take the crossbow. You're younger and stronger. Drag him in. He won't have much left in the way of brains anyway."

Fortunately for Rahl, the trooper was not all that heavy. Rahl did stagger on one step, because his boot caught on something, but he recovered. Taryl held the headquarters door for him, and they walked toward the table desk and the orderly seated behind it.

"Mage-Guard Overcommander Taryl to see the submarshal."

The duty orderly looked from Rahl and the unconscious trooper he had stretched on the floor to Taryl and then to the closed study door behind him.

"Yes . . . ser." The orderly turned, opened the door, and slipped into the study. He returned almost immediately. "The submarshal has just received . . . some disturbing news, Overcommander. He will see you in just a few moments."

"Aren't you his superior, in a way?" murmured Rahl, as they stood at one side of the outer study.

"His superior in rank, but I'm not in direct command," Taryl replied in a low voice. "He can't order either of us to do anything, but I can't order him, either."

After a time, the study door opened, and Submarshal Dettyr stood there. He was a shade taller than Rahl and broader in both the shoulders and the midsection, considerable broader in the middle, reflected Rahl. Although his expression was noncommittal, his entire being radiated displeasure and outrage, from the top of his thinning brown hair down to the toes of his shimmering black boots. "Mage-Guards . . ." He gestured for them to enter, then turned and walked into his study.

Once inside, Rahl closed the door.

"Overcommander." Dettyr did not incline his head.

"Submarshal."

Taryl's glance would have frozen boiling water, Rahl thought.

"I've just heard what happened in the courtyard, Overcommander, and I cannot say that I am pleased. In fact, that would be an understatement. I would call it an outrage. I understand your duties and brief, Overcommander, but I must protest. You have just arrived, and not even reported, when you and . . . your assistant—"

"Mage-Guard and Captain Rahl," Taryl replied coolly. "Mage-Guard Rahl was protecting my back, Submarshal. It is indeed an outrage. When an overcommander of the mage-guards is attacked by your troops, and when a mage-guard who is protecting the overcommander is belittled and attacked by your officers—that is the outrage. Were the Emperor to hear of this, I have my doubts that you would long remain as the marshal's second-in-command, regardless of any other factors."

Rahl sensed the absolute conviction and power of command projected by Taryl.

After a moment, so did Dettyr. "Ah . . . I can see your

concerns, Overcommander. Perhaps I was a bit hasty, but . . . I trust you understand . . . and, as was reported to me, much of this could be laid at the feet of a certain mage-guard. Are not those mage-guards your responsibility."

"They are, and that is why I was appointed. I also might note that Mage-Guard Rahl only initially used disabling force against my attacker and the rebel mage-guard. Your officers had only to step away. They did not."

"But were they not under the control of the rebel mage-guard?"

"Your officers could not have been under his control without their consent at some level. A mage-guard of his comparatively limited power could not compel individuals against their will. The fact that Rahl was able to overcome him so easily attests to his limits—and to the complicity of your officers." Taryl smiled politely. "Now . . . I am most certain we could trade blame and counterblame for some time. For various reasons, I would rather not. Nor should you wish to. It would be far more productive for us to work together." Taryl turned to Rahl. "If you would excuse us."

"Yes, ser." Rahl inclined his head politely, then stepped back and eased out of the study.

The orderly looked at Rahl, then to the trooper still laid out on the ancient wooden floor. "Ah . . . ser?"

"Have someone put him in confinement until he wakes up. He could be charged with assaulting an officer. Whether he is remains up to the overcommander and the submarshal. Oh . . . his right lower arm is broken."

"Yes, ser."

Rahl sat down on a bench against the wall. He was tired, not quite light-headed, but he'd definitely had an order workout. His hand touched the hilt of his truncheon. He smiled ruefully. He didn't even remember replacing it in his belt half sheath.

While Rahl waited for Taryl, the orderly kept looking at Rahl. When a messenger arrived, the orderly murmured to him, and the messenger scurried off. Within moments, two burly troopers appeared and carried off the limp form of the trooper who had attempted to attack Taryl.

Shortly after that, Taryl emerged from the study and nodded to Rahl.

As they walked out of headquarters, Taryl asked, "What did you say about the injured trooper?"

"I told them he needed to be confined for now, that he'd attacked you, and that you and the submarshal would decide upon further action."

"Good."

Taryl walked down to the wagon and the squad leader who was the driver.

"Where to, ser?" The squad leader wouldn't look at Rahl.

"The senior quarters in back." Taryl climbed back onto the wagon, and Rahl followed.

"Yes, ser."

"I hope you won't mind," Taryl said, "but you'll have to sleep on the couch in my quarters for now. There aren't any beds for captains and below. Most of them are in the field bivouacs with their men."

"Whatever you think best, ser."

Rahl had certainly considered treachery from within the mage-guards, but he hadn't thought that he'd see it so blatantly within the troopers.

Taryl said little until he and Rahl and their gear were in a modest room that held a single bed, a wardrobe, a writing deck and chair, and a couch. "Not exactly lavish, but far better than most will have." He paused. "You have a question?"

"Why would those three try to have you attacked? And why that way?"

"That way? Because crossbows are quick, and it's hard for most mage-guards to stop an iron quarrel even if they know it's coming. Also because most mage-guards never look at troops. They usually check the officers and other mage guards."

"But why?"

"The possibilities are many," replied Taryl tiredly. "The mage-guard and the overcaptain may honestly have believed that Emperor Mythalt is governing poorly. Or they may have been promised greater rewards by Golyat, then conditioned without their knowing it. Or something else." After a moment, he added, "Few people ever know themselves or truly why they do what they do. They act, or decide to act, and then they justify what they have done. That's why there are so few druids."

What did druids have to do with Hamor? So far as Rahl knew, there weren't any outside of the Great Forest in Candar. "Ah . . . ser, I . . ."

"You don't understand? To become a full druid, you have to be a black or at least a gray mage, and you have to undergo a trial. The trial supposedly requires facing the worst of yourself armed with all of the order and chaos-powers you possess. To survive it, you must know yourself, or learn to know yourself during the trial."

Rahl frowned. That didn't sound so bad.

"Would you want to face an ordermage who knew every little thing you did wrong—from what you thought when you seduced that girl in Land's End to what you thought when you first saw Saulya?" asked Taryl softly. "Or every rebellious or disloyal thought you had toward your parents?"

"Oh . . ." Rahl paused, then asked quickly, "Where did you find that out? I've never read anything like that."

"So far as I know, it's not written anywhere. I once met a druid in Diehl, when I was not much older than you are now. He showed me just the tiniest part of what their trial was like. He also showed it to a senior mage-guard. The other mage-guard died horribly right there. Several others did during that expedition as well. That's one reason why the High Command has little interest in Naclos."

"One?"

"That, and the battle cruiser·that fell apart at the docks there, and the two hundred sailors and officers who died."

Sensing the absolute directness behind Taryl's words, Rahl was silent.

Taryl forced a smile. "As for why the officers did it? Such a simple question, but like so many simple questions, we'll never know the answer. Someone will provide a simple answer, because that's what everyone wants. It will be wrong, but most will choose to believe it, because that's so much easier. Based on that incorrect simple answer, people will act, and what they will do will most likely make matters worse than if they'd admitted they didn't have an answer."

Rahl wasn't certain about that. "How can people act correctly when they don't know why something happened?"

"Think of it this way. If you admit you don't know, but you know you have to act, then you can base your acts on looking at what faces you and asking yourself what is the best thing to do. If you react to a simple and incorrect answer to your question, you risk compounding the error." He took a deep breath. "We need to get you moved to Third Company tomorrow, and we need to get them on their way."

"How will you do that? The submarshal doesn't seem like he wants to do anything."

"But . . ." replied Taryl with a smile, "he doesn't want any trouble here, and he wants to create the impression that he is doing things effectively. So I've already suggested that by immediately transferring you, he can accomplish both. After all, if you stayed here, you might find more traitors, and he doesn't want that, and by sending you and Third Company out to scout, he can claim he's preparing the way for the main body of forces. He can also blame all the trouble on you. That won't work for long. If there's more trouble, or if someone in Cigoerne High Command gets worried, Byrna won't make them happy by trying to replace you. He'll need someone higher, and the submarshal will fill the bill—and Byrna can then claim that he's doing his best to work with the mage-guards."

"I see." Rahl was getting the feeling that he might actually be far happier away from Kysha, even as miserable as he was likely to be riding a horse—if only Captain Drakeyt weren't like Helyrt.

XXV

Even after resting and eating, Rahl found that he was still exhausted, and he made his way back to Taryl's quarters. Taryl wasn't around, and Rahl just sat down on the couch. He wasn't sleepy, just tired. Was that because he'd used more order than he thought in dealing with the whole situation around the traitorous mage-guard? Was that another danger of being a natural ordermage?

He could feel the smoldering anger as he thought about what had happened in Recluce, and how even the magisters in Nylan had just decided that because he was a "natural" mage, they couldn't risk having him around. They hadn't even wanted to try doing things in a different way. By comparison, Taryl certainly didn't have that much more experience in training natural ordermages, but he had discovered ways to help Rahl.

Stewing about the past wouldn't help Rahl. He rose and walked to the writing desk, then went back to his bag and eased out paper and pen and the traveling inkwell. After a moment, he settled himself at the desk and began to write.

I am now in Kysha and will be writing this letter in sections, as I can, until I have a chance to post it, although that is likely to be some time. Already, we have encountered some unusual difficulties, but these do not bear mentioning in a letter, although in time, I hope that I will be where I can tell you in person what occurred. I am learning a great deal in areas I would not even have dreamed several years ago, and yet for all that, certain aspects of my past, as you must feel, too, still have a hold upon me.

Tomorrow I will find what assignment awaits me . . .

There wasn't much more that he could say, and he was getting sleepy.

After cleaning the pen, putting away the inkwell, and folding the letter in half and tucking it into a protected spot in his kit bag, he pulled off his uniform and took the light blanket folded on one end of the couch, then stretched out and closed his eyes. Sometime after full darkness, he heard Taryl return, but he was too sleepy to say anything.

When he woke the next morning, Taryl was already dressed.

"Ser . . . don't you sleep?"

"I don't need as much as you do. I arranged for your formal orders yesterday—and for Third Company's departure. After we eat, we'll go find Captain Drakeyt and Third Company."

"I could find him."

"I'm sure you could," Taryl replied amiably, "but it's necessary that I be there."

Rahl didn't question that. If Taryl said it was necessary, it was. But it bothered him that, again, someone had to intercede for him . . . or smooth the way.

Breakfast was served in a small room meant for less than a half score of officers. Rahl counted twice that crammed into two long narrow tables, all eating overcooked egg toast, greasy pork strips, and ale with too much sediment. About all Rahl could say for the food was that there was enough of it, and that it was passable, and better than what he'd gotten as a loader in the ironworks. He also suspected it would be far better than whatever there was to eat once Third Company left Kysha.

Everyone was crowded and hurried, and little was

said, although Rahl did notice more than a few sidelong glances, and he did catch one fragment of conversation.

". . . mage-guard there . . ."

". . . order type . . . could use more chaos-throwers . . ."

". . . don't know . . . he might be the one who laid out a chaos type, two officers, and a trooper faster than you could say what happened . . . did it all with a truncheon . . ."

". . . that what happened to Sholyt?"

". . . threw his weight around once too many times . . . could have told him that mage-guards don't take shit from anyone . . . but he never was one to listen . . ."

Another captain sat down with the two, and the conversation shifted.

Rahl couldn't help asking himself again what had happened the previous day. If officers knew mage-guards didn't put up with nonsense and arrogance, why had the captain and overcaptain acted as they had? Just because that overcaptain didn't listen? Or had the dead mage-guard picked just that kind of officer? All that just reinforced the idea that the confrontation had been planned. Or had the confrontation been the backup plan in case Taryl hadn't been killed? While Rahl hadn't exactly had much choice in dealing with the overcaptain and mage-guard, why had Taryl killed the captain? Because he didn't want any word of a plot and who might be involved circulating? Or because he'd known something would happen and knew already who was involved?

Rahl finished his breakfast quickly and headed out of the crowded mess, only to find Taryl outside waiting for him.

"I've arranged for a wagon to take us to the bivouac area, since neither of us has a mount yet. You need to get your gear. Just take one spare field uniform and leave the rest. I'll have them packed and saved for you. Or sent to your next posting, if it comes to that."

"Next posting?"

"You never know." Taryl shrugged.

"Are you sure, ser?"

"After you covered my back, I can certainly take care of a few uniforms." Taryl turned and began to walk swiftly toward the quarters building.

Rahl had to hurry to catch up with the overcommander, and he did not voice his concerns until he was back in Taryl's quarters and closing his gear bag. He had folded what he was leaving behind and placed it on the couch. "Ser . . . I've been thinking."

"That's always dangerous," replied Taryl with a chuckle. "What did you want to know?"

"Why you killed the captain."

"Anyone, officer or not, who attacks a mage-guard forfeits his life."

"Yes, ser. But . . . could we have learned something before he died? Or was there a reason why he shouldn't have been allowed to talk to anyone?"

Taryl nodded. "You're asking the right questions. Yes, there is. What do you think it might be?"

"You either already knew who was involved, or that was less important than not having lots of talk about an attempted killing of a mage-guard overcommander."

"You're right on the second part, but I don't know who was involved, except in general terms that it had to be Golyat and his mages, or those working for them. There's also another reason. Because a mage-guard was involved, we wouldn't have learned anything from the captain, and that would have been worse because we would have been shown as ineffective. Why can't we find out who was behind it? Was it because we set it up to discredit the marshal and submarshal? Those kinds of questions would be everywhere."

Was anything as simple as it seemed? Or had Rahl only thought things were simple because he'd never known what lay behind people's acts?

"If you're ready, we should be going," Taryl said gently.

Rahl donned the cold-weather jacket, but did not fasten

it closed, picked up his gear, and followed the overcommander down the steps and out to the waiting wagon. There, Rahl lifted his gear into the back and vaulted up onto the second seat beside Taryl.

"To the bivouac area, Third Company, if you know where it is," Taryl said.

"Is that Mounted Heavy Infantry, ser?" replied the driver.

"Yes."

"All of them are in the north area, but I don't know where exactly."

"That will be fine, and better than we could do ourselves."

"Yes, ser."

The drive through Kysha did not take all that long. From the sense of age, and the grooves worn in the stone pavement, Rahl could see and feel that the town was old—perhaps even older than Nylan, or even Land's End. The women on the streets all wore heavier scarves than those he had seen in Swartheld or Cigoerne, so much heavier that they might as well have worn hoods, and all of them seemed either to be in pairs or with children. The men he did see were all older, graying or white-haired.

The main street turned into a highway at the southwest end of the town, just after it crossed a small stone-walled canal. Beyond the canal were fields set out in neat squares and oblongs, but the pattern only lasted for a half kay before they reached what amounted to a town's worth of tents, tie-lines, and temporary corrals—all set on winter-fallow fields.

The driver pulled off the stone-paved highway onto an area of packed reddish dirt on the right side. "This is about as close as I can get, sers."

"That's fine. If you'd wait," Taryl told the driver, "I shouldn't be that long."

"Yes, ser."

Rahl kept a faint smile to himself as he lifted his much lighter gear bag from the wagon. The driver was not about to go off and abandon the ranking mage-guard, indeed the ranking officer in Kysha, but by making his requirement a gentle statement, Taryl was avoiding arrogance.

Rahl moved forward until he caught the eye of a trooper who was grooming his mount. "Trooper . . . if you could point the way to Third Company . . ."

"Oh . . . yes, sers!" The trooper stiffened to attention as his eyes caught sight of the overcommander's insignia on Taryl's collar. "Third Company—they're two over, that way."

"Thank you."

"Yes, ser."

Rahl could sense the man's consternation. While captains might trudge through a bivouac area, overcommanders clearly did not. That observation bothered Rahl, although he wasn't about to say anything with as little as he knew about military operations.

Captain Drakeyt wasn't hard to find because he was walking away from the tie-lines where mounts were held. He was half a head shorter than Rahl, with gray eyes, wavy light brown hair that was showing streaks of silver, although Rahl doubted that the captain was even ten years older than Rahl himself. Drakeyt was thin and muscular, but not wiry, and his smile was warm, as were the feelings behind the expression as he stepped forward. "Overcommander, Captain, welcome to Third Company, such as we are."

"Thank you." Rahl and Taryl spoke almost simultaneously.

"As a courtesy," Taryl began, "I've brought your orders to you. Captain Rahl has been assigned to you as well." He extended the envelope.

"Thank you, ser. We'd wondered when we'd be issued orders."

Despite Drakeyt's smile and politeness, Rahl could sense the captain's puzzlement as he took the orders from Taryl. The puzzlement increased as Drakeyt slowly read the orders before him. Then he studied the authorization. Finally, he looked up. "We're to leave immediately and begin scouting the main route to Dawhut. Ser, can you tell me what prompted this? Last eightday, Majer Felenyr was saying it would be another eightday before anyone was sent out."

"I can only surmise that the submarshal has been convinced that matters are more pressing than he originally perceived, Captain. But since Rahl has been my assistant, I wanted to see him off, and thought I could expedite matters by bringing your orders with me."

"Yes, ser." Drakeyt's eyes went from the overcommander to Rahl and back to Taryl.

"Now that I have," Taryl continued, "I will leave you, Captains, to your preparations." He nodded to Drakeyt, then Rahl, before heading back toward the wagon.

Drakeyt turned to face Rahl directly. "Welcome to Third Company." His smile was crooked. "We'd better get things moving. The men will be glad to get out of here, but the quartermaster will complain." He paused, then added mildly, "I didn't know we were getting a mage-guard overcommander."

"The Emperor appointed him. He used to be a Triad."

Drakeyt laughed softly. "I think we'll all be happy to get on the road." He eyed the long truncheon at Rahl's belt. "That's . . ."

"I guess you could call it a riding truncheon. A regular truncheon's too short for horseback."

"It's better than nothing, I suppose," Drakeyt acknowledged.

Rahl had to force himself not to say what came to mind—that he'd killed men with a truncheon. Instead, he nodded. "I think it will prove useful."

"How are your riding skills? Pardon my asking, but most mage-guards aren't trained to ride."

"Slight, but I do have some little ability to deal with mounts. I can probably keep one in line." That wouldn't be the hard part, Rahl knew.

"We can probably find a mount that's not too spirited."
Drakeyt frowned. "Are you a healer, too?"

Rahl shook his head. "I have been given some instruction there, and I can do a few things, like keep chaos out
of a wound if the wound isn't too severe. I can tell when
a bone is set right and when it's not, but I've only set one
or two, and that was with a trained healer looking over
my shoulder."

"That's more than most field healers."

"I can also sense people in hiding, if they're not too
far away, and I have a little ability to tell what the coming weather might be like."

The captain's puzzlement continued, and he frowned.
"Can I be a bit more direct?"

Rahl had an idea of what was coming. "Go ahead."

"Most battalion commanders would kill to get a mage-
guard with your abilities. Do you have any idea why
you're being sent out with a recon company?"

"I don't know, but I have some thoughts." Rahl paused,
then went on as Drakeyt nodded. "The overcommander
wants good reconnaissance reports. He also feels that I
need to learn more."

"There must be more," suggested Drakeyt.

"It's better if I don't stay in Kysha at the moment,"
Rahl admitted.

Drakeyt frowned, then slowly nodded, as if he had realized something. "It's not my business, but one of the messengers said that there was trouble at headquarters, and
that someone took a crossbow to a mage-guard and three
officers were dead, and no one was saying anything."

How much should Rahl say? After a moment, he
replied, "I'd prefer not to go into details. A trooper did
take a shot at the overcommander, and when I deflected
it and restrained the trooper, his captain and the captain's
overcaptain objected. So did a traitorous mage-guard—
a chaos-mage. Let's just say that none of them will be
causing more trouble, and that the submarshal is more
than happy to send out a reconnaissance company."

"With that . . . truncheon?"

"No. I used a standard short one."

Drakeyt shook his head, then smiled, more warmly. "We need to get you a mount and a bedroll . . . and lean on the quartermaster. If we both tell him that the over-commander delivered the company orders, he might cut us some slack and add a few things."

Rahl could see that possibility. He just hoped they wouldn't run into trouble before he learned more about riding.

XXVI

In the end, by midafternoon, Rahl found himself in the saddle of a chestnut gelding near the front of Third Company, riding southwest on the narrow stone highway that led to Dawhut—some three-hundred-odd kays to the southwest. Drakeyt rode to his left, and the vanguard was close to a kay ahead on the straight road. Kysha was some five kays behind them.

A space half a kay back from the road had been cleared years before, and small holdings periodically dotted the open area, with fields empty of much except browned grass and vegetation. The forest behind was partly ever-green and partly broadleaf hardwoods, but the leaves of the hardwoods were in winter gray.

"Does it snow here?" asked Rahl.

"Some, they say, but I couldn't say from experience," replied Drakeyt. "I'm from Elmari originally. I'd won-dered if you knew more about the area, but . . ."

"I don't sound like I'm from around here?"

"Sastak, maybe, or Atla, but not here. They talk flatter."

"My last duty station was as a harbor station mage-guard in Swartheld." Rahl smiled, even as he wondered whether he could have said more about where he was from. He'd tell Drakeyt sooner or later, but he worried about saying too much too soon because he couldn't help but like Drakeyt. "Where do we start the reconnaissance patrols?"

"We've been running patrols as far as five, sometimes ten kays this way out of Kysha. We haven't seen any signs of the rebels in those sweeps. The next town—one that's more than a hamlet—is Troinsta. It's about fifteen kays from Kysha. We'll set up there. If there are rebels around, there'll be some signs. While we're setting up, you and I will talk to some of the locals. Can you get some idea of whether they're telling the truth? I know some ordermages can."

"I can get some idea with most people," Rahl replied. Almost anyone except a mage with good shields.

"That will help."

Rahl glanced to the north side of the road, then beyond the small herd of sheep beyond the split-rail fence to the south. On either side, beyond the scattered dwellings, the trees were taller, and the undergrowth far thicker than the scattered forests on Recluce, but that was probably because this part of Merowey got more rain than Recluce did. While he was thinking of rain, Rahl made another attempt to see if he could determine what the evening's weather might be. The wind had switched from the northeast to the northwest, and the air felt drier and cooler. He *thought* that meant less likelihood of rain, but he wasn't about to say so unless asked.

"There's a lot of forest here, and not that many people."

"The ground here doesn't suit most field crops. The forests belong to the Emperor, but they're rented to foresters who are allowed to cut a certain amount each year. Mostly the hardwoods for cabinets and furniture. That's one reason why the main road's paved. Those wagons are heavy. Then, there are places with nothing but nut orchards when we get closer to Dawhut."

"Are there more Imperial lands in Merowey?" Rahl asked.

"There are some in most administrative districts. Usually, they're places where farmers were using the land wrong. Most of them are rented at low tariffs, but with conditions on how the land can be used. That way, people get use of the lands, but they don't get ruined again."

"I was wondering why Prince Golyat . . ." Rahl didn't finish the sentence.

"Who knows?" Drakeyt shook his head. "Merowey's not the richest district, but it's not the poorest, either."

The company continued to ride southwest, with the outriders continually returning and reporting, but there were no signs of rebels. The company had to leave the road for timber wagons a half score of times. The road was wide enough to share with the other wagons—factors and farm wagons.

In late afternoon, the company rode up a long, gradual slope that leveled off into a flat area filled with orchards, some with different types of trees. Whatever the variety of nut being grown, the trees in that orchard were old, with broad trunks, but they had been pruned and shaped so that their tops were never more than ten or fifteen cubits.

"We must be getting close to Troinsta," Rahl said.

Drakeyt just nodded.

They rode another kay before the land and the road began to descend again, and Rahl could see Troinsta. The town was set in a valley close to five kays wide. A stream meandered down the middle of the valley, running from the south but angling to the northeast, probably eventually draining into the Swarth River, Rahl thought, conceivably not all that far from where the *Fyrador* had been attacked.

"Are there any back roads that run from Troinsta more to the northeast?" asked Rahl.

"There are back roads everywhere, but the maps we've got don't show them," Drakeyt replied. "Why?"

"Some rebels had a cannon on the river, and they fired

on the *Fyrador.* Roads tend to follow water." Rahl had read that in the tactics manual, but he didn't have to admit it. "I was looking at the stream down there, and it runs northeast. It struck me that it might enter the Swarth about where we took fire."

"We'll have to keep that in mind," replied the captain. "I've already sent an outrider patrol forward to scout around the town. They won't find much, but it's good practice. The closer we get to Dawhut, the more careful we'll have to be."

"I thought Dawhut was loyal to the Emperor."

"That's what the reports we get say. Even if it is, it doesn't mean that there aren't rebels in the lands outside the city, or that there won't be attacks or raids."

The sun was hanging just above the hills to the west when Third Company rode into Troinsta. The town was laid out in the same fashion as most towns and cities in Hamor were, at least from what Rahl could determine, with a cleared area of grassy meadows, now winter brown, just outside the outermost dwellings. There was no sprawl of huts or hovels away from the town proper. The main streets and roads were laid out in a grid, with all the dwellings and other buildings with walls of either stone or brick. Troinsta had both, but the roof tiles were all the same shade, a grayish faded pink. The shutters and the doors were all painted, and most shutters matched the doors.

While a few people hurried away from the road, which after crossing a stone bridge turned into the main street, most just watched as Third Company rode into the town. By the time the company reined up in the town square, both the local town administrator and the head of the local patrollers were waiting.

The administrator was a heavyset and round-faced blond man who might normally have looked jovial, but his worried expression and manner overrode any sense of joviality. He looked at Drakeyt, but his eyes kept returning to Rahl. "Everyone here is loyal to the Emperor, most loyal, Captain . . . Mage-Guard. There's not a rebel here, not a one, and we wouldn't be having it, even if there were."

Rahl could sense both the truth and the fear in the administrator's words.

"We've been sending our reports and tariffs direct to Cigoerne, sers. You must know that."

Drakeyt glanced to Rahl.

Rahl nodded.

"Since you all are loyal," Drakeyt said, "I'm certain you will be able to help us settle in for a few days. We need a base to do some scouting. Even though Troinsta is most loyal, we'll need to make sure that loyalty extends to the lands around it."

"Ah . . . we can do that. The inns haven't been seeing that many travelers, and we've got some barns . . ." The administrator's head bobbed up and down.

Drakeyt turned to the local patrol chief, a rangy graying man wearing a pale blue uniform long-sleeved uniform shirt, a darker blue vest, and khaki trousers. "What have you seen and heard?"

The patroller glanced from Drakeyt to Rahl, then back to the captain before he replied, "We haven't seen much of anything here, sers. Some of the steadholders to the north, the ones that harvest the hardwoods—the ones that go downriver to Cigoerne and Swartheld—one of them claimed he saw wagons on the back lanes, must have been an eightday ago."

"You don't get many travelers here, I wouldn't think," offered Drakeyt. "Not in the winter."

"No, ser."

"Has anyone been complaining about their sheds or barns being raided, or things missing?"

"There's always some of that." The patroller looked to Rahl. "Not being a mage-guard, I can't always tell who might be telling what. I can't say that there's been more than usual, though, not unless someone's not saying, and that's always possible."

"We'll be talking to people, and we'll be sending patrols around, but for now, we need to get the company and mounts settled." Drakeyt smiled politely. "Where are these inns?"

XXVII

Rahl stayed with Drakeyt all through the process of getting Third Company settled into the area close to the larger inn—the Painted Pony—even though his thighs felt raw from all the riding. While he certainly didn't want anything to happen to the captain, he also didn't want to be any more unprepared than he had to be if something did happen to Drakeyt, and the more Rahl knew about what the company commander did, the less unprepared he'd be.

He and Drakeyt ate a modest meal at the inn, late, and Rahl probed gently about as much as he could about the company, while, in turn, Drakeyt asked similarly gentle questions about what he could expect from Rahl as a mage-guard.

After dinner and then accompanying Drakeyt on an inspection tour of all the areas that held the company, Rahl retired to a room in the Painted Pony, one not that much larger than the cabin on the freighter, with a single bed and little more. He had thought about adding to his letter to Deybri, except his buttocks and thighs were so sore that he doubted that he could sit for long enough on the single stool to write.

He stretched out on the bed and slept, if uneasily, waking early on threeday morning, even stiffer and sorer than when he'd gone to bed.

He eased himself to his feet and used the pitcher and bowl to wash and shave as he could, then climbed into his uniform. He packed his gear, but left it on the bed and headed down the stairs to see if he could get something to eat.

Drakeyt was already in the public room, although he could not have been there long because a small girl was standing at his table listening, and there was nothing on the table. Rahl eased into one of the other chairs.

"There's little enough choice for breakfast," Drakeyt said.

"We only have ham and fried heavy corn—and fresh bread. It's two coppers each for you."

"Do you have lager?" asked Rahl.

"No, ser. We have ale. It comes with breakfast, for you, Mama said."

"Then that's what we'll have," Drakeyt said.

"Yes, ser." The girl turned and walked quickly past the brick fireplace with its cold gray ashes and through an archway into the kitchen.

"How are you feeling this morning?" asked Drakeyt.

"Sore," Rahl admitted.

"It'll pass."

Rahl hoped so.

"I walked around some last night, talked to some of the locals," offered Drakeyt. "No one seems to have seen anything here."

"The town administrator was telling the truth about sending their tariffs to the Emperor." Rahl paused as the girl, who couldn't have been more than ten, approached and set two mugs of ale on the table.

"Your ales, ser. The rest will be here before long."

"Thank you."

The meal that arrived on orangish brown crockery platters might best have been described as hash composed of chopped corn niblets, bits of carrot, and ham chunks held together with glue and a hint of egg. Rahl just looked at it for a moment.

"It's good," the girl said. "You'll see."

Rahl couldn't help smiling as he put three coppers on the table. "You help a lot around here, I'd wager."

"Yes, ser." With that she was gone, almost scampering back to the kitchen, but not until she'd collected the three coppers from both officers.

Rahl took a bite. Surprisingly, it wasn't bad. He wasn't sure he would have called it good, but he'd eaten far worse, and the bread was hot and good. He did save the largest carrot chunk, still partly raw.

"Good bread," offered Drakeyt. "The rest is filling."

They ate quickly, and neither left anything, although Rahl did save half his small loaf of bread and slip it into his cold-weather jacket pocket.

"Wise man."

"I didn't have a chance to gather much else," Rahl pointed out.

"We'll be heading out shortly," Drakeyt offered as he rose from the table.

"I thought I might have a word with the chandler," Rahl said. "My gear is ready, and I'll get saddled and ride over there. It shouldn't take long."

"I thought we'd split the company. You want to go north or south?"

"North. I'd like to see if I can find anything about the raiders who fired on the *Fyrador*."

"I'll send Quelsyn with you and two squads. He's the senior squad leader. They'll form up outside the stables and wait for you if you're not back when I take the other squads south."

"I'll try not to keep anyone waiting."

After leaving Drakeyt, Rahl gathered his gear and walked out into the morning chill and toward the stable across the churned clay that would have been ankle-deep mud had there been any rain at all. Outside the stable he paused, looking to the north, but the wind was light and the clouds thin. He spent a moment probing the air to the north, but he sensed little water in the thin clouds. There was a hint of more, but beyond the range of his abilities.

He entered the stable, with careful steps, making his way to the third stall. There, he set down his gear and studied the gelding. If he could just remember how to saddle the horse . . . he looked at the saddle blanket. That came first.

"Be needing a hand, ser?"

Rahl turned to see a young trooper standing there and smiling. He grinned back. "I could, but I'd better do it myself. You just might not be here next time. I would appreciate it if you'd watch and tell me if I'm going wrong."

"Yes, ser." The trooper smiled.

Before even lifting the blanket, Rahl eased up beside the gelding's shoulder, patting him and projecting both control and warmth. The horse tossed his head slightly, then turned it. Rahl offered the small chunk of carrot he had brought from the inn, on his open palm. The gelding took it, gently. Then Rahl slipped the saddle blanket in place, followed by the saddle.

"Ser . . . be better if the blanket and saddle were just a touch back, maybe half a span."

"Thank you."

When Rahl finished, he turned to the trooper. "If you'd check for me, I'd appreciate it."

The trooper went over everything, and Rahl could sense his increasing puzzlement.

Finally, he stepped back and turned to Rahl. "Looks good, ser."

"You're wondering why I asked you?" Rahl smiled. "This is only the second time I've saddled a horse. I can tell a bit by how the horse feels, but that might not be a good guide, and I don't have enough experience to know yet."

"Looks like you learn fast, ser. Big thing is to make sure he doesn't puff up his belly when you're tightening the cinches. He does that, and then they're loose, and you end up on the ground when you try to mount."

"Thank you. I'll keep that in mind." Rahl fastened his gear behind the saddle and led the gelding out of the stable. He wasn't looking forward to mounting.

Mounting wasn't painful; it just reminded him of how

stiff he was in certain areas of his body. He turned the gelding northward.

Early as it was, many of the shops and dwellings were still shuttered, and whitish gray smoke rose from the chimneys into the clear green-blue sky. When Rahl rode through places where there were shadows, he could see his breath, although he didn't think it had actually gotten cold enough for anything to freeze. "Not yet," he murmured.

The chandler was just unshuttering his place when Rahl reined up and dismounted.

"You're out early, ser. What can I do for you?"

"I'm looking for travel food and information." Rahl tied his mount to the short iron railing set between two posts.

"We've got some of the first, not much of the second— except gossip, and I don't imagine that's what you're looking for." The chandler took the two steps up from the ancient stone sidewalk onto the narrow stoop with a single bound, then held the door for Rahl. "Might as well pick what you need."

The chandlery wasn't all that large, nor was it well lit. Even so, it only took a quick survey for Rahl to find what he thought would be most useful—and within his still-limited means. He brought a package of heavy biscuits, some strips of dried beef, and a wedge of hard white cheese up to the narrow counter at the side where the chandler waited.

"That'll be eight coppers, ser. We don't see many mage-guards here, ser, not even passing through."

Rahl nodded. "I imagine that's so. For the size of Hamor, there aren't that many mage-guards, and the Triad doesn't send us where we're not needed. I might be wrong, but I'm guessing that you don't have much of the kind of trouble that needs a mage-guard."

"You'd not be far wrong on that. Folks here know each other, and they know who to trust and who has to pay hard coin first."

"What about travelers? They have to pay hard coin, but have you seen any that you'd not trust if they lived here?"

"I can't say as I have, but then since the troubles on the coast began we've not seen all that many travelers, and most of them have come from the east out of Kysha." The chandler paused. "Some of those I'd not let out of my sight until they paid and left the shop."

"Did any of those come through here recently?"

"The last one was close to three eightdays past, ser."

"Is there anything else I should know?" Rahl grinned as he spoke.

"Not that I'd be thinking, except we'd be pleased if you could settle things down quick-like. Folks around here like the Emperor just fine."

"I thank you." Rahl nodded, then turned and made his way out of the chandlery. He glanced up and down the street. It was almost deserted, with two empty wagons headed south and a woman walking from the public fountain with two jugs.

After another study of the street, he mounted the gelding and rode back toward the stables south of the Painted Pony. Third Company was just forming up as he reined in beside Drakeyt.

"You were quick. What did you find out?"

"Not much that we wouldn't expect. Nothing strange. Travel has dropped off. There were some dubious travelers maybe three eightdays ago, but since then no one to speak of has been in the chandlery. The chandler did talk about the rebellion as 'those troubles on the coast.' I thought that was interesting, especially since he meant it."

"We'll see how far we go before that changes," observed Drakeyt dryly. "I'd like to finish up here today and head farther west tomorrow."

Rahl nodded.

"Third Company mounted, all accounted for, ser!" came the report from Quelsyn.

"Very well, senior squad leader. Break into patrols, squads one and two with you and Captain Rahl, squads three and four with me."

"Break into patrol groups!"

Within moments, Rahl was riding north through Troinsta beside Quelsyn. They did not stop or question anyone until they were well out of the town.

The first few steadholders knew nothing and had seen nothing.

Not until early midmorning, when they rode into the stead of a dairy farmer, just short of where the forest resumed, did they learn anything. The bearded and burly dairyman looked up at Rahl and Quelsyn with a resigned look that was mirrored in his feelings. "How might I help you, Mage-Guard?"

"We'd heard that there might have been some strange travelers out this way," Rahl said politely. "I wondered if you'd seen anything like that."

The man shook his head. "Can't say as I have, ser. Bercast was talking about some tracks, but I never saw anything."

"What does Bercast do, and where could we find him?"

"He's got a leasehold on the bottomland hardwoods. He's got a mill on the side creek that joins the Fleuver, close on to three kays out. You take this road for like on two kays, maybe more, maybe less, but when you come to the pillar that rises out of a pile of stones, you take that lane to your left, sort of west, and up the hill, and then over the rise . . ."

Rahl had the man repeat the directions twice before he thanked him, and they rode back to the patrol.

Quelsyn did not give any orders, but looked at the road ahead, dirt-packed and with the undergrowth cut back less than fifty cubits from the shoulder. "Time to send out outriders and scouts, ser."

"Send them." Rahl smiled. "Don't hesitate to make suggestions."

"Yes, ser." Quelsyn turned in the saddle. "Outriders and scouts forward!"

Six troopers rode forward.

"Scouts a kay ahead, outriders half that, but don't lose sight of each other."

Rahl and the patrol reached the turning point for the mill without seeing anyone.

Less than half a kay along the narrower lane, one of the scouts called back from the rise ahead of the main body of the patrol. "Heavy wagon coming! Driver and a guard!"

"Form up on the right!" ordered Quelsyn. "Arms ready!"

Rahl eased the gelding onto the narrow strip of brushy ground and extended his order-senses. There was a driver with a guard beside him. The guard had some sort of weapon—a crossbow, Rahl felt—but it was lowered.

"Guard has a crossbow," Rahl stated, "but he's keeping it down."

Quelsyn nodded, if skeptically.

The first pair of the heavy dray horses appeared on the rise of the lane, followed by the rest of the six-dray team . . . and the wagon. Both the driver and the guard held their hands high enough for the troopers to see them. Although the guard still held the crossbow, he held it with one hand, pointed down. Rahl noted that it was only at half tension, certainly enough to be effective at short range, but not so tight that it would put undue stress on the weapon over a lengthy drive. The wagon creaked as it passed, with wide and thick planks comprising the cargo, fastened down with wide straps of canvas.

Quelsyn looked at the crossbow as well, then at Rahl, but said nothing until the wagon was past. "On the road! Same formation! Forward!"

The patrol continued up the lane, over the rise and down, and then around a wide turn to the north and up over another rise and down, and up over yet another, before descending into a swale that had been cleared. There a squat brick-walled mill stood midway down a millrace from a large pond that had been created by a stone-and-earth dam holding a creek. South and slightly downhill of the mill were two roofed and partly walled drying barns. North and west on a slope above the mill pond was a long tile-roofed dwelling of one story, and a brick walkway led from the dwelling to a narrow bridge over the millrace.

Rahl rode down the lane, the patrol following, and the scouts and outriders continuing over the stone bridge that crossed the stone-walled creek a good hundred cubits east of the mill. Rahl and the patrol reined up in the open space east of the drying barns. The outriders continued north until they reached the top of the rise on the far side of the vale.

A wiry dark-haired man walked from one of the drying barns toward Rahl with a carriage that suggested he was more than just a worker. He stopped well short of the patrol. "Ser? Might we be of some help?"

Despite the man's polite speech, Rahl could sense the combination of fear and irritation, and he offered a pleasant smile. "You're the mill-master and forester? You don't have any lorken in those woods, do you?" As he finished his questions, Rahl could sense the surprise from both the mill-master and Quelsyn.

"I'm Bercast, and the mill's mine. We lease the lands to the north and west from the Emperor. Our leasehold payments are made, Mage-Guard. If they haven't gotten to the Emperor, that's because of the trouble on the coast, not because we didn't pay."

"We're not here for that." Rahl could sense the honesty of the miller's reply—and the worry. "About the lorken?"

"I wish we could grow lorken here," replied Bercast, still puzzled. "Would that we could, but the best we can do is black oak and walnut, and dark rosewood . . . and, of course, goldenwood."

"What was on the wagon?"

"Those were all goldenwood planks."

"We're looking for some rebels who might have taken some of the back roads around here recently. I heard that you'd come across some tracks . . ." Rahl raised his eyebrows.

"No secret about that, ser. I even told Patrol Chief Dykstat."

"He said someone had seen them."

Bercast shook his head. "No, ser. Never saw a one. We ran across some tracks, and deep they were. That was what called my eye to them. As deep as my wagons, and my first thought was that someone was timber-poaching the backwoods, but we never found any sign of that."

"Where are these tracks?"

"I can tell you where they were. Tracks aren't so clear now—we've had some rain . . . but they were deep enough that they'll still stand out, I'd think. Couldn't figure what they were hauling that was so heavy if it wasn't timber. We use that lane off and on, and never saw 'em. I'd wager that they came through in the dark. . . ."

Rahl could sense the truth of the forester's words.

"How do we get to this road?" asked Quelsyn.

"It's a good two kays from here, sers." Bercast pointed along the lane heading north. "You go maybe a kay, maybe less, until you get to the fork, where the big black stump is on the left side—that's the west side—and you take that fork over two rises and before long you'll get to the back road. Now it runs almost north and south on that stretch, and that's where the tracks I saw were, but you go a kay in either direction, and it goes back to east and west. Folks say that was once the main way, but that was a long, long time back. There are some old kaystones there. Never could figure out what they meant."

"Thank you." Rahl inclined his head.

"Glad to be of help, ser." The mill-master bowed his head.

Rahl could sense the man's relief as Quelsyn ordered, "Patrol! Forward!"

Rahl had the feeling it was more than two kays before they reached the black stump, and another kay and a half before they were on the back road—or the old road. Even the trees flanking the road were ancient, and while the road seemed to be clay, Rahl could sense that it was indeed old. He held up his hand.

"Patrol halt!" ordered the senior squad leader.

"You have someone good with tracks?" asked Rahl.

Quelsyn offered an embarrassed smile. "Ah . . . I was a scout first, ser."

Rahl gestured for him to go ahead.

The squad leader rode less than a hundred cubits before reining up.

Rahl eased his mount along the shoulder of the road until he joined Quelsyn.

"Couldn't hardly miss them." Quelsyn pointed toward the middle of the road, where two deep traces remained, sometimes diverging as if two sets of heavy-laden wagons had passed. The wheel ruts had erased several hoofprints. "See the angle there. They were heading east . . . well, north here. More than an eightday ago . . . could be two." The senior squad leader looked to Rahl. "Heavy wagon, all right."

"We'll need to patrol back along the track. There might be supply caches or other rebels," said Rahl.

"Ser?"

"The tracks are from the wagons that carried small cannon to the river. The ones that fired on our river steamers," Rahl replied. "The shore force killed or captured all but a handful. Some of them might try to get back to the rebels."

"You think they've already passed here?" asked the squad leader.

"Close to five days . . . probably not more than fifteen or twenty kays from where they were." That was a guess on Rahl's part, but he *felt* that the surviving raiders were already to the west. He didn't want to say that, though.

"A long ways on foot back to where they came from."

"Unless they can steal mounts."

"The patrol chief honestly didn't know of any," Rahl pointed out. "If any horses are missing, it's from outlying steads."

"Where the holders can't report it, or are dead," Quelsyn concluded.

Rahl extended his order-senses. He didn't feel anyone nearby—except for the troopers of the patrol. But . . . there was something.

"We'll follow this road west for a while, squad leader, and we'll look for signs. If they're trying to get back, they'll stay close to the road."

"Yes, ser."

Rahl ignored the doubt behind Quelsyn's acknowledgment.

XXVIII

The patrol had ridden at least two kays, a kay due south before the old road turned westward once more, and another kay or more after that. Although Rahl could sense something ahead, the feeling came and went, and he said nothing. Quelsyn, riding beside Rahl, was silent, but Rahl had no trouble feeling the disapproval from the senior squad leader.

The wind had strengthened and shifted, coming more out of the north-northwest, and turning the sunny early-winter day from almost pleasant to chill. Rahl kept studying the clouds gathering to the far northwest, but he had the feeling that they would not reach Troinsta before evening, if then, and that if there were to be any rain, it would not be soon.

In places, there were recent tracks in the road, but they could have been anyone or anything. Then, one of the scouts raised his hand, gesturing, before turning his mount and riding back along the old road. As he neared Rahl and Quelsyn, he turned his mount to ride alongside the two.

"What is it?" asked the senior squad leader.

"Sers . . . there's some boot prints, and they're heading west. There's what looks to be a piece of bloody cloth—could be a wound dressing—in the brush."

"We'll take a look," replied Quelsyn.

The three continued riding westward, with the patrol behind them. Rahl continued to use his order-senses, and he began to get a stronger sense of someone—or large animals—farther away.

"Just ahead there, short of where that branch sticks out." The scout pointed.

After another fifty cubits, Quelsyn reined up on the road and dismounted. He studied the brush and the ground beyond the edge of the road and then the scrap of grayish cloth. Finally, he straightened and took several steps along the road, leading his mount. His eyes were on the patches of dirt between the low weeds on the shoulder.

Rahl eased the gelding forward, following the senior squad leader.

After walking several cubits more, Quelsyn stopped and looked up toward Rahl. "There are more tracks here. Two sets of boots, maybe three, and they're all headed west."

"How old are the tracks?"

"Yesterday . . . could even be today."

Rahl frowned. He tried to extend his order-senses out beyond the outriders, and the something he had felt earlier seemed faintly stronger, but not directly ahead. Then he shook his head. Of course not. If the rebels heard or saw riders, they'd hide. "They're up ahead in the woods, I think, on the left. More than a kay out, though," Rahl said. "They're hiding."

"Hoping we'll ride by."

"I'd think so."

"What do you suggest, Captain?"

"My thought would be to ride on until we're within a quarter kay or so, then have one patrol pull up and wait while the other rides past. Once we're past, I'll take the lead patrol at them and see what we can do."

"They might be waiting for that."

"They'll have trouble shooting through the underbrush if they have bows or crossbows. I should be able to tell if they do before I get close enough for them to shoot."

Again, Rahl could sense the senior squad leader's doubt.

"You're in charge, Captain."

Rahl smiled. "You've done this more than I have, Quelsyn. What am I overlooking?"

The senior squad leader pursed his lips. "I can't say, but I don't see how they'll let you ride up to them."

"I'd wager you're right. Once it's clear that we're onto them, they'll scatter, but I think a good horseman can ride them down so long as I can sense them. We'll have to see, though."

"You sure about that, ser?"

"No." Rahl laughed. "Not absolutely, but it's worth a try. Our task is to find out what the rebels are doing, and we might find out something this way."

Quelsyn swung up into his saddle. "I'll drop back with second squad. Just stand in the stirrups and raise your arm when you want us to halt. Oh . . . you'd better have a couple of men ride back down the road so that the rebels don't try to run between us."

"I'll do that. Thank you." Rahl turned in the saddle to the first squad leader—Roryt, he thought. "There are some rebels hiding in the brush ahead on the north side of the road. Just a handful. We'll ride past and then turn and go into the brush after them. If we can, I'd like to capture at least one so that we can learn what they've been doing."

"Yes, ser."

Again, Rahl got the same feeling of polite doubt, but he forced a pleasant smile. "I'll have to lead the chase, but I'd like several men to remain on the road and cover it, in case they try to cross it."

"I'll take care of that, ser."

"I'd appreciate it." Rahl waited until the senior squad leader had ridden back to the head of second squad before he called out his orders. "Patrol forward!"

As he rode, he scanned the trees and brush on the north side of the ancient and narrow road, all the time trying to sense the rebels he knew had to be somewhere ahead. After the patrol had ridden close to a half kay and the road made a gentle turn to the west-southwest, Rahl began to get a better sense of where the rebels were. He could feel three men hidden in a depression behind a natural earthen bank. He judged that the three were some three hundred cubits ahead.

With the thickness of the underbrush, he also realized that Quelsyn and second squad would have to be far closer than he had told the senior squad leader. There was no help for that, not now, but it irritated him that the senior squad leader hadn't been a bit more helpful. It wasn't as though he hadn't asked—and politely, at that.

After he rode another fifty cubits or so, he stood in the stirrups and raised his arm, but kept riding. He led the patrol about fifty cubits past the spot on the north side where the three huddled. He could sense no weapons except sabres, and one long staff. "Squad, to the rear ride and form up!" He swung the gelding out onto the shoulder of the road and back east, reining up until the squad was in position.

"Forward!" He eased the gelding into a fast walk, not daring to ride more swiftly, not with the trees and underbrush and his own less-than-adequate riding skills. A man might be able to gain on him for a short time, but not for that long.

"First ranks on the captain!" ordered Roryt. "Last two ranks on me and the road!"

Rahl found himself using his riding truncheon as a way to keep branches from whipping into his face, but even so, he'd have scrapes from the evergreen needles and the leathery winter gray leaves of the hardwoods.

Surprisingly, the three rebels did not move immediately, not until Rahl was within twenty cubits or so. "They're directly in front of me! Flank me!"

The three sprinted away from Rahl.

He could sense that there was a low bush in the middle of the berm, and he guided the gelding through the opening between two firs and after the heavyset rebel who had been in the middle.

The rebel glanced over his shoulder, then darted to the left, between a pair of trunks, one a massive oak, the other a younger fir.

Rahl rode around the right side, losing some ground in the knee-high underbrush, but after another fifty cubits, he was within ten cubits of the running rebel. At that moment, the man turned toward an oak with a chest-high branch, and jumped to catch it. He straddled it and turned, whipping out a sabre, awkwardly.

Rahl reined up, then struck with the long truncheon. The rebel's blade went spinning into the brush.

"Don't move," snapped Rahl. "Not unless you want something broken."

The rebel froze, holding on to the branch with one hand. His eyes widened as he took in the mage-guard visored cap.

Rahl took in the rebel's uniform, khaki shirt and trousers with a jacket of blotched and faded maroon. "First squad!" Even as Rahl called out the words, a pair of troopers appeared, riding rather casually through the woods. "Over here!"

"Yes, ser."

As they rode up, Rahl said, "Tie him up and take him back to the road. Don't hurt him unless he tries something. We need to talk to him." He turned to the rebel. "If you try to escape, I'll track you down, and there won't be enough of you for the vulcrows."

"Yes, ser." The rebel's voice was steady, but Rahl could sense the fear beneath.

He eased the gelding away from the two troopers. "I need to track check on the others."

Rahl had only managed to travel another fifty cubits or so through the trees toward what he sensed was a group of troopers.

"Ser! Over here!"

He had to backtrack around a copse of saplings growing up around a fallen hardwood before he could join the four troopers.

A rebel in another faded maroon jacket lay sprawled across a crumbling log. He was dead.

"He tried to slice up my mount, ser. Wouldn't surrender."

Rahl supposed that happened. "Two of you cart him back to the road. Have the senior squad leader search him to see if we can learn anything from what he carried. Two of you come with me. Did any of you see where the other rebel went?"

One trooper pointed vaguely to the northeast. "He was running fast, ser."

"He can't run that fast for long." Rahl extended his order-senses. While he could generally sense the fleeing rebel, using his senses in the wood was harder than on the road. Why? Because of everything living around him?

Once more he set out.

Rahl thought he must have ridden more than a kay before he closed to within a few hundred cubits of the third rebel. The two troopers trailed him by more than a hundred cubits.

The man began to run, once more, but his legs were tired.

Rahl followed.

Abruptly, the rebel turned, his back against an ancient and rotting trunk.

"You . . . get close . . . and I'll take down your mount. Blade longer than yours . . . Flame me if you want, but you'll not take me alive." The words were delivered between gasps.

Rahl extended his shields to protect the gelding's legs and rode toward the rebel. The ancient long blade swung, and rebounded from the shields. As it did, Rahl dropped the shields and slammed the truncheon down across the shoulder above the rebel's blade-wielding arm. He added some order to the blow, and a dull crunch followed. The blade fell from the rebel's numb hand, and the rebel staggered, then dropped to his knees.

Rahl waited, watching, until the two troopers neared. "Truss him up, but keep him from more harm. We'll take him back. I need to question them both." He watched as the older trooper dismounted and used strips of leather to bind the wounded man's hands together.

The rebel was staggering and barely able to walk after less than a quarter kay. Rahl had the troopers hoist the man up before him on the gelding for the rest of the ride back to the road.

Quelsyn was waiting with the remainder of the patrol. His eyes widened as he caught sight of Rahl and the two troopers—and the second captive. He turned his mount to follow Rahl.

Rahl eased the wounded man off the chestnut at the side of the road where Roryt and another trooper guarded the first captive and the body of the dead rebel lay.

"There wasn't much in his gear," Quelsyn said. "Just a few coppers and a map."

"Did it show a route?" Rahl dismounted, slowly.

"According to the map, they left from Maugyta. The map showed the way to the Swarth River maybe thirty kays downstream from Kysha."

"That's where the cannon was that fired on the convoy," Rahl said, handing the gelding's reins to one of the troopers and turning to the two captives. "How many of you made the trip out with the cannon?"

"What cannon?" asked the uninjured captive.

"You're lying." Rahl smiled, coldly. "I was on the ship you hit. I know all about the cannon. We have one of your maps. You can make this hard or easy." He extended a sense—almost a compulsion for the two to offer the truth. "Let's try again. How many of you were there?"

Both men squirmed, but did not speak.

Tired as he was, Rahl extended his shields, pressing against the injured trooper. The man swallowed.

"How many?"

"A little more than a score, ser."

"Did you start out with any cannon?"

"No, ser. Didn't have no cannon. Awaiting for us in a hidden place east of Dawhut. Powder, too."

"Exactly where was this place . . ."

When Rahl finished getting what he could about the locations and the forces and the trip, he asked, "How did you expect to get back to Maugyta?"

"Plenty of steads along the way." The uninjured trooper shrugged. "They don't support the real emperor, then they'll pay."

"I don't notice you had much in the way of supplies. What stead were you headed for?"

Neither rebel said a word.

Rahl just looked at them. After a moment, he extended his shields. "Talk."

The wounded man winced. ". . . stead up ahead . . . only a pair of oxen and a donkey . . . left it alone on the way out."

"I'm supposed to believe that?"

"Squad leader Cleyn made us just sneak stuff from the back of the smokehouse when they were out in the fields. Said we didn't want to upset anyone, or let 'em know we were here till afterward. Wouldn't matter then. Then we could do what we liked. Woman looked sorta pretty."

Rahl kept asking questions until it was clear that neither man knew much more.

"What are we going to do with them, ser?" asked
Quelsyn.

"Take them back to Troinsta and have the chief patroller lock them up until someone from the campaign
can get them."

"Ser . . . waste of food," suggested Roryt.

"It probably is," Rahl agreed amiably, "but I suspect
that the Mage-Guard Overcommander will want to question them as well, and I don't think I'd want to be the
trooper who killed a prisoner he wanted to question." He
looked at the squad leader. "Would you?"

"No, ser."

Rahl could sense Quelsyn's wince behind his back.

"Good. Make sure all the men understand that before
we head back." Rahl turned and smiled politely at the senior squad leader. "I understand that sometimes prisoners are killed trying to escape. That shouldn't happen
here, but . . ." He paused. "I'll look into it, and I can tell
who's lying and who's not."

"Yes, ser."

"Now . . . let's get ready to ride back." Rahl mounted
the gelding and rode perhaps fifty cubits eastward. He just
wanted a few moments by himself. He did not look back,
but extended his hearing with the help of his order-skills.

"You heard the captain."

". . . tracked second one down like he could see
through the trees . . ."

". . . disarmed one of 'em . . ."

". . . may not be a chaos type . . . but . . . don't want to
cross him . . ."

Rahl had very mixed feelings about what he heard, but
he couldn't have troopers and squad leaders doubting his
word.

XXIX

On the return, Rahl and his patrol discovered no more signs of rebels or outlaws or much of anything except isolated and wary steadholders and foresters. By the time they returned to Troinsta in the fading light of threeday, and Rahl had officially returned the squads to Quelsyn's direction, his inner thighs were sore and raw once more.

Drakeyt appeared in the stable as Rahl was grooming the gelding.

"Quelsyn said you found three rebels." The captain's voice was calm.

Underneath the pleasant tones, Rahl could sense a great deal of concern. "We did. They killed one, and I captured two. They were part of the force sent with the cannon to attack the supply convoys. I don't think they understood that they weren't expected to return. It's clear that the idea was to slow things down and make the marshal cautious. That would allow them more time before our forces attack."

"Quelsyn said that you disarmed one man with your truncheon and broke the other's shoulder."

"He wouldn't surrender and was trying to hamstring the mounts."

"He also said you could sense where they were from almost a kay away."

Rahl shook his head. "I could sense that someone was there from that distance. It was less than half a kay before I was absolutely certain."

"He also said that you just looked hard at them, and they began to talk."

Rahl shrugged tiredly. "I let them know that I could tell when they were lying. Most ordermages can."

"Are you trying to get a field command?"

For a moment, Rahl just looked blankly at Drakeyt.

Then he laughed. "Captain . . . I'm a mage-guard. I was sent here because no one in Mage-Guard Headquarters knows what to do with me. I have no desire at all to command men in the field. I was told that, in case of injury to you, I might have to take command until another captain could be dispatched, and that I'd better learn everything I could. My thighs are so sore I can barely walk, and I had to chase that rebel at a fast walk because I was afraid I'd fall off the horse if I went faster in the woods."

Drakeyt shook his head. "Quelsyn said you acted like you'd commanded before."

"The only people I've ever commanded were lawbreakers."

For several moments, Drakeyt said nothing. Then he nodded.

Rahl could sense the other's puzzlement, but decided that anything he said, or could say, about his background would do little to reassure the captain. "What did you find out?" he finally asked.

"No one has seen anything, and no one is missing anything."

"What do you plan for tomorrow?"

"We still haven't scouted the areas west of the town."

"Can we do that while we head southwest, or do we stay here?"

"Why don't we talk it over at the Painted Pony?"

"I won't be long."

"You may be there before me. I promised the administrator I'd tell him what we found."

"He might know," Rahl said. "I put the two prisoners in the town gaol. I thought they could stay there until the overcommander or someone else could question them."

Drakeyt started to open his mouth, then stopped.

Rahl waited.

"Do you think that was necessary? They're traitors."

"It has nothing to do with them," Rahl replied. "Have you met the marshal, personally? Or the submarshal?"

"No. Captains usually don't, except on rare occasions."
Drakeyt paused. "I assume you have, from the way you
asked that. Might I ask what that has to do with the rebels
you captured?"

Rahl offered a wry smile. "Were you aware that Marshal Byrna was not the initial choice for the position?"

"I'd heard rumors . . ."

"Marshal Charynat was appointed, then died in . . .
unusual circumstances." That was all Rahl could say, because that was all Taryl had told him.

"You believe that?"

"Yes. Remember, I do have the ability to tell when I'm
being lied to. Now . . . Marshal Byrna is not exactly . . .
a commander who is swift to act, and Submarshal Dettyr
doesn't care much for mage-guards." Rahl paused. "Just
how likely is either to fully believe a report by a mage-
guard attached to the company of a captain?"

Drakeyt actually smiled. "So you've been planted on
me to make sure that good information gets back to the
campaign command."

"No one told me that . . . but that's the way the overcommander operates."

"We need to talk more. I'll see you at the inn. I'll still
need to stop by and see the administrator because I said I
would. It also won't hurt to suggest his prisoners need to
stay healthy until someone from the campaign arrives to
interrogate them. We certainly can't spare the bodies or
the time to escort them back. It's bad enough to use troopers as messengers." Drakeyt nodded, then turned and left
the stable.

Rahl finished grooming the gelding, then made sure
the horse had feed. After that, he walked slowly toward
the Painted Pony.

Just beyond the stable, he slowed. He could sense
someone ahead, lurking around the corner of the narrow
building beside the stable. He extended his order-senses,
but realized that the figure was too small to be an adult,

and sat huddled against the wall. Rahl stepped forward and peered around the corner of a narrow building beside the stable.

A small girl huddled against the wall. She looked up in surprise. Her cheeks were damp, and her eyes darted past Rahl, then down the alleyway.

Rahl didn't know quite what to say for a moment. He moved so that she could see him, but no farther. "I'm Rahl. I'm a mage-guard. You seem unhappy."

The girl looked at him, but did not move. Rahl could sense fear, resignation, and deep sadness.

"Do you want to tell me why you're sad?" Rahl kept his voice soft.

She gave the smallest of headshakes, then lowered her eyes so that she no longer looked at him.

"Do you live here?"

There was no reply, but Rahl sensed that she did.

Suddenly, a thin woman burst out of the side door ten cubits from Rahl. "Shereena! You worthless girl! Where are you?" She turned and took three hurried steps toward Rahl. "Who are you? Stay away from my daughter . . ." Her words died away as she saw the uniform. "Oh . . . I'm so sorry, ser. I . . ."

Rahl could sense the anger within the mother dying away, overtaken by fear.

"She was crying," Rahl said. "I stopped to ask her why. Perhaps you know?"

"She was upset. It hasn't been a good day, ser."

Rahl nodded politely. "Sometimes, days are like that. I hope you'll be gentle with her. She was very upset."

The woman's fear was partly replaced by irritation. "She wasn't all that good, ser."

"That may be," Rahl replied, trying to think of what to say that wouldn't cause the mother to take her anger out on the child once he left. "I don't suppose any of us were as good as we should have been as children." He stepped back, but did not leave.

"Shereena . . . it's time to come inside."

The girl rose, timidly. The mother extended her hand and took her daughter's hand firmly, but not roughly. Rahl watched as the two reentered the building. Neither looked back.

Finally, Rahl turned and continued toward the Painted Pony.

What else could he have done? He had the feeling that the child had been hurt, but no chaos had been involved, and he hadn't sensed any overt physical injury. The mother hadn't broken the Codex, not that he knew. Also, he wasn't a mage-guard assigned to Troinsta. Yet . . . he still worried about the girl.

As he neared the inn, his eyes took in the signboard—a flat piece of wood some two cubits by three on which was painted, almost crudely, a pony standing on its hind hoofs with a beaker set on a front hoof. The pony's coat was depicted in irregular splotches of faded color—maroon, black, white, yellow, and blue. Looking closely, Rahl could see that someone had tried to paint over an original signboard, using the old work as a base, but the more recent painting had been far less skillful.

The same small girl who had served breakfast led him to the corner of the public room.

"Here you are, ser."

"Thank you. The other captain will be joining me shortly."

"Yes, ser. Would you like two ales? They come with dinner."

"Yes, we would."

"I'll bring them." She turned and hurried toward the kitchen.

Rahl repressed a smile at her seriousness, even as he mentally compared her to the child he had encountered outside the stable. The inn girl might have to work, but she had a confidence that bespoke a far more settled life.

He glanced around the public room. Unlike at breakfast, there was a scattering of others in the room. He did note that neither of the adjoining tables held patrons, and he doubted that was by coincidence. Nor was the fact that the girl served them. The child could not reveal to a mage-guard what she did not know.

Rahl wondered what, if anything, the innkeeper was hiding, or if he was operating out of caution. Rahl suspected caution, but one never knew. He also realized that there was a great danger in sensing too much. All too many folks had secrets they did not wish disclosed. That had to be one reason why the mage-guards were tasked with maintaining order and minimizing chaos under a simple Codex. More than that would have been impossible for the limited number of mage-guards.

Rahl was still waiting for the ales when Drakeyt eased into the old straight-backed chair on the other side of the square table. "We have ales coming. I don't know what the fare is yet."

"Whatever it is will be better than field rations."

"How was your visit with the administrator?" asked Rahl.

"He didn't like the idea of feeding prisoners, maybe for eightdays. I asked him if he wanted to upset the Mage-Guard Overcommander of Merowey. He decided that feeding them wasn't so bad after all." Drakeyt laughed.

Before either man could say more, the inn girl returned with two of the earthenware mugs filled with ale. "Here you are, sers. Tonight the fare is mutton pie, and it's three coppers for you, and that includes one mug of ale."

Both men nodded. Rahl put three coppers on the table. So did Drakeyt.

"It won't be long, sers." She left the coppers and turned back toward the kitchen.

An older woman emerged from the kitchen archway carrying two platters. She set them on the other corner table, before two white-haired and heavyset men who could have been brothers from their appearance.

"I was thinking," offered Drakeyt. "If we check out the steads to the west tomorrow and leave first thing on five-day, we can send back a messenger then, and he can get back to us quicker. Also, the field rations will go farther. There's no place to quarter, not really, until we get to Istvyla, and that's a good three days' ride, even without scouting."

"Just little hamlets?"

"If that. The northeast of Merowey has the fewest people. There aren't that many large towns until you get near the coast. . . ."

Rahl mostly listened as Drakeyt talked, and the two ate. He still thought about the girl by the stable.

XXX

Third Company's patrols on fourday discovered no recent signs of rebels, nor did they on fiveday, sixday, or sevenday. On fourday, and on the following days during the ride southwest, Drakeyt had the company patrol separately by squads. Rahl led first squad along the narrower and more ancient old road. In more than a few places there were still remnants of deep wagon tracks, although the continuing light drizzle on fiveday and early sixday blurred those even more. After questioning more than a score of steadholders near the back road, Rahl found some who had noted the tracks but none who had actually been aware of the rebels' passing. With the heavily forested areas bordering the old road in most places, Rahl could understand how some of the holders might not have seen the wagons. But none of them hearing the wagons?

Was it just that most folk were so wrapped up in their own lives that little else penetrated unless it affected them? But then, he recalled wryly, he certainly hadn't paid that much attention to his parents' warnings about Jienela.

By late on sixday, the soreness in Rahl's legs and thighs had abated, and he could actually ride at more than a walk without feeling that he'd be pitched out of the saddle. At the same time, he was all too conscious that he was a long way from being a good rider, but he was able to get a better sense of what the gelding would do and how he responded to Rahl. Order-senses did help there.

Slightly after midafternoon on sevenday, the patrols re-formed into the full company on the main road northeast of Istvyla and then rode into the town. Rahl counted dwellings on the way, and came up with only two score or so along the road on the north side of the hamlet before they reached the square. Of those locals near the road, none fled, but all moved back and watched the mounted infantry warily.

After riding into the center of Istvyla, the company drew up in formation in the square—little more than an expanse of packed reddish brown earth somewhat more than a hundred cubits on a side. Rahl surveyed the buildings—a small two-story inn that had doubtless seen better days even a century before, a chandlery with a wide and shallow porch supported by a mixture of crude stone and brick pillars, a shuttered smithy, a small brick structure that probably held the town administration and gaol, another building that looked to have a potter's kiln in the rear, and several others whose function he could not discern because they lacked signboards or because the lettering and images on the existing signboards had faded so much.

A square-bearded and graying figure walked deliberately from the town building toward the front of the formation. He stopped and looked at Drakeyt.

"What can we do for you, Captain?"

"We're the advance party for the Emperor's forces. Are you the town administrator?"

The man shook his head. "We don't have an administrator. I'm Hyalf. I get three silvers a season to act as town clerk. Course . . . haven't gotten the silvers for summer yet. You couldn't do anything about that, could you, Captain?"

"We can send word to the Emperor, Hyalf."

"If you would, Captain, I'd be much obliged."

"Have you seen any rebels around?"

"I can't say as I have. Can't say as I've heard of anyone else who has, either."

"Has anyone had any large amounts of anything stolen,
or any horses?" pressed Drakeyt.

"If they have, they've not told me, and I'd likely have
heard. I haven't."

Rahl could sense that Hyalf was telling the truth, at
least as he saw it. So, as Drakeyt continued to talk to the
town clerk, Rahl continued to take in his surroundings.

A small group of men gathered on the front porch of
the chandlery, less than fifty cubits from where Rahl had
reined up slightly back of Drakeyt. Rahl studied them
quickly, with both eyes and order-senses. One of the men
near the back of the group glanced at Rahl, then froze for
a moment.

Rahl could sense both the man's recognition of his
mage-guard uniform, even under the cold-weather riding
jacket, and the immediate fear that followed that recognition. The man eased toward the back of the group, then
stepped off the side of the unrailed porch and vanished
into the shadows between the chandlery and the neat-
but-weathered stable of the inn.

Rahl wondered exactly what the man had done that he
so feared the appearance of a mage-guard. Most probably someone who had committed an offense in one of the
larger towns and fled before being caught. Still . . . that
much fear suggested more than a minor offense. Since
the man had been accepted by the others and since he
was attired neither shabbily nor extravagantly, Rahl suspected that he'd been living in Istvyla for at least a while.

". . . we'll need quarters of some sort," Drakeyt added,
"and food and fodder. We can pay."

"In the Emperor's script, no doubt."

"Captains do not carry golds," replied Drakeyt, "and
the Emperor's script is always good."

"But not immediately," Hyalf pointed out. "One must often wait for a season until a disburser arrives."

"You can trade it among yourselves," Drakeyt responded.

"There's some that won't take it, beggin' your pardon, ser Captain."

"That may well be, but that's their problem, and it's far better than in Candar, where there's no payment for quarters or food and fodder."

Hyalf nodded slowly, and Rahl could sense his doubt— and Drakeyt's concealed irritation.

"As you say, ser Captain, late payment is far better than no payment, but unless you wish to take dwellings, the inn and its stable and holders' barns are the only shelter available."

"We'll put up as many as we can at the inn and its stables. Then we'll use the largest and driest barns. You must know the largest barns, and you will disburse the script, except to the inn, but we will let the holders know that and how much they will receive. You will receive a small stipend for your trouble as well."

Hyalf was clearly not pleased with the arrangements laid out by Drakeyt.

After loosening his riding jacket enough to show his mage-guard uniform, Rahl adjusted his visor cap with the sunburst and eased his mount forward beside the captain. "I understand you have done a good job as clerk for Istvyla." Rahl smiled. "It would be a shame if the Mage-Guard Overcommander had to break in a new clerk."

Hyalf turned toward Rahl, his annoyance increasing— until he saw the uniform. "Ah . . . I'm certain that won't be necessary, ser. No, ser."

Rahl said nothing for a moment and just continued to smile pleasantly.

A thin sheen of perspiration appeared on the clerk's forehead, despite the cool breeze.

"I'm glad it won't be, and I'm sure you'll do your best

to work matters out so that everyone is accommodated without upsetting the people here."

"Yes, ser."

"We'll see what's available at the inn, first for supplies," Drakeyt said. "You should come with us. That way, you'll have a better idea of what else we'll need."

"Yes, ser."

Drakeyt turned in the saddle. "Quelsyn, first, third, and fourth squads remain here until we see what arrangements we have. Second squad comes with Captain Rahl and me."

The senior squad leader nodded.

The captain turned back to the town clerk. "Over to the inn."

"Yes, ser." Hyalf began to walk quickly toward the inn, giving the company formation a wide berth.

Drakeyt eased his mount over beside Rahl's so that they were almost stirrup to stirrup. "I knew that little bastard wanted to pocket script and coins, and he knew I knew," murmured Drakeyt. "But he was still going to try to do it. That doesn't make sense. I could have cut him down where he stood."

"You could have," Rahl agreed, "but it was easier this way."

Drakeyt nodded slowly. "They've never seen a war."

"But they know a mage-guard can mete out justice on the spot," Rahl replied.

"You're not a chaos type, though."

Rahl smiled. "The riding truncheon is the same length as a mage-guard falchiona. How would he know the difference?" He didn't mention that the truncheon backed with order could be as deadly as chaos-flame. He just had to get closer.

Drakeyt laughed.

XXXI

Rahl and Drakeyt sat at opposite sides at one end of a long table in the White Chalice, a prepossessing name for a modest inn, Rahl thought. Breakfast was egg toast with honey-redberry syrup and thick ham slices, with spiced pearapples on the side. Rahl had to admit that it was far better than the fare at the Painted Pony had been.

The public room was far smaller, and held only four trestle tables, all of them flanked with backless benches. Second squad had already eaten, and Rahl could sense first squad forming up outside.

"Only hamlets and small towns from here to Dawhut?" asked Rahl, spearing the last slice of ham on the wooden platter.

"Mostly smaller than that." Drakeyt took a swallow of his ale. "The next place even as big as Istvyla is Koldyrk, and that's a good hundred kays on. We'll see plenty of hamlets, and more than a few timber wagons, and probably more than a few spirit wagons. South and east of Koldyrk is where they brew Vyrna."

Rahl had never heard of Vyrna. "What kind of drink is that?"

"Oh, it's smoother than polished lager and has twice the kick of leshak, and costs half as much. Most of it gets shipped to Austra. For some reason, they like it there."

"Folks don't like it here?"

"Oh, they do, but way back one of the emperors—I think it was Dhanocyr—tariffed it to bring in golds. The tariff is levied at the ports—Nubyat, and I suppose, Sastak and Elmari. The wagons carry the kegs to the barge piers in Dawhut, and they go down the Awhut River to Nubyat . . ."

Rahl wasn't sure any of that made sense, unless the

cost of using wagons to carry the kegs anywhere else was far higher than the tariffs.

"Less than a hundred kays from the farthest still to Dawhut, and some are less than a day's drive from there . . . It doesn't cost that much more to ship Vyrna to Valmurl than to Swartheld, and the Austrans will pay twice as much. So most of it goes to the drunken northerners." Drakeyt shook his head. "They say that there are some places in Austra, like Vizyn, where the ice only melts for three or four eightdays a year. No wonder they like spirits."

"How far is it from Koldyrk to Dawhut?"

"If . . . if the maps are right, close on a hundred fifty kays."

"It'll be full winter before we reach Nubyat."

"If then."

Rahl and Drakeyt both looked up at the sound of voices. One was too high-pitched to be a trooper.

"There they are!"

Hyalf and a red-headed woman a good ten years older than Rahl walked toward the two officers. The two stopped short of the table.

"Sers, this is Edelana, and her Eskar was killed because you're here." Hyalf inclined his head.

"Because we're here?" Drakeyt raised his eyebrows.

"Eskar . . . all he said was that Suvorn wouldn't listen and that it was your fault." The woman's voice was rough and uneven, in keeping with her faded and worn blue trousers and the patched gray-wool jacket. Her eyes were red.

"Our fault?" asked Drakeyt.

"His fault." Edelana looked to Rahl. "His fault. Eskar said it wouldn't have happened if the demon-cursed mage-guard hadn't shown up. He was bleeding bad, and then . . . he didn't say anything more."

"Just a moment," Drakeyt interjected. "Did this Suvorn stab your consort?"

"That's what I've been saying. Suvorn killed my Es-kar," replied Edelana. "We weren't as like properly con-sorted, but Eskar and me, we might as well have been."

"Was Suvorn in town when we rode in yesterday?" Rahl looked to Hyalf.

"He was at the chandlery yesterday afternoon, but I couldn't rightly say if he was there when you showed up." Hyalf did not quite look at Rahl.

Rahl had an idea what was involved, yet it seemed far-fetched. Still . . . "Is your stead near the old road to Kysha?"

Edelana looked at him blankly.

"The old back way through the woods to Troinsta?" he asked.

"Yes, ser. It'd be a mite bit quicker by that road from where we are, excepting if there be rain."

"Did Eskar come into some coins, say, three or four eightdays ago?"

"Just a silver or two, ser. He did some work for Su-vorn. Suvorn said he needed help to fix an axle for some travelers."

"Do you know how many wagons they had?"

"He didn't say, ser. My Eskar . . . he wasn't one for a lot of words."

Rahl looked to Hyalf. "How long has Suvorn lived here in Istvyla?"

"He was born here, ser."

Rahl could sense that wasn't exactly the whole truth. "So he left for a while."

"Ah . . . yes, ser."

"When?"

"Mayhap, three, four years ago."

"And when did he return?"

"Close to a season ago," admitted the clerk.

"He have anyone with him when he came back?"

"I couldn't say for sure, ser."

"So you never saw anyone but him, but he bought more food and other things than one man probably ate?" Rahl pressed.

"That might be, from what I heard," replied Hyalf.

Rahl looked to Edelana.

"Could be, ser."

"I think we need to take a look at your place and Suvorn's." Rahl took a last swallow of lager from the earthenware mug, then stood.

"I don't know where Suvorn's place is, except it's back in the woods off the old road."

"Does Suvorn have a horse?"

Edelana nodded.

"It still can't be far. Wait out front for us," Rahl said.

Hyalf and Edelana had barely left when the troopers of first squad began to enter the public room.

Drakeyt stood. "You think this Suvorn was sent here just to help the rebels?"

"It's possible," Rahl hedged. "That's what I want to find out."

"You take second squad," said the captain. "Quelsyn and I will scout around the rest of the hamlet while you're gone. Send a messenger if you'll be longer than noon."

"I can do that," replied Rahl, heading to gather his gear.

Even though second squad had eaten first, it took a while to muster the squad, but before long, Rahl and Khasmyr, the second squad leader, were riding along the lane headed north out of Istvyla. Edelana was riding double behind one of the troopers. The clouds to the north had thickened again, and Rahl had the feeling that they would be in for more rain before the day was over.

Rahl had ridden no more than a few hundred cubits past the last scattered dwellings when he found that the road narrowed to a lane barely wide enough for two riders abreast—or one wagon, provided it was not a large one. Over the next kay, the squad rode past three small holdings carved out of the woods.

"There's our place!" Edelana called out.

Eskar's cot was more like a hut, with log walls chinked

with mud and moss, and crude plank shutters, although the pair of windows flanking the door were glassed. One pane was cracked. The roof looked to be made of planks covered with shake shingles green with moss.

Rahl turned in the saddle. "Khasmyr, while I'm looking here, have your scouts study the lane north for either hoofprints or boot prints, but don't have them travel out of sight of the cot."

"Yes, ser."

For several moments, Rahl studied the ground outside the hut, but the welter of old and new hoofprints only suggested that Suvorn—or some riders—had visited often. Rahl dismounted and tied the gelding to a single post. Then he turned to Edelana, who had been set on her feet by the trooper. "Who else rode to visit Eskar?"

"Lots of folk. Anyone who needed a strong back."

Rahl turned and walked to the cot door, still ajar, and looked inside. Eskar was lying on a soiled braided rag rug just inside the plank door. The front of his tunic was stiff with blood.

After several glances around the two-room cot, Rahl doubted that he'd discover anything he needed to know. He turned to Edelana. Her eyes were bright, and tears oozed from the corners of her eyes.

"Eskar was the only one who was good to me . . . now . . ." She shook for a moment.

"I'm sorry," Rahl offered.

The woman seemed not to hear him.

"How far is it to the back road?" Rahl waited.

"It's not more than a kay out the lane, but you'll have to ford the creek. The bridge wore out and washed out. The old road is just beyond that."

"Is Suvorn's place that way?"

"I wouldn't know, ser."

"Did he always ride here coming from the north?"

"Most times, unless he was coming from town." Her words were distant.

"Do you have anyone else you can stay with?"

"No, ser."

Rahl had no idea what to do next. He didn't want to leave the woman with a dead man, and he had few enough coins of his own left with hundreds of kays to ride on a campaign ahead of him.

"Do you have a spade or a mattock?"

"Oh, no, ser. Eskar wouldn't want that. Said he'd need to be buried by his sister. In the family place."

"I'm sorry. I was just thinking . . ."

Edelana looked at Rahl. "You asked. Most wouldn't. I'll do it."

Rahl wasn't certain about that. "Are you sure?"

"Hyalf said he'd send Aliva over in a bit. We'll do."

Rahl inclined his head, then stepped back to the post, where he untied the gelding, then mounted. He rode out to the lane to meet Khasmyr.

"There's one set of fresh prints," the squad leader reported, "coming down the lane and heading back out."

"Those would be Suvorn's. We might as well follow them and see where they take us."

"You think he's one of the rebels?"

"I don't know, but we'll want to check the old road for those heavy wagon tracks anyway."

"Second squad! Form up!" Khasmyr barely waited before ordering, "Forward!"

Fording the creek wasn't difficult, not with the water level as low as it was, and the hoofprints continued on the far side. Where the old lane, even more overgrown, ended at the old road, the tracks turned westward, running between two far older and deeper traces of heavy-laden wagons.

As far as Rahl could judge, they rode another half kay before the hoofprints turned up a weedy trail. He reined up and studied the road. From what he could tell, the rider had gone up the trail, then come back before riding west.

"Ser!" called Khasmyr. "Over here."

Rahl eased the gelding over to join the squad leader.

"Someone replaced the axle tree on a heavy wagon,

and tossed the broken stuff into the brush. Looks like you were right, ser."

"I don't think Suvorn's anywhere near here, but I'd like to take a look at his place up that trail."

"You want the whole squad, ser?"

"Just two or three men."

"First two ranks, follow the captain."

The four troopers rode in single file behind Rahl along the narrow trail for less than two hundred cubits before they emerged in an overgrown clearing.

From the outside, the hut looked more like a hovel, and one that had not been occupied for years, if not longer. Rahl's order-senses told him that no one was inside or nearby, but he had the feeling that the place had been lived in far more recently than appearances would have indicated. The nearly fresh hoofprints leading practically to and from the door reinforced that feeling.

Rahl gestured to the nearest trooper. "Look around behind here, follow the prints, and see if there's a shed or a barn concealed behind some of that underbrush."

"Ah . . . yes, ser."

Rahl reined up short of the doorway, dismounted, and handed the gelding's reins to the next trooper who had been riding behind him. "I doubt I'll be long."

The plank door was crude, but had been recently crafted, and the single room behind the door was neat and swept. The pallet bed was also new, and the interior walls had been hurriedly patched and repaired. A worn workman's tunic had been thrown across one end of the pallet, as had a pair of patched trousers, and a set of nearly worn-out work boots remained by the door. The ashes in the small hearth were warm, but no other garments or personal items remained.

Suvorn had definitely departed, and in haste.

Rahl stepped back out into the cool and raw morning air. All four troopers and their mounts were drawn up outside the hut, waiting.

"Sir, there's a shed out back, just big enough for a single mount. It's been used recent-like."

"Thank you." Rahl swung up into the saddle, not quite so awkwardly as he first had, but still with a lack of grace. "We'll head back and join the rest of the squad. Then we'll be riding back to town."

There wasn't much point in chasing Suvorn, but he would need to write a more detailed report for the messenger to take to Taryl. He could only hope that the rest of the campaign forces would start to follow them. Otherwise, Third Company would have to stop sending messengers before long because they'd have more troopers carrying messages than scouting.

He didn't like the way matters were going. Not at all. He and Third Company were something like eighty kays from Kysha, with almost three hundred to go left on the way to Dawhut, and he was already discovering more planning by the rebels and less knowledge by the locals of what was happening around them.

XXXII

Eightday morning found Rahl and Drakeyt riding southwest once more, through a mist that had not yet developed into rain, and might not, Rahl realized. Ever since they had left Kysha, and especially over the last few days, he'd been using his order-abilities to track the water in the air to the north, but a southerly wind he had never even sensed coming had sprung up and had met the cooler clouds from the north and, instead of rain, they had mist.

As he brushed water droplets off the oiled leather of his tan riding jacket, he wondered how any mage ever became much good at forecasting the weather. There were so many things to consider.

The night before, he'd written a few paragraphs in his narrative letter to Deybri, trying to explain to her his feelings about being unable to do much for Edelana and how the effects of one prince's greed or wish for greater power ended up in the death of a man whose only connection was that he'd accepted a silver to help fix a broken axle. What he hadn't written was his fear that incidents such as those in Istvyla would be trivial once actual battles were joined.

He also wished that he could just talk to Deybri. Would that ever happen again?

"You're quiet this morning," offered Drakeyt.

"There's not much to say," replied Rahl, "except that it's wet, and there's a long ways to go before we reach Dawhut."

"That's war for you, a lot of travel and discomfort until you fight, and then there's no travel and even more discomfort."

"That sounds like experience speaking." Rahl didn't know how the captain would have gotten much experience.

"Only a little. I was with the force that the High Command sent to Worrak to rout out the pirate crew there. They said we'd be done in eightdays. It took two seasons, and we lost three men in ten."

"I never heard about that."

"Almost no one did. The High Command is always sending companies here and there, usually in Candar. My cousin Hautyl was part of the campaign against the Southern Quarter in Nordla, but that was almost ten years back. We lost half the force, and he was lucky to come back losing only one arm and getting a stipend."

"Nordla? What did they do?"

"Oh, the local Lord of the Quadrant impounded some of our ships and claimed that our traders were cheating his traders. The Emperor thought letting him get away with it was a bad idea. So we assaulted Surien. I suppose it did the job. Between the fleet and the infantry, we destroyed

most of the merchanters and their warehouses and made
the harbor so impassable it was a year before they could
use it." Drakeyt snorted. "Golyat was in charge of the
campaign. That was before he became administrator of
Merowey. It only cost us a thousand troopers, but no one
in Nordla messed with our traders. Not for another generation, anyway."

"He was in charge of the campaign? Was he that
good?"

"I heard that the High Command complained to the
Emperor, but the Triad reviewed everything, and Golyat
submitted a report on Surien's defenses."

"Oh . . ."

Drakeyt looked sideways through the mist at Rahl.

"I wonder . . ." After a moment, Rahl went on. "We're
going to ride some seven hundred kays, when the fleet
could be outside Nubyat in an eightday or two. I couldn't
figure that out. Someone had mentioned harbor defenses
in one briefing, but . . ."

"You're thinking that Golyat studied how the Nord-
lans did it and has been fortifying Nubyat and Sastak?"

Rahl shrugged. "It's a thought, but no one told me
anything."

"As much as anything in war makes sense, that does."

"Is that why Fairhaven might be supporting Prince
Golyat? Because they want the revolt to go on and on?"

"Who knows—except that anything that ties up our
fleet and raises our tariffs benefits their traders."

"And the Jeranyi," Rahl added.

"The Jeranyi just like trouble." Drakeyt paused, then
asked, "How did you figure out what happened in Istvyla
so quickly?"

Rahl shrugged. "I suppose it was because I'd seen it
before. When we rode into the square, and everyone
gathered, one fellow—the one we didn't catch—was at
the edge of the crowd. He looked at you, then at me, and
he left, even before we said anything."

"You thought . . . from that?"

"It wasn't his leaving, but the way he left," Rahl replied. "You can't be a harbor or city mage-guard for long without seeing it. Most people can't hide the guilt at having done something. Istvyla's just a hamlet, too. Why would he leave in a guilty fashion just on seeing us?"

"You were city mage-guard?"

"A harbor mage-guard in Swartheld. Not for that long."

"What did you do before that?"

"I was a mage-clerk in Luba." Rahl didn't want to say that much more. "What bothers me about this is the planning."

"You mean that someone sent this Suvorn out here more than a season ago, with enough coin, just to be able to help the rebels with the cannon? It wouldn't take that much coin," replied Drakeyt.

"It's not the coin; it's that they found the one man whom everyone would accept without suspicion, or too much suspicion." Rahl also suspected that the episode with the cannon had been designed to play on the marshal's caution, and he wondered how many other incidents there might be that were designed to slow the campaign without much cost in men and matériel to the rebels. "There have to have been some High Command officers backing Prince Golyat."

"You think anyone's going to admit that or tell us?"

Drakeyt had a good point there. "It's not likely."

"We'll find that out the hard way." The captain frowned. "And we'll find more surprises. That's what we're here for—so that the main force doesn't find them." He shook his head. "They will anyway, but the fewer they encounter, the better."

Rahl agreed with that, but someone had planned the revolt for a long time, and they also had the help of mage-guards and some senior High Command officers.

XXXIII

Over the next eightday, little changed. Third Company followed the road as it wound through the endless high forests of Merowey, past and through small hamlet after small hamlet. Rahl saw little on the road itself except timber wagons, and few enough of those. The farther they rode from Kysha, the fewer the wagons, and the more often they held the rarer woods, such as black oak or cinnamon goldenwood. He did not see any lorken.

The locals accepted, if grudgingly, the script proffered by Drakeyt in return for supplies. They might have to wait for actual coins, but the alternatives were far worse. Actual progress was comparatively slow, because of the need to scout and to question locals, and because for two of the days, Third Company had taken refuge in scattered barns around the hamlet of Azakleth, rather than attempt to ride through rain that varied between coming down in sheets and coming down mixed occasionally with hail.

"Welcome to winter in high Merowey," had been Drakeyt's comment.

The hills became more rugged, but not that much higher, as they neared Koldyrk, and in more than a few places Rahl could make out bogs and marshy ground that might once have been lakes or actual swamps. The rocky height of some of the hills revealed patches of dark gray and light gray rock where little grew. Rahl could tell that the darker gray rock was softer because it had crumbled away from cliffs and spires in many places while the light gray stone had not. The vales and valleys were narrower and twisted more.

They had just passed one of the infrequent kaystones that bore the weathered inscription *Koldyrk—10 k* when one of the rear guards trotted forward and eased his mount alongside Drakeyt.

"Captains! There's a squad of heavies following us, and their scout rode up. They're reinforcements, and they've got a couple of pack animals and some spare mounts—and some dispatches for you."

"Just a squad?" asked Drakeyt dubiously.

"Yes, ser, and the squad leader's Fysett. Went through the Worrak thing with him."

"Might as well let them catch up with us." Drakeyt raised an arm. "Company! Halt! To the rear, turn! Weapons ready!" He looked toward Rahl. "Might as well get them used to it. Let's go meet them."

Rahl rode alongside the captain as they moved onto the shoulder of the road and headed back toward what had been the rear of Third Company. After they reached fourth squad, they could see that the squad of troopers approaching was less than half a kay away.

As they drew nearer, Rahl could also sense that the mounts were tired. He cleared his throat and looked to Drakeyt. "They've been pushing their mounts hard. They'll need some rest in Koldyrk."

"That may be."

The squad halted less than twenty cubits from Rahl, and the squad leader rode forward, reining up before the two officers. "Captains! Squad leader Fysett reporting as the fifth squad to Third Company."

"Welcome, squad leader," replied Drakeyt.

"I have dispatches. There's one for each of you, and we have some extra field rations and a half score spare mounts." Fysett fumbled in the small leather dispatch case and extracted two envelopes. He eased his mount ahead and leaned forward to extend one envelope to Drakeyt. The second one went to Rahl.

"Thank you," said Drakeyt. "We thought we'd try for Koldyrk today. Are your mounts up to another eight or nine kays?"

"At a walk, ser. We've been pushing hard to catch you. The Mage-Guard Overcommander said it was important."

"Good," Drakeyt said. "You're now fifth squad. We're close enough to make it before sundown."

"Yes, ser."

Rahl did not open the envelope until he and Drakeyt had ridden back to the head of the company and were preparing to resume the ride toward Koldyrk.

Mage-Guard Rahl—
The squad of troopers bearing this dispatch is to fulfill a twofold purpose. First, they are to reinforce Third Company. Second, they are to allow Captain Drakeyt and you the flexibility to send more frequent dispatches.

The first companies of the main advance body have left Kysha under the command of Submarshal Dettyr and have arrived in Troinsta. We will be leaving Troinsta early tomorrow—the second fiveday of winter—and look to be able to close the gap with Third Company over the next eightday. Marshal Byrna will likely be departing Kysha and following us before long.

A number of ships from Lydiar and Renklaar have been sighted attempting to make port in Nubyat, Elmari, and Sastak. So far, the fleet has driven off all of them, but our information is close to half a season old.

Rahl paused in reading the dispatch. Wasn't there any means by which any of the mage-guards could figure out what was happening on a more timely basis? What about using a glass? Rahl almost sighed as he thought about it. Screeing . . . he hadn't even practiced that, not that he'd had a glass to use in any case. Again, every time he thought about something, he seemed to remember something else he should have been doing or trying or practicing.

He went back to reading the remainder of the dispatch.

I will caution you that, because Golyat's forces are limited in size compared to those marshaled by the Emperor, his commanders are likely to attempt all manner of stratagems that will cause casualties to your company with minimal losses to their force. Always keep that in mind.

The signature was but a scrawled "T."

Rahl wanted to snort. He had a lot to learn, but the rebels' stratagems had already become clear. At the cost of a score of men, Golyat had severely damaged one steamer, killed or wounded almost twoscore, delayed the Emperor's forces, and forced more time spent on scouting—and that was before Third Company had even gotten close to Dawhut, let alone to Golyat's main forces in Nubyat and Sastak.

Drakeyt had finished reading his dispatch and was frowning. Then the captain looked up. "Anything of interest?"

"Probably nothing beyond what you've gotten. The extra squad is so we can send more messengers, and the first part of the Emperor's forces left Troinsta last fiveday and will try to close the gap between us. The overcommander warned me that Golyat will try all sorts of stratagems to cost us men and mounts without losing many of his."

"Or those he can easily afford to lose." Drakeyt glanced back at the column behind, then to Rahl. "Ready?"

Rahl nodded.

"Company! Forward!"

Rahl studied the forest ahead on both sides of the road, with eyes and senses, trying to extend his order-sensing range. The farther he could reach, the more warning the company would have.

He almost shook his head. Who would have thought he'd end up as a mage-guard and a captain in Hamor? All because that slut-sow's ass Puvort hadn't liked him.

XXXIV

Koldyrk turned out to be half the size of Troinsta—and perhaps three times the extent of Istvyla. Once again, no one had seen or heard any rebels, but that did not surprise Rahl because the older road was a good ten kays from Koldyrk at the nearest and ran well north of a range of low hills that began on the northern side of the town. At least, that was what the maps showed and what the few locals who even knew of the old road said.

After a day of fruitless scouting around Koldyrk, partly to allow fifth squad some rest for mounts, on two-day, Third Company rode out once more, early on a clear morning so chill that Rahl could see his breath. The air was still, and the sun climbed into a hazy sky.

Well before midmorning, the day had become almost pleasant, and Rahl had to loosen his jacket. Drakeyt did not.

After a time, Rahl asked, "Do you know what the overall plan for the campaign is?"

"That's something they don't tell captains." Drakeyt offered an indulgent smile. "I did ask the majer before we left, and he said that they didn't tell majers that much, either. He did say that the idea was to hold the coast with the navy and cut off supplies and arms, then attack from the northeast so that the rebels had nowhere to go."

"We're riding a long ways. Do you really think that there isn't any way that we could have attacked from the coast?"

Drakeyt frowned. "Let's say that we did attack from the sea. Let's even say that we managed it without losing a whole lot of troopers. Let's say we were successful and took over the three port cities. Then what? Where do the rebels go?"

"They retreat," Rahl said.

"Where?" Drakeyt offered a crooked smile. "Back through the lowlands, destroying the crops and taking food? Eventually, they might even get here." He gestured toward the side of the road and the stand of ancient firs, flanked by another stand of ancient oaks. "You think we could ever root them out of that? The locals don't even know what goes on in there."

"Won't some of them still escape that way?" Rahl asked.

"Of course, some will, but most of the holdings and crops will be intact. The holders will have script and coins they can use to buy seed. They'll grouse about why two brothers had to fight when both had all they needed, but it won't affect them nearly so much, and the Emperor doesn't have to keep fighting in his own lands."

"Doesn't Golyat see that?"

"I'm sure he does. He doesn't have much choice. He can't feed his forces back here, not and hold them together, and he can't maintain a large enough army to fight off the Emperor if he leaves the coast. He's wagering that the Emperor and the High Command will botch things up enough that there's a standoff. If he can do that, he becomes outright ruler of Merowey, and he's still got a claim on the throne in Cigoerne. If that happens, he'd get support from Fairhaven, Austra, and maybe even Sarronnyn. Recluce wouldn't be displeased, either, I'd wager."

If that occurred, from what little Rahl had seen in Cigoerne, he suspected that Mythalt would not remain emperor all that long. "If he does that, things could get interesting in Cigoerne."

"That they could. Very interesting."

Rahl hadn't even considered that if the Emperor did not lose, but simply failed to win—to crush Golyat thoroughly—he might end up losing more than Merowey. But if matters were that important, why had Taryl sent him with Third Company? It might be just as Taryl had told him, but Rahl had learned that very little was just what was explained. Rahl could think of a number of possible additional reasons, but he didn't know. Again, he wished people would explain fully, and not just what they thought one should know. While he trusted Taryl far more than he had any of the magisters in Recluce, he still disliked being kept in the dark.

"A man could go mad," Drakeyt went on, "trying to guess all that might happen, and a mad captain doesn't do anyone much good. I imagine it would be worse for a mage-guard." He paused, then grinned. "Not that some mage-guards might not be mad anyway."

Rahl merely grinned back. Drakeyt was far better company than all too many mages and mage-guards he'd encountered.

The road began to climb as it wound out of another long and twisty valley, but it was close to noon when they finally reached a rise in the road—almost a pass between a long line of hills that looked to run from the southeast to the northwest. The summit of the crag to the north was at least five hundred cubits above the road, and slightly farther to the west and downhill, a stream splashed down in a thin waterfall. All morning they had seen not a single wagon on the road and but a handful of holders heading into Koldyrk.

He surveyed the land spreading out to the west in the valley ahead. Beyond where the road began to level out in a wider valley, on the south side, a low meadow surrounded by hardwoods stretched for several kays. "I don't see anything grazing down there in that meadow."

"You won't. The chaëtyl and black heather won't support cattle or sheep. Mostly, when we get closer to Dawhut, you'll see them harvesting peat and chaëtyl from the bog meadows. They use them in brewing Vyrna. This is too far out, and I'd wager there are better bog meadows closer."

"You'd wager? You don't know?" bantered Rahl.

"I know that if someone could make golds from harvesting, that bog meadow would have women and children cutting the turf, and wagons would be headed down to the distilleries around Dawhut."

"Bog meadow? Does it rain that much here?"

Drakeyt shrugged. "I wouldn't know. I'd guess it rains in winter and spring here. It's not raining now, and it wasn't raining in late summer, and you don't get all these tall trees without rain."

Rahl looked to the north and the heavy clouds gathering there. He had the feeling that they'd be experiencing those winter rains all too soon. Not for the first time, he wished he knew more about the geography of Merowey than what he had learned from the few maps he had seen.

XXXV

By midafternoon on fourday, Rahl could definitely see the difference in the terrain. Instead of covering almost all the ground, the forest was much more scattered and mainly on the higher areas of the hills—except for the expanses of rocky areas—and they had passed bog meadows, swamps, and some small lakes. Some of the bog meadows had been partly harvested, but not recently.

They had lost another day, because the clouds that had been gathering had descended and pummeled them all through threeday. The road might have been clay-surfaced, but it had to have been built with sand and gravel beneath, because while it was soft on fourday, it was not extraordinarily muddy—just bad enough for Rahl's boots and lower trousers to become mud-caked.

For all of the patrols and scouts sent out, none had seen tracks near the main road, which wound and twisted around hills more than it had closer to Kysha. The older road that the rebel cannoneers had used swung much farther north, and, if the maps were correct, was more than thirty kays away at the nearest point to the route Third

Company traveled. The holders in the scattered steads they had passed had seen almost no travelers at all in recent eightdays, and no one who might have been a rebel.

As Rahl rode around a long curve that followed the base of a rocky hillside that held only brush and scattered trees, he could see an expanse of rushes and cattails on the right side of the road extending for at least a kay to the west and north.

"Do you think we should have sent a patrol on the old road?" Rahl asked.

"With the two roads that far apart? What's the point? Our forces are taking this road, and this is the one we need to scout. Besides, we'd have to split our forces before we knew where the rebels might be."

Farther ahead, Rahl could see the glint of gray-blue water—a lake of some sort. On the left side, a long ridge with scattered trees climbed gradually into a high hill, largely forested, on which he could see outcroppings of dark gray rock. He had the feeling that the road swung more to the north between the lake and the rocky hill. "I suppose you're right. If there were a road, it would still take close to two days to get from the nearest point on the old road to here, and we haven't seen any lanes or roads heading north." There had been more than a few branching off to the south over the past two days, but the handful to the north had only gone a kay or less, basically to logging camps or forest steads.

"They won't mount an attack from the old road, not from so far away and from over those hills and rocks." Drakeyt pointed to the line of rocky crags to the north. "Certainly not this far away from the coast."

Rahl tended to agree with the older captain, but then, he wouldn't have expected a cannon attack on the *Fyrador,* either.

After they had ridden another kay or so, with the marsh to the right and downhill from the road widening every cubit they traveled, Rahl could see that the road turned almost due north to circle around the rocky hill more than a

kay ahead. In fact, the road seemed to emerge from the
marshy reeds and separate the hill from the lake. The road
had actually been cut out of the hillside. For a moment,
Rahl wondered why, until he looked north once again and
realized that the middle of the lake extended all the way to
an even rockier set of hills a half kay or more away. Digging the roadbed out of the side of the base of the hill
ahead had probably been easier than it would have been to
construct a road in the rugged terrain to the south or along
the base of the rocky crags that rimmed the lake on the
north. Equally important, a level road alongside a lake
was easier on wagons and mounts than a route through the
surrounding hills.

"Good thing it's cold," observed Drakeyt. "We'd get
eaten alive by red flies in the summer."

While Rahl didn't think the day was warm, it was certainly far from what he would have called cold, and the
sun was out, if under a high haze that turned the normally
green-blue sky silver greenish. "I could do without flies."

"Their bites leave welts," the captain added.

"Remind me not to travel this road in summer."

Drakeyt laughed.

As they rode nearer to where the marsh narrowed to a
thin strip between the road and the lake, Rahl began to
study the hillside above where the road turned north.
There was something about it, but he wasn't certain what
it might be.

The roadbed at the base of the hill was a good five cubits above the narrow boggy area that bordered the southern edge of the lake and no more than ten cubits wide
from the stone retaining wall set against the cut in the
hillside to the edge of the road shoulder before it dropped
off into the marsh. In addition to the retaining wall, Rahl
could sense a rough stone wall on the steep hillside just
above the section of the road that curved back westward.
He frowned. The lower retaining wall was worked stone.
Why would the upper wall be so sloppily done? Or had it
been added later to keep rocks from falling onto the road-

way and blocking the route? Why was it just over that section of the road?

He concentrated more. The upper assemblage of stones wasn't really a wall . . . and he sensed men up there. "Halt the column."

"Rahl?"

"Halt it. Quietly, if you can. There's a trap ahead." He thought it was something like that.

Drakeyt raised his arm. "Company halt!"

"Company! Halt!" echoed Quelsyn.

Rahl pointed. "Where the road swings back west, there's a big pile of boulders, and there are men up there. I can't tell how many, but it's less than a score."

"Can we get to them without coming up from below the rocks?"

"I might be able to find a way," Rahl said. "We'd have to go back a bit and follow the ridge. Then we could come around the hill from just above that line of dark gray rock there."

"That doesn't look that easy."

"Let me take first or second squad. If we can't do it, or if it's something different, we'll at least have a better idea of what else we can try."

Drakeyt cocked his head and looked at the road ahead, then at the hillside above it, and finally at Rahl. "You lead the way, but when you get there, let Roryt handle the charge."

Much as that thought irritated Rahl, he knew Drakeyt was probably right. He'd never commanded anyone in a real battle. "I'll turn command over to him at that point."

"Squad leader Roryt, forward."

Once he eased his mount up beside the two officers, Roryt looked from Drakeyt to Rahl, then back to the older captain.

"Captain Rahl believes that the rebels have set up some sort of ambush on the section of road ahead, between the steep hillside and the lake, and that they have piles of boulders up there."

Roryt's eyes flickered westward for just a moment.

"There aren't that many rebels there," Drakeyt continued, "and the captain will lead you there. Once he's explained where they are, you'll lead first squad to take them out."

"Yes, ser."

Rahl could sense the squad leader's stolid acceptance of the order and situation.

"We'll stand by here, as if we're taking a break. Captain Rahl will fill you in on the way."

"Yes, ser."

In the end, Rahl and first squad had to retrace the path a half kay before they found a slope the mounts could climb. After that, there was enough open space, in and around the rock outcroppings and the scattered trees, that Rahl was able to find a semblance of a trail westward and upward. As they rode up the back side of the long ridge toward the hilltop overlooking the road, Rahl explained as well as he could what they faced. ". . . and it just looks like a crude retaining wall from below, but there are far too many rocks and boulders behind it."

"Roll enough big rocks down a slope, you could hurt a lot of troopers," offered Roryt.

"And we couldn't attack back from that part of the road."

"Nasty business."

The sun was hanging low in the western sky by the time Rahl reined up on the eastern side of an angled slope that rose another ten cubits over perhaps a hundred. He leaned toward Roryt and spoke in a low voice. "They're just over this rise, and down about twenty cubits. I *think* there are only about ten of them, and they're not looking in this direction." *Not yet,* Rahl thought to himself. "The slope over the rise is open, and the boulders are lined up on the right."

Roryt gestured for first squad to form up, although the space clear of scattered boulders and intermittent low pines was only wide enough for three mounts abreast.

Then the squad leader dropped his arm, and the troopers moved forward at a fast walk. Rahl let them all pass and swung his gelding in behind them, trying to stay close. He managed that well enough until they reached the top of the rise and charged downhill.

"Impies! Pull the releases!"

THRuummm . . .

Even though he was mounted, Rahl could feel the entire hillside shaking, and a cloud of sand and dust rose into the air as well as cascaded downhill.

Through the sandy dust, he could see figures in maroon jackets running toward a narrow ravine. One made it. Most of the other rebels were cut down, and by the time Rahl reached the area where the boulders had been piled, there was a single rebel standing, surrounded by mounted troopers.

"Won't tell you bastards nothing!"

Rahl reined up, slightly in back of and between two of the troopers' mounts. "Maybe you'll tell me something, then."

"Won't tell . . ." The rebel stopped saying anything as he recognized the sunburst insignia on Rahl's visor cap.

"You've been out here more than half a season, haven't you?"

"Not saying anything."

Despite the rebel's protest, Rahl got the sense that the rebels had been in the area less than half a season.

"Or was it just three eightdays?"

The man did not speak, but Rahl got a sense that his estimate was close, and he asked, "They sent out a whole company and set this up—and left a half squad of you to drop the boulders on the first full company that came down the road, didn't they?"

Rahl kept asking questions until he realized that the sun was almost touching the horizon. He turned to Roryt. "We'd better head down before it gets too dark. I'll lead the way." He paused. "There weren't any other prisoners?"

"No, ser. One of 'em got away, and another slipped in the ravine, fell fifty cubits. The others, well . . ." The squad leader shrugged. "We found their mounts and some supplies."

Twilight was shifting to evening by the time Rahl and first squad rejoined the rest of Third Company.

"You lose anyone?" asked Drakeyt.

"No, ser," replied Roryt. "We brought back one prisoner."

"We lost one outrider and one mount. I had some of the scouts farther forward." Drakeyt shook his head. "He thought he was far enough back, but one of those big boulders came this way. He didn't even see it."

"How many were there up there?" asked Drakeyt.

"Ten or twelve," Rahl answered.

"Just ten?" Drakeyt's tone was dubious. "Ten men couldn't have set up all that rock."

"They didn't," Rahl replied. "They had a full company up here for several eightdays, setting this up. They left half a squad to set them off. There's a trail up top, and it leads to the west."

"We brought back twelve mounts," Roryt added. "Sorry beasts, but they can carry supplies."

"Any tools up there?"

"We didn't see much. Why?"

"That section of the road's blocked for almost two hundred cubits. Some parts aren't that bad, but we'll have to clear it. It'll be a real bitch."

Rahl just nodded. He would have liked a little appreciation from Drakeyt for keeping the company from suffering what could have been significant casualties in both troopers and mounts.

XXXVI

Clearing the road of the rubble and stones took almost a full day. They had more than enough horses to have handled the work more expeditiously, but what they didn't have was enough rope and canvas, even after sending troopers back up to the rebel camp. In the end, the troopers carried and pushed or rolled most of the smaller boulders into the boggy area below the road. The single makeshift sling and tow was reserved for the comparative handful of truly massive boulders. One was so large that they had to leave it in place, but, by using all the stones in the area, they managed to widen the road just enough that a wagon should have been able to get around it.

Rahl wasn't certain that he would have tried it with a heavy timber wagon, but he hadn't seen any of those in the last eightday, and the main force could deal with the one huge boulder. Just to make certain, both Drakeyt and Rahl wrote dispatches with details about the attempted rockslide ambush, and the need for engineers to move the large boulder from the lake road. Rahl's dispatch went to Taryl, and Drakeyt's to his commander. They agreed on sending two troopers to reduce the possibility that one might be waylaid or injured, then traveled several kays past the end of the lake to a better bivouac.

The following day dawned misty and colder, cold enough that there was frost on the grass and the trees—also cold enough that Rahl shivered when he forced himself out of his bedroll. At least it hadn't rained again, and his boots were almost dry. After eating cold field rations, washed down with colder water, he groomed the gelding, if quickly, and saddled him. Then he mounted and joined Drakeyt at the front of Third Company. Glad as he was for the heavy jacket, Rahl was still shivering as he sat in the saddle while the company formed up.

Drakeyt turned, and said with a smile, "People who say there's no winter in Hamor haven't been in the Heldyn Mountains or in the hills here."

"I didn't expect it to be this cold," Rahl admitted. "Or this wet."

"Neither did I," replied Drakeyt, "but the majer cautioned me. He was born just east of Dawhut, and it can snow there, and that's warmer than here, he said."

"Snow?"

"Not often, but it does."

Rahl looked westward out along the road. Several thin lines of gray-white smoke rose into the clear green-blue sky. "More smoke than I'd expect. We're still something like eighty kays from Dawhut."

"I'd wager those are backwoods stills. They don't pay tariffs, but so long as they don't try to sell their Vyrna, or what passes for it, they don't owe any tariffs." Drakeyt laughed. "I imagine they trade for a lot." He turned back forward in the saddle as Quelsyn rode up.

"Third Company, all squads accounted for, ser." Quelsyn's voice was as crisp as the air itself.

"Very well, squad leader. Prepare to ride."

"Yes, ser." Quelsyn turned his mount. "Company! Forward!"

Once more, as the sun rose higher into the sky, the worst of the chill vanished, although the day was cooler than those previous, perhaps because of a northerly wind. Also, as on the day before, the road remained deserted except for Third Company.

Midmorning came, and Rahl could sense little beside occasional steadholders, if log huts in small clearings could be considered steads. The trails of smoke from the backwoods stills had vanished, perhaps because the air was slightly warmer or because the wind dispersed them.

Shortly after midmorning, while allowing a brief pause, Drakeyt dismounted and checked his maps, then turned to Rahl, who was glad for the respite, although he was no longer sore all the time.

"We should be coming to a small river before long," Drakeyt said. "I just hope there's a bridge. Fording a river when it's this cold . . ." He shook his head.

"So far there have been bridges," Rahl pointed out, "and now we're even closer to Dawhut. Why wouldn't there be a bridge? Or do you think the rebels might have destroyed it?"

"It's possible. There's not much point to destroying little bridges. We can just splash through the small creeks. This is the first really large bridge, and it's the first one that's not near a town."

Rahl almost pointed out that they'd heard nothing about bridges being destroyed and, besides that, Dawhut was reportedly still under Imperial control, but he held his tongue when he considered the two attacks he'd already experienced had been even farther from Dawhut and the rebel-held coast than where they now rode. He just nodded.

The sun had almost reached its zenith, but the day had not warmed appreciably since midmorning, not with the north wind strengthening. Third Company continued to ride westward over and around low hills. In time, they came to a longer, if gentle grade. Rahl had the feeling that Third Company was being watched, yet he could not sense anyone nearby.

At the top of the next rise, Rahl looked out over a grassy valley, no more than half a kay across, with a narrow river running down the valley. Rahl smiled as he made out where the plain stone bridge crossed the river— more toward the far side of the valley. Farther to the north, the valley widened almost into a rolling plain, with but scattered stands of trees. To the south, the valley narrowed into a gorge that had obviously been cut by the river as it descended from the higher hills there. From the brown banks of the river, Rahl suspected that much of the flow had to be seasonal, or that it dropped off in the fall and early winter, which would certainly fit with Drakeyt's feelings about rainfall. Still . . . they'd had several heavy rains in the past days, and the rainfall might well have been heavier in the hills.

"The grass looks good. It might be worth stopping for a time and letting the mounts graze," offered Drakeyt. "We'll see if it's as lush as it looks from here."

Still, as they rode down into the valley, Rahl could not get over the feeling that they were being observed, even though he could neither see nor sense any sign of anyone within a kay. Finally, he said to Drakeyt, "I can't help but feel like we're being watched."

"That's always possible, and more likely the closer we get to the coast, or even to Dawhut."

Once the company reached the valley floor, Rahl kept looking toward the river, but the grass was close to waist height away from the roadbed, more like swamp grass, and he could only see the banks, green on top, then brown below. The closer they got to the bridge, the more the roadbed rose from the grass on each side.

"That's too tough for the horses," Drakeyt observed.

Rahl looked at the grass again. There was something about it.

At that moment, he sensed something like a vast release of order, like a wave of something . . . A wave? "Drakeyt! Have the company ride for the high ground! Now! There's a flood coming! Now! Over the bridge! The hills here are closer."

Drakeyt didn't hesitate. "Company! Charge! Hold formation! Hold the road!"

Rahl bent forward, just trying to keep astride the gelding and to stay abreast of the older captain. He used his order-senses to impart urgency to the gelding, and could feel a slight increase in his mount's speed.

As they clattered over the bridge, Rahl glanced to the side. That brief look chilled him far more than the north wind had. The riverbed was close to forty cubits wide and at least five deep, and the dampness of the dark earth of the banks showed that it had been flowing at that depth until recently.

From the south, he could hear a dull rumbling roar that built with every moment that passed. He darted a quick look to the south, but he saw nothing except what he had seen before—a near-empty riverbed and marsh grasses on each side of the river. Even looking to one side unbalanced him, and Rahl had to grab the gelding's mane to keep from bouncing out of the saddle.

From that moment on, he watched the road and hung on tightly. Riding the half kay between the west side of the bridge and where the road began to climb the hillside seemed to take forever, and the gelding began to slow on the upslope. Rahl urged his mount on, conscious more that there were those behind him who might not make it if he flagged in climbing the hill. The roaring grew louder . . . and louder . . . and then began to diminish slightly.

Finally, near the crest of the hill on the west side of the valley Rahl pulled the gelding off the road and turned to look. The entire valley was filled with seething brownish water. He thought he saw some chunks of ice as well. His eyes went to Third Company, still strung out on the hillside road. He could see several mounts and riders in the water, and he began to count those clear of the torrent. From what he could see, three and possibly four squads had made it clear.

Behind him, Quelsyn's voice rose over the rushing surge of the waters below. "Third Company! Form up!"

Rahl didn't see Drakeyt anywhere nearby, but he finally located the captain near the edge of the water, where he had thrown a rope to a rider and was using his horse to drag both trooper and mount to safety.

Rahl could feel a sour taste in his mouth. Why hadn't he tried to help someone? He knew he could barely ride, but shouldn't he have tried? Slowly, he eased the gelding back down the road. Maybe he could do something else.

By the time Rahl reached the lower part of the slope, still a good fifteen cubits above the lowest point in the road between the bridge and the hill, Drakeyt had pulled another trooper clear of the water. Rahl didn't see any more troopers or horses, and the fury of the water was subsiding.

Drakeyt looked stolidly at the water, a turbulent temporary lake that was already beginning to disappear. Then he turned to Rahl. "I think we lost four or five troopers out of fifth squad, and several of the pack animals and spare mounts. Oh, and we lost the captive from the avalanche trap. Some of the spare mounts did manage to swim clear. It could have been worse." Drakeyt paused. "How did you know?"

"I didn't know," Rahl admitted. "I just sensed it. They created a dam of some sort upriver, and then broke it with an explosion or something. That was what I felt, and when I saw that there wasn't any water in the riverbed . . . when we've had rain around here recently . . . that was when I realized what they'd done."

"That doesn't make sense," Drakeyt said. "We're only one company. They'd save that kind of destruction for the main force."

"If they could," Rahl mused. "You said that it didn't usually rain that much until later in the year. It could be they were afraid that their dam would collapse before the main force got here, and they wanted to try to get something from their efforts." Rahl glanced back eastward. The water level had begun to subside, enough that he could tell that stone bridge was gone, as was much of the causeway through the marshy middle part of the valley. "Crossing that won't be easy, not unless they rebuild the causeway and the bridge. It's bound to slow down the main force. Maybe that was what they had in mind as well."

"The marshal might have to take the older road, but that will split forces. The submarshal would have to retrace his progress some as well." Drakeyt shook his head. "That will take longer. That route hasn't been scouted past Istvyla, and they won't be able to get nearly the supplies they need because there aren't many towns or steads on it. Right now, we can't even send messengers back."

"They'll have to ford the river, but the water level is already dropping," Rahl said. "By late today or tomorrow, it might be passable."

Drakeyt took a deep breath. "Let's head up." He stood in the stirrups. "Everyone to the hilltop! Form up there by squads!"

Rahl turned the gelding and rode beside the older captain. What else could he have done? He'd known that they were being watched. He'd told Drakeyt. He just hadn't expected a flood. He still wasn't certain if there had been an order- or chaos-force behind the torrent. By the time the water had reached the valley, all he'd felt had been immense natural chaos.

Even though he knew it was petty, he was also getting annoyed at Drakeyt. Although Rahl had scarcely been on a horse before, he had personally captured rebels, thwarted an ambush, given enough of a warning that most of Third Company had escaped what could have been total destruction, and the older captain hadn't even said a word.

XXXVII

During the remainder of fiveday, Rahl had taken second squad south along the hills at the western side of the valley to see if they could better determine the cause of the flood, but that had been fruitless—unless they had wanted to spend eightdays climbing rocky cliffs—because the southern part of the valley ended in sheer cliffs, and the lower part of the gorge through which the river flowed ended in the middle of those cliffs in a waterfall, with rock too steep and treacherous to climb, even on foot. Rahl had no doubts that there was a more roundabout and easier access to the upper gorge, but he could not see or sense it, and with darkness falling, he turned the patrol back. Third Company spent the night barely sheltered by a section of woods on the western rise overlooking the partly flooded valley.

Early on sixday, which dawned clear and frosty, Drakeyt sent off messengers with a report on the flood and the destroyed bridge. Once it was clear that the two troopers had safely forded the lowered river and were on the solid part of the road to the east, the captain ordered Third Company to continue westward on its scouting mission.

Drakeyt did not speak to anyone, other than giving orders, until the company had covered several kays, when he finally turned to Rahl, who rode beside him. "Have you any more warnings or concerns?"

"No. There's no one close, not that I can tell."

The older captain pursed his lips, then lowered his voice. "We're slower than we should be. By the time the submarshal's forces join us in Dawhut, it will be midwinter, if not later. The rains will come more frequently, and they'll be heavier and last longer."

Rahl forbore to point out that they really had no idea whether Dawhut lay open to the Imperial forces or the rebels held it. In the end, all he said was, "We can only do the best we can."

"And remember that the marshal won't find it good enough," added Drakeyt sardonically. "Success is due to the marshal's brilliance, failure to the shortcomings of junior officers."

Rahl was slightly surprised at Drakeyt's words. Not at their accuracy, but at the fact that the captain had voiced them. He managed his own reply. "Shortcomings being the inability to overcome the impossible and predict the unpredictable?"

"Something like that." Drakeyt gave the slightest of

headshakes. "I'd be happier if we still had Marshal Chary-nat commanding the campaign."

"Do you know who's in command of the rebels?"

"No one's said, and if anyone would know, the majer would."

Taryl might well know, but he'd not told Rahl, and there wasn't much point in suggesting Taryl knew, then admitting he hadn't informed Rahl.

Drakeyt turned and studied the road ahead once more.

The sky remained hazy, and the air cool, with a light wind out of the north. Although it was hard to tell, Rahl felt that the rolling hills were lower with each kay. There were certainly more steads—except they were estates with larger dwellings, almost mansions, and smaller dwellings around them, set amid fields and orchards. Stopping and inspecting each of the grand holdings slowed their progress even more—and seemed almost futile—since no one recalled seeing any rebel forces.

How could they not have seen *something*?

Abruptly, Rahl smiled. Magery—that might explain it. He hadn't sensed any chaos or order around the people that they had questioned, but that didn't mean some sort of sight shield couldn't have been used, and some sort of order might have made building whatever dam had held the water far easier. But that raised other questions, such as why the attacks and traps were so scattered. That suggested the rebels didn't have many strong mages and were trying to create an impression of strength while slowing the advance of the Imperial forces.

He shifted his weight in the saddle. At least he had begun to gain some skill at riding, and he had managed to stay in the saddle on the headlong charge to escape the flood. His eyes swept the countryside, now showing not only estates and smaller holdings, but bog meadows with workers in them, and a distillery here and there. It looked almost as orderly as Recluce, not that Deybri or the magisters would ever admit such.

With all the days of sleeping in the open, Rahl had not been able to add to his letter to Deybri, although he did think about her . . . and dream. Dreaming of a distant healer seemed impossible. Stupid, some might say, but he could no more not dream of her than breathe. The magisters would never let him return to Nylan, no matter how accomplished an ordermage he became, and Deybri had already said—more than once, and firmly—how much she had hated being in Hamor.

Rahl pushed his thoughts away from her and concentrated on the road.

Several hundred cubits ahead, just before the road curved gradually to the right, the brush in front of a stretch of trees had grown up to almost shoulder height within ten cubits of the road, so high that Rahl lost sight of the first outriders. Beyond the trees was a stubbled field behind a rail fence. Absently, Rahl probed that area of high brush, but could sense nothing living, except small creatures—rodents and perhaps a jay or a traitor bird. He wondered if the brush had grown up over an old fence because there was some structure inside the brush but near the front. He shook his head. Just so long as there weren't any rebels.

Suddenly, the mount of one of the second outriders stumbled. The brush shuddered, and a hail of arrows or quarrels flashed across the road. A number struck the trooper and his mount—with enough force that the horse and rider went down.

For a moment, Rahl just rode on, his mouth opening. Then he started to urge the gelding forward.

"Rahl! Are there any rebels near?" demanded Drakeyt.

"No."

"Then, hold up. You don't want to set off another trap."

Rahl reined up, scanning the area with his order-senses again. The horse was screaming, and he had to concentrate. "There's no one near."

"Company! Halt!" ordered Drakeyt. "Arms ready!"

Rahl probed the brush, far more carefully. What he had

thought was an old fence in the brush was more structured. He turned. "There's something hidden in brush.
I'm going to circle around behind it."

Drakeyt nodded. "Be careful."

Rahl eased the gelding onto the shoulder of the road
for a time, then into the brush, easing his way forward.
He could feel that the trooper was dead; his mount's
screams had died to a slowed and labored breathing.
Rahl could sense that the horse would not last long.

He could sense another section of what he had thought
was fence . . . and another beyond that, and both concealed by high brush and grasses.

"There are two others!" he called back.

Two older troopers rode up to join him.

"Can you show us where, sir?"

Rahl explained exactly where the two were, and the
troopers dismounted.

In moments, after making sure no one was near the
devices, they had sprung the traps, and then began to dis-
assemble them, quickly, and with little interest in pre-
serving them. Rahl moved closer and watched carefully.

Drakeyt joined them, then turned to Quelsyn, who had
also ridden up. "Have a detail bury Honyk, but give me
the pouch with his personals."

"Yes, ser." Quelsyn turned his mount back down the
column, returning with three troopers, who eased the
dead trooper away from his mount.

Rahl turned his attention back to the two troopers who
had disarmed the last two quarrel-throwers. While the
two troopers worked quickly, it still took some time for
them to remove all the sections of the devices. There had
been three of the traps set in a row. The construction was
simple enough—a counterweighted board on an axle of
sorts with quarrels set in wooden tubes. The counter-
weight was held by a cord running in a pipe to a trigger
plate buried a span under the road. If a horse or a heavy
wagon pressed on the wooden plate, it was depressed and
a sharpened piece of metal cut the cord, releasing the

quarrels. Rahl could appreciate the engineering of the mechanisms, because it was simple, yet could have been built elsewhere. Installing it would not have taken that long for several men.

"How did they keep it from being set off by locals?" asked Quelsyn, peering down at the hole in the ground where the first trigger plate had been.

Rahl studied the wooden box that was the plate assembly, then nodded. "There's a space here for an iron rod. They probably had a cord attached to it and pulled it out before we got here."

Drakeyt looked at Rahl. "That means someone is just ahead of us, watching us."

Rahl nodded. It also meant that whoever it was knew there might be a mage-guard with the company because they remained out of his range of order-sensing.

"It's another way of trying to slow us down. Now . . . we'll have to be even more careful."

"If we're looking for things like these," Rahl said, "I'd better be farther ahead, at least with the second outriders."

"That will make you more of a target," Drakeyt pointed out.

Rahl offered a grin he didn't feel. "Everyone's a target, sooner or later. I won't do the company much good if I'm not where I can sense things."

"Try not to get yourself killed," Drakeyt replied. "I'd hate to explain it to your overcommander."

Rahl nodded.

The captain turned to the older troopers who had disarmed the quarrel-throwers. "Just bust up that crap and toss it into the forest, except for the quarrels. They might come in useful. We've got a town or two to scout."

A town or two or more, and who knew how many more devices and traps? Rahl let his order-senses range over the quarrel-throwers again, trying to get a better feel for them.

XXXVIII

For the remainder of sixday, Rahl rode forward of the main column with the outriders, but a good quarter kay behind the scouts. The road had turned so that its general heading was due southwest, but they encountered only a few local carts and riders, and Rahl detected nothing suspicious. The half squads sent to ask local holders about rebels and armed men reported back that none of the locals had seen either. Rahl accompanied one of the groups, and the holders were indeed telling the truth. The lack of local observation bothered Rahl, but he didn't know what he could do about it except be vigilant. Once again, he'd failed to do something, and once again, it was because no one had told him what to look for. He was beginning to think that no one ever thought about telling others anything of value. Rather, they just came up with vague platitudes and thought they were being helpful. He snorted quietly.

The weather remained chill, but they'd been fortunate because they'd encountered no more rain, and Rahl could not sense any great amount of water in the air. That was encouraging for the next few days, at least. They had not sent any more troopers as messengers, nor had they received any messages from the submarshal's forces. The way matters were going, Third Company would reach Dawhut a good eightday before the submarshal—if not longer.

By sevenday, the rugged and rocky hills had gradually given way to lower, gentler, and more rounded rises, with a mixture of hardwood trees, meadows, and fields, although the tilled ground was winter-fallow. Rahl continued to keep pace with the outriders, checking everything that he could for possible traps or ambushes. He was riding beside Alrydd, an older and graying trooper.

"Still seems strange, begging your pardon, ser, to have a mage-captain riding with an outrider." Alrydd did not look at Rahl as he spoke, his eyes traversing the road and the areas on each side.

"Seems strange to be riding here, Alrydd." Rahl paused, then asked, "How long have you been a trooper?"

"Near on twelve years, ser. Was a butcher's apprentice in Sylpa. Figured being a trooper couldn't be any bloodier, and it'd get me out of consorting to the renderer's daughter."

"Did it?"

"Aye, yes, and that I never regretted."

Rahl could sense there were other regrets, but did not press. "I was a scrivener, and trying to avoid being consorted to a young woman led from one thing to another, and I ended up a trader's clerk in Swartheld, and then a mage-clerk in Luba."

"Women, ser . . . when you're with 'em, you can't do without 'em, except when you wish you could and can't."

Rahl wasn't certain he followed that line of thinking, but he laughed softly. "They can be a puzzle." Absently, he reached up and massaged the back of his neck, with his left hand. His head was already aching, and it was only midafternoon.

A low stone wall, no more than waist high, formed a neat border around a small orchard ahead on the left side of the road. With the almost-furled gray of winter leaves, Rahl couldn't tell the type of fruit trees, except that they weren't pearapple or apple.

He stiffened. Was there a hint of chaos there? He reined up the gelding and said to Alrydd, "Hold up."

The trooper complied without speaking.

"There's something about that orchard, or the wall in front of it." Rahl eased the gelding forward, but slowly, extending his order-senses.

The grass and weeds in front of the stone wall appeared and felt undisturbed, and so did the orchard, but an area a good ten or fifteen cubits wide behind the stone wall, on the end farthest north and closest to Rahl, had clearly been touched by chaos, if faintly.

"There's something here!" he called back. "Pass the word to the captain."

"Yes, ser."

Rahl inspected more closely, but still from a good ten cubits away. Loosely covered with leaves and grasses was an oblong two cubits in width and four cubits in height or depth. He guessed that it was similar to the earlier arrow traps.

He shifted his attention back to the road itself, trying to discover what mechanism the rebels had devised to set it off. There was a wide and flat space in the middle of the road, dustier than the area around it, and without any tracks across it. That had to be the cutter plate that severed the trip rope.

He turned in the saddle as the same pair of older troopers who had disassembled the first trap appeared. "The quarrel plate is behind the wall. It's fairly large." He gestured. "The spring plate is there. You can see the outline in the road. The rod is still in place. I wouldn't fiddle with it until you disarm the quarrel trap."

"No, ser. We wouldn't want to be doing that."

Rahl offered no more direction, but continued to watch as the two went to work.

What the troopers finally lifted clear of the ground between the trees and the walls was a wooden throwing plate with tubes for sixty-four quarrels, and all the tubes were filled. Once they had the plate uncovered and clear of the weighted throwing links, Rahl could sense chaos around the plate more strongly.

"There's a paste smeared on the tips," said one of the troopers.

"Poison, most likely," added Drakeyt, who had ridden up shortly before the two troopers had eased the throwing plate away from the mechanism.

Rahl almost nodded. "Why would they use poison on the quarrels?"

"To kill more of us." Drakeyt's words were dryly sardonic.

"No. The poison would still only kill a few more troopers than the quarrels without poison, but it takes more time and effort, and it's more dangerous for whoever's assembling the device."

"And it's likely to make the troopers more angry," Drakeyt added. "You're suggesting that these traps aren't being set by regular troopers or officers. They're either trying to save their troopers for actual battle, or they have something else in mind."

"Or both." Rahl had no idea what other idea might be behind the actions of the mages and crafters—it had to be a combination of both—who were setting the traps.

"That sort of treachery doesn't speak well of Golyat or those supporting him. Mythalt's been a good emperor, as emperors go," replied Drakeyt. "Why would anyone want to support someone who would poison everyday troopers? It says they don't think much of the rank and file."

"Or they think that poisoned quarrels will make the men less determined in battle."

Drakeyt shook his head. "Word about the poison gets around, and most of the troopers won't want to give quarter—especially to rebel officers."

Rahl thought it might just show the arrogance of the rebel mage-guards—and that they were the ones who felt they were above rules, decency, and being accountable for what they did. His lips quirked. They were—until or unless the Imperial forces and mage-guards defeated them.

Drakeyt turned in the saddle to the two troopers breaking up the quarrel-throwing trap. "Wrap up the poisoned quarrels. We'll want to give them to the submarshal when they join forces with us."

Whenever that might be, Rahl thought.

Then the captain looked at Rahl. "From here on in toward Dawhut, we'd better check every stead and structure near the road, and all of the side lanes or roads with tracks."

"I think that's a good idea," Rahl replied. *For many reasons.*

XXXIX

On eightday and oneday, Drakeyt put his stepped-up surveillance and scouting plan into effect. On eightday, Third Company only traveled twelve kays across the low and rolling hills, scarcely more than low rises between ever-more-extensive bog meadows and the steads on the edge of each. A number of the bog meadows looked more like mining pits, stepped downward into darkness.

Oneday was a repetition of eightday, and they still found no sign of rebels, and no one who had seen any or any tracks or other traces. By late afternoon, they had begun to encounter carts and wagons heaped with bog meadow turf creaking southwest on the road.

Ahead Rahl could see another of the old kaystones. Not until he had ridden within a dozen cubits could he make out the name and distance: *Fhydala–5 k*. As worn as the letters were on this, the "new" road, he had to wonder how much older the "old" road was.

The still and cold air carried a pungent odor. Rahl sniffed once, then again. He had no idea what the scent was. Even the gelding snorted slightly, and Rahl could sense he didn't care for the odor much, either. "Alrydd? Do you know what that smell is?"

"Can't say that I know, ser. I'd be guessing that it's from the stills. Feromyl said that was one of the reasons he left years back."

That made sense to Rahl, and, if that were so, he could see why Feromyl, whoever he was, had left Fhydala.

He rode past several oblong small lakes with dark water in them, appearing as though they had once been bog meadows that had been excavated until there was no more turf to be removed, then had filled with rainwater and seepage. After climbing another low rise, he could see the town ahead. Grayish smoke seeped from two tall brick chimneys, one almost immediately to the left of the road ahead and one more than a kay to the right. The one to the left was part of a neatly maintained brick structure. Rahl couldn't make out the structures around the chimney to the right, but he gained the impression that the structures were older and not as well managed.

Drakeyt rode forward and joined Rahl. "We'll ride into the town, and if they seem welcoming, and you don't sense anything, we'll find quarters for the men. We'll run patrols around here tomorrow and stay tomorrow night before we move on. The last eightday has been hard on the troopers and their mounts. I'm just glad you didn't find any more traps today."

"So am I," replied Rahl, "but I have the feeling that today was just a respite. What do you know about the town?"

"About as much as you do." Drakeyt laughed. "The scouts didn't see anything unusual. Did you?"

"Some of those bog meadows to the northeast looked like mining pits," Rahl said.

"They dry the best of the turf and use it to flavor the Vyrna. The rest they burn as fuel for their stoves and homes and the stills, of course."

"What will they do when it's all burned?"

"Dig it from somewhere else, I suppose," replied Drakeyt.

"Some have been abandoned for years. The ones that have become ponds don't look that good."

"That's their problem."

Rahl nodded, but he had to wonder. The vegetation around the bog-meadow ponds had looked sparse and weedy, anything but healthy, and the smoke from the distilleries wasn't exactly the most pleasant odor he'd ever inhaled.

As Third Company rode into Fhydala, Rahl concentrated on sensing anything out of the ordinary, but the folk on the road and the lanes only exhibited feelings and expressions ranging from matter-of-fact acceptance to mild surprise. Rahl could detect no signs of chaos beyond those normal for any town or hamlet.

When Third Company reined up in the town square, both Rahl and Drakeyt were pleased to see that there were actually two inns in Fhydala, on opposite sides of the square. The larger inn's signboard depicted a squarish building constructed of what looked to be enormous bricks or brown stones. The letters beneath the simple image read *The Turf Inn*.

"The Turf Inn?" Rahl wondered aloud.

"That's an old, old name," Drakeyt replied. "Centuries back, some of the poor folks built their huts from turf bricks. It's a way of saying it's an honest and modest place."

The smaller inn was narrower, and its signboard proclaimed it as *The Red Coach*. Both were without patrons, and both innkeepers were more than pleased to accept the script offered by Drakeyt for use of the rooms and the stables and sheds.

With all the arrangements for feed and food, and inspections of makeshift quarters, it was well past dark before Drakeyt and Rahl were finished with those details. After grooming the gelding and leaving the stable, Rahl went to the small upper-level room he had to himself— next to the one shared by three squad leaders. There was no shower in the Turf Inn, or any inn so far—but Rahl used two pitchers of water to wash up, and on his way down to meet Drakeyt in the inn's public room arranged for one of his uniforms to be washed and pressed. The captain had already settled at a corner table in the public room in the Turf Inn—and the troopers had already left after having been fed, leaving the two officers alone. A

slightly smoky fire burned in the hearth as a thin servingwoman appeared.

"We saved chops for you gents. That be all right, with
a bit of burhka on the side, and some late pearapple
sauce?"

"That would be fine," Drakeyt said. "And to drink?"

"Just dark ale or gold lager . . . there's Vyrna . . .
but . . ."

"That doesn't come with what we paid for," finished
Drakeyt.

"No, ser."

"Dark ale," said the older captain.

"Gold lager," added Rahl. He didn't care much for
drinks he felt he should be chewing rather than swallowing.

"Be right there, sers."

Rahl glanced around the public room. While the old
tables were oiled and clean, and the floor swept, the
wood of both was worn, and a sense of age and tiredness
permeated everything. He'd sensed age in the buildings
in both Land's End and Nylan, but not the tiredness. Did
order keep tiredness at bay? Or was it chaos constrained
by order that did that?

"You're deep in thought, Rahl."

"The place feels tired."

"I feel tired," replied Drakeyt, "and we're not even
halfway to Nubyat. We've not seen a rebel force, and
we've already lost nearly half a squad to traps and floods."

The servingwoman reappeared with two large mugs.
"Your ale and lager. Be just a moment more for your dinner."

"Thank you."

Drakeyt waited until she was well away from the table
before continuing. "It's less than fifty kays from here to
Dawhut, but we'll have to take it slower from here on in."
He took a long pull of the dark ale. "That's because there
are all sorts of back roads and hamlets between here and
there. According to the maps, anyway, and the old road

joins the one we're following some fifteen kays southwest of here. Folks don't think about it, but there are more places to hide when there are more steads and hamlets. In a place where you've only got a score of families over ten kays of road, everyone notices a stranger and whether something's missing. You can't get supplies and food if there's no one around to grow them, either."

"That makes sense." Rahl sipped the gold lager. He was famished, and he wasn't about to drink much on an empty stomach. "You think there are many rebels or supporters in Dawhut?"

"There'll be some. It's big enough to have some people who weren't happy with the way things were going. How many?" Drakeyt shrugged. "That's why the submarshal sent us."

"It would be helpful if we had some idea how far behind he is."

"Far enough to let us flush out the trouble and not close enough to help if we get in too deep. That's what recon in force is all about." The captain looked up as the servingwoman carried two platters toward them.

Neither man spoke for a time once their food arrived.

Rahl ate everything on the platter. He was hungry enough that it all tasted good.

As they were finishing, Drakeyt took a last swallow of ale, then said, "I'm going to run over to the other inn and check how things are going."

"I could check here," offered Rahl.

"I'd appreciate that."

"I need to get into more things with the company." Rahl was tired, and he wanted to write a bit more on his letter to Deybri since he had no idea when he might have another chance, but he also needed to be visible to the troopers as well, and Drakeyt could use another set of eyes.

"I'll meet you back here in the front hall, and we can talk over what you saw." Drakeyt stood.

"I'll be here." As he stood, Rahl noticed the copper on the table, and he added one of his own.

Once outside, Rahl moved across the courtyard and through the darkness toward the end of the stable and the hayloft where second squad was billeted. The door was ajar, and he slipped inside. Ahead, he could sense four men in the corner of the barn, the corner barely lit by a wicked-down lantern. He raised a sight shield around himself and eased forward quietly.

". . . never make your point, Cheslyn . . ."

". . . know when to throw and when not to . . ."

Rahl could sense the chaos around the knucklebones— except it wasn't exactly chaos—and he took several more steps until he was within a few cubits of the gamers. After watching for several moments, he realized that one of the troopers had two sets of bones and switched them when he took the bones for his throws.

"Whose bones are those?" Rahl's voice was quiet, but firm, as he dropped the sight shield.

All four troopers froze.

"I asked whose bones they were." Rahl kept his hand on the truncheon at his belt.

"Ser . . . we were just having a friendly game."

Rahl waited in the dimness, but no one spoke.

"Are they yours, Cheslyn?"

The burly bearded trooper did not speak, but Rahl got the clear sense of fear that he would be discovered.

"I think you'd better hand me the bones in your hand," Rahl said.

Cheslyn whirled and jumped to his feet, his hand on his dagger.

"Don't even think about it." Rahl's voice was like ice, and he projected order-force behind the words. He extended his left hand. "The bones."

The trooper froze. Then the hand holding the weighted bones moved back toward the slot in his jacket that held the unweighted cubes.

"You've got them in your hand," Rahl said coolly. "Just hand them over. In the morning, you can talk to the captain and me." He could sense fear and fury within the trooper. "Don't make it worse, Cheslyn. Just hand them over."

"Yes, ser." The trooper's words were even, but the rage behind them was barely held in check. He dropped the bones in Rahl's hand.

Rahl sensed that they were the weighted bones. "Very wise, Cheslyn. Come see the captain and me first thing in the morning after muster."

"Yes, ser. I certainly will."

"Good." Even in the darkness, Rahl could sense that, had Cheslyn's eyes been crossbows, Rahl would have been spitted to the wall behind him. He stepped back, then raised the sight shield.

His disappearance cooled some of the trooper's rage. Some.

"Cheslyn . . . you're an idiot . . . he's killed officers . . . think he'd hesitate a moment to put you down?"

". . . man's got a right to game on his own time . . . can't take that way . . ."

Rahl found no other problems with the other troopers in second squad or with third and fifth squad, but he also did not see Khasmyr—the second squad leader—or Quelsyn. That concerned him as well.

Drakeyt was waiting in the small front foyer of the Turf Inn. "How did it go?"

"I didn't see any of the squad leaders, and we had a little trouble," Rahl admitted. "Some of the troopers in second squad were gaming bones."

"You didn't see any squad leaders because Quelsyn had gathered them together over at the other inn, and gaming isn't really a problem, so long as they're quiet."

"The gaming wasn't," Rahl said. "But using loaded bones and switching them isn't something that ought to be going on."

Drakeyt looked at Rahl, almost expressionless. "So what did you do?"

"I asked to see the bones—when Cheslyn had the loaded ones in hand. Then I said that I thought I'd better keep them, and that Cheslyn could talk to us in the morning."

"Why not right then, if you were so intent on stopping the game?"

"The game didn't matter. Cheating your mates with loaded bones does. But if I called him then, there would have been trouble, and we'd lose another trooper, one way or another. This way . . . if you agree . . . I can tell him quietly that if I ever catch him cheating his mates again, he'll be the one investigating the rebel traps."

Drakeyt laughed. "For such an innocent-looking fellow, you have a devious way of thinking, Rahl. What if you catch him again?"

"I wouldn't say a word. I'd just send him into every nasty situation around, and when he finally didn't make it, I'd give the bones to one of his mates, and tell him that Cheslyn had to pay off on his wagers."

The smile drained from Drakeyt's face. "You mean that, don't you?"

Rahl shrugged. "I haven't been a mage-guard as long as a lot have, but one thing I've learned is that the people who don't heed the first warning don't heed the second . . . or the third—not unless they get slammed upside the head, and hard." As he finished speaking, he realized that he sounded cold, and that his words could have been applied to himself.

"What if you were Cheslyn?"

"I was," Rahl replied. "That's why I know. That's why I'm a mage-guard."

"A crooked gamer?" Drakeyt was incredulous.

"No. One of those people who didn't listen to the warnings. Once upon a time, I was a scrivener in Recluce . . ." Rahl ran through a quick summary that left out more than a few things, but wasn't misleading, he hoped, ending with, ". . . and once I got my memory back, they made me a mage-clerk in Luba."

"I thought Recluce only exiled chaos-mages."

"I'm a different kind of ordermage—the kind they didn't know how to train. So they decided I'd be better off elsewhere."

"Sounds like they thought they'd be better off if you were elsewhere."

"That, too," Rahl replied.

Drakeyt shook his head slowly. "You could have fooled me. You speak so well I just thought you were one of those Atlan merchant heirs whose family discovered he was a mage and bought him the best training possible."

"It would have been nice to have that kind of coin behind me," replied Rahl with a laugh, "but it didn't happen that way."

"We'd all like coins, but we're just poor captains of the Imperial High Command." Drakeyt paused. "Or poor mage-guards drafted to help poor captains." He yawned. "It's been a long day. I'm about to turn in."

"That was my thought," Rahl said. "Good night."

"Good night, Rahl." Drakeyt's smile seemed warmer, although Rahl couldn't have said why.

Rahl turned and climbed the creaking stairs to the second level slowly. Tired as he was, he still wanted to write at least a few lines to Deybri. Writing made him feel closer to her, and at times when he wrote, he felt she was just around a corner or beyond a door. That had to be his imagination, but it felt that way all the same. He tried not to dwell on the impossibilities of any future with her. He'd worry about that after the campaign against Golyat was over.

XL

Drakeyt and Rahl were finishing breakfast before muster when Khasmyr appeared in the public room and crossed to the table where the two officers sat.

"Sers," began the second squad leader, "word is that Captain Rahl ordered Cheslyn to see you two this morning."

"That's right," Rahl replied. "After muster. You were meeting with Quelsyn at the time when I told him."

"Captains," began Khasmyr, "Cheslyn's a good trooper in a fight. Did well in that mess in Worrak. He doesn't always see how some things might not be wise, but . . ." The squad leader paused and looked at Rahl. ". . . gaming with friends isn't a real offense."

Rahl smiled politely and extended his hand. In it were the knucklebones he'd taken from Cheslyn. "I took these from him last night. That's all I did—except I asked him to see Captain Drakeyt and me this morning." Rahl gestured to the table beside them. "Roll them. Several times."

Khasmyr looked to Drakeyt. The older captain nodded.

The squad leader rolled the bones twice, then a third time, a fourth, and a fifth, before he looked at Rahl. "Begging your pardon, ser. I didn't know."

"I didn't want to call him out in front of the others," Rahl said. At the same time, he hadn't felt much surprise from the squad leader, almost as if Khasmyr had expected something like loaded bones.

"It might be best if you were with us, Khasmyr, when Captain Rahl tells Cheslyn that there will never be another pair of weighted bones in second squad."

Rahl appreciated Drakeyt's way of conveying what was necessary. Khasmyr should be present, but Rahl hadn't thought about that. He glanced toward Drakeyt, then

Khasmyr. "I should have let you know sooner. Would you prefer to bring Cheslyn yourself after muster?"

"Yes, sers. That might be best." A faint and ironic smile followed. "If you'd excuse me, sers?"

"See to your squad," Drakeyt replied.

The squad leader nodded, then turned and left the public room.

Rahl was surprised that the squad leader felt little resentment and hoped that was because Khasmyr understood Rahl's inexperience.

Drakeyt grinned. "He's a good squad leader. He managed to let you know that you'd bypassed the chain of command without being either obsequious or offensive. You acknowledged and rectified the situation, and he accepted that."

"I won't do that again. I mean, I'd stop Cheslyn, but I'd hunt down the squad leader . . ." Rahl shook his head. "You told him, didn't you, and you told him how to handle it."

"Of course. It works better that way." Drakeyt rose from the table. "We might as well get saddled up."

Rahl followed him.

He had the gelding saddled and was waiting outside the inn stable with Drakeyt under a gray sky that suggested rain—but would not deliver it, Rahl felt—when Khasmyr appeared with Cheslyn.

The squad leader stepped back and waited as Cheslyn presented himself to the two officers.

"Sers, you wanted to see me?" Cheslyn was far more subdued than he had been the night before.

Drakeyt nodded to Rahl.

Rahl opened his hand and revealed the knucklebones. "These are very well weighted bones, Cheslyn. A man wouldn't fail to make his point often with these. Sooner or later, he might get stabbed or strangled in his sleep, but until then he'd make his points. A friendly game of bones for a few coppers isn't anything an officer needs to get upset about, but a game where someone's using weighted

bones is something else. Sooner or later, you'll end up
dead if you keep that up. Or someone else will. You're a
good trooper, your squad leader says. We don't like losing good troopers. I don't know if the squad leader told
you, but I'm an order mage-guard. That means I can tell
when someone's cheating. You're not ever to cheat other
men out of their coins. Ever. Is that clear?"

"Yes, ser."

"I'm also telling you that there won't be another warning. The next time you'll be flogged or dead." Rahl smiled
politely and extended his shields until they pressed against
the trooper for a moment. "Even when we're assigned to
the High Command, mage-guards can execute Codex
breakers without going to a court-martial or a flogging
board. Is that clear?"

Cheslyn had paled somewhat at Rahl's words and extended shields, and he did not reply for a moment. "Yes,
ser."

"Good. You can return to your duties."

"Yes, ser. Thank you, ser." Cheslyn turned.

Khasmyr escorted the trooper toward the other end of
the stable.

"About now," Drakeyt said, "Khasmyr will be telling
Cheslyn that he's lucky to be alive."

"And that he's fortunate you're his commander and
not me?" asked Rahl with an ironic smile.

"He probably won't say that."

The intimation was that Khasmyr wouldn't have to.

"Why don't you take fourth and fifth squads out along
the road to the south and see what you can find out on the
west side of the road?" said Drakeyt. "Quelsyn can go
due west with second squad, and I'll take first and third
south on the east side."

Rahl nodded. "I'll see what we can find."

"There probably won't be much, but you never know.
Don't push the mounts."

"I won't." Rahl knew too well that Drakeyt wanted an
easy day for the horses—and the men.

This time, the scouting went exactly as Drakeyt had surmised. Rahl found no signs of rebels, no tracks, and no holders or turf-cutters who had seen any sign of either.

When Rahl and fourth and fifth squads returned to Fhydala while the sun was still above the western horizon, if barely visible through the clouds that had gradually thinned throughout the day, four troopers were waiting on the narrow porch of the Turf Inn.

"Ser, Captain Rahl?"

"Yes?"

"You have a dispatch bag from the overcommander. Have you seen Captain Drakeyt?"

"He should be here before long. He was patrolling to the southeast." Rahl turned in the saddle. "Squads, dismissed to your squad leaders."

"We have command, ser."

Once Fedeor and Fysett had ridden with their troopers past Rahl and across the square to the Red Coach, Rahl dismounted and tied the gelding to the iron ring on the brick hitching post, then climbed the three steps to the porch.

"Here you are, ser." The trooper handed a leather pouch to Rahl, tied shut with a simple knot.

"Thank you."

"Our pleasure, ser."

Rahl walked to one side of the porch and untied the pouch. He didn't feel like sitting, especially on one of the hard wooden backless benches. In the leather bag were two envelopes. One bore a Mage-Guard seal; the other was addressed to him in Kysha, but in care of "Mage-Guard Overcommander, Merowey." The handwriting was feminine, and the single initial on the seal was a "D." Deybri. She'd written him. How had she thought of sending it in care of the overcommander? Did he dare open it? Was it a sweet and polite dismissal? Could he expect any more than that? He couldn't take that thought, not at the moment, and he slipped her letter inside his riding jacket.

The other had to be from Taryl, and the sooner he opened that one, the better. He used his belt knife to slit it carefully, absently noting that the edge of the blade bore a slight white sheen of chaos that he had not felt before. He read quickly but carefully.

Mage-Guard Rahl—
From our best estimates, at present, on this sevenday, our forces are less than two days travel time behind you. The submarshal has instructed Captain Drakeyt to wait for us at the town of Saluzyl, if we do not meet up with you before then. You are to scout the approaches to Dawhut, but not to approach nearer than ten kays on such scouting missions.

Several smaller high-speed frigates under the ensign of Fairhaven used the cover of a storm and darkness to enter Nubyat two eightdays ago. Given the chaos surrounding them, it is likely that several white wizards were on board. They will not be involved in action far from Nubyat, I would judge, but their presence may free other mages for more adventurous enterprises.

I have also enclosed a letter, presumably from the healer in Recluce. Should you wish to respond, once we rejoin you, such correspondence can be carried with dispatches, although the charge is five silvers.

Except for the elaborate "T" at the bottom, that was the extent of the dispatch. Rahl folded it and put it back into the envelope, then slipped the letter and pouch under his arm before leaving the porch and remounting the gelding. He rode to the stable at a walk, thinking.

White wizards supporting the rebels? It made sense if Fairhaven wanted to weaken Hamor. But would weakening Hamor really strengthen Fairhaven? Outside of trade, Hamor hadn't had that much to do with Candar, and es-

pecially with Fairhaven. From what he'd observed in
Nylan, Rahl could see that weakening Hamor didn't
benefit Recluce. Wouldn't the same be true regarding
Fairhaven and Hamor? Did Fairhaven see Hamor as a potential enemy?

He shook his head. Any land that was strong could be
considered a potential enemy. He replaced the letter in
the pouch and walked down to his mount, leading the
gelding to the stable.

Once he stabled and unsaddled his mount, Rahl forced
himself to take his time in grooming the gelding. The
mount shouldn't suffer because of his impatience. Besides, he wasn't certain he wanted to know what was in
the letter from Deybri.

Just as he finished and was ready to leave the stable,
Drakeyt led his mount in.

"How did it go?" Rahl asked.

"Same as always. No one's seen anything. No one's
heard anything, and there aren't any tracks anywhere.
What about you?"

"The same," Rahl admitted. "It's like they just left this
part of Merowey alone." He paused. "Did you get the
dispatches for you?"

"There was just one. The submarshal wants us to stop
and wait for him at Saluzyl. According to the maps, it's
fifteen or twenty kays from Dawhut, maybe two days' ride
from here the way we've been going. We're not to scout
closer than ten kays."

"Did he say why?"

"Submarshals never explain. Not this one. That's all
he said."

"I got a dispatch from the overcommander. He wrote
about the same, but he also said that some Fairhaven fast
frigates avoided the fleet and ported in Nubyat. He thought
they might have some white wizards on board."

"That's all we need—more chaos types for the rebels."

"They didn't send fleets or large numbers of troops,"
Rahl pointed out.

"Of course not. They'd prefer to cause trouble with as little cost as possible."

That description fit more than a few people, Rahl thought, and Puvort came immediately to mind. Rather than exert himself in the slightest, the magister just pushed people into exile, and some of the magisters and magistras in Nylan weren't much better. For that matter, he conceded silently, some in Cigoerne seemed the same way—especially Cyphryt, but he wasn't so sure about Fieryn, either.

"See you in the public room?" asked Rahl. "I'm going to wash up."

"In a bit."

Rahl tried not to rush back to his small room. Even so, he permitted himself a smile once he was alone there and had the letter out and in his hand. He stood beside the window, letting the last light of day fall on the envelope in his hands.

He could sense that it had not been opened and that the seal was intact. Equally important was the sense of order around the seal. Somehow . . . it *felt* like Deybri. He used the tip of his belt knife to slit the envelope— carefully—then smoothed out the single sheet of paper and began to read.

> My dear mage-guard,
> Your letter arrived today, and I am replying as soon as I can. From your words, if I do not respond soon, you may not read what I must say for a season or more. Please pardon my haste and penmanship. I almost hesitate to write you anything in reply to your elegant words and beautiful letters, yet I must.

Rahl was afraid to look at the next words, and he glanced out the window, toward the sun that was sinking below the rooftops to the west. After a moment, he turned back to the letter and continued reading.

I cannot deceive you. Although I am older than you in years, I am not that much older in my feelings. You have seen and felt those feelings, as I have felt yours. You know what I feel about you and about Hamor. At the same time, it is like I have seen the sun for the first time in years. I am half-blinded by all the light, and I cannot say what will come of what I see. I cannot promise you, not now, but your words and letters offer hope and love in a world of too much order. I must sort through all that I feel under the light of this different sun. For me either to close or open a door when I am still half-blind would serve neither of us well.

Until then, and always, my deepest affection.

Her deepest affection? Those words sounded as though she actually might recognize that she loved him. Yet . . . would she accept that? Could she? His eyes returned to the top of the page.

After rereading her letter, Rahl folded it and slipped it inside his tunic, smiling. At least, she hadn't closed off all possibilities—even if he had no idea how he would manage to see her again . . . or when.

He might as well wash up and meet Drakeyt for dinner. After that he could begin to wrap up the letter he had been writing to Deybri so that he could have it ready for dispatch.

XLI

Two days later, just past midafternoon on fourday, Third Company reached Saluzyl, another town set amid widely spaced low rolling hills. The spaces between the hills were filled with heavily worked bog meadows, many of them abandoned and filled with black water. Neither the scouts nor the outriders nor Rahl had discovered any sign of rebels or traps, but Rahl couldn't help but wonder how long it would be before they encountered either or both.

As they rode into the town, Rahl could make out several brick buildings that looked to be distilleries, with chimneys seeping gray smoke against a sky that was as much gray as green-blue. The brick houses were neat enough, but older, and the bricks were dingy, doubtless from years of smoke from the distilleries, and the air held the same pungent odor as it had in Fhydala.

The chandlery in Saluzyl was fair-sized and across the square from the Inn of the Dun Cow. As the company drew up in formation, Rahl turned in the saddle and said to Drakeyt, "Once we get everyone quartered, I think I'll go over and talk to the chandler. We're close enough that he might know something, and what he's selling or not selling or can't get should tell us something."

"The chandlers in the past haven't been too helpful," Drakeyt pointed out.

"They've told us that there weren't any rebel forces or strangers, and that seemed to be right."

"They missed the mages and saboteurs."

Rahl wasn't quite certain how to respond to that. After a moment, he asked, "Do you have a better idea about whom in town we should question?"

"You might as well question him. Then we can claim that we've done our best when the marshal complains, not that he'll listen to us. I just don't think questioning people here is going to tell us much."

"Probably not, but how will we find out if we don't try?"

Drakeyt shrugged. "We'd better get on with dealing with quarters and food."

Rahl nodded. He was still going to talk to the chandler.

As in the other towns, the proprietor of the Dun Cow was willing to take script for quartering and feeding

Third Company, but it was late afternoon by the time Rahl finished helping Drakeyt with quartering arrangements. Then he had to stable and groom the gelding. After that, he left his gear in the small room and walked to the chandlery.

The white-haired chandler was beginning to close the inner shutters when Rahl walked through the door. He turned.

Rahl saw that the man had but two fingers on his left hand. "Good evening."

"Evening, Captain. You're almost too late. You interested in some good riding fare? Or replacing some gear?"

"I might be interested in the fare. If it's not too costly. What do you have?"

"Hard white cheese wedges, and some dried beef strips. I've got some biscuits, special-like, a pack for a copper."

"Those might be useful," Rahl admitted. "Could I see them?"

"Over here, Captain." The chandler's two fingers pointed to a table against the wall. "In the tin on the left."

Rahl opened the tin. The riding biscuits were squares a span on a side and of a finger's thickness. Rahl suspected it would take strong teeth to chew them, but that they might fill his stomach at times. "How long will these last before they spoil?"

"Two seasons if you keep 'em dry."

The chandler believed what he said, Rahl could tell. "How many in a pack?"

"Five, but I'd make it six for you."

"Two packs, then." Rahl could have bargained for a lower price, but it had been a long day, and that wasn't his purpose in being there.

"Have to wrap 'em in grease paper unless you got a biscuit tin." The chandler smiled. "Got one of those, too. Old, but clean. Could let you have it for three coppers. It'll hold fifteen biscuits."

Rahl laughed. "How about half a silver for the tin and fifteen biscuits?"

"Suppose I could do that. Have to be for coin, not script. Been slower than I'd like lately."

"Coin it is." Rahl handed over five coppers. "Slow as it is, you still must get some travelers from Dawhut."

"Not many. Not these days, Captain. Just those who want to sell me the things I don't need more of because there aren't that many travelers."

"Are there any at all coming from the coast?"

"Not travelers."

"Then who?"

"Coast city traders and factors, looking for goods, or to sell 'em."

"What do they tell you about the rebels?"

"What rebels?" The chandler snorted. "Closest rebels are a good hundred kays southwest of Dawhut. The High Command garrison in Dawhut's got three companies. My cousin there . . . well, he's really Aviera's second cousin, but he's selling all he can get from everywhere else in Merowey because the rebels aren't letting any goods leave the coast."

Three companies in Dawhut? Then why hadn't they done any scouting? Or sent any scouts or messengers? Or had they, and had the rebel mage-guards captured or killed them? The latter possibility didn't seem that likely to Rahl, but he couldn't disregard it.

"What about goods here? Is anyone selling much?"

"Big thing is the Vyrna, and business there is piss poor. The Emperor won't let ships leave Nubyat, and the distilleries are stocking up Vyrna in barrels, hoping it's all over before long. A lot of folks sold their garden produce when one of the factors from Nubyat came up here last eightday. Some sides of mutton, too. Didn't think much of letting go of what they had for coin, but they will. They will. Can't eat coin, and prices'll go up come late winter and spring."

"You didn't, I take it?"

"I'm just a town chandler, but I know when I'm looking at a long winter."

"Produce wouldn't keep for that long, not on a wagon back to the coast."

"Not fresh, but he had pickling barrels in his big wagon, and lots of salt."

"There weren't any rebel troops with him?"

"Haven't seen a one. Aviera said they were staying away from the main road. Wouldn't have been surprised if the fellow with the pickling barrels hadn't already sold what he got before he'd even delivered." The chandler finished packing the biscuit tin and handed it to Rahl. "Here you go, Captain."

"Thank you. Have you seen or heard anything else that might be of interest?"

"The factor fellow was looking for bitumen. Didn't find any. The only place you can get that is in the hills north of Elmari. Other than that, haven't heard or seen anything . . . or anyone. Suppose that's of interest, seeing as we usually get more travelers this time of year than in summer or harvest."

Rahl could sense that the older man wasn't hiding anything and had said what he knew. "I appreciate the tin, the biscuits, and the information."

"I appreciate the coppers, Captain." The chandler smiled.

Rahl inclined his head, then turned and left. Even before he'd taken more than a few steps across the square toward the inn, the chandlery was shuttered and locked.

Drakeyt was standing on the front porch of the Dun Cow, looking northward at the puffy white clouds that were moving southward. "Rain, you think?"

"Not tomorrow, or not from those clouds," replied Rahl.

"What have you got there?"

"A biscuit tin, filled with biscuits."

"When a mage-captain buys hardtack biscuits . . ." Drakeyt shook his head. "That doesn't sound good."

"The chandler said a factor was here an eightday ago, buying all the produce he could get, and pickling it. Some mutton, too—salting it."

Drakeyt frowned. "So the rebels have taken steps to load up on supplies."

"That's my guess. The chandler's, too. Oh, the factor from Nubyat was looking for bitumen, too."

Drakeyt winced. "They're looking to make Cyadoran fire. Nasty stuff."

"They didn't get any here, but there's supposedly some north of Elmari."

"We'd best hope that they don't ship a lot to Nubyat."

"Did you know there were three companies in Dawhut?"

"I wouldn't be surprised," replied Drakeyt.

"Why couldn't they keep the roads open and deal with the few rebels that there are?" asked Rahl.

"Three companies three hundred kays from Nubyat are enough to hold a large town," Drakeyt pointed out. "That is, if the rebels don't send ten companies and if the companies don't get whittled down in piddling engagements."

"So these traps were designed to whittle them down?"

"More to slow and whittle us down. The rebels had to know that the majer in Dawhut wouldn't risk troopers on road patrols. He might even have had orders to hold the town. That could be why we've been ordered to wait for the submarshal."

"Because he's worried that there might be rebel forces around Dawhut? Or because the majer might attack us if we tried to enter the town."

Drakeyt shrugged. "It could be either. We'll find out when we start sending out scouting patrols tomorrow. We wouldn't want the submarshal to encounter any surprises."

"I should be with one of the patrols near the main road," Rahl offered.

"I'd thought you would be," Drakeyt replied. Then he smiled.

Rahl couldn't help grinning . . . but only for a moment.

XLII

Later, after eating with Drakeyt, Rahl retired to his small room. There he sat on the edge of the bed, using the small washstand as a desk, under the dim light of the single lamp, trying to find the right words to close his letter to Deybri so that he would be able to dispatch it as soon as Taryl and the submarshal's forces joined them.

He murmured the words, "I have just received your letter . . ."

No, that wasn't right.

"We are in the small town of Saluzyl, and I've read your letter four times already since I received it two days ago . . ."

He frowned, then shook his head. What he needed to do was to write a short cover letter expressing his feelings in response to her letter, and then enclose with it the more lengthy correspondence he had been writing a bit at a time. But how could he begin? Finally, he began to write, one slow word at a time.

Your letter was its own sunshine when it arrived, and I have savored the light brought by each and every word.

You wrote about being blinded by the sun. I also saw the sunlight, except it crept upon me like a slow sunrise, and I did not know that you were the source of that light until I realized that the days when I saw you were the brightest. Yet how could I tell you that? Then, I did not have the words or the courage.

Now, I know that there is at least a faint hope that we may share that sunlight, and that if I do not write and tell you that, then we both may lose that warm and loving light. Yet I do not wish to compel anything of you, and should you choose to close the shutters and turn from that light, I will grieve at the loss, at the thought of what might have been between the two of us, and at the dimming of the light you have brought into my life, but I will respect your decision.

I am far from wise enough to know what steps are the best for us to make sure that light endures, but I am confident that, together, we could determine what those steps might be, if that is your wish and decision. While it appears that I have found a place as a mage-guard, ordermages are welcome in at least some other lands besides Recluce and Hamor, and healers are welcome the world over.

Whatever we decide, I am obligated to finish this campaign, for I owe that at the very least to Taryl, for he saved me from Luba. Without his wisdom, his patience, his tutoring, and his perception, I would have nothing, and I would never have seen or written you again.

This time, he did sign it, "With all my love."

Was he being too bold? Assuming far too much?

He tightened his lips. He might be too bold, but he did not think he was assuming more than was warranted. Deybri would never have committed what she had to paper if she had not felt even more strongly than what her words had spoken.

After a time, he sealed the letter and addressed it.

Although he blew out the lamp, he lay on the lumpy inn bed for a long time, thinking, before he dropped into an uneasy slumber.

XLIII

When Rahl rode back into Saluzyl on sixday at the head of fourth and fifth squads, after a second day of patrols that had revealed nothing more than what he'd learned from the chandler two days earlier, he found the town filled with troopers and wagons, but no one hindered him as he formed up the two squads in the area between the stables and the Dun Cow.

Another trooper rode up even before Rahl finished dismissing the squads to their squad leaders, but he reined up and waited until Fedeor and Fysett released their men to care for their mounts. Then he eased his mount over toward Rahl.

"Captain Rahl, ser?"

"Yes, trooper?"

"The Mage-Guard Overcommander sent me to escort you to headquarters."

Headquarters? Rahl supposed headquarters was wherever the submarshal declared it to be. "Lead on."

"Yes, ser."

The ride was short, less than a quarter kay, by the time Rahl reined up in front of a moderately large but modest-looking two-story stone dwelling surrounded by a chest-high brick wall. Rahl had not seen the dwelling before, because it had not been in that part of town he had scouted. The roof was of dark gray tile, and the wooden trim was painted white. The area between the front wall and the house was a garden, not particularly well kept, Rahl noted, with more than a few wilted and dead flowers that should have been cut or trimmed eightdays before. Guards stood at the open gates that flanked a lane leading to a separate stable. Neither gave Rahl more than a passing glance as he rode past them.

Rahl dismounted at the side of the dwelling and tied the gelding to a hitching rail.

"Rahl! Over here," called Taryl from a roofed and railed side porch.

Rahl had to vault the railing because the porch had no steps down to the side yard. He glanced past Taryl at the etched-glass window beside the door into the dwelling. The image was that of two roses with crossed stems—a thorn rose and a white rose without thorns.

The overcommander followed his eyes. "Submarshal Dettyr has requisitioned this dwelling as his temporary headquarters while he assesses the situation in Dawhut. It belongs to one of the leading citizens of Saluzyl, one Shawyn. He owns the larger distillery."

"He's not around? Or he doesn't object?"

"Would you, in his position? He's wealthy and in a rebellious district, and he has offered no support to the Emperor."

Rahl just nodded.

"You look good," observed Taryl. "Your reports to me have been helpful and will prove more so in the future, but that isn't why I sent for you. I wanted to talk to you briefly before you meet with the submarshal. He has a few words for you and Captain Drakeyt. The captain arrived just before you and has been waiting. I would like to caution you to say nothing to dispute what the submarshal has to say. He is in a foul mood, and he will not be kind. After he dismisses you, you and I will discuss matters. Is that clear?"

"Yes, ser." Rahl didn't like what Taryl was telling him, but the overcommander had always been fair before, and he had reasons for everything.

"Good. We shouldn't keep the submarshal waiting." Taryl opened the door into the mansion and stepped through the doorway.

Rahl followed. The parlor inside was not much warmer than outside, but the lack of wind made it feel far less chill. Rahl glanced around the chamber—a good fifteen cubits by nine or ten. A polished rose marble mantel graced the hearth, centered on the wall opposite the door to the outside porch. To the right of the hearth, in which a fire was laid but not burning, was an archway to a center hall. The parlor held two maroon-velvet settees, set at right angles to the hearth and facing each other, several fruitwood armchairs with seats and backs upholstered in the same maroon velvet, and a small writing desk in the corner formed by the front wall and the outside wall. Under the two large front windows, whose base was some two cubits above the floor, was a low bookcase, on which rested two bronze sculptures. One looked to be a Cyadoran mirror lancer. At least, it looked like a drawing of such a lancer he'd seen in one of the histories. The other was a man in garb Rahl did not recognize. The floors were polished but worn dark oak, and a large oval rug covered most of the parlor floor.

Rahl had expected opulence in the Imperial Palace, but the casual display of such wealth in a town in the middle of Merowey somehow unsettled him.

"Rahl . . . this way," Taryl said firmly, but in a low voice.

"Oh . . . yes, ser."

Taryl crossed the center hall to the door on the other side and knocked, then opened it. "Submarshal, Captain Rahl is here."

Rahl crossed the hall and waited.

"Thank you, Overcommander. If you would have both captains join me. This will not take long."

Taryl motioned for Rahl to enter, then stepped back, leaving the door open. Rahl took three steps into the library and waited. The chamber was the same size as the parlor, but held little furniture except an ornate carved desk and chair, two wooden armchairs without upholstery, and a polished dark oak library stool stepladder. The fireplace mantel was of green marble, and floor-to-ceiling bookshelves of dark oak covered the walls—except for the area of the two front windows and an outside door to another porch. The window hangings were of dark green velvet and half-drawn. Neither the wall lamps nor the one on the desk was lit.

Before the submarshal could speak, Drakeyt arrived, and Taryl shut the door on the three, remaining outside.

The submarshal's uniform was spotless, and his boots shimmered, as did the balding patch in the middle of his thinning brown hair. His watery green eyes were cold, and he radiated displeasure. Rahl was getting the feeling that the man was never pleased with anything, and that he wouldn't know what to do if he couldn't find fault with something, if not everything.

The library remained silent as Dettyr glared at the two captains. Finally, he spoke, his voice hard. "Third Company was sent out to scout the roads and report on any enemy activity." Dettyr looked at Drakeyt. "Was this not so, Captain?"

"Yes, ser."

"And you, Captain Rahl, were supposed to detect difficulties before they escalated into major problems. Was that not so?"

"Yes, ser."

"Yet . . ." Dettyr drew out the word. ". . . all your dispatches only reported that your efforts created more problems, rather than resolving them. You killed one out of three rebels you captured, and the other two were worthless as sources of information. You triggered an avalanche that partly blocked the road, killed several troopers, and delayed our progress. You tripped an arrow trap that killed a scout, and you lost half a squad in a flood you should have stopped, and that flood destroyed the only bridge across the sole sizable river on the entire line of march. You seemed unable even to avoid a mere flood. Again, the one additional prisoner you managed to capture was drowned in the flood, and we gained almost nothing from that, except your sketchy reports on what he reputedly said." Dettyr's eyes went first to Drakeyt, then to Rahl. "Have I omitted anything, Captains?"

He'd omitted the arrow traps that Rahl had found that

hadn't killed anyone, and he'd totally mischaracterized almost everything.

"I don't believe so, ser," replied Drakeyt evenly.

Rahl could sense a combination of anger and resignation from the older captain, and he forced himself to say, "No, ser." He also managed to keep his shields in place and his face pleasant, although holding an impartial expression was difficult.

"As scouts and as Imperial officers, you are supposed to act to preserve the roads and bridges of the Empire, not to facilitate their destruction. I cannot tell you how displeased I am that I have been forced to employ troopers and fighting engineers to repair structures and highways that should never have been destroyed." Dettyr paced back and forth in front of the cold hearth, not looking at either officer.

Rahl waited.

"Your performance, Captains, has been marginal at best, and in that evaluation, I am being most charitable. Do you understand?"

"Yes, ser." What Rahl understood was that the submarshal was even less competent than the marshal, and that someone had planned for it to be that way. He couldn't imagine that either the High Command Overmarshal or the Land Marshal could have chosen an idiot like Dettyr as the best qualified senior officer to be Marshal Byrna's deputy. Then again, Rahl hadn't been all that impressed with Land Marshal Valatyr on their one brief meeting.

"Good!" snapped Dettyr. "I trust I will never have to remind you of the need for better performance and accountability again."

"No, ser."

"You may go."

"By your leave?" asked Drakeyt.

Belatedly, Rahl echoed the words.

"My leave, Captains. Close the door after you depart."

Rahl turned and followed Drakeyt, closing the library door quietly, but firmly.

Taryl motioned to Rahl from the archway to the parlor, then led Rahl out onto the side porch, while Drakeyt headed down the center hallway in the direction of the front entry foyer.

"I didn't say anything," Rahl said quietly. "Except agree."

"It took a great deal of willpower not to object, didn't it?" asked Taryl.

"More than a little."

"I'd like you to think about what he said for a bit. What did he say that was true, and what was not? How did you link them together?"

Rahl didn't say anything for a moment. Did Taryl know just how abusive Dettyr had been? And how inaccurate?

"Just tell me, gently, where he was right, and where he was wrong," Taryl said.

"He was right to be displeased about having to repair the bridges and highways, but he was wrong to blame me or Captain Drakeyt. It would have occurred no matter who was scouting, and it was all part of something larger. The cannonading of the *Fyrador* took place before I ever joined Third Company. The rockslide was built before we set out from Kysha, and even if we had not triggered it, someone would have had to have taken it apart or it could have fallen anyway. The same was true of whatever dam or levee they used to create the flood. I could have stopped the first arrow trap if I'd known what to look for, and that outrider died because I didn't have experience. Even so, I don't know how we could have avoided losing some of the troopers." Rahl frowned. "If I hadn't been thinking about the low water level in the river, it could have been worse. I don't know. Maybe I should have sensed something there, and gotten everyone clear of the flood, but I'd never seen the river before, and how could I have even known what the water level was supposed to be in early winter? Usually water levels are the lowest then anyway."

Taryl nodded. "All worthwhile experience has a price. Sometimes we pay it; sometimes others do. Most of the time, we pay but only a part of that price."

Rahl looked at Taryl. "You wanted things to be difficult, didn't you? For me."

"I didn't make them that way, but there were reasons why those difficulties will prove useful." Taryl handed Rahl an envelope. "Open it."

The last thing Rahl wanted to do after the submarshal's dressing down was to open a sealed envelope, but there was no help for it. He broke the seal and opened it. Inside was a heavy sheet of parchment with a seal at the bottom. He read the short section of parchment once, then blinked and read it again, his eyes falling on the key words— "having fulfilled the requirements, Mage-Guard Rahl is hereby promoted to the level of senior mage-guard."

He looked to Taryl, whose lips quirked into a faint smile.

"Senior mage-guard? After this?" Rahl gestured in the direction of the library and the submarshal. "I'm too young . . ."

Taryl laughed. "You are, but you need the rank and position, and I need you to have it. Senior mage-guards rank with majers."

"How did this happen?"

"The minimal requirements are much higher levels of proficiency with weapons and with control of order or chaos. You had those before we left Cigoerne. What did you think those tests were for?"

"I didn't know. I just thought you were trying to get me prepared for the campaign."

"The other requirement is an absolute. A mage-guard must have completed two tours of duty in different locales and have a position of greater responsibility in a third tour before he or she can be promoted to senior mage-guard."

"But . . . none of my tours were that long."

Taryl's eyes seemed to laugh. "The procedures don't

mention that. They just require completion with an excellent rating. You managed that."

"The submarshal won't be happy with this."

"He won't be, but that's not your worry. I'm the one who promoted you, and the worry is mine. Jubyl also agreed and wrote a recommendation for you as well. So did Mage-Captain Jyrolt." The thin-faced mage-guard frowned. "Matters will come to a head before long."

"How so, ser?"

"I'd prefer not to speculate, but you know what you did, and you know how the submarshal reacted. You have also met the marshal."

"What should I do?"

"Just keep Third Company from taking too many losses."

Rahl considered matters for a moment. "I have this feeling that matters are going to get much worse, or you wouldn't be pushing me."

"They may be even worse than you can imagine." Taryl's voice was sober and low.

Rahl waited for the explanation. There was none. "Is this because of the white wizards from Fairhaven?"

"I want you to be most alert, but I'd prefer that you come to your own conclusions." Taryl offered a sad smile. "You need to get back to Third Company and talk to Captain Drakeyt. Try to listen more than you talk." He paused, then handed Rahl a pouch. "Here are the senior sunbursts for your visor cap and the insignia for your uniforms."

"Senior sunbursts? I didn't know there was a difference."

"It's not obvious, except to those who know and who look closely. The reason is that seniors still patrol and handle many of the same duties, and it was discovered years back that citizens and merchants inevitably tried to play off the differences and discount the judgments and actions of mage-guards who were not seniors."

"Will the officers in the High Command notice?" Rahl

studied Taryl's insignia, but it didn't look noticeably different from his own.

"Only some with a great deal of experience, and not all of those." Taryl smiled faintly. "You'd better go."

"Ah . . . ser . . . I do have a letter, but not with me."

"To the healer?" Taryl smiled more broadly.

Rahl could sense a certain warmth that had not been there a moment before. "Yes, ser."

"If you'll drop it by later, or in the morning, when we meet after muster, I'll make sure it gets sent with the dispatches. I'll caution you that it will probably take two to three eightdays before it gets on a ship."

"Yes, ser."

"Now . . . I have a few matters to attend to."

Rahl inclined his head, then vaulted over the porch railing, untied the gelding, and mounted. When he returned to the inn, he stabled and groomed his horse.

As he was about to leave the stable, he saw Drakeyt finishing up with his mount and walked over to the stall. "Are you about ready for something to eat?" he asked over the low stall wall.

"And something stronger."

"It's been a long day," offered Rahl.

"Could be short compared to those ahead." Drakeyt did not speak for a time, not until he finished grooming his mount and was leaving the stall. "I saw the overcommander stopped you."

"He had a few things to say," Rahl admitted. "Not quite so directly as the submarshal."

"They always do." Drakeyt shook his head.

They crossed the dusty courtyard, and Rahl could see a number of mounts tied to the long hitching rail outside the inn. To the north, the green-blue sky looked clear—and chill—in the fading twilight.

As they entered the public room, Rahl could see three tables that held officers, undercaptains and captains, while two majers sat at another. "Do you know all of them?"

"Most of them, but mainly just in passing, except for Majer Mezlyr. He's the bigger one."

"Drakeyt! Did you have to wash out the bridge?" called out one of the captains.

"No. I did it just to give your company experience in fording rivers." Drakeyt grinned.

Rahl could sense the anger beneath the smile, but he said nothing. What could he have said that would have been better than the captain's words?

Rahl let Drakeyt choose the one unoccupied corner table, slightly away from the nearest other table. No sooner had they settled into the armless straight-backed chairs than the servingwoman appeared.

"You're the captain who's quartered here, aren't you?"

"Yes."

"You get the burhka and noodles tonight. Drinks?"

"I'll have a beaker of Vyrna."

"That's extra, ser. Two coppers more."

"I can spare two coppers."

The servingwoman looked at Rahl.

"Just good lager . . . whatever you have."

"Yes, ser." She looked at Drakeyt, almost apologetically.

The captain placed two coppers on the dark wood of the corner table.

She nodded, but left them there. "Won't be but a moment with your meal and drinks, sers."

"Thank you." Rahl's stomach felt more empty than it usually did by dinnertime. He turned back to Drakeyt. "The submarshal was hard on you. I should have told him that it was my lack of experience . . ."

Drakeyt laughed, harshly. His eyes glittered like a mirror before a brilliant lamp for a moment. "He wouldn't have listened. Or he would have blamed me for not instructing you in more detail. Or the overcommander for assigning an inexperienced mage-guard." The older captain looked at Rahl. "Besides, it isn't true."

"I've never done this before," Rahl replied. "I've only

been a city mage-guard." He looked up as the serving-woman walked back toward them carrying a glass beaker and a large mug.

"Here you are, sers. Be back with your food in a moment." This time, she did sweep up the pair of coppers before she left.

"Only a city mage-guard?" Drakeyt raised his thin and silvering eyebrows. "I've been around, and I've talked to the other captains, and I talked to the majer for a moment after the submarshal dismissed us. The majer doesn't recall any mage-guard assigned to the High Command who could tell where the enemy was from the distance you were doing. The submarshal's looking for people to blame even before the campaign gets going. The majer didn't say that, but he might as well have." Drakeyt took a sip of the Vyrna. "You're not just a plain city mage-guard. The overcommander wouldn't have planted you on me if you were. Do you want to tell me why he did?"

"I can't," Rahl admitted. "I asked him, but all he'd say was that I needed the experience, and that there were good reasons for it."

"How good are you, Rahl? Compared to other mage-guards, that is?"

Rahl took a slow swallow of the lager before answering, trying to compose a truthful answer that didn't reveal too much. "I don't know exactly. I've been tested, and I do better with weapons than all the other mage-guards of my experience. I have more control of some abilities than most of the regular mage-guards, but how that compares to the higher-level mage-guards, I just don't know."

Drakeyt grinned. "I think that says that you've been put on point in a dangerous maneuver. Dettyr doesn't know how good you are, or how capable the overcommander is, and the overcommander doesn't want him or the marshal to know that."

"How can he not know about the overcommander?" Rahl almost burst out that Taryl had been a former Triad, but stopped those words.

"What do you mean?"

"There are only a handful of Mage-Guard Overcommanders, and I'd guess that all of them are capable of becoming a Triad. Any one of them could remove or destroy Dettyr without raising a sweat."

"I doubt that thought has ever crossed the submarshal's mind. Mage-guards are just peacekeepers among civilians to him."

"Do most officers in the High Command feel that way?"

"Too many."

"Why don't you?"

Drakeyt grimaced. "I did, but I've been watching and getting reports on you from the squad leaders. They're impressed. Most officers don't impress them much. The other thing is that you've learned to ride better than most officers."

That had to do with Rahl's sense of what the gelding would do and his ability to project what he wanted to the horse . . . although he had learned to stay glued in the saddle, painful as it had been. "I had to. It hurt too much not to."

The older captain laughed, then stopped as the server returned with two crockery platters heaped with burhka and noodles. Each had a sliced pearapple on the side.

"Thank you," Rahl said. "It's been a long day."

"I thought it might have been."

Rahl knew she was angling for something extra, but he was happy to give it, and slipped her a copper. So did Drakeyt.

"Much obliged, sers. Much obliged. I'll be seeing if you'd like more to drink in a bit."

Rahl was so hungry that he took several mouthfuls of the burhka and noodles before looking up to see that Drakeyt was also eating heartily. The dish didn't even seem that spicy.

The captain swallowed, then took a sip of the Vyrna, and asked, "What orders did you get from the overcommander?"

"He said my job was to keep Third Company from taking casualties. He wouldn't say more than that."

"I can't disagree with that . . . much."

"He actually said 'too many casualties,' " Rahl added.

"That's more realistic."

"He's very realistic," Rahl said dryly. "About everything."

"It's good someone is." Drakeyt shook his head. "You know, after all that this afternoon, nothing's changed. The majer said we're to make a thorough sweep of the road to Dawhut in the morning. Then the submarshal will decide."

"Decide what? We have to go through Dawhut to get to Nubyat, don't we? We haven't found any sign of any rebels. Does he think they'll appear overnight?"

"They might be closer to Dawhut," suggested Drakeyt with a smile.

"We haven't found any in over four hundred kays, and there are three companies in Dawhut, and we're going to run into rebels in the ten kays between where we stopped patrolling and the city itself?"

"We just follow orders," Drakeyt replied. "There's no point in questioning stupid orders that are just stupid when no one is going to get killed."

Rahl nodded, although he certainly didn't like the implication. Not at all.

XLIV

After dinner, Rahl cleaned up and changed his sunburst insignia, finally comparing the old and new sunburst and insignia. Side by side, he could see the difference, but without looking for it, or knowing that there was such a distinction, he never would have seen it—and hadn't. The tips of the two sunburst rays in the middle—the ones that extended directly out from the side of the center—were straight in the junior insignia, but the very tips curved up in the senior insignia. That small difference would not even be visible from more than a few cubits away, even on the larger insignia for his visor cap, let alone on the smaller collar devices. He doubted that Drakeyt would notice, and he wasn't about to tell the captain, because that would only confuse the troopers.

He thought about writing more to Deybri and telling her that he'd been promoted, but that would have been read as boasting—and it would have been. Besides, he could always add it at the appropriate time in the next long letter he wrote, assuming he had time now that Taryl and the submarshal had arrived.

Tired as he was when he collapsed into the narrow bed, he lay awake, his thoughts alternating between Deybri, the campaign ahead, and the insinuations and implications raised by Taryl's words. Why hadn't the overcommander said more? Or was Rahl supposed to figure things out as he went along? Taryl was attempting a deep and dangerous strategy. That was obvious. It was also clear that Rahl had a part to play, but not immediately. Rahl just wished he had some idea of what Taryl had in mind. All he could figure was that Taryl was on the same side as the Emperor and Jubyl, and the other two Triads might not be, and that it was possible that one or both of them might actually want the rebellion to succeed—or at least take a long time to fail.

In time, he did drift into sleep . . . and nightmares he could not remember when he woke.

Sevenday morning dawned gray and cold, with a bitter wind out of the northeast. The clouds were high and dry, and Rahl doubted they would have rain or snow—not for several days, in any case. When he rode up to the house serving as headquarters right after he and Drakeyt had mustered Third Company, Taryl was again waiting on the side porch, wearing a heavy riding jacket.

Rahl dismounted and vaulted the railing to join the overcommander.

"Here's the letter, ser, and five silvers." Rahl didn't have that much left in the way of coin, but he couldn't think of a better way to spend it than on letting Deybri know how he felt.

Taryl took the letter, smiling and weighing it in his hand. "That's a heavy letter."

"I had a few things to say, ser."

"I hope you said them well. At your age anger is expressed too often, and gentler feelings too seldom."

Rahl shrugged, hoping he had written the right things but not wanting to say so.

Taryl slipped Rahl's letter into a leather case slung on a strap over his shoulder, then lifted out a cloth pouch and extended it to Rahl. "Before I forget, here's your pay for the time since Kysha. From here on out, as a senior mage-guard, you get five silvers an eightday. I can't promise regular pay after this, but I can promise you'll get it all in time."

"Thank you, ser." A half gold an eightday? Rahl never would have dreamed that he'd make that much. No wonder there was respect for the senior mage-guards. He slipped the pouch into the wallet he carried inside his trousers.

"I can't have a senior mage-guard without coins. There are two extra golds in the pouch. Those are for expenses—special supplies or to help Third Company. It's not much for what you'll be doing, but I will need to know on what they're spent when the campaign's over or when we hold Nubyat."

"Yes, ser." Rahl paused. "Might I ask what we will be doing in the next few days?"

"Submarshal Dettyr intends to ride into Dawhut on oneday. He wants no losses and no surprises," Taryl said evenly. "You and Third Company, as well as scouts from other companies, will spend today and tomorrow making sure there are no surprises. By the time you return to the company, Captain Drakeyt should have those orders."

"After that . . ."

"He intends to build up supplies and wait for the marshal."

Rahl winced.

"He's the kind that wants others to take the losses."

"Won't waiting just give the rebels more time and cost us more troopers?"

"That's usually what happens," Taryl said mildly. "I'm working to persuade him that losses are inevitable and that early action will reflect favorably upon him, and that he can assign the most perilous duties to those officers he does not care for so that they will incur such losses."

"Meaning Third Company?"

"And others. The officers he does not like are generally those who look to be most effective. He has his own ideas of what makes a good officer." On Taryl's thin face, the smile that followed his words looked close to predatory. "Now . . . you'd better get back to Third Company. Don't bother sending me any more dispatches. If I want to know something, I'll find you, and if you discover something I should know urgently, it's best if you come to me directly."

"Yes, ser." Rahl offered a smile, a nod of respect, then turned and swung over the porch railing.

On the short ride back to the Dun Cow, Rahl reflected on what Taryl had not said, not directly. One of the principal deficiencies of poor commanders was that they encouraged poor subordinates and discouraged able ones. Was that true in Recluce as well? Certainly, Puvort had that tendency, and Kadara had been the least accomplished of the magisters and magistras with whom he had come in contact—and she'd been the most critical.

Then he checked his pay—almost two golds, in addition to the two golds for expenses. He wouldn't have to worry nearly so much about coins, not for a while.

LXV

Over the next two days, neither Third Company nor the scouts of any other company could discern any sign of rebels or traps on the road to Dawhut or in the area around it, and on midafternoon on oneday, the long column of Imperial forces rode into the city. Under a clear and cold green-blue sky, with a blustery westerly wind, Third Company rode directly in front of the submarshal's headquarters company, and behind the array of outriders and scouts. Word had obviously spread among the locals, because the road was empty except for the Imperial forces. Every stead and dwelling was shuttered, and all the chimneys appeared cold and smokeless.

As Third Company came over the last low rise before the road descended to the bridge over the Awhut River, the odor of the distilleries enveloped Rahl. He glanced at the scattered chimneys to the south, and while half appeared to be cold, the odor from those in operation was still most objectionable.

"How do they live with it?" he murmured.

"Some people get used to anything," replied Drakeyt.

Rahl supposed so, but he had his doubts that, if he lived in Dawhut, he would ever be able to ignore the odor. Certainly, he'd never been able to ignore the aspects of Recluce that had bothered him.

Once they reached the city itself, crossing the northernmost of the two bridges over the river, the column turned south on the river boulevard. The dwellings and shops in Dawhut itself were not shuttered, but the sidewalks and side lanes were mostly deserted, and those people who watched the Imperial forces did so from windows, porches, and, occasionally, balconies. As elsewhere in Merowey, the structures were mainly brick, with a few of stucco and timber, and a comparative handful constructed of worked stone. The roofs were all tile, but the colors varied widely.

According to their orders, Third Company was supposed to form up with the others in the River Square that was the center of Dawhut. The square was midway between the two bridges, a half kay south of the north bridge. Rahl did not see or sense any mage-guards anywhere, and that bothered him.

Just before noon, they rode into the square, a paved open space a good two hundred cubits on a side, surrounded by brick-and-stone buildings, with a modest circular monument, with a statue of a man on horseback—doubtless a famous emperor or local hero. Rahl glanced ahead to the south side of the square, dominated by a large three-story redstone building with green trim and shutters. The oversized signboard proclaimed the River Inn.

From there, he surveyed the square, noting the problem almost immediately. While the square might accommodate a regiment of heavy infantry, there was no way that three regiments and a headquarters company would fit there, even with mounts shoulder to shoulder.

"We won't all fit in here," Rahl observed to Drakeyt, "even squashed together."

"We'll have to try. Those are the orders. I hope that all the scouts are right that there aren't any rebels around, because with all of us in one place, we're grounded geese."

The river side of the square ended in a low gray-stone wall. Rahl could sense that the east side of the wall dropped to a walkway, and the side of the walkway next to the river was actually the top of a stone levee that formed a river wall. There were people walking along the river, but the walkway was enough lower that he could not see them from the square.

Third Company formed up facing the river, as ordered. The submarshal and a small group rode toward the inn. Rahl could see that Taryl was with Dettyr, but the companies that followed them into the square restricted the effectiveness of Rahl's order-senses. Rahl could not follow

Dettyr's actions, except intermittently, since he was facing away from the inn, and since the growing number of mounts and men blocked his vision when he tried to look back over his shoulder.

"They can't get any more into the square," Rahl said. "Not many, anyway. There's still a little space at the edges."

"That's so the submarshal can ride around to the front and tell us . . . whatever he has in mind."

Rahl suspected Drakeyt had almost said something far less complimentary.

Before long, since the square was filled with mounted heavy infantry, the submarshal rode out from somewhere near the inn and along the south side of the square and then along the river wall toward the midpoint of the section of the wall that formed the river side of the square. Taryl rode the mount beside and slightly behind the submarshal.

Just as the submarshal and his escort from the headquarters company almost reached the midpoint of the narrow space between the companies and the square wall above the Awhut River, a man appeared on the wall, less than a score of cubits from the submarshal, carrying a horn bow and a quiver of long arrows. He wore a maroon jacket and khaki trousers—garb similar, if not identical, to the uniforms worn by the rebels who had manned the cannon that had damaged the *Fyrador.* His first shaft was away before almost anyone noticed—except Taryl, because the arrow skittered sideways just before it would have penetrated the submarshal's shoulder.

Taryl gestured, and a firebolt flared toward the would-be assassin from a mage-guard farther back in the submarshal's small entourage. Even so, the archer had loosed a second shaft, and was nocking a third when the firebolt flared across his chest.

Rahl had already urged his own mount forward and out of the front rank toward the wall, his truncheon in hand, because he could sense three others even before they vaulted onto the top of the river wall, bows at the ready, and quivers full.

Rahl's shields deflected the arrows aimed at him, but he could sense that some of the others had struck either troopers or their mounts, and that more archers had appeared on the square wall farther to the south, but closer to Taryl and the chaos-mage.

Rahl slammed the long truncheon, backed with order as well as all the force he could impart, into the nearer archer's leg. He could feel the crunch, and the man toppled forward, flailing, toward the paving stones of the square. Rahl kept his mount moving, somehow managing to swing the truncheon clear of the falling rebel, while moving to attack the next archer. The rebel loosed his shaft point-blank at Rahl.

Rahl's shields took the force, but the impact rocked him back in the saddle, and he had to struggle for a moment to hold his seat. Then he was almost past the archer, and he had to backcut, but the truncheon took the archer in the side of the knee, and he also tumbled off the wall and into the square.

The third archer had fled, scrambling down the back side of the wall and sprinting across the walkway below the wall. A firebolt flared across his back and shoulders, and he collapsed on top of the river wall, twitching but for a moment.

Rahl reined up. Even using both sight and senses, he could detect no other rebels—at least not along the square wall or the river walkway below—and he turned his mount back toward Third Company. Troopers from the headquarters company had taken both fallen archers prisoner. The second archer glared at Rahl as the mage-guard rode past. Rahl ignored the hatred, but he wondered how someone could hate so violently a man he'd never met. Rahl might hate Puvort, and the magisters of Land's End, but they had acted vindictively and dishonestly against Rahl personally. All Rahl had done was to prevent the archer from killing troopers. Several had been wounded, but he had not sensed any deaths besides those of the two rebels killed by the chaos-mage from headquarters company.

". . . still a bad idea . . ." murmured Drakeyt as Rahl edged his mount back into formation beside the captain. "If you and the overcommander hadn't been in front where you could move, there'd have been a lot more casualties."

Rahl agreed, but he only nodded.

The submarshal, unhurt, waited until quiet settled over the companies. Then he began to speak. Loud as Dettyr's voice was, Rahl doubted that many troopers or officers more than thirty cubits away could make out what he said.

". . . Dawhut is just the first step toward reuniting Hamor under the true and rightful Emperor. While some days will be long, and some battles bloody, we will persevere, and we will win. The attempt to disrupt this muster was an example of the evilness of our enemies. This evilness cannot be allowed to poison our land, and no sacrifice is too great to rid us of those who would divide us. . . ."

The beginning of what Dettyr said was trite enough, but with each succeeding word, Rahl just felt that the subcommander would have been better saying nothing— or stopping after the first few words.

Near what Rahl hoped would be the end of the submarshal's too-long speech, Dettyr said, ". . . quarters assignments for each company are being dispatched as I speak. Obviously, the compound here at Dawhut cannot accommodate all of the companies . . . do not attempt to change or to find other arrangements . . . everything has been carefully planned . . ."

If it all had been so carefully planned, then why had the submarshal tried to cram all the companies into the River Square? Good planning would have shown it wasn't possible. Rahl frowned. How had the assassins known where the companies would be—unless someone on the headquarters' staff had let them know?

At that moment, a messenger rode up and handed a folded dispatch to Drakeyt, who immediately opened it and began to read as the submarshal finished his address.

". . . the beginning of a successful effort to return all of Merowey to the order and prosperity afforded by the Emperor, and every trooper and every officer is expected to do his best at all times. You can do no less for yourselves, and I will accept no less." After a pause, Dettyr added, "Long live the Emperor!"

There was another pause before the first and closest companies repeated the words, if raggedly.

"Long live the Emperor!"

"We've been assigned quarters," Drakeyt said, looking up from the dispatch. "Such as they are."

"Not in the High Command compound, I assume?" asked Rahl.

"Hardly. We've got the equivalent of something like three heavy infantry regiments—and that's only a third of the force—and you and I are scarcely in the best graces of the submarshal."

Rahl had to convert that mentally to numbers of troopers. With five companies to a battalion, and four battalions to a regiment—if all the companies were at full strength—Drakeyt was talking about six thousand troopers in Dawhut at the moment. That meant that the land campaign from Kysha would require almost two-thirds of the entire army, possibly against twice as many men. From what Taryl and Marshal Byrna had said, only a fraction of the rebels were highly trained, but each eightday that it took for the Imperial forces to reach the coast reduced that advantage.

"We've been assigned to a stead about a kay to the west of the compound. The holder's name is Korsyn, and he's got a large barn and a shed, and some rooms in the dwelling." Drakeyt raised his eyebrows. "We're to begin scouting the south road tomorrow, and prepare for departure within the eightday. We're also ordered to maximize

supplies for the ride to Nubyat, consistent with established practices."

"Maximize supplies?"

"Scrounge, beg, borrow, offer script—anything but
actually commandeer food. And we're to send daily reports to the submarshal on our efforts."

"Where?"

"His headquarters is in the River Inn—that big place
at the south end of the square over there."

"If size means anything, it must be a good inn,"
replied Rahl dryly. "The best in Dawhut anyway."

"Would you expect any less?"

Rahl shook his head.

XLVI

On twoday morning before dawn, Rahl sat at one end
of a swaybacked trestle table in Korsyn's kitchen eating
fresh-fried egg toast. The kitchen was a long, narrow
room with tan-plaster walls—or walls that might once
have been white and that had become tan from the heat
and smoke of cooking. The big iron stove dominated the
outside wall, and hints of turf smoke escaped from the
ceramic tile that vented the stove into the hearth chimney behind it.

Drakeyt sat to Rahl's right. The holder's consort and
two older daughters were busy frying up stacks of toast
for Third Company—using not quite stale bread that
Quelsyn and the company's acting quartermaster had
gotten from somewhere on oneday afternoon while the
rest of Third Company had been setting up at the holder's
stead.

Rahl almost felt guilty eating a hot breakfast with the
holder and his consort, but Drakeyt didn't seem to have

any qualms as he quickly ate the egg toast drizzled with a thin and barely sweet redberry syrup.

"This is good egg toast," Rahl said.

"Khasia makes the best in this part of the valley," replied Korsyn.

"The best north of Dawhut," added Khasia, not turning from the turf-fired iron stove that warmed the entire kitchen. "And don't you forget it."

"You've not had any . . . trouble . . . last night or this morning?" inquired Drakeyt.

"No, ser. Your troopers been right polite to all of us."

Drakeyt looked to Rahl.

Rahl nodded, sensing that the holder and his consort were saying what they felt.

The night before, after Drakeyt had mustered the company at the stead, he had gathered the squad leaders, and he had been adamant that no harm of any sort was to come to the holder or his family. He'd even indirectly referred to Rahl, by suggesting that, if any questions were raised, there was no doubt that he'd find the truth. All five had glanced at Rahl, even though the mage-guard's name had never been mentioned.

"I wish we could pay you in coin," added Drakeyt.

"Script's better than potatoes and roots we'd have to sell in Nubyat for the prince's paper chits," replied Korsyn. "That paper'll be worthless in less than two seasons."

Rahl thought that Korsyn was being optimistic until the holder spoke again.

"One way or another. The Emperor'll defeat the prince. If he doesn't, the prince still won't have the golds to pay off his paper."

"We won't be here too long," said Drakeyt, ignoring the obvious truth of the holder's words. "I know it's cramped."

"We're not doing too bad. Norwal . . . he's just to the north. He's got two companies there. They claimed he had two big barns. Wanted to know where the second one was." Korsyn laughed roughly. "Burned down three years back. He lost his eldest and his consort and all that year's crop. Never had the golds to rebuild."

"It sounds like the quartering plans were based on information that was years old," offered Drakeyt.

"Five years leastwise."

How much other information was that dated? Rahl wondered.

"Did you ever hear any word about the rebellion?" asked Rahl. "Before it happened, that is?"

"Not a word, not here in Dawhut. I was down in Storisa last spring, and I heard one of the grain factors there saying that things were going to change, but he wouldn't say how. The fellow with him muttered something about a 'real emperor.' I just thought it was talk." The holder turned both palms up.

"Has anyone else you know heard things like that anywhere else?"

"I haven't." Korsyn glanced toward Khasia.

Even though he had not spoken to his consort, and she was working at the stove with her back to the table, Khasia replied. "Calydena was in Nubyat in early summer. She sometimes works the barges with her consort. She told me that they were building big walls around parts of the harbor, almost like a fort. No one seemed to know why."

If true, that would tend to confirm Taryl's supposition that the planning for the rebellion had been ongoing for some time.

Neither Korsyn nor Khasia had any more to offer, and Rahl hurried to finish his breakfast so that he would not delay Drakeyt and Third Company.

Once the two officers were outside the dwelling in the chill and damp northwest wind, Drakeyt stopped and looked at Rahl. "We're better off here. I wouldn't want to be at the compound right now. Not with all the senior majers and the commanders billeted there. The majer there— I think it's Zoacyr—can't be having an easy time."

"The River Inn would be worse with the commanders and the submarshal," Rahl added, thinking about their last encounter with Submarshal Dettyr. "Especially after yesterday. Why would he do something that stupid? Every junior captain in the army would know that you don't pack troops into a confined area like that."

Drakeyt shook his head. "I can't agree with you on that. Remember, the submarshal was once a junior captain, and there are others just like he was around now. There are always some of that type. They don't think; they just follow orders, and they get promoted. They keep following orders, and some of them get promoted until they become majers and commanders."

"All of them?"

"No. Just the ones lucky enough to survive."

Rahl's lips quirked, and he nodded. Was it that way everywhere? He'd seen that in Land's End, and in Nylan. No one had liked it when he'd asked questions. But then, Taryl didn't mind questions. No . . . Taryl didn't mind good questions; he was less patient with stupid questions. But then, could anyone learn to ask good questions without asking stupid ones, at least in the beginning?

In the gray light that preceded dawn, Drakeyt and Rahl resumed walking toward the stable that held but a handful of mounts. The others were either on tether lines or in a corral to the west of the barn where most of the company had bedded down.

"How do you want to handle the scouting today?" asked Rahl.

"I'd thought . . . now, I'm only suggesting . . ." Drakeyt began.

"Suggest away," Rahl said dryly.

"No one's going to be putting traps on the side lanes and the back roads, but holders back there might have seen anyone who did." Drakeyt said blandly.

Why was the captain being so indirect?

"Of course, if you don't agree . . ."

Rahl suddenly understood. "When did you notice?"

Drakeyt gave a sheepish grin. "I didn't. When we were

leaving the square, Balazyr rode over and asked if I knew
you were a senior mage-guard." He shook his head. "I
thought I'd looked close enough when you were posted
to Third Company."

"You did," Rahl replied. "I only got the promotion
when the submarshal's forces joined us in Saluzyl. I
didn't expect it."

"You never said anything. You outrank me, now."

Rahl shrugged. "You're still in command of Third
Company. It doesn't change anything. I still don't know as
much as you do about running a company." He grinned
momentarily. "What did you have in mind?"

"Like I said, no one's going to set traps away from the
main road. So . . . if you could take fourth and fifth
squads and check over anything that looks strange on the
main road, then Quelsyn and I will follow and see what
we can find out from the holders on each side, and on the
side and back lanes."

"How far out should we go?"

"Ten kays, if we can."

"I can do that, but it will take longer for you to check
all the holders. Once we reach ten kays, we can turn back
and start talking to the holders until we meet up."

"Good." Drakeyt nodded.

As he saddled the gelding, Rahl wondered why Drakeyt
had become even more deferential. Or did senior mage-
guards just have a reputation for being difficult?

XLVII

For the next three days, all Rahl and Drakeyt and Third
Company did was ride patrols on the main road to the
southwest of Dawhut, covering the first twenty kays in
depth—and finding no trace of traps and no sign of

rebels. None of the holders along the roads or back lanes could recall anything, and only a handful had even seen tracks that looked different.

When Rahl rode back to Korsyn's stead on fourday, he was still at the head of fourth and fifth squads. He had the feeling that their squad leaders were at ease with him, but that neither Roryt nor Khasmyr was that comfortable with him. That was a problem he didn't see any way to remedy except over time—because the leaders of first and second squads were uneasy with an officer who could disable or even kill an enemy with a truncheon, yet they had no problem with one who used a sabre. To Rahl, that distinction made little sense, but he was well aware that it did to Roryt and Khasmyr.

Rahl's other concern was that any more scouting within the fifteen-kay area southwest of Dawhut would not provide any additional or meaningful information, but that any more delay would certainly be beneficial to the rebels.

He'd no more than reined up outside the small stead stable as the sun touched the horizon when an unfamiliar trooper wearing the sash of a messenger rode toward him.

"Majer Rahl?"

The use of his "new" equivalent rank jarred Rahl, and it was a moment before he replied. "Yes?"

"I have a message from the Mage-Guard Overcommander for you." The trooper extended an envelope.

"Thank you."

"The overcommander requested that I return with your spoken reply, ser."

"In a moment." Rahl opened the envelope and extracted the single sheet, beginning to read immediately.

Rahl—

I'd like to have dinner with you this evening [fourday] when you return from scouting. If that is possible, please tell the messenger, and come to the River Inn as soon as you comfortably can.

I'll most likely be in the conference room. Have yourself announced if you don't see me quickly.

The signature was the familiar "T."

"You can tell the overcommander that I will be there
shortly. Thank you."

"Yes, ser." The messenger inclined his head, then
turned his mount toward the lane leading out to the main
road.

Rahl dismounted, tied the gelding to a post outside the
stable, and hurried into the stead house, where he
washed up quickly, then spotted and brushed his uniform
and jacket. He did not see Drakeyt, and when he returned to the stable area, he spent more than a few moments before he found Fedeor, the fourth squad leader,
in the barn bunking area.

"Ser?"

"I've been summoned to a meeting with the Mage-
Guard Overcommander, and I'd appreciate it if you'd
convey that information to the captain. He and Quelsyn
and the other squads haven't returned yet."

"Yes, ser. We can do that."

"I'd appreciate it." Rahl paused. "You and your men
did a good job out there today—this whole eightday in
fact."

"Thank you, ser."

As Rahl left the barn, he reminded himself that he
needed to tell the squad leaders when they'd performed
well more often.

He took another few moments to give the gelding
some water—not too much—and some handfuls of grain
before he mounted and rode out, back toward Dawhut.
By the time he neared the River Square, the early twilight had deepened into a deep violet dusk, and the brisk
breeze that had chilled the afternoon had faded into occasional light wisps of air that only intensified the unpleasant odors from the distilleries.

To his left, below the river wall and farther to the

south, he could just make out the river-barge piers. Several guards paced the piers, but the barges all seemed empty, and there were no steam tugs anywhere in sight.

The River Square itself was empty except for a squad split into four groups of five, one group at each corner, and Rahl rode across the north side of the square, then the boulevard on the west side before turning back east toward the River Inn. Once in the small courtyard behind the inn, he dismounted before the stable, then had to slip the inn's stableboy a pair of coppers to get him to find a place for the gelding.

"Thank you, ser." The youth smiled.

"You're welcome. He's had a long day, and any fodder or grain you could find . . . we'd both appreciate it."

"We'll see what we can do, ser. We will."

Rahl could sense that his gratitude was genuine. Had the officers and troopers at the inn just been ordering the staff around? "I may be awhile, but I'll be leaving tonight."

"Yes, ser."

With a smile at the young man, Rahl turned and crossed the courtyard, making his way through a side entrance and along a narrow corridor past the doors of several rooms before he pushed open another door and stepped inside the oversized but low-ceilinged foyer of the River Inn. He glanced around, taking in the dark wood paneling lit by too few wall lamps, as well as the worn dark green and maroon carpets and a number of high-backed wooden benches, all of which were empty.

Taryl was actually waiting—if talking to a dark-haired army commander. He turned and gestured to Rahl.

Rahl walked toward the two, then stopped, and inclined his head politely. "Sers."

"Commander Whelayn, this is Senior Mage-Guard Rahl. He's been working with Third Company on the scouting I told you about."

"My pleasure, Commander." Rahl inclined his head.

"No, it's mine. I appreciated your quick action out there on the square the other day."

"I just followed the overcommander's lead. If he hadn't acted so quickly, anything I did wouldn't have mattered."

"But he did, and you did, and that's what counts." The commander inclined his head. "Thank you, Overcommander, and a pleasure to meet you, Majer." With a nod and a smile, the sandy-haired commander stepped away from the two mage-guards.

"It's good to see you, Rahl. You're looking fit."

"Physically, yes, ser." Rahl was feeling worried because he really hadn't practiced enough on some of the skills that Taryl had worked him hard to develop.

"Not working hard enough on the more obscure order-skills?"

"Probably not."

Taryl only nodded, and that made Rahl feel more guilty than if the overcommander had chastised him, even mildly.

"There's a good bistro around the corner, two corners actually," Taryl went on. "The food here is less than outstanding, and that's overstating it." He turned and walked toward the double doors of the main entrance to the foyer.

Rahl had to take three quick steps to catch up.

Once they were outside, Taryl walked to the west end of the square—the southwest corner—and turned south.

Rahl studied the streets and the alleyways, looking back toward the square as well. He could only see the patrolling troopers and a few handfuls of troopers and officers on the boulevard. "There's no one out here."

"The submarshal imposed a night-time curfew," Taryl said.

"There aren't that many rebels here."

"Outside of a few malcontents, there aren't any from Dawhut. We interrogated the two you disabled. They were part of a squad that came from Sastak."

"But he imposed a curfew?"

"He did." Taryl turned westward at the next corner, then gestured toward a lit doorway ahead. "Here we are."

The bistro's front door had an etched-glass window, showing a well-endowed bull standing on his hind legs and holding a covered tray on a raised front hoof. The woodwork was varnished heavily enough that it shimmered in the light cast by the two lamps flanking the entrance.

Rahl opened the door for the overcommander.

"Thank you."

Inside, the walls and the tables were of the same varnished dark golden oak, and the hangings flanking the front window were of a pale blue. The only other patrons, not surprisingly, given the curfew, were two commanders seated at the side table just back from the window. They glanced toward the mage-guards, then quickly ignored Rahl and Taryl.

Rahl suppressed a smile and continued to study the bistro. For all that it was no larger than Eneld's cantina in Swarthheld, Rahl could see and sense that the cooking would likely be far better than what Seorya had served him when he'd been a clerk at the Nylan Merchant Association.

"Sers?" asked a trim, graying woman in a pale blue tunic. An old reddish slash scar ran from below her left ear to a point just short of the corner of her mouth.

"A quiet corner," Taryl suggested.

"This way." She smiled professionally, leading them to the far corner and a circular table that could have seated four easily. "They're all quiet, but this one is quieter."

"Thank you."

The woman nodded. "What would you like to drink?"

"A good dark ale," Taryl said.

"An amber lager."

"I'll get those, then tell you the fare for the evening."

From her bearing, and from what he could sense, Rahl had the feeling she might well be the proprietress.

"How did you find this place?" asked Rahl after a moment.

"I asked some of the staff at the River Inn."

The proprietress returned with two large crystal mugs. "Here you are, sers."

"Thank you."

"Tonight, we're a little limited. We have a cream burhka—it's richer and only mildly spicy—and we have some lamb cutlets—they're almost mutton cutlets, but they are tender, and they're served with piastoni and mint sauce. There's also a rich fowl pie with jaspard mushrooms and onions." She smiled again, the expression concealing nervousness.

"I'll have the fowl pie," replied Taryl.

"So will I," replied Rahl. The cream burhka might indeed be good, as might the cutlets, but he'd had more than enough burhka and mutton, especially mutton, since dried mutton strips were part of the field rations.

"Good choice."

Neither man spoke until she had left.

Rahl took a sip of the lager. If not the best he'd ever tasted, it was close, and he had to wonder what it might cost.

"I take it that you've found no rebels and no traps near Dawhut," said Taryl, taking a small swallow of his ale. "This is rather good, surprisingly so for a backcountry city bistro."

"The lager's good, too."

"Rebels?" prompted Taryl.

"Not a one. I did see some barges at the piers as I rode in. They were all empty."

"We'll be able to use those to move supplies," Taryl said. "That will save some of the horses and speed things up."

"Only downstream. There aren't any tugs. Golyat must have kept them in Nubyat to help defend the port."

"I'm certain he has. He may even have mounted cannon on them."

"That's another reason for a land attack?"

"Another reason?"

Rahl offered an embarrassed smile. "I forgot to mention something else. When I was talking to the holder's consort at the stead where we're quartered, she told me that one of her neighbors whose family runs the barges was in Nubyat at the end of spring or early summer. The neighbor said that they were building walls all around the harbor."

"We'd thought something of the sort, but if Golyat had already begun to build walls then, he had to have planned the construction far earlier. I'll pass that on to Jubyl and the Emperor. Anything else you forgot to mention."

"No, ser, except that it does seem we're taking a long time to travel across the part of Merowey that doesn't have many rebels."

The proprietress appeared with two white-china platters rimmed in blue, setting one before each man. "Here you go, sers."

Taryl took another swallow of his dark ale. "The submarshal and marshal believe in deliberation, very great deliberation, in fact."

"There's a difference between deliberation and stupidity, ser, begging your pardon. The other day, Drakeyt pointed out that with all of us jammed up in the square and on the boulevard, we were as vulnerable as grounded geese. We were fortunate that there were only a few men crazy enough to attack."

"And that you were prepared to act, something I've already noted in my reports." Taryl cleared his throat and went on. "Even that caused a score of injuries, because some of the horses were spooked. We lost at least four mounts, and another half score are likely to be lamed for eightdays, if not permanently."

"Why did the submarshal think we all could even get into the square? We weren't allowed to scout the city proper. What purpose did putting all those troopers in the square serve, especially in a city that's loyal?"

"I'm sure that Submarshal Dettyr will have answers for those questions when the marshal or the Overmarshal requests an explanation."

Rahl noted Taryl's certainty that the questions would be asked, as well as the implication that Dettyr's responses would be inadequate.

"Now . . . tell me your impressions of the road as far as you've scouted."

Rahl also understood that Taryl had said what he would say about Dettyr.

XLVIII

When the submarshal's forces left Dawhut on sixday, by that midmorning Third Company was already some thirty kays farther southwest along on the road from Dawhut to Nubyat after having spent two days on the road already.

Ever since the night of his dinner with Taryl, for which the overcommander had paid, Rahl had attempted to get back to practicing the order-skills he had used but seldom on the scouting missions, particularly his attempts at using a mirror to scree places away from him. He'd paid Khasia four coppers for an old framed mirror, little more than a span square, and wrapped it in fleece and rags and stowed it on top in his saddlebags.

His efforts with the glass had resulted in some images, but mostly of places where he had already been—although from the scenes displayed mistily in the glass what he saw were events that were taking place as he watched—three servants straightening up the Triad's quarters in the Palace and the Empress walking through the empty receiving room. She looked worried and sad for the few moments that Rahl could hold the image. He had no success in calling up an image of Deybri, although his head felt as if it were splitting when he finished.

He had had more success with strengthening shields, and in using order to move small objects. His efforts in shifting the balance and position of order within those small objects were limited at best. That was an area where he needed more practice. It was just that it was all so tiring after a full day of riding and using order-skills to seek out possible traps and rebel ambushes—even when he found none.

Rahl was riding forward with the scouts. The road was lumpy, but not badly rutted, if nothing to compare to the highways near Swartheld or Cigoerne—or the great highway of Recluce. He was glad that the clouds and blustery weather of the past days had been replaced by clear and sunny skies. That had resulted in clearer and colder nights, and frost by morning, but Rahl preferred frost to damp and rain. Some of the others didn't, he could tell by the murmured complaints he could overhear.

The boglands had given way to country with more hills and trees as well as with more steads and fields—except for the stretch before Third Company, which was rockier and more desolate, with trees more widely spaced on the hillsides. The road had begun to rise gradually toward a tree-lined gap between two hills more than a kay ahead. The stream on the right of the road had cut its path downward so that while the roadbed followed the slope up, with each cubit that Rahl rode, the gully looked as though it would get comparatively deeper. The hill on the right looked to have a low bluff rising almost from the side of the road.

"Scouts! Halt!" Rahl projected his voice with a slight touch of order.

"Yes, ser."

Even the scouts a half kay ahead reined up.

Rahl looked more closely at the hill on the right. The

bluff was cut from red sandstone, with some small pines clinging to the sheer stone. He couldn't tell exactly, but the bluff was no more than perhaps fifteen cubits high and flat on top, overlooking the road. Something didn't feel right, and the last time he'd ignored that feeling . . . that had been the flood.

He dismounted, then handed the gelding's reins to Shanyr, the other outrider, and carefully opened his saddlebags and took out the small framed glass. He could certainly try to see what was on the hill ahead. If it didn't work, then he'd have to get closer, perhaps scouting through the trees on the far side of the stream.

He looked down at the glass, concentrating on chaos and on the hillside ahead.

The glass, which had been reflecting his face and the green-blue sky overhead, began to show a swirling white mist, then figures—men sitting on boulders beside trees. Resting against the trees were horn bows. The men looked to be wearing jackets of various colors, but khaki trousers. A thin piercing line of agony ran from the mirror to Rahl's skull—that was the way it felt—and it grew stronger with every moment. His eyes watered so much that he could not make out the details in the glass, and he released the image, rubbing his temples with his free hand.

Slowly, he straightened, then rewrapped the glass and replaced it in the saddlebags.

"Ser?"

"Archers ahead, on the hillside." Rahl took the reins back and swung up into the saddle. "Hold here. I need to ride back and talk to Captain Drakeyt."

"Yes, ser."

Rahl's headache had only subsided slightly by the time he neared first squad and Drakeyt. He glanced back over his shoulder, then nodded. The bluff was not in sight, and that meant that the archers most likely hadn't spotted the main body of the company. He turned back to the captain.

"What is it?"

"We've got a bunch of rebel archers up ahead. They're somewhere on the hill up there, probably in the trees just behind the flat area back of that low bluff on the other side of the stream. I couldn't sense how many, but I don't think there are more than a score."

Drakeyt glanced from Rahl to the bluff, then nodded. "Up there, the ravine's too wide and deep for us to cross. What do you have in mind?"

"I'd like to try to take them, at least capture a few, without too many casualties. Once they see the company is holding position, if we don't move after a while, they'll back off. I'd suggest that I take fourth squad and fifth squad. We'll backtrack just down there where we can cross the stream. Then we'll move through the trees—the undergrowth isn't very heavy here—and circle the hill, then move up from the southwest. If first squad crosses the stream with us, but just follows the slope above the stream, if any of the archers try to flee, they'll be moving toward the squad."

"Second and third squads are to take their time moving toward the bluff on the road, I take it?" asked Drakeyt.

"After taking a break in plain sight of the archers, but well out of range of any that might have tried to sneak closer."

"That might work."

Rahl shrugged. "I'm ready for any better ideas."

Drakeyt laughed. "We could circle the hill and avoid them altogether, but somehow, I don't think the submarshal or the overcommander would be especially happy about that."

"No. We're supposed to find and remove all problems without casualties and without causing additional delays."

"And without any inconvenience to the most honorable submarshal," murmured Drakeyt in a voice low enough not to carry to the troopers reined up behind the two officers. "Your plan is as good as any, except that I'd suggest half of second squad accompany first squad. That will still leave a large-enough-looking force on the road, but give more coverage for any rebels who might flee."

"That's better," agreed Rahl.

After a short break, Rahl led his squads back down the road a good quarter kay to where the horses could easily descend the slope to the stream and then climb the other side.

Drakeyt followed with his squad and a half, while Quelsyn held the road with the remaining forces and the few pack animals. Rahl could sense the combination of doubt and puzzlement within the senior squad leader. While he did not know the actual reasons for Quelsyn's feelings, he was getting the idea that the senior squad leader was one of those men who had trouble accepting anything he could not see, touch, or experience. Since Quelsyn had no order-senses, the trooper had no understanding of why what Rahl did usually worked.

Rahl had ridden at the head of his squads through the low pine trees and up a slope that steepened gradually for almost a kay before his headache subsided into a dull ache. He did not begin to sense the archers with his direct order-senses until they were on the back side of the hill, less than half a kay from the bluff.

"Quiet riding. Pass it back," he ordered.

From what he could sense, the archers did not react or discover his squads during the entire time that they circled the back of the hill and turned back uphill.

Rahl reined up, lifting his arm to let the troopers know. "Squad leaders forward," he added quietly. "Pass it back."

Within a few moments, both squad leaders reined up beside Rahl.

He glanced from Fedeor to Fysett, then spoke. "There are less than a score of archers, but they all have horn bows at hand. They're watching the road, and, if we're quiet, we can probably get within a quarter kay without their noticing, maybe closer. The way we're approaching will allow us to ride about five across, roughly abreast. If possible, I'd like a few prisoners, but not at the cost of troopers."

Rahl's last words brought a nod from Fysett.

"We'll quiet ride uphill from here. I'd judge we'll get another hundred, maybe two hundred cubits before they notice. When they do, I'll signal, and we'll charge—as we can."

"More like a slow canter," suggested Fedeor.

"The best we can do," said Rahl.

They nodded.

Rahl waited for them to pass the word in low whispers, then started the gelding uphill once more.

They were within a hundred cubits of the nearest archer, when Rahl sensed movement among the archers. He dropped his arm and urged the gelding forward, although the pace was little faster than a quick trot, given the need to avoid the scrubby and wide-spaced pine trees. He and the other five troopers riding slightly before him were almost at the south edge of the narrow clear space above the bluff before the warning cries went up.

"Imperials! Imperials!"

Rahl had his truncheon out, but the troopers were more experienced than he was in the semimelee, and their heavy sabres were far more effective than the horn bows of the rebel archers. Within moments, the rebels were either dead or wounded or disarmed, but several had gotten off shafts—Rahl had felt them strike one or two of his troopers, but he had not sensed death.

He reined up and tried to order-sense any archers who might have fled to the north, but he could not sense anyone in the trees away from the small clearing at the edge of the red-sandstone bluff. He turned the gelding back toward the trees from where the archers had tried to defend themselves.

"We got 'em all. Don't think any of them escaped, ser," announced Fedeor, reining up short of Rahl.

"How about our men?"

"Two took shafts. Looks like they'll be all right."

"I'll need to look at them in a bit."

"Yes, ser."

Rahl looked over what remained of the rebel archers. Six lay where they had been cut down. Two were wounded, and from the fading order and chaos, one was dying. Two others stood silently, as their hands were bound. All wore the khaki shirts and trousers and maroon vests of the rebels, but each man's outer jacket was different. Each also bore the hint of chaos.

After tying the gelding to one of the larger pines, Rahl strode toward the nearest of the prisoners—a gaunt-faced man who just looked blankly at Rahl as he approached. One of fourth squad's troopers had bound his hands and stood with a sabre at the ready.

"Why did you join the rebels?" asked Rahl.

"To fight for a real emperor, ser."

"Who sent you here?"

"The Emperor Golyat, ser."

"Where did you come from?"

"The Emperor sent us, ser."

"When did you leave Nubyat?"

"When the Emperor sent us, ser."

"How did you travel to get here?"

"I wouldn't know, ser."

Rahl kept asking questions, but the answers were much the same, either a variation on the Emperor or a variation on not knowing. Rahl could sense that the archer was not lying, and that the answers were the only ones that he had. Somehow, some sort of chaos compulsion or lock had been placed on him. Rahl would have to investigate that later.

He walked across the clearing to the second un-wounded archer, beginning his questioning with, "Why did you join the rebels?"

"To fight for a real emperor, ser."

Every reply was almost identical to those given by the first archer.

He turned to the one wounded archer who was still living . . . and fared no better.

In disgust, he stepped back and looked over the surviving archers. He was missing something. Something so obvious . . . Then he shook his head. None of the archers were young. In fact, all were at least as old as his own father.

He walked over and began to check the bodies, including their hands.

"They're all graybeards, ser," offered Fysett from his mount. "Every last one of them."

Rahl also studied their hands. Several had welts and scars around the wrists, and the calluses on their hands and fingers were relatively light.

"Shackle marks, I'd wager," offered Fysett, looking over Rahl's shoulder.

After a moment, Rahl nodded. That would make sense. "I need to check our wounded. Then we'll head back."

"Yes, ser."

"Oh . . . did they have mounts?"

"Yes, ser. They were tied back in the trees. Most of them sorry swaybacks. They could carry packs, though."

"We can use them for that." Rahl walked toward the wounded troopers.

One man had taken a shaft in the shoulder, and another in the thigh. Neither wound had gushed blood, and there were only slight amounts of chaos. Rahl did his best to remove that chaos. The effort did return his headache from merely a dull ache to a more active and sharp-edged throbbing. He didn't know how Deybri and the other healers stood it, day after day. He smiled wryly. He did; he'd seen and sensed the pain and the exhaustion, and the determination to keep healing.

He looked at the last trooper he'd tried to help. "Keep the wound clean. You'll go back to the main force until you're stronger, but have the healers there keep checking it."

"Yes, ser."

Rahl remounted and rode to the front of the squads, now lined up in double file and ready to return to Third Company.

"Ready to ride, ser," offered Fedeor.

"You have all the prisoners and all the bows and quivers—and their horses?" He supposed he was being callous by not burying the dead, but the rocky sandstone wasn't suitable, and they didn't have more than a spade per squad.

"Yes, ser."

"Let's go." He urged the gelding downhill, back toward Drakeyt and first squad.

When they neared the other troopers, Rahl was careful to announce their presence. "Fourth and fifth squads returning!" he yelled, using order to boost the words through the pines.

"Squads returning," someone echoed.

Rahl still was wary until he could sense that the waiting troopers were ready with weapons but holding position. He rode through the last of the pines between him and Drakeyt. "Mission accomplished."

"Did any of them run this way?" asked the captain.

"No." Rahl reined up. That was another thing he should have noticed. "None of them tried to run at all, even when it was clear that we had them trapped."

"None?"

Rahl shook his head. "We have two of our men wounded. They should recover, but they'll have trouble keeping up with us. We'll send them back with the prisoners."

Drakeyt raised his eyebrows.

"There were three. But all of them were under chaos compulsions. They might even have been trained as archers under those compulsions. I don't know how it was done, but the overcommander might be able to find out. Also, they were all graybeards, or they would have been if they'd had beards."

"Why would . . ."

"Prisoners or roadworkers, I'd guess. Not many people in Merowey would really care if they disappeared, and those that would were probably told that the men were better off than if they'd been caught by a mage-guard."

"Would they have been?"

"By most mage-guards, probably," admitted Rahl. "Most who resist capture get flamed on the spot."

"Don't the Codex breakers know that?"

"Some do. Theft and battery and killing are all offenses against order. Everyone's taught that." Rahl shrugged tiredly. "I wasn't exactly the perfect child growing up, but even I knew that." Of course, a small voice within him pointed out, he'd still gotten away with killing a Jeranyi pirate in Land's End . . . but only because no one had cared that a pirate helping a dishonest factor had died.

"You don't sound convinced," Drakeyt said. "And you're a mage-guard."

"It's better than the alternatives," Rahl replied. Was it? Or was he just justifying things? "We'd better head back to the road."

Drakeyt nodded. "To the rear, ride! Back to the road!"

XLIX

Five more days of scouting brought Third Company within ten kays of Helstyra—another river town. According to Drakeyt's maps, perused by the two officers as they paused for a short rest, the town sat on the west bank of the Awhut River. There was a large half bow lake east of the river to the east, the ends of the lake little more than a kay from the river. Between where Third Company was and the town was a line of low hills. Beyond them, the maps showed that the road ran straight into Helstyra.

"Messengers coming forward, sers!" came the call from Quelsyn.

Rahl turned in the saddle to watch as two troopers rode along the shoulder of the road toward them. He recognized the pair as having been sent with reports and the archer prisoners, as well as the wounded, back to the marshal and Taryl five days earlier.

"Sers! Dispatches!"

"I'm not certain how welcome those might be," murmured Drakeyt.

Rahl smiled faintly at the captain's words, but just accepted the envelope extended by the trooper. Drakeyt took his dispatch as well.

After breaking the seal, opening the folded sheet, and seeing the first words of his dispatch, Rahl frowned. Why had Taryl addressed it to "Senior Mage-Guard Rahl" when all others had been addressed to him as Rahl? He continued to read, still puzzling over the salutation.

The rebel archers whom you sent for further interrogation proved most useful, not in what they revealed, which was little more than you already had determined and reported, but in confirming the precise nature of those mage-guards who have shifted their loyalties to the rebel Golyat. The means by which the rebels were trained and dispatched result from a technique developed by a most senior mage-guard. At the time of its discovery, the Triad banned the further dissemination and/or use of the technique. It has not been used heretofore, because any senior mage-guard can discover that it has been used, as did you, and, given the high-level skills required, it is unlikely that many mage-guards are capable of employing the technique. You might recall that you encountered one of originator's trusted subordinates in the course of historical research sometime back, and you can understand the delicacy of this discovery, but it is necessary that you understand fully the dangers involved in any personal meetings with such individuals, even under the guise of a truce or armistice, unlikely as that may now seem.

Rahl understood most clearly the two levels of messages conveyed. What he did not understand was why Taryl had chosen to reveal the identity of the originator— unless Taryl wanted to make sure that someone else knew. That thought chilled Rahl. He continued to read.

Because of the importance of your discovery, as well as the effectiveness and efficiency of scouting and road-clearing accomplished by you and Captain Drakeyt, I also wanted to commend you both, and to let you know that the marshal and the Emperor have been apprised of your good work, and that you should not be unduly influenced by those who do not understand what you have accomplished. Lack of understanding carries its own penalties.

With the last words and the formal full signature, Rahl understood the salutation. He looked across to Drakeyt, who was not only frowning at the dispatch he held, but seething within.

"I take it that the submarshal was less than complimentary," Rahl said dryly.

"You read it." Drakeyt eased his mount closer to Rahl and practically thrust the dispatch at the mage-guard.

Rahl took it and began to read.

Captain Drakeyt—
I am amazed and astonished that you bothered even to spend the time and effort to dispatch your latest rebel prisoners. Given their imbecilic nature, there is no question of your success, but great question as to how you managed to incur any casualties at all.

Consider this notice that further lack of competence will not be tolerated.

Rahl read it again. Could the submarshal truly be that stupid? He shook his head.

"What do you think?" asked Drakeyt.

"I'm amazed at his stupidity," Rahl replied. "I think you should read the dispatch I just received from the overcommander." He handed both Drakeyt's dispatch and the one he had received to the older officer.

When Drakeyt finished reading Taryl's dispatch, he looked to Rahl. "The overcommander outranks the submarshal, doesn't he?"

"He's not in the chain of direct command, but, yes, he does."

Drakeyt nodded, his smile faint and grim. "Machinations within machinations. I'm just a simple officer. What do you suggest?"

"What the overcommander recommended—that we ignore the submarshal and deal with the rebels. You weren't really ordered to do anything. I've never gone wrong following his guidance, and he's the one who rescued me from the slag heaps at Luba."

Drakeyt looked stunned for a moment, and Rahl realized that he'd never told the other officer that.

"I'd been drugged with something that blocked my memories and skills. I'd been slipped into the ironworks and passed off as a Codex breaker. I spent seasons as a loader before he discovered I had order-skills."

Drakeyt shook his head. "The longer I'm around you, the more I discover, and the less the world seems to be what I thought it was."

That was life, Rahl was beginning to think. "We might as well keep scouting. It'll keep us at a distance from the submarshal. I'll head back to the outriders."

Drakeyt nodded.

Rahl continued to scan the hills and the road, but the

only thing he found unusual was that there were no steads nearby, although he could see that the hills had been logged in sections, and the grasslands between the remaining patches of trees had been grazed, heavily in places.

The hills were low, and the road curved between two of them. At the end of the long curve, the road straightened, heading toward a wide swampy marsh. Rahl could see why there weren't that many steads, and he suspected that the area would be most unpleasant in summer.

Ahead, a causeway some sixty cubits wide arrowed through the swampy marsh and extended at least two kays toward Helstyra. Gray-stone riprap bordered the causeway on each side. The section of road atop the causeway was paved—the first section of paved road Rahl had seen since leaving Kysha—and was a good fifteen cubits wide.

"Ugly-looking swamp, ser," observed Alrydd, riding to Rahl's right as they neared the beginning of the causeway.

"It is." Rahl had been studying the approaches to the swamp, but could detect nothing that seemed unusual. The winter-browned swamp grass rose less than a cubit above the dark and oily-looking water that extended from the edge of the gray riprap out through the marsh grasses eastward toward intermittent scraggly clumps of low bushes. Amid the swamp grasses were open spaces of the black water. Several hundred cubits ahead on the left was a large grove of live oaks.

Rahl could see and sense the ravages of age that permeated the ancient, massive, and clearly dying ancient live oaks rising from the marshlands to the southeast of the road. Even the moss hanging from sagging and rugged limbs was a whitish gray. Despite the bright if cold afternoon sunlight, an aura of gloom shrouded the trees.

The closer he rode to the trees, the more uneasy Rahl became, yet he could detect no chaos, and nothing that seemed unusual. The oaks were so tall that he had not realized that they were not all that close to the road, cer-

tainly a good hundred-fifty cubits to the left. Then he
swallowed because he realized that he could not sense into
the swamp as far as the oaks. Why couldn't he? What was
it about the swamp? Or was it this swamp? He knew water
affected what chaos-mages could perceive, but why would
it affect him?

In one of the nearer spaces of still black water, he saw a
set of ripples radiating from one point, then recognized a
water rat swimming into the higher marsh grasses. Farther
to the south, there was a flurry of wings and two golden
cranes lifted off, skimming over the grass and past the
oaks, then to the southeast.

Then he saw a wider wedgelike head, attached to a
scaly body, swimming parallel to the causeway before
heading back toward the oaks. While he'd never seen
one before, the creature matched an illustration he'd
seen of a stun-lizard. It was smaller than the ones described as inhabiting the Great Forest of the druids, but
he had the feeling it was either the same or similar, and
a chill ran down his spine.

Rahl kept studying the swamp on both sides, but on the
right side of the causeway, there were only bushes, water,
and grass for at least a kay and perhaps twice as far. As he
and Alrydd passed even with the oaks, Rahl tried even
harder to sense what might be there, but his order-senses
did not reach that far, although they certainly had extended much farther all the time—until now. He could
see no movement in the trees, though, and nothing unnatural.

He used his order-senses to scan the bushy miniature
islands, but found nothing, then glanced back along the
causeway. First squad was drawing abreast of the oak
grove, but what could happen from a hundred and fifty
cubits away across an impassable swamp?

After another moment of studying the trees, he looked
forward again. The lead scouts were another half kay
ahead, but there was nothing except brush and grass near
the causeway where they rode.

Sprung. The sound was so faint Rahl almost didn't hear it.

He turned in the saddle just in time to see an ancient trunk drop into the swamp and a hail of arrows arch from the oaks down into the road, as well as onto the causeway and the swampy water on the left side of the causeway.

He turned the chestnut and urged his mount back toward the main body of Third Company at a full canter, hoping he didn't fall off onto the hard stone pavement.

As he neared first squad and Drakeyt, he still did not see or sense anything moving in the swamp, except for the ripples from the fallen trunk and various birds taking wing in and around the live oaks, reacting to the impact of the ancient trunk on the dark water.

"Look to Whebyt there," Drakeyt clipped, as Rahl reined up.

Rahl dismounted as quickly as he could, kneeling by the trooper who'd been lowered out of the saddle. Quarrel-like shafts protruded from his thigh and shoulder. Blood was not gushing, but his trousers and shirt showed wide dark patches.

If Rahl could stop the bleeding . . . After a moment, he concentrated, trying to erect tiny shields around the quarrels. He could sense the blood flow stopping, and he turned his head. "I can keep him from bleeding for a bit, until you can get this out and dress the wound. Then . . . maybe . . . I can do more."

A trooper appeared, then another, and between the two, they eased out both shafts, cleaned the wounds as they could, and bound them. After that, Rahl removed the wound chaos.

Finally, he stood and looked at Drakeyt, who had ridden off down the column and returned.

"I think I did enough that Whebyt will make it."

"That helps." Drakeyt's voice was slightly flat. "We lost one other, and there are three more with slight wounds."

"I'm sorry. I can't sense things as far in this swamp.

I don't know why. We didn't see anything, even after the trap was sprung."

"You can't get them all," Drakeyt replied tersely, his tone partly belying his words.

Rahl stiffened, even as he still felt that he should have done more, but how could he have gotten close enough to the oaks when there was no solid land there? How could they have avoided the swamp without going scores of kays out of their way? How could he have known?

"I'll keep doing what I can," he finally said. He walked toward his mount and climbed back into the saddle. Without looking at Drakeyt, he turned the gelding back toward Alrydd.

When Rahl reached the outrider, he just reined up and waited until the captain ordered Third Company forward. Then he eased the gelding forward. His head ached, and he rubbed his temples with his free hand. He still wondered how the rebels had managed to rig the quarrel-thrower to the falling trunk and what had set it off, but he wasn't about to try to make his way through an unknown swamp, infested with stun-lizards, to figure it out. He'd have to send a message to Taryl warning about that tactic. There were still more than a few of the oaks standing.

Rahl couldn't help breathing more easily when they reached the end of the causeway without any more difficulties. Within half a kay of the end of the swamp, the land firmed up, and Rahl could see steads, and well-ordered lines of low trees—orchards of some sort, although he did not recognize the trees. He also realized that he had regained the fuller range of his order-senses, and, again, he wondered what it had been about the swamp. The stun-lizards?

After riding another kay through the orchard steads, Rahl noted that the ground to the left of the road sloped gently upward, not even steeply enough to be considered a hill, but perhaps a rise. The orchards gave way to fallow fields edged with low stone walls, barely more than knee high.

Just ahead to the left was a lane that ran up the rise. Rahl turned to Alrydd. "I'm going to ride up that a way, just to make sure there's nothing up there."

"Best I be going with you, ser."

Rahl nodded and turned the gelding onto the lane, which was bordered on both sides by the low stone walls, and the fields within the walls had been turned after whatever had been planted had been harvested. A small house was set farther to the west, with a barn behind it. Rahl did not see anyone outside in the late afternoon, although with no wind, the clear skies, and bright sun, the day was almost pleasant, cool as it was.

Just short of the top of the rise was a hay wagon, heaped high with bales of hay, the horse tethered to a tree stump, as the farmer loaded another bale. Rahl extended his order-senses, stifling a wince as he did so, because the effort sent miniature knives of pain through his skull. He could sense no chaos in the man, who scarcely looked in his direction.

After a moment, Rahl turned the gelding back down the lane.

"Just the one hay wagon, ser?"

"That's all."

At the road, Rahl turned the gelding back toward Helstyra. He thought he caught a glimpse of water ahead— perhaps the river or the lake. After he had ridden a quarter kay or so, he looked back over his shoulder, catching sight of the hay wagon.

He frowned, then pulled the gelding off the road and looked back down the road. First squad had almost reached the place where the lane and the road joined.

Across the fallow field and low stone fence, Rahl could see the wagon heaped high with bundled hay and pulled by a bony horse now heading down toward the main road. The farmer walked beside the horse, leading it with a tether, but he was walking fast. Too fast, Rahl thought.

Could the wagon be another trap? Had he missed it because his head ached too much? Rahl had his doubts, but even as he turned the gelding back toward the road, urging him into a canter, he extended his order-senses, trying to ignore the pain. The teamster still held no chaos, and there was little around the wagon, but there was something . . .

Rahl strained to sense what he could, but it was hard trying to sense something while riding, especially after what had already happened.

The wagon had been perhaps three hundred cubits from the intersection with the main road, rolling down the gentle slope behind the horse, when Rahl had begun to hurry back. He could not sense anything else until he was within a few hundred cubits.

Barrels—there were barrels in the low-sided wagon, and they were not stored on their butt ends, but stacked on their sides, roped in place and facing forward. Why would anyone store or transport barrels that way? How had he missed them?

"Company to the rear, ride!" Rahl yelled, trying to order-boost his words to Drakeyt. He could see the captain ordering a halt, but the squads only froze in position.

Rahl kept the gelding moving.

"To the rear, ride!" he bellowed again, as he got within easy hailing distance.

At that moment, the teamster cut the horse loose from the traces—leather, not wood—and swung up onto the horse, then galloped forward just enough to get clear before turning his mount and galloping back up the lane. The wagon began to pick up speed, rumbling more loudly down the lane toward Third Company.

Rahl jabbed his heels into the gelding, hanging on. He had to get closer. He just had to.

He was almost at the intersection, almost within a handful of cubits of first squad, when he sensed a wave of chaos coming from the wagon.

All he could do was throw up shields as strong as he could, extending them as far toward first squad as he could.

CRUMP!

Rahl felt himself being hurled from the saddle, as though a giant invisible hand had swatted him.

Then a second hand—this one hot and black—slammed him into the ground.

L

Everything hurt. That was Rahl's first feeling.

"He's coming 'round, Captain."

Rahl didn't recognize the voice, and his vision was so blurry that all he could see at first were colored blotches against a blue-green haze that was probably the sky. It had to be, he realized, because he was lying on his back. His sight began to improve, but large unseen hammers pounded on his skull. From what he could sense, he didn't think he'd broken anything, but he had the feeling he was covered with bruises, especially on his right side.

After a time, he slowly sat up, then struggled to his feet, only to take a half score of steps to a low stone wall where he sat down again. His legs were wobbly.

Drakeyt rode over and reined up. "How are you feeling?"

"I'd have to say . . ." Rahl's throat was so dry and raw that he couldn't say any more.

The captain handed him a water bottle, reaching down.

Rahl's shoulders protested as he lifted a hand to take the bottle. He drank slowly, then added, "I've felt better." He took another swallow, glancing around. To his left gray smoke swirled into the sky, and he realized that he'd been smelling the acrid odor of something burning.

Drakeyt followed Rahl's glance. "We had to move you and the company—that blast set fire to the orchards on the south side of the road." He paused. "What was it?"

"It was a makeshift cammabark cannon," Rahl said slowly, "barrels of cammabark with an iron plate at the bottom and metal fragments on top."

"I thought it was something like that." Drakeyt looked down from the saddle at Rahl. "Everyone should have been shredded. What did you do?"

"I tried to shield Third Company."

"Whatever you did saved a good score of troopers. Could have been more."

"How many didn't I save?"

"About half of second squad, and their mounts," Drakeyt admitted. "I had the men buried short of the woods up there." He gestured behind Rahl. "Not much of a woods, but better than in the fields."

Rahl looked down. He'd been worn-out, in order terms, from the mess on the causeway, and he hadn't realized how much. So another ten men, if not more, had died. But what was he supposed to do? He couldn't be up in front to look to one kind of trap or ambush and also be with the main body of Third Company to prevent or protect against another kind of attack. And he couldn't just tell Drakeyt that the scouting and progress was over for the day because he was tired.

He could feel rage and frustration building, but he forced himself to take a deep and slow breath. Getting angry would only make him less able . . . but he still hated the unfairness of the situation. Slowly, he stood, looking for the gelding.

"Over there," Drakeyt said. "You up to this?"

"I won't be very good," Rahl admitted. "Better than not having a mage-guard, but not much."

"We've only got another three kays until we're in town. I didn't know how you'd be feeling. So I sent scouts out. They didn't see any rebels, and no one attacked them."

Rahl walked to the gelding, then checked the horse, but he didn't see or sense any injuries. It took all of his remaining strength, or so it felt, to clamber up into the saddle.

He rode slowly forward toward Alrydd. When he reached the outrider, he said, "We're going as far as the town." That was a stupid statement, because the sun was low enough in the western sky that the company wasn't about to go anywhere else, and Helstyra was only a few kays away.

"Tried to save 'em all, didn't you, ser?"

"I wasn't strong enough to save everyone." Rahl supposed the trooper knew that, but he felt he had to make that clear.

The trooper nodded. Rahl could sense the man was not displeased, but merely accepting, as if Rahl had stated that the twilight would be coming.

The orchards had given way to smaller and meaner steads, with the winter-tilled fields barren, and no one out or about. But then, why would they be, when there was no field work to be done? Neither he nor Alrydd saw anyone who might be a rebel, just three older women, and one mother who scurried inside with a toddler when she caught sight of the riders.

Once they reached the outskirts of Helstyra, Rahl dropped back to ride beside Drakeyt, and the scouts were less than a hundred cubits ahead on the road that had become a main street that looked to be leading toward the river. Small dwellings interspersed with occasional shops flanked the street, but both houses and shops were small and of one level. Most were constructed with oversized bricks of a brownish gray shade. The roof tiles were a dingy yellow, as were many of the doors and shutters. The street had been paved, years before, and in places the stones were missing, with gravel and crushed stones filling the space. While there were no tall stacks suggesting distilleries, a sour odor hung in the air, one that reminded Rahl of a stagnant pond.

Rahl kept studying the streets, because he saw almost no one about. Yet the windows were not shuttered. As he turned in the saddle toward Drakeyt, the captain barked an order.

"Third company! Arms ready!" After a moment, Drakeyt added in a lower voice, "Too quiet."

Rahl nodded, then once more tried to relax enough to gain greater concentration, despite the soreness in his body and the throbbing in his head. His eyes and senses looked ahead to each side lane and alley.

Ahead was a taller two-story building, with windows closed by sagging brown shutters. The roof was almost flat, with a half-wall facade around the upper level that gave the impression of even greater height. The double front doors were boarded shut with two planks nailed to each side of the door casement. Part of the odor Rahl had smelled seemed to drift from the structure, or from behind it. Had it been a rendering yard or a tannery? A dyer's facility?

They were less than a hundred cubits from the structure when Rahl sensed someone—or more than one man—crouched behind the upper facade.

"Drakeyt," he hissed, trying not to alert the rebels, "men up on that roof ahead, behind the half wall."

"First squad, charge the building! With me!" Drakeyt urged his mount forward. "Second squad, third squad! Cover the rear!"

Rahl just tried to hold some sort of order shield as he followed Drakeyt. He was more than halfway to the building when the rebels began to loose shafts at Third Company. At least one struck his shield, rocking him back in the saddle, before he was next to the building where it was close to impossible for the archers to loose shafts directly down because the facade was set back from the natural wall lines of the building a cubit or so.

Two troopers dismounted and smashed open the doors, and the remainder of first squad followed Roryt inside. Drakeyt was the fourth or fifth man.

Rahl just sat on the gelding, holding the reins to Drakeyt's mount. There wasn't much else that he could do, not the way he felt.

In moments, the shafts stopped flying. Before long, a

figure in khaki and maroon tumbled off the front of the upper level. The rebel did not move. Rahl could sense he was dead.

Shortly, Drakeyt hurried out through the ancient and shattered doors, took his mount's reins from Rahl, and vaulted back into the saddle.

"What happened?" asked Rahl.

"One of ours dead, two wounded. Six rebels killed, three wounded and captured. As many as ten might have escaped through the back alleys, because there's a wall close to the back that second and third squads couldn't get through."

Rahl turned the gelding to follow the captain up the side alley and around to the back of the dilapidated structure. Lying on the ground were five figures. From their position, they'd been tossed off the roof after they'd died.

Just in looking at the fallen rebels, Rahl could see the difference. Like the dead rebel who had fallen into the street, they were younger, far more fit, and even their uniforms looked crisper, and they wore maroon uniform riding jackets. He looked to Drakeyt. "Real rebels, this time. We'll need to send dispatches back—and about the causeway. It might be best not to mention casualties. They need to know that there are rebels in the area."

"I can't say I'm surprised. We're only a bit over a hundred kays from Nubyat. We had to run into real rebels sooner or later."

Rahl just nodded. He was having trouble just staying in the saddle.

"We're requisitioning whatever inn or inns this place has. We can do that in hostile territory, and a town that allows a rebel attack isn't friendly. You and the men need some rest. We'll re-form and take care of that."

Rahl couldn't contest that, not that he would have. He wasn't in shape to argue about much of anything.

LI

The River's Edge was an old and rambling structure, an inn that might once have been the pride of the Awhut River, with its large and paneled public room, its wide porches, and its three stories. That had been years before, and now the porches sagged, ever so slightly, and all the years of oil and polish had only dimmed the luster of the golden oak paneling. The bed frame in Rahl's room had been sturdy enough, but it creaked every time he had shifted position, trying to sleep, and the mattress was worn and as tired as the inn itself. The place was big enough to hold Third Company, if in tight quarters.

Rahl was up early on fourday to see if he could get some breakfast. Besides, he was too sore to sleep any longer, black-and-blue as he was along most of his right side. While his headache had subsided to a faint throbbing, he was hoping that the combination of food and lager might help him feel better. He managed not to totter down the unlit narrow staircase to the public room and was mildly surprised to see Drakeyt was already there, sitting at a table in the predawn gloom that was scarcely dispelled by the single wall lamp that had been lit.

The captain looked worse than Rahl felt, and Drakeyt hadn't been hurled into the ground.

Rahl sat down gingerly across the square table from the older man. "You look like you had a long night."

"So do you."

"What happened?" asked Rahl. Had he been so exhausted he'd forgotten something? Failed at something else because he'd been put in a situation where no one mage-guard could do all that was expected of him?

"Dalcayn and Whebyt died this morning."

Rahl froze where he sat. He'd been so certain that

Whebyt would recover. How could he have died? "Dal-cayn?"

"He was one of those wounded yesterday. Khasmyr thinks that some of the shafts the rebels fired were poisoned."

"I should have checked the wounded." Rahl paused. He'd been so dazed that he hadn't even thought about it. "Why didn't you wake me?"

Drakeyt shrugged. "They were already cold when Shemal and Khasmyr found them. Not even the whole Triad could do anything about that." Drakeyt shrugged. "Besides, what could you have done? You looked to be in death's foyer yourself. Could you have done that much?"

Rahl didn't have an answer and was spared for the moment by the arrival of a servingwoman, who set two ales in tall battered pewter mugs before them, and two platters of an egg hash, each accompanied by a small loaf of rye bread. Rahl really would have preferred dark bread. He couldn't recall when he'd last had any.

"Could you?" asked Drakeyt again.

"A little something, at least."

"I'm not blaming you, Majer. If it weren't for you, things would be far worse, but I can't say that they're good." The captain paused to take a short swallow of his ale. "We left Kysha with eighty-four troopers. The submarshal sent us fifth squad with nineteen more troopers. Between the ones killed by the traps, the flood, and the rebels, and those wounded, we're down to sixty-eight, and we haven't even fought a pitched battle, or even a skirmish—except maybe the one yesterday." Drakeyt shook his head.

Rahl took several bites of the egg hash, peppery and spicy, even with the cheese and scraps of mutton. Then he had more ale, hoping the food and drink would clear his head some. "We're taking casualties for others, in a way."

"That's what recon in force is all about, except the idea is to prevent casualties, especially this many."

Rahl had nothing to say to that. He'd tried to do his best, and he was getting angry at the veiled implications that, somehow, the casualties were his fault. If he hadn't done what he'd done, there wouldn't be any Third Company left.

"That fire, yesterday," Drakeyt went on. "I wouldn't be surprised if the orchard holders petition the Emperor for damages. Then the submarshal will complain to the High Command that our shortcomings resulted in the problem. They can't make us pay," Drakeyt laughed bitterly, "but I'll be a captain from now until I'm stipended out."

"I'll probably end up as a patrol mage supervisor in a backwater harbor town," Rahl replied.

"Captain Drakeyt!" A voice echoed through the near-empty public room as a trooper wearing a courier's sash appeared.

Drakeyt stood. "Over here."

"Orders from the submarshal, ser." The courier extended an envelope.

"Thank you." Drakeyt took the envelope.

"I'm to remain here with Third Company, ser, until we join forces."

"Stand by for a moment. After I read this, you can check in with senior squad leader Quelsyn. He'll get you settled."

"Yes, ser."

"I didn't expect a reply from the submarshal overnight," Drakeyt said dryly, seating himself and breaking the seal. He read quickly, then handed the single sheet to Rahl. "What do you make of this?"

Rahl took the missive and scanned it.

Captain, Third Company—
You are hereby ordered to secure the town of Helstyra, including the barge piers. No craft are to be allowed to depart downstream. You are to maintain security until the arrival of the advance elements of the Second

Army. As necessary and required, you are to scout the immediate area and to inform the advancing elements of any and all potential dangers.

There was no signature, just the seal of the submarshal.

"I didn't know we were part of the Second Army," Rahl said.

"Neither did I," replied Drakeyt. "Maybe they've split the campaign into two armies. Be nice if they told us."

"It doesn't say how long it will be." Drakeyt motioned for the courier.

The trooper crossed the room. "Ser."

"How far away are the advance forces?"

"They were about fifteen kays back when I left last night, ser."

"So they could be here as early as tonight?"

"I couldn't say, ser."

"Thank you. Get something to eat. Tell the server Third Company will take care of it."

"Yes, ser." The trooper inclined his head, then took a seat several tables away.

Drakeyt looked at Rahl and lowered his voice as he spoke. "They're moving fast. We'll need to go over the whole town today."

"I'd like to talk to the town administrator," Rahl said. "I can't believe he didn't know something, and if we're supposed to secure the town . . ."

"You'd better take part of a squad with you—or a whole squad." Drakeyt stood.

So did Rahl. "Half will do. That way, the others can help scout around the town."

When he left the public room, Rahl searched for the proprietor, finally locating him in a small study off the kitchen. The round-faced man rose. "Ser? Is there a problem?"

"No." Rahl forced a smile. "I was just hoping you could tell me where the town administration building might be."

"It's in the block behind the river piers, ser. If you

follow the main street, just turn at the avenue before River Road—that's where the piers are, River Road is."

"Thank you." Rahl nodded.

When he left the proprietor and walked out into the courtyard of the River's Edge, the sky was overcast, and a bitter damp wind blew out of the east. Rahl couldn't sense any hint of rain, not yet, at least, but he had a feeling that it would arrive before the next day dawned.

After locating Fedeor, Rahl gathered half of fourth squad, leaving the remainder with the squad leader for such duties as Drakeyt might require. With eight men behind him, he rode out of the inn courtyard and down the main street.

The administration building was a small square stone structure a block back from the river piers. The door was unlocked, and, hand on his truncheon, order-senses extended, Rahl stepped inside. The small foyer was empty except for a gray-haired woman seated at a table desk in the corner. A stack of paper was at her elbow.

She turned. "How might I—" Then she paled without finishing her sentence.

"I'm looking for the town administrator."

"Administrator Esryk? Ah . . . he's not here."

"I can see that. Where could I find him?"

"I couldn't say, ser."

"Did you know that there were rebels in town who attacked Imperial forces yesterday?"

"No, ser."

Rahl got the feeling that while she did not know, she wasn't totally surprised. "Where does Administrator Esryk live?"

"He's only an administrator part-time, ser. He also runs one of the barge services. He has two steam tugs."

"And he lives where?"

"A good ten blocks back on the street that's next to the main street."

"Tell me more about his house." Rahl projected a certain amount of authority.

"Ah . . . it's on the rise. The house has a brick wall with an iron gate. There are gables on the second level, and the front door and shutters are green."

"Thank you."

Rahl forced himself out of the small foyer and back into the chill wind. Swinging up into the saddle didn't hurt quite as much the second time, and he led the half squad back in the general direction from which they had come until they came to a gentle slope—and the dwelling of the errant administrator.

The two-story redstone dwelling was impressive, with wide windows and roofed porches, and a paved lane from the street to a stone stable and carriage house, with what looked to be quarters above. Both the lane and the paved walkway to the front entry had heavy iron gates.

Rahl was ready to pull down the gates, but the carriage gates were unlocked, and he rode up to the mounting block at the side of the mansion, well short of the rear carriage house. Although he said nothing, two of the troopers dismounted and flanked him as he walked to the main door.

A girl in a serving maid's dress opened the door, then threw up her scarf over her hair. "Ser . . ." Her voice quavered.

"Majer Rahl to see Administrator Esryk."

"Ah . . . ser. He asked not to be disturbed."

"Tell the administrator that he can either see me immediately, or these troopers, and those in the side lane, will make certain he is greatly disturbed. And leave the door open."

Her eyes widened. "Yes, ser." She backed away, then scurried out of the entry foyer and out of sight.

Rahl extended his order-senses, but he could only sense five people in the house, and four were women. Both troopers unsheathed their sabres.

A slender man with deep black eyes walked toward the open door. Esryk's jet-black hair had been dyed, Rahl realized, as had his eyebrows, but the deep blue velvet jacket was genuine, as was the gold chain around his neck, and the fharong embroidered in silver thread. Rahl hadn't seen a jacket over a fharong, and he immediately probed with his order-senses. The jacket covered sheathed twin daggers that dripped chaos within their scabbards—poison.

Esryk smiled, but only with his mouth. "This is a private residence, Captain."

"Majer . . . and mage-guard," Rahl replied politely. "The reason why I'm here is that we were attacked by rebels when we entered Helstyra yesterday."

"I cannot see what that might have to do with me, Majer."

"You are the town administrator, and it should concern you." Rahl could sense the fear and worry behind the cool words and almost-insouciant smile. "Were you aware that there were rebels in Helstyra?"

"How would I know that?"

Rahl could sense the lie concealed by the question. "Why are you trying to avoid answering me?"

"Ser . . . I don't keep track of every person in the town. I collect the tariffs and refer the delinquents to the regional overcommander of the mage-guards."

Rahl realized that he was being short with the administrator, but he hated verbal fencing and the use of words and procedures to obscure matters. It reminded him too much of Puvort. "All right. Let's make this very simple." Rahl smiled. "Are you supporting the rebels or Prince Golyat, either directly or indirectly?"

"How can you possibly charge a town administrator with such a matter?" demanded Esryk.

"Because I'm a mage-guard, and it is part of my duty to discover who is loyal to the Emperor and who is not."

"You will find that I am most loyal to the rightful emperor, Majer."

"Good. Just tell me that you're loyal to the Emperor Mythalt."

"Didn't I just say that—"

Rahl reached out and grabbed Esryk by the lapels of the velvet jacket and slammed him into the door casement, following the blow with an order-thrust. Esryk sagged, and the half-drawn dagger clattered on the stones.

"Don't touch it," snapped Rahl. "Fourth squad! Weapons out!" He stepped back, then ripped the belt from under Esryk's jacket and tossed it and the twin scabbards, one with the dagger still in its scabbard, back away from the house. He dragged Esryk down the three steps to the stone walk.

"I'll have you court-martialed and executed," declared Esryk, straightening. "Mage-Guard Overcommander Ulmaryt will destroy you."

"That's not likely," Rahl replied. "I report to Mage-Guard Overcommander Taryl." He could sense that the name meant nothing to Esryk. "Tie him up with whatever you have," he told the troopers.

"What are you doing to my consort?" A woman much younger than Esryk appeared at the door.

"Administering justice to a traitor who attempted to kill a mage-guard with a poisoned dagger," Rahl replied coolly.

Her face paled, but she did not shut the door.

Rahl turned back to Esryk. The troopers were finishing binding his hands in front of him with heavy cord.

"Have the rebels been here from the beginning of the revolt?"

Esryk said nothing, but Rahl could sense that they'd probably been there even longer.

"How many?"

There weren't that many, Rahl decided.

"Why did you support Golyat?"

"Because Mythalt is a miserable weakling, ruled by his own consort." Esryk straightened. "Go ahead and murder me. Go ahead."

"I think not. Not yet, and it will be an execution in the square. A very public execution." Rahl smiled. "How close are the nearest rebel companies?"

Esryk didn't know, but they weren't that far.

"Twenty kays?"

The administrator didn't know.

"What did you do to support the rebels . . . ?

"Who else is town is backing them . . . ?"

Rahl kept asking questions, trying to sense and judge Esryk's silent reactions. In the end, he didn't discover much more than the fact that Esryk had been supplying and feeding a squad of rebels, that the man had probably been promised a position by Golyat or Ulmaryt, and that all the town's tariffs had been sent to Golyat in Nubyat.

After it was clear that either the man didn't know any more or Rahl couldn't discover it, Rahl ordered the troopers to hoist him onto a mount, and they rode back toward the River's Edge. Rahl just hoped that Taryl would be with the advance forces and could learn more from Esryk. It might even be better if Taryl were the one to execute the traitor.

Once Rahl had arranged for the traitorous administrator to be bound and confined in what amounted to a closet in the stable, with a trooper posted as a guard, he and fourth squad made a series of patrols of the river district of Helstyra. Hard as he tried, and it was difficult enough that his head was splitting by the time they finished, he could discover no other signs of rebels. He did get the impression that Esryk was far from the only one in the town who supported Golyat—at least tacitly—and he wondered why.

The other aspect of the town that struck him, as he was riding back to the inn after the patrols, was that all the women were covered from ankle to wrist to neck, and that the scarves and head coverings were far more substantial and opaque than those he had seen anywhere else in Hamor, especially more so than in Swartheld and Cigoerne.

He had just ridden back into the courtyard, when a trooper—Reolyn from first squad, Rahl thought—rode in behind him.

"Ser! The submarshal's forces are riding up the main street here, and the overcommander wants to see you."

Rahl managed to dismount, although he staggered when his boots hit the ground.

"Ser," called Fedeor, "we'll take care of your mount."

"Thank you."

Rahl hurried across the courtyard to the inn and out onto the wide front porch. A gust of wind chilled him, but passed, as he stood there alone. Before long, a score of outriders appeared, scanning everything. With them rode Drakeyt and first squad.

With the first full company, Rahl could make out Taryl. The overcommander eased his mount away from the company, although a squad followed him, and reined up next to the porch.

"Good afternoon, ser." Rahl wasn't quite sure what else he could say.

Taryl dismounted, slightly stiffly, and handed the gray's reins to a squad leader, then climbed the two steps to the porch.

"Can we can sit in the corner of the public room?" asked the overcommander. "I could use something to drink. We've been riding harder than I'd like."

"There's no one else there right now," Rahl said. "There wasn't, anyway, a little while ago."

Taryl gestured for Rahl to lead the way, and the younger mage-guard did, making his way through the foyer and into the public room, and to a corner table. Once there, Rahl gestured to the servingwoman.

"All we have is ale."

"All?" Rahl raised an eyebrow. At least, that didn't hurt.

"There's a bit of lager, but not much."

Rahl looked to Taryl, who nodded, then seated himself.

"If you could come up with two lagers, that would be appreciated."

"Yes, ser."

Rahl sat down across from the overcommander, whose thin face looked even more drawn. "I didn't see the submarshal," Rahl finally offered, not wanting to ask.

"The submarshal is not with us. I find myself effectively acting as commander, and that's not my expertise. Fortunately, Commander Muyr has been a great help. I suggest something, and he tells me whether it is possible or wise, and then we discuss that." Taryl sighed. "I'm a little sore. I'm not so young as I used to be."

Rahl just nodded. He didn't really want to admit how stiff and sore he was.

"Before I hear what you've been doing, could you recommend where we might set up temporary headquarters?"

Rahl almost laughed. "I would suggest the rather elaborate residence of the town administrator."

"Oh?" Taryl paused as the servingwoman set two mugs of lager on the table.

"Thank you." Rahl did slip her a pair of coppers, because the lager was special, and got a momentary smile in return.

Once she left, Taryl looked to Rahl. "About the town administrator?"

"I have him in custody. He also owns and operates one of the barge businesses shipping goods up and down the river to Nubyat. He threw in with the rebels, but I couldn't find out much, except that he fed and supplied a squad, and that he's been sending all the tariffs to Golyat because he thinks Mythalt is weak and ruled by his consort."

Taryl smiled faintly. "Do you think he is that much in error on that judgment?"

For a moment, Rahl was stunned. Then he reflected on what he had seen at the Imperial Palace, and the interaction between Taryl and the Empress. There had been something else there, too. He'd seen it at the time, in the way Taryl had looked at the Empress, almost sadly, yet with something more. Rahl decided not to mention that. Whatever that had been was Taryl's business. "I'd say she influences him. I don't see that as bad."

"It is not bad. She has excellent judgment, far better than either Mythalt or Golyat, and she is more than Mythalt deserves, but what all Hamor needs." Taryl nodded, as if to dismiss the issue of the Empress. "You think this residence is suitable?"

"It's the largest one I've seen. It has some grounds, a small coach house and stable, and the owner is a traitor, not only to the Emperor, but to his position as administrator. There are two other inns, but they're smaller . . ." Rahl shrugged, then winced.

"You've been injured, I see. What else happened?" Taryl's voice was almost tart, as if Rahl were a spoiled child.

"After the problems on the causeway, there was this hay wagon . . ." Rahl went on to explain what had happened, both with the makeshift barrel cannon, and then with the rebel squad on the roof.

Taryl just nodded, but with the overcommander's tight order shields, Rahl couldn't tell what the older mage-guard really felt.

"Anyway . . . we've been following orders, and checking the town. There are more than a few rebel sympathizers, but there don't seem to be any more outright rebels."

"Have you checked to see who's not here?"

"Not here?"

"If there are a number of dwellings without men, particularly with young consorts, they've likely taken up arms with Golyat and gone to Nubyat. There can't be too many, because, if there were, they'd have mounted more resistance here. Still, that would give you a better idea of how many tacitly support the rebels."

Rahl nodded slowly. He hadn't thought of that. Why was it that Taryl always could think of something he'd overlooked?

"Because I do have experience, and because you've

gotten sloppy with holding your shields." Taryl smiled, but there was an edge to his voice.

Rahl winced. The past days had not been good, and matters were not getting better.

"Did you check the tariff books to see how much was sent to Golyat?"

"No, ser."

"What about the records of the barge business? What in the way of goods has he shipped downriver?"

"I don't know, ser."

"You should." Taryl sighed. "It could be that I'm expecting too much of you. I wouldn't have thought you'd have forgotten about commerce."

"It was difficult to remember when so many people have been attacking us."

"And afterward?"

Rahl didn't want to admit that he'd just been exhausted.

"I will question this administrator, but you will execute him tomorrow in public, in the square. That is not usually done, but there is a reason for that this time. Not a good one, but a necessary one."

"Ser?"

"I will tell you later, when it is appropriate."

Inside, Rahl stiffened, then forced himself to relax. Taryl had always acted in Rahl's best interests, and Rahl would just have to trust the overcommander. But he still hated it when people did things for his benefit without telling him why.

"And you will go over the records of the town and the barge operations."

"Yes, ser." After a moment, Rahl ventured, "I've had a few difficulties . . ."

"Most of us usually do in matters such as these." There was little sympathy behind Taryl's words.

"There was something strange about the swamp and the causeway. I didn't want to put it in a message. I couldn't order-sense anything beyond a hundred cubits there, and nothing like that has happened to me recently."

"That's because swamps are high in life force, and that provides a high level of background chaos of the type that's hard to sense. Also, that swamp had quite a number of stun-lizards, and they inhibit either order- or chaos-sensing. That's how they get close to prey. We're fortunate it's winter. They're not so active in the cooler weather."

Rahl had to wonder if he would ever be able to learn everything Taryl wanted—or to meet all of Taryl's expectations. He could meet any one, or even two or three, at a time, but Taryl seemed to expect that Rahl could handle a score of them, all at once, even after almost being killed.

For a moment, he just closed his eyes. Then he took another swallow of the lager.

LII

At midday on fiveday, Third Company rode into the small square west and south of the barge piers. The troopers lined up in formation with the statue of one of the earlier emperors at their backs. Then Taryl and a squad of the headquarters company followed and took position at right angles to Third Company. A good hundred townspeople had already gathered—the result of passing the word through the inns and elsewhere that justice was to be meted out upon the former town administrator. All the women were fully covered, and a number wore black head scarves, something he had not seen before.

Once the troopers were in place, Quelsyn and four troopers marched Esryk into the open space before the company. His hands were bound behind his back, and a

white blindfold was across his eyes. Rahl then stepped
forward, carrying his battle truncheon.

"Esryk, you have betrayed your post as town administrator. You have supported the enemies of the Emperor.
You have sent the tariffs rightfully due the Emperor to
the rebels, and you have attacked a mage-guard with
a poisoned dagger. Each of these is an offense against
the Codex, and for each the sentence is death."

Rahl looked at the troopers. "On his knees."

"I won't kneel to anyone, not to . . ."

The troopers backed away at Rahl's gesture.

Rahl had already determined what to do, even before
he struck. He used his order-skills to move order from
Esryk's neck, just below the base of his skull, then struck
there with the order-boosted truncheon. The man's neck
snapped, and he pitched forward onto the pavement in a
heap.

"The fate of all traitors."

A refuse cart, pulled by a bony swaybacked mare,
creaked toward the dead body. Rahl turned and remounted, but waited, extending his senses, despite his
continuing headache, and trying to gather reactions from
those around the square.

". . . didn't do anything a good merchant wouldn't . . . "

". . . can't risk family and business for a weakling
thousands of kays away . . ."

". . . uppity bastard . . . always thought he was above
everyone . . ."

". . . like to see 'em apply the laws to them with
golds . . . doesn't happen much . . ."

". . . killed him with a truncheon . . . and going to
throw him away like rubbish . . . insult to everyone
here . . ."

". . . like the trash he was under those fine clothes . . ."

Rahl said nothing until the two troopers picked up the
body and tossed it onto the cart, and until they had remounted. "Third Company, to quarters!"

"To quarters!"

The troopers rode silently from the square. Even the murmurs from the townspeople remained low.

Rahl turned in the saddle and addressed Drakeyt. "I have to meet with the overcommander now."

"Best of fortune."

Rahl nodded acknowledgment and guided the gelding toward the headquarters squad. By the time he was a half block away from the square he was riding beside Taryl.

The overcommander glanced at Rahl. "We'll talk once we're not in public."

"Yes, ser." Rahl tried to pick up more reactions on the ride back to Esryk's mansion, but the locals either just looked or drew back.

Once they reached the temporary headquarters and dismounted, Rahl tied the gelding to a post outside the stable and followed Taryl inside, to a study off the south side porch.

The study in the mansion was small and surprisingly plain, with white-plaster walls, blue-velvet hangings framing the windows, and but a single bookcase, and that to one side of the large pillared desk with its rows of drawers.

Taryl sank into one of the armchairs flanking the hearth, cold, but filled with ashes. "Pardon me, but I'm still weary." He gestured to the other chair.

Rahl sat, his body and head forward slightly, waiting.

"Rather impressive, the way you dispatched him," Taryl said.

"I thought it had to be quick and decisive." Rahl wasn't about to mention that the effort had intensified his headache.

"What did you learn?" asked Taryl. "You did try to observe the crowd, did you not?"

"Yes, ser." Rahl cleared his throat, then continued. "No one was satisfied. Not for the right reasons. Those with golds were angry because they see Esryk as a man just trying to protect what he had. Those with less were glad he was killed just because he had more."

"Do you think it created more respect for the Emperor or the mage-guards?"

"No, ser. Fear, but not respect," Rahl admitted.

"Aren't they the same?"

Rahl pursed his lips. "I don't think so. I can't explain why, though." He paused. "Except that fear can create respect, but I think that respect disappears when the fear does."

Taryl nodded slowly. "Those are some of the reasons why public executions usually create more problems than they solve, and why we empower mage-guards to execute sentences upon the spot. Almost the only public executions are those of mage-guards who abuse their power."

Rahl could see the reason for that.

"How do you feel about your duties with Third Company?"

"It doesn't feel like I'm helping much, not for a mage-guard."

"That sounds more like a request for a pat on the back," replied Taryl. "Very well. I can do that. Just how many of these ambushes and traps do you think most of the mage-guards assigned to the army would find? And what would it have been like without you—or without any mage-guard accompanying Third Company?"

Rahl considered. "They might find some, if they knew there were traps."

"Would it not take much longer? Would we not have higher casualties? Far higher casualties without any mage-guard?"

"Yes, ser. I suppose so."

"Now . . . does that make you feel more useful?"

Rahl smiled crookedly. "Not really, ser."

"Why not?"

"I still feel I should be better at what I do."

"Good. When you lose that feeling, you're on the road

to the worst side of chaos." Taryl coughed. "I have a few
more questions for you."

"Yes, ser." Rahl was getting wary of Taryl's questions.
They always seemed to reveal what he didn't know as
opposed to what he did.

"Are you still thinking about that healer in Nylan?"

Rahl just looked at Taryl for a moment. That was the
last question he would have expected. "Yes, ser. I'm still
writing her, but I haven't had any way to send what I've
written."

"I'll be sending dispatches tomorrow, and we can include a letter with that. Now . . . what else have you discovered, beyond what you've reported?"

"The rebels have created a fair amount of trouble for
Third Company, but they've lost very few real troopers."

"What does that tell you?"

"They've thought out what they're doing and what territory they'll defend?"

Taryl nodded, then went on. "Esryk was sending the
tariffs to someone in Nubyat, yet there are few true
rebels here in Helstyra. What does that suggest?"

"Someone had been planning this revolt for a long
time, and they cultivated the town administrators—or
some of them?"

"Good. What else?"

"We should check every administrator from here to
Nubyat. Their records—or those that are missing—will
tell more than questioning them?"

"That's true. I'm glad to see that your mind is recovering. What does it tell you about the rebels?"

"The revolt was carefully planned, all the way down
to how to obtain golds?"

Taryl nodded. "Let me ask you another question. Assume that we find most of the town administrators from
here on have done the same—or disappeared—what
does that point toward?"

"Someone knew who they were. But wouldn't Golyat
know that as regional administrator?"

"No. Golyat is the kind who gives orders and expects them to be carried out."

"So he's being supported by other lower administrators. That would mean that they weren't happy with the way things were going—or they weren't being recognized, or they were greedy."

"Or some combination of all of the above." Taryl smiled wryly. "Now . . . we need to go over what Third Company will be doing in the next phase of the operation—and what I expect from you."

Rahl had the feeling that the afternoon was going to be long—very long.

LIII

Before morning muster on sixday, Rahl and Drakeyt stood among a group of close to a hundred officers, all gathered around the south porch at the temporary headquarters provided by Esryk's mansion for a meeting of all officers. Most of the officers standing waiting were captains, and almost all of the remainder were majers.

"Do you know what this is all about?" Drakeyt asked Rahl in a low voice. "You met with him yesterday."

"All he talked about was what he wanted from me and from Third Company. I told you all that last night. He avoided saying anything about the submarshal except that Dettyr was not here and that the overcommander found himself in command."

"Found himself in command? Strange way of putting it."

How else could Taryl have put it, Rahl wondered.

A lanky commander stepped forward. His voice boomed out into the gray morning. "I'm Commander Muyr, acting chief of staff for Second Army. As some of you know, when Submarshal Dettyr was relieved of command, he killed Overcommander Haskyl and attempted to attack the Mage-Guard Overcommander. As a result, he is . . . no longer with us, and by a conditional order signed and sealed by the Emperor, Mage-Guard Overcommander Taryl is now in command of Second Army until relieved by the Emperor." He turned.

Taryl stepped forward.

"Some of you may be wondering what a conditional order signed by the Emperor is. Before we left Cigoerne, the Emperor signed an order modifying the normal chain of command. This order placed me as fourth in command, behind the submarshal and the overcommander. I do regret the unfortunate circumstances that have led to this situation, but Marshal Byrna, of course, remains in overall command, and I am only in command of Second Army until relieved by the Emperor. All other procedures remain in effect." Taryl cleared his throat before continuing. "Our task is to take Nubyat, if possible, and, if not, to make it possible for both First and Second Army to do so once Marshal Byrna arrives. I will, of course, be relying heavily on you and upon Commander Muyr . . ."

As he listened Rahl was conscious that Taryl was projecting an order-feeling—not a compulsion or anything requiring obedience, but more a feeling of openness, of suggesting receptiveness to what he said.

". . . each company will be receiving orders later today. Most of you will have today and tomorrow to rest and ready your mounts and men for the advance on Nubyat . . . Majers and captains are dismissed to your companies and commands. I'd like all the commanders and senior officers to join me in the conference room." Taryl stepped back.

"Nothing indecisive about him," murmured Drakeyt.

"No," replied Rahl.

"Well . . . we'd better head back to the company," suggested Drakeyt. "It might be easier to walk this way." He gestured to his left.

Rahl had his doubts, but smiled absently and joined Drakeyt.

As they neared the west end of the temporary tie-line for officers' mounts, Rahl realized that one of the older mage-guards was looking at him—or more precisely at his new insignia. The other mage-guard was not a senior mage-guard, not from his insignia, and Rahl could sense anger and resentment behind the man's shields. He almost frowned. Since when had he been able to do that? Or was it just that the other mage-guard's shields were not that good? He tried to strengthen his shields so that they were as impermeable as possible while projecting friendliness and walking toward the other mage-guard.

"I noticed you looking over here. Is there something I can help you with?" Rahl kept his voice pleasant.

The other mage-guard's face remained neutral. "Ah, no, ser." Behind the words was apprehension, if not mild fear.

Rahl could sense a probe at his shields, and he deflected it, then added just a slight order-push, slipping his probe through the other's shields and pressing ever so slightly on the other mage-guard's shoulder.

"Ah, Drakeyt." A majer turned and addressed the captain, who had stopped beside Rahl. The majer's eyes avoided Rahl entirely.

Rahl could sense caution, but not fear, as well as purpose, behind the majer's salutation, and he just waited and continued smiling.

"Yes, ser?" replied Drakeyt.

"Is it true that a senior mage-guard executed a corrupt town administrator with a truncheon, and that he took only one blow to kill him?"

"Yes, ser. He's also saved the company several times, as well as managing to kill more rebels than anyone else."

"Tough, is he?"

Drakeyt shrugged, almost in an exaggerated fashion. "Tough as anyone who survived being a loader in Luba could be, ser. Doesn't much go for jealousy and arrogance. Completely loyal to the Emperor and the overcommander, I mean, the acting marshal. He was the one who killed that mage-guard traitor, and two others, and the mage-guard was a chaos type."

The majer nodded. "Don't think I'd want to get in his way. Good thing he's assigned to the recon force."

"Yes, ser."

Rahl managed to keep from smiling, but he did nod to the other mage-guard. "If you need any help I can provide, please let me know."

"Yes, ser." The fear behind the other's shields was far stronger and had largely replaced the resentment.

Rahl turned to Drakeyt. "We'd probably better get back to the company."

Once Rahl and Drakeyt had mounted and were riding back eastward toward the inn, well away from the other officers, Rahl looked to the captain. "The majer was having trouble with his mage-guard, and you two set that up, I take it?"

"Yes, ser." Drakeyt grinned. "Stanyl's not the brightest mage-guard, but he'll know it was a setup and a warning. The majer overheard him talking to one of the other mage-guards, complaining about how you were too young to be a senior mage-guard and how you couldn't possibly stand up to someone like him or his friend. The majer was afraid he'd do something stupid, and then the battalion would be without a mage-guard. Stupid as Stanyl is, he can still throw a good firebolt or two." Drakeyt frowned. "What did you do to him? When he left, he looked like he'd been whipped."

"Just shielded everything from his being able to sense it. Oh . . . and I gave him the slightest push, right through his shields."

Drakeyt nodded.

Rahl could sense that the captain didn't fully understand, but there wasn't any point in explaining. He'd just sound like he was boasting. He just hoped that Stanyl conveyed what had happened to his friend. Rahl didn't need to defend himself against another jealous mage-guard, and Taryl certainly didn't need to lose any more mage-guards.

After several moments, Drakeyt cleared his throat and turned in the saddle toward Rahl. "The overcommander knew Dettyr would be relieved, didn't he? That's what he was hinting at in the dispatch he sent you."

"I wouldn't be surprised if he had been sent to make certain that the marshal and submarshal followed the Emperor's orders," Rahl replied.

"The Emperor must trust him, then."

"I don't know anyone more trustworthy." *Even if I don't know exactly what he's doing, or why.* Rahl did know that Taryl was doing what he thought was best for the Emperor and Hamor, but he had not yet been able to figure out even what Taryl's overall strategy might be.

From Taryl's briefing on fiveday, Rahl also had the feeling that he was supposed to be doing everything he had done before, as well as succeed where he had failed, then use his knowledge of trade and commerce and his order-skills to deduce some aspects of the rebel strategy from the isolated bits of information that he discovered in the course of more reconnaissance in force with Third Company.

The overcommander didn't expect much at all from him, did he?

LIV

Sevenday dawned bright and clear, and a warmer wind blew out of the southeast. Not until well past noon did Rahl see clouds, but they were not approaching quickly, not from what he could tell. Once more, he was riding forward of the main body of Third Company with the outriders, this time with Shanyr. All day long he had not seen or sensed anything suggestive of rebel forces. The lands bordering the main road had become more rugged, and the vegetation more varied, in places sparse, and elsewhere lush and almost impenetrable.

Obviously, this part of Hamor was close enough to the coast that it never felt winter, because there were no winter gray leaves, and almost no firs or evergreens. The air felt moist, and there were more small lakes and marshes and the steads and dwellings were more widely separated and set in small hamlets at irregular intervals, with almost no dwellings standing alone. Although he sensed nothing out of the ordinary and did not lose any of his order-sensing strength and range, Rahl could only surmise that there were giant cats or stun-lizards or some other predators lurking in the areas of denser vegetation.

Along the left side of the road, although several cubits below the level of the roadbed, ran a small creek, not much more than a cubit wide. In places, it had washed away the rock riprap that had been laid down to protect the roadbed, but Rahl did not sense that the lack of protection had weakened the actual road, although that well might happen before long if the rocks were not replaced.

There were no tracks in the road, and none of the holders near the road had seen any riders outside of a few wagons and guards in days. Not being able to find any trace of rebels and no sign of any order or chaos being used bothered Rahl more than a little, leaving him feeling as though he were sailing—or riding—into the proverbial calm before the storm.

"Ser . . . feels like there ought to be more signs of the rebels," Shanyr finally said.

"There should be," Rahl admitted, "but that might be the best indicator that we're getting closer to them."

"Might be, ser." Shanyr's voice conveyed doubt.

Ahead on the right, just off the shoulder of the road, Rahl could see the top of a kaystone rising out of a mossy hillock. As he rode nearer, he could make out the letters and numbers, if barely—*Lahenta*—10 k. Beyond the marker, the road curved gradually to the left, angling southward toward a gap in the rocky ridgeline perhaps three kays away.

"Never heard of it," murmured Shanyr.

Since Rahl had never heard of most of the hamlets and towns, he said nothing, just nodded and studied the road before them. There was ... something ... ahead. After another kay, it was clear to Rahl that the road was rising to a pass in the rocky hills and that some sort of force was stationed there, although he could not sense what it was or exactly how many troopers there were. He also didn't like the vine-encrusted gullies and gulches that flanked the road ahead, even if he didn't sense any forces there.

"Shanyr, hold up here. I'm going back to talk to the captain."

"Yes, ser."

Rahl turned the gelding back along the road.

"You have that look, Majer," observed Drakeyt, as Rahl turned his mount in and rode up beside the captain.

Rahl made a mental note to practice cultivating a pleasant smile under all circumstances. "There's a force ahead. I can't tell how many yet, but they hold that pass in the hills there." He nodded toward the southwest.

"Do you think it could be more than we want to handle?"

"We probably need to find that out," Rahl said, "but I don't like the terrain ahead. Both sides of the road are filled with gullies and ravines. You can't see it from here, because of the trees and the vines and undergrowth."

"What do you suggest?"

"I'd halt the company here for a rest break and let me and the scouts and outriders go a bit farther up the road and see what I can find."

Drakeyt glanced to the side of the road. "It's pretty rugged here, too."

"Not nearly so rough as up there."

"You think we should move back down while you're checking them out?"

Rahl considered. "It might not be a bad idea."

Drakeyt nodded. "We'll take a quick break, then ride back at a leisurely pace until we've got some maneuvering room."

As he rode back to rejoin Shanyr, Rahl used his order-senses to study the terrain on both sides of the road more carefully. He had the vague feeling that there were areas just beyond the range of his ability that were similar to the marsh that held the stun-lizards. Were there more of them in the small pools and marshes bordering the road? Did they avoid the spots near the road, or had the road been built to avoid them? He almost shook his head. He didn't *know* that; he just had a feeling. Not for the first time, he wished that such feelings were more specific.

Shanyr was waiting, looking intently at Rahl as he neared the outrider. "What now, ser?"

"There's probably a rebel force up there near that gap in the hills. We're going to try to get close enough so that I can tell what we're facing. We'll try to signal the scouts to hold up for us."

"They're supposed to check back now and then." Again, Shanyr's tone expressed a certain doubt.

"Then they will," Rahl replied cheerfully.

Even so, Rahl and the outrider had ridden almost a third of a kay before they reached a straight enough stretch of the road for them to see the scouts. Then, Rahl had to wait until the scouts could see him and were actually looking back before he signaled for them to halt. They reined up, waiting for Rahl and Shanyr to cover the distance between them.

"Ser?" asked the older, as Rahl and Shanyr rode up.

"We've got a rebel force ahead. We'll ride a bit closer."

"Yes, ser."

Rahl didn't have to ride nearly so far as he thought he might. They had only covered about a kay when he began to sense the rebel force clearly. He reined up and signaled for the others to do so as well. Then he concentrated intently.

The rebels were riding downhill steadily and might already have been almost a kay north of the summit of the low gap in the hills and that much closer to Rahl. Third Company was facing more than a company of lancers, perhaps two companies. The feeling of their lances was especially vivid, but the lances did not seem at all enhanced by order or chaos. He still did not sense anyone on either side of the road, but his scanning of the terrain confirmed his earlier suspicions. They'd lose all too many men and mounts trying to evade that way.

"They've got two companies of lancers heading down toward us. It's time to head back." Rahl urged the gelding forward, then turned back downhill.

When the four riders finally neared the main body of Third Company, Drakeyt halted the company and rode back upslope to meet Rahl. The two officers eased their mounts away from the others.

"What did you find?" asked Drakeyt.

"Two companies of lancers moving down from the pass toward us."

"Two, and just lancers? Usually, they've got some mounted infantry as support."

"That's all so far." Rahl didn't care for what Drakeyt had said. "I think I need to head out back the way we came. If you're right, the sooner I find out, the better." He urged his mount along the right shoulder of the road, his boots brushing the tall undergrowth that had extended into the shoulder in some places.

Rahl had barely reached the end of fifth squad, which had been leading the withdrawal, when he began to sense more troopers ahead. He kept riding until he was clear of the column, then reined up. How had the rebels managed that, when he'd never sensed any of them, except the lancers? He shook his head.

"What is it?" asked Drakeyt, reining up beside Rahl.

"We've got riders moving up toward us."

"Frigging trap."

"It's worse than that," Rahl admitted. "They know you've got a mage-guard—or they've planned this assuming that you do."

"How can you tell that?"

"They stayed farther away than I can sense—except for the lancers up ahead. Now, they're moving in on all sides."

"How many?"

"I'd guess three companies . . . could be four. The lancers look to be two full companies."

"They're planning to charge us and throw us back onto their heavy infantry."

Rahl kept trying to sense the terrain before he finally replied. "We're still not clear of all of these gullies and gulches, but there's one flat area through the trees, just ahead to the right . . . just about a quarter kay ahead, and after about another quarter kay the land leads more to the east."

"Then, that's where they want us to go," said Drakeyt. "They know we wouldn't be foolish enough to ride up the road against two companies of lancers or get trapped between the two forces. There's probably a trap there or archers or something worse."

Rahl couldn't sense far enough to determine what lay farther along that supposed route of escape, but he didn't doubt what Drakeyt said. That also suggested that there was a mage-guard somewhere with the rebel forces. "The lancers aren't nearly so effective if they can't charge, are they?"

"No. That's why they need heavy infantry or archers or other support. They carry shortswords as well, though."

Rahl began to study the road itself. His eyes fell on the stream. Then he concentrated, trying to see if he could change the order-chaos composition of things just slightly. Abruptly, he nodded. It might work . . . if he could find the right place . . . and if he had enough strength and time.

"What do you suggest, Majer?"

"I'd like to try something," Rahl said. "Just a moment, if you would."

He rode farther north until he found a spot where the road dipped into a flat area, and where the undergrowth near the road was thick and the trees were close, but wide enough for mounts. Then he rode closer to the stream, checking until he found what he was looking for, just above the flat area.

After dismounting and tying the gelding to a bush, he eased down off the side of the road and began tossing stones from the riprap across the small stream until he had a crude dam. Much of the water still flowed through the stones, but he kept adding to the dam. Next he began to concentrate on a thin line that he visualized from the exposed side of the road under it, and then around, letting the line form a large oval. Absently, he rubbed his forehead, then scrambled back onto the road and remounted.

Drakeyt eased his mount toward Rahl. "What do you want us to do?"

"When you see the lancers coming, I want you to lead first, second, and third squads off the road in the direction they expect us to go. Fifth squad will remain on that section of road on the other side of that little flat there. You position your squads just beyond them. I'll have fourth squad hidden. I don't want you to lead your squads off until the lancers are close enough that they think they might be able to reach you, and I want you to be able to reverse the withdrawal and attack, once their heavy infantry attacks fourth and fifth squads."

Drakeyt frowned. "We're going to attack three companies with a company at half strength?"

"No. I'm not being clear. If what I'm planning works, the lancers are going to be in trouble, but it will appear

that one of my squads will be caught between them and
the rebel mounted infantry. The mounted infantry will ride
forward and uphill to attack us. You circle downhill some
until you're below the lower flat, but still well concealed in
the trees. There's an area down there where you can make
the road without much of a climb for the mounts. Set up
opposite that, and let as many pass you as you can. Then
you attack the weakest point to cut through. We'll rejoin
you as soon as we can."

"What if they pursue?"

Rahl shrugged. "I'd try to string them out, then deal
with them bit by bit. But I'm hoping that they won't feel
like pursuing."

"I share your hopes." Drakeyt paused. "You don't
think we should follow that flat area through the hills?"

"My guts tell me that your feelings are right and that
it would be most unwise."

The captain nodded. "We'd better brief the men."

"If you'd begin . . . I need to get some things ready."

"I can do that."

Rahl turned his attention to his preparations. First, he
extended his order-senses and checked the position of
the lancers, but they were still more than half a kay away
and taking their time, clearly not wanting to push their
mounts. The rebel infantry was taking up a position on a
high point on the road, little more than a third of a kay
northeast and generally downslope, concealed by a rise in
the road.

Then Rahl switched his attention to the flat area. He
could see and sense the water beginning to move along
the order-voided path he had created. He extended the
order-delinking process to the entire oval within the path,
then swallowed as he sensed the soil beneath turning into
a near-instant ooze.

He turned the gelding back uphill, then reined up beside Drakeyt and in front of the five squad leaders.

The captain inclined his head to Rahl. "Your instructions, Majer?"

"Thank you. Fysett, I'd like you and fifth squad to form up on the rise just beyond the flat spot there. The first three squads will be downhill of you, and they're going to look like they're running out and leaving you. I'm asking you to be the bait for the trap. Move your squad there right now—onto the rise—and do it by not going on the road. When the lancers come down the road, have your men turn and lift their sabres and circle together as if you think that will protect you against the lancers. Don't let any of your troopers go onto the flat area of the road and the shoulder there for any reason whatever. In a little while, it could cost them their mounts and their lives. We'll join you after we've done what damage we can, and we'll follow the other squads around the mess." Rahl didn't want to get too specific because how they extracted themselves would depend on how well his order-chaos manipulations worked.

The squad leader swallowed. "Yes, ser."

"You'd better get moving now. Don't cross the flat or the shoulder beside it."

"Yes, ser."

Rah turned to Fedeor. "Fourth squad will be with me on the left, slightly uphill and off the road and behind where the lancers will pile up. You'll need to tell your men to be quiet."

The fourth squad leader nodded.

"We'll form up the first three squads downhill of fifth squad, then," Drakeyt said, "and once the lancers are in sight and close enough, we'll begin the withdrawal. We'd better get into position." He turned his mount.

Rahl looked to Fedeor. "This way."

By the time Rahl had fourth squad stationed where he wanted the troopers, Drakeyt had the remainder of Third Company set up in good order on the rise above the flat—which still looked dusty and solid . . . and was not. Rahl was beginning to worry that he might have over-done his delinking, because the ooze beneath the crusty surface was at least four or five cubits deep and a good fifteen to twenty wide, and still deepening. Rock seemed to stop it, because he could sense rocks sinking through the mess untouched, but that might not be enough.

He shook his head. Now was not the time to worry about that.

Rahl waited, peering through a slit in the bushy lower foliage. While he could sense the approach of the mirror lancers, he could not yet see them. He had decided on using a shield that merely blocked order- or chaos-sensing, something like what the stun-lizards did, because that took less energy, and the trees and underbrush would hide him and fourth squad from sight.

The sound and vibration of hoofs grew ever louder, and finally Rahl could make out the oncoming riders. He had never seen a Hamorian lancer before, but with the shimmering breastplates, helmets, arm gauntlets, and vambraces, they looked imposing, especially when the sunlight glinted on their weapons and armor. Supposedly, they were equipped similarly to the ancient Cyadorans. Was that why some of the histories referred to them as mirror lancers?

Once the rebel lancers caught sight of Third Company on the road, they began to pick up their pace, moving at a solid canter, lances lowered, and five abreast, so that they filled the road from shoulder to shoulder, their boots almost touching as they neared the flat.

As instructed, Fysett had fifth squad turn and contract into a solid wall, sabres ready. Drakeyt had the first three squads moving clear of the road, but Quelsyn was leading them, and Drakeyt remained at the end of third squad.

The last riders of third squad—and the captain—vanished into the brush and trees just as the first rebel lancers pounded down the slight grade and onto the flat area that separated them from fifth squad.

"Charge!"

Rahl thought the command unnecessary, but the lancers put on more speed at the last moment before the leading riders hit the ooze-weakened road. The first two lines of

riders were well onto the order-and-chaos-trapped flat,
and the forequarters of the mounts of the third line had
crossed the unseen edge of the trap when the crust gave
way. Almost instantly, the flat became a morass of flailing
mounts, men, and lances. The fourth line of lancers tried
to pull up, but the churning of those already trapped undercut the edge more, and they went down. The remainder
of the entire company was jammed together.

Rahl glanced uphill. There was another lancer company that had reined up, and there was no way that they'd
get caught in the trap.

"Fourth Company! With me! Through the lancers and
across the road." Rahl urged the gelding forward, aiming
toward the rear of the lancer company. The last thing he
wanted was to get ensnared by the mess that he had
created.

The lancers were so disorganized that for a time, most
of them did not even realize that they were under attack.
Rahl felt that he broke some bones, and more than a few
lancers perished under the sabres of fourth squad before
they began to drop their lances and reach for their own
shorter blades.

Uphill, the other mirror lancers waited. Why, Rahl
didn't know, but he was grateful that they did.

"Fourth squad! To me! Fourth squad!"

Somehow, the troopers—most of them, Rahl felt—
fought and rode to him. Truncheon in hand, he pushed on
to the edge of the undergrowth, just above the more gradually sloping ground uphill of his small dam, where he
reined up, using the truncheon to urge his men toward
him. At that moment, Rahl almost gagged, so strong were
the feelings of suffocating lancers sinking over their
heads into the seemingly bottomless ooze that he had created. But what else could he have done? The rebels hadn't
been about to let Third Company retreat.

He swallowed the bile and snapped, "Fedeor, take the
squad on to join the rest of the company. I need to get to
fifth squad."

"Yes, ser!" The squad leader turned. "Fourth squad!"

Rahl edged the gelding over the narrow stream, then downhill past the chaos. He could see the rebel riders beginning to trot up toward fifth squad.

"Fysett! This way! Straight across to me."

The last of fifth squad made it into the trees before the rebels charging up the road were within thirty cubits of where the squad had been drawn up.

Rahl turned the gelding and began to try to slip past the last of fifth squad's riders to reach Fysett, although the squad leader was headed in the right direction to catch up with the rest of Third Company. He tried to sense more of what surrounded them, especially since the trees and brush were thick enough that it was hard to see that far ahead.

Behind them, he could feel more deaths, and he didn't understand that. Certainly, the rebels should have figured out that all they had to do was stay out of the mess. Then, off to his left, Rahl could sense a masked concentration of chaos. Did he dare try to deal with it?

He eased the gelding forward, pressing even more, and managed to make his way around trees and through brush to catch up with Fysett. Despite the lushness of the vegetation and the moistness of the rugged grounds, twigs and small branches crackled under the horses' hoofs.

He had only covered fifty-some cubits before he reached the squad leader.

"Ser?"

"We need to make a slight detour here. There's a small force up to no good off to the right. I'll lead the way."

"Yes, ser." Fysett's professional tone did not mask the resignation beneath, not to Rahl.

Once more, Rahl managed to create a vague shield that blocked his own order-sensing, but only his own. From what he had sensed, the mage-guard had only a few troopers around him, and that suggested that the mage was powerful—or considered himself so. Going after a chaos-mage of that strength was risky, but, if Rahl could eliminate the traitor mage, that would weaken the rebels far more than the loss of a company would—perhaps more than the loss of even a battalion.

After another quarter kay—Rahl thought it was about that far, although it was hard to tell amid the trees and undergrowth—he caught sight of a more open space to his right, as well as the glamour . . . or attraction . . . that veiled the trail. He could feel how it led from the main road—the way someone had planned for Third Company to go to avoid the ambush.

"Ser . . . ?" whispered Fysett. "Over there . . . the way looks easier."

"It's not," returned Rahl in a low voice. "Their chaos-mage created an illusion. I can't see where it goes, but following an illusion usually leads to trouble." *More trouble than an honest but hard way.*

"Oh . . ."

"That's why we need to deal with him." Rahl paused, then added, "I'm dealing with him. You may have to deal with the troopers around him." He winced as a branch pushed aside by the gelding flipped up, and the tip slashed at the side of his face. He still wasn't as good in the saddle as he should have been. "Afterwards, we'll head back and rejoin Third Company." He hoped it would work out that way.

How long they paralleled the false trail Rahl wasn't certain, but the chaos feeling continued to grow.

Then, ahead was what appeared to be a clearing. It was not. Or rather, the first part of it was, but behind the illusion, after some ten cubits, the flat land ended in a broad sinkhole, concealed by wizardry. The illusory trail led right into the sinkhole. On the left side of the sinkhole, concealed behind a thin screen of trees and on a low red-stone outcropping, were the chaos-mage and a full squad of archers.

Rahl tried to gather a better impression of the mage-guard, not pressing his order-senses, but just trying to receive.

His mouth almost dropped open. He wasn't facing a mage-guard at all, but a white wizard from Fairhaven. Although he had never met one, that sense of whiteness was unlike anything he had ever felt. It had to be a white wizard. It just had to be, and Taryl had been right. The High Wizard of Fairhaven had sent chaos-mages to help the rebels.

"They're here! To the right of the trail! Loose shafts!"

"Frig!" muttered Rahl. He'd been too stunned to think.

Whhstt! An angular firebolt flared from the white mage standing on the redstone outcropping behind the trees and overlooking the gorge. At the impact a small bush to Rahl's right flamed, then collapsed into a pile of ashes.

"Keep the troopers behind the bigger trees," Rahl ordered, sliding out of the saddle and thrusting the gelding's reins at the nearest rider.

Then he turned and moved toward the wizard and the archers, using the tree trunks as rough cover, his long truncheon in one hand.

More firebolts blazed toward fifth squad, but Rahl didn't sense any deaths, only some pain. So far, he realized, the white wizard hadn't even sensed him—just the troopers and their mounts. If he could just get closer . . .

Holding his full shields behind his vague screen, he continued to hurry forward, moving quickly from tree to tree. He was less than fifteen cubits from the small clearing behind the outcropping and behind a too-slender tree trunk, wondering exactly how to deal with the chaos-mage without exposing himself to the archers who were still lofting shafts toward fifth squad. He had his doubts about how well his shields would hold against both a chaos-mage and a full squad of archers firing at short range.

Abruptly, the white wizard turned, and without speaking, flung a wall of chaos-fire at Rahl.

Rahl stepped away from the suddenly flaming tree

trunk, dropped the dissembling screen and strengthened his shields. Light and heat flared around him, but his shields held.

Archers turned in his direction, and more chaos-bolts flared toward him. He was never going to get close enough to use the truncheon. How else could he handle the white wizard? He didn't have chaos to throw. He was an order-mage.

Could he throw order?

As he kept moving forward, Rahl formed what he could only think of as a bolt of concentrated order, and recalling what Taryl had said about concentrated order seeking chaos or being sought by it, launched it toward the white wizard. At the same time, he sprinted forward and then hurled the truncheon at the chaos-mage.

Rahl watched, as if everything had slowed, as the truncheon turned end over end, arcing down toward the other mage . . . as the white wizard flared chaos toward the truncheon.

At that moment, Rahl extended his shields, slamming them against those of the white wizard, and then pressing what order he had left like a knife through the other's shields.

WHHSSSTT! . . . Crumptt!

A white wall appeared from nowhere, smashing into Rahl and slamming him into the ground. Flames soared from everywhere.

It wasn't supposed to happen this way . . .

Then . . . he felt incredible agony, as if every point on his body had been pierced by a needle, as if thousands had struck him all at once . . . and then . . . nothing.

LV

Rahl could feel the hot and dark fog lifting. Overhead, he could see stars. He turned his head, and star-points of light flashed so brightly that he could see nothing. His eyes watered from the pain. He just lay there for a time, trying to ignore the soreness across his back and shoulders and the back of his legs.

In time, he moved his head, just slightly. The star pain-points returned, but not so badly, and he could see through the jabbing needles.

"He's awake, Captain."

Rahl could barely sense Drakeyt, even when he squatted down beside Rahl. "How do you feel, Majer?"

"I've felt better," Rahl admitted. "What happened?"

"I was going to ask you that."

"There was a white wizard from Fairhaven and a squad of archers. They were loosing shafts, and he was throwing firebolts. I managed to stop him, but everything exploded. That was the way it felt, anyway." For a moment, Rahl closed his eyes.

"The explosion killed two of the troopers and left a big patch of charred ground. There wasn't any trace of the wizard or the archers. There were two of their mounts left, and Fysett brought them back. Fysett said that no one close to you was touched."

"Where are we?"

"About four kays below the fight, just off the road on some higher ground, not that I'd really want to fight anyone right now."

"What did the rebels do? Where are they?"

"They all pulled out, every last one, and scurried around that bubbling mess you created, and retreated, probably to Lahenta, if not farther."

Bubbling mess? Rahl had a very deep sinking feeling.

Slowly, he rolled onto one side, ignoring the rock that dug into his hip, and struggled into a sitting position.

Drakeyt extended a water bottle. Rahl took it, gratefully, slowly swallowing and easing the dryness in his throat.

"There's one thing that doesn't make any sense," Drakeyt said, after Rahl finished drinking.

"There are more than a few things I don't understand," Rahl replied.

"They had more than three companies waiting, and they had to know that a recon company would precede the main force. Why did they have so many troopers and a chaos-mage just to deal with one unsupported company? Seems like a waste of men, especially if they're worried about force strength."

"I can only guess. But . . . why have we only seen traps and oldsters until now? They're trying to delay us." According to what Rahl had seen and read, delays usually favored the side with more resources. That suggested to him that the rebels were stalling for time. Did they think Fairhaven or someone else would intervene on an even greater scale? Or were the rebel mages developing some technique or tool? He shook his head. There wasn't much he could do about such matters, not as a mage-guard with a recon company. "I'd judge that the idea was to kill or capture the entire company so that no information got back to the marshal. Given the marshal's reputation for caution, a missing company would certainly cause some delay. Also, if they have fewer trained troopers—"

"They'd want to use them in situations that favored their experience," Drakeyt went on. "They'll use the newer troopers and conscripts, if they have any, where they need masses of bodies, and delay as long as possible in deploying them so that they can get as much training into them as they can."

"The white wizard also fits. We weren't facing a mage-guard turned traitor. He was a young white wizard from Fairhaven." Young compared to most wizards and mage-guards, but still older than Rahl. "The rebels were more willing to risk him than one of their own."

"But you bested him."

"I almost didn't," Rahl said tiredly, rubbing his forehead.

"Most mage-guards wouldn't have, would they?"

"The overcommander wouldn't have had the trouble I did," Rahl said.

"He isn't like most mage-guards, either." Drakeyt's voice was dry. After a moment, he went on. "We can't keep doing this, not without reinforcements, not the way we have been," Drakeyt said. "Without you, there wouldn't even be any of Third Company left. As it is, we're at half strength. I've been writing up a dispatch to the overcommander reporting our status. I'm taking the liberty of suggesting that, if he wants us to continue, he supply some reinforcements."

"I'd better add some comments to your report, especially about the white wizard and what I did."

"In the shape you're in, it might be better to wait until morning. Even in the darkness you look like a white demon."

Rahl knew that Drakeyt was right, but the thought still galled him. "First thing, so that we can get off a messenger as soon as possible."

"Which will leave us with even fewer troopers."

Rahl had the feeling that whatever they did resulted in fewer troopers. At least, whatever he did seemed to, no matter how hard he tried not to put the men in harm's way.

"You could be in command, you know." There was the slightest hint of an edge in Drakeyt's voice.

"First, that wouldn't be right," replied Rahl, almost without thinking. "Second, I still don't know enough. Third, the troopers wouldn't feel right about it. . . ."

"Do you think the overcommander felt that way before he took over?"

Drakeyt's question underscored Rahl's tiredness and lack of perception. He should have sensed where the captain was headed. He would have, had he felt better. At least, he thought he would have. "Yes . . . and no. I think he felt Dettyr should never have been appointed and was wrong for the post. The man was incompetent, and everything he did endangered troopers. That makes a difference. The overcommander told me personally that he discussed everything with Commander Muyr . . ."

"The commander's a solid officer," confirmed Drakeyt. "He should have made overcommander years ago."

"He likely will now," offered Rahl.

"It's only taken a rebellion, gross incompetence by his superiors, and one of the most senior mage-guards in Hamor for him to be considered."

"What else is new?" Rahl managed a chuckle. At the end, he had to stifle a yawn. Demons, he was tired.

Drakeyt laughed, if bitterly. "Your bedroll is right there." He gestured. "We could both use some sleep."

LVI

In the end, Rahl and what remained of Third Company did not near Lahenta until oneday. A good part of that delay resulted from the time it had taken on eightday for Rahl to deal with the bubbling brownish mess that had claimed scores of rebels and had expanded even more by the time Rahl had reached it by early midmorning.

The sun had climbed overhead and dropped into the afternoon before Rahl had managed to turn the chaotic quicksandlike ooze back into clay and dirt. Part of the problem was that he was still exhausted and had to rest between efforts, because he could only deal with the ooze in sections. While he thought it had reached its limits before he arrived, he wasn't sure enough to stake anything on it, especially since the rest of Second Army would have to cross the area, or spend even more time detouring around it. He also didn't want to face Taryl if he hadn't done his best in undoing the mess.

His performance in dealing with the ooze had been embarrassing as well, because he'd barely been able to sit down at the end before he passed out again—and no one had even been attacking him. When he had come to, it had been late afternoon, and Third Company was standing by, waiting, because, after all the magery, Drakeyt had decided it was wiser not to proceed until Rahl recovered. Even after all his efforts, that section of the road was still a muddy mess, but at least it was no longer chaos-quicksand.

In the end the company only rode slightly beyond the pass before setting up camp on eightday evening. By early oneday, Rahl was finally feeling stronger and was back with the outriders, able to order-sense, if not at full strength. His truncheon had been incinerated in the blast created by the interplay of his order and the white wizard's chaos, and he was reduced to carrying his own older and far shorter patrol truncheon.

The land beyond the rocky hills was lower, flatter, and more fertile. It also seemed to have steads everywhere, but rather than cultivated or winter-tilled fields, there were rows and rows of redberries.

"I didn't know they had so many redberries here," Rahl said to Alrydd, as the two rode downhill toward the hamlet that looked to be several kays ahead.

"Best redberries in all Hamor," confirmed the outrider. "The very best they ferment and distill into the special crimson brandy."

The crimson brandy was yet another delicacy Rahl had never heard of, and probably would never be able to afford, either. His eyes dropped to the road, its churned and dusty surface bearing hoofprints obscuring other hoof-prints, the same pattern he'd seen ever since they had left the ooze-battle site the afternoon before. He had not sensed any sign of riders or chaos anywhere close during the entire ride toward Lahenta, and the scouts and outriders had seen no one. The locals they had questioned had all seen the withdrawing rebels, but the rebels had not paid for supplies or even demanded any.

Lahenta was barely even a hamlet. As they rode along the main road that was also the only real street, Rahl counted less than two score dwellings, but three overlarge storage barns and one small structure with a tall large brick chimney that he took for the brandy distillery.

The hamlet square was little more than an oblong of clay and dirt with the obligatory statue of some past emperor. There was no inn, and one shop that looked as if it were part chandlery and part something else, perhaps a cooperage. A dwelling slightly larger than the others stood on the south side of the square, set off by a fence comprised of white rails set between pillars made of stones mortared together. The pedestal and statue were both modest, with the top of the statue barely higher than Rahl's head while mounted. The weathered letters spelled out "Elycatyr."

"Elycatyr," Rahl said.

"Never heard of him," replied Drakeyt, reining up beside Rahl. "What do you suggest?"

"I've been pretty much ordered to check the town administrator's or clerk's records, and I'll need to check the records of the distillery. I haven't sensed any horsemen or rebels or wizards anywhere near here."

"I'll have second squad go door-to-door to see what they can find." The captain laughed. "There aren't that many doors."

"I'm going to start with the chandlery. Someone there should know more about who's who and where they are."

Drakeyt nodded. "I'll leave you fourth squad. You may need them for the distillery."

Rahl hoped not. "Thank you."

"My pleasure, Majer."

After discussing with Fedeor what needed to be done,

Rahl rode across the square to the chandlery, where he dismounted and tied the gelding, leaving fourth squad outside.

He stepped into the chandlery, nodding as he took in the stave blanks in crude bins and hoops hanging on one side of the single long and narrow room. The room was empty, and he walked forward.

Abruptly, a young woman in trousers and a stained leather vest appeared. Her boots were scuffed and worn. She started as she caught sight of Rahl. "Ser . . . ah . . . what can I do for you?"

"Answer a few questions." He offered a smile.

The woman did not step closer to Rahl but remained a good five cubits away, holding a wooden mallet.

"You're a cooper?"

"What passes for one, here."

Rahl wondered if she were the daughter or the young widow of the former cooper, but did not ask. "What can you tell me about the rebel troopers who rode through here yesterday?"

"Not much. Some came in here on sixday and bought some things, small stuff, mostly dried redberries. I think they were officers. I never saw any of them again." She shivered so slightly that Rahl would have missed it had he not been watching closely.

"You were worried about them."

"Why would I worry about officers?" The cynicism in her voice was barely veiled.

"Did anyone hurt you?" He tried to project concern, which was easy, because he hoped she had not been hurt or molested.

"No." After a moment, she added, "But the way one of them looked . . ."

He nodded. "I'm glad you're all right."

"Is the Emperor coming back?" She didn't want to discuss how she felt. That was clear.

"We're the vanguard of Second Army. We're here to

put down the rebellion." He paused, then asked, "Was the town clerk sending tariffs to the usurper?"

"Of course. Chyrl thought he should be so much more than a town clerk in Lahenta." The scorn was even stronger than her previous cynicism. "He must have known you were coming. He rode out to join the rebels yesterday."

"Did he leave any records? Where would he have kept them?" Rahl tried to keep his voice even.

"He took the main ledger, but there's plenty of records left. He didn't understand bookkeeping all that well, either."

Rahl was getting a very good idea who and what Chyrl was, unfortunately.

"The rest of the records are on the table there. I suppose I should have burned them or something and said I didn't know anything, but Lahenta's too small a place to cover anything up."

"You didn't support the rebels, did you?"

"No. I couldn't say much, but . . ." She shrugged helplessly.

Rahl could sense the total honesty of what she had said, but he needed to make sure about one thing. "You seem to know a lot about him."

"I should. He was . . . I guess he still is . . . my consort. He ran the chandlery part, well as he could, and that wasn't all that well, and I did the cooperage. Learned it from my da. Wouldn't have consorted, except Da was dying." She shook her head. "Don't know why I'm telling you."

"Because you believe in the truth," Rahl suggested. "And you tell it."

She looked at him more intently, and her mouth opened. "You're a mage-guard, aren't you?"

"Yes. Don't worry. It's clear you had nothing to do with what he did. I would like your help in going through the papers he left."

"I guess . . ."

Rahl could sense the doubt behind her reluctant agreement. He smiled again. "You're worried, and you don't trust me. I don't blame you for your caution, but I'm not here looking for people to punish because they didn't resist the rebels. I'm only after the ones who went out of their way to support them, and that's why I want to look over the records."

"I'm Khelra." She walked over to the shelf on the north wall that rested on two wooden brackets. "Here's his draft ledger. He had to draft everything, because he never could get anything to balance the first time. I had to check his figures half the time." She snorted. "I insisted, even from the beginning, when he was just a town clerk for the Emperor. Otherwise, I could just see the tariff enumerators visiting him with a mage-guard, begging your pardon, ser, and that wouldn't have been good."

Rahl was getting the feeling that the young woman had been far too good for her consort, and he almost hoped that Chyrl would be one of the unfortunate casualties of the revolt. He forced a pleasant nod as he turned to the last pages in the draft ledger.

After a brief study, Rahl turned to Khelra. "There are only five people who paid large tariffs, and by far the largest were paid by someone called Gorsyn. Who's that?"

"Gorsyn owns the distillery. He has the big house on the south end of the square."

"He makes the crimson brandy?"

"Grande Crymson—that's what he calls it. We don't sell it here. No one here has that kind of coin, except him and his family."

"What did Chyrl do with the tariffs he collected?"

"He gave them to the enumerator who came from Nubyat, the same as always."

"But he must have known . . ."

"He knew. He even said that he was glad they were going to someone strong." Khelra shook her head. "I'd prefer an Emperor who lets us be as much as possible . . . begging your pardon, ser."

Rahl continued through the ledger. "Who are Desytt and Shavorn?"

"They're the two biggest growers ..."

When Rahl finished, he had a list of five men he needed to visit, starting with Gorsyn. Khelra had also supplied their approximate locations. He had a long afternoon ahead.

He found Gorsyn at his dwelling. In fact, the distiller was the one who stood there when the door opened, a carved goldenwood portal, flanked by two frosted-glass panels displaying stylized redberries.

"Ser Gorsyn?" asked Rahl, standing on the narrow front verandah.

"Yes?"

"I'm here to ask you a few questions."

"Officer, I do not believe I owe you an explanation for anything." Gorsyn's voice was warm, smooth and modulated, as if it were nut oil flowing into a pan.

Rahl smiled. "It's Majer Rahl, ser Gorsyn, and since I'm also an Imperial Mage-Guard reporting directly to the Imperial Mage-Guard Overcommander for Merowey ... you do. Also, since that squad of troopers drawn up out there will do whatever I ask, I think it would be most unwise for you not to answer my questions."

Gorsyn's eyes flicked past Rahl to fourth squad, then back to the mage-guard. He smiled, but only with his mouth. "I suppose I must, mustn't I? What do you wish to know?"

"You've paid your seasonal tariffs regularly, even the last one, haven't you?"

"Of course. I'm a loyal citizen of the Emperor."

"Did you know that Chyrl was paying those tariffs to the usurper?"

"Majer—it is Majer, is it not? I wouldn't want to be disrespectful. As I was saying, Majer, my duty as a loyal citizen is to pay my tariffs to the Emperor's duly appointed representative, and to the best of my knowledge, that was the town clerk, Chyrl. It was his duty to dispatch those funds to the appropriate authority, and I would certainly not wish to second-guess any Imperial functionary, whether minor or mighty." Gorsyn smiled again.

Rahl could tell that Gorsyn had known what Chyrl had been doing. "Did you offer Chyrl any advice or suggestions once the fact of the revolt became known?"

"I wouldn't presume, Majer. I'm a distiller, not an Imperial functionary."

"Yes or no?"

"No."

"Did you offer any assistance or aid to anyone known to be a rebel, or known to support the rebellion?"

"I did not, unless you would classify paying my lawful tariffs as support."

That suggested most strongly that Gorsyn had known Chyrl's sympathies and actions, but Rahl couldn't very well discipline someone for what he knew, rather than what he had done, not in this case.

"Did anyone in your household?"

"Absolutely not."

That meant Gorsyn had forbidden it, and that suggested a very clever man. By paying his tariffs to Chyrl and winking, so to speak, he had made sure that he'd remain in a good position, no matter what happened.

"You're a very clever man, ser Gorsyn."

"I'd like to think so, Majer, but that's something time will tell, won't it?" He smiled again. "Is there anything else you'd like to ask?"

Rahl could have asked more questions, but he'd sensed enough from Gorsyn to know that he'd find little more than what he'd already discovered, and nothing that would amount to proof of treason. "No. You've been most helpful, and I thank you."

Those were the first words that created unease within the distiller, but Rahl merely smiled and stepped back. "Good day, ser Gorsyn."

"Good day, Majer." The door closed gently, but firmly.

Rahl walked back to the fourth squad and the gelding, then mounted. He still had four others to run down.

In the end, he found all four, and his conversations will all four were remarkably similar to the one he had held with Gorsyn. All insisted—truthfully—that they had given no golds or support to the rebels and that they had only paid their lawful tariffs to the town clerk, trusting in his sense of duty. That meant that they'd all talked about how to handle the situation, and that, in a way, Chyrl had been partly set up, if willingly, to be the only true rebel in Lahenta.

He did not return to the square to meet Drakeyt until close to sunset. Along the way he did discover just how highly the distiller—or the distillery—was regarded. A paved lane ran from the distillery building on the south side of Lahenta to the highway leading to Nubyat, and it appeared to Rahl that from that point on, the road was stone-paved.

"What did you find out?" asked the captain.

"The town clerk handed all the tariffs for the past two seasons over to Golyat's tariff administrator. He was active in supporting the revolt and knew full well that the tariffs went to support the rebellion, but none of Lahenta's wealthiest did anything but pay their tariffs, and none of them did anything to support Golyat or the rebellion."

"They *had* to know."

"I'm sure that they did, but you can't administer justice against someone because he didn't stop a minor functionary from abusing an official position."

"What about the clerk?"

"He rode off with the rebels. He left enough records that he can be charged with treason. That's if he survives and we ever find him."

Drakeyt snorted. "The wealthy snots knew, and they'll get away with it."

Rahl nodded. "I can't administer justice against someone who only suspected a crime and didn't look further."

"I can see that . . . but it's still wrong."

"It is, but it would be more wrong to punish them. That way, we'd have to punish all of Nubyat and Sastak, and a good third to half of all the people in Merowey near the coast around those cities."

"So they set themselves up to profit no matter who won?"

Rahl smiled sadly.

"We'll see more of that, won't we?"

Rahl didn't have to reply to the question. Drakeyt already knew the answer.

LVII

Twoday morning Rahl was up early. He hadn't slept well, even though he'd been able to lay his bedroll on some comparatively soft hay in the corner of one of the barns Third Company had taken over temporarily. He'd had nightmares about drowning in ooze while Deybri had looked on. He couldn't recall what her nightmare image had said, but he felt that she had judged him for creating so much death. Yet what else could he have done? The rebels had left him nowhere to go, and he couldn't throw order-bolts the way the chaos-mages could throw chaos-bolts. One such effort had left him so helpless that his own troopers had had to cart him back.

After he struggled out of the nightmare and into wakefulness, Rahl washed up as well as he could and ate stale field rations. He was saddling the gelding when he heard a trooper riding into the courtyard.

"Majer! Captain!"

Rahl turned, then waited as Drakeyt appeared. The two walked over to the trooper.

"Sers . . . there's a full squad coming in. They're ours."

"Thank you, Shundyr," Drakeyt said.

"My pleasure, ser. Wouldn't want it said your scouts didn't keep you posted."

Both officers had their mounts saddled and ready in the light before dawn when Rahl could sense the oncoming riders, moving at quick trot. He turned to Drakeyt. "They'll be here in a moment."

Shortly, the squad rode into the open space west of the barn and reined up. A squad leader rode forward and halted. "Squad leader Lyrn reporting, ser, one full squad for duty. We have dispatches for Majer Rahl and Captain Drakeyt."

"Welcome, squad leader," offered Drakeyt.

"Welcome," added Rahl.

Lyrn handed an envelope to Rahl, then one to Drakeyt.

"Have your men stand down and rest . . . water your mounts," Drakeyt said. "You must have left early."

"Yes, ser. We covered about six kays since we broke bivouac."

Drakeyt opened the envelope and began to read, then looked over at Rahl. "We're ordered to scout the approaches to Thalye—that's the next town—with particular concern for possible opposition from the old back road. Squad leader Lyrn and his men are to replace fifth squad, and the previous fourth and fifth squad are to be consolidated under Fedeor as fourth squad, and squad leader Fysett is to be one of the messengers returning to Second Army. He'll be reassigned as a squad leader there."

Rahl nodded. The reassignment made sense. So did the suggestion of even more intensive scouting of the route to Thalye, particularly since the rebel attack on eightday and the beginning of the metaled highway to the coast signaled the edge of territory more likely to be defended more vigorously. According to the maps, Thalye was less than ten kays from Lahenta.

As Drakeyt watched, Rahl broke the seal on his dispatch and extracted the single sheet from the envelope, immediately reading the brief message.

Senior Mage-Guard Rahl—

Second Army will be joining you tomorrow. From that point onward, you will be working more closely with the main forces, and you may well be required upon occasion to brief senior officers on both the terrain and its peculiarities and on the probable disposition of rebel forces, as well as the level of civilian support for either the Emperor or the rebel forces.

In the interim, I would appreciate a short report on the situation in the vicinity of Lahenta, to be dispatched with squad leader Fysett, before you commence the day's scouting on the approaches to Thalye.

The seal was that of the submarshal, and the single letter above it was a "T."

"You don't look exactly pleased," observed Drakeyt.

"I've been requested to write a short report. Immediately, and to send it with Fysett before I do anything else at all."

Drakeyt raised his eyebrows, but said nothing.

"In effect, he wants to know most of what I already wrote up last night, but there are one or two things I'll need to add. I'm going over to the chandlery. It'll take less time there."

"Better surroundings, too." Drakeyt grinned.

"Not my type," Rahl replied. "Besides, the one I like wouldn't be too pleased."

"How would she . . ." Drakeyt broke off his words, then asked, "Don't tell me she's a mage, too?"

"A healer, but . . . she'd know." Rahl wondered why he kept thinking about Deybri. Despite her last letter, how could they ever see each other before years passed? Was he still chasing an impossible image?

"You do make things hard for yourself, Majer." Drakeyt shook his head.

"It's a habit of mine, I've been told," Rahl replied.

"I'll finish as quickly as I can. I'd like to have my reply ready to send off right after muster."

"I'll need a bit of time to tell Fysett and Fedeor and get the squads reorganized anyway. You won't be delaying anything."

"I'll try to be quick." Rahl walked back to the gelding, untied him, and mounted.

When he reached the chandlery, it was closed, but he pounded on the door until Khelra answered.

Rahl had taken over the makeshift desk in the chandlery the night before to write out his report to Taryl, detailing the situation in Lahenta and his decision not to administer any sort of punitive action to those remaining. He had just wished he was writing Deybri, but by the time he had finished, he was too tired and too discouraged to attempt adding to his intermittently written epistle to her.

"You're back," offered Khelra ambiguously. "Early."

"Only for a little while. I need a quiet place to write a response to my latest orders."

"You weren't that quiet, Majer." She stepped back.

"I apologize. The overcommander wants an immediate reply, and there's really nowhere to write in that barn." Rahl refrained from pointing out that he could have taken over her quarters.

She did not reply that there were other places where he could write. After a pause, she inquired, "The Emperor in his great mercy has decided against burning Lahenta to the ground? Or does he just wish to spare the redberries and the distillery?"

"No one's burning anything." Rahl smiled wryly.

"And after you leave, Majer . . . then what?" Khelra was most unlike Deybri. The cooper was short, muscular, and broad-shouldered, with sandy hair chopped short enough that she could have passed for a youth at a distance . . . yet she and Deybri did share one quality that shone through both, and that was an honesty of spirit.

Rahl couldn't help but feel sorry for Khelra, trapped as she had been by circumstances into consorting with a weak and ambitious man. Was he sympathetic because the same had almost happened to him? "The overcommander is arriving, and he's even less likely to burn anything. He has to report directly to the Emperor."

"You know where the lamp is." Khelra turned and walked away, leaving the chandlery door ajar.

Rahl stepped inside, knowing the space was empty, yet still scanning it with his order-senses, even as he wondered what he should have said to Khelra. He could sense she was displeased, and it wasn't because he was leaving or not leaving. Had his very presence promised something? He was thankful he didn't have that much to add to what he had written the night before.

After he had finished his dispatch to Taryl—less than a page of additional comments—Rahl went back out to the gelding and extracted the small mirror, carrying it back into the main room of the chandlery/cooperage. Then he set it on the plank that served as the makeshift desk.

He seated himself on the stool and looked into the glass, his concentration focused on the metaled road that led from the outskirts of Lahenta to Thalye, as he tried to visualize a kaystone that gave the name of Thalye and the number 5. The glass first darkened, then began to fill with swirling mists. After a moment, they cleared to reveal an empty stretch of road, without riders, or wagons. There was no kaystone, but to one side was a low hillock, and at the top was a broken stub of stone. Rahl nodded to himself.

He concentrated once more, this time trying to reach out to find the nearest company of rebels, visualizing their maroon-and-khaki uniforms. The mists returned to the glass and swirled across it, finally parting to show a hazy group of mounted troopers slogging toward him along a paved road in the rain. Rahl could feel himself becoming light-headed, and immediately released the image, taking a deep breath as he sat on the old stool.

He turned, but did not rise, as Khelra walked toward him, her steps tentative. He could sense a combination of fear and curiosity. "Yes?"

"You were using that glass, weren't you, Majer? Like the old magi'i?"

Rahl nodded. He stood slowly, then rewrapped the glass and eased it under his arm. "I'll be going. Some of the rest of Second Army will be arriving later. Please be careful."

"As if you cared . . . ser."

"I do care. I wish you no harm, and I'm sorry that your consort threw in with the rebels. I've already reported that you had nothing to do with what he did and that your assistance was valuable."

"Like as you said about Gorsyn, most likely."

"I only said that Gorsyn paid his tariffs, most likely knowing where they were going, but not ever asking."

At that, the cooper frowned. "He owns the distillery."

"You own the chandlery and cooperage," Rahl replied with a smile, then inclined his head. "Thank you. We do need to begin scouting before the main forces arrive."

"You're welcome, Majer." She inclined her head.

Rahl could feel her eyes on his back as he left, and her feeling of puzzlement. At least she wasn't angry anymore. He didn't need to make any more unnecessary enemies anywhere. He suspected he had enough, and probably among both the Imperial forces and the rebels.

Once outside in the early light, under a cool and clear green-blue sky, he mounted and rode across the square, then south to where Third Company was forming up. The wind was blowing briskly out of the southwest and held a slight dampness.

Drakeyt turned in the saddle as Rahl approached. "You weren't long."

"The reception was cool, and I didn't have that much to write." Rahl held up the envelope. It wasn't sealed, but he'd never had a seal. He extended it to the captain. "My dispatch to the overcommander."

Drakeyt leaned to the side and took the envelope, then straightened. "Here comes Fysett. We're also sending Halamar and Jugyst with him." As the three troopers neared, Drakeyt went on, "My thought was that you and fourth squad should take the road almost to Thalye—or until you discover any signs of rebels. That will give us an idea of what might lie along the road. The other squads will fan out along the side lanes, and I'll take second squad up the lane that the map says connects with the old road. If we see any traces of rebels, we'll return to the main road, and I'll send a messenger for you."

Rahl had thought of doing it the other way, but he realized that Drakeyt was right. They needed to know what would face them on the main road first. "We can do that."

Immediately after sending off the three troopers and completing muster, Rahl and fourth squad headed straight out of Lahenta on the paved main road. Rahl sensed nothing, and the only signs of the retreating rebels were a few hoofprints on the shoulder of the road, all of them looking to be several days old.

Slightly less than three kays out of Lahenta, Rahl and the reorganized fourth squad did find the remnants of the five-kay kaystone—and the hillock was exactly as he had seen in the screeing glass. At that point, he looked across the sky ahead. He could make out what might have been clouds to the southwest, but they had to be somewhere beyond Thalye.

If . . . if he had used the glass correctly the second time, then the way to Thalye was clear—at the moment, but the riders had been headed toward Thalye, and someone wanted them there enough to dispatch them through a rainstorm.

For all that, the rest of the day brought no other signs of rebels, not even on the back road, not so far as Drakeyt and second squad had gone, and Rahl could not find any sign of rebels or traps. All the squads of Third Company returned to Lahenta, the latest being first squad under

Quelsyn, a bit before sunset. The senior squad leader did return with several yearling lambs, obtained with the promise of script from Drakeyt.

"With the rest of the army on its way, ser," explained Quelsyn, "I thought it might be best if we procured some fresh meat for Third Company while it was there for the procuring."

Both Rahl and Drakeyt smiled at that.

Taryl and two battalions of mounted infantry arrived in Lahenta late on twoday, just after sunset, although the clouds that had rolled in from the southwest had brought twilight even earlier. The overcommander had no compunctions about requisitioning dwellings—or at least none about requisitioning Gorsyn's.

Still, it was pitch-dark by the time the overcommander sent a messenger for Rahl, and he arrived in the small study at the north end of the distiller's dwelling.

Taryl said little until Rahl closed the door. "Sit down." The overcommander gestured to one of the cushioned wooden chairs set across from the desk behind which he sat.

"What did you discover today?" asked Taryl.

"At the moment, the approaches to Thalye are without rebel forces nearby. I believe that there are a number moving this way, however."

"I am most certain that there are. Is your conclusion based on surmise, or on some form of evidence?"

Rahl did not speak for a moment. Did he want to tell Taryl? Finally, he cleared his throat. "I've been trying to follow your advice and think ahead. It did cross my mind that it would be easier to plan if I could find some way to discover what was happening beyond the range of my eyes and order-senses. So . . . I've been working with trying to develop my screeing abilities."

Taryl's eyes widened, if only slightly. "How do you know you're discerning what is as opposed to what you wish to see?"

"I didn't, not at first, but this morning . . ." Rahl went on to explain about the missing kaystone, then the riders in the rain. ". . . and they were headed this way. If they're riding in the rain . . ."

"Then someone definitely wants to slow or stop us." Taryl nodded. "Could you tell how many?"

"No, ser. There was a large column, but I couldn't hold the image long."

"I'm surprised that you could tell that much. Very few mages can use a glass, and even fewer ordermages. It takes a great deal of strength." Taryl sighed. Loudly. "That brings up another point that we need to discuss. You still have this tendency not to understand your limitations. That failure could be fatal to you and costly to the rest of us as well." The overcommander fingered his chin, then pursed his lips, before tilting his head.

Rahl had the feeling he wasn't going to like what Taryl was about to say.

"I appreciated the warning about what you did to the road outside Lahenta." Taryl shook his head. "Rahl, it's a good thing you have an orderly spirit, because you have this tendency to think up extremely nasty applications of order-skills, and you don't always complete the follow-up. I had a headache for the rest of the day after stabilizing the ground there." There was another pause. "You know that over forty lancers and rebel troopers drowned in your order-quicksand, don't you? That's in addition to the ones you and Third Company killed."

"I knew some had died," Rahl admitted. How could he not? He'd felt the smothering deaths. "I thought I had stabilized the ground there."

"You didn't get it all, and it was beginning to spread again. That is a problem when you start attempting to . . . adjust order-linkages, especially when you use all your strength all at once."

Rahl couldn't help wincing at the mild-sounding reprimand. "I'm sorry." Why was it that everything he did upset someone? Why couldn't he think well enough to get things done right on the first try? Besides, what real choice had he had?

"I won't tell you that it's all right," Taryl said. "It turned out all right because I caught it. But what would have happened if I hadn't been there?"

"The rock would have limited it, but it would have been a mess, anyway."

Taryl snorted. "Not that much of a limitation. We would have had a great southern swamp and more stun-lizards than arrows in Candar."

Rahl kept his anger behind his shields. Finally, he spoke. "I understand the danger I created. I worried about it at the time. I didn't see any other way to save Third Company. Given my abilities, what would you have suggested?"

"Looking more closely at the terrain and not getting yourself into such a position. Once you were caught," Taryl's voice softened, "your choices were limited. Looking ahead is one of the most difficult things for talented mages to learn, especially natural ordermages. You have such ability that you personally could escape almost any situation. Those under your care and command may not always be that fortunate."

That Rahl already knew, and he wished Taryl hadn't reminded him.

"Your dispatch was not particularly explicit in describing how you destroyed the white wizard, but I did note a rather large area devoid of both order and chaos." Taryl's voice remained mild. "It is likely to remain life-less for generations. Exactly what did you do?"

"He was throwing so much chaos that I couldn't get close to him and still protect fifth squad," Rahl said. "I got as close as I could, and then . . . well . . . I made up an order-bolt and threw it at him, at the same time that I threw the truncheon at him. It had a little order in it as well—"

"More than a little, I'm certain, given how you've been using it. What else did you do?"

"Pressed my shields against his and punched the order-bolt through."

"I'm surprised you're still alive, given all the force you loosed."

"I managed to hold my shields around the squad. All except two troopers," Rahl amended. "Long enough, anyway."

"Captain Drakeyt noted that your squad had to carry you back. He's rather impressed with you, but he thinks—and I concur—that you risk yourself too much." Taryl's eyes bored into Rahl. "Do you think getting yourself killed will help anyone?"

"Ah . . ." Rahl had the feeling any answer was wrong.

"Do you ever want to see your healer again?"

Why was Taryl asking about Deybri?

The overcommander sighed again.

Rahl almost winced, even though he knew Taryl's gesture was as much for effect as real.

"Rahl . . ." Taryl's voice was low, gentle, and persuasive. "One of the secrets to winning a battle or a war is to make the other side overextend itself, always at a high cost, until it cannot recover. So far, only your incredible abilities have saved your neck, and your posterior. The closer we get to Nubyat, the more likely it is that you will face someone with equal strength as a mage and with far more experience. If you continue your almost-foolhardy ways, you will not survive. You need to harness your creativity in using order to somewhat more caution and greater foresight. Make them have to react to you rather than your having to react to them."

"How would you have handled the situation coming into Lahenta, then, ser?" asked Rahl.

"I would have scouted much farther ahead when it became apparent that the road was rising into a pass. Narrow passes where the defender holds the high ground are always harder on whoever has to attack uphill or defend from an uphill attack. If you had drawn up Third Company short of their entrapment, then they would have been faced with attacking you on a narrow road on level ground. Your superior mage-craft would have worked to your advantage because they would not have been able to surround you. You still could have used the same tactic with the chaos-ooze, but they would have had to cross it to attack you, and you could not have been attacked from behind."

Taryl made it sound so easy.

"Now . . . I admit that it's not always that easy, but you're very bright, Rahl. You need to think in those terms. You need to ask how many ways could the rebels attack you at every point of your patrols and how you could best respond to each attack. If such an attack might inflict heavy losses, then you need to think of a better way to approach—or make very sure that there are no enemy forces anywhere close before you employ massive magery."

"Yes, ser."

Taryl smiled, almost fatherly. "It may seem as though I'm being hard on you, but I'm trying to get you to expand your thinking and the way in which you use your brains and your abilities because matters are going to get worse before they get better."

Rahl understood that, but he still felt that Taryl had no idea what it had been like.

"One other thing, Rahl, before we get into what you'll be doing tomorrow . . ."

"Yes, ser?"

"Find yourself a staff or something longer than that patrol truncheon. I shouldn't have to tell you this. If you keep overusing your order-abilities, you're going to need it." After the briefest of pauses, Taryl went on. "Now . . . tomorrow, I'll need you to see if you can pinpoint where those rebel troops are or at least from where they're coming. . . ."

Rahl sat and listened intently as the overcommander explained in detail what he wanted. At the back of his mind, he still wondered why Taryl had referred to Deybri. Was it just to get through to him?

He forced his concentration back onto Taryl's words.

LVIII

Early on threeday, just after dawn, Rahl took out the glass once more and tried to scree exactly where the nearest rebel troopers might be. All he could determine before his head began to pound and the light-headedness threatened to overwhelm him was that close to a battalion of heavy infantry was encamped in a small hamlet surrounded by grasslands in a flat area where the grass remained green.

While he and Drakeyt sat on a bundle of hay and ate rations and strips of left-over lamb, Rahl studied Drakeyt's maps to see if he could determine where the rebels might be. Following Taryl's implied advice about assuming the worst about the enemy's tactics and position, he thought that they might be about five kays south from Thalye, just south of where a line of hills had been sketched in on the map. Supposedly, there was a stretch of grassland beyond Thalye that separated the less populated inland parts of Merowey from the richer lands along the coast.

"I'd judge they're here." Rahl pointed. "I'm not sure, but that's where it feels like."

"It'd make sense, but that worries me because nothing's made much sense so far." Drakeyt grinned.

"It still doesn't," Rahl said. "They've only got a battalion there, and the ground is pretty open, not like that pass coming into Lahenta."

"Maybe they're just trying to block Third Company. Three companies didn't stop us; so now they're trying five."

Rahl still didn't like what he'd screed, and he could sense that Drakeyt didn't either. But he didn't know what else he could do but carry out Taryl's orders. He didn't see much point in tracking down Taryl just to report that he had a slightly better idea of where the rebels were, since he was partly guessing, anyway. The important thing was that Taryl knew about where they were and that they were headed toward Second Army.

Rahl stood, carefully folding the maps and handing them back to the captain. "I need to see the cooper before we head out. I'm hoping she can make me a replacement truncheon or something like it. I should have thought about that earlier."

Drakeyt nodded. "There's always something. About the time you learn what you're doing, they promote you or transfer you, and you start all over." He paused. "Then again, if you don't learn, you get relieved or killed."

"You're so cheerful," Rahl said dryly.

"Just realistic, Majer."

Rahl saddled the gelding, then mounted. He rode northward toward the square with a damp wind at his back, under thick clouds that suggested rain. Rahl could ordersense that any rain that might fall would be light and would likely not last long. When he reached the square and the chandlery/cooperage, he reined up and dismounted, tied the gelding to the ancient wooden railing, and stepped up onto the narrow porch. He only knocked on the cooperage door once before Khelra opened it, holding it ajar.

"Yes, Majer?"

"I'd like to commission something from you, if you can do it."

"You want some sort of barrel?"

"No. I'd like a wooden truncheon, a sort of staff with

a hilt, a little longer than a sabre." Rahl gestured to the empty scabbard at his belt. He'd left the patrol truncheon in his saddlebags. "One that would fit in here."

"Out of oak or something sturdy?"

"Lorken would be best, dark oak next, oak after that."

"Come on in. You need to sketch out what you want. We'll see if it's possible. Then we'll talk coins." Khelra walked away from the door through the dim and unlit single room toward the cooper's workbench against the south wall. "When do you need it?"

"By tonight, or tomorrow morning at the latest." Rahl followed her.

"That figures." She stopped at the bench. "What happened to the one you had?"

"It got destroyed in a fight with a white wizard."

Khelra just nodded. Behind the expression, there was little surprise, as if fighting with a white wizard were the most normal thing in the world. "That why you don't you use a blade like the others?"

Rahl shook his head. "I can't. I'm an ordermage. I know how to handle a blade, but using it for long would make me unable to do much of anything."

"All ordermages like that?"

"Some can't even pick up a blade without getting sick," Rahl said.

"So you just kill them with magery and use your big stick to hold off attackers?"

Rahl smiled, sadly, before he replied, but he saw no point in lying. "No. I've killed men both ways. It's just a different kind of weapon."

"Leastwise you're honest about it." She handed him a piece of charcoal. "Rough it out on the board here."

"Can you use those barrel hoops to bind it below the hilt and at the striking end?"

"I can. Won't be as strong as forged iron."

"It'll be stronger than unbound wood."

She nodded, then watched as Rahl loosened the scabbard from his belt, setting it on the wood and using it as a rough guide as he sketched the truncheon he had in mind.

"Good hand. Could have been an artist."

"I was a scrivener once."

"They still have those?"

"In places." Rahl finished the sketch. "This is a guide. You know woods better than I ever will. Just do your best and make it so it will fit in the scabbard."

"Might have some old oak that would do. More work that way."

"How much?"

"Be at least two silvers."

"I can afford that. Can you crosshatch the hilt or something to give a better grip?"

The cooper smiled. "I'll find a way."

"Thank you."

"Don't thank me, Majer. You're paying good silvers for it."

"I'll check with you tonight."

"Be fine." The cooper did not leave her bench but watched as Rahl left.

He could sense that she was not angry, but vaguely pleased, and somewhat puzzled, but about what he could not sense.

Once outside, before he mounted, he recovered the patrol truncheon from his saddlebags and tucked it inside his riding jacket because Khelra had his scabbard, not that the standard truncheon had fit that well in the scabbard Taryl had provided for the riding truncheon.

Third Company was mustering on the damp dirt to the west of the barn as Rahl rode up and eased the gelding to a halt beside Drakeyt.

"That didn't take long. She can do it?"

"She says she can. Whatever she does will be better than having nothing." Rahl had the feeling it would be far better than just a staff with a hilt, given the underlying pride in the young cooper.

"True enough. You're taking fourth and fifth squads?"

"That what the overcommander suggested." Taryl's orders had been simple. He wanted Rahl and Third Company to check the old road and make sure that whatever side roads or lanes ran from it to the main road were shown on the maps or added to them, and that there were no rebel forces positioned to use such roads. One squad was also detailed to make another sweep of the main road all the way to Thalye. "You're handling the main road?"

"I haven't been that way. It might be good to see where we're headed next before the rebels get there."

"If they do. Maybe the ones I found are just a vanguard and waiting for a larger force to join them."

"Look who's cheerful now."

Rahl just shook his head wryly, then waited for the muster reports from the squad leaders to Drakeyt.

Rahl's squads had no more left Lahenta and turned westward on the side road that led to the old road between Kysha and Nubyat than a faint drizzle began to drift from the clouds overhead, damp and cold, and more chilling than some snow Rahl had felt. The chill and the rain might have been what kept holders and others inside, especially since it was what passed for winter in that part of Merowey, and there was no pressing need for field work. Or they might just be avoiding the Imperial troopers.

Abruptly, Rahl could feel that someone was watching him, yet he could sense no one nearby. He continued to ride along the lane leading to the old road, scanning the woodlots and the meadows, as well as the winter-tilled fields. He still saw nothing, and could sense only animals and the occasional steadholders and their families. Then, as suddenly as the feeling had come, it vanished.

That incident left him feeling most uneasy.

He tried to keep Taryl's advice in mind, checking the roads, the lanes, the wooded areas, and speculating on how he would respond to an attack from various points, not that he sensed any rebels—or even any riders—anywhere.

Slightly after noon, the same sense of being watched

struck him again, coming from nowhere. How could anyone do that?

He tightened his order shields, and the feeling vanished.

As it did, he had a sickening sense that he had done the wrong thing. He had been watched, but not by someone nearby, but someone using a glass, just as he had done that morning. Whoever it was could not watch for long, but he had let them know he could sense it, and that gave whoever it was more knowledge of Rahl and his abilities.

He took a deep breath. Once more, he'd learned something because he really hadn't thought about it. He had to wonder when he might end up paying for that mistake . . . and how.

LIX

During the remainder of the patrol and scouting on threeday, Rahl had sensed the unknown mage-guard or white wizard screeing him twice more, but he had made no effort to increase his shields when he had felt the intrusion, uneasy as that had made him. Should he have kept himself more tightly shielded? If he did, he got tired more quickly, and he alerted the other mage to his abilities. If he didn't, he revealed his position. There didn't seem to be a good answer, and he really wanted to talk to Taryl about it. Belatedly, he realized that he should have discussed it sooner . . . except that he couldn't have because he hadn't known that he could sense someone using a glass to find him.

Because Rahl and fourth and fifth squad did not return to Lahenta until well after sunset on threeday, and because Rahl felt he needed to talk to Taryl, he did not stop at the chandlery to check on how Khelra was coming with the replacement truncheon. But when he reached the barn that was serving Third Company, Drakeyt handed him a message from Taryl that said the overcommander would be unavailable until immediately after muster on fourday, when he expected to see Rahl.

At that point, Rahl wondered if anything was going to turn out as it should. He'd found no sign of rebels or their tracks. He'd been detected by a rebel mage, and he couldn't even meet with Taryl to report what little he knew or to get some advice on how to deal with the mage who was screeing him. On top of that, two mounts in fifth squad had gone lame, and Rahl still had no idea if he'd have a replacement truncheon. Drakeyt informed him that none of the other squads had found any trace of rebels, and Rahl had to wonder if he was just imagining things when he used the glass.

Needless to say, he slept less than well and woke well before dawn, shivering in his bedroll. The air was damp and chill, not quite cold enough for frost, but a dew of ice-cold water covered everything outside the barn, and Rahl's breath was like steam in the chill air even inside the barn.

Once he got himself ready and moving enough that he wasn't shivering, Rahl took out the screeing glass and hung it from a rusty spike in a corner of the barn where he was not too close to anyone and concentrated on trying to locate the nearest rebel force. As soon as the mists cleared, Rahl studied the small glass carefully. The entire grassland area looked to be filled with troops, with cooking fires glowing in the predawn gloom, and smoke mixing with a faint and misty fog that softened the outlines of everything.

He tried to imagine the image as if seen from higher and farther away. The mists swirled, and the image reappeared. There were more troops and fires than before, extending for several kays—or so it seemed. For a moment, Rahl just looked, then released the image. What he had seen hadn't looked or felt like an illusion, but the only solid indication he'd had that his visions in the glass were in fact real had been his finding the broken kaystone.

He didn't see Drakeyt. So he ate stale rations—all the rations were stale—and then saddled the gelding.

Since Taryl had ordered Rahl to report to him immediately after muster, Rahl was at the chandlery/cooperage before muster. He didn't have to knock.

Khelra opened the door even before he set foot on the narrow porch. "Figured you'd be here early. Looks like all of you are going to be moving out pretty soon."

"That's likely, but I haven't been told yet."

"It's on the bench. I've been working and polishing it. There's a way to harden it without making it brittle." She turned.

Rahl followed her through the dimness.

The truncheon lay on the workbench beside the scabbard. Rahl just looked at the smooth length of dark oak, the slightly curved iron guard, and the iron bands below the guard and at the blunt tip of the truncheon. The grip was of crosshatched bone. Rahl could sense the internal order that resided in well-crafted work . . . and perhaps more than that. "It's beautiful."

"Because it's all one piece. It's part of an old staff," Khelra explained, "I didn't use rivets on the grip. That's why there's an iron cap on the end of the hilt, and that iron circle above the grip. Some of it's crude, but I didn't have much time."

Rahl laughed warmly. "If that's crude, I'd really like to see a fine piece of your work." He lifted the weapon, amazed at its balance. It was slightly heavier than the one Taryl had given him, but that was because of the iron. The heavier weapon might serve him better in any case. He slid it into the scabbard. It fit as though the two had been made as a set.

"You said two silvers," Rahl said, reaching for his belt wallet.

"I did." Khelra's voice carried amusement . . . and wariness.

He handed Khelra five silvers. "It's worth more than that, but . . . even majers don't have a lot of coin."

"That's more—"

Rahl almost said, "My life's worth more than five silvers." He did not, realizing that would sound callous and somehow cavalier. Instead, he replied. "What you did is worth more than you asked for. I'm only being as fair as I can be." That was also true. He did have more coin, but he didn't dare give her as much as her work was worth.

He loosened his belt, then replaced the scabbard that held the new truncheon.

As he adjusted the scabbard, a faint smile touched the corner of her lips. "May your order sustain you, Majer. The Emperor is fortunate to have you serving him." She grinned for a moment. "You even sound almost like you belong in Merowey."

"I'm from much farther away, but I appreciate your words." He nodded. "I have to report for duty. Thank you. I can't say how much I appreciate it."

"You have, Majer. A crafter can tell when something's appreciated."

Again, when Rahl left the cooperage, he could feel her eyes on his back . . . as well as a certain wistfulness. He was glad Khelra couldn't see the flush on his face.

Outside, he mounted quickly, noting that his breath no longer steamed, but the air remained cold and raw as he rode back to the barn and where Third Company was forming up for muster.

Drakeyt glanced at Rahl as the mage-guard rode up beside him. "How did she do?"

"Better than I deserved." Rahl smiled, then drew the truncheon and extended it so the captain could see.

"Much better," Drakeyt agreed. "But you'll need it."

Rahl was all too certain that he would.

After muster, Rahl excused himself and rode back to

the square and Gorsyn's mansion. He had to wait in the foyer for a time, before an undercaptain appeared, opening the door to the study.

"Majer . . . the overcommander will see you now."

Rahl followed the young officer's gesture and stepped into the study, closing the door behind him.

Taryl nodded to Rahl, but did not rise from behind the desk that held an array of maps of various sizes. "I see you managed to replace your truncheon."

"Yes, ser," replied Rahl, rather than point out that he did listen to Taryl, and more than just occasionally. "I wanted to report to you last night, but it took us a while to carry out a full scouting of the old road to the south."

Taryl nodded. "What did you discover?"

"There's no sign of rebels at any time recently, but there was something else. A white wizard or a chaos-mage . . . well, it felt like one of them was looking at me with a screeing glass. I don't know that, but that was the way it felt."

"If you felt it, then it doubtless was." Taryl frowned. "If you could sense them, you're not using enough in the way of order shielding."

"More shielding takes more effort, ser. I can't seek out rebels nearby for as long or as well—"

Taryl snorted. "You're giving me the same kind of excuses you gave the magisters in Nylan. Of course, proper shielding takes effort. Proper anything takes effort. If you don't work at it, you won't get any stronger. The more you stretch yourself, the more able you become. Without me around, you're slipping back into lazy patterns, and you're failing to demand enough of yourself."

Although Taryl had not raised his voice, Rahl felt as though he had been tongue-lashed with fine order-whips. "Yes, ser. I'll work on that more."

"You should have been working on it all along." As almost always, Rahl could not sense what the overcommander felt behind his shields.

"Yes, ser. I used the glass again this morning," offered Rahl, trying to change the subject.

"What did you discover?"

"The grasslands south of Thalye—I think that's where they are—are filled with troopers and lancers. It's hard to tell, but I'd say that they might outnumber your forces."

"They probably do. The grasslands favor lancers over mounted infantry, or foot, not that we have many of those." Taryl cleared his throat. "Captain Drakeyt will be joining us shortly, and I will be explaining what Third Company will be doing in preparation for the coming battle. There will be one, you know. Golyat did not want to fight in the hills or too far from Nubyat, but the midlands are well suited for his lancers."

"They're like the ancient mirror lancers, aren't they?"

"Golyat always wanted to emulate them, but his lancers are far less capable than the Cyadorans on whom they were modeled. For one thing, he cannot formulate true cupridium. His lances are polished iron over spruce or something similar. They're heavier and not nearly so strong."

"Can anyone formulate cupridium today?"

"It's said that the white wizards occasionally expend the effort to create special blades for white wizards, but that may be a rumor."

There was a quick knock on the door of the distiller's study, and an undercaptain eased his head into the room. "Captain Drakeyt is here, ser."

"Have him come in, Smadyn."

"Yes, ser."

"Overcommander . . . Majer." Drakeyt nodded to both Taryl and Rahl.

"Thank you for being so prompt, Captain. Normally, of course, you would receive orders through the chain of command, but since you are on detached duty and will remain so, I find that it is better that I explain your orders directly so that there will be no misunderstandings." Taryl looked to Drakeyt, then to Rahl.

"Yes, ser," replied both officers, almost simultaneously.

Taryl smiled pleasantly. "Tomorrow all our forces will move forward to the south side of Thalye. There you will conduct routine scouting, but you will not initiate any contact with the rebels. They have drawn up some four kays south of Thalye, doubtless to remain clear of uneven terrain and to draw us away from the higher ground of the hills to the north of the town. At the proper time, we will allow ourselves to be drawn into battle on ground that seems to favor them." The overcommander looked at Rahl first this time, then at Drakeyt, before continuing. "Third Company has become very effective in showing initiative and in operating independently. Rather than attempting to integrate your initiative into the main plan for this coming battle, I intend to place you on the far-left flank—not out of the battle, but where you can use that initiative to make a difference." After a pause, the overcommander added, "There is also another reason. The ground there borders bogland and swamp, but there is a narrow corridor of solid ground that could be used for a feint or a limited attack. I would prefer not to have major forces diverted when we are likely to need all the companies we have." Taryl stood and pointed to the map. "Here is where the road from Lahenta enters the grasslands, and where the rebel forces are likely to be arrayed . . ."

Rahl studied the map and listened, as well as trying to get a hint of what Taryl might have in mind beyond what he said, but the older mage's shields were impermeable and let nothing slip. All Taryl radiated was concern and an attempt to make clear what he wanted from Third Company.

LX

As outlined by Taryl, on fiveday, Third Company scouted the way in advance of Second Army from Lahenta. Well behind Third Company, a long column of troopers—and behind them supply wagons—made their way along the paved main road to Thalye, the road that would eventually carry Second Army to Nubyat—if they could defeat the rebels. This time, Rahl made certain his shields were stronger. He also practiced as much as he could with his new truncheon, trying to get the best feel he could of the weapon and how it handled. Settling into Thalye that night was uneventful.

Well before dawn on sixday, Drakeyt and Rahl led Third Company out of Thalye by a side lane that skirted the hills to the north and east of the town, and then turned southward toward the boglands due south. The grasslands that stretched south of Thalye were more to the southwest. The outriders were only a few hundred cubits ahead, because there were no trees and little cover, and the grass that was usually knee high had been beaten down by winter to calf height in most places.

"It may be an honor to be trusted with protecting the flank," murmured Drakeyt under his breath, "but why do so many honors involve getting up before the sun?"

Rahl just smiled in the deep gloom. His question was different. Why was it that no matter how much he did and learned, it never seemed to be enough for Taryl anymore?

He extended his order-senses, checking the lane ahead, but at least for the next kay, it was empty of anything that could be an enemy threat, although he could sense a wild dog and several large rodents. He could not yet sense the boglands, but there was a vague feeling of what he could only have described as chaotic order ahead and slightly to the east. The air smelled of firesmoke drifting on the light breeze from the south.

Overhead, the stars were beginning to dim as the sky slowly lightened. More to the west, Rahl could make out a few puffy clouds that looked gray but would doubtless turn whiter once the sun rose. He didn't think they heralded rain, but even if they did, they were barely above the horizon and seemingly not moving, suggesting that they would not reach Thalye or Third Company until late in the day, if then.

To his right, in the distance, Rahl thought he could make out points of flickering light. Cookfires? Why hadn't the rebels just taken Thalye and settled in there? Was there something he didn't know? Or Taryl didn't?

"There are a lot of fires out there," Drakeyt said quietly.

"And a lot of rebels."

They rode without speaking for almost a kay, and by then the sky had lightened enough that only the brightest stars remained visible. Rahl had been trying to use his order-senses to determine where the swamp and boggy land began and was getting a strong feeling that the northeasternmost edge was less than half a kay ahead, just beyond the last of the low hills to the east of Third Company. The faint odor of rotting vegetation bolstered his impression.

"The swampy land starts just ahead, less than half a kay," he finally said.

"Can you tell where the part in the middle of it is that we're supposed to watch?"

"Not yet." Rahl could sense movement to the west. "Second Army is beginning to move out of Thalye and into position."

"What about the rebels?"

"I can't tell," Rahl admitted.

After riding almost another kay, Rahl began to get a very uneasy feeling, not because he sensed rebel forces but because he sensed something else entirely.

"We're almost in position," said Drakeyt.

"We've got another problem," Rahl said. "There's a road through the bog. It's not on the maps, but it goes right where the overcommander said the solid land is. It's an older road, and you can't see it from here because the grasses have grown up over the part just east of us." Rahl wasn't certain he would have noted it in full light, but he'd been using his order-senses on the land rather than looking at the vegetation.

"Frig!" muttered Drakeyt. "Odds are that the rebels know it, and if it goes very far, they could be counting on using it."

"They might not. You can't see it easily." Rahl gestured. "You see that tanglevine clump there? The road runs just this side of it."

"It's all grass there."

"That's what I said. But there's no grass covering it a half kay farther east, and I think it swings more to the south."

Drakeyt shook his head. "We're supposed to take a position that will command this rise and the possible way through the bog. That's here." He lifted his left arm and turned in the saddle, raising his voice. "Form up, squads across, first squad to the right, fifth squad to the left."

Quelsyn repeated the orders.

The rise where Third Company had halted was barely that, the top of the gentle slope being barely four cubits above the grasslands to the southwest.

In the early predawn light, Rahl could also see that the so-called grassland held more than the brown-tipped knee-high grasses that predominated. There were bristle bushes—looking like green hummocks from which protruded saw-toothed leaves as long as a man's arm—as well as scattered creosote bushes and the twisted low mounds of tanglevine. Not surprisingly, there were more of the clumps of nastier brush on the eastern end of the flat where Taryl had begun to position the companies of

Second Army, and an even greater concentration closer to Third Company.

"Drakeyt . . . I'd like to take half of fifth squad and ride down that old road a ways. I can't sense anyone for a half kay, but it's harder to sense around swamps and bogs." Rahl also had to figure out what he could do, not just to stop any attackers, but to disable or kill them. He still didn't much care for that part, but any he didn't kill could end up killing him or Drakeyt or the troopers of Third Company and Second Army.

"Might be a good idea. There's no one moving toward us from their side. Not yet. Be careful."

Rahl nodded. That also meant he shouldn't go far enough to get cut off or not to be able to get back if the rebels launched an attack. He rode to the right flank of Third Company and reined up beside Lyrn.

"Squad leader, I need five men to cover me while I'm checking for a possible route for an ambush by the rebels."

Lyrn stiffened slightly. "Yes, ser." He turned. "Astahn, you and the four others in your file go with the majer."

"Yes, ser."

After the five broke out of the squad and lined up in front of Rahl, he spoke quickly. "There's an old road through the swamp. I need to see how far it goes. All you have to do is follow me." He paused. "Unless we get attacked, and then we'll make a strategic withdrawal." He offered the last words sardonically.

Astahn smiled; the others kept straight faces.

"Let's go." Rahl turned the gelding and headed off the rise, nearly due south and toward the grass-covered end of the old road. He had the definite feeling that he needed to learn before the sun rose what might be using the road.

As he rode into the grass that covered the end of the road, he could sense that the road had not just been worn into the ground by use, but that sometime in the past it had been carefully constructed through the swamp. The clay in which the grass grew had been packed over loose stones and gravel sunk into the swampy ground. Over time, either the ancient causeway had sunk or the swamp had risen, because the grass-covered surface was little more than a handspan above the water from which grew marsh grasses, moss, and less appealing plants.

". . . how does he know . . ."

". . . don't want to know . . ."

Rahl smiled tightly at the murmured words of the troopers new to Third Company. After riding a little more than half a kay, he reined up and let his order-senses range farther south.

For a distance of almost a kay, there were only about fifty cubits of solid ground flanking the old road on each side. South of that narrow strip, the road ran through an area at least several hundred cubits wide, but for how far Rahl could not tell. On the north and grass-covered end of the road behind them, but about half a kay south of where Drakeyt had stationed Third Company, the solid ground remained a narrow strip until it reached the grasslands.

The approach that came to Rahl's mind was to see if he could find a way to isolate any rebel lancers or troopers on that narrow stretch. Based on what he had done in the hills, he could certainly turn the northern end into swampy ooze, but once the attackers discovered that, they could just withdraw and ride around the boglands.

Were there any attackers coming?

He pressed his order-senses down the narrow road, trying to focus away from the swampy area that impeded his sensing. After a moment, he nodded. Troopers were riding northward, most definitely, but they were more than a kay away, possibly even farther.

"We need to ride farther south, quickly," he told Astahn.

While they rode at a quick trot, Rahl kept trying to judge just how far away the oncoming rebels might be and how many were in the force. From what he could sense, they were only moving through the gloom at a walk, but there were far more than a single company, possibly even an entire battalion.

Rahl finally reined up after he thought they'd covered another half kay. He took a deep breath and tried to steady himself in the saddle, then concentrated on sensing the causeway just to the south of his small band.

In the end, the best he could do was to use orderdelinking on the clay beneath the rock for a section of road some fifty cubits wide and running from one edge of the swamp to the other. Then he just waited, letting the delinking process continue, trying to keep his senses on the advancing rebels.

The sky was markedly lighter when he forced himself to concentrate once more to stop the actual delinking. The ooze-building would still continue, if he'd calculated correctly, but this time Taryl wouldn't be able to fault him for not stopping the process. While it was more a matter of feel as to when the full impact would occur, Rahl believed that the crusty area on top would continue to soften, but it would take the passage of many mounts, a hundred he hoped, before it began to weaken, but the weakening would speed up with each horse and rider. With more time or more mounts, that section of the road and causeway would turn into a particularly awful swamp ooze.

Despite the chill, he was sweating heavily by the time he finished—and he was only half-done. His hands were shaking slightly, and he was light-headed. A swallow of water helped, but only a little. He fumbled some hard ration biscuits from his saddlebags, then turned the gelding.

"We're heading back. They've got troopers headed this way, maybe a whole battalion."

He began to chew on one of the biscuits, taking sips from his water bottle as he rode.

"How'd he know . . ."

"Mage-guard . . . notice how polite the captain is to him . . ."

The biscuits helped. Rahl needed to remember that he needed to eat something after he did strenuous magery. He knew he should, but he often got caught up in what he was doing and forgot.

Rahl decided to set the second ooze-trap about a third of a kay from the edge of the grasslands. Once it became clear to the rebels that the road was a trap, most, if not all of those not ensnared would have to try to make their way through the swamp, and he wanted to make sure that they had a fair amount of swamp to cross, but he also wanted to be able to see where they were headed.

This time he didn't bother with a crusty top. He didn't want anyone passing this section of the causeway without ending up in ooze that seemed bottomless. He was even more light-headed than before. He managed to swallow some water, but he dropped a biscuit into the grass because his hands were unsteady. After eating most of the rest of the travel biscuits in the second pack, his head began to clear, and he rode slowly back toward Third Company.

Rahl had just returned the troopers to fifth squad and reined up beside Drakeyt in the early light when he could see and sense the gathering of lancers to the southwest, their armor and lances glittering orangish in the early light of a sun that had barely cleared the low hills to the east of the swamplands.

"They'll be on us before long," Drakeyt said quietly. "Must be close to twice as many troopers and lancers as we have." Unspoken was the question as to why Taryl was even fighting a battle when the Imperial forces were so outnumbered, and when the marshal's forces had not yet joined Taryl's.

"We'll need to be more effective, then." Rahl knew Taryl had planned something, even if he did not have any idea what that might be, and could only hope that his trust in Taryl was well-founded.

"They're moving in good order. They don't look like raw recruits," replied Drakeyt.

Rahl shifted his weight in the saddle, then fumbled for another pack of biscuits—his last, but he had the feeling he did need to eat more. He had just finished the crumbs of the last biscuit, washed down with a hefty gulp from his water bottle, when a series of high-pitched trumpet calls rang through the air.

Rahl could sense the waves of oncoming lancers. While most of them were aimed at the center of the Imperial line, a smaller concentration had broken off and was headed toward Third Company. "Lancers headed our way." Even as he spoke, he realized the words were stupid. Drakeyt could see that as well as Rahl could.

"Third Company! Weapons ready!" Drakeyt looked to Rahl. "We'll have to let at least some of them through and catch them on the back side."

Rahl concentrated, trying to sense more than the oncoming lancers. "They've got a company of troopers behind them."

"They would. That's experience, and it means we'll have to try something like an angle charge."

Rahl tried to recall exactly what that was from the tactics books he'd read, because it wasn't what it sounded like, or not exactly, and he'd never seen Drakeyt order it in maneuvers. His eyes flickered from one body of lancers to the other while he tried to think of what he could do. He certainly couldn't hold an order shield of any size for long, and what he could hold would barely protect the front of a squad.

Since Third Company was on the left flank, and since the lancers moving toward Rahl and Drakeyt had begun farther to the southeast, the main lancer assault had almost reached the main body, while the secondary attack still had a good quarter kay to go before engaging Third Company. The front rows of the Second Army troopers began to move forward to avoid being sitting swans, and, just as the tips of the lances of those lancers leading the main assault on Second Army were within a few cubits of the Imperial forces, for little more than an instant, a massive shield flared across the middle of the Second Army. That instant was enough to flatten the entire first two ranks of lancers and to ensnare those immediately behind in the confusion of fallen men and mounts.

Rahl froze in the saddle for a moment, stunned at that burst of order-force. That had to have been Taryl. Could he do something similar—throw a wide shield for just an instant?

"I'm going to try to pile up the ones headed toward us, the way the overcommander did," Rahl told Drakeyt, "but that will only tangle the first ranks."

"Then we'll have the end squads pull and attack from the side." Drakeyt cleared his throat. "Third Company! Stand by for flank encirclement! End squads lead! Flank encirclement on my command! On my command!"

Rahl could hear the squad leaders repeating Drakeyt's commands, and he began to gather as much order as he could, trying to pull it from the air itself, forcing himself to wait as the rebel lancers thundered toward the outnumbered Third Company.

In the center of the rebel attack, three lancers angled their mounts closer together, and they and their shimmering lances aimed directly at Rahl. Following Taryl's example, Rahl forced himself to wait, trying to judge just when the right moment would be.

Just as he felt that he would be spitted within moments, Rahl extended his order shield. It lasted long enough to pile up three lines of lancers, and Rahl reeled in the saddle as his effort collapsed even before he could release it.

"Break to encircle! Break to encircle!"

Rahl's entire body felt flushed, and he was light-headed, but he managed to unsheathe his truncheon and follow Drakeyt, who had taken the lead in guiding second squad. He managed to deflect the lance of one of the lancers entangled in the mass of mounts and men as he urged his mount after the captain.

The rebel troopers following the lancers were trying to

swing wide when Drakeyt and the first two squads of Third Company slammed into them from the side.

Rahl found himself using the truncheon more to defend himself from wild attacks from the rebels than in attacking in any way. He'd hoped to use his personal order shields, but he'd expended so much order-effort already that even trying to hold them for more than a few moments sent flashes of pain through his skull. As Taryl had pointed out might happen, all he really had was the truncheon, at least until he recovered, but he did feel that he broke bones, now and again. That wasn't his desire; he just kept trying to keep from getting slashed up as he did his best in pushing the attackers back.

From somewhere came another series of trumpet calls, and within moments, Rahl found himself and the gelding almost alone amid scattered groups of Imperial troopers.

"Third Company! Re-form!" Drakeyt's voice cut through the clamor. "On me!"

Rahl straightened in the saddle, then, seeing there were no rebels nearby, sheathed the truncheon, silently thanking Khelra as he did. He studied the grasslands to the south, hoping to see the rebels withdrawing.

They were not, but rather re-forming into a different series of formations.

Rahl urged the gelding back toward Third Company, where he reined up beside Drakeyt, who was waiting for fourth squad to finish repositioning. While he waited, he extended his order-senses toward the swamp, trying not to wince at the pain-filled flashes of light through his eyes and skull.

Even so, he could sense another force approaching—down the old road through the middle of the bogland. Had the flanking lancer attack been a distraction to keep Third Company from noticing the troopers coming up through the ancient causeway in the middle of the swamp?

"We need to move to that old road," Rahl called to Drakeyt. "There are troopers moving up it quickly, and there are enough that if they get past the swamp, they could flank us on both sides."

"Can you pull that blocking magery again?"

"No. But I've already done something else that will push them into the swamp. They'll be struggling through and coming out in small numbers." *If at all.* "But there are so many that we can't let them get through and regroup."

"What did do you?"

"The road is ooze-trapped, so that once they get on the narrow part, they can't get out except by drowning in the ooze at each end of the road or struggling through the swamp."

"Good." Drakeyt stood in the stirrups. "Third Company! Left turn on fifth squad! Forward!"

Third Company arrived and reined up in formation opposite the center of the unseen old road, the squads beside each other in a line, with a five-man front on each squad.

"How long?" asked Drakeyt, glancing back westward.

"Not long. Any moment, now." Rahl closed his eyes, hoping that would ease the throbbing in his skull.

Rahl watched as the first troopers caught sight of Third Company and the grasslands and urged their mounts forward. He held his breath for a moment. Then the first mounts pitched forward into the ooze beneath the thin crust of the grass-covered upper part of the ancient road. Others followed, and in moments, a churning mass of a score of mounts and riders was struggling and sinking.

Behind them, the advance slowed.

"They'll go to the sides and through the swamp," Drakeyt predicted.

After several moments, individual riders, then squads began to leave the old concealed causeway and make their way through the marsh and pooled stagnant water.

Rahl swallowed as the ugly snout of a small stun-lizard appeared. The nearest rider and mount toppled sideways. Rahl could sense other creatures as well, although he could not see them, all moving through the waters toward the troopers trapped on the road, as well as those trying to continue the attack.

One rebel squad had figured that swimming their mounts through the clearer water might be safer, and that group was already within a few hundred cubits of solid ground. "Over there!" Rahl pointed to Drakeyt.

"First squad! Take the rebels swimming their mounts on the south side!"

"First squad! Forward!" ordered Roryt.

The troopers took station less than fifty cubits from the edge of the swampy area, waiting for the rebels to break free of the water and treacherous ground. Roryt obviously didn't want to lose men to the swamp, a decision Rahl thought most wise, especially after seeing the stun-lizards.

The first group of three rebels saw the waiting Imperials and tried to angle their way southwest—back toward the rebel forces. None of them made it.

Another pair tried to swim their mounts farther away from first squad, but one rider and his mount vanished, and the survivor and his mount lurched out and were picked off by one of Roryt's troopers.

Even so, Rahl could see scores of riders in the water, far more than the creatures and muck of the swamp would be able to stop.

"We've got heavy infantry breaking our way from the main rebel force," Drakeyt said. "You take first and fifth squads and hold the ones coming out of the swamp. We'll cover your back."

Rahl glanced at the swamp, then toward the rebel forces riding northward from the main body of the insurgents. "You'd better take everyone except first squad."

"I'll accept that recommendation." Drakeyt's voice was dry. "Second, third, fourth, and fifth squads. Wheel to the south! On me!"

Rahl turned the gelding toward the section of the

swamp to the north of where the ancient road emerged. Before he had ridden fifty cubits, eight troopers from first squad had joined him.

"We'll get 'em, ser!"

They had their sabres out, and, belatedly, Rahl drew the truncheon. In some fashion, for a moment, it caught and twisted the light, and it almost seemed as though a spear of darkness flashed from it toward the rebel trooper struggling to get his mount clear of the swamp.

The trooper spurred his mount forward, trying to escape Rahl, but a clump of thornvine blocked the rebel's way, and he wheeled his mount back toward Rahl, swinging his sabre wildly. Rahl disarmed him with a single blow, then dropped him out of the saddle with a second stroke.

After that, Rahl just found himself trying to disarm or incapacitate any rebel around. He knew there were other troopers from first squad around him, somewhere, but none even seemed to get close enough for him to verify that, and it was all he could do, it seemed, just to hold his own against the seemingly endless number of rebels riding out of the swamp.

Sometime around late midmorning—that was what Rahl thought—another set of trumpet calls echoed from somewhere, and there were even more rebels, coming from everywhere.

Rahl managed to call up a last bit of order and give some infusion to the truncheon as he thrust, parried, cut, and just plain slashed.

Then came yet another trumpet call, this one sounding almost panicky, and in moments, or so it seemed, Rahl was sagging in the saddle, alone. He looked around and found himself less than fifty cubits from the edge of the swamp, but somewhat farther southwest along its edge than where he had attacked the first rebel.

Everywhere there were bodies of troopers—mostly rebel troopers—and some were alive, moaning.

Rahl just sat there in the saddle, his sight blurred with

sparks and longer flashes of pain searing through his eyes, and most of his muscles aching and so exhausted he felt like he had a hard time breathing.

"Majer . . . ser?"

He turned in the saddle. The trooper who had reined up wore the sash of a courier. "Yes?"

"The overcommander requests your presence, ser. If you'd follow me . . ."

Rahl could sense almost nothing in terms of order or chaos, but there was a reserve in the trooper's voice. "Oh . . . of course."

He urged the gelding forward beside the courier's mount and rode slowly westward toward where the center of the battle must have been. There was no sign of any rebels, except those lying on the ground, mostly dead or dying, around which the gelding picked his way. The light breeze carried the iron-copper odor of blood everywhere. Even swallowing the last drops from his water bottle did not remove the taste from his mouth.

What had happened? He glanced at the courier, who did not quite meet his eyes. "We were isolated. All of a sudden, the rebels were scrambling to get away."

"You didn't see, ser?"

"No. Third Company was fighting off a bunch of rebel attacks. I didn't have time to look anywhere."

"The captain said . . ." The courier did not finish his statement.

"Is he all right? I didn't see him. Captain Drakeyt, I mean."

"He had a few gashes, ser. He said he'd be fine."

"What happened?"

"It was all planned. When all the rebels were pushing us back toward the town, Marshal Byrna and First Army hit them from behind. He came around on that old back road. We had the rebels trapped on all sides. Not all that many escaped."

Rahl glanced across the grassland battlefield, seeing as if for the first time all the downed men and mounts, and knowing, as order-depleted as he was, that he was sensing but a fraction of the devastation. Yet it threatened to overwhelm him. He closed his eyes for a moment, but that didn't help.

As he followed the courier, another question crossed Rahl's mind. Why had he seen no chaos-bolts, and no evidence of chaos use by the rebels? The only magery he had seen or sensed had been that used by Taryl and himself.

"There's the overcommander, ser," offered the courier. "If you'd excuse me . . . there are some dispatches."

"You're excused . . . and thank you."

The courier nodded and eased his mount away, as if in relief.

What had Rahl done? Had he failed that badly? Did everyone know it? He looked up.

Taryl was still a good fifty cubits from Rahl, but he said something to the senior officers beside him, then rode away from them, slowly making his way toward Rahl, finally reining up.

Rahl did so as well. "You requested my presence, ser?"

"I'm glad to see that you came through this." A faintly ironic smile touched Taryl's lips.

Rahl could see the blackness under the older mage's eyes, eyes that were so bloodshot that they looked pink. "So am I, ser. Things were . . . somewhat in doubt where we were for some time."

"That was true for all of Second Army. You and Third Company did remarkably well. We'll discuss things tomorrow, after you've had some rest. Convey my appreciation to Captain Drakeyt. You have mine as well." Each of Taryl's words was slow and almost deliberate.

"Yes, ser. I will. Thank you." Rahl realized that Taryl was as exhausted as he was, if not more so.

"Get some rest, Rahl."

"Yes, ser. Perhaps . . . you should too, ser, as you can."

Taryl nodded, then turned his mount back toward the senior officers.

Rahl began to ride back toward Third Company, Taryl's words still going slowly through his mind. Remarkably well? They'd bottled up an entire battalion and destroyed most of it, and all Taryl had to say was that they'd done remarkably well? Hard as it was for him even to keep his eyes open, Rahl had the feeling that, again, he had not acted as he should have—or perhaps that he had acted as Taryl expected, and that had disappointed the older mage.

Rahl turned and rode back to where he thought Third Company had been, looking one way and another before he finally made out Drakeyt, watching as troopers from Third Company recovered weapons and gear and checked for wounded amid the fallen and the dead.

The captain glanced up as Rahl reined the gelding to a halt.

"The overcommander summoned me," Rahl began. "He asked me to convey his thanks and appreciation for all that you and Third Company did. He said you did remarkably well."

"His thanks and appreciation . . . We lost another twenty-five men," Drakeyt said slowly. "Seven of them were in first squad. One of them was Roryt. He was a fine squad leader."

"I'm sorry. I did . . . what I could." What else could Rahl say? He'd used all the order-skills he'd had long before the battle was over, and they'd helped, but they hadn't been enough.

"What you could?" Drakeyt laughed, a sound that was cold and bitter.

Rahl wanted to shrink away.

"You don't know, do you, Majer?"

"Know what?" Rahl could feel the flatness in his voice.

"You and first squad—mostly you—broke a battalion.

I sent a trooper out to count. Around where you were fighting, there were fifty men down. Fifty. Some are still alive. None of them will ever fight again. You can see it in their eyes. At the end, rebels were turning and riding back into the swamp."

"Why?" Rahl didn't understand. He just knew he was almost ready to fall out of the saddle, and everything hurt. He'd been lucky because the rebels hadn't been able to attack all at once. He'd just picked them off in ones and twos while they were trying to recover from swimming through the swamp.

"Majer . . ." Drakeyt's voice softened. "You need some rest and some food. You've done enough."

"Third Company did it," Rahl said. "I didn't know what was going on or who was coming from where. I just tried to disable as many rebels as I could." Fifty? That didn't seem possible. Not with a truncheon, even the one Khelra had made. "I just helped the squad as well as I could." It probably hadn't been enough, but the battle had told him one thing—he didn't have enough experience.

"Sylarn!" Drakeyt called out. "The majer's about to fall out of his saddle. He could use an escort to the bivouac area—we've got that end cottage."

"Yes, ser." The trooper who rode up was thin and wiry, and blood was splashed across his lower sleeves.

Rahl looked down. There was blood everywhere on him.

"Ser . . . this way."

Rahl turned the gelding.

LXI

Gray light seeped under Rahl's eyelids. That was the way it felt. He was lying on his back, and everything hurt. His head still ached, and there were flashes across his eyes, but they only stung rather than knifed into his skull. Yet he had the feeling that, if he opened his eyes and moved, all those aches and pains would get much worse.

At the same time, he did need to get up—for all too many reasons.

Slowly, he opened his eyes. The pain flashes across his eyes intensified, but not by as much as he feared. He was lying near the stone wall, his bedroll on a pallet. The morning light told him that he had slept for most of the afternoon after the battle and through the night. No wonder he was sore.

Rahl didn't remember laying out his bedroll on the floor of the small cot. In fact, he didn't remember much at all after turning to follow the trooper away from the carnage of the battle.

There were voices outside, low voices, and he began to listen.

". . . you want to wake him?"

". . . commander told the captain, and he told you . . ."

". . . doesn't matter . . . scared the living sowshit outa me, and I knew he was on our side . . . closest thing I ever saw to a black demon, closest I ever want to see . . ."

"Squad leader said he killed more 'n sixty . . ."

"Rebs were throwing themselves into the swamp . . . couple of them won't ever think right again . . ."

Rahl swallowed. He'd done *that*? He couldn't have done that. He didn't even know how to do something like that. He started to shake his head, and a lance of pain slammed from his eyes through the back of his skull. His eyes watered so much that he could not see for several

moments. Then, ever so slowly, he rolled onto his side.
After a long pause, he levered himself up and staggered to
a stool, next to a table. On the table was a clay mug, and it
had ale in it. Beside it was a small oval loaf of bread.

Rahl forced himself to study the ale and bread with his
order-senses. Both were good, and he needed no more
encouragement to take a swallow of the ale and break off
a corner of the stale bread. It still tasted welcome.

He'd eaten all the bread and drunk most of the ale when
a trooper rapped on the side of the door and stepped into
the cot. "Ser?"

"I'm awake." Rahl smiled. "I think."

"The overcommander would like to see you, Majer, at
your convenience. He's at the first big barn to the west of
here."

At his convenience? Either Rahl had acquitted himself
far worse than he thought, or Taryl was feeling more gen-
erous than he had after the battle. Rahl could only hope
that it was the latter. "It will be a few moments. Thank
you."

It was probably more than a few moments before he
found a bucket of water and cleaned up as well as he
could, including sponging off as much of the blood as
he could from his uniform, then trying to blot his sleeves
and trousers half-dry.

The gelding was tied outside, but had clearly been
brushed and saddled for him. He looked around, seeing
two troopers—from fifth squad, he thought. "If you two
are the ones who took care of my mount, I'd like to
thank you. If not, please pass my thanks to whoever did."

"Ah . . . yes, ser."

"Thank you. Could one of you tell Captain Drakeyt
that I've been summoned by the overcommander and
that I'll be back as soon as I can?"

"Yes, ser."

"Thank you." Rahl managed not to wince as he swung
up into the saddle.

As he rode slowly away from the cot and the two troop-

ers, he couldn't resist using what little order-strength had
returned to catch what they were saying.

". . . just be glad he's on our side . . ."

"Where did he come from?"

"Word is that he was a laborer in Luba 'cause he of-
fended some powerful mage-guard who took all his memories. The majer got 'em back, and now he'll tear down
every stone in Nubyat to set things right 'cause that mage-
guard is one of Golyat's mages . . ."

"Might, too, if he keeps on like yesterday . . ."

Even as he smiled at the fanciful tale, Rahl wanted to
yell out in protest that it wasn't true, not even in poetic
terms. Yet he feared that disavowing it would only result
in the troopers' coming up with something even more
fantastic.

There were more than a few mounts tied around the
large barn, as well as most of the army's supply wagons,
or so it seemed. Rahl finally ended up tying the gelding
to a fence post nearby. Then he walked into the barn.
Rows and rows of injured men lay on pallets.

Rahl almost staggered at the amount of collective
wound chaos. He glanced around. He ought to do something, but there were so many wounded . . . so many.

Finally, he moved toward a group of lancers who
seemed to have thrust injuries of some sorts. None were
looking his way, not until he appeared.

Rahl let his senses range over the first man, who had
taken a lance through a shoulder, or so it seemed. There
was a pocket of wound chaos deep inside, but it was not
large. "Hold still, trooper."

The trooper looked up, his eyes widening.

Rahl let what order he could neutralize the wound
chaos, then moved to the next man. His entire insides
were reddish white. Rahl managed to keep his face
pleasant, but there was no way he could do anything. The
injuries and chaos were even worse than those of the
sailor whose lungs had been steam-burned in Nylan. All
Rahl did was project warmth and comfort. "Take care."

He managed to help, he thought, five men before he began to get extremely light-headed, and he turned away, looking to find Taryl.

"What were you doing there? Do you have—"

As Rahl turned to face the undercaptain, the young officer stepped back. "I'm sorry, ser."

"I was just trying to help some of them," Rahl said. "I was summoned by the overcommander."

"Yes, ser." The undercaptain eased back from Rahl. "He's down there."

"Thank you." Rahl stepped away. Again, he could hear murmurs, but whether they were from the wounded or from some of the officers who had joined the undercaptain, he couldn't tell.

". . . one they're calling the black demon . . ."

". . . seems young for a majer . . ."

". . . not when you see his eyes . . ."

His eyes? Was there something wrong with them? Rahl frowned, but kept walking toward the half-open plank door pointed out by the undercaptain.

Taryl was in a small room Rahl guessed might once have been a tack room. The overcommander was standing over a makeshift plank table on which were spread maps.

"Ser? You said to see you today."

"Greetings, Rahl."

Rahl could see the deep black pits under Taryl's bloodshot eyes. "Begging your pardon, ser, but did you get any rest?"

"Some, not enough. There's never enough time." Taryl coughed, then took a sip from the mug on the side of the plank table. "There are all the wounded, too."

"I know. I did what I could for some of them. When I'm stronger, I'll try more."

"That's commendable, but don't exhaust yourself. You'll need to be at full strength in the eightdays ahead." Taryl shook his head. "I might seem cold, but healing won't do much for dealing with Golyat, and that's where we—and you—have to put most of our efforts."

Rahl understood that. He didn't have to like it.

"In that regard, I wanted to ask you a few questions before you have to fight any more battles. Why do you think so many of the rebel forces were attacking the left side of Second Army?"

Rahl didn't know, and he was still so tired that he knew he wasn't thinking all that well. "I couldn't say, ser, except that they wanted to turn our eastern flank."

"Do you think it was coincidence that Third Company was there?"

"No, ser. You thought they might, and you wanted someone there who could tell if they were going to do that, and you hoped I'd be able to slow them down if it happened, ser."

"That's true enough," replied Taryl. "But what if I wanted to make sure that they'd concentrate on the eastern flank?"

"Was that to make it easier for the marshal to attack their rear?"

"Exactly. But you didn't answer my question."

Rahl closed his eyes for a moment. What was different about Third Company? Him? The fact that he was an ordermage? "You wanted their mages to sense me? But you were the one who told me to keep my shields stronger."

"I did. That was for two reasons. First, it keeps them from locating you precisely, and that will become even more important in the days ahead. Second, it shows your strength."

"And that was why they put so many forces against us?"

"I would judge so."

"What if they had overwhelmed us? Then what?"

"That was a risk, but I do have some faith in you, Rahl."

Rahl was too tired to be as angry as he might have been. He just nodded. "Could I ask you something, ser?"

"You can ask. I might not answer, or not answer to your satisfaction."

"Why did the rebels fight us here?"

Taryl laughed, harshly. "I don't know, exactly, but I can guess. First, they knew my forces were inferior, and they didn't know exactly where the marshal was, because all the strong mage-guards were with Second Army, and they concentrated on us. Second, they don't want to fight in places that will destroy crops or other valuable land or buildings or assets. That doesn't matter as much to the Emperor, because he can draw on the rest of Hamor, but Golyat has to be careful of his resources. If he fights where food or crops are destroyed, he loses much of the support of the people that he now has—and there will be more opposition. He could defeat us in every battle and lose. We don't want that because it would take generations, if not centuries, for Merowey to recover. So . . . at least in the beginning, we will fight in places like Thalye. But, as we push them back, it could get nastier and more brutal. That is why we must move with great care. It is not just a matter of winning battles."

There were several moments of silence.

"Ser . . . have I failed in some way?"

Taryl's eyes narrowed. "Do you have to ask that question?"

"I realize that I have much to learn, and I've kept trying to develop my abilities, but it seems as though, no matter what I do, it's never adequate."

"Oh . . . that."

Rahl felt as though he'd taken a staff in the gut.

Taryl shook his head. "There is one lesson, one aspect of life I cannot teach you. It is something that you must learn with every fiber of your being. It cannot be taught, only learned, and for that reason I will not tell you what it is. I will say that you have much to learn, as you have acknowledged, but you have not yet failed. Neither have you succeeded in becoming what you must in order to live with yourself. Given your potential, if you do not learn that, you will become as Golyat and those who have followed him."

"And you cannot tell me?"

Taryl's sad smile was the only answer he gave.

"Is there anything else, ser?"

"More will be expected of you, Rahl. You have the potential to be great, and of those who could be great, much is expected." Taryl's lips quirked. "Once we determine what the enemy is doing and how to pursue, I'll brief you and Captain Drakeyt on what you'll be doing. In the meantime, eat some more and get some rest."

"Yes, ser." Rahl nodded politely. "If that's all, ser . . . ?"

"For now."

Rahl turned and walked out of the small chamber.

At least he had not failed. But what was it that he had to learn that Taryl refused to tell him? And why did Taryl expect so much of him?

LXII

Oneday found Third Company on the road once more, if a different road, under a hazy late-afternoon sky that created a feel of more chill than actually was present.

On eightday, Taryl had summoned Drakeyt and Rahl. His briefing had been direct and simple. They were to take the side road, also paved, and almost as well traveled as the main road, as far as the town of Undmyn, some fifteen kays to the west-southwest. Third Company was to discover if there were any sizable forces in the area and to check the status of the mines just short of the town and determine if they were being protected by rebel forces. If the mines were not defended, Rahl and Drakeyt were to suggest to whoever might be in charge that any shipments of copper to rebel forces or to areas currently controlled by the rebels would be considered treason and dealt with accordingly. They were not to enter the town itself, nor were they to initiate any combat, but only to defend themselves were Third Company attacked. If the town and surrounding areas were free of rebel forces, Third Company was to continue onward, taking the road farther until it returned to the main road, where the company was to rejoin Second Army.

After the briefing, Taryl had transferred another twenty-five troopers to Third Company, from one of the companies so decimated by the battle that those twenty-five were all who were left alive and unwounded. One was Dhosyn, the new squad leader for first squad, a small and compact man with old scars across both cheeks and his forehead.

For some reason, Dhosyn reminded Rahl of Khalyt, the first engineer Rahl had met in Nylan, although they looked not in the slightest alike. Was it the quiet competence? Rahl wasn't sure, and he wondered exactly why he'd thought of the young engineer. Then, Deybri had that same quiet competence, and a quiet warmth that he missed even more, as much as he told himself that there was no help for it. He had tried to write her about the battle, but, in the end, he'd torn up that part of his continuing letter. He might tell her . . .

Rahl shook his head and shifted his weight in the saddle. When would he see her to tell her in person? Would he even receive another letter for seasons?

He turned his eyes to the way ahead.

The road to Undmyn didn't look that much different from the road from Lahenta to Thalye. There were steads everywhere, with fields, meadows, and woods. The grasslands south of Thalye had already begun to give way to lush and fertile fields, and the air was warmer, so much so that, although it was but a few eightdays past the height of winter in Merowey, Rahl was only wearing his riding jacket in the early morning or well after sunset. The tilled fields were showing green sprouts, doubtless because the area was warmer and the danger of frost had passed earlier in the year. The older wooden fences held a greenish shade, as if they harbored moss all year round.

The other similarity was that no one was in sight when Third Company rode by. There might be a woodpile with a stack of fresh-split wood chunks, but the splitter had vanished. There might be laundry half-hung on a line between two trees, but no sign of anyone who might have hung it.

Less than a kay before, Rahl and Alrydd, riding behind the scouts as outriders, had passed a kaystone whose worn characters had indicated five kays to Undmyn. Outside of a grittiness in the air, and a faintly acrid and metallic odor, there was no sign of either the mines or the town, and Rahl had not yet sensed the presence of large numbers of people—either troops or the grouping that suggested a town or hamlet.

"Hard to believe there's mines ahead, ser," offered Alrydd.

"Sometimes, there are more than a few things that are hard to believe," replied Rahl. *Such as what had happened in the fighting at the edge of the swamp.*

As hard as Rahl had tried to recall exactly what had happened when he and first squad had battled the rebel troopers coming out of the swamp, he did not remember much in the way of details beyond images of his truncheon striking troopers. But he could not believe he had killed all that many, and he had trouble crediting the stories he'd heard—or the belief by troopers that he broke the attack himself.

Yet . . . whenever he thought about the truncheon or let his order-senses touch it, Rahl could feel the difference. While it had been crafted from dark oak, that oak had been part of a staff. Rahl had to wonder if the staff had been one given to an exile from Recluce. There was enough order within the oak that the staff was strong enough to stand up to steel. He'd examined it more than once since the battle, and there were no marks at all on

the smooth surface. It couldn't have been that way earlier, because Khelra couldn't have crafted it. Could she?

Rahl shook his head. He hadn't sensed that kind of
order-crafting in the cooper, good as she clearly was as a
crafter. So what had happened to the truncheon? Had he
done something to it in the heat of battle? The odds were
that he had, but what, he didn't know and couldn't recall.

"Another disadvantage of being a natural ordermage,"
he murmured to himself.

"Ser?"

"Just thinking out loud, Alrydd."

At that moment, he could feel the faint and distant chill,
not in his body, but in his thoughts, that he had come to
recognize as the hallmark of some mage using a glass to
scree for him. Although Rahl could sense screeing attempts, he had followed Taryl's advice and kept holding
stronger shields—which was getting easier with each
day—and he could sense that the mages seeking him were
not finding him—at least not in more than a general sense.

Still, he had to wonder whether the Third Company's
patrol to Undmyn was really necessary, except as a tactical maneuver to keep the rebel mages off guard as to
what Taryl and the marshal were actually doing.

Whatever the reason might be, Rahl reminded himself,
he needed to concentrate on the road and the areas beside
and beyond it, and for the next kay or so, he said nothing,
just kept trying to see or sense anything that might pose the
slightest threat to Third Company. He could detect nothing.

"Ser?"

"Yes, Alyrdd."

"I been wondering, ser. You know, at Thalye, we beat
up the rebels pretty bad, but the overcommander didn't
pursue them. Well, not right away, and he's a pretty
crafty one."

"You'd like to know why?" Rahl chuckled. "He didn't
say much about that when he briefed us, but he did say
that only about one in five of their troopers escaped being captured, wounded, or killed, and they scattered

every which way. I'd judge that there wasn't much way to pursue them without splitting up our forces."

"Makes sense, ser, but I wasn't sure."

There was another reason, too, if not more, from what Rahl knew of Taryl. One well might have been that Taryl wanted word to circulate about the immensity of that rebel defeat.

Ahead to the right were several low hills, and beyond them, Rahl could make out a number of brick chimneys. But as he rode closer, Rahl could tell that those stacks were cold—not the slightest trace of smoke issued from any of them.

He turned in the saddle. "Mines ahead!"

Drakeyt immediately rode forward to join Rahl. "The chimneys beyond those hills?"

"I'd judge so. I'm not sure there's anyone there . . . but I can't tell yet."

"I'll have the company ready weapons, just in case." Drakeyt turned his mount back toward the main body.

Rahl and Alrydd kept riding.

Even before he rode fully clear of the hills flanking the smelter below the mines, Rahl could tell that the structures and the mines were empty. The buildings hadn't been burned, but Rahl could sense that no one was there.

As he rode even closer, he could see recent tracks in the side lanes and could discern a feeling of recent inhabitation. There were also no hauling wagons in sight. Doubtless, the rebels had hauled away all the copper stock or ingots or sheets and shut down the mines and smelter when they had learned Second Army was headed to Undmyn.

Had that been one of Taryl's goals?

At the moment, Rahl honestly couldn't have said he knew what any of the overcommander's objectives were, except to put down the rebellion for the Emperor . . . and the Empress.

LXIII

On threeday, Third Company rejoined Second Army just outside the small town of Secryta, just before sunset. During the entire ride from Thalye through Undmyn and back to the main road, neither Rahl nor any of the scouts or patrols had seen any sign of rebels. Nor had they seen any locals outside, which was understandable. Rahl had used the glass several times as well, but the nearest rebel force, as well as he could tell, was a good twenty kays to the south.

As Drakeyt and Rahl rode toward the inn in Secryta, to which they had been summoned to meet with the over-commander, Rahl had realized that Taryl had not asked him to check tariffs and town administrators, and in fact, Third Company's orders had precluded such. Why?

"You're looking concerned, Majer," offered Drakeyt.

"Just thinking." Then he nodded. Taryl had wanted to know the level of support enjoyed by the rebels in areas where there was some rebel presence and where local authorities had in fact had a choice in whether to remain loyal to the Emperor or to support Prince Golyat. Now, Third Company was in territory controlled by the rebels, and there was little point in verifying that. In fact, doing so might create problems later on.

"Is it the sort of thinking that might worry captains, ser?" Drakeyt's tone was light, but the feelings behind the words were not.

"Not this time." Rahl laughed softly. "I was thinking about why I had to check the records of some town administrators and clerks and not others. It wasn't about tactics or positions."

"Might I ask . . . ?"

"Supplies and golds . . . who had them, how much went to the rebels, and who was trustworthy." That was true enough so far as it went, but Rahl didn't feel comfortable saying more because he would have been speculating. He didn't actually know Taryl's reasons.

"The overcommander thinks of more than many commanders." Drakeyt's voice was bland.

"Quite a lot more, I've discovered." Rahl offered a short laugh. "There's the square up ahead."

The inn at Secryta was, as most were in Merowey, located on one side of the town square. Troopers, nearly a squad, were stationed around the inn, but there was space for Drakeyt and Rahl to tie their mounts at the hitching rail below the wide front porch. They walked up the three brick steps to the porch and into the inn.

An undercaptain straightened and turned as Rahl and Drakeyt stepped through the ancient golden oak doorway. His eyes went to Rahl, then turned just slightly from meeting the mage-guard's. "Majer, Captain, the overcommander is in the room on the left at the end of the foyer. He's expecting you."

The room at the end of the foyer was opposite the public room, which held several majers and two commanders. Rahl could feel eyes on him as he turned toward the chamber in which Taryl stood. The overcommander was looking down at an array of maps spread over an oblong table that extended nearly ten cubits, suggesting that the chamber was usually a private dining area, although Rahl had to wonder why a town as modest as Secryta would have needed such a function room very often.

"Consortings," replied Taryl dryly, as Rahl stepped into the chamber, "and you still let things slip past your shields, Majer."

"I apologize, ser." Rahl inclined his head.

"Accepted. Close the door."

Drakeyt did so.

Taryl motioned them toward the larger map on the table. "This is the area to the south of us. We have solid word that Golyat's forces—a goodly portion of them—are marshaling at Bhucyra. Here." Taryl pointed to a red dot on the map. "That is clearly an effort to stop us at a position where terrain favors them. We will appear to oblige them . . . initially." The overcommander's index finger pointed to a spot north of the red dot. "Third Company's task is to take this side road here and make a brief preemptive attack. The targets are the lead companies of the rebel battalions who are using this side road in an effort to flank First Army. You are not to attempt penetration of the enemy companies, but to make a series of attacks so that they will have to concentrate on Third Company. Your efforts will permit other Imperial battalions to strike them with far-more-damaging force. There are low rises to the north of the road—just enough to conceal your approach, until you are within a quarter kay. You will depart Secryta before dawn tomorrow, and you should reach the target area by late midmorning. If the rebels continue as they have, they will arrive somewhat after midday. You are to wait until they do arrive, or until it is clear that they will not—or until a courier reaches you with a change of orders."

Rahl knew that Taryl's information had not come from the older mage's use of a screeing glass. But how else would he have known?

"How intense an attack, ser?" asked Drakeyt.

"Enough to make them stop or pursue you. It's not likely that they'll pursue for long. You'll be attacking over a low rise that could conceal battalions, and they should be hesitant to follow."

"And if they aren't, ser?"

"Then I am confident that Majer Rahl will have planned for that, based on the situation and the terrain." Taryl nodded toward Rahl. "After your part of the operation is concluded, you are to scout the area to make sure that no one surprises Commander Shuchyl. Then you will return with the commander's force to Second Army." Taryl paused. "Any other questions?"

"How large a rebel force are we expecting?" Rahl asked.

"Between two and four battalions."

Ten to twenty companies? What had Taryl planned?

"I'm sure you understand why Third Company is required, Majer."

"Yes, ser."

"Good. Thank you, Majer, Captain." Taryl nodded to dismiss them.

As they left the overcommander and walked out of the inn, Rahl realized that something else about Taryl troubled him. Rather, it was about how Taryl had changed in his treatment of Rahl. In the beginning, and even on their mission to Recluce, Taryl had been helpful, glad to explain matters to Rahl. Now, it was as though any explanation came only if Rahl asked for it—and only then if Taryl decided that Rahl should have an answer.

"The overcommander answered a question you never asked," Drakeyt said, standing by his mount.

"Ordermages who are Triads or close to that ability can often sense unspoken inquiries," Rahl said. *Especially from careless mage-guards.* "That's one reason why the Emperor's Triad is useful and also why he must be absolutely loyal."

After a moment, Drakeyt replied, "I can see that."

Although the captain's posture did not change, Rahl could sense an internal stiffness and wariness. Rather than say more, Rahl mounted.

"Can you tell me the reason why Third Company is required?" Drakeyt asked softly.

"Because we create an impression of far greater force than we actually have," Rahl replied. "That is what the overcommander believes."

"I see," replied Drakeyt.

Rahl could also sense the half-whispered thought that followed Drakeyt's words.

". . . and who are we to question the overcommander?"

LXIV

The sun had barely cleared the woods to the east of Third Company on fourday when Rahl dismounted and handed the gelding's reins to Shanyr, the younger outrider. Rahl stepped back and eased the screeing glass and its wrappings from the saddlebag, then walked to the side of the lane that was little more than a trail, where he uncovered the glass. He took a deep breath and concentrated, trying to seek an image showing both the rebel battalions and Third Company.

The glass showed the green-blue sky, then the swirling mists. Slowly, the mists cleared and revealed an image—one that might have been seen by a hawk. In the northeastern corner was a double file of horses, little more than black dots. A trail meandered along the top of the image on the north side of several low rises. South of the first line of rises was a narrow stream, and south of the second set of rises was a wider road. Farther west on the road were much longer sets of files of horses, with some wagons—rebels, Rahl judged from the few maroon jackets he could make out. South and east of the larger force was . . . something . . . except it was blurred. The image just looked like fields and woodlots . . . but there was more there, if unseen by the eye. Rahl realized that what he could vaguely sense but not see had to be Commander Shuchyl's battalions—and that Taryl was providing magelike concealment. Those battalions had to have preceded Third Company by at least a day, which meant that Taryl had left later and ridden hard to join them. Was there another mage-guard who could have done that?

Rahl certainly didn't know of any, and he hadn't sensed any that powerful. Still . . .

He shook his head and released the image before he got light-headed. After rewrapping the glass and replacing it in his saddlebags, he remounted, then reminded himself to eat several of the travel biscuits he had purchased at the small chandlery in Secryta. He'd also added hard cheese and some dried fruit. As he ate, he rode back to the head of the main body and Drakeyt.

"We're about two kays from the attack point. The rebels are around four. If you'll gather the squad leaders, I can sketch out where everyone is and where we have to go."

Drakeyt nodded slowly, then said dryly, "That would be helpful, Majer." He raised an arm. "Company halt! Squad leaders forward. Pass it back!"

Once the five squad leaders were assembled, Rahl sketched out the positions in the dirt at the edge of the trail/road so that Drakeyt and the squad leaders could see them. "Here we are, and here are the rebels, heading toward Bhucyra. South of where they'll be shortly are our main forces, but they're concealed. They won't attack until we do." *Unless something goes wrong.* "We're about two kays from this rise, where we can wait until they get closer. We'll need to wait to attack until the rebels reach here."

"So that the commander can move his forces out of concealment and attack their rear and flank?" Drakeyt's words were barely a question.

"I'd judge so. The rise south of the road is so low that they couldn't draw up there, and that means they're almost a kay from the road. The terrain is open, but . . ." Rahl shrugged.

"We'll have to hit fast and sting hard." Drakeyt looked from one squad leader to the next, starting with Dhosyn and ending with Lyrn. "At first, and as long as we can, we'll attack by squads, one at a time. The remainder of the company will remain behind the rise, columns abreast in five-front facing the road. At some point, they'll break ranks or attack with a company or more. That's when the squad under attack will immediately circle back to the rise, and the company will form up on top of the rise.

Then we'll attack from the rise and ride southeast, across the road like scalded demons, in advance of their companies. If they advance in force, with an entire battalion, we'll clear the area and let them."

Drakeyt stopped and looked from squad leader to squad leader once again. "Our task is to get them to concentrate on us without taking any heavier casualties than necessary, so that Commander Shuchyl can hit their flank and rear. Is that clear?"

"Yes, ser."

"Good. Back to your squads."

After the squad leaders had left, Rahl edged the gelding closer to Drakeyt. "What squad will lead with the first attack?"

"First squad. Dhosyn has a good record at that."

"Where should officers fit into such attacks?"

Drakeyt smiled, wryly. "Only as necessary, according to the tactics manual."

Rahl thought he understood. "Emergencies and unanticipated events?"

"Something like that."

"Then I'll stand by with you for the first unanticipated event."

"I thought you might. I hope there aren't any, but there will be. There always are."

That was true in everything, Rahl had already discovered.

While he waited behind the rise beside Drakeyt, under a sun that seemed far too warm for winter, Rahl munched on another few travel biscuits. Between eating more and being more judicious in his use of order-skills, he hoped he wouldn't end up an easy target. He also hoped he'd be able to hold his personal shields more and longer—at least when he was in direct combat.

Before long, Rahl and Drakeyt could barely see the rebel companies, through the grass at the top of the rise. Rahl could sense that they were riding three abreast on the road and somewhat squeezed together. He could also see the dust above the rise, but farther back in the column, as if the first riders had broken up the dirt, and the hoofs of later mounts had powdered it so that the light breeze carried it into the air. Behind him and to his left were the five squads of Third Company, formed up across the back side of the rise with five-man fronts, so that, if necessary, all five squads could charge and strike the enemy as one. Or they could wheel east and move as a four-front column away from the rebels.

"They're a tight three-abreast," Rahl said quietly. "They're about a quarter kay west of us."

"First squad, stand by." Drakeyt turned to Rahl. "Let me know when they're only two hundred cubits west."

Rahl continued to use his order-senses, gauging and judging, until he turned to the captain. "Two hundred."

"First squad! Charge!" Drakeyt's voice was just loud enough to reach first squad and Dhosyn.

Following Drakeyt's example, Rahl eased the gelding farther up the rise so that he could see all of the attack. He hadn't sensed any archers or crossbowmen, but that didn't mean there weren't some.

First squad was halfway down the rise toward the vanguard of the rebels—basically a company of troopers—before there was any sign of reaction. Then sabres appeared. After a moment, a squad charged off the road and into the flat toward first squad. Dhosyn had anticipated that, because first squad split. Then each half squad turned inward and struck the sides of the rebel squad. As ordered by Drakeyt, the troopers did not prolong the attack but wheeled away.

Rahl could sense wounds, but all of first squad remained in the saddle, while several rebels had been unhorsed.

"Second squad! Forward!"

The rebel squad had broken off pursuit when first squad had apparently fled, and the rebel troopers had slowed and were trying to re-form when they caught sight of second squad racing downhill toward them. The rebel squad leader hesitated, then ordered his men to charge second squad. The command came so late that second squad's sabres struck with the impact of higher speed and certainty.

But even as second squad was withdrawing, the rebel company commander ordered the entire company onto the flat and uphill after second squad.

"Third Company!" ordered Drakeyt. "Charge through the rebels! Re-form to the south! Charge!"

Rahl managed to keep fairly close to Drakeyt for a bit, but only until he was halfway down the rise, when he had to concentrate on getting his truncheon out of the scabbard. Some actions just weren't habit yet.

As he neared the rebels, he could see three of them converging on him. Since he was still in good order-control, he just kept riding, then expanded his order shield for a moment just before the blades flashed toward him. Two of the three troopers—and their mounts—went down, but the effort shattered Rahl's control of his shields, and he had to use the truncheon on the next trooper.

"Third Company! To the south!" Drakeyt's orders rose over the melee.

Rahl managed to block another thrust and slam the truncheon into the chest of a rebel, then guide the gelding around another man, while using a backcut to stagger the other.

Then he was riding amid third squad, across the road and onto the flat. Because he could sense other riders—the Imperial forces were attacking the middle and rear of the rebel column—he glanced back over his shoulder.

While several rebels had pursued Third Company, they had broken off the chase, possibly because the rebel column was turning to face Commander Shuchyl's troopers.

"Third Company! Re-form by squad!"

Rahl turned his mount, then saw an Imperial undercaptain riding hard toward Drakeyt. Wanting to know what the orders might be, Rahl changed directions in order to reach Drakeyt as well. He reined up short of the two officers just as the undercaptain began to speak.

"Captain! The commander requests that your company take the right flank and attack their van to keep them from escaping!"

Drakeyt nodded, then stood in the stirrups. "Third Company! To the rear, ride and re-form! On me!"

As the company re-formed, Rahl rode more to the east, where he took a position at the front between fourth and fifth squads. He checked his truncheon, then concentrated on riding, still not an ingrained habit, as he and the squads flanking him moved forward to reengage the rebel vanguard company.

By the time they left the downslope and rode across the flat on the south side of the road, the rebels had re-formed and begun to charge toward Third Company. The two lines converged and . . . all order and sense of place vanished. Dust was everywhere, and Rahl was fighting as much through what he felt as what he saw. He just kept the truncheon in constant motion and tried to keep his personal shields close to him and as tight as possible.

A huge trooper with an ax rode toward Rahl. Rahl did his best to angle his shields, then duck and strike the attacker on the back of his upper arm with all the force he could manage at that moment. The ax went flying into the dust, as did the trooper, and Rahl wheeled his mount, barely staying in the saddle, but managing to deflect a slash by yet another trooper, before countering and cracking bones.

Still yet another rebel appeared out of the dust, thrusting a long blade at Rahl, who knocked it aside, then backcut into the man's face. The *crunch* and the feeling of death sent a flash of nausea through Rahl.

He urged the gelding forward and slammed aside a sabre thrust intended for Lyrn's back, then kept moving to take down another rebel from behind. Again, he could sense death, and the feeling of nausea it engendered.

Rahl's entire upper body ached, and he had swallowed bile and held back nausea more with each moment of combat, before he finally found himself at the side of the road reined up beside several other troopers from fifth squad. All he could see nearby were Imperial troopers, already beginning to re-form into their squads and companies, although he could make out several riders scattering away from the battle, presumably rebels fleeing.

"Third Company! Check for your wounded! Then re-form!"

Once the wounded had been carried to the wagons captured from the rebels, and Third Company had formed up, Rahl could see that, again, they had suffered losses, but only a handful compared to those incurred in the swamp battle.

"We won't keep doing this," Drakeyt said from his mount beside Rahl.

"Winning?" asked Rahl.

"Surprising them so badly. They counted on Marshal Byrna's tactics, not the overcommander's. They'll become far more cautious and force us to do the attacking."

"And make the mistakes?" suggested Rahl. "What if the overcommander doesn't make any?"

"All commanders do; some just make fewer than their opponents, and some opponents don't see the mistakes."

"Majer! Captain!" The call came from an undercaptain riding toward Third Company.

Rahl and Drakeyt turned and waited for the undercaptain to rein up.

"Commander Shuchyl sends his appreciation, Captain." The undercaptain turned to Rahl. "The overcommander would like a word with you, Majer. If you would follow me."

Drakeyt looked to Rahl, quizzically.

"He had to have been here. I'll explain later."

Rahl turned the gelding, letting him walk at his own pace, slowly westward on the once-grassy flat south of the road. He tried to gain a sense of what had happened, but all he could determine was that hundreds, if not thousands, of rebels had died, as had a lesser number, possibly a far lesser number, of Imperial troopers.

Taryl was talking with a commander, presumably Shuchyl. Upon seeing Rahl approach, he nodded to the commander, then turned his mount and rode over to meet Rahl, reining up less than three cubits away.

"Ser," offered Rahl politely.

"You look somewhat less the worse for wear than after the last battle," offered Taryl.

"Thank you, ser." Rahl felt he was learning, nauseated as he had felt for a time. "Your concealment was most effective."

The overcommander nodded, slightly. "It was useful . . . this time, but they will be looking for it in future battles."

"They might be, ser . . . if anyone who understood what happened escaped to explain it."

"We can't count on that, Majer. Always assume your strategies are seen and understood."

Rahl had the feeling that Taryl was talking about far more than battles. "Yes, ser."

"I will see you later. Third Company is to ride with Commander Shuchyl's forces to the main encampment for First and Second Army in Bhucyra. Golyat's forces have decided to battle for Nubyat farther south, around Selyma." Taryl nodded dismissal. "It is likely that they will force us to attack, or to make the first move."

"Yes, ser."

As he rode back toward Third Company, Rahl had to wonder why Taryl had wanted to see him at all.

LXV

By the time Commander Shuchyl had completed mopping up the isolated rebel squads and companies, as well as organizing the captured wagons, collecting stray mounts and weapons, and dealing with the wounded, it had been close to sunset on fourday. Even so, the commander had the force ride another five kays southward to a hamlet called Feoyn. Taryl had taken half a company and ridden on to return to the main body of Second Army in Bhucyra.

The commander rousted out all the companies at dawn on fiveday, and by early afternoon Third Company was settled, in a fashion, in a stead with a large barn and several sheds on the outskirts of Bhucyra. Rahl did make arrangements with the woman of the stead to wash his bloody uniform. If they stayed more than a day, he might get the other one clean as well.

He'd spent some time, and effort, trying to speed the healing of several of the less severely wounded troopers, and was crossing the space between the shed where the wounded were quartered and the main barn when a trooper rode toward him.

"Majer! There's a courier out front for you."

"Thank you." Rahl wondered what else Taryl might want, for who else would be seeking him?

He turned and headed back to the front of the stead house.

The courier inclined his head politely and extended a folded sheet of paper. "From the overcommander, ser."

"Thank you."

"My pleasure, ser." The trooper turned his mount. In moments, he was headed back toward the center of the town.

Rahl had definitely felt the shiver of fear in the man,

along with a form of respect. He wanted to shake his head. He'd never wanted to be in a war, but it seemed like his only choice, given who and what he was, was to be good at it, and from what he could tell, if he had to live in Hamor, he'd rather live under the Emperor in a united realm than under the sort of people that gathered to Golyat.

He unfolded the paper—it was just a short note from Taryl.

Meet me at the White Boar before dinner.

That was all.

Rahl took one of the spare and captured mounts to ride into Bhucyra. His gelding needed a rest. The town was large enough that he had to ask for directions to the White Boar—a modest inn located two long blocks away from the square and overlooking the Awhut River.

After finding a stableboy, Rahl had to search for Taryl, then wait while the overcommander finished his meeting with several commanders. When they left the small side dining chamber, Taryl motioned for Rahl to join him. Rahl was careful to close the door firmly, and keep his personal order shields strong and tight.

Taryl sat down in one of the chairs and motioned for the younger mage-guard to do the same. Although Taryl had not been involved in any more battles, the overcommander still looked as worn and exhausted as he had right after the battle the previous day.

"Ser . . . begging your pardon . . . but you could use some rest." Rahl turned the chair slightly to face Taryl directly.

"So could we all, Rahl."

"Yes, ser, but you make the difference, and if you wear yourself out, there's no one to replace you."

Taryl smiled faintly. "No man is indispensable, much as each of us would like to think so."

"That may be true, ser, but there are levels of dispensability, and while no man is indispensable, the cost of dispensing with some men—or some women—is far greater than with others. Dispensing with you would be most costly for the Emperor."

"I have some doubt that most in Cigoerne would agree with you."

"That is why you are here, and they are there."

"Keep practicing statements like that, Rahl, and you might yet survive in the Palace."

Rahl doubted that Taryl's words were meant as an unalloyed compliment. "It will take more time than I have, ser, for that kind of practice."

Taryl actually laughed, if briefly, and it was the first real laugh Rahl had seen in eightdays from the older mage-guard. After the laugh and smile faded, Taryl cleared his throat. "You've been very effective in the last several battles, Rahl, but, except for that one chaos-mage, Golyat's forces haven't used magery. That will change. I can't say whether it will be at Selyma or thereafter. Golyat has at least ten former mage-guards, and several are quite accomplished."

"Do you know why they haven't used them?"

"No. I can surmise, however." An ironic smile crossed the overcommander's lips. "Most mages, as strong as they may be, have only a few abilities with which they can exercise great strength and mastery. Revealing those abilities at times when it is not critical for success and victory could allow us to develop a tactic to counter them. Also, those with great power will resist hazarding themselves when it is not to their personal advantage, and . . . if they have great power, who could force them to do so?"

"A company of officers rather than troopers?" asked Rahl.

Taryl nodded. "That does not discount their potential effectiveness. For that reason, I would advise you against using anywhere near your full abilities early in any forthcoming battle. Those you may face will be more than patient, and most willing to sacrifice scores, if not thousands, of troopers to wear you out. You cannot protect

Third Company at all costs, not when that cost might be your life and might prolong the rebellion."

"I can see that, ser." Rahl didn't have to like it, but what Taryl said made an unfortunate kind of sense.

"For now, that is all I had. We'll be here tomorrow as well. So get some rest and eat as well as you can."

"Yes, ser."

"There is one thing more." Taryl rose and handed an envelope to Rahl. "You look to be most fortunate. I presume this is from the healer."

Rahl took the envelope, noting that it was addressed to Majer Rahl, Mage-Guard, in care of Third Company, Second Army of Hamor, Cigoerne, Hamor. "How—"

"The High Command makes an effort to assure any trooper or officer receives all letters," Taryl replied. "Sometimes it takes eightdays for them to reach us, but few are ever lost. I thought you might like to have it." Taryl smiled, an expression truly warm and yet wistful.

"Thank you, ser."

"Don't thank me, Rahl. She's the one who wrote."

Rahl couldn't help smiling as he inclined his head before stepping away.

Once he left Taryl, Rahl retreated to a corner of the front foyer of the White Boar and opened the letter. He wasn't about to wait until he rode back to Third Company. He forced himself to read it slowly.

My dearest,
I will soon come to a decision. Do not ask what that is or might be, or how soon I will decide. Whatever it may be, know that you are in my heart and will always be. Whatever else may come, know that is true. For now, I can only ask your patience and forbearance.

Please be as careful as you can. Remember that in all struggles, a number of men and women linked by purpose and order can always defeat the greatest of mages, whether of order or chaos. Healing and building

proceed one small step at a time. So does winning battles, I would imagine, although I claim no knowledge
of such.

Aleasya sends her best. She claims that she always
knew you would persevere and succeed in war because she had never seen an ordermage strong enough
and dumb enough to handle a falchiona. Uncle Thorl
also wishes you well.

The signature was a simple "Deybri."

What decision was she considering? He didn't like the
phrase, "whatever else may come," because that was suggesting that she loved him but could not bring herself to
commit to him. He took a deep breath, then smiled wryly.
She had asked for patience, and she would have it. What
else could he do? Besides, he had no options until the revolt was suppressed—if it could be.

Yet, as he rode back through the twilight, he thought
about her words and wondered. He dared not hope.

Nubyat

LXVI

On sevenday, Second Army moved southward under high thin gray clouds toward Selyma, a large town that straddled the Awhut River. Although the air was warmer than it had been farther inland, the grass remained green, and none of the trees sported the shriveled gray leaves of winter, to Rahl it *felt* raw and chill, doubtless because it was so damp. All the steads near the road were shuttered, and many had been abandoned by their holders, at least until they felt the fighting had passed.

Once more, Third Company was effectively the van, although Taryl had dispatched scouts ahead of the vanguard in all directions. Rahl could not sense any rebels—or any traps—but none of the holdings near the main road held any food or supplies, either, and he doubted that was solely the result of the holders' prudence.

He still didn't know what to make of Deybri's letter, and there was something else about it, something that indicated more than the words, but he couldn't exactly put a finger—or a thought—to whatever it was. Yet the words and even the feeling in the letters of her words showed that she cared. Rahl could almost feel the conflicts within her—that she did love him, but that she also felt tied to Nylan and what she did there. How would she resolve that? Could she? What could he do if she found she could not leave Recluce?

He shook his head. There was nothing he could do at

the moment, except his best for Taryl and the Emperor. Perhaps, if he did well enough . . . perhaps he could work out something, as an envoy of a more lasting nature from Hamor to Nylan.

He laughed softly, humorously. As if anyone would agree to that—either in Cigoerne or Nylan.

After a time, Drakeyt rode forward to join Rahl, and Rahl dropped back so that the two officers trailed Alrydd and Shanyr by a good ten cubits.

"How do you figure it?" asked the older officer.

"I'd judge that we're about two kays from the staging area. We just passed the stone that indicated five kays from Selyma."

"It figures that they'd make a stand at Selyma," said Drakeyt, standing briefly in the stirrups to stretch his legs. "That's the only bridge in forty kays, and there are hills north of the town, and a lake to the northwest of the hills, and the river to the southeast. The hills command the road. If we want to cross the river, and we've got to do that to reach Nubyat, we either take Selyma or backtrack thirty kays or more and then take our chances on dirt lanes that sometimes connect and sort of follow the river on the other side. Or we try to ford a river that's close to two hundred cubits wide and at least ten deep, or find barges that the rebels have mostly kept in Nubyat."

"Or we ride a hundred kays over paved roads and come back from the southeast on the road between Nubyat and Sastak?" suggested Rahl.

"None of those is a good idea." Drakeyt shook his head. "Here we've got a clear supply line and a way to move quickly. Once we take Selyma, we're less than fifteen kays from Nubyat, and we'll hold access to the river and to the coastal highway north to Elmari and south to Sastak."

If we take Selyma. But Rahl nodded, recalling what Taryl had told him.

"You look doubtful. You're the mage-guard who can do anything. Why so cautious now?"

"Because . . ." Rahl paused for a moment. "Because we

know that Golyat has a number of mage-guards, and we've encountered only one. That's going to change soon, and it could be at Selyma. If not there, it will certainly change when we move on Nubyat."

"Can't you and the overcommander handle them?"

"There are two of us and something like six or eight other mage-guards in First and Second Army. There could be fifteen mages supporting Golyat."

"How many are as good as you?"

"I don't know. The overcommander might, but he's not said much, except that there are more than a few. The former overcommander has to be strong, but beyond that . . ." Rahl shrugged. "I'm not expecting things to be as easy as before."

"We've already lost the equivalent of two-thirds of a standard company, and you're saying that's easy?"

"No," returned Rahl dryly, "just easier than what's ahead." He grinned lopsidedly. "You know that. You just want me to say it."

Drakeyt grinned back. "You did say it, Majer."

"Yes, I did, Captain." *And I hope I'm wrong, but I don't think we'll be that fortunate.*

LXVII

Even before dawn on eightday, the clouds hanging over Selyma were thick and gray, yet Rahl could sense that they did not hold all that much water, no more than enough for scattered showers. By the time the sun should have bathed the lowlands short of the town with the long light of dawn, the day remained as gray as it had been just before dawn, but First Army and Second Army began to move forward, the marshal's forces moving into position to assault the hilltop to the southeast of the highway, the overcommander's slightly smaller army advancing toward the low hills to the northwest. The highway itself was blocked with a crude and hastily constructed barricade of boulders and logs that ran two hundred cubits from the rock-and-mortar wall that lined the cut in one hillside to the other identically constructed wall in the opposite hillside.

Rahl rode beside Drakeyt at the head of Third Company on the left flank of Second Army, just west of the highway itself. There was a gap of less than fifty cubits between the troopers of first squad and those of Thirty-Seventh Company on the right flank of First Army. Through the gap in the hills through which the main road passed and over the top of the barricade, Rahl could glimpse a handful of the red-tile roofs of the taller buildings in Selyma. Farther to the northwest, from the western base of the hill that Second Army prepared to assault, stretched Lake Semayne, its waters dull gray under the sullen clouds. Farther to the northwest was a marsh that extended for several kays beyond the lake.

Rahl could certainly see why Golyat's forces had picked Selyma for a defense point. Except for the narrow gap in the hills for the road, there was no direct access to the town or the bridge across the Awhut River—and that blocked any direct Imperial access to Nubyat. What he didn't understand was why the Imperial forces were going to attack such a strongly defended point.

"You don't think there's another way to get to Nubyat without hazarding so many troopers?" Rahl finally asked Drakeyt.

"I'm most certain there is, Majer. I don't know what it might be, but there doubtless is such a way."

Rahl concealed an internal wince. Much of the time when Drakeyt addressed him as "Majer," Rahl had come to realize, it was a polite way of suggesting that Rahl hadn't thought matters through. Rather than ask another question revealing his ignorance, Rahl tried to consider the options facing Taryl and the marshal.

If they tried to avoid going through Selyma, then it

would take more time and subject the armies to battles elsewhere—and they still might have to fight another pitched battle elsewhere, and later, with fewer supplies and troopers. It also might allow Golyat to bring more troopers and chaos-mages from elsewhere. But perhaps the most important consideration, Rahl thought, was that, if worse came to worst, Taryl and the marshal could lose, and, so long as they decimated the rebels, they gained, because they could draw on all of Hamor for replacements of men and supplies. In addition, if they won, the cost might well be less than that incurred by attempting to maneuver for better positions. He'd doubtless missed other considerations, but those would have to wait.

Rahl turned his attention to the terrain ahead, trying to sense where the rebels were—besides behind the highway barricade—but discovered that one or more of Golyat's mages were using something like a shifting chaos shield to obscure the positions of the defenders. Even so, he could sense a large number of troops just over the crest of the hills. Intermittent earthworks dotted the hilltop there. A smaller number of rebels were in position behind the log-and-stone barricade. A goodly portion of those on the back side of the hilltop, Rahl felt, were lancers. Given the even and gentle grassy slope down toward the Imperial position, that made sense. The lancers would have the advantage of attacking downhill, with the attendant momentum and greater visibility.

Rahl briefly shifted his attention farther east, where the marshal's forces were also advancing, but there the rebel forces were centered around a low stone structure on that shorter hilltop ridge, constructed recently, Rahl gathered, from the feel of the stones. He turned his attention back to the slope ahead, finally saying, "They've got lancers posted just over the top of the hill."

"I would, too."

Rahl decided not to say more, but watched closely as Third Company moved forward across the flat and began to move up the lower and gentler part of the slope toward the rebel positions.

Second Army had no more taken up positions behind a series of pole-and-stone pillar fences almost a kay from the crest of the hills than cannon positioned on the northeasternmost end of the hills and less than a quarter kay from the lake began to send shells down toward the troopers.

The first shells fell well short, but the grapeshot in them ripped large oval chunks out of the waist-high grasses. The shell impacts began to move toward the first ranks of Second Army, but then stopped.

To his left, Rahl could hear the cannon firing from the stone fort, but those, too, fell silent. An eerie silence followed, broken only by murmurs, the occasional whuff or chuff of a mount, or a cough.

Rahl continued to scan the field, and before long he could sense a small force circling out from the north side of Second Army, and then back along the lakeshore—and that force contained inchoate chaos amid it.

Several cannon up on the hill to Rahl's right began to fire again, this time toward the force on the shore almost directly below the cannon. The slope there was too steep to climb—or to mount a charge directly downhill. Several iron crossbow bolts arced from the Imperial force on the lake's edge up toward the cannon.

Then a line of chaos-flame—the thinnest line of chaos—flashed from a mage-guard on the lake's edge toward one of the iron quarrels arcing toward the cannon . . . and then directly toward the cannon. At the moment that chaos struck the first cannon, three firebolts flared down on the Imperial force . . . and the mage-guard. *Whssst! Whssst! Whssst!*

The emptiness and void were enough to tell Rahl that both the troopers and the Imperial mage-guard were gone. Steam rose from the shore and the water at the lake's edge.

Thwump! Crumpt! Crumpt! Flame and smoke flared from where the cannon had been firing, followed by another series of explosions. White-and-gray smoke wreathed the northwestern end of the hill closest to the lake, and Rahl could sense another wave of deaths, and several had been chaos-mages.

Another series of explosions continued across the back of the northwest corner of the hill as powder magazines and ammunition detonated.

Drakeyt looked to Rahl.

"I don't think there are any cannon left on that hill. Not any powder, either. We lost one mage," Rahl said. "I think they lost two, maybe three."

"That's got to hurt them," said Drakeyt in a low voice.

"Not enough." Rahl had the feeling that the loss of the cannon and the powder might be more of a blow to Golyat than the loss of a few mages—if Taryl had been right about how many mage-guards had defected to Golyat. That didn't count how many might have been sent from Fairhaven to help the prince.

As if to emphasize that point, spheres of chaos-flame began to arc off the top of the hillside down toward Second Army. The first exploded well in front of the middle of the line of troopers, but driblets of flame rolled downhill, leaving long lines of fire that subsided to a thin path of dark ash. A second arched to the west, landing in a company of troopers closer to the lake, and while the screams of their injured and dying mounts were faint, Rahl could easily sense the deaths.

Rahl watched carefully, and when one of the chaos-flares looked to be headed toward Third Company, he waited until the last moment before flashing a shield to deflect it into the grass in front of the company. The heat from the chaos-fire might even have been welcome except for the acrid odor of both chaos and burned grasses that accompanied the gust of warm air.

Several other firebolts—but certainly not all—were deflected, but whether by Taryl or one of the few Imperial mage-guards, Rahl couldn't tell. To his left, across the highway, he could also sense chaos-flame being thrown against the marshal's First Army, but there cannon also continued to fire at the Imperial troopers.

Rahl's attention was drawn back to his own force as a wave of lancers rode over the top of the hill and down the long and gentle slope toward the advancing Imperial troopers. Rather than charging forward, the Imperial forces remained in their traces, as if stopped dead.

Rahl winced. Against the long mirror lances, that was exactly the wrong tactic.

The lancers thundered closer, and close to half the Imperial troopers in the front ranks broke even before the lancers neared, and those remaining seemed to mill around aimlessly. Then, at the last moment, the remaining troopers wheeled to the sides, as if trying to outflank the lancers. Out of the grass rose other troopers—and they held long pikes, dug into the ground.

The first two lines of lancers spitted themselves on the pikes, or found themselves entangled with those mounts who had struck the pikes full on, and the Imperial troopers turned back and began to cut down the lancers.

From the hilltop came quick lines of firebolts, spaced just far enough apart so that, when they struck, the chaos-fire flared and spread, turning troopers, pikes, and pikemen into writhing flames that soon became ashes. Even before those fires died away, another line of lancers charged over the hill and down toward the next ranks of advancing troopers.

Once more, if farther down the slope, at the last moment, the troopers turned, and pikes and pikemen appeared. This time, most of the rebel lancers turned, with only a few getting caught in the pikes, but the Imperial troopers were quicker and more than a few lancers went down.

From the hilltop came more firebolts, if fewer and less intense, and only a comparative handful struck the Imperial forces.

The lancers—greatly diminished—charged once more. This time a hail of arrows rose from behind the first line of Imperial troopers and poured down into the lancers' ranks. Even so, some of the lancers opened wide spaces in the Imperial formation before they retreated uphill under a hail of arrows.

Rahl hadn't realized that Taryl had brought or found so many archers, but then, from his limited experience, he doubted that archers were all that helpful in mounted fast-moving battles. But . . . in a set battle like the one unfolding before him, they were most useful—and deadly.

Again, for a time, neither force moved, but it was far from silent, not with the smoldering patches of grass and low vegetation that occasionally crackled, the moaning and low cries of wounded mounts and men, and the orders barked by various commanders. While he could not see the sun, shrouded as it was by the heavy clouds, Rahl knew that it was well past midmorning, and that it was going to be a very long day.

Abruptly, from the southeast, came a flare of chaos, and then a series of explosions. Rahl turned and glanced toward the stone fort. Part of the wall had been blown out, as if a powder magazine had exploded, but lancers poured downhill.

Rahl turned back to Drakeyt. "What next?"

"Whatever they think will hurt us worse and them less, and I have no idea what that will be, except that I don't think we'll like it."

Abruptly a large chaos-bolt arched from somewhere in the Imperial forces up and over the top of the hill. Rahl could see the flash of fire splashing off a shield of some sort, but he could also sense that troopers around the shield had been injured, and some had died.

A flurry of smaller chaos-bolts flashed from the rebel forces, striking almost at random among the Imperial troopers and archers, but, between a less-than-perfect aim and a number of shields, Rahl could feel few injuries.

Just as Rahl was congratulating himself, a pair of chaos-bolts arrowed straight down the hillside, directly at Third Company.

Rahl threw up shields, and the chaos-fire flared past and over the company. Rahl released the shields, but for a moment, had a flash of light-headedness. This time, he didn't wait, but immediately dug out travel biscuits from his saddlebags.

"Eating, at a time like this?" asked Drakeyt.

"I don't keep eating," replied Rahl through mouthfuls of very stale and exceeding dry biscuits, "and I can't keep using order."

"Is that true of all mages?"

"So far as I know, but I don't know for sure about the white wizards of Fairhaven."

Drakeyt nodded slowly. "That explains a lot."

Rahl was about to ask what it explained when another wave of lancers, seemingly as numerous as those in the charge that had opened the battle for Selyma, rode over the crest of the hill and started down toward the Imperial forces.

Another flight of arrows rose toward the lancers, but this time a wall of chaos-flame flared downhill, incinerating the majority of the shafts before they could reach their targets. A second wave of arrows, larger than the first, followed. Only two chaos-bolts flew toward the arrows, and one missed completely but fell toward the center of the Imperial force, where it was smothered by an order shield, possibly projected by Taryl.

Rahl nodded as the second flight of arrows dropped amid the lancers. He could see the tactics being used by Taryl—or Commander Muyr. As the lancers struggled to regain order, four companies of mounted troopers charged uphill into the mass of rebels.

"Companies! Forward!" came the orders.

"Third Company! Forward!" repeated Drakeyt.

Using the Imperial charge as a form of cover, the remainder of the force advanced uphill at a measured ride so that the rebel chaos-mages could not fling chaos-flame indiscriminately without inflicting even greater casualties on their own lancers.

By the time the lancers broke free and withdrew, it was clear that the majority of the most recent casualties were among the lancers, and the Imperial forces were a good third of the way up the slope in good order.

At that moment, thunder rumbled over the hillside. Then, a light misting rain began to drift downward.

"Companies! Forward!"

"Third Company! Forward!"

A single weak firebolt arched from the hilltop and flared into insignificance before reaching the advancing Imperial force.

From behind the earthworks came another group of mounted rebels in their maroon jackets—troopers with sabres, riding hard down toward the Imperial forces. One rebel company immediately swung eastward and broke toward Third Company.

Rahl drew his truncheon, then leaned toward Drakeyt. "I'll try to stop them for just a moment." He looked at the troopers in maroon, close to a twenty-man front rushing downhill with glittering sabres.

Rahl waited . . . and waited, then formed a quick shield but, against the weight and speed of the charging rebels, could only hold it long enough to stagger the first rank to a stop. The effort threw him back in the saddle and even halted the gelding. The rest of the company had already begun to cut into the stunned rebels.

That momentary advantage afforded Third Company faded as the following ranks of rebel troopers rode into the melee.

Rahl found himself with three rebels all trying to attack him, but he managed to stiffen his personal shields enough to deflect one slash that would have taken off his shoulder, then thrust the truncheon into the ribs of the second attacker with enough force—if order-boosted—to crack something and topple the trooper out of the saddle. His half parry, half thrust against the next rebel staggered the man enough that one of his troopers finished the man with a cut to the throat.

After that, Rahl lost track as he tried to keep himself in one piece while inflicting what damage he could without totally overextending himself. He had no idea if he'd been effective in reducing the number of rebels or if he'd just managed to survive.

Then, as the rebel troopers withdrew to regroup, a wedge of lancers appeared—coming around the side of the hill above the slope up from the highway—charging directly at the exposed flank of Third Company. Rahl turned in the saddle, then urged the gelding toward fifth squad, where the lancers would strike.

Two chaos-bolts preceded the lancers, and Rahl had to struggle to deflect them.

He barely managed to regain his composure and to focus his concentration on the oncoming lancers before they overran fifth squad and Third Company. As he'd done before, Rahl waited until the tips of the lancers' weapons were almost ready to strike before throwing up a shield broad enough to stop the lancers. Although he only held the shield briefly, three ranks of lancers piled into each other, and Lyrn and fifth squad immediately began attacking the tangled and fallen rebel lancers.

At that moment, Rahl could sense more chaos-bolts arcing toward him and Third Company, and he hastily threw up a shield.

Chaos flared around him, and light-knives stabbed at his eyes so fiercely he could hardly see. When he tried to shake his head to clear his vision, the pain was so great that his eyes watered, and he could see nothing at all.

In desperation, he tried to strengthen his personal shields, since he could see nothing.

He felt a lance slam into his shields, and he knew that the shields had held—but his seat on the gelding had not, and he could feel himself flying backward with such force that his boots yanked clear of the stirrups.

Then a wall of black stones fell on him and buried him.

LXVIII

Rahl woke to find himself lying on his back. Knife-flashes of light seared across his eyes. In between those light-knives he could see, dimly, two low ceilings. He closed one eye. It helped a little—one of the plank ceilings faded, but didn't go away.

"Majer . . . you awake there?"

Rahl tried to speak, but his throat was so dry that he could barely croak, "Yes . . . mostly." He turned his head slowly, very slowly. He was lying on a lumpy pallet set on the floor. Two images of a trooper with a bound arm sat on a stool beside him, looking down at him.

Rahl slowly rolled into a sitting position, then took the water bottle that had been set beside the pallet. After several swallows, he spoke again. "What day is it? Where am I?"

"It's still eightday, ser, a little before sunset. Well . . . it'd be about then, except for the clouds. This here's a shed. Mighta held sheep, 'cepting the rebs herded 'em all off afore we got here."

"What happened?"

"We're still at the bottom of the hill, and the rebs are at the top, but they lost a lot more 'n we have. I guess that means we're winning."

"What about First Army?"

"Same thing, except they got farther up their hill. Lost more troopers, too."

Rahl took another swallow of water, thinking . . . or trying to.

A thin officer stepped into the shed—or rather two images of him did, and it took Rahl a moment to recognize Taryl, what with the two images and the light-knives that occluded his vision.

"Ser . . ." Rahl began.

Taryl looked at the trooper, who immediately left the shed, closing the door hastily. He surveyed Rahl with eyes and order-senses, then nodded. After a moment, he spoke. "I hope you realize that the only reason you're alive is because you're a mage-guard." Taryl's voice was dry and contained an edge of irritation.

Rahl understood that. Without his shields—

"No. It's not that. You got yourself unhorsed in the middle of a battle, and several troopers were injured, and one was killed, recovering you. They don't care about Rahl, the person. The reason they went after you is the same reason a trooper goes after a sabre knocked from his hand. You're a weapon. But you do that again, and they might not choose to see if you're alive, especially if there are chaos-bolts falling all around."

Rahl wanted to wince, but even the thought sent light-knives slashing through the twin images that shifted in front of him.

"For a time your actions were solid, but then, when you rode out to stop that lancer attack . . . that was another example of foolhardiness. Rahl . . . you could have done the same thing without drawing attention to yourself. Why didn't you?" Taryl didn't wait for a response, but went on. "Golyat's mages knew you were somewhere near Third Company, and the lancer attack was an attempt to draw you out and wear you down, then kill you and force us to retreat."

Rahl wanted to protest that his failure couldn't have been the only reason for the retreat.

"It wasn't," Taryl replied, "but it forced us to retreat earlier than would have been optimal, before we had inflicted as much damage on the defenders as we could have." He paused and looked directly at Rahl. "Also, it wouldn't hurt to practice your shields when you're exhausted. Other mages certainly won't respect your tiredness, and merely shielding your feelings and thoughts takes little energy if you do it right."

"Yes, ser," Rahl replied tiredly, making the effort.

"That's better."

So it was better. What difference did it make? All Taryl did any more when he met with Rahl was criticize, and that wasn't exactly helpful.

The overcommander shook his head. "I can't order-sense what you're feeling, but shields don't do much good if people can read your face."

Rahl said nothing. He had the feeling that Taryl wasn't even angry, but withdrawn, and perhaps tired.

"I could provide you with greater counsel, Rahl, but counsel does not develop independence and judgment. You must make enough mistakes, while trying your best, and while someone else can deflect the blame, in order to gain wisdom. Your magisters of Recluce did you no favors, nor did they do me any, either. I ask you this—would I spend so much time with you when so much is at stake if I did not care?" After the briefest of pauses, he went on. "Now . . . get some rest and eat as much as you can. And while you're resting, try to think over the situations you might be in and the way to respond by using the least order-effort possible."

With that, Taryl nodded, turned, and departed.

Rahl lay back on the straw pallet and looked up at the twin, last-flashed images of the rough plank ceiling of the shed, all too aware, especially now, that he was out of the cold and mist just because he was a useful weapon. Was that all Taryl had wanted? It couldn't be, could it? Taryl had worked with him long before anyone knew about the revolt . . . and he said he cared, and Rahl had to admit that he was getting more attention than did most junior officers. Yet Taryl expected *something* of him. That, too, was clear.

Rahl took a deep breath. Whatever the reason, he hadn't exactly pleased the overcommander.

LXIX

The double images remained with Rahl's sight through the remainder of eightday but had vanished when he woke early on oneday. The dull aching in his head that he had not noticed because of the sharpness of the light-knives remained, as did occasional flashes. He also had bruises on his back and shoulders that were more than tender to the touch, or when he stretched, but he still managed to find and saddle the gelding.

Overhead, the same thick clouds that had darkened the sky on eightday remained, and beneath them, swirls of misty fog rose from the river, swathing Selyma and the lower part of the hillsides with thick white curtains that shifted with the barely perceptible breeze. With the fog came a damp and almost fetid odor, and a sense of decay that went beyond mere smell. Was that an effect created by the rebel mages? Or just what happened in Selyma when winter fogs rose off the Awhut River?

Once he mounted, even with his order-sensing, it took Rahl some effort to find where Third Company was forming up.

"Should you be out here?" asked Drakeyt, when Rahl rode up and joined him.

"As much as any officer," replied Rahl with a wry smile, "but I won't be able to do as much magery. I can still handle the truncheon."

"You might as well call it a blunted blade." Drakeyt shook his head. "If anyone had ever told me I'd serve with an officer who did more damage with a truncheon than most squads do with blades, I'd not have believed it. How . . . ." He didn't finish what he might have said.

"I was taught truncheon from the time I could hold one," Rahl said slowly. "Then I worked with blade masters when I was older, and . . . well . . . I can add a little strength to the truncheon when I wield it."

"You're a mage-guard, but I've served with them before, and most of them, even the ones who can handle blades, use a sabre more like an ax." Drakeyt laughed softly, but the sound carried in the foggy air. "They couldn't chop that hard, either."

"I was fortunate. I've had good teachers." Rahl looked up at the dark clouds. It seemed strange that he could see the clouds overhead more clearly than a trooper twenty cubits away.

"You think it will rain?" asked Drakeyt.

"Sooner or later, and it could be a downpour."

"Maybe that's why they've got us out early." The over-commander wants another try at the hill before it turns to slick mud."

Rahl almost asked if that wouldn't hurt the defenders as much as the Imperial forces before he realized one simple thing. The rebels only had to stop the attack, and if mud did the job . . .

"Would you like to ride out with fourth and fifth squads?"

"Of course." Rahl realized that Drakeyt was suggesting where he ought to be, and that position made sense for many reasons. He inclined his head and eased his mount eastward.

Lyrn nodded as Rahl took position even with the first ranks and between fourth and fifth squads.

Rahl could see less than fifty cubits ahead through the foggy mist. Why was Taryl continuing the battle under such conditions? Because ordermages could sense better than chaos-mages? Or because all the water in the air reduced the power of the chaos-mages? Or just because he wanted to keep pressure on the rebel defenders? Or was there something else that Rahl was missing?

"Companies! Forward!"

"Third Company! Forward!" echoed Drakeyt.

As he rode forward, Rahl had to remind himself that his task was to use his truncheon to protect himself and the Third Company troopers, while being more aware of everything that was happening and learning from it.

Farther uphill, he could sense a concentration of chaos.

Whsst! The firebolt that flew from the earthworks at the top of the hill plowed into the damp and matted grass a good hundred cubits short of Third Company. The chaos-fire barely spread at all beyond the impact area before dying away.

A second firebolt fared little better.

Rahl kept pace with the front ranks of fourth and fifth squad as they rode up the gentle slope. He kept trying to reach out beyond the misty fog with his order-senses.

Near the top of the hill and to his left, Rahl could sense riders—lancers—forming up just in front of the crude earthworks. With the fog surrounding him, he could not see the lancers, only order-sense them. They dressed their lines and began to head downhill, initially moving at little more than a fast walk.

Why were the rebel lancers heading downhill and into the fog? The slope was even enough and dry enough for the moment that footing wasn't likely to be a problem, but it still seemed foolish to Rahl—at first glance. On second thought, it made much more sense. The fog was thick enough that the Imperial forces would be hard-pressed to see a lancer and react before that lancer was upon them. The lancers could just strike and break away, and the fog would hide them from archers and what few chaos-bolts Taryl's forces could muster.

"They're bringing lancers from the east side of the hill, the same way they did yesterday," Rahl called to Drakeyt, using a touch of order to project his words to the captain.

"Third Company, to the left, half wheel!"

As Rahl swung to the left, he tried to think of what he could do.

Could he slow the charge of the lancers? Did he have to? If he couldn't see the lancers, how could they sense the individual squads of Third Company? Rahl let himself grin, then checked the lancers' position.

"Fourth squad! Fifth squad! On me!"

"On the majer!" called out Lyrn.

Rahl turned the gelding almost north, checking with his order-senses, then swung back south and halted, waiting for the two squads to dress lines. He turned to Lyrn. "We're north of their charge. Once they pass by uphill of us, we'll swing behind them." Then he turned to the end trooper in fourth squad and repeated his words, adding, "Pass it on."

"Weapons ready!"

The sound of hoofs preceded any sign of riders through the fog, and the dampness magnified the sound.

At the same time, Rahl heard a single thunderclap, somewhere to the north, he thought. He waited for another thunderclap, but he heard none—or if there had been another, it was lost in the growing rumble of hoofs beating downhill.

Rahl forced himself to wait, to check positions until the first of the rebel lancers thundered past, thirty cubits uphill, barely visible through the fog.

"Fourth and fifth squads! Forward!" ordered Rahl.

His two small squads struck the side and rear of the lancers, and in moments, close to a score of the rebels were down, and the flank attack had clearly slowed the impact of the charge on Third Company and the adjoining Nineteenth Company.

A rebel half turned and tried to swing a long lance at Rahl and the trooper flanking him, but Rahl managed to deflect the weapon, no longer shining, but dull with moisture and other encrustations. He slipped under the lance and cut-thrust with the long truncheon. The lancer gaped, then doubled over and toppled out of the saddle, one boot still caught in the stirrup.

Rahl turned the gelding to the right, trying to keep on the edge of the lancer formation rather than plunging into it. He parried another lance, but the rebel wheeled away before Rahl could deliver a direct blow.

An ominous and prolonged roll of thunder rumbled over the hillside battle.

More and more of the rebel lancers discarded the long lances and began swinging shortswords, not even quite so long as the Imperial sabres. That was fine with Rahl, because his truncheon was longer than a sabre.

A flash of lightning lit the fog, if but for a moment, and then fat drops of rain pelted the back of Rahl's neck, first intermittently, then with increasing regularity, until water seemed to be coming from the clouds as if from a cataract—or so it seemed.

Another lancer charged Rahl, who leaned in the saddle, then slashed the shortsword out of the man's hand by breaking his wrist.

As the fog began to thin, Rahl continued to concentrate on defending himself and unhorsing rebels, but he could both see and sense lancers and troopers alike being unhorsed on the muddy and slippery grass. Combatants on both sides were losing weapons as the chill rain numbed arms and hands. Even with the cross-hatched grip of the truncheon, Rahl found himself occasionally two-handing his weapon just to hang on to it. Icy water ran down his neck and spine, and his riding jacket and uniform were close to being sodden all the way through.

A trumpet call of paired triplets rang out from the top of the hills, and within moments the lancers and their mounts struggled to climb away from the Imperial troopers.

The fog had lost a battle of sorts to the cold rain, because the rain was washing the fog right out of the air, Rahl realized.

"Second Army! Hold position! Hold position!"

"Third Company! Re-form on me!"

Rahl glanced toward Drakeyt, glad to see the captain uninjured, then repeated the orders. "Third Company! Re-form!"

As the company squads straggled into line, Rahl glanced uphill at the churned mud, almost the color of the ooze he'd created before. Could he use that against the rebels? He let his senses check the ground. Then he shook his head. The entire hill was little more than soil, clay and sand piled high and deep, with little rock and gravel.

If he tried what he'd done on the road to Lahenta, and he couldn't contain it, especially now, when he was far from full strength as an ordermage, all of Selyma would end up falling into a massive sinkhole filled with ooze. Rahl didn't think either Taryl or the Emperor would exactly appreciate that, and the liquefaction process would be slow enough that most of the rebels could probably escape.

What else could he try?

"Companies! Return to quarters!"

As Rahl shivered in the cold rain and rode beside Drakeyt back down the hill through the rain that now poured down in sheets, he tried to think about what else he might be able to do, but his teeth were chattering, and his whole body was damp and chilled, and all he really wanted to do was to get out of the rain and dry off.

LXX

For the remainder of oneday morning, the rain continued. After doing what he could for the gelding, and a touch of healing for several wounded—all that he could manage—Rahl returned to the small sheep shed. He sat there in the gloom and thought about possible uses of his order-skills against the rebels. Outside, the rain poured down throughout the afternoon and well into the evening.

No matter what Rahl considered, his efforts seemed doomed to failure because he simply couldn't manipulate order on a large enough scale to affect the thousands and thousands of troopers and lancers spread across more than two kays of hillside behind various kinds of fortifications and barricades and earthworks.

That night, sharing the small shed with Drakeyt and a handful of other junior officers, Rahl slept poorly, dreaming of lancers building barricades with intertwined lances, of troopers dying everywhere . . . and Deybri looking on, clearly horrified at the carnage that Rahl had created. He was almost glad to struggle awake on twoday—except for the fact that he still had no idea how anything he could do would be of much help in defeating the rebels, and might not even be enough to keep him alive, let alone the remaining troopers of Third Company. He also wondered if there was something wrong with him that he felt more guilt when he thought or dreamed of Deybri.

After getting himself ready for the day on twoday morning, in the light just before dawn, he slowly ate some hard cheese that he'd had to scrape the mold off, and a few hard biscuits. Drakeyt was doing the same.

"They won't move," Drakeyt predicted.

"Why not?" asked Alnuyt, a company commander Rahl had only met the afternoon before, although Rahl might have seen him in passing because the young captain looked familiar.

"If they move, we take Selyma and the bridge, and the access to Nubyat. Besides, they're in the best defensive position for kays. They know they have to fight us. Why abandon a good position to fight from one that's worse?"

Rahl had to admit Drakeyt's point.

Thrap!

A trooper wearing a courier's sash eased the shed door open. "Sers? Majer Rahl? Captain Drakeyt?"

"We're both here," Rahl replied.

"The overcommander would like to see you both immediately, sers."

"We'll be there shortly," Rahl answered, "as soon as we can mount up."

"I'll tell him, sers." The courier stepped back and closed the door.

Drakeyt raised his eyebrows as he looked at Rahl.

"He has something in mind," Rahl said.

"I'm certain he does." Although Drakeyt did not say that Taryl's ideas always cost Third Company dearly, from the resigned expression in his eyes he might as well have done so. "We'd best saddle up. It wouldn't do to keep him waiting too long."

Rahl nodded and fastened his riding jacket—still damp in places, but warmer than doing without.

The two hurried through a quick brushing of their mounts, then saddled and mounted, riding down a mud-churned excuse for a lane before turning northward, away from Selyma. While the night had not gotten cold enough for it to frost, with dawn it had not warmed measurably, and Rahl's breath steamed under the gray clouds that continued to blanket the skies around Selyma.

Neither spoke on the short ride to Taryl's headquarters—a steadholder's weathered yellow-brick dwelling a kay north of the hillside battlefield. As they neared the dwelling, with its outbuildings surrounded by troopers and mounts and the tents and lean-tos—and horse-churned mud—Rahl could see Commander Shuchyl walking out of the front door, followed by several majers. Rahl looked sideways at Drakeyt, but the older officer's face was impassive.

The two tied their mounts to the railing that the commander and his staff had used, then walked up the single step onto a narrow wooden porch. After stamping his boots and scuffing them against the soiled mat to scrape off as much mud as possible, Rahl opened the door gingerly, making sure his personal shields were strong.

"Majer. Come in. The overcommander is expecting you." The undercaptain whom Rahl had seen time after time and whose name he still did not know gestured to his right, where Taryl stood facing the door with his back to the hearth.

Rahl stepped inside, followed by Drakeyt, who closed the door. The warmth issuing from the fire in the old hearth was more than welcome.

"Ser, you requested our presence," offered Rahl.

"I did." Taryl did not speak for a moment, but Rahl could feel Taryl's order-senses scanning him. Then the overcommander nodded slightly to Rahl. "Much better." His eyes went to Drakeyt, then back to Rahl. "Majer, Captain . . . I have an assignment for Third Company. You are to accompany Commander Shuchyl and his forces. You leave as soon as you can muster your men with their gear. You're not to waste time. The commander is already mustering his regiment. You'll be riding back upstream to a point just south of Bhucyra. The supply barges we sent for have arrived, and the river's narrower there. We've strung cable across, and it shouldn't take more than a day to ferry the entire force over to the south side. You'll take the most direct route possible south along the river. Your job, Majer—with Third Company—is to find that route. The hillside here will be treacherous for at least another day. Tomorrow, if we don't get any more rain, we may have to make what looks like an attack to keep the rebels from suspecting what we actually plan."

"Won't they be expecting something like this, ser?" asked Drakeyt.

"I'm sure they've considered it, but the river is high enough to be impossible to ford anywhere near here, and there are no bridges within forty kays. We assume that they'll be watching the bridges. You should be able to reach the south side of the bridge at Selyma by sunset on fourday. On fiveday, Commander Shuchyl will attack the back side of the position facing Second Army. They have little in the way of earthworks on that side, whereas the position facing the marshal is fortified on all sides." Taryl smiled wryly. "That is the plan." He turned to Rahl. "Majer, you are to use no magery beyond order-sensing and shielding—and especially not the screeing glass—until the Commander commences his attack on fiveday. The one exception is if you are attacked by a far larger force. You are to maintain full shields at all times. Is that clear?"

"Yes, ser."

"Ser . . . if I might ask . . . ?" Drakeyt asked gently.

"The majer's skills have often been all that saved the company from total destruction . . ."

Taryl's smile was colder than the weather outside the small house. "You may. The majer was knocked unconscious on eightday. Yesterday, an attack was launched directly at Third Company, but as much at the majer as the company. The majer did not and could not use any magery detectable from beyond a few hundred cubits, and a number of your troopers were killed and injured. The majer was seen to go down on eightday, and there has been no magery since then, even when Third Company was threatened. I do not wish the commander's regiment to be detected any earlier than necessary. There are no fast roads along the river, so that if he does not use magery . . . Need I say more, Captain?"

"No, ser. Thank you, ser."

"I realize that may create difficulties, Captain, but I trust you understand the necessity."

"Yes, ser."

Taryl offered a warmer smile. "You both have done well under trying circumstances. I wish I could offer some reward beyond my thanks, but for now, that will have to do." After the slightest pause, he added, "That's all I have. Report to Commander Shuchyl as soon as you can."

"Yes, ser."

Rahl and Drakeyt both inclined their heads to Taryl, then turned and left the warmth of the small dwelling. Outside, as they untied their mounts, another commander and several majers rode toward the cot.

"There are a few things he didn't say," Drakeyt said as he climbed into the saddle.

"I know." Rahl understood that all too well. "When we do attack, he wants them to think they may be facing mages on all sides."

"And a few others."

Rahl just nodded, because it was certain that more of Drakeyt's troopers would die in order for Taryl to spring his surprise on the rebels.

LXXI

Although it rained only intermittently, and that rain was more like mist than rain, the ride back northward was long and damp, and Third Company and the Fifth Imperial Mounted Infantry Regiment did not reach the encampment point until close to dark on twoday. That point was a stead on a low bluff overlooking the Awhut River, some three kays southwest of the town. The commander and his staff took the stead house, and Third Company, because it had led the column northward, managed to commandeer a long sheep shed—and several sheep as well.

The hot roasted mutton, even if provided late that evening, helped cheer the troopers, and the cookfires provided some warmth. Rahl slept somewhat better than on previous nights, if only because he had no nightmares.

At dawn began the process of ferrying troopers and mounts across the higher-than-normal water levels of the Awhut River. Rahl had to admit that Taryl's scheme was both simple and audacious. The three cargo barges were each attached to twin cables. The cables were in turn affixed to the trunks of trees on each side of the river. Then there was another cable attached to each end of the barge, and a team of horses on each side pulled that cable, one team for pulling it south, the other team for pulling it north.

Third Company was scheduled to be the first to cross, with orders to spend the day scouting out the best route southward as far as possible toward Selyma, but with the requirement that the company return to the ferry area by close to nightfall so that Rahl and Drakeyt could brief Commander Shuchyl and his staff on the route and what to expect. That would allow an early start on fourday.

Rahl was in the first group ferried across the river, and

he stood holding the gelding's reins near the bow of the barge—he assumed that end was the bow, except what he thought of as the stern would be the bow on the return trip to the north side of the river. The barge pitched some in the current, but was heavy enough—or loaded heavily enough with fifteen mounts and their riders—that it tended to plow through the gray-silver water rather than ride over it. The cables did not run straight across the river, but at an angle, so that, when the barge was heaviest laden on the crossing with men and mounts, the river's current helped push the barge across and downstream.

Abruptly, a swell or wave smacked the side of the barge, and water sheeted and sprayed up and soaked his trousers. The barge rocked, and Rahl almost went to his knees on the iron deck, his boots sliding on the wet metal. The gelding tossed his head slightly, but did not move, for which Rahl was most thankful. Several other swirling waves created spray that dampened or soaked many of the troopers before the barge reached the crude timber dock—little more than logs piled into place and held with several posts and filled with earth behind the logs, with planking on top.

Although the planking gave some when Rahl led the gelding off the barge, it did not bend unduly, and Rahl was more than glad to be off the barge.

Even under the hazy gray sky, his trousers had dried some by the time all of Third Company had been ferried across the river. Rahl had already spent some time with half of first squad locating the nearest lane heading south, and following it a ways before returning to find Drakeyt.

"I've found a solid start south, just to the left on the far end of the orchards there." Rahl gestured.

Drakeyt nodded, as if that were to be expected.

"How do you think this will work?" Rahl asked Drakeyt.

"You're asking me, Majer? You're the mage."

"You've got the experience," Rahl replied, adding dryly, "Captain."

"We won't run into any rebels for a while." Drakeyt gestured toward the lines of pearapple trees comprising the orchard around the makeshift ferry landing. "If they were anywhere near, they'd have known about this, and they would have attacked the engineers who set this up."

"So we should have at least five kays before we run into trouble?"

Drakeyt shrugged. "Three or thirty . . . who knows?" He turned in the saddle. "Quelsyn, have all the squad leaders reported ready?"

"Here comes Lyrn, ser. He's the last."

"We'll ride out as soon as he reports."

"Yes, ser."

Once Third Company left the orchard and deployed along the lane, heading south-southwest and roughly parallel to the river, Rahl felt more than a little handicapped because he could not use the screeing glass, and that limited how far he could sense ahead. Even so, he could tell that initially, Drakeyt was right. There were no rebel forces nearby.

In fact, as Third Company made its way southward, neither Rahl nor the scouts or outriders ran across any rebel forces. In some ways, that did not surprise Rahl, because he was leading Third Company along what amounted to back lanes rather than on the paved main highways. Had the rebels pulled back all the forces to key points? Was there a larger force stationed on the south side of the river at Selyma?

Rahl kept wondering that, but even by the time they needed to turn back some three kays north of Selyma, Rahl had found no trace of any large rebel forces and only a few scattered small patrols—and those had been only at the edge of his ability to order-sense.

When Third Company returned to the ferry point on the south side of the Awhut River on threeday night, Rahl and Drakeyt had mapped out a fairly direct route southward from lane to lane to a south road, and one that intersected the paved road southeast to Sastak less than a kay outside of Selyma. In three places, though, they would have to ride through fields or orchards to get from one lane to another, but none of those sections was more than half a kay in length, and they did not have to cross more than one small brook in doing so.

Bivouacking on the south side of the Awhut River on threeday night was among the most miserable experiences Rahl had undergone in at least several eightdays, if not far longer. The mist of twoday and threeday had turned into a light rain by twilight, a rain that continued well into the night. There were absolutely no real quarters anywhere, and the lean-tos created in the pearapple orchards with the tarp Drakeyt had carried was only enough for the two officers and did not keep all the rain off either. Rahl couldn't help but worry about both men and mounts, and when he did doze off, his sleep was fitful at best.

LXXII

Third Company moved out early on fourday, riding down the lane beyond the orchard under a hazy sky that Rahl sensed might well clear by midday, or at least by midafternoon. Even by midmorning, Rahl had neither seen nor sensed any rebel forces, nor had he felt anyone using a screeing glass. He rode back from the outrider's position and turned the gelding so that he was riding beside Drakeyt.

"There's no sign of anyone. No one's even looking with a glass for us. I can't help but wonder if they're just waiting somewhere."

"That could be, but if they're waiting, they're not reinforcing the defenses on the other side of the river."

"Why aren't they scouting or looking?"

"They may be. We only know that they're not scouting where we are. That makes sense, in a way. You don't move large forces on narrow roads or lanes, and you don't do it without supply wagons and logistics support," Drakeyt said.

"I can see that for the longer distances we've had to cover," replied Rahl, "but we're only talking about riding one day away from the main body, crossing a river, and riding one day back."

"They can't cover everything. The old road swings north of the lake and swamp, according to the maps, and that's an additional fifty kays out of the way. Then there's the eastern route over the bridge at Bhucyra, and that's another sixty or seventy kays going the other way. Both of those are good roads, much better suited to armies. If you were their marshals, would you be sending scouts down every side road? Remember, these lanes don't really connect. Up ahead, we have to ride for half a kay through some fields, and later, there's that apple orchard."

Rahl nodded. Even a glass wouldn't show a direct route along the river, and why would anyone try to guess at where a part of Second Army might go when it didn't take the roads?

"The overcommander's thinking like a light-horse commander," added Drakeyt. "It wouldn't work with the whole army, or if it had kept raining."

Had Taryl been able to sense that the weather would change days before it had? Just how much magery had the overcommander mastered? Rahl realized that he really had no idea, for all the time he had studied with Taryl—and that was another lesson, of sorts. But then, how long would it be before he knew enough that he wouldn't always be learning something else that proved he'd either made a mistake or barely escaped making one?

"It feels like it's going to keep getting clearer. We're done with the rain—or anything serious, anyway—for a while."

"Then by later today, they'll have more patrols out," suggested the captain.

Rahl nodded. Drakeyt was doubtless right about that,

too. "I'm heading back up with the outriders." He urged the gelding forward.

Sometime after midafternoon, Rahl began to get a sense of rebels—or riders—ahead, but they had to be at least a kay beyond the end of the road that Third Company traveled. He eased his mount back to where Drakeyt was riding at the head of first squad.

"Rebels, Majer?"

"There are some ahead. More than a kay, I think. It might be several squads, or a company. It's not any more than that. From what I can sense, they're patrolling the area where in a kay or so, several lanes join the main road into Selyma."

"Or out of it and to Nubyat or Sastak," Drakeyt pointed out. "We need to send a messenger back to the commander." He turned in the saddle. "Sienyr . . . forward."

The lean trooper drew his mount up beside the captain.

"You're to report to the commander personally that we have a rebel patrol force somewhat more than a kay ahead. Tell him that we await his orders."

"Yes, ser." With that, the trooper turned his mount and began to ride back down the lane toward the main body of the regiment.

"We need to slow to a slow walk," Drakeyt added to Rahl. "A slow and quiet walk."

"I'll bring in the scouts and outriders somewhat," Rahl replied.

The company had covered less than a kay when Rahl sensed the return of Sienyr and another rider.

"Hold here!" he told the scouts and outriders, before turning the gelding back to find out what the commander had ordered.

The courier had already reined up in front of Drakeyt by the time Rahl reached the captain. "Captain, ser, the commander requests that you circle behind the rebels. You are to hold off meeting or engaging them for as long as possible, but you are not to allow any of them to gain the town. He is sending Eighteenth Company to reinforce you, but requests that you make haste to take the main road behind the rebels so that they cannot cross the river and report to their commanders."

"Convey to the commander that Third Company has received orders and is complying."

"Yes, ser." The courier nodded and turned his mount.

Drakeyt looked to Rahl. "Do you have any ideas on how we can get past them, Majer?"

Rahl tried to reconcile the map and what he had sensed most recently. He wished he dared use the glass, but using it would reveal his existence and position, and that would defeat much of the purpose of their mission. "There's a low hill to the right of the lane, and we could go around in, but the other side is exposed for close to half a kay before we could reach the main road."

"Then we'll have to send a squad the other way, farther to the east, to see if we can tease them and keep them interested."

"I could do that," Rahl suggested.

"I'm sure that you could, Majer."

Rahl managed not to wince. "But then, that might not be the best idea."

"That's true," replied Drakeyt evenly. "It might be best to make sure that you're available tomorrow."

Rahl could almost read the exact words the captain did not speak—*since much of the misdirection of the operation rests on your using magery from the rear of their position.* Yet Rahl couldn't help but feel torn. He didn't like sending someone else to be a target of sorts.

"Sometimes, Majer," Drakeyt said quietly, "others have to take the risks. They all know what you've risked for them."

Drakeyt's words helped, but Rahl still worried. Finally, he spoke. "They'll have to be a lure, almost. If they head east and south, they'll come out to the southeast of the patrol, and they'll look more like we've taken the long way."

"That might just get the patrols racing back to Selyma," Drakeyt said.

"It might, but I can't think of any other way to try it. I'd think, if they look small enough, the rebel commander might try to find out more." Rahl paused for a moment. "I don't think I'd like to send a report that I spotted a few Imperial troopers, and I didn't know where they came from or what their objective was or how many there might be."

Drakeyt laughed. "I wouldn't, either. Let's hope their commander feels the same way." The laugh died away. "I'm going to send second squad."

In moments, or so it seemed to Rahl, he was leading the scouts and outriders off the lane and through a muddy field that held sprouts of green, not that many in the line of the company would survive. He glanced back to his left, watching as second squad trotted ahead on the lane, although shortly they would turn more eastward, then south, cutting through an orchard of short well-trimmed trees that he did not recognize.

Drakeyt was leading the main body of Third Company, only about two hundred cubits behind Rahl. While it was cool, the air was so damp that Rahl had removed his riding jacket. That hadn't helped too much, because he was still sweating, even just wearing his uniform shirt.

Once they neared that point on the northwest side of the low grassy hill—if a rise less than ten cubits high could be called a hill—where any further advance might expose the scouts and outriders to view from the main road, Rahl raised his arm and called a halt, while the four remaining squads of Third Company closed the gap.

"Forward! Quick time!" ordered Drakeyt as soon as he neared Rahl and the outriders.

"Forward!" Rahl repeated.

After riding less than a hundred cubits, Rahl could see the main road ahead and slightly to his left. There were no rebels—and no riders—on the stretch closest to Third Company, but Rahl could sense the rebels—and the fighting and deaths and injuries farther to his left, if out of his immediate sight.

"To the road, then sweep toward the rebels!" ordered Drakeyt.

Rahl had his truncheon out well before he turned the gelding southeast on the smooth stone-paved road, a highway easily wide enough for six or seven mounts abreast.

"Five-front!" Drakeyt gestured to Rahl. "When we get there, take third squad onto the far side of their formation. Keep to the right."

Rahl nodded and eased the gelding almost to the right shoulder of the road.

"Third squad! On the majer! Pass it back!"

Ahead, Rahl could see the mounts and backs of the rebel force, a full company that had already surrounded second squad. Rahl could sense that Khasmyr had withdrawn so that his rear was partly covered by a small orchard.

The rebels did not even seem aware of the oncoming attack of Third Company until Rahl was within a hundred cubits or so of the rearmost of the rebel force.

"Impies! Behind us!"

The last rank of rebel troopers began to turn their mounts, but most were still trying to re-form into some sort of order when Drakeyt and first squad slammed into their ranks.

"Third squad! On the shoulder! On me!" Rahl called, remembering not to use order to boost his voice.

From that moment on, Rahl was acting mainly on instinct, using the truncheon as much for defense as offense, but he managed to keep an eye open at least intermittently for possible rebels who might try to break free and report back to the main body on the north side of the river.

Even so, he knew he'd killed at least one rebel and injured more than a few by the time Eighteenth Company arrived and the remaining rebels surrendered.

He'd also seen several rebels riding southward in the direction of Sastak, but none headed toward Selyma. At least, he didn't think any had gone that direction.

"Third Company! Re-form!"

Rahl rode slowly back toward Drakeyt. He had to know what Taryl's orders had cost second squad.

Drakeyt looked at Rahl.

Rahl looked back. "How many?"

"Nine are left, plus three wounded. One won't make it." Drakeyt cleared his throat. "The rebels got in their own way. Otherwise, most of them wouldn't have made it."

"Khasmyr used the orchard to try to keep them from circling behind him."

"He did. Good tactic. He didn't make it."

Rahl almost apologized, except . . . that wasn't his fault. He just nodded. "He did what he had to."

"We all did." Drakeyt gave the smallest of head-shakes. "Let's see what orders the commander has."

The orders were simple enough. Take that part of Selyma south of the river. No violence against the locals, but no rebel, should there be any in the town, was to be allowed to escape.

Riding into Selyma was anticlimactic—and vaguely amusing. Upon seeing the Imperial uniforms, the locals scurried for cover. Door after door slammed shut. Shutter after shutter closed.

Long before sunset, two companies of Fifth Regiment held the arching stone bridge over the Awhut River, and the rest of the regiment was quartered in local dwellings and buildings along the main streets and roads to the bridge. No troopers were stationed on the bridge itself, but two squads stood ready on the south side, should anyone attempt to cross. Several archers were among those holding the bridge.

The commander's orders were simple. No one was allowed to cross the bridge heading north. Anyone coming over the bridge to the south was to be detained until after the attack began on fiveday.

Drakeyt and Rahl found a small inn—more of a boarding house—three blocks from the bridge and commandeered it for Third Company. They had barely settled the troopers when a courier summoned them to the River House Inn, where Shuchyl had set up his temporary headquarters.

As he and Drakeyt rode along the brick-paved street toward the square and the inn, Rahl couldn't help but wonder if almost every town along the Awhut River had a River Inn or tavern or something.

Commander Shuchyl was actually standing on the wide front porch of the inn as Rahl and Drakeyt rode up and dismounted. The commander beckoned for them to join him, and he ushered several majers away.

Shuchyl was squat, broad-shouldered, with a nose like a vulcrow and small bright eyes that reminded Rahl of a traitor bird. His voice was deep and gravelly. "Captain . . . Majer . . . your initiative and tactics in preventing the rebel company from sending word to the rebel command are greatly appreciated."

"Thank you, ser." Rahl and Drakeyt spoke almost simultaneously.

"Tomorrow, we will ride at first light. By the orders of the overcommander, Eighteenth Company will lead, and Third Company will follow Eighteenth. Once we clear the town proper on the north side of the bridge, you are to carry out these orders." The commander lifted a sealed envelope and extended it—reluctantly, Rahl could tell—to Rahl.

Rahl nodded politely as he took the envelope, only saying, "ser," politely.

"You remain in command, Captain," Shuchyl continued, "but the majer will direct you as ordered by the overcommander."

"Yes, ser," replied Drakeyt.

Rahl was more than relieved to sense amusement, rather than resentment, from Drakeyt.

"That is all, Majer, Captain."

"Yes, ser."

Neither Rahl nor Drakeyt spoke until they had mounted and were well away from the River House Inn."

"Are you going to open that envelope, Majer?"

"Once we're alone, Captain. Then, we can either laugh or be totally appalled, with no one being the wiser."

Rahl was all too certain that he was going to be appalled.

LXXIII

On fiveday, Rahl and Drakeyt were up well before first light. Rahl had not slept all that well again, although sleeping in an actual bed, lumpy as the horsehair mattress had been, had been better than a bedroll on the ground.

Taryl's orders had not been appalling in their detail, but in their lack of such. They had consisted of little more than one line:

Take the far western flank and attack with all force and magery possible short of exhaustion and foolhardiness.

"Those orders are just a way to keep Commander Shuchyl from taking control. That's all," Drakeyt had said.

That much had been obvious to Rahl, but what sort of magery could he do that would be effective and not totally exhaust him? He could protect himself, if he didn't do much else, but that wasn't an attack, exactly. The ooze-magery might work against the stone redoubt on the easternmost hill, but the rebels were too scattered along the hills west of where the main road cut through them. He couldn't throw more than one or two order-bolts, and that wouldn't be nearly enough.

Drakeyt looked from where he stood beside his mount outside the boarding house. "Ready, Majer?"

"As ready as I'm likely to be, Captain."

Drakeyt grinned and swung himself up into the saddle

with an easy grace that Rahl admired. "Then let's see if Quelsyn has everyone mustered."

The senior squad leader was waiting at the front of the formation. "Third Company, ready to ride, ser."

"Very well, Quelsyn, we'll move to the avenue and toward the bridge."

"Yes, ser."

"Company! Forward!"

Obviously, the various company senior squad leaders kept in touch with each other, because Third Company reached the avenue just as Eighteenth Company passed. Third Company swung in behind, and both halted on the wide main street, Eighteenth Company just short of the causeway approaching the bridge.

Just before the first orange light of the sun seeped out of the east, Eighteenth Company rode onto the arching stone bridge over the Awhut River, then across it and along the avenue that would become the main highway to Dawhut and Kysha once it neared the hills north of Selyma that held the rebel positions. Third Company followed.

The northern portion of Selyma was shuttered and appeared deserted, although Rahl could sense locals hidden in various buildings and dwellings. An unseen miasma of fear hovered over the town, and the impacts of iron horse-shoes on the stone pavement were as sharp as the blows of a hammer nailing shut a cheap plank coffin.

Ahead of Eighteenth Company, Rahl could sense some riders, possibly rebel officers, hurrying northward from Selyma in the direction of the two defensive positions.

Just what could he do? That question kept coming back to nag at Rahl as he rode northward and as the orangish light of dawn faded into a cold and clear day under a green-blue sky—the first clear one in more than an eightday.

Before long, he could see their objective all too clearly. The back sides of the hills to the north of Selyma and west of the main road were a welter of earthworks and tents and lean-tos, as opposed to the more orderly stone revetments crowning the top of the hills to the east of the road. Lancers and troopers swarmed across the upper part of both hills, and light glinted off the weapons and armor of the lancers.

Another question struck Rahl. Why had Taryl specified that Third Company take the western flank? Was there something about the western end of the hills? He studied the slope of the hills, then nodded.

"Quarter turn, left!" ordered Drakeyt.

Third Company came to a halt on the flat a good half kay from where the winter-bedraggled grass began to rise. From the south side, the hills looked more like a gentle ridge, and far easier to ride up than the approach from the other side. To Rahl's right, the flat began to fill with the companies of the Fifth Regiment.

On the hillside, the defenders assembled as well, and a chaos-firebolt arced down toward the center of the Imperial forces, splattering on the flattened grass several hundred cubits short of the middle of the regiment. Rahl watched, keeping his personal shields tight, and waited.

Before long another firebolt soared southward.

Rahl reached out with his order-senses and nudged it downward so that it, too, splattered short of the Imperial troopers.

At that, two firebolts flared toward Rahl.

He found those easier to divert because he didn't have to extend himself.

Another and stronger firebolt followed, and diverting it took a bit more effort from Rahl. Then, for the moment, there were no more chaos-firebolts as two companies of lancers formed up, clearly aimed at Third Company.

Rahl watched as the lancers dressed their lines, and he tried to see and sense a path that would take the company through the lancers and to the oval earthworks that held at least one mage and presumably the senior officers commanding the rebel forces. Then he edged the gelding over beside Drakeyt.

"Yes, Majer?"

"Captain, can you form the company into a five-front column behind me once the lancers start to charge down at us?"

The slightest hint of a frown crossed the brow of the older officer. "That's possible."

"Then do it. The closer everyone is to me, the less danger they face to begin with. We're going to meet their charge with one of our own, and we'll be heading through them for the center of their forces—that earthworks oval in the middle of the hillcrest there." Rahl did not wait for a reply, but rode the gelding into position right in front of third squad.

Once there, he turned in the saddle. "Shemal, we're going to break the lancers and split the rebels. The captain will be giving the orders once the lancers charge. Keep your squad as close to me as you can until we're through the lancers. They'll take fewer casualties that way."

The squad leader moistened his lips but his voice was steady. "Yes, ser."

Rahl let his senses pick up the few murmurs behind him.

". . . majer's going to break the lancers open . . . like to see that . . ."

". . . according to Clynet . . . you don't want to see him like that . . ."

". . . close to him . . . but not too close . . ."

The rebel lancers continued to dress their lines. Then a series of trumpet triplets rang out, and the lancers began to move, slowly, but gaining speed as they moved down the rise.

Rahl turned in Drakeyt's direction and raised his truncheon, then called out, "Third Squad! On me!" He urged the gelding forward.

After the slightest hesitation, Shemal echoed the command. "Forward! On the majer!"

While the squad leader might have hesitated, the

troopers did not, surging forward and tightening almost into a wedge behind Rahl.

Rahl began to expand his personal shields, slowly, and carefully; and then, at the last moment before the two forces met, Rahl anchored the expanded shield to the mounts of Third Company, so that the shield was a knife-edged wedge pushed forward by the mass of a score of mounts.

Lancers and lances sprayed away from Rahl and third squad.

Just when Third Company broke through the third line of lancers, a firebolt splashed across the shield directly in front of Rahl, momentarily blinding him, but he managed to hold the shield for a moment longer, before letting it collapse just to protect him. Even so, he felt slightly light-headed, but he urged the gelding along the ridgeline toward the earthworks at the center of the rebel forces.

As he had anticipated, Third Company's charge had caught the rebels off guard, and troopers were trying to turn their mounts to deal with an enemy that had burst through their flank and was already behind the majority of the rebel troopers.

Orders rang out from below on both sides of the hill, and Imperial troopers charged uphill.

Rahl could sense the confusion and consternation among the rebels. He hoped it lasted for a while longer.

A half score of rebel troopers swerved toward Rahl and third squad. Rahl didn't slow the gelding in the slightest, but angled to the left, then back to the right, using the motion to amplify the cut of the truncheon. The rebel sagged back in his saddle, unable to recover when a trooper behind Rahl struck with his sabre.

Less than a hundred cubits ahead was the edge of the rebel command earthworks, and standing at the edge, by an opening in the heaped turf and earth stood a white wizard, lifting his arm and pointing toward third squad.

Rahl charged the white mage, expanding his shields just as he neared the wizard, trying to throw the firebolt back at the wizard. The shields enfolded the chaos-flame and did just that, flinging it back, but it sheeted around the wizard and into the earthworks, leaving him untouched.

Rahl could sense deaths, maybe a score or more, but he concentrated on putting order into his truncheon as he rode past the wizard and struck downward. The blow was only glancing, but the order pressed by Rahl shattered the mage's shield. Then the white wizard died, his chaos overwhelmed by order.

After that, Rahl turned the gelding and just tried to do as much damage with the truncheon as he could while staying alive and trusting that the rest of the Imperial forces would continue their attacks and reach him and Third Company.

After following third squad with the rest of the company, Drakeyt had organized the squads into a half circle, backed against the earthworks. Rahl had barely guided Third Company over to the eastern edge of the formation when a wave of mounted troopers rushed them.

Rahl settled in to what he hoped was a routine of parries, slides, blocks, and thrusts.

Below him, he could sense the Imperial forces moving toward them, but more slowly than he would have liked, because more and more Third Company troopers were suffering wounds, and more than a handful had already died.

Rahl kept the truncheon moving, although he wasn't certain how he'd managed it, until, as so often seemed to be the case, abruptly the remaining rebels melted away, and he was slumped in his saddle, looking downhill at more fallen men and mounts than he'd ever seen, all too aware of the vast combined emptiness of thousands of deaths.

He just sat there in his saddle, breathing hard, then finally sheathing the truncheon and reminding himself to take several swallows from the water bottle. He glanced at the sun, nearly at midday.

Had the battle taken that long?

Then he turned and rode toward Drakeyt.

"Congratulations, Majer."

"That belongs to you and your men, Captain." Rahl could understand the barely concealed bitterness.

"We lost another eighteen men, and sixteen more are wounded. Three of them might not make it."

"I wish it could have been otherwise." Rahl still didn't see what else he could have done.

"Majer."

Rahl turned to see Taryl reined up some twenty cubits away. He eased the gelding toward the overcommander, careful to avoid several bodies and a dead horse. The odor of blood and worse was growing stronger under the midday sun, even with the cool breeze out of the north. He reined up short of Taryl. "Ser."

"I believe my orders suggested something less fool-hardy." Taryl's voice was steady.

Rahl detected no edge or anger.

"You ordered maximum force, ser. I did the best I could."

The overcommander nodded. "You did what was necessary." He turned in the saddle toward Drakeyt, who had reined up somewhat farther away. "Captain, you and your men fought well; they fought gallantly and effectively. Their losses also saved hundreds, if not thousands, of casualties. I know that such heavy losses are hard for a company commander, but I wanted you to know what you accomplished."

Drakeyt glanced at Rahl. "It was the majer's plan, ser. I—"

"You and your men bled to make it work. A plan is only as good as those who carry it out. I will be recommending gallantry bonuses for the entire company, including payment to any widows. My deepest appreciation, Captain. Thank you."

"Our duty to the Emperor, ser."

"For which he is most grateful." After a moment, Taryl turned to Rahl, but said nothing until Drakeyt had eased his mount away.

"How many casualties today in Third Company, Rahl?"

"Eighteen dead, sixteen wounded, ser."

"You killed every one of them, you know."

For a moment, Rahl couldn't believe what Taryl had said. He just looked at the older mage-guard.

"If you had held back and just let matters develop·as they did during the last battle, Third Company might have lost five men, maybe ten." Taryl paused. "By the way, before we go farther, what you did was right. But . . . do you know why I'm making this point?"

"To show that everything has a cost?"

"That's true enough, but you already knew. It's more than just that." Taryl coughed several times, then cleared his throat before continuing. "Use of great magery always has disproportionate costs at the time and place where it is used. That's true of all good weapons as well—they concentrate force. You concentrated force in the way in which you combined magery and Third Company. The cost on the enemy was terrible, but so was the cost for Third Company." Taryl waited, as if for a response.

Rahl tried to think, but he felt so tired. Finally, he spoke . . . slowly. "Is that another way of . . . pointing out that I shouldn't use magery except as a last resort, when nothing else will work?"

"That's often true, but not always. Don't get bound by inflexible rules. That's where both your former magisters on Recluce and the whites of Fairhaven always get into trouble. Each situation must be judged on its own. Rules are a useful guideline and generally should be heeded, but blindly following them eventually and inevitably leads to disaster."

"Always judge each situation on its own?"

"That's true, but then, there's always the temptation to justify what you want to do as opposed to what should be done. The more power you attain, Rahl, the greater that temptation. Never forget that."

"No, ser."

"You need some food and rest, because I'll need your help for what comes next. There's no point in killing any more of their troopers and wasting ours. Not here."

"Ser?"

"We didn't attack the other hill. That's where the senior commanders are. We have it surrounded. I have something else in mind, but we need some rest, and I'll need your help. Just follow me for now."

"Yes, ser." Especially after what Taryl had just told him, Rahl couldn't help wondering just what else Taryl had in mind, but he knew the overcommander wouldn't say. Rahl just let the gelding follow Taryl's gray.

LXXIV

After Rahl ate a large and hot meal of tough mutton and boiled potatoes, Taryl ordered him to put his still-damp riding jacket on the back of a chair in front of the fire in the ancient hearth, then lie down on a pallet in the corner of the single bedchamber in the small cottage that served as Taryl's makeshift headquarters. Rahl was still thinking about protesting that he wasn't tired when his eyes closed.

When he was next aware, he was walking through a barn where the Third Company troopers—those who were left—kept staring at him when he wasn't looking at them. But every time he turned to check, everyone smiled or looked away suddenly. Why were they acting that way? What had he done?

Then a voice startled him. "Rahl . . . it's time to get up and get to work."

Taryl's words jolted Rahl awake, and he realized that

he'd been dreaming. Slowly, he sat up, glancing around and seeing that it was still light outside, although he could tell from the angle of the sunlight that it was well past midafternoon.

"There's some ale on the table there. You need to drink some before we leave," announced Taryl. "Eat some of the bread, too."

"Did you get any rest, ser?" Rahl stood and walked to the table, where he picked up the mug Taryl had pointed out and took a long swallow. The dream still bothered him.

"Enough. Not so much as you, but enough."

Rahl had the feeling that the older mage had gotten some rest, but Taryl still looked tired. "What sort of work, ser?" He broke off a corner of the loaf and ate some, chewing slowly. The bread was stale, and crumbs flaked off.

"While we've been resting, Marshal Byrna and First Army have encircled the eastern hill, the one with that stone fortress on top. Some of the rebel companies have surrendered, but the rest are rather defiant. That may have something to do with the fact that there are a few senior officers and several chaos-mages and former mage-guards inside those stone walls."

"What exactly are we going to do?" Rahl had more of the ale. How could he still be so hungry?

"A version of what you did on the road to Lahenta, except with greater precision and for a far shorter time." Taryl smiled bleakly. "We're going to turn the ground beneath the fort into ooze, but only for a very short time. We will create a thin line of order around the hill, and each of us will do half. You'll be on the southern side, and I'll be on the north. Once the order-circle is complete, we will begin to delink everything on your side. After a few moments, it will continue on its own."

Rahl nodded. He remembered that all too well, except that it wouldn't go outside the order-boundary.

"It will, if you leave it long enough, because it will keep digging down. And you need to keep your shields full at all times." Taryl paused, and added firmly, "At all times, for the rest of your life—assuming you want to have a long and healthy life."

Rahl looked quizzically at Taryl. The overcommander couldn't mean that, could he?

"I do mean it. You've already created more enemies in a year than most mage-guards do in a lifetime, and because you're supporting the Emperor, you'll make more before this is all over. Your shields are your defense against them."

Rahl took another swallow of ale, as much to cover his confusion as because he was thirsty. "I understand about the shields . . ."

"What was Undercaptain Craelyt's reaction to you?"

"He tried to kill me, but . . . you, Captain Gheryk, and Jyrolt—Captain Jyrolt, I mean—you have all been most fair. . . ."

"The danger is never from those who are knowledgeable and good, Rahl. It's always from those who offer a facade of goodness and are not and from those who do evil while honestly believing that their deeds are for a greater good. The first will try to destroy you by catching you unawares, and the second will catch you unawares because they have no idea what they are truly doing. Because they do not, you cannot wait to shield yourself until you perceive their intentions. Your best defense is shields that will keep them from knowing anything."

Rahl understood that. What he was having a hard time understanding was why anyone would think a mere senior mage-guard presented a threat, especially one so junior as Rahl was. Still . . . Taryl's words made sense. Rahl *had* learned that. He made the immediate effort to tighten his personal shields.

"Good. Now . . . you know that once the delinking process goes on for a time, everything within the circle will sink. Once the rebel fortifications and forces have sunk out of sight, we will have to restore the links, or before long we will not have a town of Selyma, and the Awhut River will feed an ever-growing swamp. You should know when to begin restoring the links." Taryl nodded briskly. "Let's go."

Rahl reclaimed his riding jacket, which was now dry and warm for the first time in days, and fastened it before following the overcommander out of the small stead dwelling. Rahl's gelding and Taryl's mount were tied outside the small cottage. Both had obviously been groomed and fed. The late-afternoon sky was clear and looked colder than the brisk breeze that swirled around Rahl as he mounted.

Taryl did not speak as the two mage-guards began to ride southward toward the remaining rebel stronghold, accompanied by two squads of headquarters troopers, with two leading the way.

Less than a quarter kay from the grassy flat below the eastern slope, Taryl turned to Rahl. "I'll wait until you begin the circle. That way, I'll know you're in position."

"Yes, ser. How far down from the fort do you want the circle?"

"Just enough to encircle the remaining troops. Some may be able to escape once they understand what is happening. That's why our forces are drawn up below, but they're far enough away to make it hard for archers and chaos-fire. You'll probably have to ride uphill somewhat from Fifth Regiment—Commander Shuchyl is holding much of the south side. Don't go any closer than you have to."

Rahl nodded.

Taryl offered a brief smile. "Here's where we part . . . for the moment."

When Taryl turned right and began to ride directly toward the north slope of the hill holding the small stone fort at its crest, only one of the squads escorted him. The other remained with Rahl as he continued southward along the highway toward the gap in the hills. The log-and-stone barricade had been removed, and the logs and stones piled beside the shoulder of the road short of the walled cut through the gap.

Rahl glanced back. He could not only not see the older mage, but he could not even sense Taryl. That sort of invisibility to order- or chaos-sensing was what Taryl expected of him, clearly, but would he ever be able to do that so effortlessly?

As he made his way southward, Rahl was most careful to maintain shields, although he kept his order-senses especially alert when he and the headquarters troopers rode through the walled section of the road between the two hilly ridges. Nothing happened, but he breathed more easily once he was on the south side.

He turned the gelding onto the trampled grass and headed toward the Imperial companies that were formed up a good half kay downslope from the remaining rebel forces. The rebel troopers formed a barrier around the stone fortification, an action that Rahl found somehow counter to common sense. Weren't walls supposed to protect troopers, not the other way around?

The entire hillside was silent—or as still as thousands of troopers and mounts could be in a brisk breeze—with both sides poised to attack once an order was given. As Rahl neared the rear of the Imperial formation, he looked upslope. He really didn't want to try to set an order-circle from half a kay away, but he also didn't wish to have to get any too close to the rebel lancers and troopers—or any archers or chaos-mages remaining with the rebels. He also doubted that he could maintain a sight shield and set an order-circle at the same time—not to mention protecting himself from possible firebolts from the mages in the fort above.

After a moment, he guided the gelding between two companies and continued uphill. As he neared the front of the formation, a majer turned his mount and headed toward Rahl.

"Captain!"

Rahl continued to ride.

The majer reached Rahl just as Rahl was abreast of the first rank of troopers.

"We're to hold here, Captain!"

Rahl turned and looked at the officer. "That's correct. You're to hold here. And it's 'Majer,' by the way, and I'm operating under the orders of the overcommander. You might recognize the headquarters squad." Rahl smiled, but extended his order shields just slightly, with enough force to press the officer back in his saddle. "If you'll excuse me, I'd like to get on with what I'm doing so that more of your troopers don't get killed unnecessarily."

Rahl could sense both fear and anger within the majer, and he was already beginning to tire of that reaction. He forced cordiality into his voice, but projected a sense of absolute power behind the words. "You're here to do your duty, Majer, and I'm here to do mine." Then he urged the gelding forward, but only at a slow walk. Riding quickly would be one way to get the rebels charging down on him.

Behind him, the majer reined up, but Rahl could still sense anger.

"How far, ser?" asked the squad leader.

"As close as we can get without them wanting to charge us." Rahl extended his order-senses, trying to feel any indication that the lancers directly across the open grass from him—if several hundred cubits uphill—were thinking about attacking.

Slowly, Rahl continued uphill, but at an angle, away from the center of the stone walls.

Whhhsttt!

Rahl just let the firebolt splatter on the grass a good sixty cubits uphill.

The next firebolt was closer, but he merely order-nudged it so that it burned into the mud-spattered grass some thirty cubits to his left. The third one was noticeably weaker, but by then Rahl was closer than he really wanted to be to the mounted rebel troopers—a distance that seemed little less than 150 cubits.

He reined up and began to study the area around the stone fort. Then he shrugged and began to project his

thin and unseen order line. He had perhaps a third of his
half completed when he began to sense Taryl's work.

Another firebolt soared out from behind the stone walls
and down toward Rahl. He diverted it and tried to concentrate on completing his order barrier just below the surface
of the ground. He managed to get another third completed
when a single set of trumpet triplets sounded, and the
rebel lancers in the company closest to him and the headquarters squad quickly dressed their lines and began to
charge toward him. Moments later, two more balls of
chaos-flame arced toward him.

This time, Rahl hurriedly flung the chaos back at the
lancers, using order to flatten and narrow the chaos into
a thin line—almost like a chaos-whip snapped by order.

Lancers went down and piled into each other.

Using that delay, Rahl struggled to extend his order-
line more to the west to reach the section of the unseen
perimeter that Taryl was constructing.

Just as the two halves joined, three or four more
chaos-bolts flared toward Rahl.

Rahl threw them at the rebel lancers, then reached out
and began to start delinking the order-points inside the
order-perimeter, but he kept having to divert his attention to block or divert what seemed like a rain of firebolts.

Then he realized that the rebel lancers were charging
once more.

"Ser?"

"This way!" Rahl urged the gelding eastward, almost
paralleling his order-perimeter while trying to stay on
the gelding, keep distance between him and the lancers,
and continue to order-delink the ground inside the order-
line.

The lancers pulled up, letting Rahl move away from a
position directly below the small stone walls, but the firebolts kept coming, if intermittently.

Rahl could sense a far greater wave of delinking and
ooze formation on the north side of the hill, but then, he

told himself, even as he tried to keep adding to the process, Taryl hadn't been under attack all the time.

Then . . . just as Taryl had predicted, the ground everywhere under the fort and the rebel troops seemed to liquefy all at once. The fort and the higher ground began to sink. Rebel troopers and lancers started to ride downhill in every direction.

With a huge sucking sound, everything inside the order-line vanished into a grayish brown ooze. Moreover, the hilltop had vanished as well, leaving a flat expanse of ooze level with the top of the order-perimeter created by the two mage-guards.

For a moment, Rahl just looked.

Then he could sense Taryl straining to restore order, and he immediately devoted himself to that. For a time, he felt as though he were trying to hold back a wave of mud with a sieve, and he could feel the suffocation and strangulation of hundreds of men, but slowly, slowly, the edges of the ooze solidified. Then, in apparent reversal of the process, everything solidified . . . and all those thousands trapped within the hill and still alive died, crushed to death by the return of solidity.

Under that wave of death and chill, Rahl began to shiver so violently that he had to grab the saddle rim to steady himself. So many deaths . . . so many all at once.

Abruptly, he forced himself to straighten. He could sense Taryl—and there was no way he should be able to sense where the older mage-guard was unless Taryl was wounded or in trouble.

"We need to get back to the overcommander!" Rahl started to urge the gelding forward, not down the hill, but farther eastward, around the flattened and solidified hilltop that had entombed thousands of men. Then he shook his head. The flattened area above him was solid, and it provided a far quicker route.

Rahl could sense the hesitation of the headquarters squad, but he did not hold back, not when Taryl might be in trouble. He galloped across the grayish brown clay, so hard that the gelding's hoofs sounded as though he were riding a paved road.

On the other side, Taryl was by himself, a good five hundred cubits above the other headquarters' squad, as well as above the marshal's massed forces. As Rahl reined up beside Taryl, the older man was white and ready to fall from his saddle—that was the way he felt to Rahl.

"Ser." Rahl managed to extend a slight bit of order, the little he could afford.

Taryl straightened. "Riding over that was a bit much."

"It was the quickest way, and I could feel your shields collapsing."

"You could?"

For the first time in seasons, Rahl actually felt the un-shielded surprise of the older mage-guard. "Yes, ser. That's why I came the quickest way."

"I suppose I'm fortunate to have an assistant so diligent."

"You need to eat something." Rahl twisted in the saddle and fumbled some travel biscuits from his saddle-bags. "Here."

Taryl took them, saying nothing until he had eaten both biscuits and swallowed some water. "Follow your own advice."

Belatedly, Rahl did, realizing that he was not in much better shape than Taryl.

Neither spoke for a time.

"You made that circle rather large," Taryl finally said.

"I'm not as skilled as you are. I couldn't figure out how to hold a sight shield and create the order circle at the same time. I rode as close as I could, but the rebel officers were about to charge if I'd gotten much nearer. Their wizards and chaos-mages were throwing firebolts the whole time."

"I thought that might have been the case." Taryl smiled. "It was good practice for you. You'll need to learn to handle more than two mage-tasks at once, anyway. Now . . . we need to tell the marshal what happened . . . rather why it happened. He won't be pleased."

Why wouldn't the marshal be pleased? Taryl's and Rahl's effort had eliminated some of the top rebel officers and cost the rebels several thousand troopers without the loss of any more Imperial forces. Rahl could still feel that massive cold void of thousands of deaths, a chill that the riding jacket did nothing to dispel, but he knew the marshal was incapable of feeling that directness of death.

As the two rode down the slope, followed by the two escort squads, an aisle opened in the Imperial troopers, an aisle a good fifty cubits wide, as if none of the troopers or their officers wanted to get all that close. Rahl could sense a combination of fear, anger, and sadness—but mostly fear, leavened by sadness, with only a few hints of anger.

"How do you feel, Rahl?"

"Cold . . . cold all over . . . angry . . . I guess, too. So many dead, but if we hadn't done it, then . . . there would be almost as many dead, and a lot would have been ours."

"That's the tragedy of war. No matter who wins, thousands die. The only question is whose thousands."

"Better theirs than ours," Rahl suggested.

"All victors say that, and the cause of the victor is always just."

The iron-cold bitterness of Taryl's soft words cut through Rahl. He had no answer.

"We won't be doing much for a while," Taryl said quietly. "We won't have to for a few days, I hope."

Farther down the slope, Rahl could see Marshal Byrna standing on a platform some six cubits high, set in the middle of the flat area below the slope. He stood in the long shadow cast by the setting sun's drop behind the more western hill ridge. The timbers of the structure were mixed, a mark that it had been constructed hastily to offer the marshal a position from which he could watch the battle.

The two mage-guards rode directly to the raised and railed platform. After tying his mount to the railing next to the wooden ladder, Taryl climbed up first. Rahl followed.

Byrna was alone on the platform, and anger radiated from him. Taryl had barely gotten within several cubits before the marshal began. "Overcommander, could you enlighten me as to why you and your . . . assistant did not offer the rebels the chance to surrender?"

Taryl stopped and waited, saying nothing.

"Did you have a reason, Overcommander?"

"Yes." Taryl's voice was even. "First, they would not have surrendered. Second, the Emperor should not be faced with the decision of what to do with those traitors, even had they done so."

There was another unspoken reason, too, Rahl knew. He and Taryl could not have gotten close enough to create an order circle just around the fort itself, not without losing hundreds of Imperial troopers.

". . . They were all officers who had a choice, unlike junior officers and troopers. If he orders their deaths, he's heartless. If he spares them, he's an idiot. He can't afford to be either. I can afford to be merciless. He can't."

For a moment, Rahl just stood there, sensing the marshal's still-growing outrage.

"You'd take that upon yourself. You're not even in charge—"

"That's right, Marshal. That way you can tell everyone that the Mage-Guard Overcommander acted before you could countermand him." Taryl's voice was simultaneously tired and cold. "That also saves you."

Byrna flushed, and tension radiated from his entire body.

Rahl could sense that the rage seething in the marshal was well beyond mere anger.

Byrna's voice was hard, but edged with that barely controlled fury, as he replied. "Some of those men were good officers who did what they thought best."

"Exactly," replied Taryl. "They *were* good officers.

They ceased to be good officers when they violated the Emperor's trust, and any officer who would excuse or condone such behavior also risks violating the Emperor's trust. The one thing that the mage-guards can never allow, either among our own or among the High Command, is violation of that trust. Or an acceptance of those who violate that trust. Do I make myself clear, Marshal?"

"Perfectly clear, Overcommander."

Taryl looked to Rahl. "You may go, Majer."

"Yes, ser. If you need me . . ."

"I know where to find you. Thank you." Taryl's voice lost a hint of the black iron behind it on his last two words.

After he climbed down from the platform and remounted the gelding, Rahl slowly rode through the growing twilight that he had barely noticed, back in the direction of the boardinghouse, where he assumed that Third Company would be standing down. Thoughts swirled through his mind.

How could the marshal be so stupid? This was far from the first time that Rahl had doubted the intelligence of High Command senior officers. Was it that stupid officers were needed? Had Byrna been picked by Triad Dhoryk to fail? Or to allow the rebellion to drag out, as Taryl had intimated might well be part of a plan to weaken the Emperor? But whom would they select to replace the Emperor? Rahl couldn't help but wonder if Fieryn and Dhoryk were planning some kind of coup. That would certainly explain Taryl's need to rely on solid older commanders such as Muyr and Shuchyl—and his forcing Rahl to develop skills not needed that much in normal mage-guard duties. It also would account for his insistence on Rahl's maintaining his shields.

What would the conflict between Taryl and Byrna mean for the rest of the campaign?

Would there be a campaign after Selyma?

Rahl kept riding.

LXXV

Rahl and Drakeyt sat at a small table along the wall in the public room of the Tankard, one of the less prepossessing of the handful of inns in Selyma. Even though the night was barely chill, the acrid odor of smoke straying from the smoldering hearth added to the already pronounced perfume of cooking fat and overbaked bread.

Rahl took a small swallow of a bitter brew that passed for lager.

"What do you think the overcommander will do next?" asked Drakeyt.

"The marshal's the one in command," Rahl pointed out.

"The word is that the overcommander's the one making the decisions." Drakeyt sipped from his beaker.

Rahl shrugged. "I don't know what either plans, and the overcommander hasn't told me. He did say that nothing would happen for a day or two."

"Good. Our troopers need rest. Some of the troopers in the other companies are in worse shape." Drakeyt shook his head. "Ours had seen magery before. Most of them haven't."

"It's likely to get worse," Rahl said slowly.

"Did the overcommander tell you that?"

"No. Not in so many words. He's been warning me for eightdays about how I'll need to hold stronger shields once we get close to Nubyat and Sastak." That wasn't quite what Taryl had said, but Rahl thought it meant close to the same thing. Why else would Taryl have been pressing him on the personal shields so much?

"It's fiveday night. You think we'll be moving out by sevenday?"

"I don't know. I'd judge sevenday or eightday, but that's just a guess. It all might change, too, depending on what Golyat does."

"If I were the prince, I'd find a ship and go somewhere else."

"He can't," Rahl replied. "He's not worth the trouble to any land powerful enough to stand up to Hamor and too dangerous for those less powerful."

Drakeyt took another swallow from his beaker. "Means we'll lose more troopers for no good reason. Suppose that's always been the case when there's a war."

"Besides," Rahl went on, "I get the feeling that he really believes he should be emperor. People who feel like that don't usually just turn away." Not to mention the fact that Golyat was probably surrounded by people who wanted him to be emperor so that they could also have more power.

"You think you'll be a mage-guard commander or overcommander some day?"

Rahl almost choked on the bitter lager. He managed to swallow, then cleared his throat. "Me? I'm lucky to be a senior mage-guard. I think I'd be fortunate to be a city captain or something like that." Rahl would have liked to think he could be more, but his experiences to date suggested that he was exceedingly fortunate to have gotten as far as he had, and that had only happened because of Taryl.

Drakeyt shook his head. "You get out of this mess alive, and the overcommander has something in mind for you."

"Why do you say that?"

"He's given you and Third Company too many sow-shit missions, and he keeps reinforcing the company."

Why did reinforcing Third Company mean Taryl had something planned for Rahl? Usually Taryl wanted Rahl to learn or see something. But what would reinforcing a company rather than transferring Rahl to another company show? What fighting did to the troopers? Or to Drakeyt? Or how many died? Rahl was well aware of that—more than half the original company had perished.

Finally, Rahl replied. "He never does anything without a purpose, but I can't figure out what he has in mind, except to give me experience, because I didn't have all that much."

"You had a lot more than most mage-guards your age, didn't you?" asked Drakeyt.

Rahl shrugged. "That's probably true. I also made a lot more mistakes than most did."

Drakeyt laughed, darkly, then swallowed the last of the brew in his beaker. "That'd be true, too. I'm heading back." He stood.

So did Rahl. He was in need of some sleep. He just hoped he could and that he didn't spend all night worrying about what Taryl had in mind for him . . . or about all those who had died—on both sides—because of what he had done.

LXXVI

On eightday, Third Company left Selyma, heading south toward Nubyat, with the task of scouting everything within ten kays of the main highway. First and Second Army were scheduled to begin the advance on Nubyat on oneday. As before, Rahl was under orders from Taryl to maintain full shields and not to use any order-skills unless Third Company was attacked by vastly superior forces.

By midmorning, the day was like most winter days in Merowey—cool, but not cold; dampish, but not raining; and with a haze over the green-blue sky that was less than cloudy but enough to keep the sun from providing much warmth. Less than two kays south of that part of Selyma on the south side of the Awhut River, the road from Dawhut merged with the road coming from Sastak. The smooth stone surface was nearly fifteen cubits wide, with broad shoulders on each side, and it led due southwest toward Nubyat.

Everywhere were groves of olive trees, but of a type Rahl had not seen before, seldom reaching more than fifteen cubits in height. Between the tree-lined rows in the orchards was low grass with winter-browned tips. The orchards were empty, and the barns and stead houses were shuttered and barred. Many were empty, but not all, by any means. That, Rahl could sense. The road itself was empty of all riders or wagons—except for Third Company.

The company had also gotten another half score of replacements, and when they had arrived, Drakeyt had just looked at Rahl, not even raising his eyebrows. Rahl had to admit that Drakeyt had as much as predicted those reinforcement troopers. Was it just to make Third Company a stalking horse to allow Taryl to act and react in a more effective fashion? It certainly couldn't be just to give Rahl more experience. As thoughtful as Taryl could be, when the Emperor and Hamor's very unity were at stake, the overcommander wasn't about to give Rahl any experience that could threaten either. But that left the question of why Taryl continued to push Rahl to learn more at a time when the overcommander had far larger concerns than one very junior senior mage-guard.

"You think we'll ever see a clear sun, ser?" asked Shanyr.

"Not until it's hot enough that we won't want to."

The outrider laughed.

Rahl couldn't imagine the revolt lasting into summer. But then, he reminded himself, he hadn't believed Puvort had been capable of such treachery, or that Rahl himself could possibly have become a mage-guard, or—and he smiled at the thought—that Deybri would ever have admitted that he had brought a different light into her life. Still, that light might flicker out, and how and when would he ever be able to return to Recluce to see her, much less be with her for any length of time?

He pushed those thoughts away and concentrated on

trying to receive order-impressions of everything around him . . . but nothing changed.

As Rahl rode past another shuttered stead dwelling several hundred cubits to the north of the road, just the faintest hint of a chill passed across him—the chill of a screeing glass. Now, even with full shields, Rahl was coming to sense when a glass was being used to view the area around him. Since the feeling did not linger, it was likely that his shields had been effective enough that the mage using the glass had not noticed him in passing. Rahl hoped so.

After riding another kay, Rahl began to feel something, but, still following Taryl's orders, he did nothing in the way of extending an order-probe to discover what it might be.

Before long, ahead on a low rise in the road almost a kay away, three riders in maroon jackets reined up and watched Rahl and the scouts ride toward them.

"Ser . . ." murmured Shanyr from where he rode beside Rahl.

"I see them." Following Taryl's orders, Rahl did not attempt to reach out to them with his order-senses, although he could still feel that the three were not close to any rebel force. "They're alone. Scouts, probably."

One of the scouts riding a half kay ahead of Rahl turned in the saddle.

Rahl waved for him to keep riding.

After Rahl and the scouts and outriders covered another several hundred cubits, the three rebel scouts turned their mounts and galloped over the low rise and out of sight. Rahl almost shrugged. It couldn't be exactly a secret that the Imperial forces were riding toward Nubyat, not after the battle at Selyma.

LXXVII

From the saddle of the gelding, Rahl surveyed the perfectly smooth paving stones of the highway leading
down the wide and gentle slope into the circular valley
that held Nubyat, its harbor, and the fertile land to the
north bordering the delta of the Awhut River. Several
kays behind Third Company was Commander Shuchyl's
Fifth Regiment, followed by the bulk of Second Army.
As usual, Third Company was the point of the advance.

The terrain surprised Rahl. He'd expected steads with
tilled fields, or even woods, or grasslands. Instead, the
gentle slopes held orchards of the dwarf olives and occasional blue oaks interspersed in a few places with winter
brown grass. The only croplands were to the north and
east of Nubyat, along the river, and fed by irrigation
ditches. Stretching everywhere else were primarily olive
orchards, with occasional structures that appeared to be
warehouses. A kay or so ahead, the orchards ended, and
there looked to be dwellings on small plots of land between the olive orchards and Nubyat proper, where the
dwellings were more tightly clustered.

The harbor area, according to the maps, was on the
north side of the city, just south of where the Awhut River
entered the bay. Rahl was relying on the maps because
fog wreathed the harbor area, so that the lower sections of
Nubyat were hidden under a gray-white blanket. Above
the south side of the port city loomed a long, high ridge
that came to a point above the bay, each side of the penin-
sular promontory a rocky cliff that offered a sheer drop,
but whether there was solid ground or water under the
cliffs, Rahl could not have said, fog-shrouded as the lower
ground was.

Nubyat didn't seem as large as Rahl had expected, and
far smaller than Swartheld, although it was certainly

larger than Nylan or Land's End in Recluce. "It's not all that big."

"It wouldn't be this big," replied Drakeyt from where he had reined up beside Rahl, "except that it's on the river and one of the few decent ports in the west. The best olive oil comes from here, though." He looked to Rahl. "I don't see any earthworks on this side of the city."

Rahl pointed to the ridge that held the Administrator's Residence. "I'd judge that they've withdrawn to the high ground."

"That would make sense. No one really wants to destroy the town, and it'd be impossible to defend it." Drakeyt laughed, a short bark. "But I'd be surprised if they hadn't left some forces behind to give us trouble."

Rahl nodded, even while he wondered about the way the campaign had progressed. The Imperial forces had taken heavy losses, but they had prevailed in every skirmish and battle. Why hadn't Golyat seen that would happen? Why hadn't the rebels offered more resistance? Or was their strategy to withdraw and withdraw, all the time inflicting more and more losses on the Emperor's armies until they could deliver a critical defeat upon the Imperial forces? Would First and Second Army have to fight their way in two directions from Nubyat, northward to Elmari and south to Sastak? Was that where the greater resistance might be?

He looked again to the rocky ridge, one of two promontories that flanked the opening to the harbor, then to the one to the north, which held what appeared to be a neglected fort, with scraggly vines climbing stones of the wall. He shook his head. "We still need to discover where the rebels are."

"Lead on, Majer."

Rahl laughed, then urged the gelding forward to rejoin Alrydd a good quarter kay ahead of first squad. The scouts had halted on the road another half kay beyond the outrider. Once Rahl rode up to Alrydd and kept riding, if at a cautious walk, the scouts resumed their progress.

The orchards stretched farther than Rahl had realized, and he rode close to two kays before he neared their end, where, several hundred cubits ahead, a stone wall ran perpendicular to the road, ending some twenty cubits short of the shoulder on each side. Beyond the wall there were no olive groves, just small plots with neat houses and miniature fields—or large gardens—behind each.

Rahl frowned. There was something about the wall, yet he could not see what it might be, and Taryl had been insistent about his not order-probing ahead. "Scouts! Back!" He order-boosted his words, just slightly, not enough for his use of order to be detected from any distance.

The two scouts had almost reached a point even with the wall; but, when they turned and started to ride back, arrows began to arch toward them from behind the wall. One of the troopers took three shafts and toppled from the saddle, a boot catching in a stirrup so that the mount started to drag him, then stopped. The other scout flattened himself against his horse and urged it into a full gallop.

"Frig!" muttered Rahl under his breath. He should have trusted his vague feelings. Should have . . . demons, he was getting tired of learning what he should have done too late to be as effective as he could have been.

The fallen scout was dead, but the remaining trooper rode beyond the range of the archers without getting hit, then straightened in the saddle as he neared Rahl and Alrydd.

Rahl studied the wall and the ground beyond. There was no real way to outflank the archers, not easily, because the wall ran at least a kay in each direction, if not more, and for all of that length it was bordered by the orchards filled with the dwarf olives. Trying to move a company through that was asking for even more trouble.

Drakeyt rode forward and joined Rahl. "What do you suggest, Majer?"

"Let me take a squad. I can shield that many from the arrows if they stay close to me."

"We'll move up just short of their range. If there are more than you can handle . . ."

"I wouldn't think there could be too many rebels," Rahl pointed out. "There's no sign of any beyond the wall, and the wall can't hide anything like a company."

"Unless they're hidden behind those dwellings in squads."

Rahl nodded.

Drakeyt turned his mount. "I'll send Dhosyn and first squad forward."

As Rahl waited for first squad, he looked more closely at the wall, but he could see no sign of the rebel archers, although he could sense some men there, if only vaguely. The sound of hoofs on stone announced the arrival of first squad.

"First squad! Close up on the majer!" ordered Dhosyn.

Flanked by two troopers with their blades out, and with Dhosyn and first squad directly behind him, Rahl rode forward toward the wall. When they were within a hundred cubits, just past the mount of the fallen scout, the arrows once more lofted over the wall and sleeted down toward Rahl and the troopers. Rahl extended his shields. The arrows skittered off and onto the road and its shoulders. For a moment, the only sound was that of hoofs on stone.

Then another flight of shafts rose . . . and fell. But even before they skittered off Rahl's shields, a good score of archers ran from behind the wall on both the left and the right sides of the road and sprinted toward the nearest dwellings, vanishing behind them. Several entered the small house on the northwest side of the road.

Rahl and first squad rode past the wall and toward the nearer dwelling, the one on the right.

A shutter popped open, and another shaft flew at Rahl.

He reeled back in the saddle as it hit his shield. It had been a heavy iron cross-bow quarrel.

"Forward!" He urged the gelding into canter. There was no sense in riding sedately against that sort of attack, and who knew what else might be hidden inside that cot—or others along the road. He turned in the saddle and called to Dhosyn, "We'll move ahead and clean them out, house by house."

The next quarrel was off target, but still tugged at his shields.

Rahl reined up outside the barred door of the cot, a dwelling no more than fifteen cubits by twenty, with but two windows facing the road, both shuttered.

"Feragyt! Take three and clean it out!" ordered the squad leader, tossing a metal pry bar to the trooper.

Four troopers dismounted and surged toward the cot. In moments, the door was off its hinges, and the troopers had disappeared inside.

Rahl could sense the deaths—and only three of the four troopers stepped back out.

"Nasty thing, this." Feragyt held a massive iron crossbow. "There were three of the sows. They're all dead. So's Dermyt."

"Just leave the crossbow for now," Rahl ordered.

Another flight of arrows—as well as several crossbow bolts—flew toward the squad.

Rahl deflected them, then turned to the squad leader. "We'll take the next one. This time, I'll go first."

"Ser . . ."

"They're setting it up so that whoever enters gets shot," Rahl countered. "We don't need to lose a trooper for every dwelling we enter, and we can't leave the rebels here, and if we burn them out, we might as well have lost Nubyat to Golyat."

"Yes, ser." Unlike some of the other squad leaders, Dhosyn seemed inclined to accept what Rahl had said, and without resentment.

Rahl waited for the others to mount, then strengthened

his shields and rode toward the next dwelling. As before, both shafts and iron bolts flew toward him, but the combination of his shields and riding swiftly lessened their exposure. This time, a front shutter opened, but Dhosyn rode up from the side and slammed it shut.

Three troopers dismounted, and Rahl followed them, but stepped forward enough to keep his shields between them and the door. The trooper with the pry bar inserted it, and began to yank in quick powerful movements. The bolt on the other side gave way, and the door swung open.

Rahl moved forward, his truncheon in hand, as did one of the troopers with a sabre. Just when he entered the front room two arrows flew at him, bouncing from his shields. The two archers dropped their bows. Pulling long knives, they lunged toward Rahl and the trooper beside him.

Rahl's truncheon slammed the knife from the hand of one archer, and the trooper evaded the other archer and ran the sabre through his neck. After grabbing a stool in his good hand, the wounded archer swung back toward Rahl. This time, Rahl brought the truncheon across the archer's temple, and the man went down . . . dead.

He hadn't hit the man that hard, had he? Or had the archer been influenced by chaos? With so much death around, Rahl wasn't all that certain. What was certain was that there were no other rebels in the small dwelling, and he hurried out and remounted.

After that, the pattern in the next three cots was exactly the same, and none of the archers even tried to surrender, but threw themselves at Rahl and the Imperial troopers. All the rebels died.

As he rode up to the next cot, Rahl could sense a difference. There had not been quite so many arrows, and he had the feeling that there might be others in the cot beside rebels. He dismounted, careful to hold his shields firm.

Rahl held his truncheon ready as the trooper wedged the pry bar in place, then heaved, once . . . twice . . . and on the third attempt the door broke away from the hinges. Before the trooper had barely stepped back from the door, it sagged to one side, then fell back into the dwelling with a dull thud.

One of the rebel archers stood there. He held a knife to the neck of a girl, not quite a young woman. "You come any closer, and I'll kill her."

Rahl could feel the girl's terror, and the look in her eyes reminded him of Jienela. He hesitated.

"I mean it."

"Why do you want to hurt an innocent girl?" asked Rahl, keeping his voice calm.

The rebel did not look at Rahl, but at the trooper with the pry bar. "You're killing everyone else. I just want out of here."

"Let her go, and you won't be hurt," Rahl said. The rebel might later suffer, but not now, not with the girl's life at stake.

Abruptly, the rebel turned toward Rahl. His eyes widened. "No! Not one of you!" The knife slashed, biting deeply into the girl's neck, so deeply that crimson spurted everywhere. Then the archer flung the girl at the trooper with the pry bar and darted away from Rahl.

Rahl didn't even think, leaping after the rebel and striking with the long truncheon, reinforced with order and fury. The man died instantly, his skull crushed. For a long moment, Rahl just looked at his body, then turned back toward the girl. She was dead.

He could feel his eyes burning. Then he swallowed. "We need to check the cot." He stepped inside. Immediately, he could feel death. An older woman lay, half-naked, on a pallet. She might have been pretty once, but her throat had been slashed. Another archer lay dead beside her.

Rahl swallowed, then turned and stepped out into the somewhat cleaner air outside, standing there silently. After a moment, he wiped the truncheon on the tunic of the man he'd killed. "Let's root out the rest of them."

He remounted the gelding without another word and waited for the squad to re-form, then rode toward the next cot. The door was open, and there were tracks in the dust.

Rahl could see a mere handful of men in maroon hurrying toward a shed. In moments, they had recovered their mounts and were galloping southward.

"They saw what happened," suggested Dhosyn.

"They must have seen some of what we did before," Rahl said.

"Yes, ser, but it was the way you crushed the last one that broke them. You flattened the back of his head like a rotten gourd."

He had? Rahl frowned. He could have, given how angry he'd been.

After a time, he took a long and deep breath. "We might as well see what lies ahead." He turned the gelding back to the paved road.

There was no sign of any more rebels in the small dwellings along the road leading into Nubyat. The streets were deserted, and all was so quiet that the echoes of hoofs on stone sounded more like quick hammerblows. The dwellings were all shuttered, and Rahl sensed many were empty.

A movement to his right caught his eye, and he turned in the saddle. He found himself watching a scruffy black-and-brown hound easing into an alleyway.

Slowly, the squads of Third Company rode the main side streets, coming back to the main avenue that the highway had become, all reporting no sign of rebels . . . or much of anything else. Before long, Rahl rode into a square, certainly a major square, because it had a central plaza and a pedestal bearing the statue of one of the emperors of Hamor. Rahl smiled. The statue was old, but the face could have been that of Emperor Mythalt.

"We'll wait here for the other companies to close up some."

"Yes, ser."

Rahl looked around the square, much like any other square in Hamor, with an expansive inn on one side, a smaller one across from it, and shops set around the open area. The main avenue entered on the northern side, but two equally wide avenues branched out on the far side, one angling northwest, most likely toward the harbor, and the other continuing southward.

By midafternoon, Rahl and Third Company had reached the southern end of Nubyat, but instead of more olive orchards, there was an expanse of rough and grassy ground, through which the pavement ran, arcing back uphill to the west and up the side of the ridge-like promontory. The side of the road facing him was a sheer cliff, and it had clearly been smoothed with chaos-fire years if not centuries before, for it was so smooth that no one could have climbed it. Some hundred cubits uphill, at the point where the cliff-like side of the road was almost thirty cubits above the ground below, was a barricade across the road.

"Hold up," Rahl told Dhosyn.

"First squad, halt!"

Rahl studied the stone-and-timber barricade across the wide, paved road leading up to the heights and the Administrator's Residence and the walled High Command compound. He could see yet another barricade set in place a good half kay farther up the road from the first. Then he looked southward. Where the ridge turned inland, several kays away, it narrowed. Even from that distance, he could make out the earthworks across the narrowest point of the slope up from the valley. While he could not see the far side, another sheer cliff comprised the edge closest to him. That suggested that there were but two approaches to the rebel stronghold. It also suggested why Golyat had not attempted to defend the city proper all that strongly.

At that moment, a hail of arrows lofted from behind the head-high stones of the barricade, arcing skyward, then angling back down toward Rahl and first squad.

Rahl extended and angled his order shields, and the arrows clattered onto the stone pavement.

Then another flight soared toward the squad.

"To the rear, ride!" Rahl ordered. He was tired, and there was no sense trying to block arrows. They could wait for the rest of Second Army back out of arrow range.

Rahl could still see the terror in the girl's eyes. He had the feeling he might always.

LXXVIII

In the early morning light of twoday, under a green-blue sky tinted with a light haze, Rahl and Drakeyt once more studied the barricades blocking the road up to the Administrator's Residence. Neither officer was mounted, given their orders, nor was Third Company, but all the lancers held the reins to their horses and were ready to mount, if necessary. Behind the two barricades across the road were hundreds of rebels, if not more, and the road provided an easy route from above for reinforcements to reach the defenders. Third Company was stationed on the south wing of the regiment, for "contingency duty." The fog of the previous day had lifted when a warmer wind off the ocean had blown in, and a light ocean breeze still blew.

Taryl's instructions to the two officers on oneday night had been succinct. "You and Third Company are assigned to Fifth Regiment under Commander Shuchyl. Fifth Regiment is being tasked with the attack on the fortified road on the north side of the promontory. In practice, it is unlikely that you will be able to make much headway there. The real purpose is to keep the rebel force bottled up while the main body of First and Second Army attacks the more accessible slope to the south. Third Company is not to take part in the attacks, except in cases where either the battle would be lost or where you can clearly break the enemy and gain the top of the promontory."

After the overcommander had finished, he had dismissed Drakeyt and added a few words to Rahl. "You are not to attempt to protect the entire regiment, no matter what happens. The rebels have more mages, and in short order they will just wear you down. Use your magery only for significant tactical advantage. Significant, Rahl. Significant."

As he continued to ponder what he might do that Taryl would consider significant, Rahl looked back over the Imperial forces. Fifth Regiment was drawn up a good half kay below the first barricade across the road, well out of easy arrow or crossbow range, and had been since dawn.

"It'd be stupid to charge that barricade," Drakeyt observed, making conversation, because both men had already concluded that. "Wonder what the commander will do."

"He didn't tell you?" asked Rahl.

"We're directly under the overcommander, remember, Majer?"

Rahl concealed a wince. Shuchyl had barely talked to either officer, only confirming that Third Company was there to keep mages and others from escaping in the event that the rebels did break. "I imagine you talked to some of the other officers."

Drakeyt grinned. "The commander has a few tricks in his saddlebags. They might work."

"Such as?"

"He gathered all those crossbows—the oversized ones. He also has some small ballistas, and he's got some fast little wagons that carry siege ladders."

"Because they don't use cammabark or powder?" Rahl was still attempting to determine what he could do that might be effective in dealing with the rebel position. There was little use in trying to undermine the road by turning the underlying soil to ooze, because there was no soil. The road had been cut out of solid rock, and even trying to weaken those order bonds in the smallest of areas would exhaust Rahl without doing much to help Fifth Regiment. Taryl had forbidden him to use massive shields, except to prevent a disaster, and throwing order-bolts was only useful against chaos-mages. Besides, that would leave him too weak to do anything else. Charging the barricade behind his shields would have been equally futile against who knew how many mages and that many troopers. All the other order-skills he had mastered seemed useless in the situation before him.

"He's also gathered several wagons of thoroughly dried dung." Drakeyt was the one to frown.

Rahl had to think about that for a moment, then he nodded. "It's waste ordered in a way by animals, and some of it burns."

"No one I ever knew really got hurt by flying crap."

A trumpet call Rahl did not recognize rang out from the rear of Fifth Regiment.

An entire company of archers moved forward, raised their bows, and began to release shafts, lofting them over the barricade wall, if barely. Flashes of chaos-flame flicked out, but only where the arrows were heaviest. As the archers kept loosing their shafts, Rahl began to feel the injuries from behind the wall—not all that many, but some. Then, there was a death, and another.

The archers retreated just before a return volley flew from the rebel forces. Even so, several of the Imperial archers were wounded. Rahl thought one was killed.

Two wagons covered with a framework of leather soaked in water and pushed by troopers shielded largely by the framework trundled forward from the Imperial line, down the road, and then up toward the barricade. At the same time, the Imperial archers returned and began to loose their shafts once more. The rebels retaliated, and the air was filled with missiles.

The wagons moved slowly forward. As they did, a

trooper in each wagon and behind the leather framework kept dipping a bucket into a half barrel and throwing water over the leather. Rahl could sense some kind of crude mechanism in the wagon bed as well.

The wagons were within a hundred cubits of the wall before a firebolt arched from behind the barricade and splattered squarely on the leather framework of the right wagon. While chaos-fire dribbled across the framework, it did not catch fire, and the trooper with the bucket scooped and threw water even more quickly.

"They must have soaked the leather in ink or something," Drakeyt said.

"Ink?"

"Iron-gall ink, and they probably added more iron. It soaks into the leather, and with all the water, it makes it harder for chaos-fire to burn it. For a while."

Rahl had never heard of that, but whatever it was that Shuchyl's engineers had come up with, it was working— for the moment.

No sooner had Rahl thought that than the rebel chaos-mages changed their tactics. A firebolt splattered on the stone just in front of the right wagon, but it guttered out short of the wheels. So did the next one.

The troopers working the left wagon eased it closer to the stone cliff face overlooking the road, but kept moving forward.

Another firebolt exploded just under the front wheels and axle of the right wagon. Flames licked upward. Immediately, all the troopers turned and sprinted away. The entire wagon erupted in a gout of flame, with smaller globs of flame exploding away from the column of fire. One glob of flame enveloped two of the fleeing troopers, turning them into moving torches. The flame had to have held both chaos and whatever liquid the engineers had used, because the two torches flared into ashes and dust instantly.

That did not deter the troopers pushing the other wagon, who had propelled that conveyance close enough to the barricade wall that the firebolts of the chaos-mages were only occasionally striking the pavement. A trooper yanked a lever, and bladders of all sizes and shapes cascaded toward the wall. Most cleared it, although one or two splattered on the rough stones. The troopers who had been pushing the wagon sprinted back away from the barricade, trying to stay close to the shelter of the sheer rock of the cliff face overlooking the road, but the rebels seemed almost to ignore them, perhaps because the Imperial archers launched another attack.

The chaos-mages attempted to block the most concentrated flights—all of which were aimed directly behind where the bladders had struck. Falling arrows, bits of chaos-flame . . . and a section of wall, as well as the area behind it, flared into flame.

Rahl winced, even as he admired Shuchyl's success in getting the rebels to light off the flammable oils.

A series of four notes on the trumpet sounded, and a company of troopers rode forward. With them were several tall and light wagons. The charge was directed at a point immediately to the left of the center of the wall, where the flames had died away, leaving a wide area of blackened stone.

Just before the first line of mounted troopers reached the wall, a point of light flared—so brightly that Rahl could see nothing. Each eye felt like it had been pierced by an enormous needle. He blinked and rubbed his eyes gently.

Slowly, his vision returned, although stars danced across what he could see.

The charge had been stopped, and mounts milled below the wall. Firebolts dropped into the mix of troopers, and waves of chaos and death swept past Rahl.

Another trumpet signal rang out, and the troopers withdrew, leaving the bodies of both men and mounts strewn before the barricade.

Rahl glanced up. According to the sun it was approaching midmorning. Had it been that long?

"Any ideas, Majer?" Drakeyt's voice was low, concerned.

"Not yet. Anything I could do wouldn't be much help. Not here." At least, not anything that he'd been able to think up since the night before.

Drakeyt nodded.

For a time, the area between the two forces remained empty except for remnants of burned wagons, mounts, and men, but Rahl knew that would not last. He could sense movement behind the barricade, as well as activity at the rear of Fifth Regiment. Before that long, another set of wagons trundled forward from the Imperial side.

Surprisingly, to Rahl, only a few firebolts flew toward the wagons, but more than a few arrows did, and a number carried flaming tips, dipped in pitch or some similar substance. The arrows had even less effect than the firebolts had—until the wagons neared the barricade and several rebels stood near the top of the barricade and hurled what looked to be cloth soaked in oil and wrapped around a chunk of firewood under the nearer wagon.

That wagon began to burn, but the Imperial archers cut down most of the exposed rebels as another wave of troopers appeared, riding hard for the barricade.

This time the troopers who rode forward all had makeshift patches over one eye. Rahl nodded to himself. Crude, but effective. Theoretically, the chaos-mage who had loosed the first blinding flash could wait for a moment, then deliver another, but the amount of chaos required, from what Rahl had felt, made it most unlikely that any chaos-mage could do that often or in quick succession. It was also unlikely that more than one chaos-mage had that talent.

Rahl almost shook his head. How did he know that? Maybe the brilliant light flash was something from Fairhaven, where all the white wizards could do it.

There was a light flash, but far weaker, so much so that Rahl's vision returned almost immediately, and the

mounted troopers rode to the wall, dragging the light
scaling wagons into position.

Chaos-bolts flared down toward the Imperial forces
surging toward the barricade, then died away. Rahl could
sense a chill, and whiteness ran across the front of the
lower-road barricade, then began to flow down the stones,
turning into liquidlike fire moving from the barricade
wall to the pavement, then toward the attacking troopers.

The flowing chaos licked at the forelegs of the mounts,
then engulfed both the first line of horses and riders. The
screams of men and mounts were lost in the roar of
flames flaring skyward.

Rahl swallowed. He'd never seen anything like that.
Nor smelled it, as the sickly-sweet nauseating odor of
burned flesh settled around him and Third Company.

"Frig!" muttered Dhosyn from where he sat on his
mount behind Rahl and Drakeyt.

Still, Rahl could feel the chaos ebbing.

Another wave of troopers rode forward, and this time
there were only a few weak chaos-bolts, and a handful of
arrows. Scaling ladders unfolded from the light wagons,
and troopers began to climb up and over the barricade.

For a time, intermittent waves of death flowed down
and across Rahl.

Then the rebel survivors broke and sprinted or hob-
bled back up the road, scrambling up and over the second barricade, set a good three hundred cubits farther up
the road, a road that was but twenty cubits wide. The second barricade wasn't any higher than the first, but there
was a ledge cut into the cliffside above the barricade and
slightly behind it, also with a low wall, and on that ledge
were both archers and chaos-mages, Rahl sensed.

Again, a kind of quiet fell across the contested area.

Rahl checked the sun, its white light diluted not only
by the high haze, but by the smoke that had risen from all
the fires and chaos-burning, and was surprised—again—
to find that it was later than he would have believed, almost midafternoon. Bodies were everywhere, more than

several hundred, Rahl thought, possibly close to a thousand. Given the nature of the fight so far, he doubted that there were many wounded.

Shuchyl did not even consider attacking the second barricade immediately. Instead, two shielded wagons moved up to the first barricade, and figures in brown and khaki—engineers—began to use bars and picks to remove the stones in the middle of the barricade.

Rahl took the time to walk back to where one of the first squad's troopers held his mount and extracted some of his travel rations from his saddlebags. As he ate, and drank from his water bottle, he kept looking at the barricade where the engineers moved stones. He had to wonder at the danger involved, but Shuchyl had judged that the chaos-mages were so worn down that they did not want to try to pick off engineers behind stone by trying to throw chaos-bolts hundreds of cubits. Even so, Rahl was concerned, but the rebels did not even attempt more than scattered flights of arrows, few of which hit anywhere near the engineers, and the sun had dropped noticeably lower in the afternoon sky by the time there was a breach in the barricade ten cubits wide.

That suggested to Rahl that the rebels definitely had limited manpower—or that their defense consisted of efforts to bleed the Imperial forces down without losing many of their own troops. Yet, if that had been the case, why had they fought at Selyma as they had?

Once the engineers had opened a gap almost twenty cubits wide in the lower-barricade wall, they retreated, the next company of troopers moved up and stationed themselves behind the remaining end sections of the barricade as shelter from attacks from the second barricade, not that the rebels were showing much of an attack.

Just as Rahl had thought that, a barrage of firebolts cascaded down into the troopers behind the barricade walls. Then a hail of arrows followed.

Another wave of deaths surged over Rahl.

"Too bad there's no easy way to put a gap in that second

wall, or get cammabark close enough to blow it open."
Dhosyn's voice was low, resigned, coming from behind
Rahl.

"The cammabark wouldn't be any good unless it was
in a casing, like a shell or an old-style cannonball,"
Drakeyt pointed out. "Then their mages would just explode it before anyone could get close enough."

Rahl frowned. Exploding the wall . . . exploding the
wall . . . He'd once exploded a part of a wall. Admittedly, that had been the black wall separating Nylan from
the rest of Recluce, and it had only worked because of
the additional order linked into the stone . . . but natural
stone did have more order than soil or sand.

Shuchyl ordered the archers back into the fray, and, as
their shafts lofted and fell behind the second barricade,
the number of rebel arrows fell off. The firebolts continued, if only occasionally.

From the positions taken by the regimental companies, it appeared as though the commander was not about
to attempt any more assaults . . . or not soon. Considering that Shuchyl had already lost more than a third of the
regiment, Rahl could understand that decision.

Still . . . he glanced at the remnants of the carnage below the breached barricade wall and back toward the
thinner ranks of Fifth Regiment. His eyes went back to
the upper barricade. Could he do what he thought might
be possible?

Finally, he squared his shoulders and turned to
Drakeyt. "I think it's time."

"You have something in mind?" asked Drakeyt.

"Yes. I don't know if it will work, but it's worth the
effort to see." He shrugged. "If it's not, no one will know."
Except you and me, he thought.

Rahl moved more to his left, toward the base of the
cliff, but raised his sight shield before he moved away
from Third Company, navigating toward the road and the
barricades with his order-senses. Holding both sight
shield and order shields as strongly as he could, he walked

forward, then up the slope of the paved road, staying in the shadows he could not see, hugging the cliff face, and hoping that his patience had convinced the rebels that all the Imperial mage-guards were with the main forces of First and Second Army.

He had to pick his way around the troopers behind the lower barricade, then ease through the breach and back to the side of the road. He could sense an occasional firebolt, but none were hurled in his direction. His sight shield kept the light from him, and he had no way of feeling whether he was in the shade except by staying as close to the ancient chaos-smoothed stone that formed the cliff-face wall overlooking the road.

When he neared the upper barricade, Rahl could feel the presence of several mages on the walled ledge behind and uphill of the barrier. One exuded such whiteness that he had to be a white wizard from Fairhaven. Intermittent chaos-order-probes flickered around the barricade, but they felt random, almost halfhearted.

Keeping himself in the corner between the barricade and the smoothed cliffside, Rahl concentrated on the center of the barricade wall, ignoring the scores of rebels behind it, not to mention those on the walled ledge. When he had exploded the black wall in Nylan, he had merely attempted to see how the order was structured over and around the stones. Each stone had had an order framework, but that framework had been strengthened, not created, by the wall-builders. As he reached out with his order-senses and touched the crude wall before him, he knew he needed to find the knots of higher and underlying order embedded within the mixture of rock and timber.

Many of the stones were almost "dead," with barely enough order to hold them together. Amid the mixture, Rahl found bits of what he would have called "sparkling" order, and he began to link one to the next, using a thin line of order. With each link, a knotted pattern of order built, and so did the strength of the sparkling. Was the

sparkle something like order ready to release chaos? That
was the closest to how Rahl could have described it.

He forced himself to work deliberately, adding links
and strands one by one until he had an order-chaos
structure that, if he recalled correctly, had something
like the power of a small section of the black wall. As he
kept adding to that structure, he began to funnel and
channel the forces toward the middle of the barricade
wall.

Whhhsst!

A firebolt slammed against his shields, followed by a
second one, then a third.

Rahl staggered, trying to stay on his feet. So much for
remaining undetected.

He couldn't keep doing what he was doing and hold
his shields against a continuing barrage of chaos-bolts.
Or could he? What if he linked that power into his order-
chaos web? Could he?

Whhssst!

With the next firebolt, Rahl channeled the chaos into
the barricade, holding it behind order. Two more chaos-
bolts followed, and he did the same.

Then came the light flash—not that Rahl could see it
behind his shields—but he could feel the power. That
kind of chaos-force was so different from the firebolts
that he couldn't find a way to grasp it.

"Chaos-mage below! Near the inside of the road! Just
beyond the barricade!"

"Heavy crossbows! Iron bolts!"

Rahl could sense all sorts of rebels forming up, in addition to a well of chaos building above him. He had to
do what he could, and he had no idea whether it would
even work. He moistened his lips and concentrated, un-
twisting all the links he had built—all at once—then reinforced his own shields.

CRUUMMPP!

The explosion threw Rahl backward and then into the

ancient smooth stone of the cliff face. Even within his shields, he was stunned, lying on his side, his back against smooth stone. He struggled to maintain the sight shield. He didn't want anyone shooting iron bolts at him, not when he doubted whether his shields would hold much longer.

Stones pattered down around him, and more death— far closer—swept over him.

Rahl's guts twisted and turned, and he kept swallowing to keep the bile down. Officers didn't retch on themselves. They didn't.

He slowly rolled onto his knees and then staggered erect. He put one boot in front of the other and began to make his way downhill, slowly, because there were fragments of rock and stone everywhere.

Below he could hear the trumpet calls of Fifth Regiment, and he forced himself to keep moving. He didn't want to get trampled by his own forces. He finally released the sight shield when he made his way through and past the breach in the lower barricade. Two troopers from first squad were already riding uphill, leading the gelding. Behind them were Dhosyn and first squad.

Rahl just stepped back against the stone of the cliff face and gestured.

Dhosyn caught sight of him immediately. "Majer's over there!"

Once Dhosyn and first squad reached Rahl, they had to hug the cliff face as troopers from Fifth Regiment companies poured up the road in pursuit of the rebels.

Rahl climbed into the saddle, slowly and awkwardly, then turned to the squad leader. "Thank you."

"The captain and I—we thought you might be looking for a mount." Dhosyn gestured uphill. "Specially after that."

Rahl looked back toward the upper barricade. It wasn't there. Rather, a few loose heaps of stone remained, with fragments strewn for hundreds of cubits. Behind where it had stood, there was even less, and Rahl sensed that none

of the rebels within a hundred cubits had survived. Nor
had the two mages.

Rahl eased the gelding close to the stone of the cliff
face to allow another company of Imperial troopers to
gallop past first squad. He was in no hurry to join such a
charge. He'd barely been able to mount the gelding, and
his legs were shaking so much he wondered if his boots
would remain in the stirrups. Even though he had made
that charge possible, the fact that he was in no condition
to ride out immediately galled him.

He turned and reached for his saddlebags, but he was
so light-headed that he nearly lost his seat. He ate whatever he had, and slowly drained his water bottle.

By the time he thought he could stay in the saddle, most
of Fifth Regiment had passed first squad, and Drakeyt had
ridden up with the remainder of Third Company.

"You don't do things in a small way, Majer."

"Some things you can't." Rahl grimaced. He was going to be sore again. "That's what the overcommander
keeps telling me. We need to follow the regiment."

Drakeyt nodded. "Deliberately."

Rahl understood. The company had already taken
more than its share of casualties, and there was little point
in hurrying into a melee where they could add little.

The sun was low in the west, and the road up the east
side of the promontory was completely in shadow by the
time Rahl and Third Company reached the top of the kay-
long incline and came out on the flat. Park-like grounds
stretched southward, surrounding the Administrator's
Residence—a large villa of two levels—enclosed only by
a head-high iron gratework fence. Two squads of Imperial troopers had been detailed to guard the open gates,
clearly to prevent looting.

At the south end of the park was a compound with
buildings and barracks. Before the gates in its low stone
walls was another squad of troopers.

"No rebels there?" Rahl called out.

"No, ser. They saw us coming and rode south."

Beyond the compound, the mesa-like flat area on the top of the ridge began to narrow and slope downward. Rahl reined up.

Below, Imperial forces had encircled the rebels and surged inward, compressing the defenders so that many could hardly move. While Rahl could not see any fire-bolts, he could sense from the diffuse chaos that many had been thrown and that wide patches of blackened ground lay beneath the hoofs of the mounts of rebels and Imperials alike.

"The rebels had more mages than we do," Dhosyn said.

"The more troops involved," Rahl replied, "the less effect a mage can have."

"You had a certain effect, Majer," Drakeyt said.

"Only because of the way they tried to defend Nubyat," Rahl replied. "You might recall that what I did in wide field battles was far less effective."

"It was effective enough." Drakeyt's words were dry.

Effective enough? For what? For the moment, Rahl watched as the Imperial forces continued to slaughter the rebels, hoping that he would not have to contribute more to what had turned into a massacre—all because of what he had managed to do with one stone barricade.

LXXIX

After the battle on twoday, Rahl and Drakeyt had commandeered a corner of the compound barracks for Third Company. None of the other officers in First or Second Army complained, not to Rahl, at least. Amid the confusion, from what the two officers could gather, Golyat and his senior commanders had not been captured, nor had they been among the slain. Nor did any of the captured and wounded rebels have any idea where the rebel prince might have gone.

Rahl was so tired by the time that matters settled out that he slept on a pallet in an alcove adjoining the bay that held their men. So did Drakeyt. Both arose early on threeday in an effort to restore more order to Third Company, but they had barely managed to locate fodder for the mounts and arrange for feeding the troopers when a trooper arrived with a request for Rahl to meet with Taryl at the Mage-Guard Overcommander's villa immediately after morning muster.

Rahl had to hurry to groom the gelding and make himself halfway presentable. The ride was short, less than a kay, and he almost wished he'd just walked. But he would have had to have groomed his mount anyway.

Rahl tied the gelding to one of the ornate iron posts set into stone beyond the mounting blocks for the main entrance to the "small" villa assigned to the Mage-Guard Overcommander of Merowey. The villa itself was larger than most of the merchant's mansions Rahl had seen in Hamor and was built of smooth blocks of gray basalt, with gray roof tiles, unlike the Administrator's Residence, which was gray with pinkish tiles and dwarfed the overcommander's villa. Both structures had wide windows that could be opened to catch the ocean breezes—and equally wide shutters to keep out rain and chill when necessary.

Two troopers were stationed by the entrance archway. Both bowed as Rahl approached the door.

"Majer, ser . . . the overcommander is expecting you. If you take the hall to the left, it goes straight to the study. That's where he is."

"I take it that there's not much in the way of staff." Rahl smiled.

"Not at the moment, ser." Both troopers returned the smile.

Rahl extended his order-senses as he stepped through the open doorway and into the high-ceilinged entry foyer. Neither trooper said a word even after he had passed, but Rahl could sense both respect and acceptance. The left corridor was walled in soft white plaster, and several of the niches that had held paintings or sculpture were empty. He passed an archway on his right that opened onto a sitting room, fully furnished, if sparsely. The next archway was to the left and revealed a formal dining chamber with a long oval table of black oak. The corridor ended at a black-oak door, left half-ajar.

"You can come in, Rahl."

Taryl remained seated behind the simple goldenwood table desk, but looked up as Rahl entered and watched the younger mage-guard. The dark circles under his bloodshot eyes attested to the strain and effort of the previous day.

"Are you all right, ser?" Rahl blurted.

"I've been better, but I'll survive. I appreciate the concern." The overcommander gestured to the chair closest to the desk.

Rahl settled into it and waited for Taryl to speak.

"I understand from Commander Shuchyl that you sundered the upper-barricade wall. He wanted to know if it was necessary for him to lose so many troopers before you chose to act." Taryl's voice was mild.

"Necessary?" Rahl snorted. "I didn't figure out how it might be done until most of those had been lost. I also was following your advice about not getting involved until I could make a significant difference." While Rahl understood Shuchyl's feelings about the deaths incurred in assaulting the rebel position, he couldn't help but be irritated. He hadn't seen Shuchyl anywhere close to the action in any of the battles.

"How did you feel about that?"

"I didn't like it," Rahl admitted.

"Good." Taryl nodded. "There is a danger for mage-guards, especially for commanders and administrators, either to risk themselves when they should not or to avoid such risk all too readily by rationalizing that they are too important to hazard themselves."

"If I might ask, do you know what happened to Prince Golyat?"

"I do." Taryl offered a wan smile. "He was nowhere near the battle. He was in the Residence, and when he heard that Fifth Regiment had broken through, he took the cliffside steps down to the cove on the seaward side, and he and his most senior commanders, as well as Ulmaryt— he's the former overcommander of mage-guards— embarked on a steam-powered sloop with shallow draft. I imagine that he's well on his way to Sastak by now."

"What about the fleet?"

"They have to sight him to give chase, and that's un- likely with Ulmaryt accompanying him. Even if they did, they'd have to try to shell something they can't see from a distance because their draft is so much greater."

"So he'll just . . . escape?"

"For now, and if you call Sastak escape." Taryl shrugged. "I'd like to catch him, but that's less important than restoring Merowey to the Emperor's control. We've destroyed half or more of the traitor mage-guards as well as all of the white wizards sent from Fairhaven."

"How do you know that . . . ser?"

The overcommander offered an ironic smile. "Golyat and Ulmaryt wouldn't trust a white on that small a vessel with them, and none of the rebel mages left behind sur- vived. You destroyed four when you exploded the second barricade. There were almost half a score with the de- fenders to the south."

Rahl wondered how Taryl had dealt with them.

"With old age, one learns techniques that the young spurn in favor of flash and strength." An enigmatic smile followed.

"What happens next, ser? What do you need from me?"

"First, the troops and their mounts need time to rest. Second, you and I and the remaining faithful mage- guards need to screen the captives to see who truly op- posed the Emperor and who was pressed. Then we need to ready Nubyat as a port for some of the fleet vessels, so that we can receive supplies and reinforcements. After that, we proceed to wipe up the rest of the revolt. The first stage will be to send Commander Shuchyl north to recover Elmari."

Elmari? When Golyat had headed south? "Is that so that there are no rebels at our back when the marshal has to face Golyat, ser?"

"Elmari is lightly held." Taryl's tone was even.

What was Rahl missing? Taryl hadn't responded to the reference to the marshal. Rahl tried again. "Ah . . . the marshal . . . he wasn't terribly pleased with the way we dealt with the officers and others at Selyma."

"No . . . he wasn't, but he wasn't feeling that well, and he's asked to be relieved and stipended for reasons of health."

Rahl had the definite feeling that the marshal's request was not exactly voluntary. "Then you're acting marshal?"

"For as long as the Emperor wishes, and only that long."

Rahl would have added "the Empress" to that statement, but he said nothing.

"One other thing . . . Third Company has been reassigned as the Mage-Guard Overcommander's support company." Taryl smiled. "That means you'll have to move to the small barracks adjoining this villa. I don't imagine that the men will complain, except that it's a longer walk to the mess." He straightened. "We'll meet first thing after muster tomorrow morning. By then, I'll have a better idea of what you'll be doing. That all depends on who else I can trust." He paused. "I would like you to take a squad and look over the harbor, though, so that you can report on that tomorrow."

"Yes, ser."

Taryl stood. "I do appreciate what you did yesterday. It saved us hundreds of troopers, if not more."

And cost thousands of rebels their lives, not to mention the Imperial troopers who died because I couldn't figure out matters more quickly. "Thank you, ser." Rahl could sense that Taryl was withholding more than he had told Rahl, but Rahl did not sense anything that suggested Taryl was upset with him. But would he have known unless Taryl wanted him to sense that?

"I'll see you tomorrow morning."

"Yes, ser." Rahl stepped back, then turned.

As he left the study, once more, he had to wonder what Taryl was hiding . . . and why.

LXXX

Under the hazy midmorning sun of fiveday, Rahl stepped into the portmaster's building at the foot of pier two—the main fleet pier in Nubyat. Since his meetings with Taryl, all he had done was go from one minor task to another—from making sure that there would be cargo loaders back on the piers, to checking with merchants, to pressing pier guards into service to replace the mage-guards who were no longer in Nubyat, to checking warehouses and the supplies that they held. Then, almost belatedly, he'd realized that two of the piers were effectively blocked to ships.

The portmaster had clearly expected Rahl because he stood in the large open chamber outside his study looking toward the door. Several other men had frozen in place beside their table desks. The portmaster was a white-haired man with a dark face and a white mustache. His brown eyes were hard as he watched Rahl approach, then stop less than three cubits from the older man.

"Portmaster Hulym?" Rahl kept his voice pleasant, although he could sense the hostility. "I'd like to know why the chains blocking the first and third piers have not been removed."

"They were placed there by the Regional Administrator." Hulym shrugged. "Who am I to remove what he wished?"

Rahl smiled. "That Regional Administrator has been

removed. The Mage-Guard Overcommander is the acting Regional Administrator, and he wishes them removed."

"Alas . . . I have not—"

"I'm certain that you can take care of a little matter like that, can you not?" Rahl was having trouble remaining polite, given the hostility and oiliness he sensed in the portmaster.

"I am but a portmaster, not an engineer—"

"I understand that you were in charge of their placement."

"I know nothing about that." Hulym shrugged helplessly.

"Hulym, you don't quite understand." Rahl's smile hardened. "I am not only a majer, but a senior mageguard. Those piers and the channels *will* be clear by tomorrow morning."

"I can do nothing—"

Rahl extended his shields with enough force to press the portmaster against the stone wall. "Let us try this one more time. We'll start at the beginning. Are you loyal to the Emperor Mythalt?"

"Any man would be loyal to his Emperor. How could he not be loyal?"

Rahl could sense the lie behind the evasion. Now what? He released the shields. "Who is your assistant portmaster?"

Hulym staggered erect. "It was Chaulym, but he fled when . . . the revolt . . ."

"Who has been acting as your assistant?"

Tharmyl. The name might as well have been spoken. "I have none. I had to do everything myself." Hulym squared his shoulders in an attempt to regain his dignity.

"Where is Tharmyl?"

Hulym's muscles tightened, and his eyes darted toward the door through which Rahl had entered.

"Ah . . . Majer, ser . . . I am here." A younger man standing beside a battered table bowed, several times, nervously.

Rahl stepped back, his hand dropping to the long riding truncheon at his belt, so that he could watch both men at once. "Tharmyl, can you get those chains removed and the channels clear?"

"Yes, ser. We were the ones who put them there. It might take longer than tomorrow morning, but we could probably have one pier and channel clear by then. It might take a day more for piers three and four." The assistant shrugged. "We had no choice. Prince Golyat's mages threatened our families."

"It is true," added Hulym. "We had no choice."

That was also a lie.

Rahl drew the truncheon and struck—in one hard motion that caved in Hulym's temple. The body pitched forward onto the floor. "Neither did I." He looked to Tharmyl. "Lying to a mage-guard is an offense against the Codex. Lying to avoid one's duty to the Emperor and covering up treachery is worse. Do you understand . . . acting portmaster?"

"Yes, ser." There was a slight quiver in the new portmaster's voice, but he did not look away.

"The Emperor cannot change what has happened, nor can I. Nor can you. But we can all do our duties as we should from now on. I'm not interested in what happened then. I'm very interested in how loyal people are now and how well they do their duties." Rahl sheathed the truncheon. "The Emperor will reward that loyalty and effectiveness." Rahl didn't have to say that he would be the one punishing treachery. He looked to the new portmaster. "I'm sure that there are other tasks necessary to reopen the port to Imperial ships, and that you'll be taking care of them as well. I'll check back with you this afternoon." He paused. "By the way, I once worked for a very large shipping and trading concern." Then he smiled. "Good day."

As Rahl left the portmaster's building, he could already sense Tharmyl's efforts to organize the reopening of the entire port.

Rahl still had to find, sooner or later, either former lower-level tariff enumerators or clerks who could handle that task, although he had a few days there, he thought, and needed to check the schedules and structures of the pier guards and the city patrollers. For the moment, he had Third Company patrolling the streets of Nubyat in groups of five, but that couldn't continue for too long.

He untied the gelding from the iron hitching ring outside the portmaster's building and mounted. He still needed to meet with more of the remaining traders and factors to assess their trustworthiness, as well as arranging for dispatching the steam tugs back to their owners up the Awhut River. Also, if he ever had time, he wanted to write a letter to Deybri, even if he didn't know how he would get it sent until ships resumed porting in Nubyat.

He frowned. She would not have been happy at his solution to the portmaster's obstructiveness, but . . . Rahl didn't have the time or inclination to persuade traitors, nor the men to keep watch over them to see that they did their jobs. Tharmyl would take care of the port—for many reasons beside loyalty, but that was true of most people.

LXXXI

The days rushed by, and Rahl found himself getting up earlier just so that he could eat breakfast without feeling like he had to gulp it down in a crowded officers' mess meant to feed perhaps thirty officers and strained to supply more than five times that number—even when the officers ate quickly and in shifts. On threeday, Rahl and Drakeyt slipped into the mess well before dawn. Even so, the air inside was smoky with the odor of cooking oil. The windows were hazed over as well with accumulated smoke, but both officers were served within moments of seating themselves at the end of one of the two long tables, already mostly full.

Rahl took a moment to sip hot watered cider before starting the egg toast and thin mutton strips.

"You're working harder now than when we were scouting, aren't you?" asked Drakeyt.

"It's not as dangerous, but there's always something else to do. The overcommander doesn't know which of the people in charge of running things to trust, and that means I have to check everything." Rahl laughed. "We have gotten the port open, and yesterday I had to make sure that there were enough wagons and carts to shift cargoes from the river-barge piers to the deep-water piers. There were enough wagons, once I pried them away from the Residence quartermaster—"

"Why did he have them?"

"There weren't any ships porting here, not to speak of, and the rebel officers didn't know what to do with the wagons that had been carrying cargoes to the piers, so they put him in charge of storing and maintaining them until they won and opened the port." Rahl shook his head. "I really didn't have to pry them away. He was very cooperative. Finding out where they were and who was in charge was the hard part. Then I just talked to him, and we worked out the arrangements. Dealing with the local factors' council was harder. All they wanted to know was when trading vessels would start porting and whether they'd get tariffing relief because of the revolt." Rahl took a quick swallow of the watery cider. "Those aren't something that the overcommander can control. No ship's master wants to hazard a vessel, and most will wait until they know it's safe. After that, well, it's more than a few days under sail even from Cigoerne, let alone Nordla or Recluce. As for tariffs, that's up to the Emperor, but I can't imagine he'd reduce their tariffs, even for a short time. That wouldn't be fair to traders elsewhere." Rahl grimaced slightly. "Besides, none of those still here took a stand against Golyat, and granting them tariff relief would amount to rewarding them for supporting, or not opposing, treason."

"It sounds like you've gotten to know a great number of important people here," ventured Drakeyt.

"I've had to. The overcommander hasn't had time, and it takes a mage who can tell who to trust and who's telling the truth and who isn't."

"That isn't necessary in most cities."

Rahl frowned, then took a quick mouthful of egg toast, followed by a mutton strip less dry than usual. Drakeyt was right about that. Then he nodded. "That's because people learn through actions over time. If a factor charges too much, he gets less trade, or loses everything. If a tariff enumerator overcharges or pockets coins, sooner or later it comes to light. We weren't here, and we don't have any of that knowledge, and we don't know whom of those who were we can trust. But I'm learning, and one thing leads to another. The new portmaster is trustworthy, and that means that he'll report problems on the piers, and because the pier guards are also generally honest, factors can't claim theft on the piers . . . you see?"

"I see that you're being wasted as a military mage-guard," Drakeyt said. "What do you have to do today?"

"First, I have to check with the water-master about some sewer complaints, and then ride the streets to check on the patrols—not long, but enough to let them see that I am. After that, I'll have to meet one of the transports porting because we're getting replacement mage-guards and some special cargo for the overcommander. I'll have to talk to all of the mage-guards to see how they fit into the port station and the city station. Most of them are pretty junior, I've been told." Rahl paused for a moment. How could he call anyone junior so cavalierly? He was doubtless the most junior senior mage-guard in Hamor.

Drakeyt grinned, as if he knew what Rahl had been thinking. "It happens, Rahl. You get in the habit of thinking you're junior, and, then, you realize you're not, that there are others coming along behind you."

"You shouldn't be just a captain," Rahl interjected, trying to change the subject away from himself.

"No . . . I'm one of the more senior captains, but not that many majers get killed, and you don't get promoted until there's a slot."

Rahl could see that, but Drakeyt deserved a promotion more than many captains. Of that, Rahl was certain.

After leaving the mess, and well before morning muster, Rahl stopped by the quartermaster's study to confirm that there would be wagons at the pier for the mage-guards and the cargo that Taryl wanted transported directly to the Residence. Then he walked all the way to the small stable behind the overcommander's villa, where he saddled the gelding. When he rode out, he was joined by three troopers from Third Company's fifth squad. It helped to have them for more than a few reasons, one of which was simply that most people didn't consider a man riding alone of any great import. Besides, it also meant that he didn't have to worry about the gelding, and he could spend more time on dealing with the problem at hand and less with his mount.

For the past eightday, it had felt like whenever he thought he'd caught up on Taryl's seemingly endless projects, the overcommander came up with more. Yet he knew Taryl wasn't inventing things for him to do. All of them were necessary to put Nubyat firmly back under Imperial control, and by using a single mage-guard to do it, Taryl wasn't applying brute force to the city as a whole.

As he rode down from the Residence area, Rahl noted that all traces of the barricades had been removed—except for the areas of fire-blackened pavement; but a crew of rebel prisoners was working with pumice stones, and some of the darkness had been removed.

"Morning, Majer!" called the squad leader whose men were guarding the chained prisoners.

"Good morning! The road's looking better."

"Yes, ser. And it'll be better by tonight."

"The overcommander will be glad to hear it." Rahl smiled and kept on riding.

His route took him through the south square, with the two inns, but he did not see any of the new patrollers there. He made a note to ride back and check the area after he talked to the water-master or later, if necessary. He crossed through the traders' quarter on Northend and could definitely smell a foul odor in the lower-lying sections of the avenue.

Then he turned onto the South River Road, passing the barge piers just northeast of the center of the traders' quarter. After riding another two kays, he had to take a narrow, but paved, and winding lane uphill to the waterworks building. From the building beside the reservoir dam, the water-master controlled the flow of water to the sewers and aqueducts serving Nubyat proper. The dam was filled by a stone canal fed by a diversion from the Awhut River some five kays farther upstream.

Outside the low stone structure set less than a hundred cubits from the west end of the dam, Rahl reined up and dismounted, handing the gelding's reins to Naimyl, the youngest of the troopers accompanying him. "I hope I won't be too long, but water the mounts, because we'll be riding back as soon as I finish."

"Yes, ser."

Rahl had not quite reached the doorway to the building when it opened, and a lanky young man in gray stepped out. "This is not a military post—"

"I know," Rahl replied politely. "I'm Senior Mage-Guard Rahl, and the new administrator sent me to see the water-master."

The other man looked at Rahl dubiously.

Rahl projected assurance, power, and cooperation, then smiled. "I won't take that long."

"Ah . . . yes, ser. But . . . master Neshyl . . . he usually works through the administrator's staff."

Rahl laughed. "Right now, that's me." He looked past the younger man to a short, muscular graybeard. "Are you Water-Master Neshyl?"

"Unless someone has replaced me. In these times, that is entirely possible."

"I'm certain I would have heard if Administrator Taryl had done so."

"Taryl? There was a Triad—"

"It's the same Taryl. The Emperor recalled him, and he is the acting marshal of the Imperial forces who reclaimed Nubyat," Rahl explained. "He is also the Mage-Guard Overcommander for Merowey, and the acting Regional Administrator until a permanent administrator is appointed by the Emperor."

"That sounds like Taryl." Neshyl shook his head. "Come on in and tell me what the administrator wants."

While Rahl did not sense any treachery, he kept his shields strong as he followed the water-master back into the building. Inside was a small empty foyer.

"On the left is the model room. My study is here on the right."

"Model room?" asked Rahl.

"We maintain a model of Nubyat that shows all the sewers and aqueducts, and the underground water channels. Whenever something is added, or changed, we change the model. That way, anyone can see where the system goes. Of course, the buildings are just shown as rough blocks, crude but enough like those in the city so that my men can recognize where to go if there's a problem." Neshyl walked to the end of a short hallway, past two closed doors, and through an archway without a door. "Those are just storerooms for equipment."

A large table desk dominated the small room, with a wooden armchair on one side, and two armless chairs on the other side. The two windows behind the armchair were little more than slits in the stone wall. Neshyl took one of the armless chairs and gestured to the other.

Rahl took the seat offered. "You seemed to indicate that you knew Overcommander Taryl."

"Only in passing, Mage-Guard. Only in passing. Years ago, he was the one who stabilized the rock on one of the edges of the dam here. Saved us from having to drain it and rebuild a whole section. That was when Ashurmyn was the administrator." Neshyl smiled. "You didn't ride out here to talk about your overcommander."

"No, I didn't. The administrator has received a number of complaints about odors around Northend Avenue, near where it intersects the Harbor Road."

Neshyl sighed, and Rahl could sense the honest exasperation and resignation, but he waited for the watermaster to speak.

"That's the factors' quarter, mostly. The problem is that the sewers there have sunk in places, and the sewage backs up. They built that all of harbor fill years ago, and the ground sinks. We'd need to tear up the streets in three places. Every time I put forth a proposal to the previous administrator, asking for the golds to do it, I was turned down."

"Do you know why?"

"The factors near the sewers where the work has to be done claimed that it was all a ruse to push trade to their competitors in the east quarter, or to those in Elmari or in Sastak . . . or who knows where. That was what the dispatches I got back from the administrator said, anyway."

"You never talked to him?"

"Once in three years, and that was about increasing the flow in the south aqueduct that serves the Residence."

"There were golds for that, I take it?" Rahl asked.

Neshyl nodded.

"Do you have a copy of the proposal you made for repairing the Northend sewers?"

"It's in the files. It might take a moment to find it."

"I'll wait." Rahl smiled politely.

Neshyl stood. "You think it will do any good?"

"I don't know. The administrator will decide that,"

Rahl said deliberately, "but it seems that it might be best to repair them when the factors have less trade to worry about and can't complain so loudly."

Neshyl laughed as he left the study.

Sitting there, Rahl had to wonder. Taryl had never mentioned that he'd been in Nubyat before, although he'd never denied it, either.

Seemingly in moments, Neshyl returned, holding a roll of papers tied with a dark cord. "Never been unwrapped. You can keep this one. I've got the original here."

Rahl stood and took the rolled papers. "Thank you."

"We'd be happy to reset those drains as soon as we could get the golds."

"I'll let the administrator know that."

"I'd be much obliged." Neshyl smiled. "If you'd also tell Taryl that the rock is solid, I'd appreciate that, too."

Rahl grinned. "I can do that." After a nod, he turned and left.

Outside, after carefully easing the papers into his saddlebags and then mounting the gelding, he glanced to the west. From the hilly ridge that formed the western edge of the reservoir, he could see most of Nubyat as well as the Southern Ocean beyond the port. While there were a handful of puffy clouds on the horizon, the sky was clear elsewhere, and the breeze was light, suggesting that spring might not be all that far away. He thought he could make out a merchanter well to sea, but he wasn't certain, let alone whether it was inbound to Nubyat.

"Let's go. We'll take the River Road back all the way to the Harbor Road."

"Yes, ser."

Sovarth eased his mount beside Rahl's, and the other two followed.

Rahl wasn't about to miss the anticipated porting of the merchanter that was due. Taryl had been most insistent that Rahl be there, telling him to do whatever else he could around the harbor, but not to miss being there on the pier when the ship tied up because of such cargo as battle dressings, ointments, and brinn, as well as the replacement mage-guards.

As Rahl turned the gelding onto the Harbor Road, he caught sight of one of the new patrollers stepping away from a peddler. It took a moment for him to recall the man's name. "Salamyn!" Rahl reined up and asked, "How is the patrolling going?"

"Majer, ser!" The former pier guard's face lit up. "It's not bad, now that folks know that we're reporting to a mage-guard and that there will be more mage-guards coming. Some ask about them." Salamyn grinned. "Some don't."

"That's where I'm headed now, to see if they're aboard a ship that's supposed to be porting before long. Just keep at it." Rahl smiled, then nodded, before urging the gelding into a walk. While it wasn't what either he or Taryl would have liked, the city was going to have to deal with both patrollers and mage-guards for some time to come. There just weren't enough spare mage-guards in Hamor to make up for all those who had either been killed or defected to Golyat. That was just one more of the costs of the revolt that would never appear on the accounting ledgers.

Rahl recognized the faces of the two pier guards at the gates to the harbor area, but not their names. He slowed the gelding and asked, "How are things? Any problems?"

"No, ser. Not today," answered the taller one. "Hesyr, here, he caught a cutpurse yesterday."

"I was lucky," replied Hesyr.

"It counts all the same," Rahl said with a smile. "Keep an eye out. We've got a merchanter coming in."

"Yes, ser."

Rahl nodded and eased the gelding toward pier three. When he reached the foot of the pier, he was pleased to see that the three wagons from the quartermaster were waiting.

A thin line of smoke rising from the ship passing the outer breakwater told Rahl he had arrived in more than enough time, but not with enough time to attend to anything else. He dismounted and handed the gelding's reins to Sovarth. "It'll be awhile. Go on over to the harbor mage-guard station. You three can water the horses there and take a break. Check back after the ship's made fast."

"Yes, ser."

Before long, the merchanter hove into view, and Rahl watched as the *Kienelth* backed down, and the captain of the merchanter walked her into the pier. The lines went out, and before long, the ship was secured between the bollards, and the crew extended the gangway.

A tall and angular senior mage-guard walked down the ramp empty-handed while a junior mage-guard following him struggled under the burden of several canvas duffels. Seeing—and sensing—the arrogance of the senior mage-guard, Rahl checked his order shields while he waited for the other to reach him.

"I'm Senior Mage-Guard Chewyrt. I take it I'll be in charge of one of the stations." Watery blue eyes practically glared at Rahl.

Rahl smiled politely as he replied. "It's good to see you, Chewyrt. I'm sure that you'll be able to make a valuable contribution here. Oh, I'm Rahl, and Overcommander Taryl assigned me to reestablish and organize both mage-guard stations here. You'll be reporting to me until the overcommander can set up a more traditional structure. That may be a little while."

"I was the most senior at Kyalasa."

"I'm most certain you were," Rahl replied, "and I'm sure that the overcommander was well aware of that. Now . . . if you'll take your gear and put it in the first wagon there, the driver will take you to the harbor mage-guard station. That's where you'll all be quartered for the next day . . . until I have a chance to talk with each of you."

"I cannot believe—"

Rahl offered a cold and hard smile, projecting absolute power and control, even while he kept his voice mild and pleasant. "We've spent close to a season riding a thousand kays and fighting battles, and we still have rebels in two cities in Merowey that we have to deal with. You'll have to pardon the overcommander if he and I have a few matters to take care of in addition to reestablishing the mage-guard stations. I'd like to have you take over those duties just as much as you would. I should be back at the station later this afternoon, but if I'm not, it will be early tomorrow. Now, if you'd organize the others and get them and their gear in the wagon, I'd appreciate it."

Chewyrt paled. "Yes, ser."

"Thank you. I need to talk to the ship's master, and I'll get back to all of you as soon as I can."

Rahl turned and started toward the gangway, where he saw a woman in mage-guard greens—a healer—coming down. Her curly hair was light brown, and even from a score of cubits he could see those eyes—brown with gold flecks.

Deybri . . .

Rahl just stood there for a long moment. Then, forcing himself not to run, he walked quickly toward her. He stopped and just looked and let himself take in all of her, with eyes and order-senses.

Her smile was far warmer than the late-winter sun. "Just by looking, you can make a woman feel like an empress."

"Only you . . . only you."

"From anyone but you, Rahl, those would be empty words."

"You don't know how much I have thought and dreamed and thought of you." He paused. "I had no idea . . . You only wrote that you would soon come to a decision. I feared . . . much as I hoped . . ." Slowly, seemingly so slowly, he reached out and took her hands.

Then . . . both had their arms around each other.

When they stepped apart, Rahl's face was wet, but so was Deybri's.

There was so much he wanted to say, and to ask, but the first question was the safest and the simplest. "How?"

"Your overcommander arranged it. I would not have dared without his assurances." Her eyes dropped. "I am not so brave as you."

He shook his head. "You chose to come. That is brave. I had no choice. That was merely enduring." After a moment, he added, "We have to find you someplace safe to stay . . ."

"Ah . . ." Deybri flushed. "I'm supposed to report to the Mage-Guard Regional Overcommander. I'm a mage, in Hamorian terms . . . remember?"

Rahl should have thought of that, but he grinned. "I think I can take care of that. I can even provide an escort. Would you mind waiting just a bit while I talk to the ship's master? I need to make arrangements . . ."

"You're on duty." She smiled, warmly and not quite mischievously, an expression Rahl somehow had not expected. "I understand."

"I'll try not to be long." Rahl turned and strode up the gangway, but he did remember to ask the duty mate, "Permission to come aboard?"

"You're more than welcome, Mage-Guard."

Once aboard, Rahl inclined his head to the captain, standing just beyond the quarterdeck. "Ser, the overcommander asked me to confirm the cargo personally . . ."

The captain had the manifest in hand, as if he had expected no less. Even so, checking for the items Taryl had emphasized was tedious, not because it took all that long, but because Rahl was all too conscious that Deybri stood on the pier, although she was now in the company of Rahl's troopers.

After that, more time passed while Rahl made sure the priority items were off-loaded into the wagons. Only then could he afford to return his attention to Deybri, much as he would have wished otherwise.

Sovarth had taken the initiative of riding over to the

mage-guard station and requisitioning one of the two officers' mounts there for Deybri.

Rahl looked to the trooper. "Thank you, Sovarth. Both
the healer and I appreciate it."

"Be my pleasure, ser." The trooper flushed.

After loading her rather large duffel behind her saddle,
Rahl held the reins while she mounted, then mounted
himself and led the way out from the harbor.

He did address the pier guards as they passed, although he had to remind himself because his eyes kept
drifting to Deybri. "There will be cargo wagons coming
from the *Kienelth*."

"Yes, ser."

Once on Harbor Road, Rahl and Deybri rode side by
side, and he could not help but notice that the three
troopers lagged behind them at a greater distance than
they usually followed him.

He finally said, "I still cannot believe you're here, that
you're really here."

"I am." She smiled again, both warmly and tentatively, then added, "You've grown."

"I think I had to."

"Except for those few moments when you saw me and
held me, I haven't been able to sense anything . . . nothing."

"Taryl insisted on it. He said I'd never survive if I
didn't."

"And when you addressed that other mage-guard, I
could feel the power. He just wilted, and you never raised
your voice. . . ."

Rahl shrugged, somehow embarrassed. "I was just trying to get him to understand." He flushed. "Not just that,
but he walked off the ship as if he were doing everyone a
favor, and he had that junior mage-guard carrying everything. Thousands of men died taking Nubyat from the
rebels, and . . . somehow his attitude didn't seem right."

"It wasn't." She grinned at him. "But it did remind me
of someone else several years back."

Rahl flushed more. "I wasn't that bad . . . was I?"

She shook her head. "But you did have some unthinking arrogance."

Rahl kept his face calm, but winced inside. "I'm fortunate you saw beyond that."

"I didn't. I was attracted to you despite it. Aleasya was the one who insisted you'd get over it. She said I'd be a fool to avoid you because of that."

Aleasya? The muscular arms instructor? *That* did surprise him. "Then . . . what changed your mind?"

"You'd already changed a great deal when you returned to Recluce, and I could see more of that in your later letters. And that you wrote. Uncle Thorl told me that each one cost you at least three silvers to send. You spent more on letters than some earn in half a year. I'm not sure I'm worth that."

"You're worth far more than that," he said quietly.

"I'm glad you think so."

They rode for a time without speaking. While Rahl had so much to say, little of it was what he wanted to blurt out on horseback and in public. But he did keep looking at Deybri. In the mage-guard greens, she was more beautiful than he had recalled.

"Your hair is shorter."

"It's easier to take care of that way. I also thought it might be better for a mage-guard."

Rahl paused as he studied the southern square ahead. Then he caught sight of one of the new patrollers, striding along the south side, and he nodded. They needed to be seen, especially now, although having some real mage-guards in place would help in the days to come. The patroller turned at the sound of hoofs, then raised his truncheon in acknowledgment. Rahl lifted his arm to acknowledge the greeting, and the patroller stood and watched as Rahl and the others rode past the ancient Imperial statue and through the square.

When they reached the base of the road up to the Residence and compound area, Rahl could see that the crew of rebel prisoners was still working on scrubbing the blackness and soot off the paving stones around where the lower barricade had been.

As he neared the guard squad, the squad leader nodded. "Afternoon, Majer."

"They've almost got it taken care of, I see."

"Another day or two, ser. Be more, weren't for you."

"You're kind, squad leader, but it took all of us." Rahl projected appreciation.

Once they were well past, Deybri turned and glanced at him inquiringly.

"They're rebel prisoners. They'd built some barricades to keep us from taking the Residence and compound up there. They're cleaning up the mess." Rahl gestured.

"You were here, weren't you?"

"Yes. We lost hundreds just on this stretch of road."

"How did you take it?"

"Commander Shuchyl's engineers got oil bladders, and catapulted them onto the wall. They caught fire, and that cleared the wall enough so that they could storm it."

Deybri turned in the saddle. "There's more, isn't there?"

"Yes, but I'd rather not talk about it now." Somehow, Rahl felt that telling her what he'd done would have been bragging, and he didn't want to do that, not when he recalled how many had died. "If you don't mind."

She nodded.

Again, there was a silence between them.

Rahl waited until they reached the top of the road and had turned back southeast. "The large villa ahead—that's the Administrator's Residence, and where we're headed. It's more than that, really, because the lower level is mostly for his staff. There aren't many now, of course. The next villa is the overcommander's, but Taryl is using the Residence right now because he's both administrator and overcommander. Then, the buildings with the low walls behind them—that's the permanent compound for the troopers normally stationed here. All the tents and shelters are what we're using for quarters for those who can't fit in the compound. Some are quartered in the city as well, of course."

"The grounds—they're beautiful, almost like a park. I hadn't expected something like this."

Rahl laughed. "Neither did I when I first saw it. There is some beauty here in Hamor."

"I don't believe I ever denied that."

"You were just too miserable to see it when you were here before?"

"Too frightened."

Rahl could sense that some of that fear remained, if held in check. "We'll just ride to the north portico over there. That's the administrative entrance, not the formal one."

"You could fit all of the magisters and trainers in Nylan in half of one level of that building," Deybri observed. "You'd still have room for more."

Rahl smiled as he reined up at the first mounting block. There he dismounted, handed the gelding's reins to Faslyn, then offered a hand to Deybri. She took it, although she did not need it in dismounting. Then, belatedly, Rahl recalled the proposition from the water-master and extracted it carefully from his saddlebags.

Neither of the two troopers on guard duty moved as Rahl and Deybri approached.

"Good afternoon," Rahl said. "Majer Rahl and Mage-Guard Healer Deybri to see the administrator."

"Yes, ser."

Once inside the small circular foyer, Rahl led Deybri up the side staircase to the upper level, then to the rear of the Residence.

After the first few days, Taryl had moved his headquarters from the overcommander's villa to the Administrator's Residence, which made sense to Rahl. It also meant that to get to Taryl, Rahl had to announce himself to Falyka—a stern-faced former mage-guard who had been stipended off after thirty years of service, but whom Taryl had found somewhere to serve as gatekeeper and personal aide. Falyka sat behind a wide table desk in the foyer outside the administrator's study. Every time Rahl had been to see Taryl, the table had been filled with neat stacks of paper, and this time was no exception.

"I see you did manage to find the healer," offered Falyka, even before Rahl could say a word. "The administrator is expecting you both." She nodded toward the door to her left, then picked up her pen from the blotting pad where she had set it and continued making entries in the ledger before her.

Rahl managed to keep his mouth shut. How many people had known that Deybri was coming to Nubyat?

Deybri looked at Rahl and raised her eyebrows.

He smiled helplessly, then opened the door.

Taryl immediately stood from behind the enormous wide desk, and Rahl could sense his quick appraisal of Deybri. He smiled warmly and broadly. "If anything, Rahl underplayed your beauty and ability. I cannot tell you how pleased I am to see you, Healer Deybri." He gestured. "Please have a chair. You've had several long voyages."

"Thank you." Deybri slipped into the rightmost of the three chairs before the desk.

Rahl took the second one, not only to be beside her, but because the sunlight pouring through the wide west window bathed the leftmost chair and might have distracted him when he wanted to concentrate on Deybri— and needed to watch Taryl.

"How was the trip?"

"The voyages were both long, but the quarters were more than I could have expected. I'm very grateful. I'm also happy to be on land again. I'm not really a seafarer, as Rahl may well know."

"You look to have borne up well," Taryl replied. "I imagine you would like the chance to clean up and get settled. There are quarters here in the Residence for the administrator's healer," Taryl said. "Since the officers' quarters are already overfilled, you'll be quartered here until matters settle out more."

Deybri looked squarely at Taryl. "As a healer, I do intend to accompany the force attacking Sastak."

"I would not have thought otherwise." Taryl offered a faint but warm and amused smile. "As a healer, however, you will be assigned to the headquarters company. You cannot do much good as a healer if a rebel trooper spits you on a lance or blade."

Deybri inclined her head in acquiescence.

"Now, Mage-Guard Healer, while you are getting settled, I need to discuss some matters with Senior Mage-Guard Rahl. Falyka—the aide outside—will help you. Later, in view of your situations, I have arranged dinner for the three of us here in the Residence this evening, and I will discuss anything you wish and answer any questions you may have."

"You've been most kind, Overcommander, and I'm most appreciative."

"I'm serving my own interests as well, Healer, but I appreciate your words." Taryl rose, adding more gently. "And I am glad to see you here safely."

Rahl stood as well. Much as he understood Taryl's reasons and requirements, he didn't want to let Deybri out of his sight—or senses.

"I'm glad to be here." Deybri's eyes turned to Rahl. "Until later."

Her words were almost a caress, as evenly and calmly as she uttered them, and he could not help but smile widely. "Until later."

"How did you get her to come?" Rahl asked, several moments after the study door had shut behind Deybri. "She wouldn't even entertain the idea when I hinted at it."

"Age does have certain advantages, Rahl. I did point out that I could offer her a position as a full mage-guard. I also sent her the golds for passage and agreed that, if she did not find Hamor to her liking, she could return at my expense."

"*You* paid her passage?"

Taryl smiled. "Why not? Good healers are hard to come by, and so are good mage-guards. I have no children, and it is most unlikely that I will. My legacy will be how well the mage-guards perform after I am gone. Unless I'm mistaken, you will be a better mage-guard because of the healer, whatever may happen—"

"Whatever may happen?" Rahl didn't like that thought at all.

Taryl held up a hand. "You have thought of her ever since you came to Hamor. Don't tell me you have not. There is only one way to deal with that. Now that she is here, you two will decide whether you belong together or whether you do not. If you do, then you and the mage-guards, and Hamor are all better off. If you do not, then you will not waste time and effort pining for what cannot be, and you will be more effective. The healer will also understand what she is and is not." Taryl's shields were as firm as ever, but the overcommander did smile.

Rahl could not argue with Taryl's logic, cold as the words sounded.

"What else do you have to report?" asked Taryl quickly.

Rahl had the feeling Taryl did not wish to say more about Deybri at the moment.

"Oh . . . I met with Water-Master Neshyl . . ." Rahl went on to recount his visit, concluding, ". . . and he gave me the proposal that Golyat had turned down." He extended the proposal, still tied in the dark cord.

Taryl raised his eyebrows. "Neshyl?"

"He said to tell you that the rock is still solid, ser."

Taryl laughed. "He would. We'll find his golds, but it will have to wait a bit."

"Have you heard anything from Commander Shuchyl, ser?"

"He's still almost an eightday from Elmari, but the fleet is standing by off the port there. Once he takes the town, they can transport Fourth Regiment back here in a few days. We'll leave Fifth Regiment in Elmari to keep order. By then, we should be ready to move on Golyat in Sastak."

What Taryl said made sense, but the overcommander had certainly not been that cautious in attacking Nubyat. Or was Nubyat of such importance that Golyat and Sastak were effectively only afterthoughts? That couldn't be . . . but Taryl always had his reasons.

Taryl's eyes dropped to a dispatch on the corner of the table desk. Then he looked up at Rahl. "That came in with the transport. Regional Commander Chaslyk is dead. He was inspecting the warehouse of the city station in Swartheld, and part of a wall fell on him. Another mage-guard with him was killed."

Chaslyk? The mage-guard who had commanded the entire area around Swartheld? Rahl could still remember the tall and muscular officer with the black eyes, olive skin, and angular face who dominated any room he was in—unless Taryl happened to be there.

"That wasn't an accident, was it?"

"I don't think so, but it will be awhile before I know. What else?"

"I met the mage-guards. There's one senior mage-guard—Chewyrt. He tried to lean on me, but I think everything will be fine. I do need to get back there and talk to them. The sooner I can put him to work, the less trouble he'll be."

"Cyphryt sent him because he's always been trouble. Do you think you can keep him in line?"

"I think so. He's the kind who respects power and little else. I didn't raise my voice, but I just projected absolute authority at him. He might do better if I could make him an acting undercaptain and tell him that whether the position is permanent depends on how well he gets things working without using unnecessary force and authority."

Taryl smiled, if briefly. "You'd better go deal with him so that you can devote some attention to dinner and the healer. Oh . . . you can make him an acting undercaptain, but it is your responsibility."

In short, Rahl had to make sure that Chewyrt understood.

He was about to leave, but realized he had one particularly nagging question. "Ser? How did you know how to reach her?"

Taryl laughed. "Who posted many of your letters?"

Rahl shook his head. So simple, and he'd never even thought of it.

LXXXII

When Rahl returned to the harbor mage-guard station, still accompanied by the three troopers, he found Chewyrt was standing in the corner of the small front foyer. With the suppressed anger and energy within the older mage, he might as well have been pacing furiously back and forth across the foyer.

"Mage-Guard Chewyrt," Rahl said pleasantly, "I thought we'd walk around the area, and I could fill you in on some of the things particular to here."

"I'd be most pleased." Beneath very leaky shields, Chewyrt was anything but pleased. He was angry and felt that Rahl was being unfair and disrespectful. He jammed on his visor cap.

Rahl said nothing, but walked out the doorway, letting the senior mage-guard catch up. Rahl walked deliberately along the stone-paved walkway that led directly to pier one, saying nothing until Chewyrt had joined him. "You know, Chewyrt, I find myself in a rather unusual position. I don't imagine you know my background, do you?"

"No, I can't say that I do."

Nor did Chewyrt care, Rahl sensed. "It might prove useful to you, although I'm most certain that you have no personal interest. You can see by the truncheon that I'm an ordermage. What you can't see is that I'm an exile from Recluce who survived a year or so in the ironworks of Luba and who worked his way back to becoming a mage-clerk after someone dosed me with nemysa." Rahl smiled.

"I see."

Chewyrt didn't.

Rahl shook his head: "I seem to be able to sense, even behind shields, what most people are feeling. You, for example, feel that I don't respect you, that I'm being unfair, and that there's no reason that you should care about my background."

Chewyrt almost hesitated in taking his next step.

"You also feel that very few in the mage-guards understand what you've endured and that you should have been given more responsibility long ago." Rahl stopped, just short of the wide paved street that served all the piers, and turned to face the older man. "I've talked it over with the overcommander, and he told me that you'd been sent here because, despite your abilities with chaos, you're so difficult that no superior in the mage-guards really wants to deal with you."

"That's not true."

Rahl shrugged. "You have solid abilities. You've been a senior mage-guard for years. If it's not true, then why has no one ever recommended you for a position of authority?"

Rage erupted within Chewyrt, barely held in check. He tightened his lips and did not speak for several moments. "Because they don't want to put people with real ability in those positions. They just want lackeys."

That, unfortunately, was at least partly true, at least from what Rahl had seen. "You have real abilities, and I'd like to see you make use of them." Rahl paused.

"But what? There's always a 'but.' "

"But . . ." Rahl drew out the word, "you've gotten so bitter and angry that your abilities haven't been recognized that no one wants to work with you or for you. I'll give you a chance at that position of responsibility—"

"You?"

Rahl smiled, then wrapped his shields around Chewyrt, contracting them. The older mage-guard tried to break free, but found himself immobilized. Rahl waited until the other stopped struggling before he eased the pressure.

"Me. For better or worse, the overcommander has made me his acting deputy. Despite your outburst, and your lack of respect for me, I'm still willing to make you the acting undercaptain of the harbor station. If . . . *if* . . . the overcommander and I are satisfied with your performance, we'll make the rank permanent."

Rahl could sense the faintest glimmer of hope amid the anger and bitterness, although Chewyrt did not reply.

"What we expect are what is expected of every undercaptain—that you be diligent, that you be effective in carrying out your duties, that you be open and fair, and that you do not abuse your position in having others do things for you that you should be doing for yourself. And that you stop arrogating yourself over others."

Rahl waited.

"I only . . ." Chewyrt broke off what he might have said. After another long pause, he asked, "Might I ask, ser, why you are only a senior mage-guard?"

Rahl was relieved to sense that at least some of the other's anger and bitterness had receded, if only because Chewyrt had realized Rahl's true power and position, and that the question was the only way that Chewyrt could admit that he would try to meet the terms.

"Because I haven't been a senior mage-guard long enough to prove that I'm worthy of being more." That was the most honest answer Rahl could offer.

The directness of the reply clearly stunned Chewyrt.

After another silence, the older mage-guard said, "I appreciate your honesty, ser. I would like to try."

"I'd like you to try. More than that, Chewyrt, I'd like to see you succeed." Rahl paused. "So would the overcommander." Left unsaid, but understood, was the fact that Chewyrt would never get another chance if he failed.

"So would I, ser."

Rahl nodded. "I don't have much time now, but across from us is pier one. That's for smaller fleet vessels. Pier two, over there is for the cruisers and larger ships. Pier three and four are for merchanters. . . ."

As he continued to walk and explain, Rahl wondered if he'd handled Chewyrt correctly, but he thought that the man needed a combination of force and understanding. Rahl just hoped his feelings about the older mage-guard were right.

LXXXIII

Rahl managed to get back to his small room in the over-commander's barracks with enough time to wash up and don a clean uniform. He did walk the distance to the Residence, if at a leisurely enough pace that he would not arrive overheated. No one questioned him—but no one had in days—when he entered the staff doorway and made his way to the upper level on the south end. He couldn't help but note that the green carpet runners in the staff quarters had seen far better days, and that the plaster walls could have used a fresh coat of whitewash.

He cleared his throat, squared his shoulders, and knocked on the goldenwood door. Then he waited. When Deybri opened the door, Rahl couldn't help but stare, thinking how truly alive and luminous she looked in another set of immaculate greens.

"The way you look at a woman makes her the center of the world."

"Not *a* woman," he protested, taking her hands. "You. Just you."

"I would say that you tell all the women that," she said gently, "and you say it well in Hamorian, but I know better. That's almost frightening."

Rahl was afraid he knew what she meant, but he didn't want to talk about that. Not yet. Then he realized something else. "Your Hamorian is much better. You barely have an accent."

"Uncle Thorl's doing. He said I always had the ability, but that I really didn't want to learn it perfectly."

"I've always known you had many hidden abilities."

"I didn't know you were that interested in my less obvious attributes," she teased.

"I always have been. I must be. I haven't even kissed you."

"I know."

Sometime later, Deybri eased back out of his arms. "We are supposed to have dinner with our superior officer."

"I came for you earlier than we're expected," Rahl confessed.

"You have a devious mind, Senior Mage-Guard."

"Not at all devious," Rahl admitted. "Hopeful."

"We still should go."

"Yes, Healer. Oh . . ." He extracted the thick envelope from his winter uniform shirt and extended it to her. "This is for you. It's the latest letter—or letters—the ones I could never post because there was no way to send them. I kept writing . . ."

She leaned forward and kissed his cheek, then took the envelope. "I will read them. You write so well, and your hand is so beautiful."

The two walked down the long corridor from the staff quarters and into the formal area of the Residence.

Taryl was standing outside a large archway. He smiled sheepishly. "I forgot to tell you that we'd be eating in the private dining chamber. We'd be lost in here." He stepped aside and gestured toward the darkened formal dining chamber, not that the dimness was any barrier to the three, which held a table that stretched a good twenty cubits, if not longer. Then he turned, and the three walked another fifty cubits and around a corner and through a far smaller archway.

The private dining chamber was still large, holding an oval table that could easily seat ten. Three places had been set at one end. The pale green china plates had silvered edges, and the crystal goblets shone in the light of the polished-bronze wall lamps. The cutlery was also silver.

"This is less pretentious, but not as warm as I'd prefer." Taryl gestured to the seat to his right.

Rahl seated Deybri, even if it was probably against some protocol, since he outranked her, technically anyway. The three had no more been seated than an orderly appeared with a pitcher of wine, half-filling each goblet.

"It's Seblenan, supposedly very good." Taryl smiled. "Prince Golyat did keep a fine cellar, and most of it is still here. It's been years since I've had the privilege of good wine." He lifted his goblet. "To your safe arrival, Healer."

"Thank you."

There was something about the formality with which Taryl addressed Deybri, but Rahl could not quite put a finger on it. Instead, he lifted his own goblet, then sipped the wine, a vintage that was the palest of ambers, holding a flavor that reminded Rahl of roses and pearapples.

The orderly returned with three small bowls of soup. Rahl had never tasted anything like it.

"That's a winter gourd cream soup, isn't it?" asked Deybri. "It's very good."

Rahl had no idea that there were even winter gourds, or soup made from gourds in winter. He just nodded his agreement.

"I promised I would answer any questions you might have, Healer." Taryl looked at Deybri.

She tilted her head slightly, as if thinking, then smiled. "Why is Rahl so important to you?"

Taryl laughed, then shook his head. "I would not wish you opposing me in anything."

Deybri waited.

"I could offer evasions, but you would know them, even behind my shields," Taryl finally replied. "The simple answer is that he is powerful and honest, and that while there are other powerful mage-guards and other honest mage-guards, there are far too few who are both, and Hamor needs those desperately in these times."

"Why is that so? Why now?"

"You know about the revolt. It occurred because powerful and less-than-honest mage-guards persuaded Prince Golyat that he was far better suited to rule Hamor than his younger brother. It also occurred because other powerful and less honest mage-guards wanted a revolt to occur, but to be unsuccessful, and to use it for their own ends. Without Rahl, we would not have accomplished near so much so quickly, and without him, the future is far less certain."

"Is that why you offered me a chance to join him?"

"That is one reason. Another is as I wrote you. Also, you must already have noted that Hamor has far fewer skilled healers than does Recluce. There are other reasons as well, which I will not reveal, but which are honorable, and for which you must take my word for now."

She nodded. "What plans do you have for Rahl if you are successful in quashing the revolt?"

It surprised Rahl that Deybri did not press Taryl on his other reasons, but he said nothing.

"I would like to see him advance as far as he possibly can in the mage-guards."

"Enough to assure that?"

"I will not press others to promote him beyond his abilities or what he has earned, but I will support him fully for what he has earned."

"And for me?"

"The very same, Healer."

At that moment, the orderly removed the soup and replaced each dish with a plate on which were thin slices of beef laid between thinner slices of pastry and covered with a dark mushroom sauce.

"Beef Fyrad," Taryl said. "It's not all that popular these days, but I enjoy it."

So did Rahl, perhaps because he'd been so involved in thinking about Deybri and watching her that he'd forgotten how hungry he was.

"You did read the *Mage-Guard Manual*?" Taryl asked after several mouthfuls.

"Yes, ser," Deybri replied. "Some of it was . . . difficult."

Taryl nodded. "It is for most healers. You would not be healers were you not inclined to believe that there is at least a chance to heal most wounds. The *Manual* as much as states that some individuals can never be redeemed and that they must either be executed or work their lives away in the ironworks, the quarries, or the road crews."

"I can see that. Most in Recluce avoid thinking about that because we exile many and leave their fate to others. We do execute some few, but their offenses are usually great."

Rahl still had his doubts about that latter statement, especially given his experiences with Puvort and the magisters in Land's End, but he saw no point in contradicting Deybri.

"Rahl might disagree," Deybri added, "but I have to believe that his experiences are colored by his own uniqueness."

"Because he is a natural ordermage of the kind Recluce is unable or unwilling to train?" asked Taryl.

"And because he is potentially far more powerful than any of them—or any mage-guards here, possibly with the exception of the Triads. You know that. Wasn't that one reason why you saved him?"

"No," replied Taryl. "When I made him a mage-clerk, he only had a fraction of his true abilities. Later, it became very clear."

Deybri looked at Rahl.

"It's true. I could barely order-sense more than a few cubits away, and I could do nothing else."

"To be honest, however," Taryl added, with a wry smile, "I suspected more because usually only strong mages survive the amount of nemysa that he had to have been given. But I didn't know that."

From that point on, through the dessert of pearapple tarts in flaky crusts, Taryl was careful to keep the talk casual.

After the dessert, Taryl stood. "I must say that I've enjoyed this, and now I must pay for that by getting back to what remains on my desk."

Rahl and Deybri rose:

"Thank you, ser," offered Deybri.

"Thank you," added Rahl.

"It was my pleasure." Taryl smiled, warmly, and anything but mechanically.

Rahl offered Deybri his arm, and they left the small dining chamber and walked slowly down the long corridor toward the staff section and her quarters.

"He was very formal with you," Rahl said.

"It's both a message and a habit, I would say. He didn't strain to remind himself to use my title," mused Deybri.

The Empress?

"You have that look, Rahl. Your face reveals what your shields conceal."

"I don't know, but I think he was once in love with a woman who was consorted to someone else very powerful. I don't think he's ever forgotten her."

"You're being mysterious. Please don't be."

"I'm sorry. It's just . . . I owe Taryl everything . . . Everything but you, and now, in a way, I owe him for you. For your being here. I wouldn't want to say anything when I'm only guessing . . . but you should know. You probably could guess . . . You know, he was once a Triad. I think I wrote you that. Well, when we were in Cigoerne, I saw him once with the Empress . . ."

"The Empress of all Hamor? You met the Emperor and Empress?"

"It was at a reception. Each of them spoke to me for just a moment. The Emperor thanked me for helping with the mission to Nylan."

"What was she like?" Deybri's voice was soft.

"She's a healer, but she doesn't look at all like you."

"A healer . . . of course. The poor man. The one woman even a former Triad could never have. Not one as honest as Taryl."

"No one has ever said anything," Rahl said quietly, "but I wonder if he gave her up so that the Emperor would be a more able ruler."

"That's . . . horrible . . . as if she were . . ."

"There's more to it than that, but I don't know what. Maybe she loved them both. I can't believe Taryl would trade anyone."

"Maybe she gave up Taryl," suggested Deybri.

"I don't know. He's never said a word. It's only what I saw and felt."

"That's enough, most times." Deybri stopped outside her door and turned to him.

He leaned toward her and kissed her tenderly. She returned the kiss, warmly, lovingly, but also gently, then eased back from him. He could feel her entire body trembling.

Looking at him, she smiled sadly. "Rahl . . . I would like that more than anything . . . but we can't. Not now."

He could sense both the longing within her, the sadness, and see the brightness in her eyes. "Could you tell me why?"

"You've become so much more powerful. None of the magisters in Nylan could stand against you now, and you desire me so much . . ." Her words broke off.

"A child? Is that it?" He'd almost forgotten what she had told him so long ago about how almost any love-making would immediately lead to a child . . . the same mistake that had begun his exile and the long way he had come.

She nodded, her eyes dropping from his for a moment. "I'm almost sure that we should be together, that it's right. But . . . with you . . . almost isn't enough . . . and it would never be fair to the child. Please . . ."

He stepped forward and put his arms around her. Demons, it felt so good even to hold her. He still couldn't quite believe she was with him—in Hamor, where she had said she would never return.

Their faces were damp with tears when he stepped away and opened the door for her. He did not leave until it clicked shut.

LXXXIV

For the next three days, Rahl did not see all that much of Deybri—except at dinner, twice in the staff quarters at the Residence and once more with Taryl in the private dining room. All three times, she was close to exhausted from her efforts with the remaining wounded—those who would likely not survive without the ministrations of a healer. While he enjoyed being close to her, and she was warm and looked at him with affection, that affection was restrained—and those restraints chafed at Rahl, no matter how much he told himself that he could appreciate Deybri's exhaustion and caution.

Sevenday was not that much different from any of his recent days. He'd begun by meeting with Taryl and briefing the administrator on the shortages of goods identified by the factors' council, primarily foodstuffs, as a result of the need to feed First and Second Army, as well as the difficulties caused by low water in the Awhut River, which limited the amount of cargo that could be carried downstream to Nubyat, and the timetable for repairing the sewer drains. After leaving Taryl, he'd ridden out to

Water-Master Neshyl and conveyed Taryl's approval of
the sewer project.

Then he'd returned to Nubyat and spent more time
with the portmaster, arranging to have the channel
dredged near the end of pier two, where one of the merchanters had almost grounded leaving port. That meant
that none of the warships would be able to dock without
risking getting hung up.

Following that, Rahl had made a riding tour of Nubyat,
accompanied as he had been all day by three troopers
from Third Company, checking on the patrollers and
stopping to talk to crafters and shop proprietors, all as
part of his efforts to get a better feel of the city as well as
to reassure them that there would be no retributions
against those who had not raised arms—or coins—in
support of the revolt.

Although he did not spend that much time with any
one crafter, the sun was barely above the masts of the
trading schooner tied up near the foot of pier three when
Rahl reined up outside the harbor mage-guard station.

Chewyrt was actually waiting when Rahl stepped into
the front foyer where one of the younger patrollers was
handling the duty watch.

"Ser." Chewyrt inclined his head.

"Undercaptain, a few words."

"In the study?" asked Chewyrt.

Rahl nodded. "It won't take long."

"Yes, ser."

Rahl followed the undercaptain to the small study,
where he closed the door behind himself. As he glanced
around, he could see that Chewyrt had rearranged the
room, and that everything was spotless. There were neat
stacks of paper on the table desk, and the draft of a duty
schedule that the undercaptain had obviously been puzzling over. Rahl took the armless chair by the corner of
the table desk and waited for Chewyrt to seat himself before he began.

"The administrator has indicated that you will get two more mage-guards sometime before the turn of spring."

"That will help, but we will still have to rely heavily on the patrollers and pier guards." Chewyrt gestured to the half-completed schedule. "It's hard to come up with a duty roster that doesn't exhaust everyone."

"You could reduce the number of pier guards on eightday, at least for a while," Rahl suggested. "If you haven't already."

"I'd thought about it . . ."

"See how it works out and let me know." Rahl cleared his throat. He still felt awkward, at times, although those moments were fewer, acting as if he were the regional mage-guard commander, but there wasn't anyone else. "From now on, you will also be responsible for discovering beginning mages here in Nubyat. Because your mages don't have that much experience, they're just to refer any incidents of magery to you for action."

Chewyrt nodded. "That makes sense."

"If you have questions, or would like someone else to observe such youngsters, just let me know."

"I can do that."

"You assigned Dhemyn, Perguyn, and Saol to the city station," Rahl went on. "How is that working out?"

Chewyrt frowned, then pursed his lips. "I worry about Dhemyn. I've watched all three, and Perguyn and Saol are good at projecting authority so that they don't have to use chaos much at all. Dhemyn . . . he wants to be liked, and there's a difference between being polite and likable and needing to be liked."

Rahl understood that. "What do you think might help?"

"I'd thought about switching him back here and sending Vhoral to the city station. It wouldn't matter as much on the piers because here, things are more . . . definite, and he'd have a chance to see more about how people use both the implication of chaos and charm. I'd also be able occasionally to point things out to him."

Rahl nodded. "Go ahead and shift him. What will you tell him?"

"That I had to decide who went where in a hurry, but now that I've had a chance to get a better look at matters and schedules, I think he'll be more valuable here at the harbor station."

"That's a good approach. . . ." From there Rahl went over the ledgers with Chewyrt, both the supply ledger and the payroll ledger, and it was close to dinner by the time he finished and rode back to the small stable beyond the overcommander's villa.

When Rahl finally dismounted and led the gelding inside for grooming, he was thinking about how he was looking forward to having dinner with Deybri. Over the past few days, he'd managed to spend as much time as he could with her, but that depended on her free time—which was at dinner and little enough—given that she was often exhausted from dealing with the scores of injured who might not recover at all from their wounds without a healer.

Drakeyt was already grooming his mount outside the third stall, and he turned to Rahl. "Majer, I finally saw your healer." The captain shook his head and laughed. "Now I can see why you wrote so many letters to her. . . ."

"Was it that obvious?" Rahl was a little chagrined.

"Perhaps not that obvious, but I noticed. That's because I don't have anyone worth writing, and even if I could, I doubt that I'd be able to put it on paper well enough for anyone to want to read."

"I'm sure you could."

"Not like you."

Rahl only laughed, then turned his attention to the gelding. He forced himself not to shortchange the grooming, but after he finished, he hurried to wash up and get to the staff dining chamber so that Deybri wouldn't feel that he'd forgotten her.

When he hurried into the dining chamber, she was sitting alone at a corner table in the chamber that held ten tables, although there were only ten or eleven others in the room. She set down the beaker of golden ale she had been sipping, and a slow smile crossed her face as he neared. "You don't have to hurry. I would have waited."

Like Taryl, she had deep circles under her eyes, but Rahl only smiled in return. "When I can help it, I never want to keep you waiting."

"You're kind."

"No, you're the one who's kind. You're probably starving." He slipped into the chair across the battered wooden tabletop from her, belatedly noticing the beaker of lager awaiting him. "Thank you."

Almost immediately, the assistant to the cook set two platters on the table, along with a basket of bread. Each platter held four biastras—the Hamorian pepper-beef tubes that were floured and fried. "These are lamb, Healer . . . ser."

Rahl had the definite impression that she still did not know how to address him, but he wasn't certain what title fit him. "Majer or ser will do," he said after a moment, making sure his words were warm and kind.

"Yes, ser."

Rahl could sense her relief. He could also sense more than a few pairs of eyes directed at the two of them.

"We're confusing them," Deybri murmured. "We should either be eating here all the time, or with the administrator all the time."

"We wouldn't eat half the time," Rahl replied in a low voice. "He takes most of his meals in his study—or with the commanders at their mess."

"He drives himself so hard, and he expects much," murmured Deybri. "Those around him either wish to leave or to be as good as he is."

"That can be rather difficult," Rahl replied dryly.

"Would you have it any other way?"

Rahl flushed, but did not reply. Neither spoke more for several moments as they ate, hungry as they both were. Not until Rahl had finished the second biastra did he ask, "What did you do today? More healing?"

She nodded. "I can only offer healing to so many each day. There are some who died before I could get to them. There have been every day."

"I'm sorry. That sounds like a long day. You must be tired."

"I am tired," she admitted. "There are still so many wounded. So many." She straightened. "One of them knew about you. Not by name. He kept talking about a battle near someplace called Thalye, and about an officer with a long black truncheon who broke an entire battalion and killed scores single-handedly."

Rahl winced. "That . . . there was at least a battalion coming down the road through the swamp, and if they'd gotten through, they could have turned our flank. Third Company had to stop them. I just did what I could." Her question brought back images of the swamp, the ooze-traps he'd created, and the scores who had died, either at his hand or through his magery. He managed not to shudder.

"Rahl . . ."

He could sense the warmth behind that single syllable, but he still had to explain, even if the explanation wasn't enough. "It's just . . . I feel like you're trying to undo the damage that what I've been doing has caused. I know it's not true. I mean . . . I didn't cause the rebellion, and I'm not the one who wounded or killed our troopers, yet . . ." He shrugged, almost in frustration. "I'm supposed to be keeping and restoring order, and it seems as though what I'm best at is using it for killing and destruction."

"What were you doing today?"

"I briefed Taryl, then rode out to the water-master to complete getting the sewer repairs started, made sure that the portmaster started on dredging out that sandbar near the end of pier two, checked on the mage-guards, talked to several crafters and shopkeepers, looked over what the new undercaptain was doing . . ."

"All that builds order." She reached out and laid her hand on his.

The warmth of her touch gave him the courage to ask something that he had pondered more than once. "You've been most cautious with me, and I'm trying to understand and be patient, but at times . . . I feel as though . . ." How could he express what he felt? He swallowed and forced himself to go on. "I sometimes feel that it's not even between you and me, that there's something else, almost . . . someone else . . ."

Deybri nodded slowly, her eyes meeting his. "There was. Not anymore, not for years. The reason I went to Atla, one reason, was for Bhulyr. He was exiled, except he wasn't a mage. He wasn't much of anything, now that I look back. He was a junior trader, and he was assigned to the Merchant Association in Atla, and I thought I was in love with him. I begged, and I pleaded, and Uncle Thorl finally worked out something, and when I got there, Bhulyr had already taken up with the daughter of a local factor—and I had to stay for almost five eightdays. It was half a season that lasted a year."

"You'd only told me that you were a healer for a trading company," Rahl said evenly.

"I was. I needed more healing than anyone there. I was so in love with him. I would have done anything for him." Her voice turned thoughtful, with just a touch of bitterness. "Young women in love, girls, can be so stupid."

Rahl just listened. Had he taken advantage of Jienela in the same way? He tightened his lips. He had. He'd never thought of it in the way Deybri had put it.

"Rahl? You look so distant. What is it?"

"I was thinking. You must have heard how I ended up in Nylan, didn't you?"

"Not really. Leyla said that you'd gotten in trouble with a magister and used order in ways you shouldn't have."

"I did." Rahl didn't want to say more, but he had to be honest, especially after what Deybri had told him. "I also got a girl with child. I didn't mean to, but it was . . .

I didn't want to consort her, but I agreed that I would if she and her parents insisted. It never came to that. Her brothers attacked me—they were much older, and then, I didn't even know I was an ordermage. Magister Puvort actually used some sort of order to lower their self-control. Taryl thinks he did that because he didn't want to deal with a natural ordermage." Rahl forced himself to look squarely at Deybri. "In some ways, maybe I'm not any better than Bhulyr."

"Do you regret what you did? Honestly?"

"I am sorry I led Jienela on. Even though it was as much her doing as mine, it wasn't fair to her." And after what Deybri had said, and what he had sensed, he was even more regretful than he had been before. "I can't say I'm sorry about defending myself against her brothers or hurting them. I was trying to explain that we'd already arranged to talk to her parents. They didn't listen."

"Rahl . . . Bhulyr was never sorry. He wasn't capable of regret. He couldn't understand someone else's pain." Deybri put both her hands around Rahl's. "I could see what you felt just from my words. I didn't know why until you told me. So long as you feel like that, you'll never be like one of *them*."

"I . . . how can . . ." Rahl wasn't sure what to say. He had been one of them. He hadn't meant to be, but . . .

"Rahl . . . do you remember what I said to you when we first met . . . about your being almost a pretty boy?"

He could hear the quiver in her voice as well as feel the uncertainty and the anguish, and it tore at him. He nodded slowly, unwilling to trust his voice.

"I was so . . . surprised . . . taken aback . . . by what I felt in seeing you . . . that . . . I said what I felt. After Bhulyr, I'd been so cautious. I never thought I'd ever again see anyone who attracted me, and then to see you . . . and realize how much younger you were, I wasn't thinking, and I couldn't believe what I'd said." Her eyes dropped for a moment. "I just tried to pass it off. You knew better, and that frightened me. I'm supposed to be a grown healer, but, maybe, someplace deep inside, we're all still barely grown girls and boys."

"Maybe we are." He managed a smile. "Maybe we could still grow up together."

Her laugh was shaky, but it was a laugh, and he lifted his other hand to take both of hers in his.

LXXXV

Oneday morning was far more like a spring day than winter, although winter had several eightdays yet to run, with a warm and gentle breeze flowing through the open windows of the administrator's study. Taryl did look more rested, finally, and the deep circles under his eyes had disappeared, but he was more angular than he once had been—and Taryl had never carried any fat.

". . . and the patrollers will just have to put some of the troublemakers and cutpurses in one of the station gaols until one of the mage-guards can question them," Rahl concluded his summary of the mage-guard/patroller situation in Nubyat.

"Once the younger mage-guards get more experience, Chewyrt can change that."

Rahl nodded. "What can you tell me about Prince Golyat and the rebels?"

"As for the situation with regard to the rebels . . ." Taryl coughed, then continued, "Shuchyl should be in control of Elmari by now, but we haven't gotten any dispatches yet, either from the fleet offshore or from Shuchyl himself."

"If he has, when will we move on Sastak?" asked Rahl.

"Shortly," replied Taryl. "I expect we'll be able to begin mobilizing within a few days."

Taryl was waiting for something. That was clear. But

what? And why? "I've certainly appreciated the time here, but I almost feel guilty, ser, just waiting."

"Every tactics manual cautions against both unnecessary delay and impatience, but none of them define either one except in generalities, Rahl. That's because the terms can only be defined in context of the particular situation. Right now, both supplies and tempers are getting short in Sastak."

"We're blockading the port, but we're not cutting off their access to the surrounding land."

"You're right, and the land is fertile," Taryl pointed out. "It's one of the breadbaskets of Merowey and Hamor."

Rahl frowned.

"All their surplus grain and tubers were shipped out for hard coin after last fall's harvest. It is every year. There's not enough left for both the port and the troopers and their mounts."

Rahl wasn't certain that was the only reason for delay, but Taryl wasn't about to say more. "What will you be having me do?"

"Third Company will be utilized as it was in the attack on Nubyat."

"Standing by until needed, or until I figure out what to do, later than I should?"

"Something like that," Taryl said amiably. "Your abilities and the support Third Company provides are still largely unrecognized."

"After the wall?"

"Anyone on the rebel side who understood what you did is dead. Those on our side who know you did it won't be able to explain how it could have been your doing in any fashion that is believable to those who were not there. Thus, the credit, if one can call it that, will go to me or be attributed to someone of greater experience who is currently elsewhere, but who will be rumored to have been here." Taryl laughed, a sound that combined humor with a sardonic cynicism without being cold. "Feats of great and stupid strength are always attributed to the young, and those of skill and devastation to the old because that is what all, except the young, wish to believe." He stood, signifying that it was time for Rahl to head out on his daily duties.

Rahl rose quickly. "I'll see you tomorrow, ser, unless there's something urgent."

"Let's hope there isn't."

After offering a smile, Rahl left the study. He had only taken three or four long strides away from the study door and from Falyka and her ledgers and neat stacks of papers when he saw Deybri coming down the long corridor. He smiled and kept walking toward her. "Good morning." He stopped short, just looking into her golden brown eyes.

"Good morning, Rahl." An amused smile played around her lips, but beneath it was both warmth, and preoccupation.

"You have some problems? Besides me, that is?"

"Some of the troopers are getting something like a chaos-flux. It's not too bad, but when it gets warmer . . . more of them will start getting it. They really should be in real barracks."

"They'll probably be moving out before too long. That might help."

"It might."

"You could help my chaos, too," Rahl bantered, offering a grin he hoped was disarming. "You could accept my offer to consort you."

"Did you actually propose?" Her smile was amused, but he could sense the worry behind it.

"Several times, as I recall, if not exactly in those words." He paused. "You're worried about my proposal?"

She sighed. "A woman can't keep many secrets from you."

"I can sense how you feel, but not necessarily why," he pointed out.

"You know how I feel. I can't hide that from you.

Much as I want you, I still worry that your loins are playing a larger part than your head or heart." She leaned forward and kissed his lips, gently. "It's all very strange. In some ways, we've known each other our entire lives, even from before the first time we met. In others, we don't know each other at all . . ."

"If that's so . . . why did you come here?"

"Rahl . . . isn't it better to look for your heart's desire than to turn your back on it? I *think* and feel that you are, that our spirits could become one, but I want to *know* it, and I want you to know that as well."

"That's why I wrote you . . . and gave you the letters I never had a chance to post . . . the letters I wrote hoping I could send . . ."

"I've read them, and they help . . . They help a great deal." Her eyes were bright again.

He took her hands. "I'm sorry. You are my heart's desire—and far more than that." He swallowed. "I won't press you again, not because I don't want you for my consort, but because you know what I want, and I'll wait for your decision."

"Rahl . . . don't . . . don't look at me like that."

"Like what?"

"You know what."

He offered a contrite smile. "I'm sorry."

"How do I know? You're so self-contained."

Rahl just looked at Deybri, then dropped all his shields, letting her sense everything—the longing, the love, the fear that she would reject him—even the desire.

"Rahl . . . please." Her face had gone white.

"You wanted to know." Rahl eased his shields back into place. "How else could I tell you?"

The smallest of tears oozed from the corners of her eyes. "It's hard, Rahl. Being around you is like either being in pitch-darkness or blinded by the sun. With your shields in place, I don't sense anything about how you feel. Without them in place, what you feel overwhelms me."

What could he say? Finally, he just took her hand and squeezed it gently. His own eyes burned, and he swallowed.

She squeezed his hand back. "I'm sorry. That's not fair. You try so hard. It's me, not you. Please . . . I do love you. Please?"

He nodded.

"I should go. I have to tell Taryl what we need before he starts meeting with all the commanders."

Rahl released her hand, then turned and watched her as she walked past Falyka and into the administrator's study. After a moment, he made his way to the stairs, then to the stable.

After saddling the gelding, Rahl gathered his three troopers and went through his morning rounds, then made his way to the harbor to see if Chewyrt had anything to report. He hadn't even reined up outside the mage-guard station when Pemyla, one of the junior mage-guards, hurried toward him.

"Big cruiser coming in, ser," offered Pemyla. "It's flying banners, the Triad banners, it looks like."

"It is? I need to see." Rahl urged the gelding past the younger mage-guard and toward pier two. "If it is, the overcommander will need to know immediately."

After reining up at the seaward end of the pier, Rahl studied the banners, then turned and rode back to the waiting mage-guard and his three-trooper escort.

"Sovarth, you ride back and find Captain Drakeyt. Tell him that we'll need a squad to act as an honor guard for the Triads. And we'll need a carriage or a fancy wagon. Faslyn, you ride to the Administrator's Residence and tell his aide that both the High Command Triad and the Mage-Guard Triad are aboard the cruiser."

"Yes, ser!"

Rahl turned to Pemyla. "You need to inform Undercaptain Chewyrt immediately. Tell him that I've taken steps to inform the overcommander."

"Yes, ser."

Once Pemyla had hurried off, Rahl looked back at the cruiser, with its dark hull and white superstructure. Two Triads in Nubyat? That worried him.

He didn't like the idea of meeting the Triads personally, but someone had to, and he dismounted and handed the gelding's reins to Naimyl, the remaining trooper. "Go and tell whoever's on duty at the mage-guard station that we'll probably need a wagon for baggage or cargo and to have one ready. After that, just stand by where you're out of the way but can see when I'll need you. I'll wait here at the end of the pier for now."

"Yes, ser."

As Naimyl rode toward the mage-guard station, Rahl looked back at the incoming cruiser again, then shook his head.

Drakeyt arrived with first and second squads just as the *Ryalthmer* was doubling up the lines to the bollards on the pier. "The Triads?"

"Two of the three," Rahl replied.

"The administrator's carriage isn't far behind."

"Good . . . and thank you."

"I always did want to see the Triads. That way I can tell everyone that they pull on their boots one foot at a time. We'll form up here at the foot of the pier, one squad on each side. That will leave space for the administrator's coach at the end of the squads."

"And I can greet them and lead them to the coach."

"You sound most enthusiastic, Majer."

"I will be by the time I greet them." Rahl turned and hurried toward the cruiser.

He stood waiting until the gangway was swung into place. Then he waited some more until the two Triads appeared on the quarterdeck. Behind them were other mage-guards, aides of some sort, predominantly women, Rahl noted.

Finally, Fieryn strode down the gangway, followed by Dhoryk.

Rahl bowed his head politely. "Triad Fieryn, Triad

Dhoryk, welcome to Nubyat." He let nervousness play across the surface of the shields he was trying to keep hidden, as well as some worry. "As soon as we saw your banners we sent word to the overcommander and acting administrator."

"Taryl is handling three positions, again, then?"

"I beg your pardon, ser?" Rahl projected the slightest bit of confusion.

"He's always overworking himself and those around him." Fieryn's words carried amusement and condescension. "I'm amazed that there was even a senior mage-guard here to greet us." He glanced to the end of the pier. "And an honor guard as well."

"All Triads merit an honor guard, ser, as they should." Behind his shields, Rahl hoped he was treading the line between simple conscientiousness and worry in his projected feelings while not revealing how much he was concealing.

"That is something a few others should remember." Fieryn paused. "I've met you. You're Rahl, the one from the ironworks."

"Yes, ser."

"You've been in most of the battles, have you not?"

"Yes, ser."

"As Taryl's assistant, or with the troopers?"

"With Third Company, ser."

Fieryn's eyes dropped to the overlong truncheon at Rahl's belt. "That's right. An order mage-guard with skill in arms." He looked up. "Ah . . . I see that the administrator and his coach have arrived."

"For Taryl, that is positively punctual," murmured Dhoryk.

Rahl decided against commenting. "If I could escort you . . ."

"Lead on, Mage-Guard Rahl."

Rahl turned and set out to cover the two-hundred-plus cubits at a measured pace.

Taryl had indeed accompanied the coach, and he stood

beside it, waiting as Rahl led the way through the honor guard and to the coach. Taryl glanced at Rahl. "Thank you, Rahl. Report as usual before dinner."

"Yes, ser." Rahl stepped back.

"Greetings, Fieryn, and you, Dhoryk. You do us great honor in coming to Merowey . . ."

Rahl slipped away and back toward the *Ryalthmer*. Nor was he looking forward to dealing with either Triad's aides.

LXXXVI

With some relief, Rahl did discover that the aides to Fieryn and Dhoryk seemed to have no overt agendas but did insist on a greater briefing on the situation in Merowey than Rahl had expected. After dealing with them, he had to hurry through the rest of the day, trying to deal with the usual—the fact that no matter what he and Taryl had done, it never seemed to be enough. Even so, he did manage to return to Taryl's study well before dinner. That need had been clear from Taryl's words on the pier, since Rahl often did not report in the evening.

"Did either Fieryn or Dhoryk say anything of interest?" Those were Taryl's first words when Rahl entered the chamber.

"Fieryn asked if you were handling three positions. I asked what he meant, politely, but naively, and he replied that you overworked yourself, with the implication that you overworked everyone else as well. He said he was surprised that there was even a senior mage-guard on the pier. Dhoryk murmured something about your lack of punctuality, and Fieryn asked if I'd been in the battles, then remembered that I came from the ironworks and promptly seemed to lose interest in me. That was all."

"You didn't ever relax your shields?"

"No, ser." Rahl didn't mention that he wouldn't have dared after all of Taryl's emphasis on keeping them solid around older and more experienced mage-guards.

Taryl fingered his chin, then glanced out the window at the early evening clouds gathering out over the ocean to the west. "After Thalye, you asked a question. Do you remember it?"

Rahl managed to conceal a frown. What had it been? Oh, he'd asked if Taryl had been dissatisfied, and Taryl had told him that he had a lesson to learn, one that could not be taught. "Yes, ser." His words were polite.

"Good." Taryl continued to glance out the window.

"Did the Triads reveal anything new?" Rahl finally asked, knowing that Taryl did not intend to say more about that lesson but wondering why Taryl had brought the issue up now.

"Scarcely," replied Taryl. "We only talked in the coach, and they were more interested in finding out the situation here. They were pleased that you recognized the requirements of their status but suggested that Nubyat does need a permanent honor guard, among other things." The overcommander laughed.

"That would not be the highest of my priorities, ser."

"Nor mine, as you well know." After another pause, Taryl went on, "You handled the shields well enough. Neither of them realized that you actually had shields. But don't get too confident. They had other things on their minds, and had they really been concerned about you, they would have sensed more."

Rahl was both pleased and slightly irritated, but he kept the irritation behind his shields. How many times had he had to hold shields against powerful mages besides Taryl? "I'm still learning. I haven't been around many mages with abilities like yours, ser."

"That may be, but when you are, it may be too late to learn."

"Did they say anything else, ser?"

"They allowed me to pay my respects, and they'll be

joining me for dinner. We have a longer meeting scheduled for tomorrow when they're more rested. They feel
that they should be present when we confront Golyat in
Sastak."

That bothered Rahl, although he could not say why,
especially since that would place more strong mage-
guards against Golyat.

"That will make matters interesting, although it will
strengthen the forces we present to Golyat."

"I would not have expected them to come here," Rahl
temporized.

"They could not do otherwise once the port was open,
not and claim that they supported the Emperor." Taryl
glanced toward the door. "I need to prepare for dinner,
but I'd like you to plan on meeting at this time every day
while the Triads are here, in addition to the morning
meetings."

"Yes, ser."

After he left Taryl, Rahl went to find Deybri, but she
was not in the staff dining chamber, nor in her room. He
finally found her sitting on one of the stone benches in
the walled garden below the balcony off the grand dining
salon.

"I've been looking for you," Rahl said quietly. "Might
I join you?"

She nodded.

"I'm sorry about this morning," he said as he settled
onto the backless stone bench, straddling the end so that
he faced her.

"You have nothing to be sorry about. I'm the one . . ."

Rahl took her left hand, gently. What could he say? "I
didn't mean to overwhelm you, or upset you. The
shields . . . Taryl told me again, just a few moments ago,
that I needed to do better."

"Rahl . . . you do . . . but don't follow Taryl all the
way. . . ."

"You know something about him, don't you?"

"I asked him the other day why he had been so good

to us, and I told him that it couldn't have been just for the mage-guard and Hamor. He gave me a sad smile. Do you know what he said?"

Rahl could imagine, but he shook his head.

"He said that he'd once been too young and too driven. He almost said more. He didn't have to."

"That makes it so hard," Rahl said slowly. "I feel like . . . if I do what I must to survive . . . I'll lose you. If I don't, I'll lose you another way."

"You . . . you have to work on your shields. I can't . . ." She dropped her eyes.

Rahl could sense the effort she made to avoid tears. "I could just use partial shields," he offered, "when I'm with you, but I worry about that, too."

She lifted her head, and her eyes met his. "You can't do that. In time, I'd wonder what you were hiding, even if you hid nothing, and you'd try to protect me, and that would make me suspicious."

Hard as it was, Rahl just held her hand and waited, taking in her gold-flecked eyes and the warmth behind them.

Deybri turned more toward him and extended her other hand. She swallowed. "This is hard. I never thought I'd find love, and I never thought it would be so wonderful and so painful."

"I didn't, either."

She straightened slightly. "I've asked you to be honest, and I have to do the same."

Rahl winced within. Was she going to refuse him, to say that love wasn't enough?

"I'm not a great healer or a great mage, and you will be one, but you aren't yet." Deybri pursed her lips, and her eyes dropped, but only for a moment. "The kind of love we have, and will have, is not halfhearted. Nor is the kind of magery you possess."

As if a sudden light had illuminated the fading glow in the garden, Rahl understood where Deybri's words were leading, but he forced himself to listen, because Deybri needed to voice those words herself.

"You won't be complete, and who you should and must be, not until you finish what you've begun with Taryl. You don't do anything halfway, not anymore. If I become all of your life, now . . ." She shook her head.

"What do you see, then?" Rahl barely spoke the words.

"I . . . don't know. I only know that consorting you now is wrong, and not consorting you is even more wrong."

"You will consort me, then, when the time is right?"

"I can only say that I will consort you—but not until after whatever happens at Sastak."

I will consort you. Her thought was even stronger than her words.

Rahl could feel the burning in his own eyes, and he eased forward and enfolded her in his arms. Their lips met.

LXXXVII

Twoday passed rapidly, doubtless because Rahl felt as though he walked and rode without effort. Almost from the moment he had first seen her, he had known that Deybri was the only woman for him, but that had not meant that she had felt the same—or wanted to. Still, as he went about his duties, he did have to make an effort to keep from smiling all the time. He'd also had to promise Deybri that he would not talk about what the future might bring for the two of them until after the revolt was completely put down.

The joy of knowing of her love had momentarily distracted him from Taryl's inquiry about Rahl's question after the battle of Thalye, but he knew that Taryl had asked to jog him into thinking about it. As he entered the Administrator's Residence on threeday, Rahl was reminded once more. How could he have forgotten? He still recalled his reaction and how he had felt—as if he could never do enough to satisfy Taryl.

Taryl had just said something like, "Oh, that."

Why was Taryl bringing it up now, when Rahl was riding from point to point trying to get more things working throughout the city, when everyone wanted his or her problems resolved . . . ?

Rahl suddenly stiffened and stopped. That was it! No one, especially not an officer or an administrator, could ever meet everyone's expectations. After the past eightdays, that had become more than clear, but he just hadn't related it to what Taryl had said.

His smile was ironic as he started up the stairs. When he finally eased past Falyka and into the Regional Administrator's study, he found Taryl standing by the window, looking out at a gray sea under a greenish gray sky.

"Quite a good view, ser," Rahl observed.

Taryl half turned. "I actually would prefer the villa of the regional overcommander of the mage-guards, but people believe in symbols, and they need the symbol of a regional administrator in the Residence, temporary as that may be, since we'll be leaving to deal with Sastak and wiping up the last part of the revolt." Pointing to his left at the villa with the blue-tile roof, Taryl snorted. "That was more than large enough for me. It's considered quite modest, even if it is large enough for two families, with room to spare, not that the overcommander here has ever had a young family before."

Rahl looked. The overcommander's villa still didn't look modest to him—except in comparison to the massive Administrator's Residence. The smaller villa was still two stories with a blue-tile roof and a covered balcony terrace overlooking the harbor. It had its own carriage house and a walled garden, not to mention the nearby barracks with the quarters for three officers, one of which Rahl had been enjoying—and feeling guilty at times when he thought of how poorly the other officers were quartered.

"We've gotten confirmation that Golyat has indeed arrived in Sastak. Also, some of the forces that were to the southeast of here have withdrawn to Sastak. The fast frigate that arrived in the harbor early this morning carried a dispatch from Commander Shuchyl. Elmari is back under Imperial control. Even though he had Fourth Regiment as well as the Fifth, there wasn't much resistance, and the locals had actually captured some of Golyat's lackeys before the commander reached the city. . . ."

Something about that bothered Rahl, but a lot of things seemed somehow wrong to him, and he couldn't say why.

". . . the Fourth Regiment has been embarked on two cruisers and will be here tomorrow, and we will be setting out for Sastak on fiveday. Rather, you and Third Company will be, with the bulk of First and Second Army to follow on sixday." Taryl walked to the table desk, where he picked up a short sheaf of dispatches, which he then handed to Rahl. "I'd like you to go over these and sort through them. Set aside any that you think reveal a problem. I'd like your thoughts and recommendations on those." Taryl paused. "Those are the only copies, and I'll need them. Just use the table in the adjoining chamber. That was Golyat's aide's study. Leave both doors ajar, the one to the corridor and the one to this study."

"Ser?"

"I'm certain you've already noted that few indeed are to be trusted. While you're going through those, you're to keep full shields—the kind that only suggest you're a minor mage-guard at best." Taryl offered an ironic smile. "Try not to be more than that while you're looking them over."

Rahl barely concealed the wince he felt.

"Sometimes, Rahl, it's better to conceal power than

reveal it unnecessarily. That way you don't warn your
enemies." After a pause, Taryl added, "At the same time,
I'd like you to observe anyone who comes to see me, but
in a way that they don't notice."

"Yes, ser." Rahl didn't like the assignment, but he
smiled pleasantly, keeping his feelings behind shields.

"Good." Taryl stood.

Rahl walked toward the aide's study, and Taryl followed, closing the door after Rahl until it was ajar barely
a crack. Then Rahl settled into the wooden chair at the
table to read the dispatches.

The first was one Taryl had mentioned before—
Shuchyl's report on the taking of Elmari. The events
suggested that the port town had never been that strongly
supportive of Golyat, nor had it been that heavily gar-
risoned, even with the reinforcements of the harbor fortifications. Hadn't Taryl known that? Rahl frowned. Why
hadn't Taryl just attacked Elmari in the beginning? Then
he smiled wryly because he was thinking that Taryl had
been in charge of the campaign at the time. But Taryl had
not been and had not had that choice.

He set aside the first dispatch and began to read the
second, a short report from Commander Muyr relaying a
longer request from an engineer about the need for oils
and wax for fire-bladders to replace those expended in
taking the barricades.

Rahl read through five dispatches and picked up the
sixth, his eyes widening and his patience further evaporat-
ing as he read the long and pedantic harangue by a Commander Duchym, whom Rahl did not know, about the lack
of adequate quarters for senior officers in Nubyat, followed
by a recommendation that "appropriate" local dwellings be
requisitioned for said officers. Rahl set that aside and was
about to pick up the next when he sensed the approach of
powerful chaos-forces—the two Triads.

Rahl immediately allowed his surface feelings and
thoughts to dwell on the pettiness and the stupidity of
Commander Duchym, while still receiving what order-

chaos thoughts and impressions that he could. He also used his own order-senses to boost his hearing, a use of order within himself that should not be detectable, although in his experience even the strongest of chaos-mages were not so perceptive as order-mages in sensing order-usage.

"Triad Fieryn . . . Triad Dhoryk, please go in." Falyka's voice was coolly pleasant. "The Regional Administrator is expecting you."

"Most kind of him," murmured Dhoryk.

"Greetings, honored Triads," Taryl's voice was warm and welcoming.

Rahl could detect nothing beyond that, and he had to admire the fashion in which Taryl not only hid what he thought and felt but covered it with feelings to match his words and inflections.

"Greetings, most effective Acting Regional Administrator," returned Dhoryk.

From that point on, Rahl concentrated on trying to pick up information he did not know or words or phrases that did not quite ring true.

"You asked to be briefed on the schedule . . . will be heading out on sixday . . . Third Company leading with reconnaissance in force . . . anticipate two eightdays to reach the outskirts of Sastak . . . barring changes in the weather . . ."

". . . rather optimistic . . . I would say . . ."

"Taryl has been known for making his optimism work out, Dhoryk . . ."

"Most fortunately . . ."

"Would you prefer to join the advance, honored Triads, or to arrive by ship once we control the port there?"

". . . proceed with First and Second Army . . . would seem most efficacious in the case of unexpected magely opposition . . ."

". . . especially given the loss of mage-guards on both sides . . ."

". . . we have most of those with whom we set out . . ."

644   L. E. MODESITT, JR.

"Arms-mages of order, such as the fellow who met us on the piers, may well be overmatched in Sastak."

"That is always possible, and your presence will certainly strengthen our forces. . . ."

"What do you recommend for dealing with Prince Golyat?"

"That is a matter for you as Triads to determine, assuming that he is not killed in the attack or that he does not flee as he did from Nubyat. . . ."

". . . you plan to remain as Regional Mage-Guard Overcommander after this is resolved?"

". . . my future lies in the hands of the Triad and of the Emperor, as it always has . . ."

"Oh, you might be interested to know that Thasylt died rather unexpectedly several eightdays ago . . . just received word . . . might you have a recommendation for a successor?"

"You are doubtless more aware of those regional commanders who would work best with the current Triad, but I will most certainly give that some thought."

"Is there anything to which you do not give thought?"

"Very little . . . it's a bad habit of mine . . ."

Before all that long, the two Triads departed with more meaningless pleasantries.

Although Rahl gathered a vague impression of chaos-tinged dissatisfaction toward the end of the conversation from one of the Triads, he could not tell which one it had been. Even with his order-boosted hearing, Rahl had not been able to catch all that passed between the three in the Regional Administrator's study, ranging as the conversation had from mere routine civility to Taryl's brief outline of the planned advance on Sastak.

Rahl couldn't help but be pleased that neither Triad had even so much as directed a probe in his direction, and that they didn't seem to recall him, but it also suggested that they either didn't need to because they could sense who he was without trying—or that they were so arrogant that they felt everyone except Taryl was unworthy of notice. Neither possibility was particularly attractive.

As Taryl did not summon him, and since he had not finished with the dispatches, he went back to reading those remaining in the sheaf. In the end, he had five dispatches that he thought revealed matters requiring action beyond what he would have called routine.

He stood and walked to the door, still barely ajar, and knocked. "Ser?"

"Come on in, Rahl."

When Rahl stepped into the capacious study, he found Taryl leaning back slightly in the chair behind the table desk, but the older mage-guard immediately straightened. "You heard the conversation. What do you think? Honestly, and without either excessive caution or unnecessary vituperation."

"They both strike me as arrogant, particularly Triad Dhoryk. They talk as if the only force that matters is magery."

"Chaos-magery—or your kind of order-magery—can be rather effective."

"As I discovered at Thalye and Selyma, it is far less effective in many situations than large numbers of troops with sharp weapons, ser. It's most effective in limited areas."

"That is so. What do you suggest I do?"

"What you can, ser, without ever exposing yourself to what they might do."

"You do not trust our honored Triads, Senior Mage-Guard?"

"No, ser, but you know I am skeptical of those who hold power as an absolute right."

"You have mentioned that, if not exactly in those words. Now, what are you recommending on the dispatches I gave you?"

Rahl picked up Commander Duchym's dispatch. "Commander Duchym seems even more arrogant than the Triads. I would not wish his regiment to be the one left here to hold Nubyat. You might have to retake the city on your return."

"What else would you do?"

Rahl frowned. "Stipend him off, if possible. He doesn't sound like the kind who would listen to an explanation of how one doesn't sack one's own cities, even after a revolt, if one wants prosperity and the tariffs that come from it."

"He's Dhoryk's cousin."

"Have him lead the first charge in Sastak," Rahl said dryly. "Otherwise, keep him from any position where he has to exercise initiative or control."

"What else?"

"The fire-bladders. I suppose they should be replaced, but there will be more chaos-bolts in Sastak, I would judge, and I wouldn't recommend having them anywhere close to you or to large numbers of troopers."

"I would agree with that. What else?"

When Rahl had finished noting his observations and concerns and returned the sheaf of dispatches to Taryl, the older mage-guard set them on the table desk, and said, "Triad Fieryn wanted me to know that the Mage-Guard Overcommander for Matlana died unexpectedly. He asked if I had any recommendations for a successor. I told him that he was doubtless more aware of those regional commanders who would work best with the current Triad, but that I would give it some thought."

Matlana—that was the eastern region administered from Atla. "I heard him mention the death of someone called Thasylt, but I didn't know who that was. Was the overcommander that old?"

"He didn't die of flux or old age, I'd wager," replied Taryl.

Nor would Rahl.

"You need to spend the rest of today and tomorrow finishing up with all your duties around the city, and letting Chewyrt and the others know that they'll be acting on their own until you return. Don't forget to let them know that you will expect an accounting when you return."

"I won't, ser."

"You're having dinner in the private dining room, with your healer. The Triads and I will eat in the formal salon."

"Thank you."

Taryl smiled for a moment. "You'd better get on with winding matters up."

Rahl nodded, then turned and departed. Outside the study, he glanced down the long corridor but did not see Deybri. So he headed down the steps.

LXXXVIII

Dinner with Deybri on threeday evening was the most enjoyable Rahl could remember since he had eaten with Deybri seasons before, not so much because of the perfectly seasoned lamb burhka or the cream sylazas that constituted dessert, but because the question that lay between them was no longer one of consorting but of when that would happen. Rahl just enjoyed looking at Deybri and listening to her. Although he would have preferred more than that, he had those pleasures to look forward to, and he could still recall when even seeing Deybri's gold-flecked eyes and the warmth and intelligence behind them would have seemed the most impossible of dreams. Unfortunately, the dinner was too short, and fourday arrived too soon and was far too long, because Rahl had far too many loose ends to tie up—before getting ready to ride out with Third Company on fiveday.

He was up early on fiveday, early enough to catch Deybri in the staff dining room, he thought, but she had already left to make a last round of the wounded she would be leaving behind in Nubyat. So he ate quickly and headed to the stable to ready the gelding.

Even so, the stable was empty except for the gelding, and he had to hurry to saddle his mount and load his gear.

After he mounted outside the small stable, he sat in the saddle for a moment without urging the gelding toward the road to the east of the overcommander's villa, where Third Company was forming up. For several moments, he studied the overcast sky, both with eyes and order-senses. From what he could tell, the clouds were moving northeast, but there wasn't much water in them, and the breeze that caressed him was warm, but dry.

Then he urged the gelding forward, riding slowly to the front of the column and reining up beside Drakeyt.

Shortly, Quelsyn, the senior squad leader, rode up and reported, "All squads, all troopers, present or accounted for."

"Very well. Prepare to ride out."

"Third Company, ready to ride, ser."

"Third Company, forward!"

As the company rode past the Regional Administrator's Residence, Rahl glanced to the left to see if Deybri might be watching from somewhere. He neither saw her nor sensed her presence, and his eyes went back to the stone pavement before him. After riding past the Residence and the northern end of the parklike grounds that surrounded it, Rahl neared the wide turn in the road before it turned almost a full half circle and descended. From there, he could see Nubyat spread out below the promontory, a city of gray and green, although the light gray of the paved streets was almost white.

In the early morning, the loudest sound was the echo of hoofs off the stone and the sheer cliff face to the right of the road.

"Word is that you're going to consort the healer, Majer," Drakeyt said, as he and Rahl followed the outriders and scouts down toward the southern part of Nubyat.

Did the walls have ears? Probably eyes as well, Rahl reflected. "That depends on what happens in Sastak."

"If you return?" Drakeyt laughed. "If anyone is likely to return, I'd wager on you."

"She's with the overcommander's headquarters company as a healer," Rahl said. "Healing in and after battles isn't risk-free."

Drakeyt nodded. "And there may be attacks on the overcommander's position in Sastak. Is it true she came from Recluce?"

"Yes. Some of us have, over the years." Rahl wasn't about to explain how Deybri had come—or why.

"I can't say it makes sense to me," Drakeyt mused. "What you've done here is worth a couple of companies, if not more, and they just threw you out?"

"Not exactly." Even as he began to explain, Rahl had to wonder why he was defending anything about Recluce. "They felt that they couldn't train me without too much risk to Nylan, and Nylan has a few less people than Nubyat, although the harbor and port facilities are larger."

"Did they have to train you in Nylan?"

Rahl checked the paving stones as they rode past where the barricades had been, but the prisoner crews had finally removed all traces of the blackened residues. "I was already banned from the rest of Recluce because magisters in Land's End didn't like the way I'd used order, and Nylan is actually not much larger than Nubyat in size."

"They knew you had that kind of ability and tossed you out?"

"They thought I did, and they didn't want to find out." Rahl glanced ahead as they neared the southern square, his eyes searching for any patrollers who might be around. At least one should be. He saw several people on the covered porch of the larger inn, and he was pleased to see that none of the shops were shuttered.

Then he nodded, as he caught sight of the familiar mage-guard uniform.

From across the square, Saol raised his falchiona in a salute.

Rahl returned the gesture by lifting the battle truncheon, if briefly.

"Word was that you were the one really running the city." Drakeyt's voice was casual, but the curiosity behind the words was not.

"I just did what the overcommander wanted." Rahl offered a laugh. "And he wanted a lot done. He always has."

"They say—you told me—that he doesn't do anything without a reason."

Taryl never had. That was true, but . . . "He has more to worry about than Nubyat right now. I really didn't have much else to do except the duties he delegated to me."

"That's probably true."

Drakeyt wasn't convinced, but neither was Rahl, but he was afraid to hope that Taryl's assignments were to familiarize him with the city and might lead to his promotion to undercaptain or captain—perhaps in Nubyat. Still . . . it was possible.

"We'll just have to see." That was all Rahl dared to say, especially with the battles that still lay ahead determining the fate of the revolt—and his own destiny.

LXXXIX

Over the next three days, as Third Company scouted the road to Sastak, as well as the surrounding roads and lanes, neither Rahl nor any of the troopers and scouts found any recent signs of rebels. Every morning Rahl received instructions from Taryl, and every evening he reported on what he and Third Company had discovered and observed. The countryside and the steads were peaceful, with the buds beginning to open on the dwarf olives, foretelling the imminent arrival of spring. Rahl couldn't help but think that it would still be chill in Land's End, with frosts and even rimes of ice on the edges of the few streams.

On oneday evening, just after sunset, Rahl rode up to the White Stag—the larger of the two inns in the town of Cheystak and the one where Taryl had made his headquarters for that night. Even before he had tied the gelding to the hitching rail just below the inn's slightly raised and roofed front porch that overlooked the main square, he could sense the faint presence of both Triads.

Undercaptain Yadryn—whom Rahl had only met once or twice in passing—stood in the inn's foyer. "Majer, ser, the overcommander and the Triads are in the small dining area down the hall on the left. The overcommander said you were to report immediately."

"Thank you, Yadryn." Rahl offered a smile in passing, although he didn't relish the idea of reporting to the Triads as well as Taryl.

As he reached out to knock on the age-darkened oak of the door, Taryl said, "Come on in, Rahl."

Rahl stepped inside the chamber, closed the door firmly behind himself, and turned to face the three men seated at one end of the oval table. He inclined his head to Fieryn, then to Dhoryk. "Honorable Triads." He let concern seep from his shields, and a hint of apprehension, then choked it off.

"Proceed with your report to the overcommander, Senior Mage-Guard." Fieryn's voice was firm, but Rahl sensed something between boredom and indifference.

Barely concealed skepticism seeped from around Dhoryk's shields.

Rahl looked to Taryl.

"Go ahead, Rahl."

"Third Company has reconnoitered to a point fifteen kays south of here, some eleven kays short of Semistyd. The last rebel force passed through this part of Merowey more than an eightday ago, on the sixday preceding the last, and that was a loose grouping of riders in rebel

uniforms riding toward Sastak. They took supplies from
the local chandlery and left a form of script, but they did
not physically injure anyone. There have been no wagons or shipments of goods headed south on the road for
roughly two eightdays, and the last barrels of flour were
sent to Sastak almost four eightdays ago."

"*Roughly* and *almost* are rather general terms, Mage-
Guard," noted Dhoryk. "Is it possible to be more accurate in your reporting?"

Rahl paused for just a moment, keeping his astonish-
ment at Dhoryk's arrogance and lack of understanding of
the record-keeping, and lack of it, in small towns, well
behind his shields. "I could only be more accurate, honored Triad, if those whom we questioned—and their
ledgers—were more precise. When a ledger merely notes
that a shipment of flour was included on a wagon sent
from Sastak in the sixth eightday of winter, rather than on
threeday or fiveday of that eightday, and when no one
remembers exactly which day it was half a season past,
the precision that we all seek is rather difficult to obtain.
Only in one case was an actual date posted, and that was
for a wheel of cheese. That was, I recall, on threeday of
the seventh eightday of winter." He inclined his head politely.

Dhoryk turned to Taryl. "You really should think
about having the regional tariff enumerators crack down
on such sloppy bookkeeping."

"I appreciate your suggestion, Dhoryk," Taryl replied
pleasantly, "but you might note that those dates precede
my taking over as acting Regional Administrator. Not
even all the Triads acting together could change what has
already been shipped or how it was entered in ledgers, but
once this revolt is over, assuming that the Emperor de-
sires that I remain as Regional Administrator, I will certainly instruct the tariff enumerators to request more
accurate dating of all records applicable to tariff collection." He looked at Rahl. "What else did Third Company
discover?"

"None of the rebel forces have ever attempted to collect grain or other goods from steads, towns, or hamlets more than five to six kays from the main road. Nor are there any tracks or traces of rebel forces in those areas. This is likely to change, I would judge, once we reach Semistyd, because the east–west roads there are paved and well traveled. . . ."

"You would judge?" Fieryn raised his eyebrows.

"I can only make a calculated judgment, honored Triad, until we reach those areas and can actually scout and determine what has in fact happened."

"Then why guess? It is a guess, you understand?"

Rahl forced a smile. "I do so, ser, so that the overcommander can see what I plan and inform me if I am proceeding in a fashion contrary to his expectations."

"Why would you even consider proceeding contrary to his expectations?"

"I would not, and do not, honored Triad." Rahl inclined his head again. "But I have discovered that at times words and directions that seem perfectly clear have differing meanings to different people, even when both have the same goals and aspirations, and I would not wish to undertake any action where there might be a misunderstanding that could be avoided by my merely indicating the course of my actions under the overcommander's orders."

"Such caution is commendable." Fieryn's words were dry. "If not always possible. Initiative is sometimes preferable to caution."

"Could we obtain supplies without leaving the locals short through the spring and early summer?" asked Taryl.

"Here in Cheystak there are enough stocks of flour and oils, but the flocks and herds seem thin. There are more herders farther south, and their herds appear fuller, with yearlings and calves."

Taryl nodded. "I think that will do, Rahl. I will have further orders in the morning."

Rahl inclined his head. "Ser." He added, "Honored Triads."

Neither spoke or acknowledged his words.

After leaving the dining chamber, Rahl walked out through the foyer, across the front porch, down the two steps, and stopped, looking through the gloom of twilight toward the statue of an ancient emperor on his pedestal in the square. After a meeting such as the one he had just endured, he could understand why the magisters of Recluce thought so poorly of Hamor.

He glanced back at the inn, wondering if he could locate Deybri. He shook his head, realizing that he had no real idea where she might be and that searching for her would subject him to possible further scrutiny by the two Triads. That was not something to risk, not at that moment. With a sigh, he turned toward the gelding. He needed to return to the stead outside Cheystak where Third Company had billeted itself. He was more than glad for the distance between the company and the Triads.

XC

Early on twoday morning, while Third Company was gathering for muster, Rahl reined up in front of the White Stag. He had no more than dismounted and tied up the gelding when he sensed Deybri. He turned. She was standing on the porch in her healer greens.

He bounded up the two steps, but stopped short of embracing her when he sensed the worry and anger within her.

"Rahl . . . you know the Triads are here?"

"I had to give my report to Taryl last night with them present. It wasn't pleasant."

"They're . . ." She paused, as if unable to come up with a word or phrase.

"They're like everything the magisters said about Hamor?"

Deybri nodded.

"Taryl told me something interesting when I first was introduced to them," Rahl said quickly. "He said that they were the first chaos-mages to be Triads in ages. Most of the past Triads were order types, even though most mage-guards tend to be chaos-mages."

"Why did that change? Do you know?"

Rahl shook his head. "I think it had something to do with why Taryl had to step down or was replaced as a Triad, but I don't know that for certain, and no one whom I've met who knows will speak of it. I've heard scores of rumors, but—"

"Scores?"

"Several," he admitted, "and they're all different, and I've been told by those who should know that none of them are correct."

"Be careful around the Triads, Fieryn especially."

"Taryl's already suggested that. I think they're one of the reasons he was so particular about my working on my shields."

"He may be more dangerous than the Triads." Deybri had lowered her voice. "He sees more than they do, and I can't read him at all. He and you are the only ones whom I can't."

Rahl nodded. "Yet he's the only one who has never steered me wrong."

"He may be preparing you to use as the tool to regain his power as Triad."

Rahl had thought of that. It was more than possible. "What other choices do I have? Do you want to return to Recluce?"

She shook her head. "I find I trust him . . . and you. That is the most frightening aspect of it all."

"Trusting a disgraced Hamorian Triad and an exiled natural ordermage." Rahl forced a grin. "Kadara and Leyla would say that you're not in your right mind."

She reached out and took his hands, squeezing them warmly, but only for a moment before withdrawing them. "Please be careful."

"I will." He paused. "I need to report to Taryl."

"You'd better do it now. The Triads left him a few moments ago. Their shields were tight, but neither looked pleased, and I could sense some buried anger."

That alone reassured Rahl. He leaned forward and brushed Deybri's cheek with his lips. "Until later."

"Much later, I fear."

"Why?"

"There haven't been any battles, but there are so many troopers that someone is always getting injured, through accidents or quarrels or mishaps with mounts. And there are the cases of flux, and we don't want that spreading. The other healers are pressed. How could I not help them? It is either late before I'm done, or I've already fallen asleep."

"I have to report to Taryl most mornings," Rahl pointed out.

"I'll try to be around in the mornings . . . dearest."

Rahl hung on to that last endearment as he entered the inn.

Taryl was alone in the small dining chamber, seated at the table and surrounded by maps.

"Good morning, ser," offered Rahl as he closed the door behind himself.

"Good morning, Rahl. The Triads departed a short while ago. Fieryn in particular expressed that he was less than pleased with your report last night and your attitude toward the Triads." Taryl's words were pleasant and without chill.

"I was most polite, ser."

"Without speaking a word of description and without an unpleasant word or tone, you very politely and calmly conveyed that the most honorable Triad was the hindmost part of an unclean quadruped."

"Ser . . . what was I supposed to do? His questions

were designed in a fashion that any reply would either show total ignorance or total subservience."

Taryl smiled. "Actually, you behaved perfectly for the situation. Fieryn now believes that you are a third-rate mage-guard with delusions of superiority, and he has decided that I was absolutely correct in returning you to duty as an arms-mage with Third Company."

"I'm happy to follow your instructions, ser, but . . . do you think my future should lie as an arms-mage?"

"For now, that is where you will prove most useful, and out of the direct way of Fieryn and Dhoryk. As you should recall, I have noted that it is always useful to be underestimated by those in power who may not be either friends or allies."

"You honestly believe they have underestimated me, ser?"

"I do, and we had both best hope that is the case. They could be as much a danger to you as could Golyat and his mages."

"Because they seek greater power and because you stand in their way and I am your aide and ally?"

"There is great accuracy in that observation, but you need to observe even more." Taryl cleared his throat. "Your healer is most accomplished, and I hope that she will choose to remain in Hamor."

"She would like to do so, ser, but that will depend on what happens at Sastak."

Taryl softly barked a laugh. "Much will depend on that, perhaps the future of all Hamor and the world."

"The world?" asked Rahl.

"If the Emperor loses at Sastak, Hamor as it is will fall. That will strengthen Fairhaven. Recluce will rejoice to its eventual sorrow."

"Why would the Emperor's defeat lead to sorrow for Recluce?"

Taryl offered a crooked smile. "I leave you to think about that one. We had best concentrate on how to best avoid that possibility."

Rahl could tell that Taryl had said, as was often the case, what he would say. "What do you require of me and Third Company?"

"Continue the same duties as you have been doing. Unless you see signs that would indicate otherwise, you need not scout in depth up all the smaller side roads. It is becoming clearer and clearer that matters will be resolved in Sastak, and that it is unlikely that much of import will happen before."

"The rebels have not really prevailed in any battle, ser."

"That is true, but the winner is not the one who wins the battles, but the one who remains standing and in control when all the battles have been fought. Usually, that is the one who wins the battles, but not always."

"I'm to report to you this evening."

"As always." Taryl stood.

"Until then, ser." Rahl inclined his head, then turned and took his leave. He did not see or sense Deybri—or the two Triads—anywhere near.

As he rode back to Third Company, Rahl thought over Taryl's words, particularly his phrasing—"If the Emperor fails . . ." The more he thought, the less he liked the implications behind those words, and the more he understood what Taryl had meant beyond what he had said.

XCI

The next five days varied little. Third Company scouted, and First and Second Army followed after the scouting. There were no signs of rebels or mages or mage-guards, but there were fewer and fewer foodstuffs available from the local steads and growers. Because he was assigned to Third Company, Rahl was nowhere close to Deybri—or Fieryn and Dhoryk—during the course of the day. He usually managed a few words with Deybri in the morning, but only once in the early evening. As she had predicted, because there were too few healers for First and Second Army, she seldom returned to wherever Taryl had set up his headquarters for the night before Rahl had already reported and departed. Rahl had tried twice to wait for her, both times unsuccessfully, and resigned himself to their brief morning meetings.

Eightday morning, Rahl entered the less-than-impressive Growers' Inn on the main square in Gherama—a town known for onions so powerful that there was a regional description about them: "so hard-hearted a Gherama onion wouldn't bring tears to his eyes." While the inn seemed clean enough, the oak of the plank floors had been scrubbed and cleaned and washed—and then oiled—so much that the golden grain was lost behind years of labor and oil that left the floor a nondescript and shimmering brown. The glass of the windows was so old that looking through the panes, clean as they were, left Rahl with the impression of seeing the stable yard as through a fog—despite the fact that the morning sun was pouring light down through a clean blue-green sky.

Taryl had commandeered a corner of the public room and was talking to Commander Muyr. He looked up as Rahl entered. "Rahl . . . if you'd wait outside, the commander will let you know when we're done."

"Yes, ser." Rahl stepped back and glanced around the foyer outside the public room. There was not even a bench to sit upon, and the space felt uncomfortably warm, perhaps because he was wearing his riding jacket. Besides, waiting there might give the impression he was eavesdropping.

After a moment, he crossed the foyer and pushed open the door to the side porch. Once outside, he took the bench on the right end, the one farthest from the street and closest to the spice garden—as well as across the yard from the inn stable. As he sat there, letting his order-senses gather in impressions, he gained an increasing sense of the two Triads approaching. Could he observe them without being seen or detected . . . or at least without their realizing what he was attempting?

He tightened his shields and let a certain concern about scouting and what might lie ahead in Sastak swirl about above them. He added a worry about having to wait to meet with Taryl. Before long, Dhoryk and Fieryn strolled beyond the board fence on the back side of the spice garden, heading toward the stable.

Both held firm shields, but Rahl gained impressions of amusement, supreme self-confidence, and concern. He felt that the concern was focused on Taryl, but he had no way of actually determining that, and that feeling might well have been what he thought the concern might be, rather than what it was.

As the two reached the end of the board fence and began to cross the stable yard, Dhoryk's eyes flicked back to Rahl and the porch, but Rahl ignored the glance, as if his thoughts were elsewhere. Then the faintest of order-chaos probes touched him, and he ignored it, letting Dhoryk take in his worries about scouting and about why Taryl was making him wait. After several moments, the probe vanished.

Rahl let his order-abilities extend the sharpness of his hearing.

"He's more worried about Taryl than anything. Not all that many other thoughts in that head . . ."

"More than you might think, Dhoryk. Taryl has little patience for ignorance or incompetence."

"He's a more-than-competent scout and city mage-guard, and that makes him better than most mage-guards in this force—except for our assistants, of course."

"How could it be otherwise?"

"It could have been," Dhoryk replied, "if Taryl had cared more about himself."

"We're fortunate he didn't, but there's little point in speculating on what might have been. . . ."

At that point, the two Triads had walked beyond Rahl's order-ability to catch their words.

If Taryl had cared more about himself? More about himself than what? The Emperor? The Empress? Hamor?

Behind and to Rahl's left, the door to the inn opened, and Commander Muyr leaned out. "The overcommander is ready to see you, Majer."

"Thank you, Commander." Rahl stood and headed for the inn doorway and the day's scouting assignment, not that it would vary much until they were closer to Sastak— and that was still at least three days away, according to his calculations.

XCII

Scouts! Halt!" Just before midmorning on twoday, Rahl's order boomed out from the low crest of the main road that led to the port city of Sastak. He had just reined up, taking in the long ridge ahead and to the left of the road.

He and Third Company had left the marshy lands surrounding the town of Taskyl immediately after morning muster, heading south. They didn't have that far to go, given that Taskyl lay less than ten kays due north of the outskirts of Sastak, and that he'd just passed the kaystone that indicated the edge of the city was but five kays farther to the south. Until just a few moments before, Rahl had not seen or sensed any rebels, although he and the scouts had discovered that, until two days before, the rebels had been commandeering rice from the warehouses in Taskyl as well as other provisions from the holders within fifteen kays of Sastak.

A kay or so to the south, the long ridge ran from the northeast to the southwest, its flattened top a good sixty cubits above the drained rice paddies that stretched along the eastern side of the road for almost two kays and ended directly below the ridge. A grassy slope less than two hundred cubits wide ran from the far side of the drainage ditch bordering the road up to the top of the ridge, a distance of perhaps four hundred cubits. Rahl estimated that the ridge extended a good kay from the top of the grassy approach to a similar slope on the southeastern end. A third of a kay to the southeast, Rahl could make out what clearly had been a narrow watercourse, where some of the exposed stone was damp.

He shook his head. Of course, the rebels had dammed the stream, doubtless from a spring. That might have been another reason for choosing that ridge.

What was of greater concern to him was the sense of hundreds, if not thousands, of rebels located on the ridgetop—that and the three-cubit-high stone-and-earth wall across the top of the grassy slope. He could also sense at least two chaos-mages near the earthworks. Yet the road below and northwest of the earthworks was not barricaded or blocked in any way, although a strong chaos-mage could certainly have splashed a firebolt on anyone using the road.

As he waited for Drakeyt to join him, Rahl surveyed the area to the west of the road, but so far as he could tell, it consisted mainly of scores of rice paddies, many of which had been planted and refilled, and all of which were separated by dikes anchored by trees of a kind whose leaves never shriveled into silver-gray for the winter. He thought he could see the glint of sunlight off the ocean ahead and to his right, but it might have been the sun reflecting off more rice paddies.

Before long, Drakeyt reined up beside Rahl. "I see that they're dug in up there, some of them anyway."

"Close to a thousand, but it could be more." Rahl pointed. "I'd guess that they can reinforce the position from the far end there. I'll have to ride along one of those paddy dikes to get close enough to see about that."

"You'll take a squad with you?"

"It might not be a bad idea. Could you send Quelsyn or a squad leader to look over the paddies to the west? We don't need to find that there's a hidden road there."

"Like Thalye?"

Rahl nodded.

"Lyrn's pretty solid, and he's familiar with wetland growing. I'll send out fifth squad." Drakeyt glanced back at the ridge. "What do you think about the earthworks, Majer?"

"They've fortified the approach, and probably the one at the other end, but it's not as strong as the barricades at Nubyat. Stronger than what they had at Selyma. The north side above the paddies is too steep for a horse and too exposed for troopers on foot—unless we could attack along the entire perimeter, and I don't think we have enough troopers for that, especially if they have more than a few chaos-mages."

"I don't like this," murmured the captain.

Rahl didn't either. They'd seen no opposition for nearly two eightdays, and now they faced a fortified position that didn't even block the main road into Sastak. To Rahl, that suggested great confidence by the rebels. Had the whole campaign just been designed to lure the Imperial forces to this particular battle, well out of the way? Was something else going on in another part of Hamor?

"After I look over the southeastern end of the ridge, I'll see what else is down there. I'd appreciate it if you'd find out what you can from any of the growers around— if you can find any."

"We'll see what we can do." Drakeyt paused. "I trust you'll be careful, Majer?"

"As I can," Rahl replied.

Rahl didn't have to wait long after Drakeyt rode back to the main body of Third Company before Dhosyn and first squad rode forward to join Rahl.

"Ser."

"I'll be leading the squad on one of those paths on top

of the paddy dikes. We need to get far enough east to find out what the rebels have at the other end of that ridge."

"Yes, ser," replied the squad leader.

Rahl turned the gelding toward the dike that looked the widest and most solid, and that took him another two hundred cubits closer to the ridge before he could start eastward. He wasn't exactly comfortable leading Dhosyn and first squad in a single file along the top of the dike that paralleled the ridge. While the paddies held no obvious water, the exposed soil was clearly wet and muddy enough that a mount might well sink half a cubit into the mud—if not more.

As he rode, Rahl concentrated on picking up any signs of possible attackers or traps. While he kept checking, he neither sensed nor saw either. Nor were there any boot prints or hoof prints on the narrow pathway he followed. What he did pick up was the unmistakable fetid odor of waste or sewage, and he had the definite feeling that more than one kind of manure had been used over the years to fertilize the paddies.

The sun was warm, almost hot, and the combination of the stench and the heat left him sweating heavily and more than ready to leave the paddies behind when he suddenly experienced a chill—not a physical chill, but an order-chaos chill, the kind that came from the use of a screeing glass. After several moments, the chill passed over Rahl and the squad, suggesting that whoever was using the glass had not been looking for Rahl specifically, but for Imperial forces. Still . . .

Rahl kept riding and finally reached a wider area of ground where the dikes of four paddies intersected far enough eastward that he could see and sense the earthworks on the southeastern end of the ridge.

"Looks just the same, ser, doesn't it?" asked Dhosyn, who had moved his mount up beside Rahl's.

"They're almost identical in length, height, and construction." Rahl continued to study the approach. "There's a road to the base of the slope, and it looks to run straight south to the city and up to a flat space a half kay or so south of us." He wanted to take a deep breath, but decided against that as he eased the gelding onto another dike pathway, heading south. He didn't sense any rebels, and he needed to get closer.

He just hoped Lyrn hadn't run into any trouble in the paddies west of the main road.

XCIII

Late on twoday afternoon, Rahl dismounted outside a white-stone villa on a hilltop just to the southwest of Taskyl. Two headquarters troopers stood outside the small entry portico of the country estate. It had belonged to one of Golyat's local supporters who had fled, presumably to Sastak. Both the portico and the villa itself were roofed in a tile so light a gray that it was almost white. The outer walls were of a white stucco over stone, and the window shutters, though open, were of the same light gray shade as the roof tiles.

"Afternoon, Majer."

"Good afternoon. I assume the overcommander is here."

"Yes, ser."

Rahl stepped into the welcome shade offered by the portico roof, then through the doorway into the villa. Another undercaptain Rahl did not recognize sat behind a small table inside the foyer. He took one quick glance at Rahl and jumped to his feet. "Majer, ser!"

"Is the overcommander free for my report?"

"Yes, ser. He said to send you in whenever you arrived." The undercaptain pointed down a white-walled corridor.

"Thank you." Rahl smiled and turned down the corridor, wondering why an undercaptain he'd never seen was nervous and even frightened by his presence.

The study door was ajar, and Rahl called out, "Ser?"

"Come in, Rahl, and close the door."

Rahl did so, stepping into a small chamber no more than ten cubits by twelve. The white walls were bare, but the lighter patches of white suggested that paintings or hangings had been recently removed. The wide windows overlooked a walled garden. Beyond and below the lower wall was an expanse of rice paddies that had been drained for planting.

Taryl looked up from the map spread on the table desk before him, leaning back slightly in the wooden armchair. "You're back earlier than I expected. What did you discover?"

"We could take Sastak with minimal casualties and without confronting the rebels."

Taryl said nothing.

"There's a long ridge about six kays south of Taskyl and four north of Sastak . . ." Rahl went on to explain what he and Third Company had observed, using Taryl's map to point out the disposition of the enemy forces. He finished up with, "They've fortified the southwest end of the ridge at the top of the gentle slope that leads down to the main road, and there are embankments on the north side above the gentler slopes. But they haven't blocked the road to Sastak. We could ride past them and into the city. We might take a few losses, but not many. I worry about attacking their position on that ridge. We'll lose hundreds, if not thousands, if they fight as well as they have before."

"Unfortunately," Taryl replied, "you're probably right."

"We could just take the city," Rahl suggested again.

"I'm certain we could," replied Taryl. "And then what?"

"They'd hold the high ground behind us," replied Rahl, "but we'd still control the roads and the supplies."

"Rahl . . . how long has this revolt been going on?"

"Since last summer."

"We're now into spring. That's more than half a year. What would happen if we followed your suggestion and avoided fighting them in a pitched battle?"

"They couldn't stay on the ridge. They'd have to retreat in-country."

"Exactly. Through all those rice paddies, and those near-tropical swamplands farther to the southeast. How long would it take to chase them down? How many troopers would be tied up watching them? How many would sicken and die of swamp fever? How much in the way of supplies would we have to ship here to support the armies? Would we lose any fewer men that way?"

Rahl didn't have an answer to those questions.

"The Emperor can lose two ways," Taryl went on. "He can lose if we fight the rebels here and lose. He can also lose if we choose not to fight the rebels here, and the revolt drags on for another half year . . . or longer."

"But why doesn't Golyat retreat into the lands to the east, then, and drag matters out?"

"Because he loses as well, then. He won't be able to claim the support of the people and the merchants and factors. Both he and the Emperor lose that way, and that means that Hamor as a land loses even more."

"So Golyat's wagering that we have to fight and that he can win?"

"Exactly. If Golyat wins tomorrow, the Emperor's support will crumble. It's never been that strong—"

"Ser . . . he's the Emperor, isn't he?"

"Rahl. I think I pointed out before that no one rules except through others who carry out their will. The Emperor's present problem is that he needs the support of two of the three Triads. While Jubyl will support him, if we do not crush this revolt quickly, Dhoryk will turn from the Emperor because he believes that the High Command has not been given the coins and the resources to protect Hamor effectively, and many of the senior officers in the

High Command have already expressed those very concerns. Likewise, Fieryn has expressed concerns that there are more offenders against the Codex than previously because there are fewer mage-guards for the number of people, and without either a greater use of non-mage patrollers or a greater use of magely powers, order cannot be maintained. Either alternative is costly, one way or the other."

"Those sound like excuses to turn from the Emperor," Rahl suggested. "We've been using patrollers in Nubyat."

"Only as an emergency measure. Institutionalizing that across all of Hamor would create great unrest among many of the mage-guards, and it would upset the people as well. They know that a mage-guard can tell what is true and what is not, and they would fear patrollers who could not and who might be bribed. Fieryn's and Dhoryk's reasons may sound like excuses," Taryl continued, "but many with power and coins would support such excuses if the Emperor does not show himself as strong and effective. Letting a revolt continue when one has a chance to end it decisively would reinforce the concerns of both Triads. While neither has spoken to me of this, I believe that they are here to see if I will, as the representative of the Emperor, act decisively." Taryl offered a wry smile. "There's also the practical consideration. If we let Golyat escape and refuse a decisive battle, we'd have to ship in rations on a massive scale, and that would please no one, or we'd have to seize grain, livestock, rice, and tubers from the local growers over an area of close to a hundred kays by a hundred kays."

"Seize? We've offered script before . . ."

"After a few eightdays, the food becomes more valuable than the script, and if we paid what it would be worth, the cost would be as much as shipping rations, if not more."

Was war always a matter of coins? Or did the coins just provide the measure of what was lost in war? Rahl leaned toward the second, but he wasn't so certain that some favored the first.

"Now . . . how many men are on this ridge?"

"Earlier today, there were no more than two thousand, if that, but there are two roads from the south—the main road from Sastak and a farm road. They both can be used to reinforce the ridge, and while we were scouting I could see another battalion moving into position. They have one mage using a screeing glass as well, and his detection of Third Company—"

"You didn't try to find out anything, did you?"

"No. I just kept my shields tight and took in what I could. He kept coming back to us when we got close to the southeastern earthworks, then seemed to lose interest once we headed back north."

"Was he focused on you?"

"No, ser. It seemed to be on the entire squad, at least from what I could tell."

"Let us hope so. What else?"

"The rice paddies to the west of the road are flooded, but we could see no trace of rebels or encampments there. . . ." Rahl described the total lack of rebel presence north of the ridge, giving as many details as he could. "That's what makes this all so strange. They've collected food and supplies, but there are no outlying posts or forts and no sign of scouts."

"Given Golyat and Ulmaryt, that's less than surprising. He's rather good with the screeing glass. Besides, what's really the point of scouting when we have to attack them?"

"To see how many troopers we have," suggested Rahl.

"They either destroy us, or they don't. Our force is more than a third smaller than when we set out, and that must give them confidence."

"Why hasn't Dhoryk sent reinforcements?"

"Because there aren't that many to send, and those that there are wouldn't add a great deal."

No more to send? Rahl found that hard to believe.

"Hamor can support a mighty fleet or a mighty army, but not both," Taryl said. "The fleet keeps us prosperous because it protects our trade. The army regiments, while necessary, are a drain on the land, because the mage-guards keep order with fewer coins." He paused. "Is Recluce any different?"

Rahl knew Recluce followed that philosophy, but he hadn't considered that Hamor did as well.

"I can tell that I've made you think," Taryl said dryly. "Go and do so elsewhere for a time. But stay around the villa, because I've arranged for you and Deybri to join me for a short evening meal before the commanders' briefing, and it won't be that long before we eat. You will be the one to brief them on the disposition of the rebel forces. Do not voice any conclusions whatsoever. Just point out what is where and what is not, and only answer any questions from the Triads by repeating the facts, and saying that those are the facts, and that decisions about how and why are to be made by those in higher authority."

"Yes, ser."

Taryl gestured toward the study door, and Rahl inclined his head, then slipped out.

Once in the corridor, he debated what he should do until they ate. He wouldn't have had enough time to ride back to the stead housing Third Company, and yet, just standing around seemed . . . wasteful. At the same time, he had the feeling that the dinner with Deybri was more than a gesture by Taryl, but even if it were not, he appreciated the invitation.

He surveyed several rooms, all of which retained the majority of furnishings, but none of the artwork or hangings, and finally settled himself in a comfortable chair in the front parlor to try to puzzle out what lay behind Taryl's words, because something always lay behind the overcommander's words.

Golyat—or his advisors—had obviously known that the High Command was well provided with warships and less well provided with troopers, but the troopers Rahl had encountered were all well trained and able— far more so than the rebels they had fought, even given that at least some of the rebel forces had to have been former High Command troopers. Under those circumstances, several things made more sense. Sending Rahl out with Third Company had been designed to reduce unnecessary casualties. By the same token, the traps set by the rebels had been planned with the idea of reducing the number of troopers while not reducing the rebel forces. Fieryn and Dhoryk were present, not because they cared for Taryl or even for the Emperor, but presumably because, if Taryl failed, they also risked losing power and position, either because they would be linked to the inability to subdue the rebels or, in the worst case, because Golyat would not retain Triads ostensibly loyal to the Emperor. That also suggested that the two Triads and Taryl were aware of far more mages in the rebel forces than had appeared heretofore, and that meant the result of the coming battle would be anything but as certain as those that had preceded it.

Rahl was trying to consider what he had not seen, his eyes directed out the windows into a small walled garden, but not really seeing the early spring flowers, thinking over what Taryl had not said when he heard steps and sensed Deybri. She'd barely crossed the foyer when Rahl met her.

A warm smile appeared. "Taryl said you'd be here."

Rahl embraced her, and for a time they were lost in each other.

Deybri was the one to slip back. "I'm a mess."

"I didn't notice." Rahl heard a set of chimes in the background, but he concentrated on what Deybri was saying and feeling.

"I'm grateful for that."

"It is time for dinner." Taryl stood behind them, beside the parlor door.

"Oh . . ." The most fleeting feeling of embarrassment

and confusion accompanied Deybri's inadvertent syllable. "I didn't know . . ."

"I can understand why." Taryl gestured. "We are limited to the main dining chamber." He turned.

Rahl and Deybri followed, holding hands.

The dining chamber was modest—for a villa—with
the same white walls and a green-tile floor that had once
been covered by some form of carpet—and a table that
had six chairs on a side and two chairs with arms at each
end. The end farthest from the archway off the main hall
was set for three. All three settings had pale cream porce-
lain platters, rimmed in green, with a crystal wine goblet
for each as well.

Taryl took the seat at the end of the table but waited
for Deybri to seat herself. "It's very much a treat to have
a beautiful woman at dinner."

Deybri inclined her head slightly. "You say that with
such gallantry."

"That does not mean it is not sincere, although I need
gallantry because I cannot express my pleasure merely
by looking in the way that your intended does. I can tell
you," Taryl finished as he seated himself, "that I have
never seen him look at any other woman that way, even
the Empress, and she is most beautiful."

While there was nothing in the tone of Taryl's voice
nor any indication of feeling other than pleasantry, Rahl
wondered just what emotion lay beneath the overcommander's shields.

"You are kind to include me with the Empress, but I
doubt I merit such comparison."

"You do," Rahl said quietly. "Although she is most
beautiful, so are you."

"That is something I would not argue with Rahl about,"
added Taryl with a laugh. He lifted the crystal pitcher and
poured the amber wine into Deybri's goblet, then Rahl's,
and finally his own. "I'm told that this is a fair wine. The
best of the cellar departed with the previous owner."

At that moment, an orderly in a trooper's uniform

brought in a large platter, setting it before Taryl, then returned with two other casserole dishes, and a basket of a thin hard bread, broken into irregular chunks.

"It's a southern pickle-spiced fowl, with crispy-sticky rice and orange sauce," noted the overcommander, serving Deybri, then himself. "The bread is a local specialty. It helps in scooping the rice around."

"I've never had this before," Rahl admitted, taking a healthy portion of the fowl and rice.

"Neither have I," replied Taryl, "but the cook here insisted that no one should visit the southwest without having the best southern fowl—and hers is the best. She was most insistent upon that."

Deybri smiled faintly, but Rahl could sense apprehension behind the smile.

The orderly reappeared, but only to light the bronze oil lamps in the wall sconces.

Rahl attempted to use a bread fragment to scoop up the orange sticky rice, but the rice was more solid than he had thought, and fragments of the hard and thin bread—more like a smooth cracker—splintered across both his platter and the table.

Deybri smothered a smile.

"It is sticky and solid," Rahl admitted. "Tasty . . . but solid."

"I don't think I'll mention that to the cook," Taryl said.

The conversation remained confined to the food for the rest of the meal because Taryl only discussed the food and how it differed from cooking in the north of Hamor and because Rahl would have felt most uncomfortable bringing up some of the questions he had, especially since he knew Taryl was unlikely to answer them.

The main course was followed by pearapple-lime tarts.

"That was most satisfactory," Taryl said, after finishing the last morsel of his tart. "And now . . . to the briefing." He looked to Deybri. "I would like you to take the chair by the archway, as if you were monitoring and watching, but I would ask your concentration on those at the briefing."

"Yes, ser."

Rahl could sense both her willingness to observe and her curiosity at Taryl's order.

"And after everyone leaves, just return to my study and wait for me."

Rahl and Deybri nodded.

The three did not have to walk far to reach where the briefing would take place—just down the dimly lit hallway to the large salon in the villa, where several chairs had been added to the settees and armchairs already in place. A map board had been set up on what had been a dining table and propped at an angle with heavy square stones. All the wall lamps had been lit, imparting a warm glow to the salon.

"Take a good look at the map, so that you can easily point out where the rebel forces are," Taryl said to Rahl. "Then sit in the straight-backed chair on the end there and wait. Practice looking polite behind your shields."

"Yes, ser."

The first officer to enter was Commander Muyr, and the second was Shuchyl. Neither more than glanced at Rahl in passing, although he did sense a certain veiled curiosity from Muyr. The other seven commanders followed quickly. Only after the nine commanders had arrived did Fieryn and Dhoryk make their appearance, walking to the two armchairs that constituted the middle of the semicircle of chairs.

Taryl waited several moments, then stood and addressed the senior officers. "Before we discuss the plans for the attack on the rebel positions north of Sastak, Majer Rahl will brief us on their positions and disposition of forces." Taryl nodded toward Rahl.

Rahl stood and walked to the map board, then half turned, taking a position from which he could both point to the map and still address the commanders and Triads.

"The rebels have fortified this ridge four kays north of the outskirts of Sastak. The ridge extends a kay from one end to the other and runs from the southeast to the northwest, with the northwest end sloping down to the main road between Nubyat and Sastak. . . ." Rahl followed Taryl's instructions as precisely as he could, providing the geography and the facts as he knew them and offering no opinions or judgments. When he finished, there were a number of questions.

"How does the eastern farm road compare in the ability to hold riders to the main road?"

"Are there any obvious sources of water on the ridge?"

"Exactly how steep are the approaches?"

After answering the last of the questions, Rahl inclined his head to Taryl.

"That will be all, Majer. Stand by in the event some factual issues about the terrain arise."

Rahl returned to the end seat, thinking about how intently both Dhoryk and Fieryn had followed his description. Yet neither had asked a question.

Taryl stood once more. "Golyat is challenging us to a battle. That much is clear. While there is some risk attached to attacking, the position that the rebels have chosen limits their capabilities even more than it does ours. The slopes to the ridgeline are comparatively gentle and easily traveled by mount. They are narrow enough, however, that our mage-guards can provide some protection against chaos-bolts. . . ."

Rahl listened as Taryl described the plan, if a direct attack up two open slopes could be considered a plan. The overcommander did propose a series of smaller attacks initially, both to draw out the archers and chaos-mages and to minimize the impact of chaos-bolts, then the use of spread formations because chaos-attacks would have far less effect when the troopers were spread apart until they reached the earthworks.

After he finished, the first question came from a gray-ing commander Rahl had seen but never met personally. "I will submit that, if we intend to attack, Overcommander, your plan is the best that is possible. I question why we need attack at all. We can bypass the ridge, take the city, and wait."

"For how long?" asked Taryl softly. "Every day that the fleet must patrol costs hundreds of golds. Without such patrols, Fairhaven will send more mages, like those who have already killed hundreds of troopers. In addition, I have been reminded that Jeranyi pirate attacks against our merchanters are increasing, especially in the Eastern Ocean, because of the warships tied up in the blockade of the rebels."

"Overcommander," offered Fieryn, "perhaps you might explain some of the other losses involved."

"Thank you, honored Triad." Taryl inclined his head. "As a result of the rebellion, the Jeranyi have taken ten more ships in the past season than ever before. Each of those ships carried an average crew of twenty, as well as close to twenty passengers. That amounts to four hundred innocents dead. The loss of ships and cargoes to our factors from just those ten vessels exceeds fifty thousand golds. The loss to the Imperial treasury is estimated at more than five thousand." Taryl's words became harder. "Even with healers, for every half season, a force in the field loses a minimum of one trooper in twenty to disease, desertion, and accidents. Following your recommendation will require at least an additional season, and will not necessarily end the revolt, since we cannot patrol that effectively a perimeter of over three kays night and day for a season with the manpower we have. In addition, occupying Sastak will result in additional costs, not to mention that it will result in less support for the Emperor from an area that has not been that supportive, and that will require even more golds in the future."

"Begging your pardon, Overcommander—"

Rahl could sense a whiteness around and within the

commander, something not present in any of the other commanders.

"Commander Hyksyn, we will attack tomorrow. Since you are clearly uncomfortable with that decision, you are hereby relieved, and Majer Deolyn will assume command of Third Regiment, effective immediately."

"You can't—" Hyksyn abruptly swayed on his feet, then sat down hard, shaking his head.

Rahl could only admire the speed and force of the unseen order-bolt that Taryl had projected.

"Majer Rahl, please escort the commander to the protective detail waiting in the foyer. Captain Healer Deybri, I'd like you to check the commander before he is confined to assure his health."

"Yes, ser."

Rahl moved beside the shaken commander, then grasped his arm and eased the older man to his feet. "This way, ser."

Hyksyn tried to speak, but could not manage a word until Rahl had him in the hallway outside. "You . . . you're . . . one . . . of them."

"I'm a mage-guard and a majer, ser, and I'm loyal to the Emperor and the overcommander."

". . . so many will die . . ." whispered the commander, shaking his head. "So many . . ."

Rahl caught a glimpse of the man's unguarded thoughts and feelings—and froze for a moment. While those feelings were indeed Hyksyn's own, they had been twisted and turned by chaos, then further scrambled by Taryl's order-bolt, so much so that Rahl had the feeling that the man was but a shadow of his former self. Who had used so much chaos on him? And when?

Rahl understood Taryl's actions because a vacillating regimental commander could be a disaster.

"Let me see him, Majer." Deybri's voice was cool as she appeared beside the two.

"He's been hammered by both order and chaos," Rahl whispered.

Deybri order-probed the still-dazed commander as Rahl continued to walk him toward the main foyer. Rahl could sense her anger and consternation.

Rahl recognized the captain who led the guard detail waiting in the foyer—Alfhyr, the older and perceptive captain he'd met at the High Command headquarters south of Cigoerne.

"Ser, is this the officer requiring a protective detail?"

"The commander suffered some sort of seizure," Rahl improvised. "He'll need to be confined and watched until he recovers. He may need a healer now and again."

"Yes, ser. We can take care of that."

"I'll need a few moments with him," Deybri said.

"I'm fine . . . just need some rest . . . have to get ready for tomorrow," insisted Hyksyn. ". . . be just fine." His words slurred.

"We'll make sure you get that rest, Commander." Alfhyr's voice was reassuring.

Deybri rested her hands on the commander's forehead, and Rahl could sense the order, and the sense of calm. Abruptly, the commander slumped, and Rahl barely caught him.

"He should sleep for a while," Deybri said. "I don't know how long."

"We'll make sure he won't hurt himself, Majer . . . Healer." Alfhyr turned to the two burly troopers behind him. "You'll need to carry him."

"Yes, ser."

Rahl and Deybri watched as Alfhyr and the four troopers departed with the unconscious commander.

"Why did they pick him?" murmured Deybri. "Because he was the most concerned about his troopers?"

"That made him vulnerable," suggested Rahl.

"That's horrible. I know it happens, but it's still terrible."

"It is, but the magisters in Nylan aren't any better." Rahl paused, thinking about the guard detail that had been waiting. "He *knew* something like this would happen," Rahl murmured to her. "He knew."

"He's able to foresee, almost as if he had the same powers as Ryba." Deybri's voice was low.

Rahl wasn't certain of that, or that the legendary Ryba had even had such powers, but Taryl had certainly anticipated both the question and the commander's reaction.

They returned to the archway into the salon and listened while Taryl answered the remaining questions—all about logistics and implementation. Then, as the commanders and the Triads rose, they eased away to the study Taryl had been using.

After fumbling with a striker, Rahl did manage to light the lamps, then offer Deybri a quick embrace, but only that, before Taryl returned.

The overcommander sank into the chair behind the table desk. He cleared his throat. "What did you think of the briefing?" His eyes went to Deybri.

"The commander was twisted with chaos," Deybri said. "It was done recently. It might have been done today. That was why he was confused. It was also why your order-bolt had such an effect. I managed to soften the worst of both. He'll probably sleep well into tomorrow."

"Good." Taryl nodded. "He won't be able to do any more damage to himself, one way or the other. I'd appreciate it if you would just report his sudden collapse as a form of brain flux or something like it. That way, there won't be any question about his getting a stipend."

"Who did it, ser?"

"Whom do you suspect, Rahl?"

"It was chaos-based, and it was recent, and I haven't sensed any strong chaos presences except for the Triads."

Taryl offered a wry smile. "Do you wish to accuse a Triad?"

Rahl wanted to, but he had no proof of which of the two it might have been.

"Exactly," Taryl replied. "By the way, Third Company will be held in reserve, just forward of the headquarters company, but farther on the flank so that you will have a clear line at the rebels. I've already sent the orders to Captain Drakeyt. Do you think he would make a good battalion commander?"

"Yes, ser."

Taryl nodded. "That will have to wait." After the briefest pause, he asked, "What else did you notice?"

"Both Triads paid great attention to me and to you and to what we said," Rahl replied.

"Neither one reacted to what happened to Commander Hyksyn," added Deybri.

"But they wouldn't," mused Rahl. "If one of them did it, he wouldn't react, and neither would the other because . . ." He knew there was a reason, but he couldn't find a way to say it.

"Precisely," replied Taryl. "What about the commanders?"

"From what I could sense," Rahl said, "the others agreed with you, not just on the surface, but deeper, that your plan makes the best of a bad situation."

Deybri nodded. "Commander Muyr is saddened by that, but committed to support you. Commander Joarsyl just wants to punish the rebels."

"His consort died unexpectedly sometime after we left Dawhut," Taryl said. "His anger will be . . . useful. Sixth Regiment will be the one to make the second full attack. Did you notice anything about Commander Shuchyl?"

"He has little love for the rebels. He'll back whatever he thinks will end the revolt quickly," offered Deybri.

"Commander Pioll?"

"He is very reserved, but loyal . . ."

After a time, Taryl yawned. "I need some sleep, and so do you two. You can stay here, but don't talk too late." He stood.

So did Rahl and Deybri.

Taryl closed the door on his way out.

Rahl turned to Deybri.

"Not . . . not yet." She smiled nervously in the lamp-light. "Uncle Thorl . . . he told me when I left Nylan that I was taking a great risk. He said he loved and respected me for that because one seldom found great love or happiness or achievement without risk." Deybri's golden brown eyes caught Rahl's. "He didn't tell me that it could hurt so much. I knew it could, but knowing isn't the same as feeling. What if you don't come back?"

Rahl choked back the first thought that came to mind—that if he didn't come back, he didn't come back. Instead, he said, "We wouldn't have had even this if you hadn't come."

"I want more than this." Her words were quiet, but the intensity behind them burned through Rahl. "I want you. I want you, and me, and our child, but I can't and won't raise our child—your child—by myself. . . ."

"You're saying that I'd better survive."

"You can do more than that. You have to." Her words held hope—over a buried desperation.

Rahl stepped forward and enfolded her in his arms, then kissed her gently.

Her fingers dug into his back, so tightly was she holding to him.

"I'll be back, and you won't have to worry."

"How can I not worry? Even Taryl's worried."

"You can tell?"

"Not with his shields, but from the way he looks, the way he forced himself to eat at dinner."

"He worries about everything." Rahl kissed her again, gently. They had so little time, and yet . . . he had to respect her wishes and her feelings. He had to act as if there would be a future, when, for the first time, he truly had doubts.

XCIV

Rahl, Drakeyt, and Third Company joined up with Taryl's headquarters company just at dawn and began the ride to Sastak. Rahl thought he could sense Deybri somewhere behind him, but where, he could not have said.

"What do you think we should expect?" asked Drakeyt.

"More magery, more chaos-bolts, and high casualties." Rahl glanced up at the sky, now a deep green-blue with a touch of a silvery haze ahead to the south. "They want to destroy us, and we have to destroy them."

"Like always," snorted Drakeyt. "Someone's not happy that he doesn't have what he wants and thinks he should have. So he'll kill thousands trying to get it, and if he succeeds, he's a great conqueror and hero. . . ."

"Of course," replied Rahl. "The ones who win are the ones who hire the scriveners and the printers, and they're not interested in the facts, just in what they believe to be true."

"Do you think what anyone believes to be true is indeed true?"

"Seldom, if at all."

"It sounds like you don't believe in truth, Majer."

Rahl had to think for a time as they rode. He certainly believed that one had the choice between telling the truth or a falsehood, but he had trouble with the whole idea of "truth." The magisters of Land's End had an idea of what truth was. So did the magisters in Nylan, as did Taryl and what he believed about the *Mage-Guard Manual*. Doubtless, Golyat had his own ideas of truth, and so did the Emperor, but how many of them would agree on what the "truth" was? If the rain fell, and Rahl said it fell, that was truthful, and all the magisters, and rulers, and mage-guards would agree on that. But was it "truth-

ful" for Taryl to say that the Imperial forces had no
choice but to attack the rebels on the ridge? Taryl hadn't
said that, only that it was the only feasible option, but
Commander Hyksyn had disagreed. Had his thoughts
not been scrambled, he would have agreed, burying his
doubts.

"You're being pretty quiet," suggested Drakeyt.

Rahl forced a laugh. "I was thinking about truth and
not getting anywhere with those thoughts."

"Thinking too much isn't good for a trooper. The secret of being a good officer is knowing how much to
think and when. When you're an undercaptain, it doesn't
matter what you think; no one will listen. As a captain,
the only thinking they want is on how best to carry out
your orders." Drakeyt paused, then went on. "I suppose
that's true of senior officers as well."

Rahl merely nodded.

As they rode closer to Sastak the sun rose over the
drained rice paddies to the east and the low rises that
were barely hills. The water-filled paddies to the west
shimmered bluish in the long morning light. By the time
Rahl could see the ridge that lay between the Imperial
forces and the town, he could also sense a massing of
men and of chaos, although the chaos seemed to be
greatest at each end of the ridge, just above the grassy
slopes leading up to the rebel earthworks.

The number of rebel troops seemed to be far greater
than that of the Imperial troops moving into position.
Based on what Taryl had said, it seemed likely that many
were effectively conscripts and not so well trained, but
poorly trained conscripts could be used effectively to
weaken mages and overwhelm archers.

The bulk of the Second Army—under Taryl—formed
up along the road to the north of the western end of the
ridge, while First Army under Commander Muyr moved
into position near the eastern end of the ridge. Third
Company took a position on the right flank, forward of

the headquarters company, and then received orders to stand down.

Rahl could sense the controlled and muted chaos-forces of the two Triads somewhere behind him, probably under the two canopies used by Taryl. The air was still, warm, and heavy, so that, early as it was, Rahl was already sweating as he stood beside the gelding, waiting, as were all the troopers in Third Company. He took a long swallow from his water bottle, then corked it, and replaced it in its holder.

Beside him, Drakeyt murmured, "We wait too long, and we'll all sweat down to nothing."

"It could be that's what Golyat hopes." Rahl doubted that, but Drakeyt had wanted some sort of response. It was far more likely that the rebels would follow the same strategy as always: Let the Imperial forces make the first moves and then try to carve away the Imperial forces until they could no longer press the attack. Once that happened, the rebels would try to use superior numbers and chaos-magery to annihilate the Imperials.

A series of trumpet triplets ordered the first charge, and a company of troopers rode up the slope at a measured pace, spreading apart as they advanced. They continued to close on the earthworks. When the leading riders were less than three hundred cubits from the earth and stone ramparts, arrows began to sleet down, and the troopers immediately turned their mounts.

From what Rahl could tell, only a handful of the troopers had been wounded, with one death, but the advance had achieved part of one of Taryl's goals because it had cost the defenders hundreds of shafts.

Before long a second set of trumpet signals rang out, another company of troopers began to ride upward toward the earthworks. This time, the rebels did not offer a hail of arrows, but scattered shafts clearly aimed at individual troopers. Those missed, and the troopers continued up the slope. Rahl noticed that, attached behind the saddles of the second ranks of the troopers were bladders of some sort, filled with liquid. The bladders weren't likely to be seen from behind the earthworks.

The front ranks of the Imperial riders slowed just slightly, enough for the second wave of riders to catch up to the first, then both charged toward the earthworks. As they did, the riders with the bladders produced devices that looked like a cross between a forked branch and a child's catapult, and Rahl could sense the tiny points of chaos that had to be burning fuses. The bladders arced toward the earthworks. Many felt short, but more than a score slammed into or over the earthworks. Almost instantly, bluish orange flames rose from the point of impact.

Thin screams quickly died away.

"Sticky oil!" Drakeyt shook his head. "Nasty stuff, burns hot, then pops out in globules and sticks to everything and keeps burning. Still, they only landed a half score or so."

The bladders that had fallen short also burst into flame, incinerating the grass and creating a shifting smoky veil between the rebel and Imperial forces. Rahl had to believe that wasn't totally accidental.

Even before the second company of attackers returned downhill, a third company passed through them on its ride up toward the earthworks, and the second rank held riders who weren't mounted infantry. The mounted archers reined up a good two hundred cubits short of the earthworks and began to loose thick-shafted arrows—not at random or at the larger concentrations of defenders, but at the areas where the sticky oil still burned. One of the arrows landed in a pool of flaming gel, immediately catching fire, and then spewing a stream of liquid flame skyward and back down over the nearby defenders.

Many of the thick shafts missed, but a number did strike where the sticky-oil flames still burned or smoldered, and more flame fountains spewed over the defenders at the earthworks, thickening the haze of smoke.

Then an entire company that had been creeping up the slope on the far-left flank, partly shielded by the smoke, burst into a full gallop toward a section of the earthworks where the flames were dying away.

Whhstt! Whsst! Chaos-bolts flamed over the earthworks toward the charging troopers.

Rahl couldn't help but wince as one of the firebolts exploded across the front rank of one squad and turned close to a half score of men and mounts into momentary torches, then fine ashes. The remaining troopers reached the section of the earthworks where the defenders had been decimated by flame, but by that time more defenders had appeared. Several of the troopers dropped iron grapples over the top line of stones, and then began to ride away. In places two courses of stones tumbled forward, leaving a low spot in the wall.

Rahl had been watching that so closely that he almost missed another attempt of the same type near the southern end of the wall and earthworks.

A handful of troopers were so close beneath the wall that the chaos-bolts that were aimed at them were bursting farther downslope. Taryl's archers were arcing arrows into the area just behind the wall. The trooper-engineers were beginning to pull out the top course of stone that stood on the earthworks base. If the stone work could be removed, Rahl calculated, then a trooper could remain mounted and cross the wider earthworks base. He had to wonder why they hadn't put a ditch under the earthworks, even lined it with stakes or something.'

A well-placed firebolt dropped on one of the laboring engineers, engulfing him and the base of the wall in chaos-fire. When it died away, Rahl had his answer. He could see whitish stone, stained black and brown by the chaos-fire. The soil was barely thick enough to support the grass, and digging a deeper ditch would have taken seasons.

Whhhstt! Whssst!

One of the rebel chaos-mages had moved forward and

to the north so that he or she could angle firebolts down onto the engineers. The handful of Imperial troopers who survived galloped away downhill, chased by two more firebolts.

Rahl had been able to identify four different mages, and all were fairly powerful, if not of the strength of the two Triads or of Taryl, and it was unlikely that the mages being used in the early stages of the battle were the most powerful available to Golyat.

Third Regiment was moving up into position at the bottom of the slope.

A set of double trumpet triplets rang out, and the battalions of the regiment began to move forward, slowly at first, and then more swiftly. A firebolt arced from behind the earthwork ramparts and splattered across the grass a good hundred cubits short of the first riders.

Then, just as the leading riders began to near the point where the firebolt had struck and splattered chaos-flame, waves of arrows sleeted down into the defenders.

Rahl looked around, because he had seen no archers, before he realized that the shafts had come from the north, and that Taryl had placed the archers below the steeper part of the ridge, out of sight of the rebels. That didn't keep them from arcing the shafts up over the ridge toward an unseen target.

A series of wide chaos-flares appeared in the air just beyond the earthworks, incinerating most of the shafts, although Rahl could sense the chaos-tinged iron arrowheads falling like dark hail. More shafts lifted and in turn were incinerated. A third volley suffered the same fate.

The troopers of the two lead battalions of Third Regiment were almost at the earthworks, when a line of chaos-bolts wiped out close to two entire companies, and the massive waves of death rolled downhill and through Rahl, chilling him deep inside.

The chaos-bolts had done more than kill those troopers they had struck, because the loose chaos-fire also ignited the thick-shafted fire arrows that had previously fallen short of the earth-and-stone ramparts, as well as several sticky-oil bladders that had not previously ignited. More Imperial troopers and their mounts died a fiery death.

Gray-and-black smoke rose from all around the earthworks, slowly roiling downhill toward Third Company, burning eyes and throats alike, and carrying a sickening odor of roasted flesh. Defenders poured over the earthworks, many bearing falchionas and hacking at disabled and burned or blinded troopers. The troopers in the companies following swept in at an angle, cutting down the defenders on foot.

A scattered volley of arrows tore into Third Regiment, and more firebolts ripped into the battalions leading the assault.

A trumpet recall echoed uphill, and Third Regiment withdrew, leaving an expanse of blackened ground and stone before the defenders' earthworks, where the charred forms of men and mounts lay strewn. Yet all those dead forms represented but a fraction of those killed, Rahl knew, because the chaos-fire left no corpses, only blackened ground and ashes.

Rahl could sense a welter of death behind the ramparts as well as he watched Third Regiment return to lower ground and re-form. Was the use of Third Regiment for such a punishing part of the attack because Commander Hyksyn had been relieved? The former commander had certainly been right about the cost to his former regiment. Or would they all suffer that much before it was all over?

"Do you know what we're standing by for?" asked Drakeyt.

"No. I'd guess that we're going to be part of the final assault—or the overcommander's rear guard if the attack fails."

"I'm not certain which I'd prefer less." Drakeyt's voice was low and dry.

Rahl studied the ramparts. Whether from the engineers'

work, the continued assaults, or even the chaos of the defenders' mages, the stone work of the upper levels had been destroyed or tumbled in a score of places, and he could see the defenders trying to lift stones back into place.

Rahl glanced up through the smoky haze. The sun was past midmorning and headed toward noon.

The trumpet ordered another attack, and Third Regiment started riding back up the slope.

Another flight of arrows arced into the defenders, but those shafts were far fewer, far fewer indeed. Even so, more firebolts slashed down toward the half-concealed archers on the rugged north slope. While most missed, a few did strike, assuring that the next volley would have even fewer shafts coming down at the rebels.

Rahl became aware of something, moving closer, but he could see nothing. Why couldn't he see or sense anything but a vague sense? Shields and sight shields! He'd have wagered that a strong chaos-mage was shielding a force coming around from the south for a strike at Taryl and the Triads. "There's a mage-hidden side attack coming," he snapped at Drakeyt. "Have the company mount up."

"Third Company, mount up and form up! On the double!"

"Form up on the double!" echoed Quelsyn.

Belatedly, Rahl realized he needed to mount the gelding. He scrambled into the saddle, then tried to get a better idea of where the rebel mage was. Even with the additional height from being mounted, he was having trouble locating the other mage.

He kept looking where he thought the attacking force might be . . . and saw nothing, except he could feel his eyes almost skip at one point. He looked back there. He still saw nothing except a more rugged slope with scraggly vines and thornbushes that looked almost like dwarf olives. He watched as a fragment of smoke drifted down and westward from the high ground where chaos-bolts continued to arch into the troopers of Third Regiment as they advanced toward the earthworks once more. Rahl continued to watch the smoke until it rose in an arc.

That had to be it.

Rahl turned the gelding and rode toward the right end of the company. "Third Company! On me!"

"On the majer!"

Rahl had only ridden a hundred cubits or so—just off the flatter grass and into the rougher ground flanking it—when the sight shield vanished. Rahl and Third Company were facing two companies, if not more, but a ragtag two companies, with lancers in the front ranks and troopers behind.

"Charge them!" ordered someone.

The lancers aimed the shimmering polished lances and spurred their mounts forward on the rugged ground. One mount slipped, but regained its footing. Rahl felt that the lances were all aimed at him, and he began to ready himself to extend his shields when a firebolt flared toward him.

He deflected the chaos down into the path in front of the lancers, causing one to slam into the lancer next to him. The other lancer and his mount could not avoid the chaos and flared up into a column of flame that subsided to gray ashes.

When the second firebolt flashed toward Rahl, he was ready, and cast it back toward the white wizard in the middle of the lead company. While the wizard's shields held, the chaos splashed around him, taking out another rebel lancer.

Rahl had managed to get out his riding truncheon just before the first line of lancers neared Third Company.

In the moment before their lances would have struck, Rahl extended his shields, this time anchoring them to the ground. All but one of the front line of lancers pitched from their mounts, and several mounts went down as well. Rahl immediately contracted his shields, then rode past a fallen lancer and toward the next rebel, who did not manage to level his lance before Rahl swept past it and struck with the long riding truncheon. The lancer reeled and dropped his lance, then toppled out of the saddle.

Beyond the second lancer were regular mounted troopers, with their sabres out. Using the gelding's weight and motion, Rahl disarmed the nearest by breaking a wrist.

With rebel troopers surrounding him, Rahl just concentrated on holding on to his truncheon and inflicting damage upon as many rebels as possible.

Whssst! A firebolt flared against his shields, followed by a second one.

He turned the gelding to face the white wizard, conscious that, of the two rebels who had been attacking him, one was horribly burned and the other was backing away.

A narrow chaos-lance slashed toward Rahl, and he let it slide off his shields, even while he tried to figure out how to turn the chaos against the white wizard. The greenish blue tip of a second chaos-lance pressed into his shields. Rahl contracted his shields ever so slightly, then expanded them to fling the chaos back at the wizard. The greenish blue point flared into a brilliant white that cascaded across the wizard's shields, destroying the two rebel troopers behind and flanking the wizard.

Although the wizard remained untouched, Rahl could sense both anger and desperation, and he urged the gelding forward, toward the thin-faced and long-haired white wizard. Rahl leaned forward, gathering order around and within the riding truncheon.

Whssst! The firebolt was aimed at the gelding's legs, but Rahl caught it with his shields and hurled the chaos back at the white wizard, now alone on his mount, as the others in the rebel companies struggled to escape the energies created by the fight between mages. The wizard's shields shivered under the impact but held.

Rahl struck those shields with the order-reinforced truncheon, and chaos flared, lines of fire streaking in all directions as the white wizard's shields disintegrated.

With the next move of the truncheon, Rahl managed a
short slash up at the wizard's right arm.

The wizard opened her mouth—and Rahl understood
that he had been fighting a woman just as the order and
chaos exploded, giving her figure an incandescence that
lasted but a moment before a whirlwind of ashes
whipped around Rahl and the lancers. Stars flashed before Rahl's eyes from that burst of brilliance, and it was
several moments before he could see clearly. When he
could, he and Third Company held the area. The remaining rebels were riding back to the east, and Rahl had the
feeling that many would not be trying to return to the
rebel lines.

"Back to position!" ordered Drakeyt.

As Third Company re-formed and turned, Rahl rode
toward Drakeyt. Just as he neared the captain, a massive
chaos-bolt flew toward him—and it had come from the
west. Rahl managed to extend his shields just enough to
slide the fiery mass of chaos more to the rugged southern
side of the hill. It struck, and a massive column of flame
surged skyward, then subsided.

"That was close," said Drakeyt.

"Closer than I would have liked," Rahl replied. Had
that been an accident, with one of the Triads reacting late
to the attack? Or had it been an attempt to get at Rahl and
Third Company? Whichever it might have been, Rahl
didn't relish having to watch for chaos from all directions. But then, did he have any choice?

During the time that Third Company had been fighting
off the two companies attempting to reach the headquarters area, another regiment had joined Third Regiment on
the slopes below the earthworks. The troopers were already pouring through and over the weaker spots in the
defenses, and slowly pressing back the defenders. Rahl
thought that someone in charge had realized that the
sooner the Imperial forces were locked in combat with
the rebels, the less effective firebolts and archers could
be. But then, Taryl had probably known that all along. It

just took time and enough weakening of the defenses before that tactic could be implemented.

Just as Rahl thought that, a firebolt arced down from high on the ridge, smashing down into one of the gaps in the earthworks through which and over which Imperial troopers were attacking, pushing back defenders. The chaos fire-storm cleared the gap, incinerating Imperials and rebels alike, and leaving swirling ashes and blackened stone and earth.

The gap did not remain clear for long as another squad of troopers charged uphill and through the space, unimpeded by defenders until they were a good ten cubits uphill of the earthworks. As the Imperial forces pressed uphill, firebolts continued to fall into the individual melees, flaming Imperials and rebels alike.

Rahl had never seen so many chaos-bolts in one place and time. Were Golyat's mages so desperate that they had no choice but to kill their own troopers in their efforts to slow or reverse the Imperial attacks? The desperation suggested that Commander Muyr's forces had not made similar headway on the south side. But had Muyr even attacked, or was the role of his forces merely to hold and keep the rebels from escaping? Since Rahl had not heard the entire briefing because he'd had to deal with Commander Hyksyn, he had no idea.

What he did know was that it was now midafternoon, and the ridge was wreathed in smoke and the stench of burned flesh, and that the approach slope to the rebel earthworks was littered with the bodies of men and mounts.

An undercaptain rode toward Rahl and Drakeyt, reining up. "Sers . . . the overcommander requests that, as soon as the Second and Third Regiments clear the earthworks, Third Company move forward on the flank as far uphill as possible without being in the front rank of combat."

"Third Company hears and will obey," snapped Drakeyt.

The undercaptain looked to Rahl.

"You heard Captain Drakeyt. Tell the overcommander his orders are being carried out."

"Yes, ser."

Drakeyt turned in the saddle. "Third Company! Forward!" Once they were headed up the slope, he looked to Rahl. "Thank you, Majer."

"You're in command," Rahl pointed out.

"Mostly." Drakeyt laughed.

The brief conversation brought home to Rahl how comparatively few words were exchanged in the course of a battle. With a shake of his head, he went back to scanning the battlefield for possible uses of chaos against him and Third Company, but the nearest concentrations of chaos were those near the center of the ridge, still a third of a kay or more to the southeast, and those of the two Triads.

He frowned. The Triads were moving. He glanced back over his shoulder. Although it was difficult to determine, he could see and sense that the entire headquarters force was following Third Company, including the Triads, and presumably Taryl. Was Deybri among them? He knew she'd accompanied Taryl earlier. He hoped she remained well in the rear. Although she had training with a staff, as did all healers from Recluce, he didn't know whether she'd kept up with it—or even if she had a staff with her.

He forced himself to concentrate on the swirling eddies of rebels trying to hold back the advancing Imperial forces. There was something about the pattern of those forces, and there should have been more defenders, rather than a thin line of rebel troopers giving ground, almost as if to delay while a counterattack of some sort was being developed. Yet with all the swirling chaos, and the chill rushes of widespread death, Rahl was having trouble seeing where or what that counterattack might be.

"We need to get on top of the ridge now! Something's about to happen!"

"Third Company! Forward on me!" ordered Drakeyt, urging his mount into what Rahl thought was a slow canter.

What with trying to ride over and around bodies, with acrid smoke still swirling everywhere, and with the gelding nearly stumbling and lurching as he went over and through one of the gaps in the earthworks, Rahl couldn't concentrate on sensing and seeking what bothered him. He had to concentrate on riding, and being ready to defend himself in the case of a rebel attack.

Whhhstt! A small firebolt flared seemingly from nowhere toward Rahl and Drakeyt and the lead riders of Third Company. While hanging on to his seat on the rougher ground above the earthworks, Rahl managed to deflect it into the ground ahead of them because he could see no rebels nearby where he could have redirected the chaos-flame to help the Imperial advance.

Whhsstt! Another chaos-bolt followed the first.

Again Rahl deflected it, although that took more care because Third Company was nearing the rear ranks of Second Regiment. At least, he thought the troopers he saw just ahead were bringing up the rear of Second Regiment.

When the third firebolt came his way, and he had not seen or sensed any others being sent forth from the rebel side, he deflected it and made a greater effort to tighten his shields. He waited for a fourth chaos-bolt, but none came, not then, at least.

When he extended his order-senses farther behind Third Company, Rahl could pick up the feeling of the two Triads, but not of Taryl. He nodded.

The rebels fighting off the two Imperial regiments were still giving way, but Rahl could see that the bulk of the rebel forces had regrouped in front of the unbreached earthworks on the southeastern end of the long ridge, hurrying past the stone redoubt that still held hints of chaos and chaos-mages—but there were no troopers stationed outside the roofless redoubt, set as it was near the back side of the ridge.

"Drakeyt! Send a trooper back to the overcommander! The rebels are massing at the earthworks to the east, but all the mages are in the redoubt on the back side of the ridge up ahead."

Drakeyt turned as he rode. "Alrydd! Take a message to the overcommander! It's urgent! Tell him the rebels are massing . . ."

Alrydd repeated the message, then turned his mount, urging the horse into a longer stride.

Rahl just hoped that the message reached Taryl in time. He didn't know what he could do about the regiments ahead. Even if a messenger could find the commanders, what could he say? Don't pursue the rebels past the redoubt? But was that what Golyat wanted, so that his forces could have time to regroup? Or was something else being planned?

Whatever might happen, the commanders should know what the rebels were doing. Rahl started to open his mouth, but closed it as he sensed that the remaining rebels in front of the Imperial regiments had broken— scattering in all directions and leaving the way open for a charge toward the main rebel force.

The troopers of the regiment on the northern side of the ridge surged forward.

Rahl winced. In those moments he'd deliberated, he'd lost his chance. Although a messenger might not have found the commanders, they might have.

The troopers on the southern side actually reined up and began to re-form.

Just before the northern regiment—the Third, Rahl thought—drew abreast of the stone redoubt, with the nearest troopers and their mounts a good three hundred cubits from the stone structure, chaos-flame flared out across the ridge.

Despite himself, Rahl reeled in the saddle with the wave of deaths that chilled the afternoon, despite the heat of the sun. From what he could see and sense, the entire regiment had been wiped out. "Company halt!" he yelled at Drakeyt.

"Company halt!"

All five squads drew up in a line abreast, first squad to the south, and fifth to the north. Ahead of them, no more than a quarter kay, the commander of the surviving regiment had ordered a withdrawal, and the regiment reversed itself and then re-formed just before Third Company—almost five hundred cubits from the redoubt.

Whatever means the rebel mages had used to project that searing blast of chaos-flame, it had taken great effort. Rahl could easily sense the decrease in the amount of chaos-power within the stone redoubt.

A ring of blackened ground surrounded the small circular stone redoubt, no more than thirty cubits across. Rahl sensed close to a half score of mages within the redoubt, although he felt that three or four were either not that powerful or so exhausted that they had little more that they could contribute. After the attack on Third Regiment, Rahl could understand that.

An eerie quiet began to settle over the ridgetop. Rahl looked back northwest along the ridgeline. Taryl and the headquarters company, as well as the two Triads, continued riding toward Third Company. Another regiment had moved up the slope and was drawn up in formation just above the breached northwestern earthworks.

Why was Taryl exposing himself and the Triads? All that was between him and the rebel mages were Third Company and what remained of Second Regiment.

Drakeyt looked back as well, then at Rahl.

Rahl shrugged. He couldn't say that he understood, unless Taryl felt that the battle would end up being resolved by an order-chaos struggle with Taryl and the Triads pitted against the rebel mages.

As the headquarters company rode closer, a captain cantered ahead and called out, "The overcommander requests that you move more to the south, covering the flank, Captain!"

"Third Company! Right turn! Ride!" At that moment, Drakeyt's orders were the loudest sound on the flat of the ridge.

Shortly, the second command rang out. "Third Company! Left turn and halt! Left turn and halt!"

First squad was less than thirty cubits from the south edge of the ridgetop, and the slope to the right was steep enough that it could almost have been called a cliff. No one was going to ride down or across that sheer expanse.

Rahl watched intently as Taryl and the Triads rode past, just behind the first rank of troopers. Once most of the company was passed, he leaned toward Drakeyt. "I need to move up, but keep the company here."

Drakeyt nodded.

Rahl eased the gelding forward, keeping abreast of the middle of the headquarters company, but remaining close to the south edge of the ridgetop.

Taryl was only slightly less cautious than the commander of Second Regiment. He and the headquarters company reined up a good three hundred cubits from the circular stone redoubt. Rahl moved forward for a few more cubits after Taryl had stopped, then reined up and waited.

Again, near silence dropped over the ridge.

"Hear me!" The words rang out from the redoubt, chaos-boosted, and shivered the air. "Hear your rightful emperor before you destroy yourself with your foolishness." The man who spoke had to be Golyat. He stood within a space on the northwest side of the redoubt that resembled an archer's niche, with stone on both sides, and stones piled roughly to waist height. Even from more than two hundred cubits away, by using his order-skills to boost his physical senses, Rahl could see that Golyat was not especially tall, a span less than Rahl. Unlike his younger brother the Emperor, Golyat's black eyes were not friendly, but portals through which he angrily observed the world. Gray strands streaked his black hair, and heavy frown lines creased his forehead.

"I will not be denied. I am the rightful emperor of Hamor, and a mage, as all emperors of the Cyadoran lineage should be. Unless you yield to me and accept me as emperor, you will discover my power."

Rahl frowned. He could sense that indeed Golyat was a chaos-mage of sorts, but not a particularly strong one. On the other hand, at least one of the mages within the redoubt was as strong as either of the Triads. That was doubtless Ulmaryt.

Taryl did not step forward, but his voice, quiet and calm, without the thunder, still filled the air. "You are not the rightful emperor, Golyat, and no amount of magery can make that so."

A line of white chaos-flame issued from the redoubt, burning toward Taryl. Just before it reached the troopers in the rank before him, Taryl diverted it—almost half a kay to the southeast, where it slashed across the front ranks of the massed rebels.

Following that flame, another unseen wave of deaths swept through Rahl.

Two lines of white flame flared toward Taryl, but this time blasts of chaos-flame that moved almost as fast as the white flame flashed from the Triads back at the redoubt. The head-high walls in the rear shook, and several large rough stone oblongs flew from the top of the roof-less walls across the structure. One smashed into Golyat, crushing his skull.

No one seemed even to notice.

The chaos-mages on both sides hurled forces back and forth at each other, and Taryl blocked and diverted those forces, sending many of them against the rebel troops. Once more the smoke thickened, as did the acrid and sickly-sweet odors of all manner of burning substances.

Rahl could sense that more than a few of those troopers were slipping away and sliding down the steeper north and south sides of the ridge above the earthworks.

Should he enter the magely battle?

Not yet, something told him as he edged the gelding closer to the headquarters company and to Taryl.

Chaos welled up from the very ground, like a fountain of molten rock, or like the white-hot streams of molten metal from the ironworks at Luba, and a tall figure—Ulmaryt—focused that molten-metal-like chaos into a massive shaft and hurled it toward Taryl.

Taryl staggered as his shields diverted the massive chaos-shaft, and the ground shook as the shaft slammed into the rocky soil between Taryl and the redoubt. Another shaft flew toward Taryl, almost reaching the over-commander before he dropped it into the ground.

For a moment, there was another silence.

Then the twin firebolt shafts of the two Triads ripped into the redoubt—one striking the remaining white wizard behind and beside Ulmaryt, the other hitting a Hamorian chaos-mage. Both the white wizard and the rebel mage-guard collapsed into a pile of ashes.

The next-strongest rebel mage launched a greenish gold chaos sphere at Dhoryk. The Triad's shields barely held, and chaos splashed over the three troopers nearest him, instantly incinerating all three.

Just after the rebel mage had attempted to strike at Dhoryk, Fieryn had slammed another firebolt shaft into the rebel—killing him.

In all the exchanges of various forms of chaos, three of the weaker rebel mages had been killed as well, Rahl realized, leaving Ulmaryt and one other renegade mage-guard.

Rahl could sense the exhaustion of the former Mage-Guard Overcommander. So did the two Triads, who flung another set of firebolts at the flagging Ulmaryt. At that instant, Taryl struck with an order-bolt.

The combination shattered the shields of the last two rebel mages and turned the interior of the redoubt into a mass of heat and chaos that reminded Rahl of the interior of the iron blast furnaces of Luba.

Rahl caught a sense of . . . he didn't know what, but he urged the gelding toward Taryl.

Another chaos-bolt flew toward Taryl—except that chaos had come from Fieryn. Taryl diverted that bolt, as well as the next from Dhoryk.

The troopers of the headquarters company—those that could—spurred their mounts away from the three mages, leading them and their mounts away from all others nearby . . . except for Rahl.

Rahl managed to rein up and divert Fieryn's next firebolt back toward the Triad. Fieryn brushed away Rahl's effort as if it were nothing, slamming the chaos back at Rahl's shields, and nearly flinging Rahl from the saddle.

Fieryn was far stronger than he was, Rahl realized, and with both Triads against Taryl . . . What could he do?

He blocked another near-incidental chaos-blast that nearly shivered his own shields.

Think! He had to think. There was no way he could breach Fieryn's shields. The Triad was far too strong, and Rahl knew that one order-bolt wouldn't be enough, and he could only cast one against a mage like the Triad.

He couldn't get through the other's shields. He couldn't . . .

Rahl would have grinned had he not been so busy fending off stray chaos from both Dhoryk's and Fieryn's attacks on Taryl . . . who was clearly feeling the strain. He didn't have to get inside Fieryn's shields to strike.

He immediately began to probe for any sort of rock beneath the Triad's feet. Sweat was pouring down his face from the effort of fending off Fieryn's incidental attacks and from his own searching, but he had found what he needed.

He began to order-move parts of the rock, and then to loosen the order-links . . .

KRUUMMMPT!

Even though he'd been expecting the explosion, and had strengthened his shields against it, he found that he'd been thrown to the ground. But so had Fieryn, Dhoryk, and Taryl.

Rahl drew the truncheon and bounded toward Fieryn. The Triad struggled to move, and Rahl could feel the other's shields beginning to rebuild as he struck with the truncheon, strengthened with order, its force fueled with anger.

The dark oak shattered the Triad's skull.

Rahl whirled as a chaos-bolt slammed into his shields, staggered at the force, even though it was not so powerful as those thrown by Fieryn.

Taryl still lay stunned on the ground, barely a half shield around him.

Dhoryk smiled, slowly gathering chaos, knowing that Rahl could not break the Triad's shields.

Rahl threw everything into the last unlinking, just trying to delink anything he could beneath Dhoryk's feet, stripping order from order, from dirt, from clay, and then from a section of a broken blade.

The late afternoon flared white, and Rahl could hear nothing.

Then, he saw nothing.

XCV

Rahl looked up into the darkness. He was lying on his back, and he thought he saw stars, but then he realized that someone was looking down at him. The face was blurry, but the healer greens and the warmth that flowed into him told him that the healer looking over him was Deybri. He tried to smile . . . and couldn't. He could barely move.

"Oh . . . you're here . . ."

Where else would he have been?

Drops of rain fell on his cheeks, except that they weren't raindrops, but teardrops.

"What . . . happened?" he finally asked.

"It's all over. The rebels who were left fled or surrendered, and Taryl has already sent battalions to take over Sastak."

Taryl was well. Rahl breathed easier. That left one other question. "What happened to Dhoryk?"

"He died," whispered Deybri.

"I killed him, too?"

She shook her head.

"Taryl?"

Rahl could sense the sadness. How could she have done it? "You?"

"He was stunned, but he was going to wake up before you or Taryl did, and he would have killed you both. I couldn't . . . I couldn't lose you again, and . . ." She shook her head once more. "I couldn't touch all the chaos in him. It burned too much. So I just . . . moved the order out of him, enough anyway, that his own chaos killed him."

"Are . . . you all right?"

"It helps . . . to heal, and to see you."

He could still sense the sadness and unshed tears, and he finally rolled onto his side and sat up, ignoring the dirt and soot on his uniform. He did wipe his hands on his trousers before he reached out and took her hand. What could he say?

"It helps to know you care and understand. I'm glad your shields are down right now."

Rahl doubted he could have raised a shield if he'd had to.

"I know," Deybri replied, "but it still helps."

"Where's Taryl?"

"He recovered sooner than you did. He was just knocked out. You used almost every last bit of order and strength you had against the Triads."

What else could he have done? He'd just been trying to keep them from killing Taryl.

Rahl slowly stood, and Deybri rose from her knees as well. Rahl squeezed her hand.

"I need to go."

"Now?"

Before Deybri could say more, someone else came forward, leading a mount. In the darkness, Rahl made out Drakeyt, leading Rahl's gelding.

"Glad to see you on your feet, Majer. We got here as fast as we could, but without the healer . . ."

Drakeyt didn't say more, but he didn't have to.

"I'm glad you were here." Rahl stepped forward and just held on to the edge of the saddle for several moments.

"You took out both Triads, didn't you?" asked the captain.

Rahl could sense the restrained awe and fear and started to say that he hadn't done it all alone, but he caught the sense of pleading from Deybri. "I took out Triad Fieryn . . . and Dhoryk. I didn't want to, but they wanted to kill the overcommander and replace the Emperor."

"I wondered about that when they turned on the overcommander at the end."

"Rahl . . . others need me," murmured Deybri.

Rahl looked to her. "You're leaving?"

"Just for now. You'll be fine, and there are so many others . . ."

"Could I help?" He didn't want to leave her.

"Rahl . . . you have so little order . . . please don't even think about that, not for days."

Rahl could sense the stark fear behind her words. Drakeyt's words had suggested he'd been in danger, but had he come that close to dying?

"Yes."

Rahl swallowed. "Please . . . don't do more than you can." He knew he was pleading, but he also understood what she needed to do now, what she had to do. At least, she could heal, to atone for what she—and mostly he—had done.

"I won't. I'll see you later. I promise."

Rahl slowly climbed into the saddle. He had to leave it to Drakeyt as to where they were going. He was so tired he could sense nothing.

He glanced back once he was mounted, but Deybri was already moving away, her stride purposeful, but he was glad to see the two troopers flanking her. He wished he could have been one of them.

XCVI

In the late afternoon of fourday, Rahl walked along the polished white-marble floors of Golyat's mansion in Sastak. Taryl had taken over the mansion as a temporary headquarters, while he and Commander Muyr organized the return of the port city to Imperial control and arranged for the sea transport of the High Command troopers to Swartheld . . . and then to Cigoerne, or to wherever their previous station had been.

Rahl hadn't seen Taryl since the afternoon before, when he and the overcommander had fought Golyat and Ulmaryt—and the two Triads. Nor had he seen Deybri since the night before.

Taryl had sent an undercaptain to find Rahl, and it had taken the officer half a day in the chaos and confusion to run down Third Company. Still . . . Rahl wasn't all that sure he wanted to see Taryl. What if he had misjudged the situation, and Taryl could have handled it without his ill-advised attempts to help? Had he just made matters worse?

The undercaptain outside the study door bolted to his feet. "He said for you to go right in, ser."

Rahl didn't have to be reminded to close the door. He didn't want anyone overhearing what Taryl had to say.

The overcommander sat at a broad table desk with neat stacks of paper set around him in a nearly perfect semicircle. The double doors to the balcony to the left were open, and a gentle breeze cooled the study.

Taryl looked up. His bloodshot eyes were set in deep black circles, but his shields were as tight as ever, and his first words did not offer Rahl any great comfort. "As usual, Rahl, you did the right thing in the wrong way, and someone had to clean up after you." Then the angular and stern-faced mage-guard smiled warmly. "And I'm very glad that you and Deybri were there. Without the two of you, Hamor would be in sad straits indeed."

"I did my best, ser." Rahl swallowed. "Without Deybri . . . it wouldn't have been enough."

Taryl nodded. "I'm glad to see that you recognize that. But, without your efforts, hers would not have been possible."

"Fieryn and Dhoryk were conspiring to remove the Emperor, weren't they?" Rahl looked at Taryl, hoping to change the subject.

The older mage-guard nodded again.

"That means . . ." Rahl paused. "Jubyl, he couldn't have been part of it. If he had been . . ."

"Why do you say that?" Taryl's tone was almost idle. Almost.

"If all the Triad agreed, then why would they have needed a rebellion? They could have removed the Emperor without fighting."

"Could they? Was that the reason for the revolt?"

What else could have been the reason? Rahl knew Taryl was testing him in yet another way. What else would make sense? Then he thought about Captain Gheryk, Regional Commander Chaslyk, the regional commander in Matlana . . .

"They wanted a revolt in order to conceal their removal of mage-guards loyal to the Emperor?"

"Who could prove that?" asked Taryl. "But yes, that fitted into their plans."

"Couldn't you have . . . ?"

"How?"

Rahl understood, then. "You ran the whole campaign in a way that drew the two Triads here because you couldn't have checked every regional officer—not in time—and not without alerting them, and you hoped that you could do something against them when they acted against you. And if you hadn't succeeded, they would have named Cyphryt to replace Jubyl."

"Possibly. Or perhaps Welleyn."

"Not the Mage-Guard Overcommander?"

"That has always been almost a ceremonial post, and Kurtweyl was loyal to . . . the Emperor." Taryl smiled, still tiredly. "When he wasn't involved in his musical compositions."

"What happens now, ser?"

"That is up to the Emperor and the new Triads."

Once again, Taryl was not really answering the questions, and Rahl still wasn't thinking as clearly as he would have liked as he asked, "Who will be the Regional Administrator for Merowey?"

"That hasn't been decided, but I'm certain it will be some cousin of Mythalt's."

"After all this? They wouldn't consider you?"

"Mage-guards are never permanent regional administrators. The position will be filled with a pleasant man with the proper connections who understands fully that, when in doubt, he is to ask the Mage-Guard Overcommander of Merowey for advice, and who will understand that he is never to cross his regional overcommander. Who that administrator will be is not for either of us to say."

With the firmness of Taryl's tone, Rahl decided not to press that issue.

"What about Deybri?" Taryl asked, almost idly, although Rahl doubted that there was anything idle at all about the question, since Taryl's shields hid whatever the older mage might be feeling.

"Deybri . . . you know how I feel. We're going to be consorted properly when we . . . well, when we can work out wherever we'll be." Rahl paused. Surely, Taryl or the Mage-Guard Overcommander wouldn't separate them? "I'd hope . . . that we wouldn't be separated."

"I can see that." A faint smile crinkled Taryl's lips. "I don't see that such a separation would serve anyone well."

"At our consorting . . . will you be there?"

"That, Rahl, I can promise, provided you don't wait too long."

"No, ser." After a pause, Rahl asked one of the questions he'd wanted to know for a long time. "I've inquired before, but you've never really answered. Why did you go to such lengths to persuade her to leave Recluce?"

"You need her. She needs you. You'd both be wasted in Recluce. Besides, Hamor needs you both. So it seemed like a good thing to do, and it was something I could do."

Even behind Taryl's shields, Rahl could sense the pain. At least, he thought he could. But what could he say? After a long silence, he finally spoke. "Thank you. I cannot tell you how much that means to me, but . . . I know you understand that."

Taryl just nodded. "There is one other matter. . . ."

"Ser?"

"What to do with a mage-guard who is so powerful that all the others shiver when they think of him."

Who was Taryl talking about? "Ser . . . how can the Emperor not reward you?"

The older mage-guard laughed. "That's already been decided, but I'd trust that you not mention it since plans for my departure have not been announced."

"You're going to be Triad again, aren't you? Mage-Guard Triad," guessed Rahl.

"That is most likely."

Rahl laughed, if softly. "The Emperor needs you. So does Hamor." He realized he was quoting Taryl's words back at him, but that seemed only fair.

Taryl nodded. "I wasn't talking about myself when I asked that question."

The mage-guards shivered when they thought of Rahl? "Ser?"

"Although you, Deybri, and I know the full story, what everyone saw on that ridge was you take on and vanquish two of the most powerful mage-guards in Hamor, perhaps in the world. Were you older, and wiser, there would be no question that you would be selected as a Triad. Even so, I wouldn't do this, not if Deybri had not agreed to come to Hamor, and not if she had not agreed to consort you," Taryl went on. "But she's older, and wiser, and you listen to her." His voice turned wry. "More than to anyone else. So . . . from here on in, you're acting Mage-Guard Overcommander of Merowey. You and Deybri will be departing within the eightday on the *Tyrsalelth* to return to Nubyat. You'll also be temporary acting Regional Administrator for me, but that will be very temporary, I am most certain. Once the Emperor convenes the Triad, you will be confirmed as Mage-Guard Overcommander of Merowey and servant to the Emperor."

"Me?"

"You could never go back to being a regular mage-guard, even a city captain. Your reputation would terrify everyone, and what superior would dare to discipline you? As a regional overcommander, you report to the Mage-Guard Triad and the Emperor. Besides, returning you to a lower level would be a waste of what you've accomplished. Your reputation will help keep Merowey loyal. The Emperor and I know that you and Deybri will not be corrupted. Because you will not be, neither will the next administrator, nor the mage-guards of Merowey. Besides, it's the easiest way to make sure you and the healer are together."

"But I'm only a senior mage-guard."

"That's all *you* have to be after the Great Battle of Sastak," replied Taryl dryly. "Why do you think I gave you all those duties here earlier? Besides, who's left to complain? You're more powerful than anyone who's left in the mage-guards."

"Except you," Rahl pointed out.

"Don't let that go to your head," added Taryl, clearly ignoring Rahl's interjection. "You still need to develop more skills and strength."

"Yes, ser."

Taryl looked at Rahl. "You'll pardon me if I don't stand. That's all I had to tell you."

"What about Drakeyt?" blurted Rahl.

"He'd be wasted in Nubyat with Third Company. You'll have to break in a new captain. Drakeyt's already been promoted to majer to take over the battalion that Commander Deolyn commanded before his promotion. I trust you do not object." Taryl coughed. "There's one thing more. I asked Deybri to wait on the upper verandah. I didn't tell her why. I thought you should have that pleasure."

After leaving Taryl, Rahl walked from the study and down the wide marble-floored hallway to the double doors to the verandah. The warmth of spring surrounded him, even though the upper verandah was on the north side of the mansion and shaded. Below the stone railing was a walled garden, and Rahl could hear the splashing of fountains.

Deybri rose from the cushioned chair and smiled, tentatively. She did not move toward him. "You've seen Taryl?"

"Yes." Rahl smiled, keeping his shields tight. He would surprise her.

"Rahl . . . are you all right? What did he say?"

"You'll still consort me, no matter what happens, or wherever I'm posted?"

Her face darkened. "What have they done?"

Rahl grinned and dropped all his shields. "Taryl named me as acting Overcommander of Mage-Guards for Merowey. The Emperor is supposed to confirm it as a permanent appointment once Taryl returns to Cigoerne and becomes a Triad again."

"You're too young for that." Her face warred between worry and joy.

"Taryl said that. He said he wouldn't have done it except for you. He said that you were the wise one, and that I'd best listen to you. He also said that I still had much to learn, but that there was nothing else he could do."

"You've already learned a great deal." Deybri smiled fondly.

"I have," reflected Rahl. "One of the problems is that too many other people helped to pay for that learning." He couldn't help but think of the outrider who'd died because he hadn't even considered an arrow trap without people around, or the troopers in fifth squad who drowned because he hadn't reacted quickly enough, or the girl whose throat had been slashed before his eyes, or the thousands and thousands on both sides who had died . . . Or Deybri, who had sacrificed comfort and come to a strange land for him. "You're one of the ones who paid a great deal."

"No. I don't think so. You've given me a different kind of experience. I couldn't go back to Nylan now."

"Why not?"

Her eyes dropped. "Yesterday . . . I did what I had to, just as you did so long ago in Land's End. Healers in Recluce don't use order that way." She looked up and at Rahl. "The other reason is that people need me here. The difference is that I wanted everyone to tell me I was needed. Here it doesn't matter because I can see the need."

"There aren't any really good healers in Nubyat, or not many," offered Rahl.

Her eyes darted to the north. "We'll live . . . there in Nubyat in that villa?"

"At the overcommander's villa." Rahl couldn't help but smile even more broadly. "I hope you don't mind. It is a little larger than your dwelling in Nylan. Oh . . . and Taryl will be at the consorting ceremony. He promised—if we don't wait long."

Her smile was all he could have hoped for, and so was the embrace, and the kiss that followed.

XCVII

When he finally left Deybri, Rahl knew he had one more person to seek out, but the sun was low over the harbor before he reached the barn northwest of Sastak and walked toward Drakeyt. He looked at the older officer, pleased to see that Drakeyt already wore a majer's insignia on his collars. "I just found out that you're now a battalion commander. Congratulations."

"Thank you." Drakeyt nodded.

Rahl could sense the other's mixed feelings, but he didn't know quite what to say. After several moments of silence, he finally added, "I don't think anything turned out quite the way we expected, but I wanted you to know that I appreciate everything you taught me. I owe you more than I can repay."

Drakeyt smiled ironically, but warmly. "That's true, but you'll repay it to others, just like the way I'll try to repay what you taught me."

What had Rahl taught Drakeyt, besides foolhardiness? He didn't even want to ask.

"That's the way it works," the newly promoted majer went on, "or should work. Besides, your healer wouldn't have it any other way, would she?"

Rahl smiled. "No, she wouldn't."

"You're fortunate to have her, you know? Not many

women, especially healers, would follow a man across two oceans."

"I know. It's hard to believe she's here. I'd hoped you'd be at the consorting. It will be on eightday at head-quarters here in Sastak."

Drakeyt grinned. "The overcommander said that might be soon."

"Very soon." Rahl flushed.

"I wouldn't miss it. She and the overcommander are the only ones who'll ever be able to tell you what to do."

"Not quite," Rahl protested. "I listened to you, espe-cially when you added my title, and I always will."

"A mere majer's words?"

"A trustworthy majer of good judgment who won't al-ways be a majer," Rahl suggested.

Drakeyt shook his head, then, after another moment of silence, added, "I asked the overcommander to make Lyrn the Third Company undercaptain. He agreed. I'm taking Quelsyn to be battalion squad leader."

Rahl nodded. "Lyrn will do well at that. He's solid and thoughtful."

"What about you, Majer?"

Rahl could see a twinkle in Drakeyt's eyes. Despite that, he still felt sheepish in answering. "Well . . . it seems . . . you were right. Taryl did have something in mind . . ."

"More than city mage captain, I'd wager." Drakeyt was grinning again.

"Acting Regional Mage-Guard Overcommander of Merowey," Rahl said, managing to inject a note of wry-ness into the words. "It seems that I'm unsuited to be a mage-guard city captain."

"Might it have something to do with the fact that no one besides Overcommander Taryl would dare to be your superior?"

"Something like that was mentioned," Rahl admitted. "It was also mentioned that he wouldn't have considered it without a certain healer's presence as my consort."

"Wise man."

"There's something else," Rahl said. "If you ever need the help of a mage-guard . . ."

"I hope the Emperor and the overcommander will make sure that I wouldn't, but . . . I'll keep that in mind."

As he left, Rahl just hoped that Drakeyt would.

Epilogue

Rahl and Deybri stood before the desk table in the study. A warm breeze barely moved the air, but the stone walls of the overcommander's villa kept out the worst of the summer heat.

Rahl opened the case that had just been delivered—all the way from Cigoerne. Inside was a roll of parchment, a smaller folded sheet of parchment, and a deep green enameled box that, despite its unmarred exterior, exuded great age. Rahl unrolled the document with the Emperor's seal.

"That makes it official," said Deybri, as she read the words over his shoulder. "Mage-Guard Overcommander of Merowey." After a moment, she pointed. "You need to read the other one."

Rahl unfolded the smaller sheet and began to read.

Please accept this antique badge of rank as a token of my deepest appreciation and esteem. The badge reputedly came from a distant ancestor. May it provide an inspiration for your son to come and a reminder to you both of the costs and triumphs of love.

The signature was a single name: Emerya.

Rahl handed the note to Deybri and eased open the green-enamel box. Inside was a lambent cupridium and lacquer pin displaying three crossed miniature items: a lance, a jagged lightning bolt, and a sheaf of grain.

"What is it?" asked Deybri, leaning toward him.

"A token of esteem and inspiration," Rahl said quietly, turning the pin over. There was a name inscribed in tiny letters. Cyadoran, he thought. He squinted and puzzled them out. "Lorn'elth'alt'mer. That must be the name of her distant ancestor."

Deybri smiled sadly. "The poor woman. Poor Taryl."

Rahl thought so, too. But Hamor was the richer for that doomed love . . . and so were he and Deybri. He reached out with his free hand and drew her to him, feeling the swell of her body against him . . . and the life force of their son.

Turn the page for a preview of

IMAGER

L. E. Modesitt, Jr.

Available now from Tor

TOR® A TOR HARDCOVER

ISBN-13: 978-0-7653-2034-6   ISBN-10: 0-7653-2034-7

On Jeudi afternoon, I was in the work shed powdering red ochre, using the ancient mortar and pestle that looked as though they had been in Master Caliostrus's family for generations. Despite the sunlight outside, a chill breeze seeped through the bare plank walls. Powdering hard red ochre was sweaty work. The chill made it even less pleasant, especially if I crushed it and twisted the pestle too hard, because then some of the powder seeped into the air and then stuck to my sweat. Later, it got cold and itchy, and scratching just made it worse.

I consoled myself that the situation was only temporary because Stanus had finally run off, after throwing a bucket of hot ivory-black scraps at Ostrius. The scraps had burned holes in Ostrius's shirt and given him several welts on his neck, but it would have been worse had not Ostrius been wearing a leather working vest. If the civic patrollers caught poor Stanus, he'd spend at least a year in the mines, but, in the interim, assuming that Master Caliostrus could find and accept another apprentice, everyone expected me to do all the apprentice chores as well as my own, not to mention painting whatever commissions might come my way, not that I had any at the moment.

Still . . . the Scheorzyl portrait had turned out well, and I'd even gotten a half-gold bonus. I had to wonder how much extra the Scheorzyls had paid Caliostrus. But my name was getting around—at least to families with daughters who liked cats.

Everyone in the household was edgy that morning. As I'd left the table after breakfast, Madame Caliostrus had murmured something to her husband that had sounded like "your worthless brother skulking around here again." I'd known Caliostrus had a brother, and I'd even seen him a few times over the years—and smelled him, reeking of plonk so cheap that not even the poorest apprentice would have drunk it. That morning, Caliostrus had snapped back, but I hadn't heard what he'd said. I'd just wanted to get away before Ostrius made another comment about my lack of foresight, especially since it was really his short-sightedness, not that he'd ever admit it.

I checked the powder. Still too coarse, but getting closer to what was necessary to mix with the oil and wax that were melting over the small iron mixing stove in the corner. I went back to grinding, wishing that Stanus were still around, or that Caliostrus would get another apprentice so that I didn't have to do everything.

The shed door opened, and a gust of wind swirled ochre powder up around me, and I began to sneeze.

Ostrius stood there, glowering at me. "How long will it be before you can mix up the pigment?"

After I could stop sneezing, I just looked at him, noticing that he'd replaced the dressing covering the burn on his neck.

"Answer me. When will we have red ochre pigment?"

"Not until tomorrow. I won't have enough powder until later today, and then it will have to be blended and cooled . . ."

"You should have gotten to this earlier." He glared at me. "We're both waiting for the pigment."

"No one told me until this morning." I didn't point out that talking to him slowed me down—or that he'd been the one to use all the red ochre pigment for his portrait of High Chorister Thalyt and that he hadn't bothered to tell anyone that there hadn't been more than a palette knife's worth of it remaining.

"You should have known."

What could I say that wouldn't make him even angrier? Especially since Ostrius had never been the type to listen to reason or consider himself the cause of anything. He'd been the cause of the problem with his attitude and his mistreatment of Stanus, not that he'd ever been pleasant to me, either, but I had the advantage of having parents who had some position, unlike poor Stanus, whose father was dead and whose mother was a seamstress.

With a last glare at me, he stalked off, leaving the work shed door open. Of course, the wind gusted again and blew some of the finer powder I'd just ground right out of the pestle and up around me. I began to sneeze more, and by the time I got the door closed, I'd probably lost half a cup's worth of ground ochre powder. At that moment, I would have liked to strap Ostrius to a worktable and then slowly pour fine ochre powder down his throat and nostrils until he choked to death.

I recovered some of the powder from the bench top beside the mortar, and then went back to work. But I kept having to stop and sneeze. There was no help for it. I needed to brush the fine grit and powder off me and wash my hands and face, or I'd never get much done.

After carefully and quickly opening and closing the shed door behind me, I walked toward the service pump house in the corner, past the low wall that separated the garden from the more mundane and less attractive working areas of Master Caliostrus's establishment.

Despite the chill and the wind, Shienna was pruning the bare-branched grape vines—even the leaves were used, mainly for the dolmades her mother made and which one enjoyed the first several times they were served, but which became less than entrancing by the onset of spring. Some of the less perfect leaves were used with copper plates for making verdigris, but that green pigment was used only for quick treatments, because it was so fugitive if exposed for long to bright light.

Shienna was a sweet girl, unlike her elder brother, but to say that she was plain would have been an exaggeration that not even an imager could have transformed into truth.

Still, she was sweet, and I did smile. "Mistress Shienna, how lovely your cheeks today, like the paleness of a fresh white peach . . ."

"They're wind-chapped and red, but you're always so dear, Rhenn. I don't believe a word, but the kindness is appreciated."

"And your hair shimmers with a lustre beyond that of the greater moon in the fullness of harvest." I have never held myself to be bound by the dictates of foolish consistency, particularly when dealing with young women— except, strangely, for Seliora—since most so often professed what they esteemed in a man, and then bedded his exact opposite, while refusing the man who embodied what they said they professed.

Inconsistency I did not condemn, nor even foolishness, but the hypocrisy of professing an ideal, whatever it might be, and defending it verbally and vociferously, while secretly betraying it by behavior, I generally found disgusting. Unless such betrayal was accomplished with such wit and grace that it might be termed admirable, and then it was what one might call "polished" evil.

"Rhenn!" Ostrius called from one of the studio windows overlooking the rear courtyard. "You are not grinding or powdering when you are jawing!"

I looked up and smiled politely. "I can't powder when I'm sneezing because someone opened the door and blew powder all over me."

Caliostrus appeared in the window beside his son. "No excuses, now, Rennthyl!"

"Yes, sir." I managed not to grimace or grit my teeth, but I would have liked to submerge both of them in powdered ochre.

"Don't mind Father," Shienna murmured. "He likes to shout because it proves he can."

"He is the master portraitist," I replied.

"Well, don't just stand there!" Caliostrus shouted down.

I kept my lips together and resumed my progress toward the service pump house, imagining both Caliostrus and his worthless elder son being consumed by an explosion of paraffin from a container heated too hot on the studio stove because Ostrius was too lazy to check it . . . flaming wax everywhere, and fire washing over them . . .

Whhoosshh!

I turned to see flames exploding through the open window where Caliostrus had been a moment before.

For a moment, I just stood there, frozen.

Crumpp! Some sort of explosion, a small one, shook the upper level. As fragments of glass and some tile fragments pattered on the pavement, my mouth dropped open. The entire second floor of the building—the studio level—had become a mass of flame, and the flames were rising higher.

"Mother! Marcyl!" screamed Shienna.

I ran toward the outside steps and sprinted up them, trying to ignore the heat radiating past me as I scrambled upward past the second level up to the family quarters.

Olavya stumbled out of the upper doorway. "Father!"

"Where's your mother?" I demanded.

"Inside . . . Marcyl's sick."

I only took two steps into the kitchen area before I almost ran into Almaya, who was half-pulling, half-dragging Marcyl. I just grabbed him from her and staggered back outside and down the steps. I could feel and smell my hair being crisped as I hurried down past the second level. I could also smell another sickeningly sweet smell, and I could barely keep from retching as I carried Marcyl into the far corner of the courtyard, where I set him down.

Somewhere in the distance I could hear the fire bells ringing. I knew that nothing would stop the conflagration already raging through the building. Then . . . I did retch.

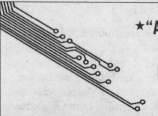

★"An excellent showcase
of a very fine writer's
highest quality work."

—*Publishers Weekly*, starred review

VIEWPOINTS CRITICAL

selected stories by L. E. MODESITT, JR.

Featuring a new Recluce story

This is the first story collection from bestselling fantasy and science fiction writer L. E. Modesitt, Jr.! It includes selections from his entire career, as well as three new stories: "Black Ordermage," set in the world of Modesitt's bestselling Recluce series; "Beyond the Obvious Wind," set in the Corean Chronicles universe; and "Always Outside the Lines," which is related to the Ghosts of Columbia books. *Viewpoints Critical* is an excellent introduction to the work of one of the major SF and fantasy writers publishing today.

"L. E. Modesitt's character development is top-notch.
If you haven't read anything by him, pick up this book
and introduce yourself." —*SFRevu*

"Modesitt is an extremely intelligent writer, possessing
remarkable ingenuity at creating systems of magic and
a real gift for characterization." —*Booklist*

TOR®
tor-forge.com
978-0-7653-1858-9
In trade paperback April 2009

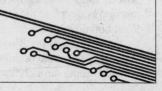